Praise for the acclaimed Rai-Kirah saga by Carol Berg

"Vivid characters and intricate magic combined with a fascinating world and the sure touch of a Real Writer—luscious work!"
—Melanie Rawn

"A spectacular new voice. . . . Superbly textured, splendidly characterized, this spellbinding tale provides myriad delights."
—*Romantic Times*

"This well-written fantasy grabs the reader by the throat on page one and doesn't let go. . . . Wonderful." —*Starburst*

"Both a traditional fantasy and an intriguing character piece. . . . Superbly entertaining." —*Interzone Magazine*

"The prince's redemption, his transformation, and the flowering of mutual esteem between master and slave are at the story's heart. This is handled superbly."
—*Time Out* (London)

"Vivid characters, a tangible atmosphere of doom, and some gallows humor." —*SFX Magazine*

"Wonderful. . . . Carol Berg hooks the reader with vividly drawn characters. . . . Her heroes come alive on the page . . . and the magic is fresh and full of purpose."
—Lynn Flewelling, author of *The Bone Doll's Twin*

Also by Carol Berg

Transformation

Revelation

RESTORATION

CAROL BERG

A ROC BOOK

ROC
Published by New American Library, a division of
Penguin Group (USA) Inc., 375 Hudson Street,
New York, New York 10014, U.S.A.
Penguin Books Ltd, 80 Strand,
London WC2R 0RL, England
Penguin Books Australia Ltd, 250 Camberwell Road,
Camberwell, Victoria 3124, Australia
Penguin Books Canada Ltd, 10 Alcorn Avenue,
Toronto, Ontario, Canada M4V 3B2
Penguin Books (NZ), cnr Airborne and Rosedale Roads,
Albany, Auckland 1310, New Zealand

Penguin Books Ltd, Registered Offices:
80 Strand, London WC2R 0RL, England

Published by Roc, an imprint of New American Library,
a division of Penguin Group (USA) Inc.

First Roc Printing, August 2002
10 9 8 7 6 5 4 3

Cover art: Matt Stawicki
Designer: Ray Lundgren

Printed in the United States of America

PUBLISHER'S NOTE
This is a work of fiction. Names, characters, places, and incidents either are the product of the author's imagination or are used fictitiously, and any resemblance to actual persons, living or dead, business establishments, events, or locales is entirely coincidental.

To all true heroes and heroines

CHAPTER 1

I was living in the land of demons when I first came to believe that the god-stories of the Ezzarians were true. Being Ezzarian myself, I had heard tales of Verdonne and her son Valdis from the time I was cradled, my faith in their relevance waxing and waning as I progressed along the journey of my life. But by the time I had survived sixteen years of slavery and reclaimed my life. I had discovered undeniable evidence of the gods. I had seen the feadnach—the light of destiny—emblazoned on the soul of an arrogant Derzhi prince, which told me that the heir to the most brutal of empires was destined to transform the world. Beside such a wonder, how could I doubt my growing suspicion that I had some part to play in the story of the Nameless God?

"You know planting," said the woman from behind my shoulder. "You've a deft hand with seedlings."

Wiping the sweat from my brow with the back of a dirty hand, I shifted myself and the basket of rista shoots down the newly tilled row. Though the early spring air was still cool, the morning sun on my back was broiling. "My father worked the fields of Ezzaria," I said. "He took me with him every day until I started my schooling. It comes back."

I picked off the lower leaves of the plant, then scooped out a hole, inserted the tender shoot, and repacked the cool black soil snugly about the feathery roots and stem, winding about them the simple enchantments of steady growth and resistance to disease. Rista seedlings were fragile, but with a little nurturing and a nudge of sorcery, they would provide a harvest far more bounteous and reliable than wheat.

I was a guest of the woman and her husband, repaying a night's stay in their quiet green valley by helping with spring planting. For most of my life I had been caught up in the death and violence of a war that could not end. Now that I had done what

I could to change the course of that conflict, a quiet morning and a little dirt under my fingernails felt very close to happiness.

The woman came around to the other side of the double row, set down her own basket, and went to work. Her shining black braid draped gracefully over her shoulder, and her long fingers made quick work of setting the plants. Elinor had a lively intelligence and a wide knowledge of the world, despite the isolation of her current home. But she knew very little of Ezzarians. "So your father was not a warrior as you were, a . . . what is it called?"

"A Warden? No. He had no melydda, thus he had no choice in his profession. Ezzarians without true power must do whatever work is required of them." Those of us found to have power for sorcery were nurtured and trained and allowed to choose our own way to fight the demon war. Until one learned new truths and betrayed it all.

She glanced up at me without pausing her quick fingers. "I'm sorry. I don't mean to bring up painful matters."

I sat up to ease the cramp in my right side—one too many knife cuts in those muscles, the last injury deep and unskillfully repaired. After eight months I feared the painful tightness was caused by internal scarring and might never leave me. An unwelcome reality for a warrior—even one who has no intent to raise a sword ever again. "There's no pain in remembering my father, Mistress Elinor. He was as fine a man as ever lived. Though farming was not the life he would have chosen, he was well content. I learned more of true value from him than from any of my more scholarly mentors."

The tall woman sat back on her heels and assessed me as boldly as any queen. Reddened hands and a coarse, worn tunic could not hide her mature beauty. Dark, slightly angled eyes, along with lustrous red-gold skin, were the telltale of her own Ezzarian heritage, though she had grown up far from our rain-swept hills and forests. "It's just that you speak so little of Ezzaria, Seyonne, and I know the love Ezzarians bear for their homeland. I thought perhaps it was uncomfortable for anyone to bring it up now that you're reviled there." Elinor was nothing if not direct. Ordinarily I liked that in my friends.

Of course, to call Elinor a friend was presumptuous. We had spent some hours in one another's company, talked of the weather and her brother Blaise's retired outlaw band. But, in truth, we knew nothing of each other save a few superficial facts. She had once been an outlaw herself, a rebel against the Derzhi Empire, but was now settled in this lovely valley, where she and her husband fostered a two-year-old child. I was a sorcerer, a retired warrior of thirty-eight years who had a demon living in my soul.

"If I were to avoid everything uncomfortable about my situation, I would have very little to talk about," I said. I moved down the row again and set another plant. Though I enjoyed Elinor's company a great deal, at that moment I wanted nothing more than to lose myself in sweat and dirt and unthinking labor. Duties were awaiting me, truths to face, some of them terrible and dangerous, some of them more personally painful; but every day I could put them off and absorb such peace as this green valley could provide gave me time to be ready.

"My brother says you'll be executed if you return to Ezzaria."

"It is no matter. There's nothing for me there anymore." I wished she would leave it.

"But—"

I smiled at her, trying to apologize for my poor company. "A man cannot become something his people have abhorred and feared for a thousand years and expect them to be swayed instantly into acceptance by his charm and good manners." Especially when he was having the devil of a time accepting it himself. I dragged the basket closer and carefully pulled apart a tangled clump of roots and moist soil. Abomination, my people called me.

"I've been trying to decide how to thank you. Words seem so impossibly inadequate. You've saved my brother's reason . . . and our child's and our friends' . . . but at such cost to yourself . . ."

My skin began to itch. I felt her eyes searching to see the demon that now lived inside me, not an inborn element of my nature as were the demon aspects of her brother Blaise and the child she fostered, but a separate conscious being with voice and emotions and ideas of his own

"I have no regrets," I said. Just worries. Just fears. Just terrifying uncertainty about the future and my place in it.

Elinor could not know how well she repaid me for my deeds of the previous year. Even as I shifted down the row and fixed my attention on my work, hoping to escape her scrutiny, I heard the faint music of my solace from the far end of the valley—a child's laughter, giggling, bubbling, making the golden noonday magic. Before very long, footsteps came pounding across the meadow—tiny bare feet on short sturdy legs, followed by the galumphing boots of someone much taller, someone who was holding back just enough to keep up the merry chase.

"Da!" squealed the little one as he streaked across the fields toward the sod-roofed cottage tucked into the edge of the trees. In the cottage doorway stood a large, square-shouldered man—a bearlike Manganar with brown curly hair and only one leg. He set down a heavy barrel and leaned his crutch against the door frame just in time to catch the boy and rescue him from the tall, dark-haired man giving chase.

"Have you outwitted your uncle Blaise, Evan-diargh?" said the one-legged man, rumpling the boy's short dark hair. "Have you played the clever fox to his hound, then?"

"He has indeed," said the pursuer, a spare, large-boned man of thirty. He patted the boy's back. "I've never seen a mite could run so fast. Especially after we'd been working hard all morning to catch these few paltry trout." He pulled a canvas bag off his back. "As it is, I still need to clean them. The boy was falling asleep on the bank, so I thought I'd best get him home."

"I'll wager he's ready for a bite to eat and a rest," said the big man, reaching for his crutch.

"Then I'll take care of our supper and be back in a bit." With a quick glance and a nod to my companion and me, the dark-haired man started back across the flowered meadow toward the stream that meandered through the valley.

The kindly rescuer nudged the boy, who clung to his neck. "Give a wave to your mam, child." The boy loosed his grip just long enough to waggle a small hand at Elinor. The child's dark eyes, their blue fire hidden only by distance, sparkled happily over the man's shoulder. With one arm around the clinging child and the other expertly maneuvering his crutch, the man carried the boy inside the house. A child could have no safer haven than Gordain's arm.

I turned back to my work, swallowing the uncomfortable knot of joy and grief, gratitude and loneliness that lodged in my throat whenever I watched Elinor and Gordain and the child that fate had given into their care.

"Night's daughter." The woman was staring at me, her hands

fallen limp and lifeless on her knees, the blood drained from her strong and lovely face. "How could I have been so blind? All these months Blaise has brought you here to visit . . . to help you heal, he told me. I've seen you watching Evan . . . devouring him with your eyes. But I never caught the resemblance until now. He's your son, isn't he?" Her eyes darted to the shabby cottage. "Why are you here?"

I shook my head, trying to think of what to say. "Elinor—"

"Why would you hide the truth? You and your cursed, wicked, vile Ezzarian ways . . . You left him out to die, willing to murder a child because he was born different from you. Because you were afraid of him." She wrapped her arms about herself and rose slowly to her feet, her eyes on fire. "And now you've learned that you were wrong to do it. Are you here to appease your conscience? Do you think to make it up to him that you were willing to let wolves tear him apart? Or did you plan to sneak him away? You've never even touched him. How dare you set foot within a league of him?"

"Mistress Elinor, please—" How could I explain all the reasons I dared not touch him, that it was the most difficult thing I had ever done, and that only her goodness and her husband's made it possible? "I've no intention— You and Gordain—" My blundering inability to respond quickly exhausted her willingness to listen.

"You'll never have him. Go away." She spun on her heel and strode toward the cottage, crushing the newly set plants under her feet.

I jumped up to follow her and cursed the catch in my side that stopped my breath for a moment, as if Ysanne's knife were still buried in my flesh. The sun glare dazzled my eyes, making my head throb as I limped across the rista field. Sweat dripped beneath my coarse linen shirt, and clouds began to gather on the horizons of my mind. Creeping darkness . . . With growing misgiving, I halted at the fenced corner of the goat pen next the house, not daring to go closer. Gordain stood in the cottage doorway, his face fierce, determined. Pitiful . . . as if a mortal human could block my way if I chose to summon power. I gritted my teeth, banishing these hateful feelings that were not mine, though they seethed inside my head like boiling tar. I forced my tongue to obey my own will, stammering as I searched for the right words. "Forgive my secrecy. I never intended— I could never—"

But before I could get out the explanation, the storm of rage exploded in my mind, thundering fury that threatened to split my skull. My hands flexed, demanding to grasp Gordain's thick neck and twist it, to hear him scream and choke until the muscles snapped and the bones cracked. My feet were ready to kick the cripple's leg out from under him, my hands to snatch the ax on his wall, and my eyes to watch his face pale as I hacked off his remaining limb.

My hands were shaking as they gripped the fence post, my knees trembling. "Please, get Blaise. Hurry. I'm so sorry . . . so sorry . . ." Only a moment's hesitation and a blur of green and brown streaked past me. Shouts faded into the pandemonium of fury and raging death.

Running feet. Anxious voices. "Get in the house, Linnie. Bar the door! I'll explain later."

Rumbling . . . growling . . . erupting in a roar of madness . . . The fence post dissolved in fire, and a cloud of blackness obscured my sight. I was lost . . .

". . . Listen to me, my friend. Hold on to my voice. I'll not leave you. We're going to bring you back, Seyonne, and get you away from here safely. I know you don't want to hurt anyone. Remember who you are: good friend and teacher, guardian of a prince, most honorable of warriors, loving father. This sickness is not you."

Determined hands gripped my shoulders, and I wanted to rip them from their puny arms. I bit my lip and tasted blood, and it gave me strength. I would kill him for keeping me captive. Only his voice—this vile bondage of calm words and reason—held me in check. As soon as he stopped speaking, I would strangle him. Snap his neck. Pluck his eyes. Eat his heart.

"Did you see him running? He runs like you, easy and light and very fast. He spent the morning digging in the sand by the stream and scooping water in his hand to fill up the holes he made. So patient— No, listen to me, Seyonne, my friend. You are not going to hurt me or anyone. Every time the boy scooped water in his hand, he spilled most of it before he got it to his little holes. But he would squat down beside the hole and pour his tiny bit of water in and watch it disappear into the sand. Then he would sigh and go back to the stream to try again. You see? He is patient like you. How often have you tried to teach me to cast a vermin barrier? Am I the stupidest Ezzarian ever born? Yet without reproach, you try again and again to teach me these simplest of skills. You, who can see the patterns in the world, who can unravel mysteries that no one else can begin to understand. I've never known anyone who sees so clearly . . ."

The man was a fool. I couldn't see. Everywhere I turned was darkness. Terror lapped at the fires of my blood thirst and soon became a flood. At any moment I would take that dreadful step where there would be nothing under my foot, and I would plunge into the abyss. I would become the one I feared . . . the one who held sway over my dreams and visions.

But the strong hands did not let go, and the calm voice did not stop. Before long the tide of fear began to ebb, and I allowed the strong hands and the calm voice to guide me back into the light.

". . . Apologize. I thought you were ready for a longer stay. You seemed so much better."

The world began to come back into focus . . . a dappled woodland, a dusting of new green on the bare branches. The smell of damp earth and new growth. A steep angle to the sunlight. A stream mumbling beside the path, half hidden behind a tangle of willows.

"Here. Let's stop and have a drink. We could both use it, I would guess. Are you ready?"

Numb, unspeaking, I dropped to my knees where he pointed. The rippling water was cold on my scarred and bony hand, still soiled from Elinor and Gordain's garden. I scooped out a handful of the clear, cold water and scrubbed at my hands, letting the muddy dregs drain into the new-sprung grass. Splashed another handful on my face, and then another on my neck, cleaning off the sweat of sun and madness. I looked at the water in my cupped hand and imagined a tiny bronze fist carrying water so carefully across the sand to a childish enterprise. Evan-diargh—son of fire. Smiling, I drank down my own treasure and three more besides, and then sat back, leaning my head wearily against a tree.

"You're getting very good at this," I said to the dark-haired man who sat cross-legged beside me, having drunk his own fill of the sweet water. "How long until you tire of preventing mad Wardens from destroying the world?"

Blaise smiled his crooked smile. "I will do whatever is necessary. So my mentor has taught me."

"I can't go back there again."

"You'll go back. He'll not grow up without knowing you. I've promised you that already. We'll just have to work some more before you do. What set it off this time? Have you had more dreams?"

I ran my fingers through my damp hair and pondered the question. "The same dreams come every night. Nothing new." Dreams of an enchanted fortress and a mystery that terrified me. "Elinor and I were talking about farming. About my father. About Ezzaria. And then you and Evan came . . ."

"We were running. Were you afraid for him? Was that it?"

"No. Just the opposite. I was so grateful for your sister and Gordain. I couldn't ask for a better home for him. No. It must have been something else . . ." I hated that I could never remember exactly what set off these attacks—the storms of violence that had riven my soul ten times in the past eight months since the first one in Vayapol, when three beggars had tried to rob Blaise's foster brother Farrol. I had come near killing them all, friends and robbers alike, as if they somehow deserved it by their very act of breathing.

My demon was the cause, I believed. Angry. Resentful. Trapped behind the barriers I had built in some vain belief that I could control my own soul long enough to understand my dreams and face their consequences. I was sure this waking madness was my demon's raging.

But as I searched my memory for the key, I ran across something more immediately distressing. "Oh, Verdonne's child! Elinor guessed that I'm Evan's father. She thinks I'm planning to take him away. Blaise, you've got to go back. I was trying to reassure them, and then I go mad in front of their door. They must be terrified."

"Stubborn Ezzarian—seems like I advised you to tell them everything." Blaise jumped to his feet and offered me his hand. "As soon as you're safely asleep, I'll go back." We started walking briskly down the trail, Blaise working the enchantments that took us farther than the number of our steps and true geography would admit, the sorcery that kept my son's location hidden from me. Much as I longed to be a father to Evan-diargh, I could not trust myself with the most precious thing on earth. And even if I were cruel enough to uproot him from the only home he had ever known, I had no place to take him.

My life as a Warden of Ezzaria, a sorcerer-warrior in my people's thousand-year battle to save the human world from the ravages of demons, had almost ended before it had begun, when I was enslaved by the Derzhi. But after sixteen years of bondage, the Prince of the Derzhi had returned my freedom and my homeland, and I had taken up my Warden's calling once again, only to discover that the secret war we Ezzarians had fought with such diligence for ten centuries was a war against ourselves. The rai-kirah—the demons—were not wicked beings bent on destruction of human reason, but fragments of our own souls, ripped away by an ancient enchantment and banished to a frozen, bitter land called Kir'Vagonoth. The birth of my son and my meeting with Blaise had convinced me that whatever the reasons for this ancient sundering, it must be undone.

My child had been born joined to a rai-kirah. Possessed. As it was impossible to remove a demon from an infant, Ezzarian law demanded that such children be killed. But before I even knew of his birth, my wife had sent our son away until he was old enough for us to heal. My search for the child led me to Blaise, an Ezzarian also born demon-joined, a young outlaw of generous heart and inner peace—a wholeness, a completion, that led me to understand our nature and the terrible split that had occurred so many centuries before. Blaise taught me what my race and the demons were meant to be, and so I set out to free the rai-kirah from their exile by unlocking the way to our ancient homeland called Kir'Navarrin. To accomplish this task, I was forced to put my new beliefs to the test and join myself with a powerful demon named Denas.

But my own people could not accept what I tried to tell them. A possessed Warden was an abomination, the ultimate corruption and an unimaginable danger. Once they understood that the change I had undergone was irreversible, the Ezzarian queen, my own wife, Ysanne, had stuck a knife in me and left me to die.

As I lay bleeding, I was tormented by visions of a dark fortress that lay deep in Kir'Navarrin. Demon memory and crumbling artifacts told us that someone powerful and dangerous was imprisoned there. Fear of this prisoner had caused my ancestors to reive their own souls, to destroy all evidence of their history, and to lock themselves out of Kir'Navarrin. My death visions, so vivid as to bear the patina of truth, showed me the face and form of that prisoner—and they were my own. Unfathomable mystery, yet I believed . . . I feared . . . that I dreamed true.

If the prisoner in the fortress endangered human souls, then my Warden's oath, my training, and my history demanded that I be the one to confront that danger. But for eight months my dreams had held me paralyzed, and now, I seemed to be going mad.

CHAPTER 2

Just after sunset Blaise and I came onto a dirt lane on the shabby outskirts of Karesh, a town in the southern Empire where the remnants of the outlaw band of the Yvor Lukash were working garden plots and learning trades, waiting to see if their truce with the Prince of the Derzhi would come to anything.

"Do you want to stop and wash?" Blaise paused outside the local washing house, a dank and dismal shack built around a sporadic little spring of marvelously pure warm water. For a copper coin, the corpulent proprietor would give you half an hour of access to a pool lined with cracked tile and use of a towel that had likely not been clean since Verdonne was a mortal maiden.

I sighed and tried to ignore the stink of farmwork and madness. "It would be delightful, but you need to be on your way."

So instead we hurried down an alley and up a dusty wooden stair to a room on the third floor of a locksmith's shop. There I sat on one of two straw-filled mattresses and munched sour cheese and bread, while Blaise mixed a sleeping potion. I didn't trust my own fingers to do it, as if my resident demon might alter the formula to prevent my safe sleep. I was a sorcerer of considerable power and a warrior of long experience. If I set my demented mind to murder, it was no simple matter to prevent it. But once I had slept a sound night after one of my attacks, I seemed to be myself again. Until the next time.

"When will you go to Kir'Navarrin and be rid of this?" said Blaise as he crushed a few leaves and dropped them into a cup with a spoonful of wine and a few pinches of white powder. "You know what I was—a raving, drooling idiot, more beast than man. I couldn't even feed myself, and in less than a day there . . . Stars of heaven, even after all these months I can't explain the difference. To be whole again. To see clearly, as if someone had popped my eyes back into their proper sockets. Surely it would help you."

Confined to the human world, Blaise and the few other

Ezzarians born demon-joined had faced a terrible choice. Their demon natures allowed them to shift their forms at will—a talent those of us born unjoined had never even suspected. But after a number of years of shapeshifting, their bodies lacked some essential component to remain stable. A day would come—some sooner, some later—when they would shift into beast form and be unable to shift back again, quickly losing their human intelligence. I had come to believe that entering Kir'Navarrin would solve their problem, and it was for this—for my child's future and for Blaise, as much as anything else—that I had joined with Denas to unlock the gateway. But I had not yet passed through the gate myself.

"Your problem was something normal—a natural progression of your life," I said. "Mine is not. I can't risk the passage until I understand what this cursed Denas is up to."

"The demon is a part of you already," said Blaise, "joined as you were meant to be. Gods above, man, you walked your own soul and saw the truth of it—there was no separate being inside you. You've told me fifty times how you long to enter Kir'Navarrin. So go there and be healed before you kill yourself or someone else."

I pulled at my hair, as if to let some light and air into the thickness of my head. "He is not me. Not yet. He sits in my belly squirming, as if I've eaten something that wasn't quite dead. I think he's the one that's so determined to get there"

The golden demon who called himself Denas and I had relinquished our separate lives for common purpose, and for the few hours it took us to accomplish that purpose, we had reached an accommodation. But it would have been hard to gauge which one of us had been more reluctant. He had suffered in a frozen wasteland for a thousand years, believing my people had destroyed his own. I had been trained to believe demons devoured human souls in unending lust for evil. Neither intellect nor pragmatism could overcome my sense of violation, of corruption, of certainty that Denas was waiting for one moment of weakness to enslave my will to his.

I raised the bread and cheese to my mouth and put it down again. I wasn't all that hungry. "Whatever is causing these episodes, I daren't let down my guard. If Denas can drive me to do murder now, what would I be if we were fully joined?"

Blaise handed me a clay cup, and I downed the purple-gray

liquid it contained, followed by water to drown the foul taste. "You will be the man you have always been. The rai-kirah will bring you memories and ideas, talents, perhaps new ways of looking at the world. But it can't be so simple to corrupt a human soul. Not one such as yours." He smiled and threw a wadded blanket at me. "You're far too stubborn."

I wasn't so confident. Even if I dared cross into the demon homeland, there was a finality about passing through the enchanted gateway—so I had been told. Once that step was taken, Denas and I would be completely merged, all barriers between us dissolved forever. My visions implied that I was the danger that raged in Tyrrad Nor, threatening to destroy the world. If I could not control my own hand, my own soul . . . That could be the very circumstance that caused the danger. Occasional bouts of madness might be better.

Five minutes and my limbs felt like they belonged to someone else. As my vision blurred and my head spun, Blaise donned his black cloak and a slouched hat and blew out the candle. "Joining with the rai-kirah was the right thing to do. You'll learn what you need to solve this."

"One more thing," I said drowsily as he opened the door to go. "Tell your sister that we did not lay Evan out to die. I was off fighting demons, and Ysanne . . . Ysanne sent him to you. We didn't—either one of us—want him dead. Not for a moment. Not ever."

"I'll tell her everything, Seyonne. Sleep well."

As a disturbing result of my condition, most of Blaise's people—even the few like Blaise with inborn demons of their own—were a bit afraid of me. Certainly everyone respected my privacy. Thus, it was a surprise when someone burst into my room not a quarter of an hour after Blaise had left. When the visitor's feet accidentally kicked over an empty water jar, my descent into drugged stupor was temporarily suspended. Light flared in my face.

"Spirit's flesh! Dak was right. You're still here. I thought you'd gone off with Blaise again." The intruder, a short, round-faced man with thinning hair, was Farrol, Blaise's dearest childhood friend and foster brother. Farrol, a man neither subtle in action nor temperate in opinion, had been born as well with his demon nature intact.

"Only a moment and I'll be safely out of the way," I mumbled, letting my eyelids sag. My body felt like river-bottom mud.

"But it was you the messenger wanted. Said it was urgent."

"Messenger?" I wedged open the gates of sleep.

"Said he'd come from Prince Aleksander. Cursed Derzhi bastard—acted like we were some kind of vermin. Blaise had only just left, so I sent the fellow after him . . . and after you, I thought."

"From the Prince?" I dragged myself up to sitting. Blaise and I had been scheduled to meet with Aleksander on the day of the spring equinox. But the Prince, bearing the burden of his father's empire if not the crown as yet, had sent word that he would have to delay until midsummer. That was still more than two months away. "What did he say exactly?"

"Said he was to give the message directly to the Ezzarian what was the Prince's slave, the one with the slave mark on his face. Said the message couldn't wait. Had to deliver it himself."

"The Prince's slave . . . Those were his exact words?"

"Aye. Arrogant, sneering fellow, he was."

Aleksander would never refer to me as his slave. Not anymore. Not to a Derzhi messenger whom he would wish to treat me with respect. "Tell me what he looked like, Farrol. His colors . . . a scarf or a crest on his shield or his sword or somewhere on his dress . . . And tell me about his hair. Did he have a braid?" I reached for the cup of water Blaise had left on the table by my bed and poured the contents over my head to force my foggy mind awake.

"Looked like any cursed Derzhi. Armed to the teeth. Riding an eighteen-hands bay that Wyther or Dak would kill for. No scarf, but a tef-coat over his shirt. An animal on it—a shengar, maybe, or a kayeet. I don't know. His braid was like any of the arrogant bastards. Long. Light-colored. Tied with a blue . . . no, it was a purple ribbon on the left side of his head. Why do you care? What's wrong?"

I jammed the heels of my hands into my eyes, trying to think. "The braid—which side of his head was it?"

Farrol kicked at the empty water jar. "I don't know. What does it—?"

"Think, Farrol. You said left. Which was it?"

The round man threw up his hands. "Left, I think . . . yes, it was the left. That's how I saw the color of the ribbon because the fire was on his left."

Left . . . spirits of darkness! I staggered to my feet and grabbed Farrol's arm. "We've got to go after them. Hurry. Help me wake up, and get me a sword."

"What's wrong?"

"He's no messenger. He's a namhir—an assassin." And Blaise was leading him straight to my son.

By the time Farrol had poured enough strong tea down me that I wouldn't fall off a horse, we were a half hour behind Blaise and the Derzhi assassins; namhirra always traveled in threes. As we raced through the moonlit woodland, Farrol traversing the enchanted ways as Blaise did, all I could think of were the murderous warriors venting their fury on Evan, Elinor, Blaise, and Gordain when they realized they could not fulfill the death vow they had made to their heged lord. Unless Blaise noticed them and shook them off, they could follow him right through the paths of enchantment just as I did. And Blaise was tired and worried, and even in the best of times he lacked a warrior's instincts.

Through the open forest of oak and ash, down into stream-cut gullies thick with willow and alder, over a rocky ridge. Each time the route was slightly different, enough that even an experienced tracker could not duplicate it or detect the signs of an earlier passing. By the time Farrol raised his hand in warning, I was grinding my teeth.

"It's a direct way, now," whispered Farrol. "Over this ridge will take you in behind the house. How do you want to work this?"

I dropped lightly from the horse and yanked my sword from its scabbard. "Circle left and get to the house through the goat pen. Your task . . . the *only* one . . . is to get the family away." I gripped his leg. "Don't think you can fight these men, Farrol, nor can Gordain or Blaise; namhirra are extremely skilled and failure is worse than death to them. I'll try to draw them away." And then I would find out what in the name of night they were doing here. "Go!"

I left my horse at the top of the rise, and then crept silently down the dark hillside through a thick stand of pines. When I was no more than halfway down, orange light flared from the valley and a man screamed in mortal agony. Piercing the black wall of the night came the terrified wail of a child. Abandoning stealth, I ran. A dark form lay sprawled on the ground just at the edge of the trees. Blaise . . . and I could spare no time to see if he lived.

The cottage was already burning when I reached the base of the hill, and one of the Derzhi was standing in front of the door, sword drawn. Evan's whimpering cries came from behind the man. Gods of night, he was still inside! But I could not take on the door guard, for the other two namhirra were also in view. In the wavering shadows beyond the fire was a small group—a man huddled on the ground, another man—the second Derzhi—behind him bending his head back and holding a knife to his throat. The third namhir, tall, thin, his arms folded calmly in front of his chest, stood in front of the two, barking a question. The crumpled man responded with a harsh, sobbing curse.

Gordain was going to die. No matter what enchantment I cast or what feat of arms I might be able to muster, the distance between us was too great. I could not possibly move fast enough to halt the knife of a namhir.

"They will live, Gordain," I cried, offering the good man the only gift possible as I sent my dagger spinning through the night to catch the door guard in the heart, and then raced the heartbreakingly long steps to plunge my sword into the second namhir's back. As I yanked the blade from the lifeless Derzhi, I glimpsed Farrol's stocky form streaking from the woods toward the burning house. I had no choice but to trust him to do what was needed, for the third assassin drew his sword and attacked.

"The sorcerer slave himself!" he cried gleefully as he met me stroke for stroke. "Flushed you out like a hungry kayeet."

I had fought few humans in my career as a warrior—my opponents had always been the monstrous manifestations of demons—but I learned quickly that the namhir was among the most skilled of his kind. Simple illusions—itching, boils, crawling spiders—would not disrupt the focus of such a killer. He knew I was a sorcerer. And my son's terrified wailing fed my anger so sorely that I could not allow myself the time for more impressive, and thus more difficult, workings. I had to rely on my sword and my fists. Once, that would not have been a problem—I was very good at what I did—but the badly healed wound in my side was proving treacherous. Every time I raised my sword, my right side felt as though it were tearing open.

I tried to back the warrior into the fence of the goat pen, but he seemed to have the lay of the farm imprinted on his mind. Just before I had him trapped, he ducked and rolled and leaped to his feet behind me. I pressed him again, toward the flames, ripping my blade across his chest. Not deep enough, for he did not falter. Rather he worked me sideways toward the new-plowed field, hoping, no doubt, to tangle my feet in the soft earth. I whirled about and landed my boot solidly in his back. He stumbled, but did not go down. My son's crying became short bleats of terror, and I dared not think why Farrol's shadow was still flailing about between me and the fire.

"Get them out," I screamed, and brought my sword down on my opponent's shoulder. Dark blood gushed from the wound.

Still the namhir fought, dodging my blows and kicking at my knees, smashing a thick wooden stave into my back. The blow staggered me for a moment, and only a desperate recovery prevented his sword from following. But the namhir was human, and I had been trained to fight demons. With my next blow, I shattered his blade. The tall Derzhi stumbled backward, holding only the hilt and stub of his sword.

"More will come after me," he snarled as I kicked the broken sword from his right hand and pressed him to the ground with blow after blow, parried only by his wooden stave. "You will no longer interfere in the affairs of your betters, slave."

I kicked him in the gut so hard that blood ran out of his mouth, and then set my boot on his chest. "Who sent you? What Hamrasch lord cares enough about Aleksander's freed slave to send namhirra?" The wolf crest on his bloodstained tef-coat identified him as a member of the Hamrasch heged, one of the twenty most powerful Derzhi families.

"All of my lords . . . every one of them." He coughed and grinned through the blood. "The puling Aleksander will never rule this empire."

"All of them . . ." The absolute assurance of his taunt shook me to my boots. For every lord of a heged to take a share in an assassination . . . I bent down and twisted his bleeding shoulder, my voice hoarse with fear and fury. "Tell me, namhir, have they spoken kanavar?"

He neither flinched nor answered me. Only laughed until he choked on bloody spittle.

My hand fell away, and I stood up slowly. Kanavar . . . a swearing so deep, so dreadful, so solemn that every man, woman, and child of an entire Derzhi heged would die to see it kept. The Hamraschi had sworn on the very existence of their family to destroy Aleksander.

The namhir scrabbled weakly backward across the firelit grass. "You'll die, too, slave," he croaked. "And any who shelter you . . ."

I raised my sword to finish him, but my eyes were distracted by the shifting firelight and my caution by the import of his words, and so I missed the movement of his left hand. The wooden stave smashed brutally into my right side.

My breath stopped. Red streaks of light shattered my vision as ripping, paralyzing agony exploded in my side. My right arm fell limp, and the sword slipped from my lifeless hand. Another blow, this time to my ankle. I scarcely noticed it, for I was fighting to get a breath. Doubled over, left hand fumbling in the dirt for my dropped weapon, I staggered backward. *Head up, fool. The next one will crack your skull.*

The namhir was a dead man, no matter what. The injury I'd done him would have seen to it, whether I survived another moment. But to his mortal regret—and my own—I stumbled over Gordain's body and saw what they had done to the good Manganar. They had ripped his throat to finish him as I knew they would, but earlier . . . before I'd come . . . they had cut off both of his hands and seared the stumps in fire so he wouldn't die too quickly. Unimaginable horror for any man, but for a man who already lived without one leg . . .

"He wept like an old woman" came the rasping whisper. "I thought Manganar had more bile."

Darkness thundered in my blood. The remnants of my day's madness surged anew, and I forgot the kanavar, forgot Gordain and Aleksander, Blaise and my child, forgot everything. Somehow I managed to lift my sword again, but I did not kill the namhir quickly. With strokes as precise as those of a gem cutter and so vicious they shivered my own bones, I took off the screaming Derzhi's right hand . . . and then his left . . . and then the rest of him piece by piece until there was nothing left to cut.

CHAPTER 3

I stood panting harshly, trembling and bent over with the searing pain in my side. I could not think what I needed to do next or remember why the silence seemed so strange. When a hand fell heavily on my shoulder, I almost shed my skin.

"The boy's all right, Seyonne. And Elinor, too. They're safe."

Dully I stared up into Blaise's pale face. He had a monstrous purple bruise on his temple, and even his sincere concern could not mask disgust. My arms were covered with blood, my clothing soaked with it and spattered with bits of flesh and entrails. What lay before me on the ground was no longer recognizable as a man. I dropped my sword and sank to my knees, pressing the back of my bloody hand against my mouth.

"Are you injured?"

I shook my head. Not injured. Diseased.

The garish orange flames were already dying, only the blackened stone finger of the hearth marked that a home had once nestled at the edge of the trees. A short distance away stood Elinor, pressing Evan's dark head fiercely into her neck, muffling his sobs and hiding his eyes from the carnage.

"I'm sorry," I whispered. Although I spoke to the iron-faced woman and to my weeping son, they could not possibly have heard me. "I'm so sorry."

"You saved their lives." Even the kindest of friends could not sound convincing. Not on that night.

It was a measure of Blaise's heart that he did not recoil or run away.

"Take me away from them," I said. "Never let me near them again."

"Soon. For now they have to come back with us. Without Gordain, they can't stay here." He dropped my abandoned cloak over my shoulders.

The night breeze swirled smoke, obscuring the stars and the strangely peaceful valley. Tendrils of flame crept toward the fences and newly budded trees, only to die away in the damp. Farrol, his round face blackened, his shirt half scorched away, holding his hands in the rigid posture that told me how severely they must be burned, was trying to prevent Elinor from approaching Gordain's body and the horror on the ground beside it.

"Tell me who they were, Seyonne. What further danger do we face?" Gingerly Blaise picked up my fouled weapon, made some effort to clean it, and stuffed it in my scabbard. Then he got me to my feet with a hand under my elbow, nudging me away from the dead. Even as we retreated, Elinor shoved her way past Farrol's quiet pleading and knelt on the blood-soaked ground beside Gordain, still clutching my child to her breast. She did not scream or cry out at the sight of her husband's mangled body, but only touched his broad shoulder tenderly and closed his eyes with a steady hand. When she rose at last, her glance swept the gruesome earth about her and came to rest on my face. She stared at me as if she were unable to comprehend that such creatures as the namhirra and I could share the same earth, much less the same blood, with those she loved. She tightened her embrace of the whimpering child, then turned her back and walked with Farrol up the hill into the woods.

"They were assassins," I said. "Sent by Aleksander's enemies." I pulled the cloak about my trembling limbs, as if wool could warm the night's chill. "They knew where to find me." An ominous mystery in itself, for I had believed that only Aleksander and my friend Fiona knew that secret, and neither of them would willingly reveal it.

"But why? What possible—"

"The assassin said Aleksander was under a kanavar . . . a heged oath . . . that he will never rule the Empire. The entire Hamrasch family has sworn it. Maybe other hegeds, too. No way to tell." It was as if the light had gone out of the stars, and the deadness in my own soul had infected the universe itself. I could think of only one way anyone could prevent Aleksander from inheriting his father's throne. "They're going to kill him." The hope of the world. The friend who had shared his soul with me. The brother so unlikely. The consideration was so painful and the night's events so disturbing, I could not think.

"Then why are they trying to kill you?"

I shook my head. It made no sense. I had scarcely seen the Prince for three years. "But if they want me dead, they won't stop.

I don't know how they found me, but when these don't come back, they'll send more. I'll leave Karesh, but even then—"

"So the rest of us will have to hide. We've done it before. Let's go."

I was away from Karesh before Blaise had all his people out of bed. I stuffed my meager possessions in a cloth pack, and into a pocket of my cloak I dropped a few of the zenars I had earned by reading and writing for local merchants. Unable to face those who would soon hear the tale of my savagery, I bade farewell to no one but Blaise.

"You must give me a way to find you," he said as I pulled on my spare shirt, fastened my cloak about my shoulders, and gave him the little leather bag that held the rest of my earnings to use for Evan and Elinor. "I've never opened the gate to Kir'Navarrin without your help. What if one of the others needs to cross and I can't open the way?"

"I've taught Fiona everything. Without being demon-joined, she can't open the way herself, but she can remind you of anything you forget, help you use your power." My fiery young friend was off and digging in ruins, searching for remnants of Ezzarian history.

"Your son needs you, Seyonne. I'll keep him as safe as I can, but—"

"He needs no one capable of what I did this night."

"You know better. You'll find the answer. This is a sickness. It is not you. And you saved their lives as you've done so many others." He followed me down the stairs and into the night-shuttered lane where my horse stood tethered to a post. Lights were beginning to flicker behind the dark walls, like fireflies disturbed from the grass. "You must give me a way to find you."

"I've got to warn Aleksander," I said, strapping my small pack onto the saddle. "I'll tell him about the kanavar, and then get away again before I go mad again. When I figure out where I'm going, I'll send word here to the locksmith."

"And if you need me, I'll—"

"Don't tell me anything!" I untied the horse and mounted, the urgency of my leaving driving my leaden limbs. A Warden was sworn to protect the world from evil. I could not even protect my own child from myself.

But Blaise would not allow me to go yet. "If you need me,

leave a message at Dolgar's shrine in Vayapol. Tell me where you are, and I'll come to you. I promise I won't tell you where to find the others unless I judge you're well." He stayed my horse until I nodded in agreement. "I owe you more than life, Seyonne. If you're in the pits of Kir'Vagonoth itself, I'll come."

There was no answer to such friendship. I clasped his hand and rode away.

The red fingers of dawn were just touching the sky when I first glimpsed the spires of Zhagad in the distance, rising from the shadows of the dune sea. The Pearl of Azhakstan. The seat of imperial power since one of Aleksander's great-grandsires had outgrown his desert kingdom and decided to order the world according to his whim. For five hundred years the warrior Derzhi had proven that they could kill, enslave, burn, starve, or mutilate anyone into their grand design. Their Empire had grown into an uneasy prosperity of roads and trade, anchored on the rocks of tyranny and fear, bound into a whole with the chains of slavery.

Why did I believe that one cocky prince could alter the bleak landscape of such a world? What arrogance was mine to believe that the bright center I had seen in Aleksander was the gods' answer to its brutality? But I did believe it. When Aleksander bought me at the Capharna slave auction, I had been resigned to death in bondage, bereft of hope and faith after half a lifetime of degradation. When I saw the feadnach in him, I had cursed my Warden's oath that bound me to protect my cruel and arrogant conqueror. But our journey together had changed us both. I had shared Aleksander's strength and refreshed my spirit at the fountain of his unquenchable life. He was our hope. I could not let him die in some tribal spat. I tugged on the reins and headed down the rocky promontory toward the golden domes that glittered in the growing light.

An extraordinary amount of traffic bustled on the wide, paved road that led from the travelers' well at Taíne Amar to the outer gates of the royal city, the last league of the Emperor's Road that stretched from Zhagad east and west to the boundaries of the Empire. One would have thought it was time for Dar Heged, the twice-yearly gathering of Derzhi families to present grievances before the Emperor. Troops of scowling warriors occupied the center of the roadway, escorting finely dressed lords toward the city, consigning everyone else to the peripheries. And everyone else seemed to be leaving Zhagad that day; vast merchant caravans lumbered outward like traveling cities, the horses and chastou straining under the drovers' urgent whips. For so many to depart the city before the evening market was very odd. And seldom had I seen so many clumps of people gathered at the roadside talking, rocklike obstacles for the herdsmen screaming at their flocks of goats and the hurried travelers lashing at beggars who pawed at their stirrups. The din of shouts and hooves, clattering wheels, dangling pots, snapping whips, and bleating animals was deafening. I hated cities, and the noise and stink and crowds of this one had polluted the peaceful desert.

It had taken me three anxious weeks to get to Zhagad. I had traveled the harsh desert road alone, thankful for my well-trained sight that allowed me to move safely at night, avoiding bandits and the worst of the sun. Once I had put some distance between myself and Karesh, and felt the brutal impact of the Azhaki desert, I sorely missed Blaise. With his help I could have traveled the grueling distance in a single day. But he had needed to get his people to safety, and not even for Aleksander would I slow him. I would give much to change the world, but not my son. Never him.

I had hoped that my joining with Denas would give me the ability to follow these magical pathways as Blaise did, but I'd not yet grasped the trick of it. Blaise had suggested that my failure was of my own making. "You need to let go of your physical boundaries," he said whenever I complained of my inadequacies. "But you won't do it. It's the same with your shifting; the reason it's so hard for you to change form is that you try to hold on to too much of yourself."

Blaise had little formal schooling, but he saw things clearly. Now that I was joined with Denas, I was capable of shapeshifting at will, transforming myself into an eagle or a chastou or a fleet-footed kayeet, the fastest runner on earth. But unlike Blaise and his fellows, I found the act excruciatingly difficult. Perhaps Blaise was right, and it was my reluctance to yield control. Or perhaps what I had done to myself—sharing body and soul with a rai-kirah who had no kinship to me—was not the right ordering of the world as I had hoped.

In the early days of my recovery, Blaise had convinced me to let down the magical barriers I'd built to isolate myself from the demon. He said I should talk with Denas, learn of him. Knowledge and understanding would surely make coexistence easier. The rai-kirah had never spoken, not once. I wondered if my coming so close to death had destroyed him, if perhaps his anger was all that was left, the fading rumbles of thunder as a storm moves out. But then I'd started attacking people, and I quickly rebuilt my barriers.

Preoccupied with my continuing dilemmas, I pushed my horse through the crowd, taking advantage of a large party forging a path toward the gates. Five warriors rode in a wedge, opening the way for a richly dressed noble. Two columns of soldiers rode behind him, protecting heavily laden pack animals. The troops were Hamrasch warriors, along with a few dark-skinned Thrid mercenaries, but the lord did not wear the gold tef-coat and wolf crest of the Hamrasch. I could not see his own heged symbol.

"Clear the road of this offal," commanded the noble, a soft-bodied man with a sleek blond braid. "Cut them if they won't move aside." The party had come to a standstill, the fault of several caravan outriders who were trying to use the same space to move several heavily laden sledges pulled by slaves. From a long cylinder strapped to his saddle, the Derzhi noble yanked an arm-length stick of polished wood and struck at a slave who had fallen to his knees when the sledge he was dragging caught the wheel of a cart going the opposite direction. The slave cried out and fell backward, blood blossoming on his forehead. He got tangled in the leather traces and pulled the sledge further askew, spilling its poorly lashed contents onto the roadway.

The noble's troops drew their swords and began to force other travelers to step aside. As he waited for the path to be opened, the Derzhi lord paced his horse back and forth beside the slave. Each time the bleeding man tried to rise and untangle himself from the traces, the lord, his face composed, struck him deliberately and viciously with his stick—on the face, on the elbows, on shoulders already raw from the abrasion of the leather harness.

My bones ached with each blow. My back was scarred from years of such mindless cruelty, and no matter what I told myself of necessity and danger, I could not walk away. I dropped from the saddle, tied my mount to an abandoned tinker's cart, and shoved my way through the surging crowd. Crouching low, ducking my head, and using the cover of the overturned sledge,

I grabbed the tangled straps and snapped them with a word of enchantment. Grasping the fallen man's bloody hand around the corner of the sledge, I gave him leverage to get his feet under him. As soon as he was up, I backed away into the crowd.

"*Tas vyetto*" came a breathless whisper from the other side of the sledge.

You're welcome, I thought, already too far away for him to hear me say it. *Would I could do more.* I would have left him my knife, but his overseers were too close. If caught with a weapon, he'd lose a hand or an eye.

I never saw the slave's face, but I made sure to note that of the Derzhi, who was back among his guards and riding coolly toward the gates. He was perhaps fifty-five years old, tall and straight in the saddle. Women likely called him a fine figure of a man, handsome for his age, unscarred by weather or battle. But I thought his soft face vicious: his wide brow empty, his full lips gluttonous, and the round eyes set close beside his narrow nose devoid of human sympathy. Or perhaps I saw only the habitual cruelty in his hand and the lack of expression on that fine face as he beat a man to breaking while waiting idly for his path to be cleared.

As I pushed back through the crowd to where my horse waited patiently beside the tinker's cart, I felt a light touch upon my back. I whirled about. No one. But far across the passing crowd a tall woman stood staring my way, her dark eyes so penetrating, I would have wagered she could see the scars beneath my shirt. Her gown and veil were a brilliant green. Among the sea of shabby browns and grays, she stood out like a sprig of new grass in the desert. A party of riders came between us, and I scrambled into the saddle and rode onward. I needed no one to notice me.

I reached the outer gates still unsettled with the incident, sure I should have done more, yet knowing that I could have used every scrap of my power and skill and changed the outcome not a whit. The slave and I would both have ended up dead.

"Hold up there! Yes, you. Get off that bag of bones. Come here and let me look at you." The mounted Derzhi who was patrolling the throngs of beggars, travelers, and beasts at Zhagad's fortresslike outer gate waved his spear at me.

Stupid. Stupid. Distracted by the incident with the slave, I had forgotten to mask my Ezzarian features when I approached the gate. Aleksander had revoked the law that required Ezzarians to be enslaved, but Ezzarians still caught the eye of soldiers, and the slave marks burned into my face and my left shoulder would forever leave me vulnerable to suspicion. The gate guard moved closer, and people fell away, leaving a path between us.

I felt for the leather packet tucked into my shirt, and, trusting that Aleksander's paper would prove sufficient as it had in the past, I dismounted and approached the warrior.

As did all the Derzhi guards in Zhagad, he went shirtless in the heat, exposing massive, bronze-colored shoulders, one of them crossed by a dreadful scar. "Zakor! Over here," he called to one of his fellows. "I believe I've found me a runaway." The guard's spear point pricked my neck, forcing me to turn my head to show him the falcon and the lion burned into my cheekbone on the day I had been sold to Aleksander. The Derzhi smiled and licked his lips, no doubt anticipating the pleasure of hacking off the foot of a runaway slave and the rewards of delivering him to the royal slave master.

Controlling the fury that welled up at his bloodthirsty glee—and a gut-gnawing anxiety that had not quite vanished in the years since my release—I reached up with my right hand and grabbed the shaft of his spear, holding it away from my throat. With my left, I held out the worn parchment, making sure the imperial seal was clearly visible. My voice remained even. "Indeed you have not, your honor. I am a free man by order of the Crown Prince. Find a scribe and have this read. You'll learn the consequences of interfering with me."

The guard squinted at the paper in the sun glare. "The Crown Prince . . ." He shrugged his bare shoulders as he yanked his spear from my grasp and used it to poke at the writing. ". . . I Suppose he is still that. And for the moment his seal will get you off, but by tomorrow sundown, I'd advise you not rely on it. The Twenty will have something to say in the matter." He spat onto the dusty paving stones and wheeled his mount.

In a single heartbeat the insistent frenzy of the mobbed travelers took on a more ominous cast: furtive conversations, racing troops, shouts. From inside the walls came a constant wailing that grated on the spirit like steel on glass. On the stone towers where the red banners of the Derzhi lion hung limp and heavy in the hot air, something was missing—the gold banners with the silver falcon that always hung in place beside the red, the banners of the Denischkar heged, Aleksander's family. In their place were banners of solid red. Everywhere solid red banners . . . mourning banners . . . Sweet Verdonne!

I bulled through a knot of beggars to follow the mounted Derzhi. "Please tell me the news, your honor. I've been deep in the desert and not heard."

He looked over his scarred shoulder and sniggered. "You must be the only man in the Empire, then. The Emperor is dead by an assassin's blade. The Twenty are gathering to see to the succession." The man stabbed his spear into my freedom paper, which had fluttered to the paving stones, and offered it back to me. "I've heard it was Prince Aleksander himself who did it."

CHAPTER 4

Aleksander was not dead. The tale of the streets, that the Emperor's murderer—what was left of him—hung in the marketplace, had frozen my heart. But it was a Frythian slave who had been found kneeling on the Emperor's vast bed, bathed in royal blood, and who now provided a vultures' feast in the heart of Zhagad.

Frythia was likely already in flames. Soon there would be nothing left of the dignified little mountain kingdom, no structure, no artifact, no animal, and certainly no human with any identifiable drop of Frythian blood. But all that was no matter to the people of Zhagad. Every man and woman of them was convinced that the slave but did Prince Aleksander's bidding. Certainly those who stood gaping at the grisly remnants of treachery had no doubts about whom to blame. *... couldn't wait for the gods to crown him ... I heard they argued ... threats were made ... Not enough his father let him rule ... the Emperor was ready to revoke his anointing ... I was beginning to think he'd come to manhood ...* No rumor of a kanavar, no supposition drifting through the streets that perhaps Aleksander was the target and not the arrow. The finest imperial torturers had succeeded in eliciting only one word from the assassin, so observers said. "Aleksander." After seven hours they'd had to stop, else there would have been too little of the prisoner left to do sufficient screaming when they disemboweled and dismembered him in the marketplace.

I needed to fly into the imperial palace of Zhagad. To enter the walled inner ring of the royal city, much less the palace, one needed a Derzhi sponsor, and I doubted Aleksander was available. Despite my dislike of alien cravings and the feelings of vulnerability as the senses I had honed for thirty-eight years were altered, bird form had its distinct uses. So I crammed myself into a deserted alcove—a stifling, nasty place at the end of a beggars' alley—and considered shifting. *Settle yourself, fool, I thought. Find him, warn him, and get away before you kill him.*

As always, I constructed the shape of my desire inside my head, summoned melydda from the deep center of my being, and tried to release my physical boundaries. The change should have happened easily . . . an effortless merging of my limbs and torso with the image in my mind, a chilly shudder as I gave off heat, the natural result of shifting to a smaller form, a momentary adjustment of the angles and sensitivity of vision and hearing, and a breathless rippling pleasure as I touched the truest nature of my race. Thus Blaise and Farrol, and others like them, experienced shapeshifting. So I had felt it once when Denas and I had taken wing in the storm-racked demon land of Kir'Vagonoth. But on that hot morning, I felt as though my bones were cracking, as if my eyes were being squeezed out of my head, as if my skin were being peeled away by a Derzhi torturer's knife. Three rats hurriedly buried themselves in the rotting refuse, as I sank to my knees in groaning misery and forced myself into the shape of a bird.

My silent demon lurked within me like the worm at the core of a ripe fruit.

The Imperial Palace was ominously quiet. Its graceful cloisters and cavernous halls should have been bustling with gold-clad chamberlains and leather-clad hunting parties, with legions of slaves and servants, with white-robed warriors newly arrived from the desert, with stewards and clerks, their shoulders hunched with the burdens of running an expansive empire, with weapons makers and tailors, musicians and priests, and everywhere beautiful women dressed in silken gowns. But on that morning, as I fluttered through the latticed courtyards and shaded arbors, perching on balcony rails, listening at windows and doorways, I glimpsed only a few fearful slaves scouring footprints from the tile floors; every one of them had bruises and bloody streaks on face or shoulders. Nervous slave masters have heavy hands.

Here and there in corners, small knots of courtiers huddled whispering, their verdict the same as in the streets. A slave could never have done such a deed alone. Someone had drawn off the Emperor's bodyguards and ever-present courtiers. Someone had left a dagger in the Emperor's bedroom, where weapons were forbidden, and had told the slave where to find it. Someone powerful had thought to profit from this death, and it was clear who looked to profit the most—the same one who had been summoned to answer charges of conspiracy not two days previous, the same one who had been the object of the Emperor's screaming rage when closeted with him before last evening's meal, the same who had refused to sit at his father's table a mere three hours before the deed was done.

The rustle of my wings quickly scattered the gossips. The falcon was the symbol of the Emperor's Denischkar house, and those who noted me cast their eyes nervously to the heavens beyond my wings, as if expecting Athos himself to follow and render judgment on the cowardly villain responsible for this most heinous of all crimes—regicide, the murder of the god's own voice on earth.

I found Aleksander in the Hall of Athos, a vast columned temple dedicated to the sun god, built in the heart of the palace gardens. The soaring dome was sheathed with gold inside and out, and pierced with slits and delicately etched windows so that on every moment of the sun's path, sunbeams fell like fine lacework upon the floor. The thick stone walls held the coolness of the night just past, and the high windows and broad doorways drew in whatever fair breeze wandered over the city. I settled in one of the slots in the gilded dome. Far below me spread a vast floor of shining white marble, inlaid with patterns of cool green malachite. On it lay two bodies, one draped in gold and one in red, both mortally still. As if Athos' own beams were insufficient to the day, the two were surrounded by a thousand burning lamps of gold and silver, some set upon the floor, some hung on the forest of columns that supported the dome and the arched vaults of the side temples, some dangling from lamp stands of wrought silver and bronze. Among the lamps were braziers, burning sweet herbs and incense, so that wafting gray-green smokes obscured the mingled light of morning and the flickering death flames. At the great arched doorways that opened onto the Emperor's gardens stood guards, their naked backs rigid and their spears crossed. The silence was absolute.

My falcon's heart racing, I shot downward toward the two still figures and took a closer view. Raptor's instinct told me that only one of the two was dead. Ivan zha Denischkar, the one in gold. He lay upon a golden bier, four rampant lions with amethyst eyes holding up the corners, and he was draped in cloth of spun gold, adorned by a falcon worked in silver thread. The long white braid that lay over his right shoulder was unadorned, and a finely crafted sword, well used and plain, lay lengthwise on his body, hilt upon his chest. His face was cold and still. No sign of death terror for this man, stabbed by a gelded bodyslave as he was prepared for bed.

Aleksander lay facedown upon the stone floor, his long, lean form laid out square to his father's body. His arms were stretched to either side, the scarlet robe of mourning spread gracefully like the plumage of a fallen bird. His long red braid—the outward symbol of a Derzhi warrior's manhood—was gone, cut off, leaving just enough fiery red hair to touch the floor, like a shaggy curtain to protect his private grief.

I settled on the floor close beside the bier, behind a giant bronze statue of the sun god's horse. Shielded from view by the statue's massive base, I shifted back to human form. Again it took far too long, and I was near prostrate after, sweating as if I'd run ten leagues in the desert. My senses were near overwhelmed by the thickly scented smokes and perfumes, and I felt as if someone had slapped on blinders and stuffed my ears with wool as I reverted to my own sight and hearing.

I leaned against the block of marble and waited, trying to shake off the unhealthy disturbance of my shifting. The Prince had not moved since my first glimpse of him. How did he mourn his cold and ruthless father? The father who had indulged his every boyish whim, and then given him to his harsh uncle to raise as a warrior. The father who had condemned his only son to die when Aleksander could not prove his innocence of that uncle's death, and who had yielded only one fierce embrace when at last the truth came out and the executioner's ax was stayed. The father who had been unable to face the rigors of ruling after so close a brush with disaster and laid the mantle of empire on a young man who scarcely knew himself. This day would be very hard for Aleksander, far beyond treachery and danger and duplicity. If they had parted in anger, as rumor had it, things would likely be worse.

"Time gives us no indulgence, my lord," I said at last, speaking softly from my hiding place. "And so I must intrude upon your grieving. I wish I had no need." His enemies were moving.

A long while passed before he answered, as if he had a very

long way to come from wherever his thoughts had taken him. He did not shift a muscle, thus leaving his voice half muffled by the floor. "Have you a wish to die this day, Ezzarian?"

Despite the somber circumstance, I smiled. Whatever threat an observer might have noted in those words was belied by their history and the particular dry tone in which he voiced them. When I was a slave and the demon Khelid had afflicted Aleksander with an enchantment of sleeplessness, I had made a choice to venture the half-crazed Prince's presence to tell him of it. On that day he had spoken those words and meant them . . . and come very near fulfilling their mortal promise. Now they were a symbol of the gifts we had given each other.

"There seems to be a surfeit of death," I said. "That's why I've come."

"I cannot leave here before sunset." His quiet voice was slightly hoarse. It was almost midday, and he had likely taken up this vigil in the middle of the night. "It would do him dishonor."

"Then I'll wait until sunset. Though I've no cause to love the dead, for the sake of the living I would do him no dishonor."

"Oh, gods, Seyonne,"—the quiet words ripped through the suffocating scents and smokes of death—"what cause have I to love the dead? And yet I would neither move from here nor have the hours pass, because the next thing will be his burning, and nothing will be left of him." The Prince remained prostrate, as if bound to the cold stone.

I could say nothing to ease him. My own beloved father had been as different from Ivan zha Denischkar as lush, green Ezzaria was from the Azhaki desert; his death in the Derzhi war of conquest was still my own deepest sorrow. And so I could not guess how much of Aleksander's loss was love and how much was emptiness. Ivan had been ruler of all the known world for thirty-four years—a lion, a terror, a ferocious and intimidating warrior, the blazing, inescapable sun in Aleksander's sky.

Creeping darkness stirred within my head like a cat disturbed from afternoon sleep. *No. No. No.* Terrified that my murderous madness might explode so near the Prince, I called upon every mental discipline I knew to quell it. I had no time for madness. Kanavar had been spoken. Aleksander was going to die if we couldn't find some way to stop it. A man needed no prophet's gift to know this.

The Prince did not speak again through all the long afternoon, and I would not do so until he gave me leave. Perhaps even enemies and mortal danger needed to wait on grief. But I stayed with him and watched his back. My duty . . . and my desire . . . was to protect him. It was an unnerving thought that his nearest danger was likely my own hand. I watched that, too.

When the last remnants of the daylight had faded, leaving only the pale circles of lamplight in the smoky haze, Aleksander stirred. He pushed himself up to his knees, mumbling a soft curse as he stretched his shoulders and neck that must have been as stiff as unoiled leather. Then he turned around, sat back against his father's bier and glanced over at me, running his fingers through his short hair, as near embarrassment as I had ever seen him, more naked without his warrior's braid than when he was unclothed.

Though my instincts were screaming at me to hurry, I waited for him to begin.

"You're here to warn me of the kanavar, aren't you?"

I felt a bit of a fool. "You know of it?"

"In the past three months, my five most trusted advisers have died—one from rotten meat, one from a septic wound, two in drunken falls, one at the hand of his wife, who claimed to know nothing of the dagger in his throat even as she was hanged. During the same time, my three most reliable bodyguards have been discovered in intolerable disciplinary infractions—falling asleep on guard, dicing, thieving. All have been reassigned by their commanders. And the commanders themselves? Kasko has retired to his Capharna estates, suddenly deaf. Mersal has recently found a yearning to guard the frontiers instead of his prince. And when I summoned Mikael from Capharna, a man who would have considered himself blessed to lay down his life for me, he got himself dead in a paraivo. It seems he forgot his childhood lessons and set his tent in the dune path. When the storm came in the night, he was buried alive. Does it not seem a strange coincidence? The Hamraschi are so anxious to see me impotent, they make themselves ludicrous."

"But none of these deaths are provable as murder, and none can be linked to the Hamraschi." Derzhi were masters at such intrigues, Aleksander not least of all.

"They're clever enough. I'll give them that. They smirk when none but I can see it, while expressing concern to all that I am too whimsical and ruthless with those who dare disagree with me. To stand by me has become a death sentence."

"What of your wife, my lord?"

"Well out of the way. Once I understood their foul game, I took Baron Gematos' daughter to my bed and a slave girl or two—all of them quite willing, you'll be glad to know. You can well imagine how Lydia took to that. People thought the walls of Zhagad would fall at last. Then I put on my own display of temper. Three years wed with no heir . . . everyone was expecting it long ago." Someone would pay for forcing Aleksander into this. In only a few fatal instances had I heard his voice so soft and deadly. "I named my wife barren in front of half the nobility of Zhagad and dismissed her to her father in Avenkhar."

"Stars of night . . . and you didn't tell her why?"

"It's safer this way. Her father can protect her better than I at the moment. Kiril is safe, too. My idiot cousin had a brush with a poisoned dagger and a maddened horse before he believed my warnings and contrived a public falling out with me. I . . . persuaded . . . Sovari to go with him, and they are now guests of some crone of a Fontezhi baroness who enjoys hearing them complain about my cruel humors. Yours is the first friendly voice I've heard in months, and you don't sound too cheerful."

"They tried for me, too."

"Bloody Athos. Were you hurt?"

"A good man was killed instead. And others . . . it was a close thing."

Aleksander examined me carefully, and then his fists clenched and his cheeks flamed the color of his robes. "Your son . . . ah gods, Seyonne. Not your son." No one could read a man's unspoken words as Aleksander could.

"He's safe for now, and the namhirra are dead."

"How in Druya's fires did they find you? I'll swear I told no one but Lydia, and no matter what she thinks of me, she would never betray you."

"I never thought it. I understand about palaces and servants, rumors and spies . . . a messenger could have followed me when I picked up your message in Vayapol . . . any number of slips."

"I'll find him . . . whoever it was. I'll have him dead for it."

"What's done is done. Blaise has hidden the boy so even I don't know where he is now." I leaned closer and dropped my voice. "But you . . . this business of your father . . . it's part of it?"

He closed his eyes and shook his head. "No. Not even the Hamraschi could be such fools. Why make me emperor when they are bent on undoing everything I've tried to accomplish?"

So he didn't see the truest danger. "My lord Prince, in the streets they are saying you commanded your father's death. They're saying the Twenty will—"

"These matters are not settled in the streets. I am my father's anointed heir. It will take more than peasants' prattling to undo it." Even on that dismal night, the Prince could not unmake himself. His scorn could wither a healthy oak.

"But you quarreled."

Aleksander grimaced. "A month ago I was on the Suzaini border. Bandits—damned villains threatening ruin across the whole eastern Empire. Twenty villages already destroyed, granaries ravaged up and down the border, horses stolen or slaughtered. In the midst of the campaign, my father summons me back here to answer 'unnamed charges.' If I'd left right then—"

"You refused an imperial summons?" No wonder Ivan had been furious with him.

The Prince was twisting the hem of his mourning robe, a long red cloak, fastened about his neck with a band of silverwork. "We'd lost nineteen warriors already, chasing the cursed bandits. I wasn't going to waste their deaths to answer some pissing accusations no one would explain."

And abandoning the mission would have left the Suzaini to starve. Their granaries and horses were their life. When Aleksander was twenty-two, he wouldn't have considered that.

"So I finished cleaning up the mess, then rode like a paraivo. Got here yesterday at dawn. Found the paraivo was already here."

"No doubt." A god-raised desert sandstorm would be nothing to Ivan's rage.

Aleksander leaned forward, his face ruddy with remembered anger. "And who was with him but Leonid, the Second Lord of the Hamrasch, so concerned at the insolence and insubordination of my delay, the very one who had brought 'certain matters' to my father's attention . . . All of it stupid. Contrived. It would have taken only a day to clear it up."

But the Prince had been tired and angry and headstrong as always. "You weren't given a day."

He glanced up sharply. "No. It's only *my* neck they want. Murdering my father as well is not going to get them anything. We don't do things that way. Until I have a son, my heir is my father's cousin Edik, a puling coward who makes me look scholarly and temperate. But the rest of the Denischkar would fight for him anyway, and the other hegeds would never allow old Hamrasch to say who sits the throne. It would be the end of the Hamraschi; the entire heged would die."

But of course that was the very problem. Clearly the Hamraschi didn't care if they died. What in the name of the gods had Aleksander done to raise a kanavar from one of the most powerful Derzhi families?

From outside the room came the droning of a mellanghar and a powerful male voice beginning the Derzhi mourning song, a winding, wordless lament that could make a mountain weep. Rage drained from the Prince's face. He shook his head slightly and waved his hand, as if to silence his own thoughts, and then got slowly to his feet, turning his back to me. "I'll be occupied until dawn. Come to my apartments then and we'll talk. Be discreet, Seyonne. I'd not lose you, too."

"My lord, I need to go . . ." I'd not yet told him all I'd learned. Did he even know that the Frythian had accused him? But the time was not right to tell him anything. As Aleksander stood beside his father's body, his broad shoulders grew rigid. Curious, I slipped quietly to the edge of the marble block where I could get a broader view of the hall to see what had alerted him.

No unseemly disturbance or untimely intrusion had caused Aleksander's tension, however, but his own act. Beneath his red and silver cloak, the Prince wore black breeches and a sleeveless shirt of embroidered red silk, and now he had used his father's sword to cut three long gashes in his bare left arm. As I watched, he did the same to his right and began drawing circles about his eyes and on his cheeks with the blood. He had already forgotten I was there.

I withdrew into my niche, trying to convince myself that I could manage shifting form again. If I was going to stay through the night, then I might as well be useful and keep up my watch. And no non-Derzhi was going to get near Ivan's funeral rites. As

I sat there in the smoky dimness, trying to summon the will to shift, someone in soft slippers hurried across the vast room.

"Your Highness, the procession is engaged." The gold-clad chamberlain dropped to his knees behind the Prince, whispering just loud enough to hear. "The bearers await your command . . ."

Aleksander, eyes fixed on his father's body, gave a slight nod. But the chamberlain did not go.

". . . and, Your Highness, please forgive me for carrying any other message than those required by this most mortal . . . most dreadfully grievous . . . and I would not speak it if not commanded by my lord High Chamberlain, who was himself commanded by His Highness, who waits outside . . . demanding . . . insisting . . . most kind lord that he is—"

I winced. The servant's craven, crawling stuttering was just the quality to put an edgy man violently out of humor. And Aleksander was a very edgy man. The Prince did not raise his voice, but might have bitten the words out of the stone floor. "Speak or I'll rip out your useless tongue."

"I am bade to tell you that His Highness, Prince Edik, has arrived in Zhagad and says he must see his beloved Emperor and cousin laid out before the rites begin."

Before Aleksander could answer, a clattering of boots and unmuted voices violated the reverent stillness of the temple. No servants this time. I could hear the clink of gold chains around their necks and feel the steel menace of their weapons. The very air carried the assurance of royal privilege. The newcomers stood on the far side of the bier, just out of my line of sight.

"Shades of Druya, Aleksander. You look like some barbarian priest calling up gods to protect his village. No one's done this kind of silly blood-marking in three hundred years." The visitor had a lilting voice that curled around its edges, as if he were forever on the verge of sneering laughter. "One might think you were actually mourning the old devil's passing."

"Have you come to lick at the trough now he's dead, Edik? Do you think I've forgotten that he forbade you to stand or speak in his presence?"

"Ah, my young cousin, this is the time to draw up the ties of blood, not—"

"On your knees, Edik, and hold your coward's tongue! You are in the presence of your Emperor, and until he is ash, you will obey him." Aleksander strode to the end of the bier. "Bring in the bearers!"

No one in the palace could have failed to hear Aleksander's scornful rebuke of his visitor. But only I, with a Warden's hearing, could have heard the visitor's whispered response, buried as it was beneath the shuffling clamor of those who came to carry Ivan to his pyre. "And afterward, dear cousin Zander . . . once my cousin is burned and only you are left . . . then what?"

I crept along the floor far enough to glimpse the three on the far side of the empty bier, and the odor of danger was so strong, it almost gagged me. Two Hamrasch lords stood smiling at Aleksander's back, and before them, kneeling on the floor, was a middle-aged man. His sleek blond braid fell to the side of his placid face. No anger twisted his full lips; no offense or indignation marred his wide brow or glinted in his narrow-spaced eyes. But he had ridden into Zhagad with a troop of Hamrasch warriors, and he propped his hands and his chin on a stick of polished wood, still stained with the blood of a clumsy slave.

CHAPTER 5

Derzhi inheritance was strictly through the male line. Horses, land, titles—and in the case of the Denischkar heged, the Lion Throne—passed from eldest son to eldest son. Fortunately or unfortunately, the most recent generations of the royal branch of the widespread, powerful Denischkar family had produced few children of either sex. Aleksander was Ivan's only child. Ivan's only brother Dmitri, Aleksander's harsh and well-loved likai, had been childless when he was murdered by the Khelid. Aleksander's closest cousin Kiril was of the female line, the son of Ivan's widowed sister Rahil and therefore unable to inherit, dependent upon the Emperor for his position and fortune. And so to find the man who stood next in line to Aleksander, one had to look back another generation, to Varat, a younger brother of Aleksander's grandfather. Varat himself was long dead in some Derzhi war, as was his youngest brother Stefan, but Varat had left an only son, Prince Edik. It appeared that the Hamraschi had no intention of wresting the throne from Aleksander's family . . . only from Aleksander.

Though I had served in the Emperor's summer palace in Capharna for some five months, I knew little of Edik. One of my previous masters, an elderly Derzhi baron, claimed that Edik had once abandoned fifty warriors to be slaughtered by the Basranni, and was therefore a proven coward whose braid should be shorn. Perhaps true, perhaps not—the baron was not always the most accurate in his history. But I knew that Edik did not change expression when he beat a helpless man.

I did not leave Aleksander that night. There were few enough honorable people in the imperial court. I knew of none save his wife, the Princess Lydia, his personal guard captain, Sovari, and his cousin Kiril who understood Aleksander well enough to truly love him. No others could he trust to guard his back.

Derzhi custom required the disposition of a corpse no more and no less than one day after death. Desert life demanded quick resolution, but the gods had to be served, too, and by allowing the sun to rise on the lifeless body, one allowed the gods to see clearly what had come to pass. Perhaps it gave them a chance to intervene if they desired.

Such speedy disposition precluded most of the powerful from attending Ivan's rites, as it would take weeks for the principal heged lords to travel from their widespread holdings. But every heged was required to maintain a household in Zhagad and to have at least one male relative in direct line of its first lord living there at all times. These were not hostages, of course; the idea of hostages from their own houses was repugnant to the Derzhi. They were informants, conveyors of the Emperor's pleasure to their honored families. And each household had its own garrison, sized in proportion to the importance of the house and available to serve at the Emperor's command. But whatever the reasons and explanations, as a result, all Derzhi families were represented in the funeral procession. As soon as I had shifted into falcon's form and made accommodation yet again with altered senses, I flew through the deserted palace toward the sound of the singing, hunting for those I needed to know.

A torchlit procession wound slowly through the streets of Zhagad toward the desert. Following a row of singers and priests rode troops of Derzhi warriors, from grizzled lords to youths with new braids, all of them wearing the patterned scarves or colored tef-coats of their hegeds. Small groups of red-robed women walked or rode alongside the men, as was their heged custom. At the front of the procession came representatives of the Ten—the most venerable of the two hundred or more Derzhi families—the kayeet-crested Fontezhi, the highly traditional, blue-coated Gorusch, the despicable Nyabozzi, who controlled the slave trade, the Marag in their long green-striped scarves, and the rest of them. The Marag were the family of Aleksander's wife, and it was the Princess's downy-cheeked, sixteen-year-old brother, Damok, who led the Marag warriors. Behind the Ten rode the remainder of the Council of Twenty, hegeds not so ancient as the Ten, but some of them even wealthier and more powerful, like the Hamraschi. The Council had little true power; the Emperor's word was absolute in every instance. But every heged had its legions of warriors, and strength was everything to the Derzhi.

After the Twenty, some fifty or sixty people marched chained together—one for each of the lands and peoples subject to the

Empire. The sullen prisoners—some young, some old, all gaping stupidly at the crowds—were people of no significance. The kings and nobles, wisewomen and chieftains of the conquered lands had all been slaughtered, their noble lineage vanished into history. Many of the long-defeated peoples like the Suzaini, the Manganar, and the Thrid were no longer enslaved, and now formed the working heart of the Empire. But the Emperor kept one prisoner of each race, picked at random and held until death in his dungeons as a symbol of his domination, and they were paraded through the streets on occasions such as this.

The Emperor's heged, the Denischkari, followed the prisoners. Beside Edik rode the short, square-shouldered Kiril, his face like stone, and a handsome older woman dressed in flowing red—Kiril's mother, no doubt, the Princess Rahil. Rahil had married for love, so Aleksander had told me, to the younger son of a minor house. The marriage was an intolerable disgrace to her family. On the day Kiril was born, Rahil's brother, the Emperor, had sent her husband into a battle where the young noble was certain to die. Rahil had never spoken to Ivan again, though the Emperor had lavished on Kiril the father's fondness he had withheld from Aleksander. Kiril was permitted to ride with the Denischkari, as a concession to his royal blood, rather than being consigned to the roadside, as were other nobles of minor houses.

Behind the Denischkari came Ivan, laid out on a gold-draped wagon pulled by ten fine horses. Ivan's own mount, a magnificent bay, followed riderless, nervous, as if he knew he was to be slain and burned beside his fallen master. And after them all strode Aleksander, tall and proud, his red cloak billowing behind him in the chill night breeze risen off the desert. His feet were bare, his blood-marked face cold and haughty, his gaze wavering not one mezzit to either side of him. He might have walked right off the etched and painted stone tablets that decorated Derzhi halls. No bodyguard rode beside him or behind him, yet I doubted anyone would dare strike at him directly. For that moment the Prince wore the mantle of empire, given him by the fierce old warrior still very much in view. As long as Ivan existed in Derzhi eyes, any hand that touched Aleksander must surely risk the gods' wrath.

I flew from one perch to another, seeking a place from which to observe the Hamrasch lords. At last I settled on a monument to some long-dead emperor and sat among the stone vultures who were pecking out the eyes of the emperor's vanquished foe. From there I could stare into the grizzled face of Zedeon, the First Lord of the Hamrasch, a short, craggy, gray-braided veteran of the Basran war. He wore a golden tef-coat with no shirt underneath, the sleeveless garment exposing a broad chest and upper arms as thick as Kuvai oaks. A narrow red scarf was tied about his bare left arm with something held in the knot. It was a sprig of nyamot, the tiny white flower that bloomed after a desert rain.

Flanking Zedeon were his middle-aged sons, Dovat and Leonid, the two who had accompanied Edik to the palace. Their stern faces were no comfort for one who cared for Aleksander. I'd had occasion to observe Leonid when I was a slave. Intelligent, I had always thought him, well-spoken, always a surprise among a warrior race that prided itself on illiteracy. Ruthless, as were most powerful Derzhi, but not exceptionally cruel. Dovat, the younger of the two brothers, squat and rough like his father, I didn't know at all. Leonid and Dovat also wore red scarves and the incongruous nyamot about their arms, as did every other warrior of their heged. Odd. Their family symbol was the gold tef-coat sewn with a howling wolf.

The procession passed beyond the gates of the inner ring of Zhagad. Inside the wall the onlookers, members of the lower houses, had been solemn as their betters passed them by, not mourning Ivan so much, I guessed, as weighing the chances for the future. A disputed succession was a fearful prospect, only slightly less disturbing than being ruled by a Derzhi son who would murder his father. Once the Emperor's body passed into the outer ring, the crowds to either side of the roadway surged forward, women wailing, men hoisting sons and daughters upon their shoulders to see. The din grew deafening, and I fought the urge to streak for a nearby rooftop. As I passed back and forth above the procession, I was distracted by a glimpse of brilliant green among the crowd—a woman standing between two of the torchbearers that lit the way, the same woman I'd seen watching as I helped the fallen slave on my arrival in Zhagad. Were her eyes following my flight through the murky light? I circled closer, but she had already vanished into the crowd.

I maintained my watch upon the Hamraschi until the procession passed through the outer gates, traveling along the Emperor's road between the paired stone lions that guarded the approaches to the city. On the desolate plain stood a massive pyre, built with trees dragged by chastou from the sparse forests of the eastern uplands. They placed Ivan's body on a platform atop the pyre, and a giant Lidunni warrior wielded the sword to kill the Emperor's horse bound near the foot of it. With torches carried from the temple of Athos, the acolytes set the base of the pyre to burning.

Derzhi funeral rites were magnificent—wild music and singing to wrench the soul, pageantry and customs that drew on centuries of heged traditions. Unlike their Basranni kin, the Derzhi did not engage in long-winded storytelling, but rather reenacted the glorious deeds of the deceased with dancing.

To the murmured astonishment of the assembly, Aleksander himself stripped off his mourning garments and, clad only in a loincloth and blood, danced the story of his father's journey into the afterlife. With ferocious grace his long, lean body evoked the ritual battle with the sun god—a demonstration of the dead warrior's strength and worth—and then a final acceptance of a seat at the god's right hand. The dancing did not stop when the Prince returned to his place. Rather it became wilder as the night grew late and the flames grew high, the dezrhila dancers whirling in the rapture of ancient deities nearly forgotten in the glory of the young sun god Athos.

I fluttered through the smoke, watching Aleksander, watching the crowd, watching the Hamraschi. The hegeds sat in a circle about the burning mound. Old Zedeon sat cross-legged in front of a hundred Hamrasch warriors, his sword laid across the sand in front of him, as was the custom in times of war. Leonid and Dovat were no longer beside him, but rather sat with the representatives of other houses. As the night wore on, the two Hamraschi moved about the circle, always respectful, but eventually sitting with every one of the Twenty hegeds, whispering quietly with the lords. Aleksander, seated at the front of the Denischkar family, kept his eyes fixed on the pyre, but I suspected he had noted the Hamrasch brothers, too. Prince Edik sat behind Aleksander, his soft face expressionless. When the pyre caved in upon itself, exploding in whorls of sparks so that the heavens were adorned with a whole new array of stars, Edik smiled. And when the crowd began to wind its sleepy way back toward Zhagad, Edik, Leonid, and Dovat rode together.

* * *

"Horns of the bull, Seyonne, what are you doing to yourself?"

I knelt in the corner of a flower-decked balcony, retching into a stone planter and holding my head, praying my skull wouldn't crack before I emptied my stomach. "Haven't got the hang of this shifting business yet," I said as I slumped back against the balcony wall, shivering in the dawn chill. "A useful skill, but no pleasure at the moment." Another factor in my problem—the longer I stayed shifted, the worse was the return.

"So it *was* you hovering about all night." The Prince stood in the open doorway, the rosy light revealing the haggard truth of his blood-marked, unshaven face. We must have looked a dismal pair.

"Thought I ought to keep an eye on things."

Aleksander disappeared into the dim room for a moment, and then returned to the balcony with a crystal carafe and two silver goblets. He tossed one of the cups to me, and then sank heavily to the stone floor and poured wine. "So you saw the Hamrasch wolves on the prowl. Observing Edik safely in their grasp, I am forced to concede your point. It appears they have decided that another branch of the family must rule the Empire."

"What is their grievance, my lord?" I sipped the wine. Though I craved water more than wine, I could not refuse the Prince's hospitality, certainly not when I was asking an exceedingly uncomfortable question.

"Will you leave if the matter is not to your liking?" Aleksander downed his wine in one long pull, and then threw the delicate cup hard into the corner. Not the same corner where I sat, which was better than I might have hoped. His anger was not directed at me.

"If I can help, I will."

The flare of temper was quickly extinguished. Elbows propped on his knees, Aleksander massaged the center of his brow. "I told you last year that I'd have to bring the Hamraschi into line. They challenged my authority."

The Empire had seen increasing unrest in the previous year, at the time I was a prisoner in the demon realm. Blaise's outlaw band had rubbed the hegeds raw, causing havoc by their pursuit of justice for the Empire's populace. Several hegeds had declared their own war on the outlaws—and on Aleksander if he blocked their way. The Derzhi had stood at the brink of civil war. We had found a solution but had never believed it more than temporary.

"I planned to wed their children into loyal houses," said Aleksander. "It's the way of things among us . . . you know that. So I married Leonid's eldest daughter to Bohdan, the son of the Rhyzka first lord. The match was suitable. Rhyzka is a venerable house. The bride gifts were paid—fine horses, gold. No shame or disgrace save that I did the choosing instead of Leonid." The Prince leaned back against the wall. "Only I didn't know Bohdan. A brute. The worst . . . bloody Athos, a rai-kirah would have been better. And the girl . . . she was only ten. Bohdan didn't wait. Within a month, the child was dead. The Hamrasch custom is to bury their women, so Leonid went to retrieve her body, and he saw what had been done to her. Her name was Nyamot."

Thus the delicate flowers worn on the arms of the Hamraschi. A beloved daughter of a mighty house. "You are the arbiter of justice, my lord. Even for Derzhi, there are limits."

"Well, you see, that's been the problem with my position. My father would not rule his own empire, yet everything I did was subject to his decree. Publicly he sympathized with the Hamraschi, ruing my misjudgment in arranging the match. Privately he forbade me to punish Bohdan, as the Rhyzka hold the border beyond Karn'Hegeth—the most dangerous frontier in all the Empire. I could strip him of titles, burden him with taxes and horse levies—petty annoyances—but I could not touch a man who would brutalize a child. I could not give him to the Hamraschi for justice. I could not allow him to be harmed." The carafe followed the silver cup into the corner, shattering into glittering pieces. "I've defied my father's will in many things, but the safety of the border . . . it would have been legitimate treason." Aleksander looked up at me, clear-eyed and bitter. "The worst part is that I believe he was right. My duty is to the security of the Empire."

And so Ivan had reaped the result of it, as would Aleksander and thousands of others. Nothing useful could be said. "Now the Hamraschi are courting Prince Edik," I said.

"No surprise. Jackals find the weak in any herd."

Voices murmured from inside Aleksander's apartments. The Prince jumped up and stepped inside, motioning for me to stay where I was. "Yes, I'm still awake," he said. "Not likely to be anything else today. Certainly not with all of you standing in here gabbling."

"Your Highness, messages have arrived."

"Send them up, and tell Hessio I want a hot bath."

"Aye, my lord, and something to eat . . . ?"

"Something . . . yes . . . anything . . . Enough for two."

He stepped out again and dropped his voice. "Will you stay? I might need a strong sword arm today. I'm going after the Hamraschi." It was spoken diffidently . . . yet he had asked. He must be truly worried.

But it would be a grave mistake for him to rely on me. "Today, yes. I'll stay. But I can't—"

"After today, one way or the other, I don't think it will matter. You can turn yourself into a bird again and fly back to your friends."

To confess that my sword arm was no longer reliable would be no easy matter, and attempting to explain my madness would be worse. I tried to begin, but Aleksander gave me no opening. He thought I was trying to dispute his decision. "My lord, I cannot—"

"The Hamraschi have murdered the Emperor of the Derzhi. There's no question as to their guilt; Zedeon brought me a Frythian dagger as his funeral gift. Whether or not anyone else believes my accusation, I have to take them down, and I have to do it immediately, before negotiations, before investigations, before the Council of Twenty convenes to crown me . . . or someone else . . . Emperor. If I do nothing, I'll be admitting my own guilt or my weakness, which is much the same."

No wonder he needed a strong sword arm. "Have you the men to do it?"

He shrugged and ran his fingers through his ragged hair. "Old Zedeon likely has more than a token garrison at his Zhagad stronghold. To take him I'll need at least a thousand warriors. The bulk of my own troops are still in the desert somewhere between here and Suzain—do you begin to see the beauty of their plan? So I've had to call upon the other hegeds who have garrisons here in the city. I sent out the command to all of them before I came back from the rites. Shall we go inside and discover who sees fit to support their Emperor-in-waiting?"

It would have been exceedingly convenient if I could have shifted easily into a mouse or a plant or one of the hundred cats that slunk about the royal palace. As it was, I had to face the curious stares of Aleksander's gentlemen attendants and courtiers as I followed him into the richly furnished apartment. The floor was sand-colored tile, shot through with the deep blue of lapis.

Silk cushions and couches of red and blue were positioned throughout the large airy room, with lamps of brass and crystal set on low, round tables of exotic woods inlaid with ebony. Traditional Derzhi sand paintings of exquisite artistry hung on the walls, and silver wind chimes hung beside the open windows. But the fairest decorations were the window prospects themselves. Aleksander's apartments occupied the highest reaches of the north tower of the palace, where the slightest breeze would find its way under his high ceilings, and between the sitting rooms and bedchambers, he would command views in every direction. One window after another displayed the graceful arches of Zhagad and, beyond them, the purple and gold vastness of the desert. To the north one could see the distant shimmer of snowcaps, the mountains where lay Capharna, the Empire's summer capital, where, on a winter's day five years before, Aleksander had bought me for twenty zenars.

"The scribe is on his way, Your Highness," said a chinless, high-voiced courtier who held a silver tray stacked with small rolls of parchment.

Aleksander, who was allowing a slight, fair-haired slave to remove his red cloak, snapped his head around to me and waggled his eyebrows. "No. I think not." He waved off the bodyslave, who was attempting to unfasten his shirt. "I've engaged a new scribe. I've heard he is quite capable, if not particularly refined. We'll have to induce him to clean himself, or the chamberlains will think he's a slave and lock him up." Indeed I was a filthy, stinking mess. "So you agree to the position, whatever your name is?"

I bowed low, shaking my hair to the side of my face where it might help hide my slave mark.

"Give him the messages, and show him where the writing materials are to be found. And pass him flatbread and some of these figs. I can't bear a servant who looks as though he'll eat my carpets."

Before I had broken the first seal, the Prince was naked, reclining on blue silk cushions and eating dates while the fair-haired Hessio, his longtime bodyslave, tended the angry wounds on his arms. Another soft-faced youth washed his face, hands, and feet. The position was so familiar, an echoed memory, that I found myself checking my wrists to make sure no slave rings had been sealed about them while I wasn't looking.

"So tell me the news, my scribe. Time gives us no indulgence, as a wise man told me quite recently. Malver here is waiting to take the message to his captains—shall we have a thousand warriors or two hundred to destroy a nest of murderers?"

Three unsmiling soldiers stood attentively before the Prince. One of them, a short, wiry man with a scar on his chin, bowed slightly to Aleksander. I could not guess his ancestry—his skin was the color of old leather, and his close-trimmed hair and beard were mottled gray and black. From his lack of a braid, his plain dress unmarked with any heged symbol, and his air of unassuming competence, I judged him a professional soldier—a lowborn man who had risen to a post of responsibility through hard work rather than family. His companions were bigger, typical ruddy-faced Derzhi warriors with full beards, long braids, and sun-darkened shoulders protruding from leather vests marked with the Denischkar falcon. Hovering by the door were a handful of chamberlains and messengers, as much a part of the royal furnishings as were the tables or cushions. And beyond them, standing in the shadows of the great arched doorway, was a tall woman in brilliant green. Her hair was hidden by her filmy veil, but her eyes were dark as desert midnight and riveted on my own. Her mouth formed words I could not hear.

"Have you lost your voice, then?" Aleksander was frowning at me. "Read the replies."

I started and bent my head to the stiff page.

The first message was terse. *Twenty warriors of the Fontezhi garrison are available at Prince Aleksander's command.*

"Twenty!" one of the bearded men bellowed. "The Fontezhi garrison numbers three hundred. My lord—"

"The next, scribe." Aleksander ate another date and allowed Hessio to begin shaving his chin.

I unrolled the next stiff paper, glancing briefly across the room to the doorway. The woman in green was gone.

The Rhyzka heged will supply a hundred and twenty-five warriors at the Prince's pleasure. The house stable master will also be alerted to supply twenty-five extra horses, three armorers, and two surgeons.

"Ah, my loyal Rhyzka. What prince dares offend such an ally?" Aleksander sat up abruptly, causing the fair Hessio to yank the razor-knife away and lose what color he had in his boyish face. All royal bodyslaves were gelded; the slave master in

Capharna had told me that Hessio was, in fact, almost forty. The Prince grimaced and waved at Hessio to continue. Or perhaps it was to me. The next message was longer.

> *My lord Aleksander,*
> *I have heard your command to supply a suitable levy of warriors by midday to carry out justice for your most honored and glorious imperial father's untimely death. Before I commit Gorusch men, I must beg indulgence to appear before you and submit questions which I know my first lord would require be answered before engaging in such a dreadful enterprise. In short, there are disturbing accusations which bear upon the honor and rightness of this cause—*

"Read the next." Aleksander was as red as the cushion under his feet, and Hessio's delicate hand trembled as he quickly finished his risky enterprise with the razor-knife.

I nodded and broke the next seal. Every response was similar. A token offering, sure to be the dregs of the house legions, stable boys, or unbraided youths. Or an excuse—rampant flux among the garrison or their lamentable absence at this exact time—or specific orders of the heged lord to commit the troops elsewhere on this particular day. For some, as for the excessively traditional Gorusch heged, some question needed to be answered before commitment. Unspoken was the real question—had Aleksander truly murdered his own father as reliable reports had it? Aleksander's brother-in-law, the young Marag, sent a terse "none," with no excuse or explanation. A bold lad.

By the time I finished reading the replies, Aleksander was standing up, half dressed in leather breeches, white shirt, and thick leather vest. His fists were clenched, his face a storm of humiliated rage. But when he spoke, his voice was controlled, marred only by bitter irony. "We must assume that my Denischkar troops will not arrive from Suzain in time. By my tally we have two hundred sixty warriors, give or take a pittance. If we strip the palace garrison and use the damned Thrid hirelings, we might muster five hundred seventy men. See them ready, Malver."

The dark wiry man was about to explode. "But, my lord, that's nowhere near—"

"Do not question me, Commander! I said see them ready. We ride for the Hamrasch stronghold in one hour. The Emperor will have his justice, whether his subjects think it fit or no." Slaves were waiting with Aleksander's boots, sword belt, and a white cloak, embroidered in gold. A Derzhi prince did not wear the haf-fai—the all-encompassing desert robe—lest his enemies mistake him for a common man and hold back the ferocity that was his due.

Malver bowed and withdrew. Behind his back, where no one but I could have seen it, his right hand made the village-bred man's sign against ill luck.

The two bearded warriors and the rest of the attendants hovered about Aleksander. "All of you, get out of here and see to your own preparation. I'll be down when I have my boots on. The assassins will not win this day."

I dawdled long enough, cleaning up the broken wax and stack of papers, that only Hessio was left. Aleksander stood stiff and silent while the bodyslave buckled on his weapons and fastened the cloak to brass rings on the shoulders of his leather vest. As the slender man finished his work, he knelt, bending his head toward the blue-veined tiles. Aleksander touched the slave's shoulder, stopping his obeisance before he could get all the way down. "You've done me good service, Hessio. Since I was ten years old, I think."

"It is and will ever be my honor to serve you, Your Highness." The soft, high-pitched voice expressed surprise. Bodyslaves were rarely spoken to. They lived their unending degradation in silence, always gentle and courteous, required to know what needed to be done and to do it with minimal intrusion . . . always afraid, for such intimate service lent itself to danger. Naked royalty was prone to irritation.

"You remember Seyonne, do you not?" An unsettling note charged the Prince's casual words.

"Yes, my lord." The slave's eyes shot toward me, a hard glance that nearly knocked me off the stool. Hatred. The bitter, unrelenting hatred of one who wore slave rings for one who no longer did so. Aleksander saw it, too, and he nodded ever so slightly. I didn't understand.

"Do you know that you are the only man in the palace who also served me in Capharna three years ago?" said the Prince. "The only man in Zhagad, save my cousin Kiril and Captain Sovari, who knew the name of the Ezzarian slave who saved my life or could describe him to another. The only man in all the world who could have heard me tell my wife where my friend Seyonne could be found if she needed him . . . and I never breathed that secret to another soul, and she the same." The hand on Hessio's shoulder gripped tight. The colorless slave winced and tried to shrink away, but the hand would not allow it. "This is the day for justice, Hessio. And it shall begin here." With a movement unimaginably quick, the Prince's knife ripped Hessio's throat. Skillfully Aleksander pushed the dead slave away, so that the blood pooling darkly on the sand-colored tiles did not stain his white cloak.

The Prince wiped his knife on Hessio's garments, and then sheathed it and walked to the window without looking at me. "You disapprove."

I resumed breathing and chose my words carefully. "The man who died for me had only one leg. The Hamrasch assassins cut off his hands to make him tell where I was. There is justice and there is mercy, and when I think of Gordain, I can see only one of them." Of course, none of that had anything to do with the fate of a slave whose manhood had been stolen along with his freedom. The sweet flavor of justice so often sours into vengeance. I wished he had not done it, and he knew it without my saying so.

"It's likely the only battle we'll win this day. Pitiful, eh?"

"The gods will have their say in that, my lord."

"Did you know that the last time it rained in Zhagad was the day of my birth?" Aleksander swung around, gazing bleakly into my eyes, seeking answers I could not give him. "My father said that to my uncle once, on a day when I was showing off my sword work for my father and accidentally killed my sparring partner. They'd had me stripped naked and beaten in front of them for my poor control. I heard Dmitri answer him, 'I think the gods were weeping for the Empire on that day. Tell me, brother, do you think they were tears of grief or tears of joy?' "

"And what did your father answer?"

Aleksander turned his back to the window, leaving his face in shadow. "I was fifteen and angry. I didn't listen to his answer."

CHAPTER 6

The battle was lost before it was begun. By the time Aleksander approached the Hamrasch stronghold, a massive fortress set atop a rocky bluff an hour's ride from Zhagad, he had no more than three hundred fifty warriors, half of them the despised Thrid mercenaries. Some of the promised heged levies never appeared. Some melted away in the noonday heat—groups of five or ten, riding west or east instead of south toward the confrontation. Some laggards complained of tired horses or lack of water or insufficient time to prepare, and returned to Zhagad as soon as the main body of the troop moved on. Fortunately it was still spring, else the desert would have taken its own toll upon the rest.

Aleksander had not come to lay siege to the fortress. He stopped well before the gates and sent his challenge to the heged lords, naming them guilty for the crime of regicide, offering no terms but death in combat or execution. To accept his challenge meant that only the warriors of the heged would fight and die—a mercy he was willing to offer because of the untimely death of their beloved daughter Nyamot. To refuse the Prince's challenge was to admit Hamrasch guilt in the Emperor's murder, leaving every member of the heged liable to his judgment—forfeiture of all property, execution or enslavement of every man, woman, and child. It was a prideful challenge for one whose army was outnumbered five to one.

The messenger returned with a bundle of nyamot, tied with a red ribbon. The Prince wheeled his mount and returned to confer with his commanders and to wait patiently in the blazing sun for the sortie from the fortress.

I did not ride with Aleksander. We had walked together from his apartments down to the bustling yards where the palace garrison was preparing to ride out, and he had pointed to a burly Manganar who was commanding a legion of scurrying armorers. "Fredovar can give you a sword. I'll tell him to find one that pleases you. And you can have your pick of horses. Whatever nag you're riding, I doubt it's good enough for this."

"My lord." I stopped on the last step, forcing the Prince to turn back to hear me. "I've been trying to tell you. I cannot go with you today. Anything else . . ." I suspected what was going to happen with the levied troops, and he did, and I knew he would see my refusal as but the first betrayal of the day.

Aleksander's face burned scarlet. He had humbled himself to ask for my help, but hadn't bothered to listen to my reply. "Ah yes. I forgot. Ezzarian Wardens fight no one but demons . . . and *you* don't even do that anymore. I misunderstood your offer." The Prince strode toward a groom who was holding his prized horse, Musa.

I could not let Aleksander go into battle believing I had deserted him. "My lord, please listen. I *will* be there." Just not at his side.

The Prince did not slow down or even turn his head. "You can write the story of it then."

Aleksander gave me no time to tell him of my unhealed injury, I told myself. And yet how long would it have taken to say I was no longer the man he had seen defeat the Lord of Demons? That I could not fight beside him because I was afraid my weakness would endanger him? No words are more difficult for a warrior, and before I could force them out, the sea of Derzhi warriors had parted to let him pass, and then closed up again behind him. "I'll be there, my lord," I called after him, but I couldn't tell if he heard me.

I stood watching the mustering troops without seeing them, my desire to run after the Prince and tell him that of course I would stand with him, battling with my need to come up with a sensible alternative in a hurry. But as my eyes drifted over the teeming crowd, a patch of bright green drew me out of my thoughts—the woman in green again, an island of stillness in the center of fifty warriors who were checking saddle girths, attaching waterskins to their saddles, settling weapons in sheaths, donning padded leather vests under their haffai. As if drawn by enchantment, I jumped down the steps and hurried toward the woman, determined to find out who she was and why she was watching me.

Before I could get near her, five warriors rode through the courtyard gates in a spurt of red dust, pulling up at the side of the yard not twenty paces from me, ready for the Prince to assign them a position. Their leader was short in the saddle, but broad shouldered and hard muscled. His braid was blond, and his square face was dusted with freckles, making him appear much younger than his twenty-seven years, even with his current severe countenance—Lord Kiril Rahilezar Danileschi zha Ramiell, Aleksander's charming and honorable cousin.

Aleksander walked past the young lord without a glance, stopping to speak to Malver for a moment. Then the Prince strode briskly among the assembled garrison, inspecting their arms as they stood beside their horses. As he nodded his approval at each warrior, the man would mount up. Malver rode over to Kiril and bowed his head respectfully.

"I've brought a levy of my personal guard," said Kiril coldly, "though the Prince's summons seems to have gone astray. I'll not have it said that I failed in loyalty to my fallen Emperor."

"Your warriors are not needed, Lord Kiril," said Malver.

"Not needed?" blurted Kiril. "Has Prince Aleksander such a surfeit that he can pick and choose? I *will* fight for my uncle's honor." Kiril urged his horse forward, as if to force himself into the Derzhi column, but Malver positioned his own mount across the young noble's path. "You will not, my lord. The Prince says he will have women carry swords at his side before he will permit you to do so."

Kiril flushed the color of a desert sunrise. Setting his jaw, he jerked on the reins and spoke a single harsh word to his men. The party started toward the gates. I slipped around the edge of the yard and caught Kiril's ankle before he could follow his warriors out of the gates. He snapped his head around, his hand flying to his knife.

"Keep moving, my lord," I said. "And look away."

"By Athos' head! Seyonne!" Even in his surprise Kiril kept his voice low, and he quickly averted his eyes, fixing them on his warrior's backs and holding his horse to a walk. I moved alongside him, keeping out of sight between his horse and the wall.

"He's going to lose today, my lord. You know it."

"Damned prideful donkey." The young man's voice was near breaking. "He won't let me go with him. If he's going to die anyway . . ."

"Prince Aleksander will not die," I said. "I'll see to it. But his men . . . whoever is left . . . they'll need someone to handle their surrender. I must be able to tell him that they are not abandoned. Do you understand me?"

Kiril glanced down at me, his blue eyes wide. "I think so."

"I'll send news when I can."

Kiril nodded thoughtfully, and I saw the beginnings of strategies play across his face. "Who's with him?"

Quickly I recited the results of Aleksander's summons. "I'm uncertain of one," I said, glancing at the woman in green who remained an island of stillness in the shifting crowd. "Who is the woman standing next to the Fontezhi warriors? The handsome one in the green veil. She seems to be everywhere today."

"I see no women but the water carriers. None in green and none near the Fontezhi. Wouldn't expect it; they don't allow women near their horses."

I glanced up at Kiril, who was scanning the crowd with a puzzled frown, and then whipped my eyes back to the Fontezhi. The woman was gone, not a glimpse of green anywhere in the yard. Prickling unease danced across my skin.

"Tell Zander I'll find out who's loyal after today. And I'll be waiting for his word. Go with Athos, Seyonne." After giving me his hand, Kiril kicked his horse and tore out of the courtyard.

Aleksander had finished his inspection. With a motion to an unbraided youth to raise the Emperor's banner, he threw himself onto his warhorse. Then, with a bellowing war cry, the Prince of the Derzhi led his pitiful army into the desert.

I put the mysterious woman out of my mind. Events were moving quickly. I considered shifting to bird's form and flying over the battlefield to get a clear view of what came about. But the day's outcome would not depend on positions or flanking maneuvers or reinforcements. A bird could not do what I needed to do. I needed a larger form, and because my shifting was too slow and too debilitating, I couldn't afford to shift twice. As soon as the troops had ridden out, I prevailed upon the arms-master to provide me the horse and weapons Aleksander had offered, and I raced out of the city after the warriors.

As the Derzhi stood poised before the Hamrasch fortress awaiting an answer to the Prince's challenge, the heat shimmer rising from the iron-hard plain, I sat atop a nearby outcropping, fighting to keep my head and stomach intact while I shaped wings. Not a falcon's wings this time, but my own.

When I was eighteen and engaged in the worst demon battle of my short Warden's career, I had been backed up to the brink of a chasm. Wounded, desperate, facing certain defeat, I had taken the biggest gamble of my life and jumped off the towering rock face. For months I had been sensing something extraordinary in myself, a persistent burning in my shoulders and an irrational conviction that I could fall off a cliff and not die. I was never fool enough to try it in the human world. But on that day in the realm of a possessed soul, faced with a monstrous being who was about to carve out my heart, I managed to shape wings of gray gossamer out of wrenching fire and breathless incantations. From that day on, I fought winged, glorying in the wonder of it, never understanding that it was but a remnant of my true heritage. Even when I became capable of changing to any shape after my joining with Denas, I wanted only wings.

I emerged from my difficult shifting to the distant clamor of battle: screams and shouts and pounding hooves, crashing steel on steel. Behind and below and between every sound was the unceasing drone of the dying. The hot, dry wind that filled my wings tasted of blood, and the dust raised by a thousand horses dimmed the sun.

I had told Aleksander many times that my aim was not to protect his empire, only his life and his soul. My intent was certainly not to avenge his father, the tyrant. Yet if I had thought I could make a difference with a sword, I would have fought for my friend that day, duty or no, pain or no, come death or madness. But he led a few hundred reluctant warriors against a heged who'd sworn kanavar. He was going to lose, and I had to be ready to save him, whether he liked it or not.

I tore my eyes from the conflict, forcing aside the noise and the stink and my fear for those embroiled in the bloody chaos. Instead, I submerged myself in the eerie silence of sand and rock that stretched unbroken to the horizon behind me. A sorcerer cannot weave enchantments from emptiness, but must twist and knot and intertwine the fabric of the world close by his hand. My heart soon beat with the desert's slow, throbbing pulse; my senses embraced its sere touch. Seated on my rocky hilltop, I bent my mind to the work, only looking up again when I held the spell poised at the brink of thought. Timing would be everything.

As the Prince had surmised, the Hamraschi were well prepared. No less than twelve hundred warriors had flooded out of the fortress and now surrounded the royal troops on three sides. Whatever plan of battle Aleksander had set was already broken, the fighting close and confused, impossible to tell where the Prince's lines began or ended. Only the Thrid flankers held firm, preventing the attackers from completely surrounding the Prince's men. Soon even the flanks would be irrelevant because the Hamraschi would have pushed through the center, all the way to the rear of the imperial army. But in the very heart of the melee was a hard center, a knot of flying blades and wheeling horses that held unmoving while the tide of battle surged around them. That's where Aleksander would be.

I could not move too early. The cowards had already run away or surrendered. Those still fighting and those already dead deserved their chance for victory, no matter how unlikely. And the outcome had to be sealed, else Aleksander would languish forever in the realm of might-have-been. To live beyond defeat would be bad enough. So I had to sit on my rock and watch men die, their bodies trampled, their blood soaking quickly into the wasteland. It was one of the hardest things I'd ever done.

But my Warden's oath still held. No matter that my people had declared it void and violated fifty times over. No matter that I had chosen to reinterpret its meaning in light of the truth of demons. For twenty years it had been the cornerstone of my life, and it demanded that I do everything in my power to save the young man at the heart of that valiant knot, no matter that he would despise me for doing so.

The knot at the center of the fighting grew smaller. The Hamraschi tightened around the imperial troops like a coiled snake, its head raised to strike. Here and there, clusters of Aleksander's men, trapped in rings of Hamraschi, were forced to dismount and kneel upon the ground while their horses were led away, and even as I watched, the wave of surrender flowed through the imperial army. Even Derzhi warriors were not eager to die for a prince they mistrusted. The Prince's standard bearer fell, a spear tearing him off his horse as his protectors died, and the toppling Denischkar falcon was snatched away by a Hamrasch rider as his fellows cheered. He carried it back toward the fortress and threw it to the ground in front of Zedeon, who sat his horse alone before his gates, watching his vengeance bear fruit. I hoped Kiril was nearby, ready to do what was needed.

I summoned the wind and streaked toward the battle, holding

my enchantments on my tongue. Aleksander was engaged in a ferocious duel with a squat warrior wearing Hamrasch colors. The Prince's white cloak was ripped and stained with blood, and his golden arm rings glinted in the sun as he swung his sword, shivering the hot air with the force of his blow. The blood-streaked Hamrasch, his left arm hanging limp, shifted back as he parried, but did not fall. The man's snarling face told me he would endure much to gain this victory. Dovat zha Hamrasch, the dead girl's uncle.

Five warriors, including the wiry Malver and the two bearded Derzhi from Aleksander's apartments, were positioned around the Prince, holding a space large enough for Aleksander to maneuver and fending off those who were trying to attack him. But their protective ring was collapsing as the imperial troops were disarmed, freeing more Hamrasch warriors to concentrate on the Prince. Even as I swooped in, one of the bearded Derzhi fell, shredded by three Hamrasch swords. I circled, and another of the five defenders, a giant Derzhi who had roared in warrior's glee with every swing of his outsize sword, stiffened as a spear point was buried in his back. The big man swung his weapon lazily and then toppled from his mount as four more spears found their mark in his massive body.

A tall Hamrasch warrior forced his way through screaming horses and crowding troops toward the Prince. Leonid. The dead girl's father paused at the edge of the chaos, watching Dovat hammer away at Aleksander, ready for his brother to yield him the final blow. I had only moments to get Aleksander out.

I spoke the first word bound to my enchantment, drew my sword, and flew in a circle about the collapsing ring, leaving a wall of silver fire in my wake. Carefully I wove the essence of the desert noonday—no illusion, but true flame—around Aleksander's protectors, trying not to harm those I was hoping to save, trying to exclude as many Hamraschi as I could, for we would have to deal with any left within the ring. As the wall of fire grew, wonder spread across that battlefield, transforming the din of battle into cries of terror. A few brave souls tried to ride through the flame, but realized quickly that it was nothing like the fakeries produced by Derzhi court magicians. The men screamed as they burned, their terrified horses rearing and causing worse havoc in the ranks.

When my circle was complete, I dived into the center, almost too late. Aleksander's beloved Musa lay dead in the center of the ring, and the Prince himself was on the ground, struggling to extract his left leg from under the fallen beast while desperately holding off a scowling Dovat with his sword. At least ten Hamraschi besides Dovat and Leonid remained inside the ring. Only their stunned confusion at the silver fire and my appearance prevented disaster, for by this time only Malver and one other man were left to aid the Prince. For the moment, they, too, held tightly to their rearing mounts, gawking at me as if the gods had suspended time.

"Look at my face, Malver," I yelled over the roar of the flames, disabling two awestruck Hamraschi in as many swings, praying that the soldier would remember that he'd seen me in the Prince's chambers. "Get Aleksander on a horse. We're going to take him out."

"Druya's horns, it's the Ezzarian!" The second defender, wearing the red and gold of the imperial guard, sprang to life first, driving his horse between the Prince and the stunned Leonid. Skillfully he blocked a blow from behind him, even as he dared the bewildered Hamrasch lord to take him on. As I drove another Hamrasch into the wall of flame, I caught a glimpse of the guardsman's face—craggy, intelligent, familiar, a wide and wondering expression of dawning hope on his weatherworn face. The warrior was Sovari, the longtime captain of Aleksander's personal guard. The efficient, experienced Derzhi was devoted to the Prince, and I could only imagine what threats Aleksander must have used to force the loyal guardsman into safe exile with Kiril. I was immensely thankful that Sovari had seen his duty at Aleksander's side that day. "Am I dead?" he yelled, letting a dagger fly at a huge, black-bearded Hamrasch who was aiming a spear at the Prince. "Or just seeing visions?"

I laughed and kicked the sword from a gaping warrior's hand before sweeping him from his mount with my wing. "Visions. Your aim's too good for a dead man." The black-bearded Hamrasch toppled from his horse, Sovari's dagger in his heart.

Captain Sovari's words unlocked Malver's stupefaction. As I swung my sword at a new attacker, Malver slid easily off his mount and ran to the Prince's side, fending off a blow from Dovat that was about to split Aleksander's skull. Beneath the roar of flame and terror, I could hear Malver muttering. "Holy goddess mother protect us . . . holy goddess . . . holy mother . . ."

Leonid, his sure vengeance cast suddenly into doubt, shook off his astonishment, bellowed at his warriors, and attacked Sovari. While Malver worked to free Aleksander, I touched earth and distracted Dovat with a slash to his legs. From behind me Malver's steady stream of invocations was replaced by a steady stream of curses, along with a harsh command. "Get me on my feet and get out of the way." Pain twisted the Prince's voice almost beyond recognition. "I will not die groveling."

"Get him on a horse," I yelled over my shoulder. "Throw him over the saddle if nothing else. By the count of twenty." My wall of fire would not last much longer. I could feel the melydda draining from me, the pain in my right side was threatening to tear me apart, and the most difficult part of the enchantment was yet to come. I disarmed the stubborn Dovat, and he slumped to the hard earth as if his sword had been the only thing holding him upright.

From behind me came an agonized groan, followed by a rasping curse. "Damn your eyes, I said on my feet."

"I've got him up," cried Malver.

In a way it was much easier that Aleksander was wounded. I had no time to argue with him. "Malver, follow me. Sovari, stay close and guard his back." I took a breath, countered two slashes, and summoned the wind.

It had been waiting on the horizon at the boundary of the dune seas a league away, a roiling monstrosity of such power as could flay a man. At first, in the sudden void left by the dying of the silver flames, it sounded only like the lowest note of a droning mellanghar, a quiet rumble felt deep in the belly. But in moments it devoured the western sky, and the rumble became deafening thunder, shaking the ground beneath my feet.

"Paraivo!" Five hundred voices cried at once, and, as the first stinging sand whipped across my face, the field erupted into madness.

We had to move quickly. Holding such an enchantment more than a brief time would leave me a dried-out husk. I had thought to carry Aleksander away in my arms, but I could not abandon his two valiant defenders. They would not survive Leonid's rage long enough for Kiril to claim them when he bargained for surrender terms as I had asked him to do. Enough men had died that day. And so, with my wings spread wide to create a sheltered breathing space for those who followed, I forged a way through the raging wind.

The sand cut through cloth and flesh like slivers of glass, and threatened quick suffocation. My garments were soon in shreds, scarcely enough of my haffai scarf left to wrap around my nose and mouth. My watering eyes were narrowed to slits, and what scraps of melydda I could spare were dedicated to protecting them. I had planned to head southwest, as that would get us through the bulk of the storm soonest and keep the scouring sand between us and the Hamraschi, but I quickly forgot such details in my struggle to keep breathing and to move in any direction at all. *Gods of night and day, could you not have come up with a better idea?* I berated myself as the wind blasted through a small hole in one wing, leaving an excruciating tear. Though truly, how many things did I know to distract two armies? On further consideration, I decided I'd done well enough.

It seemed only moments until I reached the limits of my endurance. My lungs were on fire, my wings about to rip from my screaming shoulders. Red lightning threatened to crack my skull from the inside as I fought to push through the wind and hold my working together. All we needed was distance. Every mezzit was precious. A few more sweeps of the wings. A few more thrusts into the wind. A few more steps for the racing beasts behind me. At first I had been able to glimpse the dark outlines of panicked men and horses on the peripheries of my vision, but either the whirling sand was hiding them or we had made it past the boundaries of the battlefield. Enough. Let it be enough. One more breath, and then I would stop. Another. I reached down deep for yet one more, until at last I had nothing more to draw on. Then I touched my feet to earth and cut loose my tether to the wind, leaving the world enveloped in profound silence.

CHAPTER 7

"How is he?" I croaked. I sat on a hill of hot sand, my forearms resting on my knees, hands dangling limp, head hung forward where the westering sun could not touch the raw flesh of my face. I had been in the same position for at least two hours, forced to hear Aleksander's muffled agony as Sovari and Malver worked on his shattered leg, but unable to help, to watch, to advise, because I was absolutely incapable of movement, reasoning, or speech. Now silence had fallen over our little patch of desert, I had rested awhile, and I was anxious to know the outcome of their activities.

"Two breaks that we could tell, one of them with the bone sticking out. We did our best, but I don't know if . . . damn all . . . damn all . . ." The nervous man kneeling in the sand just down the hill from me—Sovari, it was—held quiet until he had controlled the shaking in his voice. It had taken him a number of stammered beginnings even to answer me. "He's insensible. Just as well, as we've got to splint it better if we can find the means to do it. All we had was our scabbards to work with. It was wicked for him."

I knew that much. I'd heard the bones grinding as the two grunting warriors had pulled and twisted to set them back straight.

"And we've got nothing to dress the wounding in his flesh. Malver has seen hot oil poured in the wound save such a limb . . . but we've none, so we've had to leave it . . ."

"You can only do your best." I tried fruitlessly to moisten my lips. They felt like tree bark, and my tongue like slate. No moisture existed anywhere within me.

I felt the instant relief of shade as the big man squatted in front of me and stuck a sliver of something warm, moist, and pulpy in my mouth. "Carroc," he said. "You should suck on it. We've only a bit of water, so Malver's gone scouting. There's good prospects. We've found the carroc, and this kind of wasil usually has springs."

"Thank you. Where are we?"

"We're not sure. From the sun, we estimated we rode at good speed for almost an hour, which would put us some eight or nine leagues from Zhagad. But in what direction we've no idea. The storm wiped out our tracks. We're in wasil, more sand than rocks, and dunes in every direction." He hesitated. "We were hoping you'd know."

My gratitude for the sweet, life-giving flesh of the thick-skinned desert plant was matched only by my respect for Captain Sovari. The captain's hand displayed only the slightest tremor as he touched a man who had just raised a storm that Derzhi lore attributed to the wrath of the gods. Stars in the heavens, I'd held it an hour. No wonder I *felt* like the wrath of the gods.

"We've made a bit of shade over by the Prince. Of course you are welcome to it and everything we . . . everything."

"Not yet. Thank you." I was doing very well just to exist. Moving was out of the question.

"Anything else I can do for you?"

"New shoulders, perhaps," I whispered. "Maybe the loan of your skin." My wings had disappeared with the last of my melydda, so thankfully I didn't have to shift, but the muscles that had held them were still quivering. "A little time." Maybe a year.

"I've never seen . . . the fire ring . . . the storm . . . I don't even know how to say it . . ." His deep voice shook a little.

"Not all ex-slaves can do such things, you know." I wasn't so sure how I had managed all of it. "Takes a bit of doing even for those who can."

His awe was diluted by a rueful chuckle. "The Prince is going to be as angry as a trapped kayeet at being pulled out of that battle. Seems you can take care of yourself, but I hope you'll have a thought to protect Malver and me."

I managed to lift my head enough to glimpse the long body lying motionless in the sand, shaded by a bloodstained white cloak stretched between two swords. "I'll be happy to hear him go at us."

Sovari's voice sobered quickly. "I, too. I, too." Only a living man could yell at us as Aleksander was like to. The captain went to check on Aleksander, and I drifted off to sleep.

When I woke, the cold desert night had me shivering. Someone had thrown a haffai on top of me, but the robe had blown off and was bunched up near my head, exposing everything but one arm. I was deciding whether it was worth the effort to retrieve it, when I heard voices.

". . . Horses over there at first light to bring the water. They could carry the wood, too, but I haven't a notion how we'll get it cut fit to make a sturdy splint. If I'd just not lost the bloody ax . . . Cursed Hamraschi." The terse, weary voice belonged to Malver.

"Maybe Seyonne can manage the cutting," said Sovari. "I don't know that he'd need tools."

"The dark gods save us, Captain." Malver dropped his voice. "What is he?"

"I think you just said it, friend. The god must be in him. I've never believed in such . . . not truly . . . but I saw this man a slave in Capharna. They say Ezzarians are sorcerers, but back then he couldn't so much as save himself from old Durgan's lash."

"That fire was real . . . and the storm. Never seen any magician who could do such. And wings . . . I've ever been Druya's man, but I thought I was looking on Athos himself."

"Tales were told back in Capharna, after Lord Dmitri was murdered and the Prince was accused . . . tales of a man turning into a shengar, of someone helping the Prince escape through a barred window too small for a sparrow. This one, slave though he was, vanished at the same time as the Prince escaped. And last year, on that night we chased the Hamraschi into southern Manganar, the night of the terror when the troops all went mad, I saw something . . . The Prince has never been quite the same since those days in Capharna, and I've wondered . . . If the gods wanted to change a man, make him better than he was—"

"Shhh," said Malver with a nervous hiss. "Rein your tongue, Captain."

But the captain was not deterred. "—they might send someone to watch him . . . to teach him . . . one of their own."

The two men fell silent, and I lay there with my skin on fire and every bone aching and thought that if I were ever to be a god, I would damn well work out things a little better. The wind raced across my skin, causing me to shiver and catch my breath, which set me coughing. With all that misery, I decided that maybe I could move after all and get myself a bit more comfortable, maybe even find a drink if the two soldiers had come up with so blessed a thing. So I stumbled to my feet and hobbled toward the flickering gold of their tiny tarbush fire. No one seeing me limping across the rocks and sand, my ragged clothes flapping in the wind, coughing and spitting out a quarry's fill of dirt, was ever going to mistake me for a god.

Aleksander woke up later that evening as Malver was telling me about the sink he'd found—a depression in the wasteland of rock and sand where the scant rainfall and a spring had left a few spike-leafed nagera trees, some date palms, and a good water source. I'd said that with a few more hours' rest, I should be able to ride, at least, and could probably come up with a way to cut wood to make sturdier splints for Aleksander's leg. Malver kept his gaze fixed somewhere in the vicinity of my boots, and his left hand fidgeted with what looked like a piece of bone hung around his neck, a luck charm I guessed. Interesting that he called himself Druya's man but had invoked the goddess mother during the battle.

Sovari was watching Aleksander. I had just downed a cup of nazrheel—the bitter, vile-smelling tea the Derzhi so prized—and between that and the sleep, I was feeling a good deal livelier, when the Prince began to mumble. "Dead men . . . kill you for this . . ." A moment's rustling and a massive groan, and Sovari and I had him pinned to the ground so he couldn't even squirm.

"You've got to stay still, my lord," I said. "You won't like the consequences if you try to move."

His lips were bloodless, his muscles rigid under my hand. "Traitors," he whispered through clenched teeth. "All three of you."

"We've nothing to give you for the pain, my lord, and you know I've no talent for healing. I wish I could tell you other. But Galadon taught me a few things when I was in training—"

"It was my father's honor." Pain and fury had him trembling. "*My* honor."

"You lost the challenge, as you knew you would. Your dying would have changed nothing, and that was all that was left."

He wasn't ready to hear those things. "My warriors—gods avenge me—abandoned. How could you do it?"

I told him about Kiril, then, though I knew what bitterness it would raise to hear how we had planned for his defeat. I told him what I had seen of the battle, every detail I could remember that might show him how hopeless it had been. I hoped he would argue with me, yell at me, spill out the gall so it would not eat at him, but he clamped his teeth shut and turned his head away.

Sovari risked his wrath to give him water, and we got enough in him that even when he spit it out, we knew he'd got some benefit from it. For a long while I saw him forcing his eyelids open, as if somehow refusing to succumb to sleep would be his fit punishment for living, but the exhaustion of his long ride from Suzain, two nights without sleep, the battle, and his injury soon overcame his will. Pain dogged his dreams, and the two warriors and I took turns restraining him through the night, lest his restless shifting make it worse.

By first light I had gotten a little more sleep, and, after a chunk of carroc and another cup of stinking nazrheel—somehow always available in a Derzhi camp no matter how sparse the circumstances—I was feeling well enough to ride with Malver to the sink. To be surrounded by an eternity of sand and gravel—wasil, the Derzhi called this particular kind of desolation—and then to ride over a slight rise to see a small basin filled with lush green was astonishing. The silence of the wasteland was broken by a thousand chittering birds—pipits and grass birds and yellow-tailed finches—and the heady smell of moisture soon had me intoxicated. The grass was cropped close—goats had been here within a seven-day—the trees were sparse, a few thorny acacias among the thick-boled date palms, scrawny doums, and stunted prickly juniper, yet the grassy basin was as beautiful as anything I'd seen in weeks.

Malver filled the waterskins and said he would work on trapping some dinner, while I walked down among the trees and set about the task of cutting splints. My old friend Garen had always been good at shaping wood without tools, and I tried to remember how he'd done it. Something with rope, I thought, and I sat on the cool grass for a time, idly fingering a loop of rope from Malver's saddle and staring at the tree.

So many years gone . . . Garen was a miller's son who had gone into the world as a Searcher, one who sought out possessed souls for us to heal. When his father had died, Garen had come home to see to the mill, only to have the Derzhi invade Ezzaria two days after his return. Ill luck, indeed. But he had survived it, escaped into exile with the Queen and a few others, and gone home again sixteen years later when I brought them Aleksander's gift—the return of our homeland.

Garen was still living in Ezzaria, along with my wife, Ysanne, who had tried to execute me, my friend Catrin, the intelligent young woman who had taken her grandfather's place as a Wardens' mentor, and so many others. How did they fare? Were the demon Gastai still hunting, requiring Ezzarian warding? I didn't know. I had opened the way to Kir'Navarrin, but I had no idea how the rai-kirah fared, either—whether their presence in that ancient realm had eased their cravings for physical life or whether my efforts to put things right for them had been for naught. But on that sweet morning, with the sun still teasing the sky with pink, my thoughts refused to stray from Ezzaria, my own true home. I had tried to shut them out of my mind—my beautiful, rainswept forestland and my stubborn, honorable, blind people who would slay me if I stepped beneath its oaks again. What was it about this green island in the desert that caused such an assault of homesickness that I could scarcely contain it?

I snapped the loop of rope about my hands, forcing my thoughts back to the present dilemma. Fire. Garen had wrapped rope about a tree and made it burn without consuming the rope, and then tightened the noose and burned it again, slowly cutting its way through the tree. That was a start.

By the time Malver came and found me, the sun was high and murderously hot. He had a brace of sand grouse hanging around his neck, and I was drenched in sweat and staring down at a stack of rough, splintery shards of nagera wood. "Earth's bones!" he said, blinking. Then he raked me up and down with his hooded eyes, astonishment getting the better of his shyness. "Never thought the gods' magic would be all that much work. How, in the name of all things, did they ever get the world put together?"

I started laughing then, and picked up several of my ungraceful shapings and shoved them into his arms. "I've been trying to find the answer to that question forever, Malver. But I keep getting farther away from it."

I was appalled when Malver removed the blood-soaked wrappings on Aleksander's leg to examine it before we set the splints. Swollen, grotesquely purple, the jagged rent just below his knee, where bone had punctured flesh, still slowly seeping blood, the limb resembled nothing human. *Oh, my Prince,* I thought. *What have we done keeping you alive?* It was the first time I'd had doubts about what I'd done. I did not see how it could be possible to save such a leg, and the thought of Aleksander maimed, hobbling on a crutch as Gordain had done, unable to ride his beloved horses . . . He would fall upon his sword first. And the pain of it . . . No wonder his face was the color of old linen.

"We're going to have to shift it, my lord," said Sovari grimly. "Splint it better so we can move you."

"Get on with it," whispered the Prince through clenched teeth.

Sovari handed me the Prince's knife sheath. It already had teeth marks in it. When I offered it to Aleksander, he closed his eyes and jerked his head, and I slipped it between his jaws. I knelt behind his head and placed my hands on his shoulders, nodding to Sovari. "Listen to me, my lord," I said as the two warriors began to strap the new splints about his leg, and I had to press down upon his shoulders to keep him from rising up off the sand in his agony. "Remember how we did this when you became a shengar. How you held onto my voice and took yourself out of your body, letting it transform as it would. Do that now. Take hold of me and let me draw you away. I've experience of my own with this recently. Blaise has been my guardian spirit as you said I was for you . . ."

Sovari and Malver were as gentle as they could be in binding his limb into its cage of wood, but the business took a great deal of time. For that endless hour I told the Prince of my madness and my fear of Denas and Kir'Navarrin, not for self-indulgence, not thinking he might help or believing it was anything he needed to be worried about. Indeed I would far rather have kept it to myself. But I knew that every other subject of importance to him would lead us back to his father and his battle and his failure and his wounding, and he needed to be thinking of something else. Likely he would not even remember what I said.

By the end, Aleksander was gray and near collapse. I pulled the knife sheath from his mouth. He had almost bitten through it. As I blotted his face and dribbled water on his lips, he kept his eyes closed and took shallow, trembling breaths.

We needed to determine where we were, to consider our position and resources, to plan what to do next, but all of us were weary beyond telling and the cruel sun sapped our strength as a smith's fire softens steel. We squeezed into what scraps of shade we could contrive with haffai and swords and slept away the noonday.

* * *

Flying . . . over green hills sculpted by the steeply angled light, past meandering rivers of glinting bronze, above stands of trees, their rich green edged with gold . . . golden, glorious light . . . a promise of the fiery magnificence hiding just below the western horizon. Why did I fly away from the light? What beauty lay in the shadowed east that I hurtled so desperately toward it? But of course it was not beauty that drew me . . . the wood, yes, the twining, yellow trunks of the gamarands, the loveliest of all woodland trees . . . that was beauty, but beyond it . . . Even as I flew inerrant, my eyes wanted to turn away. Yet even if I were to shut them tightly, seal them with enchantments so they could not look beyond the gamarand wood, blind them to all seeing forever . . . even then I would see. The smoldering edges of the woodland. Knee-deep ashes and skeletal trees. The bleak, forbidding wall, its leaking blood stanched only for the moment. With the next breach, the fortress on the mountainside would spew forth blood again, a river that would set fire to all it touched. The woodland would burn first, and then the hills and rivers and all the worlds beyond its holy boundaries. On I flew . . . past the graceful walls of gray stone . . . past gardens and courtyards filled with flowers and fountains . . . past crystalline windows, for the fortress was as beautiful as it was dreadful . . . and onward to the shadowed ramparts where the prisoner waited, wings unfurled, ready to wreak havoc on the world . . . "Don't turn around," I begged as I touched my feet to the stone. "Don't turn . . . I don't want to see . . ." But as ever, he turned, and, as ever, he wore my face . . .

The flat, silver desert sunset was fading when I woke drenched in sweat. I swiftly buried the dread raised by my dream. Though fear owned my sleep, I would not allow it to rule my waking life. I would find another path. I had to.

Malver sat plucking his birds, readying them for a smoky tarbush fire. From where I lay stretched out on the warm sand, I whispered an enchantment that soon had the coals brighter without consuming his meager fuel any faster. After a few minutes he blinked and examined his little conflagration, and then cast his eyes about him uncertainly. I couldn't hear what he was muttering as he spitted the birds on a long dagger, shaking his head all the while. I smiled to myself. I hated raw fowl.

I rolled over to sitting, yawned, and stretched out my shoulders. Malver ducked his head awkwardly in my direction as he poked his birds at the fire, trying not to stare at me. No doubt he was wondering if I would sprout wings again any time soon. I rose and checked on Aleksander. The Prince was moaning softly in his sleep, his skin hot and dry. I couldn't tell if he was feverish or just overheated from the lingering day.

"I gave him some water and carroc, but he never came awake for it," said Malver. "Captain Sovari's gone to fetch more water. He thought we'd best be traveling tonight to find shelter, unless . . . unless you were to have another plan."

"Tell me what we'd find eight leagues from Zhagad, Malver," I said as I returned to the fire, cut off a piece of carroc, and sucked on it. "In every direction." The Azhaki desert was not a hospitable place for lost travelers. Indeed we needed to find shelter—not only from the elements, but from the Hamraschi and the Emperor they were going to make. I could not imagine where Aleksander might be safe.

"Me and the captain talked of it a bit. We're likely not north of Zhagad. From the city north along the road to Capharna and westerly, we'd see naught but wasil most anywhere until we were far enough to get into grasslands and the river country. On the other side of the road, where it branches easterly toward Avenkhar, we'd be set in the middle of Srif Polnar; but Srif Polnar's not so wide as what we see from here. And anyways, I don't think we could have gone through Zhagad in the storm . . ." He glanced up at me as if to ask whether I'd done some sorcery to make such a thing possible.

"No. Not likely."

Malver set a stone in the sand to represent Zhagad, and then, with his finger, drew a ring around it to represent the distance we had traveled from the Hamrasch fortress. As he spoke of towns and roads and desert features, he marked each one on his diagram. "Straight south is the Manganar road out of Zhagad. At eight leagues you'd look west to Srif Balat, the widest stretch of dunes in Azhakstan. A bit more west and you'd find the Merat Salé—the Sea of Salt. There's some high country around there—two big Fontezhi fortresses guarding the salt—and some stretches of wasil. We could be somewhere here or here." He sounded dubious as he stuck his finger in the sand. "Wouldn't want to ride into Fontezhi holdings just now. They're intermarried with the Hamraschi. Farther west is more high country looking out over Srif Naj, some of Prince Aleksander's lands, but this doesn't feel right for being Srif Naj. I've been that way often enough, and the captain more, and he doesn't think it so."

The Hamraschi would be watching all of Aleksander's holdings, I guessed. No sanctuary there. With Kiril's surrender terms binding what loyalists might remain from the Zhagad garrison and with the bulk of Aleksander's personal troops still straggling in from Suzain, the Prince would have no one to protect him. "What if we're east of the Manganar road?"

"Eight leagues out and nearby the road, we'd be in heged lands: the Ramiell—Lord Kiril's hold—the Fozhet, and such like smaller houses." Every heged had its traditional holdings in the desert, as well as its more productive fiefdoms in the fertile conquered lands. "Beyond those, more easterly yet, we'd be in Srif Anar, a treacherous land, haunted some say"—Malver's glance flicked to my face and back to his drawing very quickly—"as that's where Drafa lies." Drafa was the ruin of an ancient city, born and dead long before the Empire grew out of the heart of desert Azhakstan. "Straight east from Zhagad and you're on the trade routes to the eastern provinces . . ." He continued to move his finger about his circle, telling me of towns and villages, roads, wasils and srifs, the empty dune seas where there was too little life to share with the desert.

I thanked him for his lesson and even more for the roasted birds; the few mouthfuls that were my share were exquisite. The men were right; we couldn't stay where we were. No matter where along the ring we sat, the fertile sink would attract herdsmen and travelers who would carry news of anyone camped nearby. I had cut two long poles extra from the trees. We would need to craft a litter and carry Aleksander, a frighteningly slow way to travel.

Once Sovari was back with the horses and full waterskins, I told the men I was going to scout a bit and then we would get moving. They looked curious, but didn't question how I might do such a thing in the growing darkness, merely said they would try to get the Prince to eat and drink to give him strength for the journey.

I walked into the night toward the sink, just far enough to be out of view. Then, sitting with my back against a rock still pulsing with warmth, I set myself to transform into a night bird's shape so I could survey the land from above. But I had not even begun the transformation when a movement from the darkness caught my eye. I flattened myself to the sand beside the rock, expecting to see a dune-runner, perhaps, or a gazelle or a sand-deer startled from the sink by the scent of men upon the wind or nervous at the lurking presence of a kayeet. But the form that walked out of the darkness was tall and slender, and, if the starlight had burned brighter, her gown would have shown bright green.

I rose and waited for her to come, listening for the words she had been trying to tell me for so many days. My skin prickled. Who was she who could melt in and out of crowds and palaces, who had been able to recognize me in my falcon's form, who could appear in the desert night with no obvious transport? Her beauty was not the ethereal perfection of Vallyne, the rai-kirah who had tried to steal my soul in Kir'Vagonoth, nor was it the cool and dusky elegance of my wife, Ysanne. Rather this woman put me more in mind of Elinor—her loveliness more in bearing and spirit than in fine features. She stopped a few paces from me, and after studying me from head to toe, she smiled with a radiance that warmed the night.

"A comely form, my darling." Her soft voice caressed my soul like the sweet winds of Ezzaria. "Strength and grace as ever were your raiment." A step closer and her hand brushed the scar on my left cheek. "And this . . . ah, dear friend . . . but one mark of so many sorrows."

I dropped my eyes and sank to my knees, unable to view such a depth of grieving as I glimpsed in her luminous countenance. "Lady, what is it you want of me?" Tears welled in my eyes. Longing . . . devotion . . . old, old sorrow . . . though I could not explain any of it.

"You must remember, my darling. He reaches for you, thinking you've forgotten."

The braying of a chastou ripped through the quiet night at my back, the noisy desert beast drowning the woman's soft words, breaking the spell she had laid upon me. I leaped to my feet, my sword drawn ready to protect her, and I was nearly blinded by flaring torchlight.

"There you are!" called an elderly voice. "I knew we'd find you beside the spring. What did I tell you, boy?" Some twenty paces away, an old man clutched the arm of a slender boy of twelve or thirteen. The old man's hair was perfectly white, twisted into two braids that reached below his waist, one on each side of his head. He was unmistakably Derzhi. Though sun exposure had withered his face into myriad tiny wrinkles, age had neither stooped nor shrunk his long bones nor made flaccid the arms revealed by his sleeveless tunic. His nose was long and slightly arched, and from his ears dangled hooped earrings of gold. His eyes flashed amber in the torchlight, though it was apparent from their aimless wandering that they saw nothing of the world. He carried no stick, as blind men usually do, but only held the boy's arm.

"He's not beside the spring, Gaspar," said the boy quietly, leaning toward the old man as if to keep his correction private between the two of them. "It's still five hundred paces away." The boy was slim and wiry, every movement quick and graceful. He had long light hair, unbraided, and was mostly naked, wearing only a loincloth, silver arm rings, and silver hoops in his ears. Neither boy nor man wore shoes.

The old man snorted. "Boys! Who can teach them? I say that out of all the Srif Anar we will find them at Taíne Het, and Qeb quibbles about five hundred paces." Somewhere behind them the chastou bawled its displeasure.

My head was still filled with cobwebs of green enchantment, loving words that flitted through the night like fireflies, dark eyes filled with a world's sorrows. I could scarcely comprehend the odd newcomers and their noise and bright light. "Lady," I said, turning back to confirm her safety . . . but she was vanished again, and I wanted to cry out the loss.

"We had no intent to interrupt your prayers, sir," said the boy in great solemnity. "Gaspar was in a great hurry, believing your injured companion to be in grave danger."

"Prayers . . . no," I said limply. Madness, more likely. They had not seen her. I shivered. "I just . . . who are you, and who is it you're looking for?"

"You and your fellow," said the old man. "The one of darkness and the one of light. We've come to take you to Drafa to prepare you for the last battle."

CHAPTER 8

Drafa. Had the gods ever contrived so unlikely a haven? So perishingly hot and dismal a scar on the majestic desert? A holy city, Gaspar said, once beloved of the gods who were old before Athos went to live among the stars, the gods who had built the world from sand and water and fire.

Certainly the city itself had been built from sand and water—mud bricks—in some ancient past when water was more abundant. The old man said that at one time ten thousand people had lived there, that Drafa was the true heart of Azhakstan when the Derzhi king still dwelt in a billowing tent, hundreds of years before a Derzhi emperor dreamed of Zhagad's rose-colored arches. Lemon, almond, pomegranate, and hazelnut trees had blossomed in abundance, and thousands of sheep had grazed on hills of sweet grass bordered by the boundless desert.

What palaces or hovels had graced the heart of Azhakstan were all the same now, collapsed into a maze of half-walls and broken paving. A few gaunt pillars and a fallen statue of a lion marked a slight rise in the center of the city. The lemon and almond groves were gone, and the sweet grass. Only the unceasing wind remained, a soft and hollow wailing that stirred the sand, covering and uncovering the crumbling walls and toppled towers, stealing a bit more of the ancient city's bones with every pass. A dusty lemon tree stood alone beside the walled courtyard where we barricaded the horses and Gaspar's scrawny chastou to protect them from prowling zhaideg and kayeets. A row of spreading blue-green tamarisks marked the eastern approach, where they had once offered welcoming shade to all who approached the holy city. Now they held back the dunes, preventing the desert from claiming the ruin completely. And a small grove of the ever-present, ever-useful nagera palms stood just beyond the sheltered corner of broken walls where we laid Aleksander to see if he would live or die.

It was difficult to believe any humans actually made a home

amid such desolation. One would expect the scorpions half as big as my palm, the lizards, the jackals that whined outside the boundaries of our fire at night, and the vultures that circled over the dunes. But the old man Gaspar and the boy Qeb were two of five people who squeezed out a living from the spring and the trees and a few goats. The other three were women—Sarya, Manot, and Fessa—all of whom appeared to be even older than Gaspar. I was curious about the boy. If he was a slave, then it was a benevolent bondage, as he was unmarked and wore no slave rings. The four old people obviously doted on him. His features and coloring hinted at Derzhi or Basran ancestry.

The journey from our bit of wasil had been very slow. The jostling could have been nothing but agony for Aleksander, and by the time we reached Drafa, he was glassy-eyed and feverish. No sooner had we laid him under the shade of the nageras than the three old women began hovering about us like flies on drying blood.

"Get away from him," Sovari snapped at the wizened little woman Gaspar named Sarya. Her skin was the color of the baked mud, all cracks and crevices, and she appeared to have no more than three teeth, those in precarious condition. "No filthy desert vermin will touch him." All through the long night's trek I had watched the guard captain's hand drawn to the heavy sword at his belt, only to see him snatch it away a few moments later. A seasoned warrior like Sovari knew how dangerous it was to let a limb mortify. He was steeling himself to save Aleksander's life. I prayed to every god I knew that we would not come to that.

"Have you any medicines?" I asked Sarya quietly as Sovari bathed the Prince's face and tried to get water down him. "We have nothing, and the only remedies I know come from forestlands." No oak trees in this desolation, and none of the herbs or roots Ezzarians used to care for wounds.

"Manot knows well of healing. Fessa knows more," said the old woman, nodding her head to her companions. A tall, angular woman with a tangle of wispy white hair stood peering at Aleksander, her leathery nostrils flared, testing the air for any whiff of putrefaction, I guessed. The third old woman, round-faced and fluttering, darted around Sovari and Aleksander clucking her tongue. "But they need to see the wound and tend the damaged parts so it can heal cleanly. We must be quick."

Gaspar and the boy walked slowly down the dusty path.

"Your other friend is seeing to your horses," said the old man. "How fares the warrior?"

"Very ill," I said, drawing the old man aside. "These women . . . ?"

"They know what they're about. There's healing in the desert" —he winked at me and smiled conspiratorially—"for all kinds of injury." I had the uncanny sense that his sightless eyes saw far more than was comfortable. I had not forgotten his greeting . . . *one of darkness and one of light . . . the last battle* . . . And how had he had been able to tell the women of Aleksander's injury before he came to find us in the desert?

As the sun crept over the edge of the dunes, I squatted next to Sovari. The veteran sat with his chin on his fists, staring hopelessly at the sleeping Prince. "We need to let these women see to him, Captain," I said softly. "They're not royal physicians, but they'll know what remedies are available hereabouts. You and I have only the one thing to offer, and he'll not welcome it."

Sovari shot me a hard glance, and then looked away. "My duty is to protect his life," he said. "Who knows what poisons these people would concoct?" Fessa had tiptoed close again, and the captain angrily waved her off. "What could ignorant beggars know of healing? Might as well have the jackals come gawking, or some Thrid witch-woman. Leaving him with a mortified limb will kill him for certain."

I was set to argue with him, but a panting whisper from in front of us silenced the dispute before it began. "You will not take it. You will not." Aleksander's eyes were not open, but his fists were clenched as if ready to take us on in battle.

"Of course not, my lord," said Sovari. "Only if absolutely—"

"You . . . will . . . not . . ." The words were edged steel. ". . . ever."

"As you wish, my lord. Of course."

I raised my eyebrows at the captain, and he grudgingly shrugged his shoulders. Though Sovari had scarcely moved, the women descended on us and gradually eased us aside. Before we knew it, they had a small dung fire burning, woven mats unrolled and baskets laid out with various roots and dried leaves in them, and our crude bandages cut open to expose Aleksander's leg—looking far worse than the day before. I hadn't thought it possible. The Prince took no notice. The effort of speech seemed to have sent him into a stupor.

"Qeb," called Sarya. "We need fresh chosoni." The boy nodded and ran off, leaving Gaspar sitting against a wall, where the old man soon nodded off.

Sarya ground dried roots of the sticky milkweed that grew in the cracks of the mud walls, boiled the gray powder, cooled it, strained it through coarse cloth, and then boiled it again. While Manot used the steaming liquid to wash the dirt and blood from Aleksander's wound, Fessa heated nagera oil in a small earthen vessel, adding crumbled tarbush leaves. For two hours she stirred the mess, sniffing the acrid fumes and touching her tongue to drops she sprinkled on her hand.

The sun rose higher, baking away the night's coolness. Qeb brought Sarya a handful of grayish spiky weeds, and then squatted down beside Gaspar, telling the old man he would help him to bed to finish his nap. Gaspar protested drowsily, trying to sit up straight. "It's been too long since we've had visitors. As soon as the healing's done, I want to talk." He pushed away a goat that had wandered close, interested in the patch of thistle behind Gaspar's back.

"As soon as the healing's done, Qeb will bring you back," said Sarya, glancing up from peeling the bark from three pine branches. "You'll have your time to babble as you will." Her crinkled eyes were smiling.

"Not much time." The old man scratched his beard. "No. Not so very much."

Sarya's smile fell away, and her eyes darted to the boy. Qeb, his tanned face serene, helped the old man to his feet and maneuvered him gently and safely over the broken ground. The boy returned after a while, silent as he watched everything that was done, helping however was needed.

The women pressed me into service, too. I chopped two onions from Manot's basket, while Fessa strained her oily mixture through the cloth into another earthen cup. Sovari and Malver returned from caring for the horses, and the round-faced Fessa bade the two men hold Aleksander's shoulders. It was well-done, for Fessa dripped her concoction right into the raw wound. Aleksander's scream ripped the day's stillness.

"Curse you, witch," yelled Sovari. "Ezzarian, we should send for a real phys—"

"The pain is necessary," said Sarya, laying her withered hand on my arm. "We must kill the poisons before the wound can heal."

The Derzhi would sear such a wound with a hot iron, and then bind it up until it festered or healed. Even in the best cases, the victim ended up lame. Surely this treatment could be no riskier. I breathed again and resumed my chopping. "He is very important," I said.

"We know."

I looked up quickly, but Sarya had returned to the fire and set a small vessel of water ready to prepare Qeb's gray-leafed chosoni. Another hour and they had placed an onion poultice on the wound and covered it with leaves. The chosoni was steeping in a pot, and the resin from Sarya's bark had been cooked and mixed with nagera oil to make a sticky, pungent ointment. Now we waited.

Manot watched the Prince first, her light-colored eyes scarcely blinking. After a few hours, Sarya relieved her, while the tireless Fessa brought us something to eat: a few of the red-fleshed fruit from the nagera, cups of goat's milk, and flatbread baked from ground almonds and sweet nagera butter. After sharing this generous offering—three healthy men were going to tax such a meager subsistence—Malver and Sovari went scouting, saying they needed to get the lay of the city and find the best place to set a watch. For the next two hours I sat in the stifling shade and watched Aleksander's fever rise. His cheeks were flushed, his breathing shallow and rapid, and he grew restless, so that whichever woman was caring for him had to keep a hand on his chest to keep him still. We would need no fire to warm him when the cold night came.

Fessa took up the watch. I could sit still no longer. As the ruthless sun traversed its course, I paced the sandy rubble and stared out at the sculpted dunes Aleksander so prized. The desert's changes were subtle. Blue shadows stretched slowly across its face. A dusting of sand shifted in the wind. I had grown up in deep forest, and loved few things better than the smell of rain on spring earth or the touch of autumn sun on my cheek while red and gold leaves spoke fire above my head and beneath my feet. Yet I could not conjure an image of my homeland as I gazed upon the evening desert, nor could I fasten my mind on insidious demons or perilous dreams or failed love. The peaceful emptiness was very welcome.

"This is a holy place." Gaspar's voice was as spare as the desert. Qeb and the old man had come up the path as the sun slipped into the west, spreading night upon the desert like a cloak.

"I feel it," I said.

"There was a time when all Derzhi warriors made pilgrimage to Drafa," Gaspar said. "Just after they earned their braids, they would come here seeking visions. A young warrior newly steeped in blood must find his center of balance."

"Sometimes older ones need the same," I said.

The old man stood at my shoulder, almost of a height with me, and beside him stood the slim and graceful boy, his silver earrings catching the last stray beams of day. About the two hung a heady sweetness of smoke and unfamiliar herbs. "We can help you, warrior. Few remember we are here, but we've not fallen wholly out of practice."

"Is that why you stay in this ruin?"

"There have been ones like us in Drafa since it was new-built from the sand. As long as there are warriors, we will be here."

So Gaspar was some kind of tribal mystic. Every race had them—wise men or women who watched the stars or claimed to see visions or to find portents in clouds or beast entrails or worm droppings. That would explain the boy. Gaspar had likely found Qeb in some backward village and brought him to Drafa to be his acolyte, training the child to serve some priestly function for Derzhi who no longer came to find balance in Drafa. Before I could learn more, I heard a hoarse shouting from the shelter.

I hurried back to find Sarya taking the pot of chosoni tea off the fire, while Manot and Fessa gripped Aleksander's arms. The Prince's amber eyes were open, flaring hotly in the firelight, though seeing nothing of the women or of me. "Out of me, demon! I'll not have you! Oh, mighty Athos . . . he burns . . ." His ravings were fragments of memory: of arguments with his father, of love and longing for his wife, of the time when the Lord of Demons had ravaged his soul to make himself a dwelling place, of confusion and uncertainties long held private.

"Raise his head and hold him steady," commanded Sarya, holding a steaming cup. "We'd hoped to let this fever burn itself out, but it's too fierce." Careful not to spill the hot liquid on Aleksander's bare chest, she forced him to drink the vile-smelling chosoni tea. He gagged and fought and raved, calling us demons and traitors, threatening every sort of mayhem. When he had drained the cup, the old woman brought another and we forced that one into him, too. And another, and again, until Sarya's pot was empty. The Prince was limp and quiet when we laid him back on his cloak, and soon he began to sweat. Sarya nodded in satisfaction and gently blotted his face and chest and limbs with rags, while Manot renewed the poultice on his leg.

For two more days the Prince's fever soared and was sweated out again. Sovari and I took turns sitting with him as the women plied him with their teas and potions. With Malver we shared the watch, the care of the horses, and the hunting to supplement the food supplies. We snatched sleep in hour-long bits. By dawn of our third morning in Drafa, our tempers were short, and my eyes felt like sand had been ground into them. After a frustrating morning trying to shoot something that was edible, I threw Malver's luckless bow onto the sand and fell to the ground beside Sovari, asleep before my empty stomach could complete its hollow rumble. Malver was on watch.

Sun glare seared my eyes when I cracked them open. Cracked was an apt word, I thought, perhaps a crack right through my forehead. And the murderous sun weighed heavy on my shoulder. *Dangerous. Stupid.* What kind of fool was I to fall asleep unsheltered? Yet I was sure I had lain down on the woven mat under the nagera trees, three steps from Sovari and the Prince.

". . . Left him here. Don't expect the ropes to hold him, but the blow seemed to take him down well enough." The speaker's brave words did not hide anxious undertones. "Didn't know if it was possible to kill him . . . or wise. Makes no sense after all he did before."

"Have the women see to your arm. I'll hear what he has to say." Both speakers were nervous.

"Be wary, Captain."

Only when I tried to crawl out of the brutal sun and found it impossible did I comprehend that the talk of ropes and blows pertained to me . . . and that the flashing steel of Sovari's sword was poised at my neck. I was lying on my side, hands tied behind me and lashed to my ankles with ropes much too short. With my back strained into such an arch, my right side was beginning to throb in time with my head. But none of these discomforts was as painful as the understanding that banished my confused wakening.

"I'm all right now," I said, gasping a bit to get the words out. "I won't hurt you."

"Tell Malver that."

"What happened? I truly don't know." Well, I knew in general what had happened, of course. Only details were lacking.

"Malver says you came up here raving, swearing to 'kill the cursed humans.' You had a knife in your hand and didn't seem like you cared who it was got stuck with it. He hid behind one of the pillars. When you came close, he bashed you on the head with a brick. When he tried to bind you, you almost cut his arm off, so he had to whack you again."

"Gods . . ." No matter how troubled my dreams, sleep had always been my refuge from this madness. "I'm sorry. Tell Malver . . ." Tell him what? Not to be afraid? ". . . I'm truly sorry." Pitifully inadequate words. "Please step back now, Captain. I've got to get loose, but I promise I'll not harm you."

After only a moment's hesitation, Sovari stepped far enough away to remove any danger that he would slice my neck while I got myself untangled. He didn't lower his sword, however. I understood his reluctance.

I grunted with the jerking release of the strain when the ropes binding my wrists and ankles snapped. "The others . . . I didn't hurt anyone else, did I?" I sat up slowly, pressing a hand to my aching side, doing my best to appear nonthreatening.

Sovari shook his head, staring at the charred ends of the ropes I had burned through with a word. His answer provided me more relief than the broken bonds.

I rubbed my wrists and my aching head, keeping my breathing shallow while the pain in my side subsided. "This is something I can't seem to control," I said more calmly than I felt. "A mind-sickness that has nothing to do with Malver or you or anyone here. I should have warned you."

I should have stayed away from people . . . *Humans*, I had said. Was that it? Never in my life had I thought of Ezzarians as other than human. Yet it was true that my deadly, inexplicable rage had never been directed at an Ezzarian, never at anyone demon-joined. Gordain, the first three beggars in Vayapol, Blaise's friend Dian, the namhir . . . all were humans.

"My only purpose has been to see the Prince out of danger," I said to the wary Sovari. "And you still need me for that. But I'll leave as soon as he can ride. Until then, if you or Malver see this happening again, you have my full permission to do whatever is needed."

"We'll see to it."

I glanced up to see him wondering. No more thoughts of me being Athos' messenger, I guessed, unless the gods were something altogether different than he had ever learned. The point of his sword had sagged to the broken paving. "Don't try to be easy with me if it happens again, Sovari. I'm good at what I do. You've seen it."

"Aye. I've seen what you do." He reached out a hand to help me off the ground.

I limped slowly down the gentle slope. When we reached the spring and its companion, a solitary pomegranate tree, I stopped to drink and cool off in the shade, allowing Sovari to go ahead of me and speak to Malver and the others.

After savoring a few mouthfuls of the warm, murky water, forcing myself not to gulp down the entire contents of the slow-to-replenish pool, I lay back under the glossy green leaves of the ancient tree and tried not to think. No use. I needed to walk away; I couldn't even protect Aleksander from myself. I closed my eyes and threw my sweaty arms across my face. If only I could recapture the peace of the desert evening.

As if in answer to my desire, Gaspar's slow footsteps approached, stopping just beside me. The boy was not with him. "You're not afraid?" I said when I felt him sit down beside me. The leaves rustled tiredly in the hot wind.

"Not so much as you." The old man's voice was different than I'd ever heard it. Not teasing, not querulous, not reverent, but sharp. Resonating with authority. "My hand does not hold the life and death of the world."

I sat up and stared at him. In an instant the day was swallowed by a star-shattered midnight, so cold that I yearned for the sun's harsh blaze. "What are you, Gaspar?" I said.

"I could ask you much the same." His blind, golden eyes were fixed on me. Though his voice did not quaver, whatever he envisioned beyond the realm of human sight was indeed frightening him. "But then, you know already what you are. I have named you."

"The one of darkness."

He did not agree or disagree, only pressed on as if his words were in a hurry to be spoken. "To strike terror into the hearts of those you love is a difficult thing. One of many difficult things. To embrace the darkness of your dreaming is the most difficult of all. To give name to the nameless and stand across the fathomless gulf from the light."

"It is not me," I said as my heart shrank, not asking how he knew, not questioning his surety, not bothering to think how foolish it was to beg the universe to change what I had known all these months. "Please, it is not me."

"This is your true path, the one you have chosen. For good or ill, for death or life."

"No. Say something else." As if his saying would change it.

"I cannot unsay these things or pronounce a lie that might sound more pleasing. To protect a soul from the moment's evil oft condemns it to an eternity of evil."

But if I could not protect those I loved or those I had sworn to defend, then what was the point of anything? If I was truly destined to destroy the world, then perhaps it would be best to end my own existence first. And yet of all things, I abhorred self-murder—the ultimate denial of life's worth. "Help me understand," I said. "I don't know what to do."

"You walk the path you've chosen. For the light to triumph, there must be darkness."

And so, in the end, this moment's mystery gave me nothing new. Whatever the source of his words—gods or prophecy or an old man's ravings that happened to touch upon a festering sore—matters still came down to yielding control of my future, to setting my foot upon the path and following wherever it led. But I knew where it led. Through a pillared gateway into a fortress that bled, to where a man with wings . . . a man with my face . . . raged and swore to destroy the world.

"We can help you find balance, warrior. Before you begin the last battle, you must end this war with yourself."

But I did not want to hear any more. I buried my head in my arms and fortified the barriers I had built to hold my demon at bay, smothering him with spells and enchantments, locking him in a fortress of my power. Surely if I could remain myself, hold back the demon and remain on this side of the portal, refuse his craving to return to Kir'Navarrin, none of this would happen. *It is not me. I will not. It is not me.*

When next I looked up it was early evening and I was alone. Scented smoke hung faintly on the air. I must have been asleep or stricken by the sun, I thought. Gaspar was just a blind old man. No bone-reader or stargazer was going to give me answers.

"He's asking for you, Ezzarian!" The call came from Sovari down beside the nagera grove. I waved a hand in acknowledgment and hurried down the path.

CHAPTER 9

Aleksander was propped up on one of the Derzhi saddles, grimacing as Sarya fed him some thick brownish liquid with a wooden spoon. "Demonfire, woman, have you nothing that doesn't taste like dung? If I'm going to live in this cursed world, then decent food might be pleasant."

"Cassiva will nourish you well, warrior. Better than meat for the wounded. Heals the bones." The old woman jammed another spoonful in his mouth before he could complain again. Despite his belligerent manner, he could not seem to muster the strength to push her hand away. He glared at me ferociously over the old woman's head.

I sat beside one of the walls that formed the sheltered corner and waited. Sovari had vanished after summoning me, and Malver was nowhere to be seen. Likely the quiet soldier was planning to stay out of my way until he saw I wasn't going to kill him at the next opportunity.

When the cup was empty, Sarya set it aside and pointed to a clay bowl that sat next to the Prince. "Shall I help you with this now you're awake, warrior, or do you prefer your friend to do it, or will you lie in your own puddle?"

"I've been pissing on my own for a fair number of years. I need no wretched hag and no cowardly Ezzarian to manage it."

"I think we have his blood running again," said Sarya, flashing her three brown teeth at me. "They never name me wretched hag until the fever's fair gone. Manot will come see to the poultice after a bit."

Aleksander mumbled at her retreating back. "What kind of healer leaves a man smelling like a beggar's hovel? Next thing they'll be bandaging me with goat liver or rotted cabbage." He began fumbling with the bowl and the tail of his filthy, bloodstained shirt, but in trying to maneuver, he jarred his leg, bound tight into its cage of wood from thigh to foot. His head dropped back onto the saddle, and he closed his eyes. "Bloody Athos," he whispered, losing the bit of healthy color he had regained.

"You wanted to see me?" I said, moving around to where I could support his splinted leg and roll him smoothly to his side so he could take fair aim at Sarya's bowl.

Even in this less than dignified position, with his jaw clenched at the effort of movement, he managed to sound like a Derzhi prince. "I wished to tell you that you're free to go. Take wing, fly away, whatever it is you do."

"A bold dismissal from one who can clearly not take a piss on his own at the moment."

"Your duty is done. You've always told me that your interest is not to protect my empire. Good enough. It might take me a little while to regain the confidence of my nobles after running away from a fight like a peasant farmer." He grimaced and swore as I rolled him back and adjusted the saddle to support him more comfortably.

"You were going to die. That wasn't going to inspire much confidence, either."

The pain in his eyes told of more than a wounded body. "You've put this damnable burden on me—to see the world as you see it. I tried, and where has it left me? When I take back what's mine, do you think I'll be able to afford the slightest suggestion of weakness? Do you know what I'll have to yield to pull in allies?"

I had no answer, of course, and he well knew it. What use to argue alternatives, when none had existed for either of us? So I let him yell at me for as long as he had strength to do so, regaling me with how little I knew of Derzhi warfare and how stupid I had been to think that just because the Hamraschi had encircled his men and killed half of them, he had been destined to lose the battle. Then he told me in gruesome detail how he would punish the traitors who had failed their Emperor.

Only when he finally lay back and closed his eyes did I speak again. "So what will you do now, my lord?"

"Go begging, I suppose. Grovel before the Gorusch and swear I did not kill my father. Grovel before the Fontezhi and tell them they can have half of my horses, my lands, and my firstborn son if they will but do their sworn duty. Tell the Nyabozzi I was mistaken—they can take whomever they please as slaves again and cut out the wretches' eyes and sell their children if it makes the first lord happy. Then perhaps I can get them to skewer Edik before he gets thinking my empire is his for the taking. But here I am laid up like a kayeet in a leg trap, while the snake is likely sleeping in my bed. By Druya's horns, has ever a man been in such a vile predicament?"

"You should probably sleep a bit more before you go groveling." I pulled his stained white cloak over his legs.

"Weeks . . . it will be cursed weeks before I can ride."

"If you want the limb straight, you must stay off it until it grows together."

"There's a man in Zhagad who makes riding boots for broken limbs . . . steel bars in them, foot to thigh. I'm going to send Malver to have one made for me. He can take my old boot to use for the measure."

"But, my lord, you can't allow—"

"Malver knows how to be cautious. And he and Sovari will have to carry my messages until I can get moving again. I've got to find out who's with me."

Night had fallen as we talked. The moon was new and rising late, and soon Aleksander's face was but a pale smudge in the darkness. Our conversation dwindled away, my mind returning to the strange midnight I had experienced that afternoon, when Gaspar had spoken of light and dark and fate and choices. As I watched the glimmering sky above the spiked silhouettes of the nagera grove, I longed to be among the stars, cold and detached from all this pain. I needed to be about my leaving. But worries kept nagging and I could not begin. If Aleksander dispatched Sovari and Malver on errands, he would have no one left to protect him . . .

"Malver told me what happened with you this afternoon." Aleksander's voice came softly from the shadows. I had thought he'd fallen asleep. "Was it what you told me of, this mind-sickness that has you so worried? The demon?"

I should have known he would remember all I told him on the day Sovari and Malver set his leg. "I need to get away from Drafa before I doze off and cut your throat," I said, bitterness welling up within me like the stinking octar that seeps from desert rocks.

"Was that why you didn't fight beside me? Were you afraid you would kill the wrong people?"

"There were a number of reasons."

"Tell me, Seyonne. I believed you would stand with me if I

asked. For me, not my father. Why would you not help until the day was lost?"

The question was born of love, for his pride would never have allowed him to ask it. And so I overcame my own pride and gave him the answer, the thing I could not and would not tell any other person in the world. "Yes, I worried about this cursed demon and my annoying habit of attacking anyone who happens to be within reach. But even without that . . . I can no longer wield a sword without pain, my lord. A well-placed blow to my right side, and I cannot even raise my arm, much less hold a weapon." A difficult thing for a warrior to reveal, especially to a friend who believed that strength was everything.

"Ah, bloody damn . . . the knife wound." Aleksander had seen Ysanne's work. He and Blaise and Fiona had rescued me from the brink of death that day.

"The namhir nearly took me with a stick of wood. Fortunately he was mostly dead when he got in his hit. You could say this madness saved me; I don't seem to feel the pain when I'm hacking bodies apart. But if you had relied on me in the battle, it could have cost you everything. I had to wait and be ready to save your life."

"You won't mind if I withhold my thanks for that?"

"I never expected your thanks."

"I'm sure not." He laughed a bit, but when he spoke again, he was very serious. "You'll stay with me now? We'll have the others keep wary—they don't know what to make of you anyway—and it's been months since I've slept without a knife in my hand. But I don't believe you would ever do me harm, even if you were mad."

His trust was humbling, but only the conviction that he was a dead man otherwise held me there. "If you're willing to risk it," I said, "unless I get worse, I'll stay."

The days in Drafa were very long and very hot. The season was moving toward summer, when even the dune-runners and sand-deer came out only after dark. We slept a great deal in the daytime, especially Aleksander, for the women plied him with herbs and teas to ease his pain and heal his wounds. In the days following my attack on Malver, the swelling in the Prince's leg began to recede and the dreadful tear in his flesh to knit. No further sign of sepsis showed itself, and Manot replaced her poultices with ointment made from pine bark.

As he had planned, Aleksander dispatched Sovari and Malver with well-crafted messages for the lords of several powerful hegeds. I persuaded him to have the two men speak first with Kiril. That he held out so long against this was a measure of his unspoken pessimism.

"Your cousin awaits your word, my lord," I argued for the tenth time. "He may already know the information you seek. You've no stronger ally."

"I don't want Kiril dead. If old Hamrasch gets the slightest idea—"

"You shame Lord Kiril by not accepting what he offers. Even I know enough of Derzhi honor to understand that."

With deep misgiving, he at last relented, sending Sovari to Kiril and Malver to the boot-maker. Malver left me his bow, and I shouldered all the hunting duties, taking the stringy chukars feeding at the spring—no more than one in ten, Gaspar told me, else the birds would stop coming—and a sand-deer. The old ones could no longer hunt easily, and Qeb would not leave Gaspar's side. At least we were able to repay some of their kindness with provisions.

The old women flitted about us day and night, cleaning and dressing Aleksander's wound and re-splinting his leg as the swelling went down, making sure to pad the wood carefully with leaves and ointments to prevent skin sores. They held very little conversation beyond the moment's business, leaving the difficult task of Aleksander's amusement to me. In less than a day our blades were in danger of disappearing from his excessive honing. He fidgeted and cursed and complained at my attempts at distraction: discussions of geography and weather, my recent employment as a scribe in Karesh, and how difficult farming was when landlords refused to give their tenants any tools. Peasant farmers were among the most courageous of his subjects. Ezzarian sword making and the differences in fighting demons and humans interested him somewhat more. But the only thing that truly intrigued him was the story of my banishment from Ezzaria: the search for my son that had led me to Blaise, my long sojourn in the demon realm of Kir'Vagonoth, the Warden Merryt, long-captive in the demon realm, and the accumulation of evidence that had led me to believe that my people and the demons had been split apart in fear of something or someone imprisoned in Kir'Navarrin.

"And you don't know what's inside this Tyrrad Nor?" he said one wakeful midnight.

"To my mind, a fortress is more likely to hold a prisoner than some formless danger," I said. "Merryt certainly believed so and called him 'the Nameless,' referring to the Nameless God, a figure in Ezzarian myth. I suppose it's not out of possibility that our god-story has grown from some real incident in our history."

So then I had to tell Aleksander the story of Verdonne, the mortal maiden beloved of a god, and how the god had grown jealous of their half-human, half-divine son, Valdis, and tried to kill him and all the humans who loved the child. Despite her husband's rage, Verdonne had stood firm between the god and the mortal world, protecting her child and her people. "When Valdis was grown to manhood," I said, "he defeated the god in single combat, but could not bring himself to kill his own father. So he imprisoned his father in a magical fortress and took away his name so that no one could worship him anymore. The story concludes with a warning: 'Woe to the man who unlocks the prison of the Nameless God, for there will be such a wrath of fire and destruction laid upon the earth as no mortal being can imagine. And it will be called the Day of Ending, the last day of the world.' Not a warning to take lightly."

Aleksander paused in the middle of devouring a fist-sized chunk of deer haunch. "So you think that a god is sitting in this fortress called Tyrrad Nor, waiting to destroy the world. And you believe that somehow he is you."

"He's not a god. No. Nor a rai-kirah. He understands how to use dreams, and rai-kirah don't dream. A sorcerer, perhaps, one of my own people—a joined rai-kirah and man." I tapped my knife idly on the haunch bone. "Sometimes I think he's taunting me . . . telling me that what I've already done will allow him to be free . . . or that somehow he can force me to do his work for him. I don't know."

"Do his work . . . destroy the world? I won't believe it." He started eating again. If appetite was any sign of healing, Aleksander would be riding within a month. "It's your blasted care for all the world that keeps tearing up my life. You held onto yourself through everything we Derzhi did to you, and then through torture and enchantment in that fiendish Kir'Vagonoth. What could make you alter the very nature of your soul? Nothing." He waved a piece of flatbread at me to make his point. "As you said, he's likely taunting you, trying to make you doubt yourself. Perhaps he knows you're the only one who can destroy him."

But, of course, I *had* altered the very nature of my soul. I didn't remind the Prince of that, and I didn't tell him of my strange encounter with Gaspar at the spring. I was still trying to convince myself that Gaspar's insights were naught but an old man's ramblings, and my odd perceptions merely sun exposure.

"Look," he said, "I'll make you the same promise that you swore to me on the day I cut off your slave rings. If you ever become this monstrous villain, I'll come after you. You'll die by my hand and no other. Does that make you feel better?"

I laughed. "Much better." I didn't mention that if I became the thing I feared, neither prince nor warrior nor sorcerer would be capable of facing me.

The old man and Qeb came to sit with us every evening, unrolling their mats when the breathless furnace of the day yielded to shivering night. Gaspar drank endless cups of nazrheel and told us endless stories of Drafa and its history, of the days when the Derzhi were wandering warriors who protected the other desert peoples from the invasions of barbarians. "The wild men came looking for our horses and our sheep, our salt and our women," he said, inhaling the stinking fumes of his tea with deep satisfaction. "But the warriors chased them away and kept vigil in their wanderings throughout the land. The desert people named the Derzhi tribesmen lords in thanks for their protection, and they named the greatest of them king of their land that they called Azhakstan."

"Did Seyonne bribe you to recite this fable?" said Aleksander in irritation. "It sounds just like him. But I am not a wandering tribesman who was given a throne by sheepherders. I am the rightful Emperor of all the lands my grandsires have conquered, including Azhakstan, and I will have my inheritance if I have to kill every Hamraschi that breathes." As Gaspar rambled on, unfazed by this outburst, the Prince threw his arms across his face and pretended to sleep.

"As the kingdom grew, the warriors remembered Drafa and made pilgrimage here for the siffaru—the rites of balance. Every king of Azhakstan would come here seeking his vision upon the day of his anointing. It's been a long while since we've seen a king here, and never have we seen an emperor, but there are still a few who come—"

"Lidunni," said Aleksander, his voice muffled by his arm. "I'd wager my soul on it. Damned good in a fight, but their asses are bound up too tight with all their traditions. Something like my Ezzarian friend here."

The Lidunni were the most formidable warriors of all Derzhi—members of a sect who combined religion and the art of hand combat. They never carried weapons, but it was said that they could snap a man's spine with one hand or catch a thrown spear before it struck.

Gaspar sighed. "I will not say who seeks us out—truly there are not so very many—only that they often come naked and broken and leave here whole. I have tried to persuade your troubled friend to seek the siffaru before he fights again, but he struggles on unaided. Perhaps you could influence him?"

Aleksander pulled his arm from his face and wrinkled his brow at me. "Maybe you ought to try it. You like mystical sorts of things, and, no matter how much they gabble on about matters of no consequence, these people do seem to know this healing business. If the Lidunni see value in their foolery, maybe it would help you with your problem."

I shook my head. I wanted no more visions.

Sovari was back in ten days. He rode in at dawn, bringing saddle packs full of blankets, wineskins, dried meat, flatbread such as Derzhi carried on long campaigns, some blessedly clean clothes, and a head full of news, none of it good.

"Lord Kiril was about to go mad with worry about you, my lord," said Sovari, dropping from the saddle and bending his knee to the Prince. He did not rise, but kept his head bent, even when Aleksander motioned him up. "Forgive me bringing vile tidings, Your Highness, but Lord Kiril bade me speak all of it without pausing for breath or your interruption, and so I shall do. You have been named Kinslayer and regicide, my lord, stripped of all your titles and lands, condemned by the Twenty to be flogged, hung up in the grand market of Zhagad, to have your entrails pulled out and set afire while you yet live—"

"Gods, Captain, consider your words!" I said. No man recovering from grievous injury needed to hear such grotesque elaboration. Aleksander knew what his people were capable of.

"As I said, Ezzarian, Lord Kiril bade me tell all without holding back so that my lord would understand the danger of his position. You are not safe anywhere in your empire, my lord Prince." Sovari swallowed uncomfortably. "They have put a price on your head."

A price . . . like a common thief. Aleksander was silent for so long, I was afraid his heart had stopped. When he spoke at last, his words could slice flesh. "I hope they've made the price a worthy one, at least. So tell me, how do they value my entrails?"

"Ten thousand zenars, my lord."

"Ten thousand . . . You were a bargain, Seyonne. I paid only twenty zenars for you and never burned your entrails once." He leaned back on the mound of sand we'd piled behind him, but the air yet quivered with his anger. "So have they crowned my father's cousin?"

Sovari faltered, his hesitation confirming what his tongue dared not. "My lord . . ."

"I see." Rarely had I felt so deadly a chill. "And who has died for it?"

"Siva, Walthar, Demtari—all of your personal advisers and bodyguards and servants were executed on the coronation day. Some seventy men. The only ones left living were a few who are kin to the Fontezhi and those willing to witness against you. Some testified to your disagreements with your father and hinted at plots against him; others claimed that your decrees moderating the slave trade and changing terms of indentures were purposed to weaken hegeds you disliked. The order was given that your troops were to be intercepted and your captains slain, but Lord Kiril had already sent word to Stepok to avoid Zhagad and take your men directly to Srif Naj. When matters got worse, he commanded Stepok disperse the troops, hide in the village, and await your word."

Aleksander was livid, his hands trembling. "And my wife . . . what news of her?"

I'd thought Sovari's sunburned face could burn no hotter. "Safe enough for now, my lord. Her father, Lord Marag, has publicly denounced the Emperor's murderer, though without naming you. He has returned to Zhagad to protect young Damok; times are too perilous to leave a boy with the Zhagad house. My lady has returned to Zhagad with Lord Marag, but remains in seclusion in her father's house and has let it be known that she will not hear your name spoken in her presence."

"As well we made no child. That's the only reason she yet lives. How does Kiril keep safe?"

"His lady mother, the Princess Rahil, has maintained silence on Lord Edik's ascension, which disturbs Lord Edik greatly. Lord Edik has made a great show of wooing the Princess's blessing, claiming that his concern for Denischkar honor has forced him to these hard choices, and that his authority will not be complete until his own heged closes ranks behind him. Even so, Lord Kiril himself has made public witness against your folly in attacking the Hamraschi. He begs you understand that it scalds his tongue, but it is the only way he can uphold your interests. He negotiated the surrender of your legion after the battle and was able to get favorable terms, claiming that most were unwilling conscripts. But he is also in contact with several houses who clearly detest Lord Edik and the unseemly haste with which he has proceeded."

Aleksander leaned forward. "So they will support me? Which houses?"

Sovari bent his head even farther. "Ah, my lord . . ."

"Come, tell me. If it is only three or four, so be it, so long as they are of the Twenty. Every powerful heged has its own alliances that can be brought to bear. Which ones will join me?"

"None of them, my lord. Lord Kiril says—"

"None! How in the name of the holy gods is it possible that no heged will support their rightful Emperor? What of the cursed Rhyzka, the most loyal of all?"

Sovari flinched, as if the Prince's words were tipped with steel. "Prince Edik has given the Rhyzka charge of your personal holdings, my lord, to prevent your using them as a base for rebellion."

"Get out. All of you. Get out!" Aleksander was shaking with rage. I believed that if Sovari or I had said another word right then, we would have found a dagger between our eyes. So we left him, and I warned Sarya that the Prince was not to be disturbed until I gave her leave.

"Perhaps he also needs the siffaru," she said, peering through the glaring sunlight at the figure huddled in the stifling shade.

"It will take more than visions to put his life back in balance," I said. "And I don't know where we'll find what's needed."

"Gaspar seeks answers for the warrior of light, but just when he feels this urgent purpose, his sight is clouded." Sarya's overwhelming sadness distracted me from Aleksander's distress. "Gaspar's time grows short. I can't think whether it is a mercy or a burden that he knows it."

"Gaspar's sight . . ." I touched Sarya's rounded shoulder as she turned away. "Tell me of a blind man's sight, Sarya."

Bits of moisture beaded her red-rimmed eyes. "Gaspar was fifteen when his day came to look into the smoke. He had shown the signs since he was a child, of course, and had been brought to Drafa to await his time. Dyomed had only fifty summers, so Gaspar thought he would have a long waiting. But Dyomed was bitten by a cycnid—a poisonous scorpion—and died within a day. Since that day, Gaspar has been the Avocar of Drafa. For sixty summers he has held answers, but so very few have come to ask. And now it grows late."

Avocar. Oracle.

CHAPTER 10

Ezzarians were not the only sorcerers in the world. Though we believed that we alone understood enough of melydda and possessed enough of it to fight the demon war, we knew that every race and tribe had its seers, or prophets, or those who wove love charms or healing spells or wards against evil, and that, on rare occasions, those people wove true.

On a blistering morning a few days after Sovari's return, I asked Aleksander if he had ever heard of the Avocar of Drafa. I was helping the Prince shift his position, propping him up with mounds of packed sand and rolled blankets. His leg still pained him, though not so much as Sovari's report. The Prince had spoken scarcely ten words in the preceding days, save to the captain, whom he quizzed unendingly on the fates or the public and private positions of every lord in the Twenty hegeds. Sovari was to leave for Zhagad that very nightfall to discover the answers he had not been able to supply.

"An oracle? I don't remember hearing of such. Could have saved me a lot of trouble, couldn't it? Told me not to bother with a number of things." I grieved to hear Aleksander's bitterness.

"Surely there was some mention of Drafa. You've been taught by people who revered Derzhi traditions—your uncle . . ."

"Dmitri would have killed anyone who tried to predict his future. He'd have said they were plotting against him, and the only way to be sure they failed was to be rid of them. One of many lessons I should have learned from him."

"Oracles don't predict the future," I said. "They make no claim to see true events or to interpret or influence what you should do about them. They only report the insights that come from their visions. You must make your own choices as to what they mean. Sarya says that Gaspar is called the Avocar of Drafa."

"Tell the old man to preach me none of his nonsense. Our future is written nowhere but in our deeds." Aleksander threw his arm across his eyes to shut out the light—a gesture I had learned meant dismissal.

"Perhaps," I said and left him to his sleep . . . or more likely to brood.

I could not shake my unease. My life had been intertwined with prophecy. Every time I denied it and charged off in a different direction, I ended up right in the middle of it again. Prophecy had caused my ancestors to close the way to Kir'-Navarrin, and I had judged them wrong to have done it. They had not understood the consequences of their deeds: the existence of the rai-kirah and the torment of the demons' exile that had led to our unending war. That same prophecy, recorded in an ancient mosaic, had depicted a winged man walking toward the fortress of Tyrrad Nor with a key in his hand, and had warned of an overwhelming catastrophe that was one possible result of his deeds. I had done what I believed right, come to an interpretation that justified my actions to reopen the gateway, but I could not escape doubts, not when my dreams told me that the face of monstrous catastrophe was my own. Thus, it was more difficult to thrust aside Gaspar's words, now that I heard there was a tradition of mystical truth in Drafa.

I took my unease with me as I walked up the rise to our watch point and sent Sovari off to get some sleep before his night's journey. Sarya was sitting with the sleeping Prince, for Malver had not yet returned from his mission in Zhagad. The day was murderously hot. I sat under a lonely nagera tree, sipping occasionally from a waterskin, watching the lizards scuttle from one bit of shade to the next. To persuade myself to leave the shade and circle the rise every hour, in order to scan every direction for signs of pursuit, was a monumental effort. Kiril had sent warning that Edik would not sit comfortably on his stolen throne until he had proof that Aleksander was food for vultures, but it was hard to imagine the Derzhi would seek the Prince in Drafa out of all the vastness of Azhakstan.

The air throbbed with the heat. I felt myself nodding off. Only a short time had passed since my last round, but I pulled up the scarf of the flowing white haffai Sovari had brought me and stumbled to my feet. I picked a few juicy red pomegranate seeds from a fruit I had just cut open, popping the sweet little nodules in my mouth as I walked the dusty path again. The midday light was flat, the sky a hard silvery blue. The silence was unbroken by any bird or insect or whisper of wind. Yet in the north where Zhagad lay, I glimpsed a telltale puff of dust. I stopped and squinted. The dust was moving . . . southward toward Drafa.

"Riders!" I yelled, running down the path toward our shelter.

As I had learned from hard experience, even powerful sorcery could not counter sheer numbers. No matter what enchantments I worked, Sovari and I could not kill fifty Derzhi by ourselves, and leaving any one of them alive to report Aleksander's position would be failure. I had no time to shift. Nor could we run, not until Aleksander was well enough to ride, which meant we had to let the riders search Drafa. The women had told us they had a place to hide us if the time came, but had refused to reveal it unless it was needed. Faced with no reasonable alternatives, I prayed that it was secure. The Derzhi would arrive in moments, not hours. "Qeb," I shouted. "We need the hiding place."

Standing in the dusty path, the boy stared north into the desert. "Sarya will show you," he said quietly, folding his arms across his thin brown chest. "I'll go to Gaspar. We'll take care of this."

"Tell Gaspar these are Derzhi warriors," I said. "They're not coming to seek balance. They're hunting my friend who's injured. He's the heir—"

Qeb waved off my concerns. "We know who he is. You needn't worry. Take him to safety." I wanted to shake the boy from his strange detachment. Torn between the desire to get Aleksander away and the certainty that this quiet boy and the old man were going to do something foolish, I stood stupidly in the dirt, doing nothing. But then Sarya beckoned from beside a crumbled wall, and I had to move. "They'll show no mercy, Qeb," I called after the boy. "They want him badly."

As he walked slowly toward Gaspar's house, he nodded calmly. "We understand."

Sovari had set our crude litter beside a snoring Aleksander and was shaking the Prince's shoulder. "My lord," he said. "My lord, we must move you." Aleksander mumbled drowsily, but did not wake.

"We can't wait for permission," I said. I grabbed the Prince's middle and rolled him toward me, while Sovari slipped the litter underneath his back.

Aleksander grunted as we laid him down, and then, as I carefully lifted his leg and placed it on the litter, his color fled and his eyes flew open. "Demonfire, what do you think you're doing?"

"Riders, my lord. We're not sure who they are, but there's a goodly number of them. We've got to hide you."

"So I'm to run away again."

"We've no time to argue," I said, tossing Aleksander's sword, dagger, and blankets on top of him. I nodded to Sovari, and we hefted the litter.

Manot had joined us, gathering up her medicines, the waterskins, and blankets scattered about our little shelter. She kicked sand and brush about, and soon the corner by the nagera grove looked like any other part of the decrepit ruin. Meanwhile Sarya had pulled aside a tangle of weeds and mud bricks, exposing a low doorway in the side of a mountain of rubble where a number of houses and walls had collapsed, one upon the other.

Sovari and I had to stoop as we stepped through into a dark passage. The air smelled smoky and sweet, and the walls and ceiling seemed a great deal more stable than the overlay of crumbled brick would suggest. What I could see of the path led steeply downward, disappearing into pitch-black after the glare of noonday. I whispered a light to augment Sarya's sputtering torch. It wouldn't improve our fortunes to stumble and drop Aleksander.

What we found at the end of the passage was astonishing—a cool, dry room, its walls of solid rock—a cave room, long buried by desert and city. As we set down the Prince's litter and turned to marvel, time itself seemed to roll backward. This place was not a part of Drafa, but far older. On every surface of the room were paintings, depicting neither the sophisticated abstractions of faces and figures that graced Derzhi sand paintings, nor the detailed representations of life and myth I had seen in other cultures of the Empire. These were simpler works, created by hands that believed in the power of what they drew. Kayeets, sand-deer, herds of dune-runners and gazelles—the creatures of the desert—all of them moving, running, leaping, painted in deep reds and ochres and browns and blacks—the colors of the desert. And everywhere were horses, the graceful horses that were the very soul of the Derzhi. The room was alive with their power.

"Holy Athos . . ." The Prince gaped at the sweeping majesty, and I wondered at it, too, but only for a moment, as the horses reminded me of the hooves racing toward us across the dunes.

Manot had followed us down the path, but there was no sign of Fessa, Gaspar, or Qeb. I ran back up the passageway to fetch them, but Sarya stood in the bright rectangle of the outer doorway and caught my arm before I could go out. "Stay here. Qeb will close the way when he comes." The sunlight illuminated her withered face. She was weeping.

"What are they going to do, Sarya?"

"Gaspar believes that not all of us can hide. The hunters will know someone lives here in Drafa. Best they find someone."

The old man was right, of course. Much as I wanted to drag them to whatever safety this hidden room could provide, the absence of residents in a place that showed signs of recent habitation would goad the pursuers to tear the place apart. "He knows what these men will do?"

Sarya nodded. "For half his life he's known. Only the day was the mystery."

We had to respect Gaspar and Fessa's choice. The gift was theirs to give, and to refuse their generosity would have been cruel, for it would not have saved any of us.

The old couple was sitting in the nagera grove. Qeb was kneeling beside them, his head bowed as a smiling Fessa stroked his shining hair. Gaspar laid his hands on the boy's wiry shoulders and kissed him, and then motioned for him to hurry. Clouds of dust rose beyond the tamarisks.

Qeb walked away from the old couple slowly, stopping several times to gaze out toward the desert and up at the sky. At one point he crouched down, scooped up a handful of sand, and watched it trickle through his fingers. I was about to split my skin with his dawdling.

Gaspar called out to the boy, "Go, child! You won't forget!"

Qeb stood up again and waved to Fessa, and then ran lightly toward our hiding place. Before moving aside to let the boy through the door, I raised a small whirlwind to mask our footsteps. In the nagera grove, Gaspar laughed and raised a cup in my direction. Perhaps the blind man felt the wind and knew it was not of the desert. I helped Qeb pull bricks and scrub into place, we retreated down the dim passage, and there we sat. Waiting.

* * *

Deep layers of sand and rubble separated us from what occurred in Drafa that afternoon. Ordinary ears could not hear the shouts and curses of frustrated searchers or the agonized cries of the two old people who died a cruel death to keep our secrets and save our lives. Though I would much rather have remained deaf like the others, I chose to listen. To share the event in some fashion seemed a matter of respect for Gaspar and Fessa's sacrifice. I hoped that the old ones guessed my ability and thus knew that, in some ever so small a way, they were not alone.

The others watched me, but did not ask what I heard. Likely my muttered curses and clenched fists were enough for them to surmise that they did not want to know. Sarya and Manot held hands, resting their gray heads on one another's shoulder. A solemn Qeb sat in the corner of the painted room, his slender arms wrapped about his knees, light brown eyes fixed on the ancient paintings. His tanned skin seemed to glow with a light of its own. In some unfathomable way the boy belonged in that room. A holy place. His place.

Eventually I heard the hunting party depart, murmuring of their unease at staying in "haunted" Drafa after nightfall. Their captain claimed satisfaction with the afternoon's results. The old people had held longer than he would have thought possible, but had clearly revealed their secret: Prince Aleksander had sheltered in Drafa long enough to recuperate from a twisted ankle, but had disappeared into the desert ten days previously.

Once the murderers had gone, the silence held absolute, and after another hour's listening, I believed that if soldiers had been left to stand watch in the city, they were few enough that I could kill them. I relished the chance. "Stay here until I tell you," I said. "I'll make sure they've not left a sentry."

"The old ones?" said Aleksander.

"Dead," I said. "They told a good story and held it until the end."

Carefully I shoved aside the rubble at the doorway and crept out into the late afternoon. I slunk up and down the pathways of the dead city, listening for the shuffle of a boot or a cough or the muffled ring of weaponry, watching for the gleam of metal where it had no place or a shadow that was darker than the usual. I wanted to punish someone for what had happened; I craved a Derzhi neck to throttle, a smug jaw to smash, a well-fed belly in which to embed my dagger. But a thorough inspection convinced me that every horse that had galloped into Drafa that afternoon had galloped out again, and that the only creatures abroad were rats and scorpions and a single nervous sand-deer at the spring.

Before calling the others from hiding, I debated whether to take Gaspar and Fessa down from the nagera trees where they had been bound and tortured. Though it would have been a kindness to Manot and Sarya, I was not feeling particularly kind, and instinct bade me leave the dreadful scene so that all of us could bear witness to the vileness one human could work upon another. And so it was that Sovari and I carried Aleksander out of the painted room, and the Prince saw what had been given to save him. He did not avert his eyes, but said nothing, which was perhaps the truest measure of his horror.

Sovari suggested that we leave the dead couple in place so that their absence would not give witness to our presence in case the hunters returned. But the women would not hear of it, claiming that the souls could not take their leave of the tormented flesh until the bodies lay on the sand. So, once Aleksander was settled again, the captain and I took Gaspar and Fessa down, leaving Manot and Sarya to tend the ruined bodies.

Sovari left for Zhagad an hour after sunset, afoot, for the Derzhi scouts had taken his horse and killed the chastou. ". . . and I want to know who rode here today," said the Prince after reviewing his long list of messages and inquiries. "Every man's name."

"Aye, my lord. I would do it for my own knowledge, even if you had not commanded it."

I helped Sovari fill his waterskins and saw him on his way. When Sarya was ready, I carried the two cleaned bodies into the desert, the gods having had their due with the daylight, and laid the corpses out on the dunes for the jackals. Wood was scarce in the desert. Only emperors could afford burning. When all this was done, I sought other occupation. I offered to keep the night's vigil with Sarya and Manot, but they declined. Qeb had not yet emerged from the cave. Perhaps the boy was afraid to see what had come down on his friends. He was very young. I returned to Aleksander.

The Prince claimed he wished to sleep, but I sensed his need to be alone. I understood that. I had always needed time alone after a demon battle to regain balance and perspective. But on that night I was afraid to be alone. Darkness and violence seethed within me, fed by the horrors of the day, and I wasn't sure I was capable of holding them off. I warned Aleksander to sleep light, then rid myself of weapons and walked the dusty ruin, trying not to think, trying not to stare out into the empty night, fearing I would see a woman in green tearing at my divided soul with grief I could not understand. In search of stability, I tried again to strengthen my barriers—the protections against demon infestation that I had learned in my youth—but the melydda would not shape itself to my will. I was on the edge of bursting, ready to spew violence and danger and madness across the silent ruin. In the end, sometime just after moonrise, I sank to my knees in the sand, burying my head in trembling hands. I felt ragged and crippled and afraid.

"I can help you, warrior." The scent of herb-laden smoke and the quiet voice, just on the edge of manhood, told me who had come. The boy's bare feet had made no sound.

"Unless you can stand with me in a place I fear to go, I don't think that's possible."

"The siffaru is a journey of the spirit. The gods can take you where they will, teach you of what you fear, while reminding you of the strength you possess to face it. You know already the worth of seeing what is painful. Now you must prepare yourself for the task you have chosen. Will you not allow us to help you?"

"I can't indulge my fears right now. The Prince . . . in such danger . . . he is everything . . ."

"Gaspar and Fessa have given you this time. The hunters will not return here, and Sarya and Manot will care for your prince as he heals. Right now his greatest danger is your own hand."

I shuddered at this eerie echo of my own thoughts. "How can you know these things . . . a child who has lived here in the wastes since before you can remember?"

"It is my gift to know." The strangeness of Qeb's voice yanked my eyes up, but the boy was already walking away from me toward the dark doorway that gaped in the pile of rubble. His steps were slow and awkward, tentative, altogether unlike his graceful quickness. He stumbled on a bit of rubble, and something about the way his hands flew out seeking balance tore at my heart.

When I was in bondage to the Derzhi, an old slave woman had advised me to be content with my lot, saying that those who climb to the greatest heights have the greatest price to pay. Here again was evidence of her wisdom. What price to gaze into realms of mystery, to seek out visions and hold them ready for those who came naked and broken?

I rose and walked down the path, following the blind youth into the darkness.

CHAPTER 11

How many days did I exist in the cave? Once I convinced myself to let go the demands of duty and attempt the journey, I also made myself forego the captive's imperative to tally his days of bondage. I might have numbered my sleeping periods, but lost in a haze of smoke and mystery, I could not be sure that I slept only once a day or that I ever slept at all. Fruit or bread and goat's milk appeared on the flat rock by the entrance door when I wasn't looking, just enough to quiet the physical cravings while leaving my inner hungers untouched. I was not a captive, of course. I could have walked out of the caves at any time. But I was on the verge of disintegration, and I prayed this mystery would help me hold myself together.

From the first hour, when Qeb led me to the bare inner room, sat me on the dirt floor, and bade me forego speech and all connection to life for the duration of the siffaru, I was never sure exactly what was happening. Every time my head began to clear, I would blink and find Qeb sitting cross-legged beside me. He would smile, throw a handful of dried leaves in a brass bowl, and light them from a taper, cupping his slender fingers about the bowl to guide his actions. Then, as the pungent blue-gray smoke wafted from the bowl, he would take my hands and force me to look into his sightless eyes, still raw and seeping from whatever he had done to ruin them.

To loose the bonds of the world was difficult. Vague worries plagued me: about Aleksander, about Sovari, about Malver who had not yet returned from Zhagad, about my wife and the Ezzarians lost in their denial of truth, and about Blaise and his sister and my child, hidden somewhere in the increasingly dangerous world. When I ate, the flavors burned my tongue like acid, and I was overwhelmed with memories: a sip of wine from my father's cup . . . a ripe peach shared with Ysanne on the first day of our pairing, when I was fifteen and loved her with the focused passion of youth . . . the dry, maggot-infested bread that had gagged me when I first succumbed to hunger as a slave. Sometimes I found myself kneeling in the center of the roughly circular room, knees aching and muscles stiff, as if I'd been there long hours, and my body demanded my attention, crying out its hard history as warrior, slave, and prisoner.

But gradually, as I was immersed in silence and solitude and smoke, the clamor of these things—appetites and anxiety, pain and memory—faded into a murmur no louder than my heartbeat. My mind began to wander freely . . . in a vast nothingness, it seemed. Only then did I truly begin the journey.

I sat cross-legged in the center of the circular room as always. My hands lay relaxed on my knees. I had adopted the position Wardens used when preparing to battle demons, finding the attitude of peace and contemplation eminently suitable to this strange exercise. The still air of the cave room smelled faintly of Qeb's herbs. My eyes were fixed on the smudge of light that was my candle flame, and I was so drowsy, my heart seemed scarcely to be beating.

The light faded, replaced by a now-familiar blue-gray nothingness. Yet something was different . . . a thickening . . . a texture to the swirling cloud . . . shadowy forms . . . trees . . .

. . . A ghostly landscape. A blackbird shrieked . . . the faint scent of ash on a warm breeze . . . the flat metallic taste of blood on my tongue . . .

I blinked, long and slow, and Qeb was there with his bowl and his taper. The blind youth, no longer smiling, nodded and touched his tiny flame to the crumbled leaves in his brass bowl, and I drifted deeper yet . . .

Raindrops spattered on the gravel path, glancing off the white stones like beads of crystal, joining their fellows in thready rivulets that drained into the garden. Leaves of rambling honeysuckle dipped with the brisk pounding, and daylilies were turned in upon themselves as if to protect their tender petals. So green it was, narrow swaths of grass encircled by exuberant stands of yellow, white, and blue flowers. A towering willow centered one swale, the graceful arcs of its branches brushing the green. What sound was so delightful as that of soft rain, bounteous life itself, so generously, so tenderly given from heaven to earth? Absorbed in my contemplation of the rainy garden, I strolled along the white gravel path, noting only in passing that I did not seem to be getting wet.

What place was this? I stopped, puzzled, trying to think where I had just come from and where I was going. Beyond the field of flowers, scarcely visible through the curtain of rain, was the dark line of a wall. Like the twang of a broken harpstring intrudes upon a sweet melody, so the sight of that wall infused the day's beauty with a piercing sadness.

"So you've ventured a visit at last. An interesting way you've chosen." The bemused comment came from behind me.

I spun about and almost stopped breathing. A tall, spare, elderly man, dressed in a plum-colored shirt, green breeches, and knee-high boots stood between two rosebushes at the edge of the path, staring at me. A worn leather bag hung from his wide belt, and a gray cloak was thrown carelessly over one shoulder. His clothing and his short gray hair were dripping, which emphasized the oddity of my own dry state. Yet what had stolen my breath was not the man's sudden arrival, nor anything related to his appearance, which was generally unremarkable. Rather it was what I saw behind him.

The garden was part of a walled parkland fronting a castle of gray stone, a turreted palace built on a broad, gently sloped green shoulder of a craggy peak. Beyond the encircling arms of the black wall, the land fell away precipitously, revealing hazy vistas of distant mountain ranges. From within the castle, candlelight shone through windows of colored glass, making them gleam and sparkle in the soft gray of the day. And far above me, where graceful towers soared into the clouds alongside the mountain's pinnacles, were the lonely ramparts . . . the walkways where a prisoner strode back and forth, raging at the world. Oh yes, I knew where I was.

"It is not as you expected, is it?" My gaze returned to the lean figure, who was turning his back to me. "Well, I'm not going to stand out in the rain while you decide whether you would rather gawk or converse. You can come if you wish." He set out briskly along the gravel path toward the castle.

"Wait!" I called to his rapidly disappearing back. He was almost at the wide steps and pillared portico before I caught up with him. Even then he kept moving up the steps, into a wide hall where muted light from high glass windows left a sheen on smooth columns and marble statuary.

How to begin? Ask him if the one imprisoned here truly wished to destroy the world? Have him tell me what was my connection to the prisoner's dreadful plan? I had not passed through the gateway at Dasiet Homol, so how was it possible that I walked Kir'Navarrin? I had once touched a painted image that convinced me this fortress was the source of profound darkness; why did I not feel that now I was here? Was this lean old man the jailer of an angry god? "I would very much like to speak with you," I said, hurrying alongside him.

"If you don't mind, I would like to get a dry shirt first. Not all of us are so fortunate as you to escape a soaking." He strode into a finely appointed room: patterned carpets of dark green and red, tall windows that opened onto the portico and the garden, a marble hearth three times the height of a man, carved so that the tall, slender figures of a man and a woman who gazed down serenely upon the well-proportioned room seemed about to emerge from the stone. Around the walls were lamps of crystal and painted glass, gleaming with soft light. A small table beside the fire held a checkered game board of black and gray glass and on it the carved game pieces for warriors and castles.

"Kasparian, where are you?" the man called out in annoyance as he threw his cloak onto a padded bench and hurried to the fire, pulling off his soggy, plum-colored shirt to reveal a broad chest covered with gray hair. Almost before he had the word out, a man and a woman bustled through a door beside the hearth. The man carried a towel, a green shirt, and a dark green cloak, while the woman set a tray of porcelain cups and teapots, crystal goblets and carafes on a side table. The serving man—for so he seemed to be—retrieved the wet shirt and began fussing with the towel about the man's head and chest. The old gentleman snatched the towel and threw it to the floor, motioning for the dry shirt and the green robe, grumbling, "I am not a child needing to be blotted." The serving man did not seem to notice the comment, as he stooped down, recovered the towel, and began to dab at the old man's boots.

The woman poured hot liquid from the pot into the cup and proceeded to stir in sugar and fragrant spices. "No, no. I want wine," demanded the old man. My host—I had no other name to call him—soon dry and dressed, began tapping his foot while the serving woman ignored him and went on with her preparations. Only when she had the cup steeping and covered with a thin glass plate did she pour wine—three varieties into three goblets—and what appeared to be dark brown ale into a silver tankard. As the two servants withdrew, the old man sighed and snatched a wine-glass from the table, speaking to himself as much as to me. "One would think I'd get used to such petty annoyances. I've become so accustomed to the general way of things, I'd almost be willing to stay put, as so many seem to wish, but truly it is the trivial that creates the greatest burden. And Kasparian, who devotes himself to relieving those burdens, cannot understand why they exasperate me so." He sipped pale wine and darted a sideways glance at me. "You are not so big as I expected."

Never had I been so utterly bereft of words.

The old man shook his head slightly, as if coming to himself. "You are uncomfortable. I had no intent to be rude." He motioned to a chair beside the fire. "Do come and sit. You wanted to talk."

Abandoning all expectation, I blurted out the mad, impossible whimsy that had taken shape as I watched and listened. "You are the prisoner."

His dark eyes widened in mock amazement. "A day replete with surprises. I would celebrate if I could remember how to do such a thing." His features were fine: high cheekbones, jaw and brow that might have been formed from the same granite as his mountain prison, thick gray hair and beard trimmed close. A dignified, aristocratic look about him, but no evidence of ill nature, save his peevish humor. Nothing of hatred or cruelty written on his visage, though I hunted carefully for the signs. And his dark, intelligent eyes told no different story. They were deep and clear, like snow-fed mountain lakes on a moonlit midnight, eyes that seemed far younger than his body. I did not shift my own sight to look more deeply. I could not think his was a soul to be probed without consequence.

He sat in a high-backed wooden chair beside the hearth, drawing his green cloak close about him and stretching his boots toward the flames.

This man, this place, could be but creations of my diseased mind. This experience was certainly some type of dreaming . . . only in dreams and visions could one walk through rain and remain dry. Yet I did not believe any dream could be so contrary to the dreamer's preconceptions. "Who are you?" I demanded, as if a simple answer would make everything clear.

"You're a blunt sort of fellow." Again he waved me to the

chair. "Well, I suppose I am the same of late, as you see. But at least do me the courtesy of pretending politeness. Allow me to demonstrate that I recall a bit about civilized behavior."

Dreamlike, I moved to the hard, straight-backed chair facing him. The table with the glass game board sat between us. About half of the pieces of each color—black and white—sat to one side, as if a game had been interrupted.

"Do you play?" The simple question was spoken gruffly, like all his speech.

"I know how. I'm not proficient." He had not answered my own question, but I could not think what else to say.

He fingered the black pieces . . . obsidian, the black glass found near old volcanoes. The white were alabaster. "I persuaded Kasparian to learn, but he sees no more use in games than he sees in conversation. Every few days, he steels himself and offers to play, but I thank him and refuse. I get no pleasure from tormenting him. I often wonder if I remember the rules correctly."

"I'll play if you like."

His eyes popped up, and for the first time he looked me full in the face. "That would be fine. Quite fine." Remarkable eyes.

And so we pulled our chairs close to the table and set the pieces in their squares. I, as white player, began, and we exchanged several moves before he spoke again. "You can call me Nyel."

Nyel. In the language of the rai-kirah, the word meant "forgotten."

"It seems you know me already," I said, pushing one of my castles two squares forward.

He dipped his head in acknowledgment and contemplated my move. After only a few moments, he moved a black rider and captured one of my warriors. "I've had no wish to frighten you."

"No wish to frighten . . . I don't believe that." His assertion was so absurd that it shook me from my careful reticence. I thought of the dreams he had touched: my death visions of this very fortress that haunted my nights, and the dreams that had lured me into the demon realm—the image of a black and silver warrior whose power filled me with despair and dread. Both visions implied that I was to bring destruction to everything I valued. What man or woman would not be frightened?

"Power is frightening," he said. "Great power extremely so. But fear was never my intent."

"Then you miscalculated."

"Your fear does not diminish my estimation of you. I know how I am perceived in the worlds. Even the staunchest heart must blanch in the face of uttermost evil." He might have been speaking of a preference for onions over radishes.

This dry poke at himself did nothing to restore my equilibrium, thrown off so badly by this strange visit. I took a moment to survey the game board and gather my wits. I laid a finger on one of my warriors . . . then took it away again as I saw the danger in the move. Instead, I shifted one of my priests to protect my lady queen. "If not to intimidate me, then why any of it?"

Without hesitation he used his rider again to capture another white warrior. "Because I want to be free. I am not immortal, despite what stories say of me. I am coming to the end of a very long life, most of which has been spent locked away in this place. Pleasant though it be, it is still a prison. So—this is not so difficult a concept—there are a few things I would like to do before I die. Perhaps to walk the world beyond these walls."

I shifted a rider to threaten his. "You've been trying to escape. Using others, manipulating them . . . with dreams, I think, as you have with me." I could not even begin to tally the names of the dead that lay at his feet—rai-kirah, Ezzarians, Khelid, the uncountable victims of the demon war—yet the dead seemed so very remote beside the consuming reality of this moment.

"Every captive has the right to yearn for freedom. There is a certain madness in bondage . . . you know of it. We are driven to make compromises that we would abhor in other circumstances."

Disconcerting to think that he knew so much of me, and I so little of him. My demon and I had both made compromises to be free, and our choices had not been guiltless. Yet surely Nyel's crimes must outweigh my own; my ancestors had riven their souls for fear of him. What had he done? And what did he see in me that made him think I would be his tool? I could not allow myself to be mesmerized by disarming frankness and a friendly game. "Why me?"

He kept his eyes fixed upon the game and drew his obsidian priest halfway across the glass to threaten my king. "Your power, of course. That's what I've been trying to tell you. Of all beings in the worlds, you have the power to release me. You have power enough to do a great many things."

This was the first lie I had heard from him. Not that what he said was untrue. Now that he laid it out, it was obvious that my dreams had been crafted to tell me exactly that—I had power beyond telling. But I also sensed that his words were not the truthful answer to my question.

As I contemplated the game board and this odd discourse, the woman servant returned, bringing hot water to replenish the teapot, a plate of frosted cakes, and a bowl of plump red grapes.

Nyel jumped up from his chair and strode to the window, peering out into the misty afternoon. "Where is the cursed Kasparian? I've no mind for sweets and dainties. I've climbed the mountain path today and would dine early."

The woman did not respond. She left the room and returned with a silver salver piled high with sugared dates. The manservant poked up the fire, turned up the lamps, and drew the curtains against the failing light. Nyel might not have been in the room for all the note they took of him. They performed their duties without speech or deference. When the manservant brought soft slippers, he did not approach Nyel or ask if he was ready, but knelt in front of Nyel's empty chair. He waited there motionless until the old man sighed in exasperation, sat down, and allowed his damp boots to be removed and replaced with the softer shoes.

Just as the two servants left the room, another man hurried through the door, buttoning a high collar about a neck as thick as my waist. Unlike the servants, he addressed Nyel directly, bowing with respectful familiarity. "I am shamed, Master. How could I have missed his coming?" His shoulders and chest were in proportion to his neck—a giant of a man. Wet brown hair, long and thick, was threaded with gray. His apparel, apparently thrown on carelessly, was simple—dark brown vest and breeches, white shirt, and worn boots. He had not been in so much hurry as to leave off his weapon, however, a formidable sword in a battered sheath. On observing the hard-edged patterns of his face, I surmised that the weapon would always be the last thing he left off.

"His arrival was unconventional, as is his continued presence," said Nyel, acknowledging the newcomer's respectful address with a slight nod. "It seems he needed no admission to our charmed fortress."

The man's wide hands, freed of occupation now that his collar was fastened, settled to his hips as he stared at me in frank appraisal. After a moment his eyes widened. "He isn't really here at all!"

Nyel propped his chin on his hand and raised his eyebrows. "Perhaps it is more accurate to say that he is with us in spirit only. He has yet to take the more decisive step of passing through the last breach."

"So he is still human." The derisive hatred with which the newcomer spit out this accusation threw Nyel's amiable sparring into darker context.

"No," snapped Nyel. "He was never that. Mind your tongue."

The man dipped his head. "We differ, as always, Master. I can say only as I see."

"Before we set off arguing again, will you tell your benighted minions that I am ready to dine? I climbed today and am like to wither away altogether without sustenance."

The man bowed and withdrew. Nyel slumped in his chair, staring at the game board. I didn't think his mind was on our game—certainly not the one we played with black and white pieces.

"I never thought to see others in this place," I said. "Who are they?"

Nyel glanced up. "The servants are . . . creations . . . neither human nor anything else. Made to serve my comfort, though, as you see, I cannot command them. Nor can I kill them." He grimaced ruefully. "I must confess, at times I've been driven to try. When I die, they will vanish as if they had never been."

"But this other man . . ."

"Kasparian. Like me, a captive in this gracious house. Though, unlike me, he chose it freely."

"He chose to be imprisoned?"

"Extraordinary, is it not, such ferocious loyalty? And still undimmed, for his is a noble spirit. Could you do such a thing for anyone? I don't think I could." The old man sighed. "It is not his fault he has the dullest mind ever woke of a morning."

Extraordinary, indeed. Someone had cared enough for Nyel to share his captivity for untold years—far more than a thousand, for it was a full thousand years in the past that an Ezzarian prophet had foretold the release of the prisoner of Tyrrad Nor and the catastrophe that it would cause. "Is he a kinsman?"

"He was my *attellé*—the son of a very good friend sent to live with me and learn from me, though not very successfully even then."

"Your student."

"Much more than that. What student chooses to lie ill when his master is diseased?"

"More like a son, then."

And here I believed that I had stumbled close to the heart of the matter, for though Nyel sat very still and made no show of anger, his dark gaze pressed down on me until I was almost suffocated. "No. Not a son. Never that."

Even Kasparian could not match Nyel as a source for wonder. I had expected to find a being kin to the Lord of Demons, the vile and murderous rai-kirah I had battled in Aleksander's soul, and what had I found instead? A tired old man—petulant, lonely, wryly humorous, aggrieved. Though I had seen no direct manifestation of it, I did not discount his power. I was utterly fascinated.

"Will you tell me your story, Nyel? I'd like to understand."

He rubbed his forehead absentmindedly. "And what would that accomplish? You judged me long ago. You think that those who put me here must have done it for good reason, and that a friendly game of warriors and castles will change nothing."

"I am not afraid to listen." Wary, but no longer afraid.

He glanced across the room, where the manservant was bringing in a covered dinner service. He rose to his feet and looked down at me. "I need to eat and rest for a while. You can ruminate upon your confounded expectations and decide if you truly mean what you say. If you're still here when the sun rises, perhaps I'll tell you.

CHAPTER 12

I walked in Nyel's garden under a double-sized moon, hung in a canopy of unfamiliar stars. Like a ghost, I left no footprints on the wet grass, nor could I feel the rain-washed air nor smell the honeysuckle. Far in the back of my mind, like the tiny, clear images sighted through a spyglass, were a blind, half-naked boy and a brass bowl. I believed that I had but to reach for them to go back. My true life waited for me there, but here . . . what was here?

Danger, certainly. Just as in the days I had walked portals into the realms of human souls, I had journeyed far beyond the boundaries of intellect and experience. But because of the demon inside me, I could no longer trust my Warden's instincts. I felt vulnerable. Exposed. History, legend, and suspicion proclaimed this mysterious man's wickedness, yet I was drawn to him in ways I could not express. He was an answer to questions I had not asked. He was a memory I could not capture, a word poised on my tongue, ready to be spoken.

In my sojourn in Kir'Vagonoth I had been enchanted, enveloped in a spell of romantic attachment to a beautiful rai-kirah named Vallyne. With confusion and stolen memory, Vallyne and her charming partner Vyx had tried to trick me into yielding my soul to Denas, not understanding that I was ready to do as they wished for my own reasons. But my fascination with Nyel was something far deeper—an attachment developed while my eyes were open and wary, and thus far more worrisome. Denas could not help me. At the time of our joining, Denas had known no more than I of the danger in Tyrrad Nor.

Reviewing every word of my strange discourse with Nyel, examining them for snares and signs of treachery, I walked for hours. I did not watch where I wandered, so that when a shadow blocked the angled moonlight, I was surprised to look up and find myself about to stumble headlong into the wall. The barrier was twice my height. Though built of smooth, solid black stone so finely joined, one could scarcely see the edges of the blocks, it looked as if someone had taken a hammer to it. Chips of stone lay on the ground, and cracks as deep as my second knuckle wandered here and there across the flats. In a few spots the top was ragged, crumbling.

When I had been bleeding away my life on a hillside in southern Manganar, my death vision had shown me this very wall breached by a jagged crack that leaked blood, a deadly flow that threatened to consume the world of Kir'Navarrin in fire. In that same vision, I had seen Vyx insert himself into the breach to seal it. I believed what that image had shown me—not so much that a good-humored rai-kirah had truly become a part of the stone, but that Vyx had somehow sacrificed himself to keep the fortress secure. I ran my fingers over the black stone, trying to sense something of its enchantment, to learn of Vyx's fate or what he might have done to heal the breach. But my ghost hand could feel nothing but the hard surface. "I wish you were here to advise me, rai-kirah," I said, walking alongside the barrier, dragging my palm along its rough solidity. "This is not at all what I expected."

I walked along the wall all the way to the juncture where it merged seamlessly with the mountainside; then I walked back again past my starting point to the other end. No tree grew within fifty paces of this dark barrier, and I found no gate or other opening in the black stone. Nowhere did I see any possibility that a man, sorcerer or no, could scale or breach its smooth face.

The hours passed quickly. As the darkness after moonset yielded to dawn gray, I hurried back through the garden toward the castle, where I found a green-cloaked Nyel sitting on the wide steps and watching the watery sun rise over the mountains. He nodded—in satisfaction, I thought—when he caught sight of me. "The grounds are not so large as they seem, are they?" he said, gesturing to his domain. "Do you mind walking awhile longer? I'm a bit stiff from the damp."

"If you like," I said. "Did you rest well?"

"Indeed. I find it so annoying to require sleep. When I was young, I could go entire seasons without. There was so much to do—exploring, enjoying games and conversation, building, devising those things humans call magic, contemplating the world . . . worlds, as we discovered."

We strolled along the same paths that I had trodden in the

night, but I was not watching the scenery this time, only listening and formulating questions. "When you say 'we' . . ."

"We called ourselves Madonai, and we had lived in this world we called Kir'Navarrin for seven ages—thousands of years to those who count time. I cannot describe the glory of my people—their beauty and intelligence and goodness of heart. To see Kasparian and myself so fallen . . . to think we are the last . . . it is a bitter ending."

I thought he was going to stop with that, for his voice was shaking. But though his steps slowed, they never stopped, and soon he began to speak again. "As I told you, we are not immortal, but we live a very long time compared to humans or your own kind."

He did not quite spit and curse when he said the word human, as Kasparian had done, but from the beginnings of this story, I felt his loathing for humankind. "As with everything in the natural world, there was a balance to be maintained," he continued. "And so it was with our long lives. Only rarely did we birth children. No Madonai could parent more than one, and when I came of age, it had been a great many years since the last Madonai child was born. This was a great sorrow to us, as we missed sharing our learning and adventures with children.

"There came a time when my good friend Hyrdon and I came into a great enchantment—a mode of travel that took us to a place that we did not know existed. To a different world, where beings lived who were something similar to ourselves, though weak and fragile and unendingly contentious." He glanced my way. "They called us gods, Hyrdon and me."

"You found the human world," I said.

We had wandered through the garden and onto the wild grass at its edge, but never did we approach the wall. Whenever our path threatened to take us near it, Nyel would alter his direction. "Hyrdon was uncomfortable in this new world and soon returned home, but I explored further and came upon a land so marvelous . . . a warm forest land of healthy trees and abundant rain . . . of smooth hills, and leaves that took fire with color in the waning season . . ."

Ezzaria. He had fallen in love with my homeland. His voice trailed away, and I took up the story for the moment, reciting eagerly as for a well-loved schoolmaster. "You helped the people tend the forest. Taught them how to live in it, how to nurture it and love it as you did. And eventually you met a human woman, fell in love with her, and she bore you a child."

Nyel laughed, but without mirth. "You learned your lessons well. Yes. That all happened. But I was never jealous of the boy. I was elated. All Madonai rejoiced. When they learned that I had produced a child after only a short time mated, others sought partners among the humans. Men who had produced a Madonai child could also father a half-human child. A Madonai woman who had seen her only babe grown long years before, could have three more if she mated with a human man. And the children were so beautiful and marvelous . . . we called them 'rekkonarre' . . ."

"Children of joy," I said. Rekkonarre . . . rai-kirah . . . I wanted him to stop there. To let me savor the revelation, the answer to the puzzle of my people's origin, the bits and pieces of truth that I had seen, now snapped into their proper positions within the mosaic of history. "They could shapeshift," I said. "These children had power something like that of Madonai."

"Greater in some ways," said Nyel as we climbed a narrow track that led from the grassy slope up onto the rocky face of the mountainside behind the castle. "They lived in both worlds easily. Indeed they needed to spend time in both worlds, for their nature was of both. They could have many children of their own, and they aged more slowly than the humans, though much faster than we did. We grieved sorely to think we might see them die."

We walked faster as he told the story, up the track that grew steeper and narrower as we climbed, the land falling away to one side. "But something else happened. Something terrible. My own people began to die, far, far earlier than should have been their time. Those who stayed too long in the human world grew weaker until they could not breathe, as if something had drawn the heart from them. We tried to find the cause—some disease, we thought. But it was not disease . . . not as you think of it. We discovered that those who died soonest were those of our people who had produced many children with their human partners. The more children, the sooner the Madonai parent faded."

And so it came. The reason for everything.

"I had risen high within our ranks, and I told the others of what I had learned. We had to stop, I said, or we would extinguish our race. No one would listen. No one wished to hear that our joy was killing us."

We had reached a ledge and could go no farther. A sheer cliff rose behind us, soaring skyward to the rocky peak, and before us was a precipitous drop to the palace ramparts. Nyel was breathing hard. I stood beside him and gazed on the green country in the distance, bathed in waking sunlight. A sheet of water shimmered on a distant plain. Nearer to hand was the walled shelf of green that was Nyel's prison, the precipice beyond the wall, and far below, at the mountain's foot, a ribbon of pale green and brilliant yellow. Gamarand trees—trees with twin yellow trunks that twined about each other like lovers. Denas had told me that the gamarand wood was a holy place to those who lived in Kir'-Navarrin, that it somehow helped to protect them from the danger imprisoned in Tyrrad Nor.

"I tried to barricade the way to the human world," said Nyel. "That was my crime. I said we had to leave our mates, abandon our children with their human kin, and destroy the passages between us, before we destroyed ourselves. I begged them to heed me, to let me save them." He threw a rock into the vast nothing that surrounded us. "Some agreed with me. Most did not. They called me murderer, monster, child-slayer, for we could see that our children needed the life of both worlds to survive. The argument was long and terrible. I lost."

"And from your prison, you watched your people die."

The wind I could not feel caught Nyel's green cloak and whipped it about his tall form. "One who is not Madonai cannot comprehend the bond we shared. Through all those years I felt their joys and sorrows, and every time one of them died, a part of me died as well." He folded his arms tightly across his chest. "By the time of their fearful prophecy, our children's children had forgotten their own history. They called the Madonai 'gods' or 'myths,' and remembered only that the prisoner in the fortress was anathema. Frightened by their seeings, they destroyed themselves, left this land, and closed the way back, not knowing the price they would pay when trapped with their folly in the human world. Is it not a wicked irony?"

But he could not be as innocent as his story claimed. "Yet you invade our dreams and cause upheaval," I said. "You have used the rai-kirah—the demons—goaded them to torment the world. In your name Tasgeddyr, the Lord of Demons, tried to take power in the human world. Perhaps you want to avenge yourself on the descendants who caused the death of your people. How can I possibly let you go free?"

"How could I wish to destroy our children? Your race—the rekkonarre—is all that is left of my own. Besides, you have done worse to yourselves than I ever could have done. What need have I for vengeance?" Nyel started down the path.

But Ezzarians were not the ones he hated. "It's humans, isn't it?" I called after him. "Not the rai-kirah who are the 'Madonai' part of us nor the Ezzarians who should properly be joined with them—your children. It's humans you despise."

His expression was everything of disgust as he shouted back at me. "Yes. I freely confess it. Humans twist and destroy and ruin everything they touch; they slaughter each other like maddened beasts. I curse the day I walked into their world. But you needn't worry about them, either." He shrugged his shoulders and started walking again, slower this time, allowing me to catch up. "Their own violence and disharmony cause the upheavals you lay at my feet. You, of all the rekkonarre, have lived in their world and seen their cruelties."

"The human world is my world. How can you expect me to release one who threatens the very people I have spent my life protecting?"

"Humans are a disease; eventually they will kill themselves. I have no need to hurry it along. I wish only to walk in woodlands and sit beside rivers, to listen to songs of noble deeds, to speak with people who speak back to me of matters other than what fruit I want for supper. I will not apologize for what I have done to gain my freedom. If you have doubts, so be it. I will die here."

We walked quickly and silently down the path, as if hurrying to some final destination now that the story was told. Yet I wanted to linger awhile, to consider his tale, to find the flaws in it . . . to find a solution. The boundaries of his prison were so narrow, and the wide and lovely lands beyond, so close as to almost touch them, were empty of everyone he had known and loved. Perhaps it was better to be captive in the dark pits of the Gastai or the slave houses of the Derzhi, where you could not see so vividly what you had lost.

"What do you know of my life, Nyel?"

He stopped in the garden, hesitating before he spoke. "I touched your mind as you lay dying. I cannot read your thoughts, but a dying man's visions give a fair image of his life."

"Then you know that when I was a slave, I despised humans as much as you do, even though I believed myself one of them."

"Yes. I saw it. That's why I thought you might understand."

"But I learned that even in a heart that seems irredeemable, there are wonders . . ." I told him briefly of Aleksander and our journey together.

And though Nyel listened patiently to my tale, when I was done, he expressed only contempt. "Of all things I have seen in you, this one I cannot fathom. Your regard for this human weakling . . . crude, bestial . . . it is inexplicable. You are a rekkonarre, a child of the Madonai, of so much more worth than any sniveling human beast. You claim he has a grand destiny, yet there is no destiny that is not better filled by the least of our blood than by any human. Come to Kir'Navarrin in your own form. Walk this land that is ours and feel the power that flows in your veins. Your birthright. Then stand before me and tell me of human destiny."

"Their power is different from ours," I said. "I want to make you see it."

We had come full circle on our journey. Nyel stood at the top of the palace steps, and I stood on the white gravel path below. "So you will come here again?" he said.

I wondered he did not know the answer already, so strong was my desire. "We need to finish our game," I said, bowing ever so slightly. I told myself it was not in deference, but only in respect for age and grief.

For the first time since I had stepped into Tyrrad Nor, Nyel smiled . . . and he was transformed. For a single, marvelous instant, I glimpsed a lord of the Madonai, tall, dark-haired, commanding, melydda shimmering, singing in the air about him. His physical beauty was matched only by that which dwelt in his dark eyes, the deep, clear eyes that held everything of wisdom, everything of power, everything of kindness and joy. I sank to one knee and dropped my gaze. One might easily mistake such a being for a god.

I waked from my visioning clearheaded, hungry, and alone. When I staggered into the blazing sunlight, wobbly from the slender rations and stiff from inactivity, Aleksander and Sovari and the two old women paused their activities as if I were an apparition that might well strike them down where they stood. I waved. "I'm all right," I called. "Everything is all right."

Though Aleksander mentioned no less than three times in that first hour that I seemed more at ease than I had been since my arrival in Zhagad, and though he waggled his eyebrows in invitation, I held Nyel and his strange story close. To discuss such things in glaring daylight or to speculate upon their meanings in casual conversation seemed somehow profane. I volunteered only that the siffaru had yielded visions that were quite unexpected and that I needed to think about them. But I agreed that I felt more balanced for having ventured on this journey. Indeed, for the first time in months, I felt hopeful.

The prisoner of Tyrrad Nor was very dangerous. Though not yet able to number his talents, I was not blind to his power; he could touch my dreams. Yet long before I had learned the truth of the rai-kirah, my people had believed that killing a demon would diminish the universe. When a Warden fought a demon battle, his first aim was to banish the rai-kirah from the possessed soul, to prevent it doing harm, not to kill it. Even my brief glimpse of Nyel's glory told me that his death would be an immeasurable loss—knowledge, beauty, and power that could never be replaced. Every event of my life had led me to this point, shaped me into one who might understand this strange and magnificent being, and I refused to believe that it was only coincidence. As soon as Aleksander was safe, I would venture the passage to Kir'Navarrin. To prevent Nyel from flaying the world with his hatred, I would need either to heal him of it or kill him. Yes, I would be wary, but I hoped . . . prayed . . . that I could heal him.

CHAPTER 13

"Tomorrow," said Aleksander, hobbling over to where I sat stuffing myself with a second roasted chukar and a fistful of dates. "Tomorrow we ride for Karn'Hegeth. Kiril sent word that the First Lord of the Mardek is willing to give me audience. 'Willing' . . . insolent bastard."

"The Mardek are not of the Twenty," I said through a mouthful of tough, stringy fowl. My stomach rumbled in pleasure.

Aleksander's healing had progressed rapidly while I was in the cave—a span of three weeks, I discovered. By the time I emerged, the Prince was already forcing himself up and down the dusty paths of Drafa on crutches Sovari had fashioned from the wood poles of his litter. Malver had arrived with the riding boot on the day after my return. The heavy boot, soaked and shrunk as the maker instructed, fit closely about Aleksander's leg and thigh. Sturdy laces allowed it to be put on and off when required, and the steel rods built into it kept his limb straight and stretched for proper healing. Sovari had brought new horses from Kiril, and after two weeks of wearing the boot and a few days of riding practice, Aleksander was ready to bid farewell to Drafa. On the next morning we were to set out to raise support for a bid to reclaim his throne.

"None of the Twenty will hear me." Aleksander leaned against the broken wall, used a crutch to bat aside several bags of clothes, weapons, and foodstuffs, and lowered himself awkwardly to the sand, settling his back against the wall. "I'm left to build an army of weaklings."

"Powerlessness will be your strength." Though the sun had long set over the dunes, the night was changed when Qeb joined our conversation so suddenly. The hard-edged starlight took on a softer glow, the sky grew muddled like an ink-scribed page when water is spilled on it, and the air fell still, as if the wind had withdrawn deep into the dunes. The boy stepped from the nagera grove, the silver hoops of his earrings catching the light of our small fire.

"Powerlessness will be my death," said Aleksander, aiming his knife and his attention at the remaining chukar. "If I march on Zhagad with a straggling legion of minor houses, I'll be spitted like this damned bird, and my father's cousin will have his pleasure with my entrails."

"You will find no kingdom in Zhagad," said the boy, his voice resonating with authority beyond his years. "The Empire of the Lion Throne is rotted. Diseased." The rings that banded his outstretched arm and fingers pointed into the dunes of Srif Anar like a silver arrow.

Aleksander paused in his activity and stared at the youth. "So I am to be emperor of nothing? Is this some 'seeing' of yours?"

"A worthy warrior must strip himself bare before he rides into battle, yield those things of most value. A worthy king must be willing to slice off a portion of his own flesh, destroy it, though it be his very heart."

The Prince shrugged and resumed carving off a portion of the roasted chukar. "It seems I am to be mutilated no matter which direction I choose. So forgive me if I pursue my own plans instead of yours."

"My lord . . ." I wanted to tell him to heed the boy, who knew more of his business than one might suppose. But if I chided Aleksander to give credence to Qeb's pronouncements, then the Prince could rightly ask what Gaspar had told me on a dark afternoon beside Drafa's muddy spring. I didn't want to think of that. I had buried the old man's ramblings beneath my newfound hopes, reasoned them away by telling myself that everything had changed when I had faced my enemy. So with only moderate twinges of guilt, I kept silent while Aleksander continued his scornful grumbling.

In the cool hour before dawn, we took our leave of Drafa. The two old women saw us off with prayers and admonitions, patting our ankles and giving us instructions for Aleksander's continued care. When they were done, Aleksander bent down, and into Sarya's hand he placed a small bundle, tied with a strip of gold-embroidered cloth cut from his ragged white cloak. "*Na salé vinkaye viterre*," he said. *Salt gives life its flavor*. The custom was as old as the Derzhi, and even Manot beamed. I looked back as we rode away. Qeb stood beside the fallen lion at the top of the rise, the wind shifting his shining braids as his ruined eyes stared into the empty desert.

One of life's truest pleasures is to watch a person do what he or she was born to do—to observe a fine sword maker fold and shape hot steel, to watch a skilled harp player brush her fingers on bare strings and birth a heart-stirring melody, to gape as an artist lays down three strokes with a bit of charcoal and makes a bird take wing. Aleksander was born to ride horses.

"Damned plow horse," grumbled the Prince as he shifted his weight yet again on the balky chestnut, trying to accommodate the stiff boot that had his leg sticking out to one side, iron straight save for a slight flexure at the knee. "How in Athos' name does Kiril expect me to command respect, riding a beast with a head like a brick and legs like posts? Bad enough that I'm locked in this cursed leg trap." Neither Prince nor horse ever looked anything but miserable when Malver helped Aleksander get his leather-bound limb across the beast's back. Once in the saddle, Aleksander would curse and swear how it was impossible to command any horse properly one-sided. Yet on this morning some seventeen days after leaving Drafa, as on every morning of our journey, I watched the Prince lean forward to speak to the beast, lay his hands on its thick neck and his right knee on its barrel-shaped flank, imposing his discipline like a lute player tuning his instrument. In that moment, man and horse became one.

Sovari grinned, his teeth white in his sunburned face. A smile was just detectable beneath Malver's stolid demeanor. The three Derzhi wheeled their mounts, gave a whoop, and raced across the dunes of Srif Anar against the fire-shot sky. I sighed and abandoned our resting place at a traveler's well, resigned to another endless day of starting and stopping as we journeyed westward across the desert toward Karn'Hegeth and a meeting with the First Lord of the Mardek.

The Mardek were a minor house who had but a single claim to honor in the Empire. A lord of the Mardek was always the First Dennissar of the Imperial Treasury, overseeing local tax collections in the city of Zhagad itself and certain special levies for the Emperor's wars and pleasures. Although such administrative positions were mundane for a warrior people, this one was potentially quite profitable. There were always bribes to be had, collection fees to be assessed—and deposited in one's own treasury—and judgments to be rendered that could cause pain and annoyance in more powerful houses. But the Mardek prided themselves—and pride was almost as significant a part of the Derzhi character as battle experience—on their ethical purity. In more than a hundred and twenty years, no Mardek official had ever been known to enrich his own coffers with illicit gains, accept a bribe for delaying collections or reducing levies, or render judgments that were anything but strictly in the Emperor's interest. But in the first week of Edik's ascension, the office had been snatched away and given to one Yagneti zha Juran, a dissolute brother-in-law of Leonid zha Hamrasch. Kiril had reported that the Mardek were ripe for rebellion. Honorable rebellion, of course.

At midday, Malver returned from a scouting trip. "The Karn'Hegeth road lies just over the next rise, Your Highness. We needs must take the road from here, as it's too odd otherwise. They've got lookouts all about the walls and only the main gates open, with at least fifty soldiers manning them. I asked a drover why the heavy watch, and he said there's rumors coming in from traders about bandit raids, and they've been alerted to look for . . . ah . . . particular outlaws."

"Then let's get to the road," said Aleksander, nudging his mount. "I've no time to dawdle."

Though I could scarcely lift my eyelids for the breathless, glaring heat, I caught the hesitation in the soldier's report. "Wait," I said, squinting in the glare. "These 'particular outlaws' . . . They're watching for Prince Aleksander, is that it, Malver?"

Malver ducked his head in acknowledgment. He still refused to look me in the eye.

"My lord, you must not be recognized," I said.

"These rags aren't fit for a slave and haven't been clean in two months. My chamberlains, servants, and warrior legions are conspicuously absent. And I've neither banner nor herald to announce my coming. I could hardly be mistaken for a visiting Emperor, riding on this cart horse."

Indeed Kiril had been wise enough to send us mediocre horses, offering his apologies along with his conviction that mounts of Aleksander's preference would be too conspicuous. But clothes, horses, and servants were only part of the royal personage. Aleksander couldn't see that even his annoyance was revealing.

"You must unbraid your hair," I said, "you and Sovari both. And, my lord, you must remove your ring and cover the hilt of your sword. Captain Sovari—"

"Unbraid my hair?" Aleksander pulled up sharply. "You jest."

I continued, hoping he would get my point soon, so that we could move on and find shade and something cool to drink. The gritty dregs in our waterskins would scorch the tongue. "Captain Sovari, you must remove your imperial sash. It didn't betray you in Zhagad, where imperial troops are common, but everyone will know what captains are garrisoned here. We must display no imperial connection and no heged identification for a man with a broken leg. Better if neither of you can even be recognized as Derzhi. Give them no reason at all to associate this boot with Prince Aleksander. Do you understand me?"

Sovari grimaced and dragged the embroidered sash bearing the Derzhi lion and his badge of rank over his head. He stuffed it in his saddle pack, and then untied the strip of leather that bound his long braid. Malver sat quietly watching the Prince, who glared at me in fury.

He had to hear it. "You've a price on your head, my lord. You must act like it or you'll suffer for your folly. All of us will."

Aleksander's red hair had only just grown out enough to make a stump of a braid on the right side of his head. His whole posture had changed on the first day he had managed to twist it into something that would stay put—the way a man walks when he steps onto his own land after long journeying. He wasn't going to enjoy being a fugitive.

I sighed and made a futile swipe at the sweat that dribbled endlessly down my neck. "There are other things. We must agree on a story . . . tell him, Malver. You know how Derzhi guards behave, and what they're likely to do when hunting a king-slayer."

Malver nodded slowly. "We must ride no more than two together. Gate guards will likely question any man of fighting age, as will any warrior of the local houses we chance to meet in the streets. With four together they'll have swords drawn before asking—"

"As well they should," said Aleksander. "I'd not have my warriors fail in their duty."

Malver threw me a quick glance and continued. "The

Fontezhi have the greatest holdings here. Their warriors are among the most . . . They may strike you at any time, my lord, if they don't like your answers or the words you use to make them, and they'll cut you or give you a taste of the lash if you so much as look at them crossways."

"And if I do anything untoward, I might as well stick a crown on your head and shout your name to all," I said. "I'm going to have to mask my features as it is—try, at least. You daren't be seen with an Ezzarian. If they recognize any of us, we're dead men."

Aleksander tugged his horse's head about furiously as if to ride back the way we'd come, but he stopped as soon as he was facing away from us. After a long moment, he reached up and yanked out the thong holding his braid. "You would have me unmanned."

"We would have you live, my lord."

Karn'Hegeth was a sprawling city, built on the steep slopes of a broad and barren ridge in the territory of Basran, just beyond the western border of Azhakstan. Basranni were close kin to the Derzhi, related by intermarriage, culture, and long alliance, but a misdirected assassination had doomed Basran towns and villages to destruction and its people to enslavement some thirty years before. Karn'Hegeth had survived the razing of Basran because there was so much wealth to be had nearby—gold and silver mines, salt deposits, major trade routes that led deep into the western Empire—and the Derzhi would only have needed to build the city up again. Aleksander's uncle Dmitri had battered the palace of the Basran warlord into rubble, mounted the heads of Basran nobility on pikestaffs at the city's ten gates, enslaved the Basran people, and called it good enough.

We emerged from our sheltered dune just as a long caravan passed out of sight along the broad Karn'Hegeth road, a well-traveled strip that stretched straight across the desert to the hazy heights just visible in the west.

As my horse plodded dutifully along behind my companions, I let the scarf of my haffai droop down low over my face, and I considered transformation. Eyes first—Ezzarians were instantly recognizable by eyelids that made our eyes take on a downward angle. And then skin color—even in a city of desert dwellers, our copper coloring and lack of beard were distinctive, and I would need to mask the royal mark burned into my left cheek. I drew up an image of Ezzarian eyes in my mind and worked out what changes would make them appear like those of other races: tighten the eyelid, draw the outside edge upward and inward, reduce the prominent cheekbone and brow that set them off. With a quick estimate of the variance needed in skin color and a determined avoidance of my proclivity to think too much, I summoned melydda and relaxed the boundaries of my flesh.

A cool prickling rippled across my face and neck, spreading quickly to torso and limbs, redefining the edges of my physical being as it touched air or cloth . . . easy . . . little more than the flush of long exertion in cold weather. Grinning in relief at this unexpectedly pleasurable experience of shapechanging, I nudged my horse a little faster. I wanted to catch up with Aleksander so he could tell me if I'd done enough.

Get to the gateway . . . The whisper came from inside me, along with a sudden swelling pressure of anger and frustration. One of my hands jerked brutally on the reins, while such a conviction of imminent catastrophe filled me that my other hand flew instinctively to my knife, caressed its hilt, considered its balance. My arm and eye readied themselves to judge distance and speed and angle. These were a warrior's instincts when confronted with danger, but not my own instincts at that moment. *While you play with these useless companions, waste our time . . . the danger grows . . .*

I recognized this voice, unheard since I lay dying at Dasiet Homol. I forced my hand away from my knife and refused the demand to kick my horse southward toward the entry to Kir'-Navarrin. "So tell me, demon," I said, gritting my teeth against the nauseating intrusion. "What danger do I face? Tell me its name if it is not yours."

It's from the past, he said. *And inside you. It is the reason for everything.*

"Why now? All those weeks I listened for you. I left myself open, tried to talk, to come to some resolution"—left myself exposed, vulnerable to corruption until I had been almost sick from it—"but you never deigned to answer."

I told you that you'd win. You have the soul. What more was there to say? But now, after seeing the prisoner . . . hearing him. Listen to me. When you pass through the gate, you must yield control of this body. Let me guide you. His hurried words grew louder, more desperate, a trickle grown quickly to a flood. *It's something about the prison . . . it's so close . . . let me remember . . . you are already compromised . . .*

Even as we spoke I felt the storm building, the paraivo on the horizons of my mind ready to flay any human within the reach of my hand. "You want me to trust you, yield to you, when you've driven me to murder?" I could scarcely squeeze out the words for the rage hammering my skull, deafening me, driving me to violence and madness.

. . . wasting time . . . I won't apologize for it . . . your own mind's weakness . . .

The din grew louder. My eye fell on Aleksander's back, and a flush of hostility burned my skin. Humans were so stupid, so ignorant. Captives of their flesh.

Listen to me!

My hand crept toward my knife hilt. I needed to rid myself of these distractions. Hot anger boiled and surged . . . the heat thrumming . . . the glare of sand and sky blinding . . . confusing . . . while cold, creeping darkness gnawed at my soul . . .

"No! You will not have me." I squeezed the words through clenched teeth. Appalled at what I was about to do, I threw every protection I knew between my soul and my wakened demon, wrestling him into silence, stilling the cacophony in my head. At last I understood, and with clarity, my newfound hopes came crashing to earth.

Denas's anger fueled my madness. His outrage drove me to bloodshed, and his fury shredded my self-control. But Nyel surely chose my victims. The Madonai's long grieving had turned into virulent poison that tainted everything he touched. He had infected my dreams, and like dry cedar in a lightning storm, his hatred of the human race had become tinder in my warrior's hand. I had fed on his hatred: when looking on Gaspar and Fessa's bodies, when watching Edik beat the slave, when seeing how the namhir had mutilated Gordain. It had festered in me as I watched Aleksander suffer from the folly and injustice of his own kind, until it burst like a suppurating boil to foul my sleep. Creeping darkness.

Your strength will be your downfall, fool, cried the demon's fading voice.

"I've not forgotten how you feel about those who wear flesh," I muttered under the cover of my scarf, shoving my half-drawn knife blade back into its sheath, commanding my trembling hands still. "When we ventured this joining, you claimed that the danger in Tyrrad Nor was your enemy. But even if you don't share his purpose, your anger does nothing but feed his power. You caught me napping today, Denas, but never again. I control my own soul, my own hand. Neither you nor the one in Tyrrad Nor will shape my future." Now I knew it was both of them, doing battle in my soul, each trying to manipulate me to his will. I would not yield to either one, not now, not if or when I ever ventured Kir'Navarrin.

"Seyonne?" My eyes blinked open, and I found Aleksander not three paces from me, his hand poised casually above his own dagger. Malver and Sovari were just behind him, looking puzzled.

"I'm all right," I said. "Doing no more than I asked of you." I threw back my hood and stared the Prince in the face, thrusting my pale bare arms out from the dusty haffai. "Is it done fairly?"

Startled, wary, he examined me as a Derzhi horse-broker reviews his newest purchase. "Done," he said at last. "But not fairly, I think. You look as if you've eaten something off."

We rode for a while in silence. I felt my heart settle back into its normal rhythm. The sweat dried quickly. When the two soldiers pulled ahead of us, Aleksander spoke quietly. "Is it the rai-kirah, Seyonne?"

"It is nothing."

"Always you've been a private man. I respect that." He wrinkled his face wryly. "A new thing I've been working on. But these things going on with you— When you lay so ill after the matters at Dasiet Homol, you asked me to look at you and tell you what I saw, as if you valued my word on it. I told you then that despite this demon joining, I saw only the man I knew, the one who fought with the hand of the gods to save my soul."

Despite the sunlit noonday, my skin grew cold. I wished he would stop.

"You've not been the same since this siffaru. Healthier, I've thought, more at peace than any time since you came to Zhagad, and I'm glad of it. Yet I've realized that since you came out of the cave, I see only the seeming and not the truth. Three weeks you were buried in that cave, yet you've said not a word of it. I can't read you anymore."

"The seeming is the truth," I said. "Denas is silent and will stay that way. The prisoner is still locked away. My . . . problem . . . is under control. When you're safe, I'll settle it once and for all." Exactly how, I wasn't sure. I could not speak of the sif-faru. Nyel and the feelings he had raised in me, my conviction that somehow I was destined, not to destroy, but to salvage something marvelous—I buried deep. I didn't trust my feelings anymore, and I had other business to attend.

We did not enter Karn'Hegeth until sunset. Though we lingered outside the gates all afternoon, as if we thought to camp there for the night like the scores of others who disdained roofs or could ill afford the price of an inn, we merged back onto the road as soon as the shadows grew long. Night might mask our features better, but it would cause closer scrutiny by the troops of Derzhi warriors who patrolled the gates and streets. We stood a better chance of losing ourselves in the confusion of late-arriving caravans at the outer margins of day.

Malver and Sovari ventured the gates first, leading our four horses. Malver's dark features blended easily with the crowd as the two soldiers pushed their way into the noisy press. But even though he was afoot—unlikely for any Derzhi—Sovari's height, light hair, and confident bearing marked him out of place in the streams of peasants and merchants, horsemen and slaves, chastou, goats, chickens, beggars, carts, and wagons. Malver must have noted the same, for he stopped, held a quick conversation with a ragged herdsman, and then threw a bleating goat across the Derzhi captain's shoulders. The two soldiers moved slowly with the crowd and disappeared through the gates. We noted no disturbance among the guards who stood stiff and alert on the gate towers above us or on the ramparts to either side, and no mustering of the mounted warriors who bulled through the milling travelers, staring into faces and poking their spears into carts.

"Time to venture forth, my lord."

"Must I, too, carry a goat? Perhaps I could take it to Mardek as a bribe."

"Though the goat would add a certain charm," I said, unable to control a grin at the thought of it, "your crutches will be enough to manage. Hunch over them, as if your back were twisted, too. And remember to keep your eyes down. Never look a Derzhi in the eye, especially when he challenges you. Keep your hand away from your weapons, as Malver told you. Remember our story, and let me talk."

"Is my education quite complete now?" The Prince jammed the crosspieces of his crutches under his arms.

I picked up our two grimy cloth packs from the ground and dropped their rope ties around his neck, tied an old rag of Sarya's about his head to mute the telltale of his red hair, and yanked on the folds of his filthy haffai to make sure its long folds covered the unusual boot. Then I motioned him toward the gate, mumbling to myself. "I don't think we've even begun."

CHAPTER 14

The girl was no more than seven or eight, a thin, leggy sprite with sparkling eyes, brown curls, and bare feet, a dirty, ragged, dancing child lost in her own fancy. She was with the man just in front of Aleksander and me—a gaunt Manganar dragging a two-wheeled cart to the gates while herding five small girls and three goats alongside it. The long-handled cart was crammed with two emaciated pigs, a flour barrel, an iron pot, and a pile of dingy bundles, one of which was producing a thready wailing.

"I've naught for such a fee, your honor," the man said to the burly Derzhi tax collector who was inspecting his pitiful cargo. "The childer's mam died birthing, and I've brung them to her folk. Her kin won't take the childer without the goats to feed 'em. My pigs are most dead, but if you'd take one for the fee . . ."

Two imperial officials were collecting entry tribute on any carts or livestock passing the gates, assessing the value of the goods and requiring a proportional fee or a share of the merchandise. This was profitable duty for a tax collector, but with Karn'Hegeth's other nine gates locked against the threat of bandits, and more and more stragglers trying to get into the city before the gates were closed for the night, the two Derzhi were harried and short of temper.

I cursed my timing. Sovari and Malver had moved straight through the gates, but the Prince and I had gotten snarled in the hot, stinking crowd, crammed between the poor Manganar and the agitated horses of a Fontezhi baron's traveling party. After a tedious hour's delay while a massive caravan was assessed and its gonaj argued every zenar of his taxes, we were only now getting close to the gates. The annoyed baron's servant pushed forward to have a word with the gate guards, and soon the party was let through without stopping for the tax collectors.

"A Fontezhi sixth-degree," murmured Aleksander, keeping his head down and his voice low. "Likely a half-wit. The Fontezhi are so inbred they can see up their own asses. They're afraid to lose a bit of their property as bride gifts, so they marry their own sisters."

The baron's place was quickly taken by a prosperous-looking and very impatient Suzaini rider and a pair of Kuvai lute players on donkeys, who decided to while away the time teaching themselves some annoyingly repetitive passage of a popular saga. For a while I thought the lute players were most likely to get us in trouble, as Aleksander began muttering something about smashing their instruments and inserting various small pieces into the musicians' ears, noses, and other bodily openings. But that was before the burly tax collector began eyeing the little girl.

His neck was as wide as his head, and a hairy bulge of belly hung out below his embroidered vest and imperial sash. He wore no braid. "What do you think, Vallot?" he called to his fellow, a soft, moonfaced man who was inspecting the bundles on the Manganar's cart. "We could have one of the brats and sell her. This one might be pleasing if she was fattened up. Better than a half-dead pig." The big man caught the arm of the spinning child and drew her close, running a thick finger along her shoulder. Though smudged and grimy, the child's tanned skin was not yet coarsened by relentless sun and poverty. The little girl frowned and tried to pull away.

Aleksander raised his head to see. I edged in front of him.

The father shook his head, his weariness like another companion standing beside his bent shoulders. "Take her if you will, your honors. I'd sell her myself, but I'm told she's too young to be of much use. A year or two and she'll fetch a good price . . . if she lives so long. You'll have to feed her until then." He held out a single silver coin that he had carefully unwrapped from a bit of rag. "I've no more than this bit to pay. Is it worth more than a hungry child?"

The second tax collector, the younger, moonfaced Vallot, had just allowed the Suzaini rider to pass after pocketing a well-stuffed purse. He glanced at the restive crowd, noisy and pressing in the failing light. "I think we've more profitable prospects for our Emperor than a knob-kneed starveling. From the look of this beggar and his cart, she'll have the crabs already." He snatched the Manganar's coin. "Get on with you." He tossed the coin to a sallow-faced assistant who was standing just behind the two, jotting the official tally of the collections—not to be mistaken for the actual sum—in a cloth-bound ledger. Vallot motioned Aleksander and me forward.

All might have ended well enough, save the brutish official shrugged, licked his lips, and reached his hand under the girl's tunic. The child grabbed his other hand and bit him. He roared and shoved her away, shaking his bleeding finger.

"Stupid girl!" The distraught father slapped the child to the ground just as the injured Derzhi recovered enough to raise his fist. With the girl out of reach, the vicious blow felled the father, and the tax collector's heavy boot kicked over the cart, scattering pots and bundles and crying children from hither to yon.

It was over quickly. The moonfaced Vallot shoved the wailing children aside and motioned the rest of us forward impatiently. "See to your proper business, Felics. I've supper waiting."

I had a silver piece ready to slip into the Derzhi's hand. Having sent our horses with Malver, we had no goods or livestock, but that never stopped a tax collector from assessing a fee. "Name's Arago," I said, ducking my head respectfully. "Smith's man come from Avenkhar to find work in the mines. This be my cousin Wat."

The moonfaced official gave us only a cursory look. We were dirty, shabby, and had contrived to appear unarmed. Sovari had bound the Prince's sword to his back under the loose haffai, and I had done the same with mine. Not unheard of among desert people, but Vallot had no time to undress us. "Lame is he?" Vallot jerked his head at Aleksander.

"Fell into a shaft as a boy," I said, sensing the hundred unfortunate retorts boiling inside Aleksander.

To our left I saw the bleeding father right his cart, silently urging the little ones to gather their bags and bundles quickly. The furious Felics flexed his bitten hand and cast sidelong glances at the family, while bellowing at the lute players and threatening to close the gates entirely if people didn't stop crowding too close.

"Can Wat not speak for himself?" said Vallot, his small eyes glaring at the Prince suspiciously, as if he, too, felt Aleksander's hostility.

"Fell on his head," I said, trying to keep my mind on our business as well as the looming disaster. "Tell him your name, Wat."

"Name's Wat," growled Aleksander. He was rigid under his shabby haffai.

"Being impudent with me, cripple?" The Derzhi poked a

fleshy finger at Aleksander's chest, requiring the Prince to shift his crutch to keep from falling over.

"Not a bit," I said. "Are you, Wat?"

Aleksander leaned slightly away from me. As I was on his right, that meant he was leaning onto his good leg. I feared he was bracing himself to deliver a blow.

I grabbed his arm as if to steady his clumsiness, but I held on so tight that he would have had to break his own limb to get it loose. "My cousin has only the highest respect for the Emperor's men, doing the Emperor's work as they're sworn to do. Aye, Wat? Answer his honor and speak respectful, now. He's just thick in the head, your lordships." I moved aside and jostled Aleksander forward, as if to make him speak for himself, leaving me standing directly in between the brutish Felics and the scrambling Manganar. In the process, I dropped ten silver coins into the dirt.

"Aye, only the highest respect for the land's true Emperor and his loyal servants," said the Prince, jerking his head in what might be construed as a measure of respect—or a dry imitation of spitting.

"Are these yours, sir?" I leaned toward Felics, pointing at the silver, pretending a whisper, though just loud enough that my own interrogator might hear. "I didn't see who dropped them." The big man tore his gaze from the Manganar, shifting it slowly from me to the ground.

Before he could grab the coins, a noisy party of young Derzhi noblemen rode up beside us, laughing and joking about an evening horse race. They were well into their wine, and impatient with the tax collectors and gate guards. "My lord Mardek will have your teeth for these delays!" cried a blond youth with a newly sprouted beard. "He had a wager on this race and is waiting to hear of his luck. Move these oafs aside." The prancing horses crowded the tax collectors to the side, and the Prince and me also, until we were stumbling over each other. The tail of the young lord's horse flicked into Aleksander's face. Behind the riding party was a large caravan, chastous bellowing and straining at their traces as if they had smelled the water inside the walls. Drovers screamed and cracked their whips to keep the unruly beasts in check.

"May we go, sir?" I said.

Vallot motioned us forward impatiently. "Be off and teach the cripple more respect, or I'll throw him down a shaft that has no bottom." With a quick eye and a quicker hand, he elbowed his dull-witted partner aside, scooped up my dropped silver for himself, and attended to the urgent—and presumably profitable—business of the young noble. His broad face red and swollen, the bullish Felics backed away, bumping into the sallow-faced clerk and his ledger. Felics mumbled something to the clerk and jerked his head toward the gateway.

Without releasing my grip on his arm or slowing my pace to accommodate his injury, I dragged Aleksander into the passage under the gate towers. At last glimpse the two tax collectors were arguing with each other.

"Bloody, insolent vermin!" muttered the Prince, trying to wrest his arm from my hand, but succeeding only in stumbling awkwardly and painfully over something in the road. It was difficult to see anything in the deep shadows under the gate towers. I caught Aleksander before he fell, only to have to shove him against the brick wall when the Derzhi noble's party came tearing through the arched gateway. The pale-haired young lord threw an empty wineskin at us, splattering us with the musty dregs.

"Gods of earth and sky!" Aleksander was shaking.

"Get your balance," I growled into his ear, not knowing who might be lurking in the darkness. "And keep silent. We need to get away from here."

"I'll kill them for this."

I didn't know which "this" he was talking about, or, to be sure, which "them." "It will have to be later," I said. "We need to get moving."

"Unless you plan to break my arm," said Aleksander through clenched teeth, "I would appreciate your letting go of it."

My fingers were clamped almost to his bone. "Sorry." I was no more settled than he.

We had to wait while a wagon rumbled past, and after it two riders in striped robes, prodding a group of three slaves dragging a sledge loaded with cut blocks of stone. Before us, through an archway illuminated by lingering dusk, was the city. Behind us, where the ironbound wooden gates stood open, slaves were setting torches in high sconces. As my eyes adjusted to the shadows, I picked up what had tripped the Prince—one of the bundles from the Manganar's cart, a leather apron wrapped around a pick, a small saw, a steel-headed hammer, and a few chisels of various sizes. A man's livelihood. I rewrapped the bundle and hooked its rope tie over my shoulder. "Let's move," I said.

We hurried as fast as Aleksander could manage into the outer ring of Karn'Hegeth, a cramped street of stables, warehouses, and slave quarters grown up between the inner and outer ramparts. Beggars waylaid every traveler who passed the gates, and slack-mouthed children with dead eyes shuffled here and there in the crowds, begging bowls raised. A skeletal woman of indeterminate age, shrunken breasts hanging out of a loosely tied bodice, smiled and rubbed a bony hip against my side. "Two coppers, traveler, and I'll do the cripple for naught extra." I pushed her away, and we made our way through the inner gates and into the cobbled streets.

Sovari and Malver were nowhere to be seen. It was not a worry; we had agreed to meet in the marketplace as soon as we were sure we'd not been followed. But just ahead of us, disappearing into an alley, was the two-wheeled cart, and sidling through the crowds watching its progress was the sallow-faced clerk from the gates. Petty vengeance was the most dangerous sort.

"Come on," I said. "We need to get these back to the Manganar. He'll likely starve without."

Aleksander swung himself forward on the crutches. "Let the cowardly villain starve." He spat on the dusty pavement. "He was going to sell the girl . . . his own child . . . or kill her. Even animals protect their young. Weaklings deserve what they get."

"And the Derzhi who started it?"

"Even brutes have their duties." He could not yet see the whole of matters, nor how the brute planned to carry out his "duties."

"Is it duty has brought the clerk away from the gates just now?" I said, drawing Aleksander into the dark alleyway. "Or does good Felics think to get the tithe he wanted all along?" I stopped just far enough inside the turning that we could not be seen from the street and pointed out the man pushing his way through the stream of traffic.

Aleksander remained skeptical until the clerk hurried into the alley. "Bastard!" Before I could take care of matters, Aleksander slammed a crutch into the clerk's middle, knocking the sallow-faced man into me. "Stealing children is against the law of the Empire, you misbegotten jackal!"

What I had not noticed in the street was that the sneaking fellow had brought a friend with him, a big, efficient, but otherwise unremarkable thug. The brawny fellow rammed a fist into Aleksander's jaw, and then kicked the other crutch out from under him. The flailing Prince toppled into the dirt. Before the thug's massive boot could connect with Aleksander's head, I shoved the clerk to the ground and tackled his big friend. Aleksander retained enough wit to cover his head and roll toward the wall, releasing a stream of curses and epithets entirely appropriate to the occasion.

The thug was easily dealt with. I left him sprawled in a pile of offal with such a knot on his head that he would not remember how he came to be there. Unfortunately, the clerk scuttled away before I could teach him any similar lesson.

"Damnable, cursed blight of a world . . ." The strength of Aleksander's diatribe relieved my concerns as to his physical well-being.

I retrieved his crutches and helped him to a wobbly stance. "I think our stay in Karn'Hegeth has just been cut short," I said. "Someone is going to be looking for us."

The Prince rubbed the bleeding split on his jaw and wiped his fingers on his soiled haffai. "I won't run away. But I've no mind to stay longer than to see to my business."

We picked our way down the fetid alley. Night had already arrived there, long before it reached the wider streets. A beggar with only half a face and no tongue grunted and pawed at my feet as I stepped around a yellow-faced woman slumped against the mud-brick wall, her skirts pulled up around her waist. Aleksander coughed and spat, and I pulled the scarf of my haffai across my nose. The stink of yaretha—the mind-numbing weed that left such women dead by age twenty—and its companion scents of excrement and vomit was overpowering. A little further on, sitting next to a pile of refuse that included a bloated mound which had once been a cat, we found the Manganar and his children.

The bony man sat against the wall cradling his little daughter, muffling her sobs against his ragged shirt and dabbing at the small bruise on her forehead. "It'll pass, child. It'll pass. Only a little ways to go, now we've rested a bit." His battered, bleeding face looked fifty, though he was likely not more than twenty-five. While the goats bleated weakly and nosed about in the refuse, the other children huddled next to the man, eyes wide and frightened in their thin faces. One of the girls clutched a gray bundle almost as large as she. She kept staring at it and jiggling it with tiny shakes. The father glanced at her, his expression an artwork of pain. "It's no use, Daggi," he said softly. "Leave him be till we find Potters' Lane. He . . . sleeps."

I could not fathom how the man could find strength to spare for grieving. "Good day, sir," I called out. "You left this behind at the gates."

The man jumped to his feet and shoved the children behind him, fumbling about to produce a large, old-fashioned knife that he waved about inexpertly. "Who's there?"

"We found this at the city gate. Thought you might need it." I tossed the tool bundle at his feet, while keeping a respectful distance. I didn't need to grind his nose in the dirt.

He stared at the bundle as if it had walked back to him of itself, and then shifted his astonishment back to me, squinting into the darkness and craning his head to see Aleksander, who was leaning heavily on the wall. "A kindness on a day with none else, save . . . I wondered . . . you dropped the coins that snatched the villain's eye from us."

"A loose knot in my purse," I said.

"May Panfeya bless you with healthy children, goodman."

"And Dolgar grant you sturdy walls," I said. The Manganar low gods provided useful gifts for their petitioners. "And you might need them. You were followed from the gates. The scrawny one with the yellow face was given a commission . . . you understand?"

The Manganar sheathed his knife and lifted his daughter again, gently pulling her head onto his shoulder. "I'll watch, then. If I had ought to repay you . . . Tell me how you are called, so I can at least name you in my prayers."

"Arago out of Avenkhar, and this is my cousin Wat. If luck holds, we'll have no need of your repayment."

"I'm Vanko of Eleuthra, soon to be of Potters' Lane with my brother-in-law Borian. My hand is ever at your service, Arago, and those of all my family."

I bowed. "Dolgar guard you, sir, and comfort your child."

The man bowed in return and proceeded to gather his children and his goats, and take up the long handles of his cart.

Aleksander and I headed back the way we'd come. Torches soaked with octar—the tarry seepage found among desert rocks—were already filling the streets with stinking yellow smoke. We saw no sign of the sallow-faced man.

"We'll have no need of this Vanko or any other peasant," said Aleksander as we made our slow way through the streets. His movements were becoming increasingly jerky, and he could only take a few steps at a time without stopping. "My uncle gave the Mardek their house here and at least two silver mines. And my local dennissar Tosya and I spent three weeks opening up the silver trade routes from Karn'Hegeth when your friend, the Yvor Lukash, had the place strangled two years ago. Tosya will harbor us if Mardek is too cowardly." We stopped again, and Aleksander leaned heavily on his crutches, grimacing. "Druya's horns, it will be fine to get in the saddle again. I'll apologize to that wretched horse for everything I said about it."

"I wouldn't count on anyone's loyalties," I said. I wasn't so confident that Mardek's gratitude would extend to a man with a price on his head. "Vanko might be the more useful friend."

I kept my eye moving over the throngs in the streets, watching for any gaze that rested on Aleksander for more than an instant. He wasn't likely to be recognized by just anyone; few commoners ever caught a glimpse of royalty. But the Derzhi tax collector would not be happy that his nasty little plan had been foiled by a man on crutches.

"Are your slave's ears deaf? The child-beating coward talked of selling the girl. He would probably have worked a deal for her right there in that alley."

I pressed the Prince into a dark doorway and stuffed myself in on top of him while two mounted Derzhi rode past, peering closely at the passersby. "Your head is grown thick, Wat," I whispered, "and your eyes dim. He saved her life with the only weapons he had. The bruise on her face likely pains him far more than the blood on his own." And though I did not say it, I knew that the child's bruised face hurt Aleksander as well. He had not forgotten Nyamot.

CHAPTER 15

Any doubt Aleksander might have borne as to the Emperor's intentions vanished when we came to the grand marketplace of Karn'Hegeth. At first we couldn't understand why the evening's activities of eating, drinking, buying, and selling seemed to be confined to the eastern half of the paved expanse . . . not until we moved to the edge of the crowds to watch for Sovari and Malver and saw the bodies.

From a succession of gibbets that lined the western boundary of the marketplace hung at least twenty men. Three of them were rough-looking fellows—branded, flogged, and hanged by the neck as thieves. But the rest were Derzhi, some dressed in fine clothes as if dragged from feasting or temple rites, and all of them hung by their feet, with lips and noses cut off and their braids shorn and tied to their swollen tongues in mockery—a traitor's punishment. Most were dead. Hungry rats had already found their way down the chains. But as Aleksander moved awkwardly down the row, drawn to the gruesome display in a horrified fascination that my nervous cautions could not deter, we heard piteous moans from a few of the blackened faces, even as the rats fed on them.

"Tosya," he whispered, heedless of the imperial guards who stood watch at either end of the dreadful display to assure that no one would succor the dying. "And Jov and Laurent . . . oh, holy Athos . . ." Aleksander turned to me, his stricken face yellow in the sickly torchlight. "If ever you would do me a service, Seyonne . . . With whatever sorcery you can work, I beg you finish them. They are honorable men, noble warriors whose only crime was to serve me."

"Ah, my lord, don't ask—" It was not the Ezzarian way to hasten a death.

He gripped my shoulder with fingers of iron. "You listened to Fessa and Gaspar, staying with them through their ordeal in the only way you could. I can do no less for my warriors. I will not leave them like this."

My whole being wanted to refuse him. To intervene, even in such horror, was to rob a man of his last breath, his last thought, his last hope, no matter how impossible. Yet I could not dismiss Aleksander's threat to stay. Alone in the deserted part of the marketplace and gaping like nasty urchins, the two of us stood out like silk on a beggar. My oath . . . my desire . . . my hopes demanded that I keep Aleksander safe.

"They crave death, Seyonne. They hunger for it. It is our way."

A wretched, despicable way to ease suffering—murder. Yet, I had no skill to heal the dying Derzhi, nor any sorcery that could ease their pain, and no one was going to save them. Of all the deaths held to my account, these few . . . surely their tally would be very light. "Gods forgive me," I whispered, and gathered my melydda.

"The dennissar said you are to come through the postern gate and wait in the olive grove until someone comes to meet you." Sovari kept his eyes cast down as he reported on his foray into the walled estate of the Mardek heged.

"The postern? Wait outside? You told them this was their sovereign and not some churl of an envoy?"

We had been waiting at the lower end of a steep, twisting roadway for most of an hour while Sovari informed the Mardek that their Prince had come to speak with First Lord Vassile. With admirable diplomacy the captain had persuaded Aleksander that it would be wise to give the lord some warning.

"Truly, my lord," said the captain, "it took some doing even to get a message sent in so late in the evening. I thought the steward might swallow his tongue when I said I brought word from the rightful Emperor."

After what we had seen in the marketplace, I was not surprised.

"But he did take the message and then someone more responsible came to speak with you?" said Aleksander.

"Aye, my lord."

"I suppose I must be grateful I wasn't left entirely to the steward." Aleksander knew he faced an humiliating interview, yet, after the sight of Edik's handiwork and my unholy completion of it, he had held his temper grimly in check. He had spent the wait reviewing every detail of the Mardek position in the Empire, their holdings and history, down to the jewelry and perfumes preferred by the sixth lord's favorite mistress. His memory for such details was astonishing. "A nervous junior dennissar played intermediary, I would guess."

Sovari nodded. "He, too, was very frightened. My lord, I think it is a measure of success that you are received at all."

Aleksander snorted and nudged his thick-necked mount. "Well, then, let's see if sufficient groveling can increase the spoils of our victory. After such a day as this, my expectations can only improve." Though his words were light, they were devoid of humor.

Aleksander might be forced to slink through a postern gate, but he would not arrive in disguise. He had rebraided his hair, replaced his signet ring, and removed his haffai, exposing his sword hilt and his damaged limb. "They'll see I'm being honest with them," he said when Sovari tried to persuade him to keep his injury hidden. "And that nothing will hinder me." There was nothing to be done about his bruised chin, the mediocre horse, his sweat-stained shirt, or the breeches cut raggedly to accommodate the boot, but no one who gave him more than a casual glance would mistake him for a mere envoy.

We left Malver at the foot of the roadway and Sovari to stand watch at the narrow back gate that had been left unguarded for the hour. "They consider me no more than an old toothless dog to be allowed in and out at will," said Aleksander as we rode between the twisted trees to the crossing path where he had been instructed to wait. The olive grove was scented with summer blooming, the perfumed clusters of white blossoms scarcely visible under the dark leaves. Through the branches we could see lamplight from a stone house that sprawled across the ridge above the city, where the breezes could cool its courtyards.

The wait seemed interminable, but with no apparent effort, the Prince held his mount perfectly still. With a great deal more trouble, I kept mine from bolting. I had never claimed to be a horseman, and the beast seemed to have smelled something he liked better than olive trees.

At last a few of the lights about the house began to move our way. "I'll be nearby," I said, ready to withdraw into the trees. "Shall I listen?"

"I've nothing to hide from you."

His gibe stung, but I told myself not to dwell on it. At the city gates, in the fetid alleys, and in the cursed marketplace, I had indeed felt the familiar rage rising within me—stirred by human cruelty that drew my hand to violence and murder, threatening to corrupt my gifts. I could not speak such darkness as I felt that night, for, of course, Denas's anger and Nyel's disgust were mine, too. But my head remained clear and my hand under control. I knew what I was doing now.

Dearest one . . . you must remember . . . deceived . . . The whispered words drifted through my mind like the perfumed breeze. I snapped my head from side to side, peering through the dark branches, expecting . . . fearing . . . to see a glimmer of green. But the only other souls in the olive grove were the two men who came riding through the trees from the direction of the house, their way lit by a young torchbearer who jogged alongside.

In the lead was a straight-backed, bulky warrior, whose nose and cheeks and incipient paunch spoke of too many skins of wine since he had last ridden to war. His sleeveless shirt and cofat—a short cape fastened at one shoulder with a silver brooch—were expensively fashioned, and on the arm left bare, he wore a silver arm ring set with emeralds. He stopped at the edge of the road and examined Aleksander, motioning the slave boy to hold up the light. The other rider remained out of view, to the man's side and slightly behind him.

"Your Highness," said the florid warrior, his eyebrows slightly raised. He made no salute with his sword and no bow, not even a dip of the head. His greeting was not quite a question.

"Mardek." Aleksander held his horse motionless while extending his left hand, allowing his signet ring to gleam in the light.

Lord Vassile's full lips were drawn into a disgruntled frown. To refuse his Prince's proffered hand—and the ring that was the symbol of the Empire itself—would be an affront far more serious than a cold reception. The older man nudged his restless mount forward slowly until he could touch Aleksander's fingers, and then he bent stiffly and kissed the ring. "My son Hadeon," he said as he withdrew, waving his hand at the second rider.

Aleksander's back stiffened; the man who rode into the flickering light was the young nobleman who had splattered us with his wine dregs earlier that evening.

My hand moved to the hilt of my sword, and once again explored our surroundings with my heightened senses. No one else was in the olive grove.

Hadeon, elegantly garbed in purple silk shirt and gold-embroidered cofat, followed his father's lead and kissed Aleksander's ring, but as he lifted his head he cast a calculating glance at the Prince's damaged limb. Luckily for young Hadeon, Aleksander had resolved to keep his mind on his business.

The proprieties established, the Prince became a gracious supplicant. "My lord Vassile, I have come to affirm the strong bond between our families. Both my father and my uncle had nothing but the utmost respect for the Mardek and their service to the Empire. The honor of your house is renowned throughout the land. Thus I come to you in our gravest hour, trusting you will see fit to join our effort to bar the usurper from the throne, where my father's murderers think to put him."

The portly Vassile sat stiff and wary. "Fine words, my lord Aleksander. We hear many words. The Mardek have no love for this Edik, nor for Hamrasch dogs who squat upon other people's rugs . . . but you, sir . . ." He raked Aleksander with a practiced eye. "What are we to make of you?"

"I am your rightful Emperor-in-waiting, proclaimed on the day of my birth and anointed by your sovereign in the year of my majority. No honorable Derzhi can make anything else of me."

"But our Emperor lies murdered. We hear there were arguments between you, disagreements of long-standing. Your impatience is well-known . . . your intemperate hand. And now you come to us in this state . . ."

Lord Vassile shifted his hand on his horse's neck to still the agitated beast. Only a small movement, but Aleksander and his mount remained absolutely motionless, perfectly controlled. "On the day of my anointing, my Emperor named me as his Voice and Hand. For more than two years I spoke for him and wielded his authority as he intended. Every man, Lord Vassile—even an Emperor—has occasion to argue with himself. As to my father's death, here is the truth of it: the Hamraschi rebelled against my legitimate authority. When the time came to reap the consequences of their perfidy, they plotted against your Emperor and his son in fear that my 'intemperate hand' would raise up honorable houses like the Mardek at cost to their own domains. Would you have me serve temperance and permit them to succeed in such a crime? And as to my state . . . cowards and usurpers fear a worthy warrior."

Aleksander's strategy was a gamble. The minor houses had grumbled for years at the excessive influence of the Twenty, but, of course, if an Emperor's whim could exalt a loyal heged, his next whim could as easily diminish it. Vassile hesitated, scrutinizing Aleksander as if to weigh his appearance against his words.

"What worthy warrior abandons his troops and then dares flaunt his defeat?" Hadeon blurted into the heavy silence, thrusting his narrow chin at Aleksander's boot. "And what murderer is better than another?"

"What worthy warrior plays at horse racing when brother Derzhi hang in living torment in his city?" said Aleksander, releasing his pent-up fury. One might have imagined the very stones beneath the olive grove rumbling in answer to him. "Brothers whose only crime was service to their anointed Emperor and whose blood cries out for vengeance as did my father's blood. I wear the mark of my service to honor. Where is yours, boy?"

A red-face Hadeon touched hand to sword hilt, but quickly removed it when Lord Vassile raised his hand and spoke sharply. "Please, please, my lord Aleksander. My son is concerned only that we risk what remains of our family security. Any who dare gainsay this Edik are quickly silenced, as you have seen. Indeed no evidence, no rendered justice, but only this false lord's command condemned our brothers. To see you in the flesh and hear your claims is a powerful warrant of your truth. But we have also heard that none of the Twenty will support you. For a small house to risk its very existence in an unwinnable pursuit . . ."

"Edik is buying the Twenty with the fortune of every other house," said Aleksander. In cold calm he detailed the stories of bribery and treachery that Kiril had collected and sent to him: lands confiscated, horses appropriated for the Emperor's service, and then found in another heged's herds, long-held mining rights and trading monopolies revoked and shifted to a more powerful rival's control. "Do you think the usurper will allow you to keep your mines when the Fontezhi wish to increase their silver hold? What do you protect by your restraint?"

"But what do you offer that is different, my lord? To regain your position you must have the Twenty, and we will again be inhaling their dust."

"Never again, Mardek," said Aleksander in ferocious quiet. "Never again will the Twenty hold me hostage, nor will they treat my allies as lesser men. Tell the lords of the Fozhet and the Kandavar, the Naddasine, and the Bek, all of the worthy houses that have been ignored for too long . . . I will find a new way. By my father's blood and sword, by my dead warriors in Karn'Hegeth market, I will."

The old Derzhi's nod of approval was almost imperceptible, yet it signaled that Aleksander had won a monumental victory. Unfortunately, victory bought him very little. Beneath his fleshy exterior, old Mardek was as hard as the rocky foundation of Karn'Hegeth. "We mourn your father's passing, Lord Aleksander, and would honor his will to see you crowned. Come back to us with evidence that others trust your word and your prospects, and the Mardek shall ride with them and you to Zhagad. Until then, we do nothing, and you are not welcome here. Your presence in the city endangers us all, and my family must come first." With a generous bow, the first lord bade farewell. "Safe journey, Your Highness." As if Aleksander could ride out from Karn'Hegeth openly and in the state to which he was born. The old warrior clucked to his mount and rode back the way he had come. Young Hadeon followed his father's example, though less gracefully and without words. A curt bow and he, too, was gone.

Aleksander yanked the signet from his finger and the tie from his braid, wrapped his filthy haffai about his head, shoulders, and boot, and then wheeled his mount, riding past me without a glance or a word. I spurred my restless beast and caught up with him. Though he had acquitted himself well, I, too, remained silent. I couldn't think of any words that he would welcome.

Aleksander did not want to accept Vanko's offer of his relatives' hospitality, claiming he would as soon sleep in an alley as share a roof with a sniveling coward, but I convinced him that we would be safer off the streets. I didn't like imposing our danger upon the Manganar family, but we were desperate for rest, and we needed to see to Aleksander's leg. I was afraid of what we might find. After weeks of constant improvement, he seemed scarcely able to move it.

Truly I wanted nothing more than to get out of Karn'Hegeth that night, but one of the younger Fontezhi lords who resided in the city had fought alongside Aleksander in his first battle, and the Prince thought to visit the man in the hour before dawn. If the nobleman would hear him, perhaps the Prince could splinter one of the Twenty Hegeds. The strategy was unpromising at best, but despite his brave words to Lord Vassile, Aleksander remained convinced that he could not fight the combined might of the Twenty with only the minor hegeds.

Within an hour of our arrival at his brother-in-law's door, Vanko and his brood moved into a goat shed behind the pottery shop, leaving the tiny balcony just off the second-floor family rooms—the house's prime guest quarters—available for Aleksander and myself. I protested that my cousin and I would gladly sleep with the goats; for my part, I could have slept in a thornbush. But Vanko insisted that there was not room enough for all his children on the cool balcony.

"Daggi still cries for her mam all the night, and Olia walks in her sleep. She'd as like fall off the balcony," said Vanko. "Best we stay together near the privy on level ground. I'd not visit the dead handlers again this night." The ominously silent bundle in his daughter's arms had been the Manganar's infant son.

Malver volunteered to spend the night prowling the market quarter. He claimed to have acquaintances among the traders and caravan drovers who frequented Karn'Hegeth, and in the market, where they were loading, unloading, and drinking away their profits, he would devise some way to get Aleksander out of the city. Sovari remained abroad in Potters' Lane to keep watch until I came to relieve him later in the night.

The Prince and I were soon sitting in a small hot room above the potter's shop eating a late supper. The stifling room was furnished with a long plank table, a blazing hearth, and sixteen people, most of them wriggling, and at least half of them talking at once. Besides Vanko and his five, the wiry potter Borian and his plump wife, Lavra, had at least six children of their own, aged two to fifteen.

"I'm sorry for your loss, Vanko," I said, trying not to gobble Lavra's thin soup too greedily. Though we had arrived late, the harried woman had insisted on stretching her pot far enough to accommodate us. We contributed the remnants of our traveling provisions—a lump of goat cheese far past its prime, a handful of dates, and a packet of flatbread—to the lively meal. I sat in the middle of a long bench, crammed between Vanko and one of Borian's sons, a pimple-faced boy of fifteen who seemed to have an excess of elbows and knees.

"Lavra's milk grows fine sons, as you see," said Vanko, trying in vain to get a small green-glazed bowl to his mouth with two little girls on his lap, one jostling his elbow, and another hanging on his bony shoulders. "I'd hoped to get the babe to her breast before he sickened. He never found the knack of suckling with any of the village women. But truly childer so young and weak don't take to traveling. Eight days we had to come from Eleuthra. My girls did well, though." Vanko stroked his daughter's curls, though he could not mask his wistful sadness. He was, after all, a Manganar, whose gods mandated that his place in the afterlife was determined by the number of his sons. "If not for the Derzhi at the gates—"

"The braidless brute at the gate only finished what was already done," said Aleksander. "A man must shoulder his own blame." The Prince was perched on a stool in the corner, where his awkward leg was out of the way of the sweating Lavra and her rosy-cheeked daughter, who hurried between hearth and table, trying to keep the many-colored bowls filled. Aleksander had spoken very little in the hour since I had knocked on the pottery shop door and inquired if Vanko meant what he said about helping us.

"'Twas no one but a cursed Derzhi baron as killed the boy," said Borian, the shy, nervous potter speaking up for the first time. "Tell them as you told me, Vanko. The blame falls on the Rhyzka bastard who would not allow my sister to rest when he decided that the men of Eleuthra were not enough to plant his fields this year. From sunrise to sundown for a seven day he forced her and the other women to kneel in the sun to seed his rows. When she asked to rest for a while and see to her childer, the overseer would not allow her to drink for the whole day as punishment. And so the same every day until the planting was done. Though they gave her water each night after sundown, the child withered in her. By the eye of Dolgar, that's what killed them both." Borian turned red after this outburst and ducked his head toward his bowl.

"No Rhyzka baron has land-bound peasants in Eleuthra," said Aleksander scornfully. "Those are Bek lands, held by grant from my—from imperial properties."

Vanko looked at Aleksander as if the lame visitor had indeed fallen on his head. "What Derzhi ever cared if a man was land-bound to force him to do his work?"

The Prince swallowed the dregs of his soup and shook his head. "The law of the Empire says—"

"Is your head stuck up a goat's ass, friend Wat?" said the gaunt Manganar. "If the lord refuses to sell you wheat and forbids any transport of another lord's wheat through his lands, then you work for him or starve. Though I'd give no Derzhi credit for a decent bone, at least Bek paid a wage for forced labor. The Bek still hold the manor at Gan Hyffir, but the new Emperor—curse all Derzhi now and forever—has given all the land in northern Manganar to these Rhyzka, who wouldn't know the law from the shit on their boots."

"Bloody thief!" Aleksander threw his bowl to the floor, scattering shards of blue crockery everywhere. "I'll have his balls for this." As he fumbled for his crutches, Lavra and her daughter glanced in alarm at the Prince and began shooing the younger children into others' laps so they wouldn't cut their bare feet.

"Hold, Wat," I said, trying to restrain Aleksander while suddenly tangled in the warm, wriggling limbs of a two-year-old boy. "Wat has no love for this new Emperor, either. His injury was—"

But I had no time to give them a story, for a noisy pounding on the shop door below us was followed by running steps and the appearance of Sovari, flushed and panting at the top of the stair. "An imperial search party headed this way—five warriors. And you"—he nodded to Vanko—"you'll want to know that the clerk from the gates is with them, and the fat tax collector."

"An imperial search party?" said Borian, turning a puzzled face to me. "Why? Who are you?" Before I could answer, his glance drifted to Aleksander and the sword that the Prince was buckling about his waist—the fine sword with the simple hilt, engraved with a falcon and a lion. All color deserted the potter's face.

"My cousin has had a mortal dispute with the servants of the new Emperor," I said, jumping to my feet and plopping the little boy on the table. "I'm so sorry, Borian, we had no reason to believe they could follow us here. We'll go. And you, Vanko, tell them—" Gods. What to tell them . . .

"We'll every one of us be dead before we let them take Olia," said Borian in quiet anger. "Now, get you gone the two of you. Vanko owes you his sustenance—as good as his life for a Manganar in this Empire. And anyone at dispute with our new Emperor—no matter who you are—deserves a life for a life. But we'll deal with our own trouble as we have ever done."

"We won't forget," I said, bowing quickly.

"Neftar, show them the back lane." Borian shoved the pimple-faced boy toward us. Sovari was already helping Aleksander down the back stairs.

The potter's yard smelled of goat and ash, and everywhere were broken or misshapen oil jars and water jars, pots of dried paint, and barrels of sand. The goat shed was little more than an earth-roofed vestibule built over a scrape dug into the hillside. Sovari had brought the horses on his way up, and as the captain and I shoved Aleksander onto his mount, I heard the crash when the front door of the shop was kicked in.

"Go on," I said to Aleksander and Sovari. "Find Malver and get yourselves out of the city. Take my horse. I'll catch up. Fly if I have to." I could not leave the two families in such danger. They didn't understand what kind of trouble they were in.

"Where's the cripple?" The warrior's bellow was almost unhearable above the screams and wails of the children. "Get these brats out of my way."

"Go!" I said. The pimple-faced Neftar had dragged open a section of wooden fence, revealing a weed-choked lane that led into the darkness beside the goat shed and the hill. The boy waved his arm frantically for us to get through it. Sovari hesitated, but Aleksander nodded and disappeared quickly into the lane without looking back.

"If you want to save your family, come to the shed with me," I said to the boy once he had shoved the gate closed and flapped his arms at the goats so they would mill about and cover the horse's tracks. "And listen carefully to everything I say." I didn't tell him not to be frightened. A good show of terror was exactly what I wanted.

We slipped into the close warmth of the goat shed. In one corner, scarcely discernible in the darkness was the tumbled pile of bundles that were the entirety of Vanko's household. I pulled off my haffai, shirt, leggings, and boots and stashed them behind the bundles along with my sword belt. Dressed only in breeches, my knife in hand, I took a breath. "Give me a moment."

With care and discipline, I let the shaping I had carried with me throughout the long evening fall away. Though I could not see the change in the angle of my eyes, nor even the altered color of my skin, I felt the nagging constriction of held enchantment lifted, the relief a snake must feel when shedding its papery skin. But I had no time to enjoy the release, nor the fact that I maintained my barrier against my angry demon as I changed, for I needed to work an illusion—one that was very easy to create as its component parts were disturbingly familiar. A moment's concentration, and then, with full sympathy for young Neftar's choking terror, I dragged the boy into the corner of the little shack, twisted his arms behind him in a secure hold, and put my knife to his throat. When the searchers came and lit the goat shed with their torches, the slave bands on my wrists and ankles shone like evil talismans to lead them straight to us.

CHAPTER 16

"Where's the girl?" I growled. "I told you I wanted the dark-haired girl-child, not this pustule-covered lackwit that a maggot wouldn't mate with."

"Well, what have we here?" The voice boomed heartily from behind the gaping Borian, who had just stumbled into the goat shed. One of the potter's eyes was purple and almost swollen shut, and he was clutching his left arm tightly to his ripped shirt.

I tightened my hold on the quivering Neftar and made sure my own hands were visibly shaking. "This Felics wants a whore, not a catamite. It's my freedom—" Then, as if just noticing the three Derzhi crowding in behind the bewildered Borian, I screamed, "You bastard! I spared your lives. I spared your children. All I wanted was the one girl to buy my freedom. He promised me." I nicked the boy's chin with my knife, a neat little wound that would dribble a goodly bit of blood down his neck and leave only a small, manly scar. "Stay back or I'll kill him."

"Please, your honors, my son . . ." Borian's voice cracked.

"We care naught for your scrawny offspring." The warrior captain shoved Borian to his knees, and his two companions moved to either side of me, awaiting his word to take me down. Sovari had reported only five Derzhi, but my ears told me there was one man standing just outside the door, and at least four more people in the yard, two with drawn swords, and two scrabbling up the hill behind the goat shed. "Come in here, clerk!" bellowed the captain.

The sallow-faced clerk sidled into the shed, his hands in his pockets.

"What's your game, you little rat's ass?" said the captain, not taking his eyes from me as he snarled at the clerk. "Instead of the kin-murdering Prince, you've hauled us from our watch to catch a runaway slave who couldn't walk five paces from the walls without getting caught."

"But this isn't the one," said the clerk, his smug expression quickly sagged into confusion. "There were two of them, a cripple that wore a braid and a ring and rode like a lord, and the fellow what was with him—a Kuvai, I think. And they met up with two others—at least one of them Derzhi—outside the house of the Mardek. Just as I told you."

"That's the filthy devil what made the deal," I yelled, pointing to the clerk as I pulled the quivering boy deeper into the corner. "His master promised me my freedom for the girl. Did you think to play a double round, devil? Pocket both the money for the girl and the reward for the runaway? Your master's likely pinching the girl for himself even now. You're too stupid to know the truth from the shit on your boots."

Borian jerked his head up and stared at me, ignoring the six goats that were nosing about him.

I didn't see much after that. With a jerk of his head, the warrior captain had his lieutenants pull Neftar from my hands and throw me to the straw, exposing my accumulation of scars, including the slave mark burned into my shoulder. Then they laid in to me with their boots for a goodly while before one of the heavy feet came to rest in the middle of my back.

The captain approached, his well-crafted boots stopping perilously close to my face. He crouched down and used a handful of my hair to pull my ear close to his mouth. "Now, what's all this about Felics?" he said.

Before I could catch a breath to spin out my story, the potter blurted out, "This slave sneaked in here earlier tonight and took my son captive. He said a tax collector promised to let him out through the gates if he would steal my sister's child for him. This Felics lusted for the child, he said, but couldn't take her himself as it was against the law and he would lose his post." The captain shoved my face into the dirt and moved away as Borian babbled on. "I didn't know what to do, your worships. The slave said he'd kill my son if I reported him to the watch, and kill us all in our beds if we didn't give him the child." My smile was hidden by the filthy straw. Not an impregnable story, but it would do.

The clerk regained his wits as quickly as had Borian. "Felics is mad for the girl-child, your honor. Ask Vallot, who worked the gates with him today. The fat bastard had me chasing 'round the city this whole night to find her. He's such a coward that he forced me to tell the lie of the villain Prince being here. He thought that if he came here with the watch, he could snatch the girl without danger from her kin. I feared to cross him when he's witless over the girl."

"Bring me this Felics," said the exasperated captain, who sounded ready to wilt under the barrage of changing stories.

Felics was evidently found inside Borian's house, attempting to dismember a defiant Vanko, who was shielding little Olia from the tax collector's paws. When dragged into the yard and questioned, Felics vehemently denied all knowledge of the clerk's accusations. His denial rang somewhat true, since he was clearly confounded by my appearance and the general turn of events. Unfortunately, he gave the Derzhi quite an accurate description of Aleksander.

It took the Derzhi watch captain well over an hour to get things sorted out. Somehow all the neighbors had got wind of the story that Prince Aleksander had been found in Borian's goat shed, and a goodly number of them stepped forward to tell the guardsmen how they had seen the Prince in other parts of the city. Their descriptions were not quite so accurate as the tax collector's, though every one of them mentioned that the Prince was lame. All swore that Borian had told them to summon the guards, so he should not be blamed for harboring a runaway slave. The potter could not possibly have gone to give the news himself, they said, as all Manganar were known to be half-crazed about their sons.

In the end, irritated and confused, the captain sent everyone packing with threats of mayhem if he was called out again, whether by false tales of fugitive princes or true tales of child stealing. By the time he dispatched two of his warriors to discover who in the city was missing a slave, the crowd had dispersed. No one needed to witness the dismal departure of a runaway slave bound for a night of beatings and certain mutilation. For I, of course, had not been sent home, but leashed to the captain's saddle by ropes around my wrists and to his hand by a rope around my neck. My bonds would not last long; a little way down the street, away from the Manganar's house and into the dark lanes where the Derzhi would relax, the slave bands on my wrists and ankles would vanish, and the ropes would snap to set me loose. I just hoped I'd not be forced to kill any of the guardsmen as I escaped, inviting Derzhi retribution on the slaves of Karn'Hegeth.

As the captain and his men mounted up, I stood barefoot in

the muck, bent over to ease the throbbing in my side where a warrior's boot had come too near my old wound, and waiting for the uncomfortable jerk on my wrists and neck that meant I was to keep up or be dragged. Through the open door of the pottery shop, I saw Vanko watching me, holding his bright-eyed daughter. It would be up to Vanko and Borian to keep the little girl safe from the lascivious tax collector. I had no great hopes for them. But then, I wasn't counting on Aleksander.

About the time the captain spurred his mount and I stumbled forward, familiar laughter echoed from Potter's Lane. "Ah, Vanye, the wine was sweet tonight, was it not? And the loving so full of charm! You have no such succulent roses in the north, I think."

My ears pricked. Vanye was the name of the dead man who was the root of my history with the Prince. We had used the name once before when working a deception.

"Did you see her father's face when she saw you were a Derzhi? I've heard chastouain lock their girls in cages if they lie down for Derzhi." I would never have guessed Sovari for an actor. "Speaking of fathers, we need to get home before yours has us beaten. He warned you after the races."

"My father is a noble ass." The slurring baritone began singing in wine-endowed fervor. "Desert roses are passing fair; no rain-fed bloom will ere compare. Mark my words, all ye who dare; my love is true, though I be . . . drunk! What comes next, my good Vanye? I've forgotten the cursed words."

All but one of the torches had gone with the Derzhi messengers, and the sleepy neighbors had returned to their beds, so only one sputtering flame and a few windows cast any illumination on the dark street where two haffai-clad riders were weaving their drunken way down Potter's Lane.

"What ho, Captain?" Aleksander pulled up abruptly, about the time I was scrambling to my feet after tripping over a rut. I could mistake neither the form nor the voice, though the haffai scarf was wound about his head. "Did your horse just shit an Ezzarian turd?" The Prince and Sovari burst into raucous laughter. "Whatever are you doing with Lord Vanye's slave?"

With scarcely concealed irritation, the captain gave an abbreviated version of the evening's confusion.

"A girl-child!" Sovari kicked me in the shoulder, sending me sprawling in the street muck. "Come, come, vermin, I thought

Ezzarians only lusted after pigs." As Sovari leaned toward the captain to offer him a swig from a wineskin, his haffai fell open to reveal his red imperial sash. "My slave doesn't like it here in the desert because the pigs stink too much in the heat."

"So this is your slave, Lord . . . Vanye, is it?"

"House of Mezzrah, from Capharna." Sovari nearly tumbled off his horse as he swept a bow. "Visiting my Fontezhi cousins. And yes, this squirming little vermin is the slave that my father charged to be my wet-nurse. I commanded him to wait at the gates until I came back from—"

"Shhh," said Aleksander, with exaggerated gestures. "Mustn't tell the captain where the roses can be found." His haffai was wrapped just enough to cover his boot, but expose a gold-wrought tef-coat embroidered with the Fontezhi kayeet. "So where is this girl-child?"

"In the potter's shop just behind me, my lord." The captain's voice was stiff. Anyone would have grown impatient with their reeling silliness.

"Is she fair?"

"Quite pretty for a Manganar whelp. Shall I have her brought out to you? If not, I'll—"

"Do you need another rose, Vanye?" said Aleksander, clapping his hand on Sovari's shoulder. "Or have we been pricked enough this night?"

"I think we're the ones have done the pricking!" More hilarity. "My slave will do nicely. I'll have him bathe me with rose petals before I take his foot."

Sovari flipped a coin in the air toward the guardsman, but it fell in the dirt out of the Derzhi's reach. The officer had either to bend over to pick it up, risking an appearance of avarice, or ignore it, risking the "noble's" wrath at his ingratitude. I could have sworn I heard a murmured oath. After bowing with strained politeness, he attached my ropes to Sovari's saddle, and then asked if there was anything more he could do for the two lords.

"This fair girl-child," said Aleksander, wagging his finger at the captain. "We mustn't have our roses plucked by slaves or tax collectors. You put it about that any man who touches this house will hang in the marketplace without his balls—right beside the cursed traitors. Do you understand me, Captain? By the honor of my father's house, you are commanded to see to it. And don't think I'm too drunk to remember. Is it understood?" Even with his wine-soaked slur, the command was clear. Derzhi nobles had a certain way with words, and Derzhi guard captains recognized it.

The Captain bowed his head. "Understood, my lord . . . I didn't catch your name . . ."

But Aleksander and Sovari had already spurred their mounts to a fast trot and broken into song again. I stumbled along behind them into the dark.

"I knew you were going to do something stupid," said the Prince as Sovari unhooked the ropes from his saddle and hauled me up behind him. "When are you going to leave off this damned playacting? Do you *want* to be a slave again?"

With the tail of Sovari's scarf, I blotted a cut on my forehead that was bleeding enough to blind my right eye. "I can't ever seem to think of anything else at the time," I said, vowing to improve my repertoire of deceptions as soon as I could think clearly again. "The results are always predictable, and people notice the slave rings before they notice my face. Gives me time to figure out what I'm doing. Where in the name of the gods did you get the Fontezhi tef-coat?"

"After I watched your little performance—"

"You watched?" Of course he had watched. I remembered the scrabbling noises behind the goat shed. No wonder he had gone off without arguing. Damned, hardheaded fool of a Derzhi.

"As I said, I knew you were going to do something stupid. The back of that shed is built right into the hill. Easy enough to crawl up and take a look inside. Thought I was going to have to come in after you. You didn't have a rabbit's twitch of a chance to convince them of that story—"

"Until Borian confirmed it."

"The potter did well. Indeed he did." Aleksander shrugged. "Anyway, when I saw the guardsman getting different tales from all sides, I knew we needed to prevent your having to do anything too extraordinary to get away."

"You roused the neighbors!"

"Easy enough. Gave us time to go hunting. I've had some good times in Karn'Hegeth. So I knew where to look for some stupid young bastard who had drunk too much and was seeking pleasures where he oughtn't. Found one, too. Sovari bashed him on the head and left him in an alley. He'll wake without a clue as to where his clothes got off to." Even as he told me, Aleksander stripped off the tef-coat and threw it into the muck.

"I'd recommend you keep your leg well covered, my lord," I said. "They're going to be looking everywhere for you."

We rode quickly through the streets and into the unsleeping caravan quarter, seeking Malver among the wagons and chastou, casks and barrels and boxes, slaves and sledges. We threaded our way between two teams of mountain oxen, their wickedly pointed horns wider than a man's arm span, only to be brought to a standstill by a herd of pigs. The beasts squealed in frantic chorus as they were herded into a torchlit slaughterhouse, there to be hacked into slabs or ground into sausage to hang in the meat merchants' stalls at dawn.

"Where is the blasted fellow?" said Aleksander, peering into the crowds of merchants and vendors of every race who were haggling with each other over accounts and market spaces and screaming at their slaves and bondsmen who were loading and unloading their merchandise. "How can you find anyone in such chaos?" He cursed as two brawny men, carrying a wooden booth on their shoulders, bumped his leg.

"How does a warrior tell his enemies from his brothers in a battle?" I said. "You just have to know where to expect them. Besides, Malver said he knew some cloth merchants." I pointed to a knot of men and women arguing and gesticulating as they clustered around an open chest. A tall woman with braided hair and skin the color of ebony stood serenely in the middle of the small crowd. She wore a purple loobah—a graceful Thrid garment made of one long strip of cloth draped about the body—and a necklace of interlaced rings of ivory or bone. Every once in a while she would point to one of her agitated customers, and the one so favored would pull a length of colored fabric from the chest and drop coins into the woman's slender hand. She transferred the coins into the folds of her richly colored garment. Watching the proceedings from the seat of a long wagon hung with scraps of fabric was Malver.

Sovari raised a hand, and Malver jumped down from the wagon, surveying the milling throng anxiously as he motioned us to ride around behind the knot of cloth buyers. "Wasn't expecting to see you here tonight, my lord," he said, pulling our horses into a shadowed nook. "Something's not gone quite to plan?"

"We need a place to stay out of sight for a few hours," said Aleksander. "I'm still seeing Kestor before leaving the city."

I could think of few worse ideas than for Aleksander to meet with a Fontezhi noble, even if the man was bound to him by the blood of their first battle, and if I could have worked some sorcery to remove the Prince from Karn'Hegeth in that hour, I would have done it. But I was in no condition to be of use. I'd been holding on to Sovari's waist with my left arm, because I could scarcely move my right, and indeed the numbness was affecting more than my arm. When I looked down, the ground seemed very far away. Sovari got himself off the horse gracefully, while I sat there wondering how I was going to manage my own dismount.

"W'Assani will transport you, my lord," said Malver, moving close and keeping his voice low. "She's joined up with a caravan that leaves after tomorrow's evening market. I told her only that I had a friend—pardon the presumption, my lord—who needed to get out of the city discreetly. She has moved goods that were perhaps . . . not properly taxed . . . in the past."

"What kind of fool are you to trust the Prince to a Thrid smuggler—and a woman?" said Sovari. "I thought you had sense. Thrid take whatever position pays them best, and the usurper can pay better than we can at the moment."

Malver was not ruffled in the least. "I've fought beside Thrid half my life. They hold to their bargains. Once paid, no one is more trustworthy. She—"

I heard no more of Thrid virtues, for just then a ripple of unease passed through the throngs in the streets: here and there an edgy glance cast toward the center of the city, a noisy conversation dropped to whispers, a hand reaching out for friends or children, drawing them out of the center of activity. I passed the back of my hand before my eyes, forcing my senses alert. The source of the disturbance was a distant knot of Derzhi warriors moving slowly through the crowd in our direction. A second group rounded a corner at the opposite end of the long street. Farther away, horses were galloping through the main streets of the city. Hunters.

"We can't wait for evening market," I said, my tongue thick. "And we can't wait to see the Fontezhi. We need to go now." The night was closing in. "With the Thrid woman or without."

Aleksander inspected me from bruised head to bootless feet. "Perhaps we've done all we can do here."

Malver ran to speak to the woman, while Sovari helped Aleksander from his horse. I gripped the lip of the saddle with my left hand and swung my leg over, but the horse was very tall, and I was suddenly very dizzy, and the ground was very hard when my face met the dirt.

CHAPTER 17

I didn't meet W'Assani until the chest she dropped on my arm waked me abruptly from a dead sleep with a vow to dismember whomever had done it.

"You've had the free use of my home all morning. I'll not apologize for reclaiming a bit of it."

I pulled my left arm out from under the hide-covered box, relieved to find the limb intact, and I tried to disengage my head from a pile of colorful woven goods. I scarcely had time to glimpse the flat silver light of desert noonday before a wad of coarse gray linen hit me in the face.

"Put this on." The woman was not at all in good humor.

Her command was easier spoken than obeyed, as first I had to untangle myself from the unending folds of the garment, and one of my hands seemed to be firmly attached somewhere else. And even beyond these difficulties, my head ached so ferociously I could scarcely see.

Someone released the immovable hand by untying the ropes that bound it. A similar activity in the region of my ankles told me they had been tied, too—a disconcerting discovery.

"Sorry for the bindings. We said you were W'Assani's new slave who had misbehaved." Malver's dark face swam in a blur of sunlight and gray cloth. "Didn't have time to see to you. Here." He shoved a waterskin into my hand. "W'Assani will look at your head."

"Where are the others?" I had only vague recollections of falling and whispers and hurried jostling. Someone had told me to keep my mouth shut or she would sew it that way.

"Captain Sovari's been sent off to Tanzire to set a meeting with the Bek. The Prince is up forward. Safe for now." Malver backed away into the dazzling sunlight.

I wasn't sure I wanted anyone to look at my head, much less a woman who had dropped a chest on me. But as I sat up and began to assess the damage, trying to resist draining the entire contents of the waterskin, I realized that part of my vision problem was that blood had congealed over my left eye. From the feel of the rest of my face, there was likely a good deal of dirt crusted in with it. And manure and considerable other filth. I was rank.

"Bloody Athos, woman, were you trained in healing arts by a shengar?" Aleksander's bellow sounded quite healthy. I dribbled a few drops of water on a corner of the gray haffai and dabbed at my eye, more convinced than ever that I had best tend to my own problems.

"Forward" was the half of a large, deep wagon bed that was exposed to the brutal sun, as opposed to the semi-shade provided by the roof of woven cloth scraps above my head. Once my eyelid came unstuck, I crept toward the light, threading my way between stacked barrels and chests and overflowing baskets of cloth, slightly nauseated from the heat, my head, and the stink.

The wagon wasn't moving. We seemed to be sitting on the edge of nothing; to my left, as far as I could see, were rocks and sand. Four donkeys harnessed to the well-built wagon were nosing at a mud hole on my right, where the last remnant of a stream had cut through this rocky apron of the desert. Jutting out of the jumbled rocks on the far side of the cracked mud were a few dusty tamarisks and a tangle of brown and brittle weeds. I could not see Malver.

Aleksander was sitting just behind the wagon seat with his back braced against the side of the wagon and his arms stretched out along the rim. The unlaced riding boot was tossed on top of a pile of ropes and harness, and someone in a white haffai was kneeling beside him, bent over his bare leg. Her long black hair was tied into a hundred tiny falls, each of them wound tightly with purple and blue thread.

"Look," said Aleksander, jerking his head at me, "here's a fellow so wounded he gets off a horse face first. Can scarcely move his sorry bones. Why don't you go tend him for a while?"

The woman straightened up and pointed a long finger at the Prince. "One more word from you and the both of you are out of my cart." Her brown eyes sparked like dry tinder lit in a desert midnight. As the sunlight bathed the fine planes and angles of her narrow face, I could not but think of the exquisitely carved obsidian game pieces on Nyel's game board. "You cost me a day's profits in the best market west from Zhagad, and instead of having a pleasant evening's journey to Khessida, where women appreciate fine weaving, I'm in the middle of Srif Naj on my way into Manganar, where people think they're god-blessed to wear goat hide. And who is like to be chasing me but every blood-handed Derzhi in your cursed Empire's service? No more push than a moth's wing on my backside would convince me to put bakza thorns in these wounds instead of this ointment that costs me fifty zenars a box. So you, my Derzhi friend, had best curb your proud tongue." With a single movement of her finger that directed every word of her diatribe to me as well as the Prince, she went back to work.

Aleksander's expression was such a perfection of astonishment that I grinned, thinking that perhaps I liked this woman after all. "Is he all right?" I said, crawling forward where I could see what she was doing. "Other than his tongue, I mean."

She was wrapping a thin strip of clean white linen just above the Prince's ankle. Two other strips were already in place beside the dreadful red-and-purple scar just below his knee. "Sores from this boot," she said. "Ate right through his tender royal skin. One almost to the bone. Has he no cleverness at all?"

"His cleverness has always been a matter of debate," I said. "But no one can fault him for lack of persistence."

The woman glanced up. She kept a smile at bay, except in her wide, dark eyes, where it settled as if in a familiar place. "I am W'Assani. How is your head?"

"Seyonne," I said. Her qualifications as guest-friend were unquestionable; thus I did not chafe at exchanging names. "It feels like your donkeys kicked it."

"Looks like it, too," Aleksander mumbled, pulling his haffai scarf down low over his face.

"Leave off the boot until these heal, lord of princes, or you'll have no need of boots." With a quick rip of a small knife, W'Assani trimmed off the end of the bandage and turned her attention to me. The line of her lip immediately informed me that I should not have used the gray haffai to clean my eye. "I thought Ezzarians were a cleanly people," she said. Before she could get started on another lecture, urgent hoofbeats and a choking shower of red dust announced Malver's return.

"Caravan!" he shouted as he slid from the saddle.

W'Assani slapped her hand on a wooden chest. "I knew Kavel would come this way." She thrust a ragged square of clean linen and a small brass box into my hand. "Use *this* to clean it.

Then put a bit of the ointment on it; only a bit, mind, or I'll take payment from your hide. When we stop again, I'll make mavroa to ease your head." She jumped down from the wagon, grabbed the donkey harness, and hauled the beasts away from the mud hole, cursing at them in a mixture of Thrid and Aseol, the common language of the Empire. Malver leaped onto the wagon seat and grabbed the traces just as the wagon lurched forward.

"I'll make the arrangements," W'Assani yelled to Malver. "You get the cart to the road." She snatched a trailing fold of her purple loobah, pulled it up between her legs, and tucked it somewhere in the other folds. Moments later she was astride Malver's horse, riding off the way from which he had just come, her beribboned black hair flying and her haffai streaming behind her like white wings.

I crawled over beside the Prince, leaned my back against the side of the wagon box, and closed my eyes, hoping that I wasn't going to have to wait for W'Assani's tea to ease my head, content for the moment to contemplate her striking image behind my eyelids.

"Have you had a woman since you left Ezzaria?" I had thought he was asleep.

Even under the dirt and crusted blood I felt my color rise.

"I thought not."

"I thought you couldn't read me anymore."

"The donkeys could read this."

"I have a wife—"

"—who tried to murder you, and will do it yet if you should cross her path. Worthy wives do not drop their wedding tokens into their husband's blood."

Fiona must have told him about Ysanne and the ring. "I vowed to be faithful until death," I said. "It makes no difference what she's done."

Aleksander pulled his scarf lower and settled as if to sleep. "Well, if you should ever change your mind, I'd not start with this one. She would devour you as a kayeet eats a rabbit."

An hour later, I was sitting in the back of the jostling wagon, dreaming of a bath. I had made one swipe at my face and was trying to find a clean spot on the square of linen to start on my hands. Unfortunately I made no progress on the stink, which seemed to be getting worse. A number of things had come to mind that were worth wishing for—food, rain, boots—and other nonsensical yearnings seemed to be written on my face for all to see, but I would have traded the prospect of any of them for a sliver of soap and an hour in a tub, pool, or river.

Aleksander had moved underneath the shade of the colorful canopy also, but had not shown any further inclination to talk. He sat across from me, his fingers tracing the engraving of his sword hilt. No pleasant thoughts there.

"I told Pujat Kavel that you were my new bond-servants," said W'Assani, who rode up beside the wagon and matched the horse's pace to the donkeys' plodding. "He thinks M'Alver there is my new partner, and I have acquired you—a cripple and a freed slave—to strip and clean the bones. You must show your diligence, or he won't believe me. When we stop at midday, you can start on those in the basket." She spurred the horse and left us spitting dust, but not before I saw the crinkle in the corners of her eyes.

Aleksander had seen it, too. "Damnable smirking Thrid witch. I'll let Edik have his way with me before I do her bidding."

"Bones?" I said. My head had eased considerably, but I was still confused.

Aleksander grimaced and shoved his sword belt back under an oaken chest. "Cast your sorcerer's eye inside the basket. No, the long one just behind you."

The object to which he was referring was about the length and width of a coffin, but twice as deep and made of tightly woven reeds with handles of rope. The moment I cracked the lid, I realized that the dreadful stench I had assumed my own was from quite another source—two animals, very dead. "Foxes?"

W'Assani had gotten us out of Karn'Hegeth through one of the closed gates, so Aleksander told me. Evidently she regularly needed a quiet way out of the city and knew several guardsmen who were willing to let her pass for a share of her profits. This time she had paid a man with Aleksander's horse and mine. The guardsman had poked around her wagon to see what was worth such an expensive bribe, finding only one battered, insensible slave, supposedly acquired in trade, her usual baskets and chests of woven goods, and a large, vile-smelling basket that held two fox carcasses. The foxes were sufficient explanation.

Ornaments of fox bone were prized by a good many men across the Empire, for they were believed to enhance virility.

Derzhi from those hegeds that permitted multiple wives, and Suzaini who often had three or more, had been known to pay handsomely for fox-bone arm or finger rings, pendants, bracelets, or brooches. Especially valued were the bones of the elusive red Azhaki fox. As a certain Fontezhi lord who resided in Karn'Hegeth maintained his own supply of them, captive, the guardsman had no difficulty understanding W'Assani's hurry. He was not in the least inclined to poke around in the smelly basket, so he failed to discover that just below the quickly ripening carcasses were a false bottom and his anointed Emperor.

"I thought I was going to cook in my own vomit," said the Prince. "If she thinks I'll do any more playacting . . ."

But of course she did. And we did. W'Assani was very clever.

We rode with the caravan of one Pujat Kavel, a Hollenni trader in olive oil, spices, and dried fish. Though oil and spices were immensely profitable items, the trade in them was controlled by Derzhi hegeds, the Jurrans for spices, Gorusch for olive oil. By the time Kavel paid imperial taxes, the required heged shares, and bribes enough to keep his caravans moving, he earned barely enough to support his own business in dried fish. And he knew that if the dried fish business were ever to become truly profitable, one of the Derzhi families would take it over, probably killing him in the process. Though he was not yet thirty, the hard truths of the world had already sapped his hopes, and he wore a perpetually morose expression. Even his dark mustaches drooped.

At our first stop Malver—M'Alver as W'Assani called him in the language of Thrid—helped me carry the basket of fox carcasses out of the wagon. The moment we left the basket to go help Aleksander out of the wagon bed, the caravan dogs were on it. W'Assani screamed at them and threw stones, and then grabbed one of Aleksander's crutches and beat them off.

I suggested that it might be clever to let the dogs do the disgusting job of removing the decaying flesh from the prized bones, but W'Assani said she could not have her precious stock ruined by teeth marks or cracks. Bad enough our urgent departure had prevented her skinning her prizes right away. The delay had likely ruined the pelt. Once the pelt was removed, we were to carefully cut away the meat and gristle. That should distract the dogs and vultures while we finished the job of stripping the bones. Whenever we made camp for the night, we would boil an earthen pot of hali—the bitter powder that the desert sun leached from bad water holes—and clean away the remaining bits from the day's harvest of bones.

In the midday heat, such tasks were no pleasure, but I had done much worse many times. W'Assani would feed, shelter, and transport us for only a few days, but long after we were gone, she would ply these roads and towns, where informers would sell her life for a few zenars. To hold up our end of the deception seemed a fair exchange for her risk.

Aleksander did not so much object to the task—he had hunted the desert since he could draw a bow, and even Derzhi princes skinned their own kill. The unpleasantness resulting from three days' rotting in W'Assani's basket was only a matter of degree. But to take orders from a woman . . . and from a Thrid, the most despised of all races . . . to labor at her command while others took their leisure, and to suspect how perfectly she must be enjoying her moment's dominance over the Derzhi Emperor-in-waiting . . . *that* left him near bursting.

"She's a devil." His knife slid expertly along the inside of the fox's legs and down the centerline of the belly, detaching the soft pelt from the decaying muscle. I had a feeling that the dead fox wore a Thrid woman's face at that moment.

"She's clever."

"What's she doing now?" Aleksander was sitting with his back to the wagon, his leg stretched out stiffly in front of him. To shift his position in order to observe his tormentor would be awkward and obvious.

"Drinking ale with Malver."

"Gods, I'll flog him for this. She's laughing, is she?"

"Not at all. She's showing him some of her weavings." Malver was easy with W'Assani as I had not seen him with anyone else. I had thought him a man of few words, but the two seemed to find a great deal to talk about. I was surprised that he had revealed Aleksander's identity to her, but it seemed to have worked out for the best. She was taking her commission very seriously.

"You're enjoying this." The Prince's glare was hotter than the sun.

"I can think of many things I'd rather be doing."

Pujat Kavel strolled by, his hands clasped behind his back. He nodded to W'Assani. "Another hour and we'll be on our way, mezonna." *Mezonna* was the honorific for a businesswoman. Though the drooping Hollenni had been willing to accept W'Assani's fee and her story of a broken bargain with another caravan, he took care to make sure the Thrid woman was what she said. When the train of nine wagons and twenty chastou stopped to rest and eat and sleep through the hottest part of the day, he strolled by our position no less than four times an hour.

"She'll send Malver hunting to bring us more carrion to play with, won't she?" said Aleksander after Kavel had passed by.

"I would expect so. Gazelle or kayeet bones won't fetch the same price, but someone will buy her trinkets. At least we'll be able to cook fresh meat and eat it." Though at the moment, with my hands buried in rotting fox flesh, eating meat was about the last thing I could desire.

We maintained our roles carefully as we traveled with W'Assani. Aleksander and I rode in the wagon and worked whenever the wagon stopped. W'Assani rode our horse and laughed and talked with Malver, who drove her rig. She held no discourse with the Prince or me, only commanded us where everyone could hear. Sometimes she rode beside Pujat Kavel during the day, and she spent every evening at his cook fire. Her mellow laughter echoed through the camp as we skinned and boned, cooked and ate her kill, and sweated over her boiling pots.

My eyes would not leave her graceful form—walking, riding, speaking everything of life; they brushed her lusciously dark skin, and I imagined how it might be to loose her thick hair from its windings and let it fall about her shoulders . . . or mine. While Aleksander brooded and plotted strategy, I smiled to myself at her wit, and admired her cleverness, and wondered if the tales she told Kavel of her smuggling exploits were true.

But when the night grew late and I finished my work, I lay under the stars and tried to clear my head of this woman who had no rightful place there. I had a wife. Ysanne had been my very heart since I was fifteen, everything I wanted, everything I could imagine wanting. How could I consider intimacy with anyone else? Yet the only memory I could summon of my wife were the last words I'd heard from her lips. *Find the demon . . . bleed him until he's dead.* The wounding of those words was far deeper than the scar in my side.

CHAPTER 18

The caravan crawled along the Vayapol Road, a well-traveled route that led southeast from Karn'Hegeth across Srif Naj toward the distant trading city where I had first met Blaise. Well before we got to Vayapol, however, W'Assani planned to turn our wagon south and head for the fertile wheat and barley fields of Manganar, lands that Aleksander had once called his own. The Prince had granted a number of estates to the Bek heged at the time of his anointing, as he had done for every other Derzhi family. The knowledge that the hated Rhyzka now controlled his own vast holdings had been bad enough, but to hear that Edik had revoked his gifts came near driving him mad. He saw only one bright spot. Surely the Bek and other hegeds subjected to such humiliations would join him to throw down Edik.

Someday I would remind him that neither Rhyzka nor Bek nor Denischkar held true claim to those lands. Manganar had once had a king of her own.

On our third day with the caravan, we heard tidings from Karn'Hegeth. A fast moving party of Senigarans passed us on the road, and, as was the custom, rode alongside the caravan long enough to exchange news. The three were hired swordsmen, I guessed, from their confidence in traveling alone. And, too, the quality of their weapons was much finer than the quality of their dress. "We were lucky to get out of Karn'Hegeth," said the swarthy spokesman for the three. "They've locked the gates and are allowing no one in or out."

"How's that?" said Kavel.

"Prince Aleksander was seen there—all over the city, you'd think—in the noble quarter, in the craftsmen's quarter, in the market quarter. There's rumors that he came to avenge the murders of his friends that were executed by the imperial governor. Rumors that he came to save the common folk from the new Emperor. Rumors that he's going to kill the Fontezhi second lord. No man could do so many deeds as the talk would have him doing, nor be so many places all at once. You've heard the story of his battle with the Hamraschi? How a winged god came and took him out? As if that wasn't wonder enough, now they say the Prince himself can change his shape. The Fontezhi lords are furious at the talk, searching every house. They've vowed to gut the Kinslayer in Zhagad market and see if any god comes to save him."

I reported the conversation to Aleksander.

"Everyone would be quite disappointed to see the truth, wouldn't they?" he said.

Indeed we were a sorry case, caked with sand and sweat, our skin and garments hopelessly stained with blood and worse. I was still without shirt or boots, and my skin was blotchy green and black with fading bruises. Aleksander's leg was grotesque with sores, his healing wound, and patches of pale withered flesh. Later that same day, when he thought no one could see him, I watched him try to put some weight on his leg. It crumpled immediately and left him scrabbling for a handhold on the wagon. He smashed his crutch into the dirt, then leaned his forehead on the wagon side, one fist pounding on the unyielding oak.

On our fifth day out of Karn'Hegeth the hunters came. The caravan had stopped at Taíne Dabu, a lush green sink with a well so prolific it merited a long stop, though the hour was earlier than usual for a rest. Aleksander and I were grateful, for not only was it a somewhat cooler part of the day for our bloody work—a sand-deer to dismember on this day—we could actually have a bit of shade to ourselves. And deception or no, desert custom or no, I was determined to have a wash.

Most of the caravan halted near the well, the easier to tend their beasts and fill their water barrels. But we pulled W'Assani's wagon away from the other wagons and set up under a spreading tamarisk outside the lip of the green sink so our activities could not foul the well. As I cut into the deer and cast a small enchantment to keep the dogs and vultures away until we were ready, I heightened my hearing to listen to the gossip throughout the caravan. I had gotten into the habit of doing so to make sure no suspicion attached to W'Assani or her bondsmen. As always, the chastouain were cursing their recalcitrant beasts. The leather merchant was beating his slave for spilling a cup of nazrheel on his new haffai. W'Assani was telling Kavel how she had smuggled a load of untaxed nazrheel through the gates of Zhagad itself on a dare. The two were sitting by the well beyond a grove of nagera trees, and I let my investigation linger there for a while. Old Talar, the guardian of Ezzarian purity, would have been horrified at such use of my gifts. But because I had indulged my fascination and left my hearing sharp, I heard the Derzhi horsemen coming well before they reached Taíne Dabu.

"Riders!" I said to Aleksander, then I whistled long and loud, a prearranged signal to warn W'Assani and Malver of nearby danger. I leaped into the wagon to make sure that Aleksander's sword belt, ring, and telltale boot were safely hidden in the false bottom of W'Assani's basket, then returned to the Prince. Aleksander had wound his haffai scarf around his hair, and I did the same, making sure it drooped over the scar on my face. Nothing else to be done. We went back to work.

"Who is the gonaj here?" demanded the Derzhi officer as the five warriors rode up, their horses kicking dust all over our fresh meat.

I ducked my head and pointed toward the well. "Pujat Kavel of Hollen, your honor."

Aleksander kept his eyes on the sand-deer, but his hands, bloody to the elbows and gripping his knife, were very still.

The riders proceeded down the path into the sink.

"What heged—?"

I motioned Aleksander quiet and listened to the questioning. The Derzhi spoke of reports that the Kinslayer had been smuggled out of Karn'Hegeth. All the roads were being scoured. *Every wagon and cart must be searched. The villain prince is supposedly in company with three men, one of them Derzhi, the other two of unknown race. The Fontezhi first lord has added five thousand zenars to the price of the murderer's capture—but only if he is taken alive. And, oh yes, the Prince has been injured. He wears a thick leather boot on one leg, such as nobles wear for a broken limb.*

"Nothing new," I said. "They're going to search the caravan." I dragged the sand-deer pelt over Aleksander's scarred leg and crutches and cursed myself for not thinking to hide them earlier. What if the soldiers had noticed? "No need to have anyone wondering about you."

Aleksander shifted awkwardly. "I don't like this."

I felt the same. Sitting with our backs exposed. Unable to run.

Unable to fight to any good purpose. I could perhaps take on five Derzhi if I had a sword in hand—as long as none of them struck me in the right side. But there were at least twenty men of fighting age in the caravan, and fifteen thousand zenars would let a man and his family live like lords. Even had I been willing to sacrifice W'Assani and Malver and fly away with Aleksander, I could not carry him far enough to see him safe. Nor would stealing a horse help us, as it was so difficult for him to mount, and no horse in the caravan was good enough to outrun those the Derzhi rode. So we sat. Waited. Pulled bleeding muscle from bone as if it were important that it be done right.

Half an hour passed. I considered enchantments. Paraivos and walls of fire needed time and concentration to prepare, so I tried to come up with some smaller working. I dared not do anything that would draw attention unless we had no other recourse. Better to let this storm pass over us.

"You're ruining my cloth, you flea-brain," W'Assani yelled, running up to her wagon as a ham-handed Derzhi clambered in and started dumping her chests and baskets. No mistaking the crack of a solid blow on flesh.

I dropped a half-stripped leg bone and leaped to my feet. Aleksander clamped an iron hand about my ankle. "Sit down," he said through clenched teeth.

"What kind of witch are you?" The Derzhi held up a handful of kayeet bones. "My lord! The Thrid savage has got a basket of bloody bones in here! Animal bones, I think."

A rider approached the wagon. "Has someone paid you for your devil's magicking?"

"I fashion bone ornaments, good lord, as well as weaving cloth," said W'Assani, rubbing her bruised face and showing them her necklace, bracelets, and rings. She made a good show of defiance subdued . . . until she opened her mouth again. "My bondsmen strip and clean the bones, but even such dull-wits as they know to keep the blood from off my cloth."

"We care naught for your trinkets, Thrid witch," said the rider, a noble, so said the fine cut of his clothes. "We hunt the coward Aleksander, and I would strip your black flesh from your bones if it would find him." Something was vaguely familiar about the nobleman's voice, but I was looking into the sun and could not recognize him from the back.

"If these bones are those of your royal father-killer, you may have them and good riddance," said W'Assani. "Even Thrid savages do not bleed their fathers."

The Derzhi in the wagon grabbed and twisted W'Assani's hair, pulled her head close to his mouth, and growled at her. "Mind your barbarian tongue, witch."

The noble snapped his reins. "Let's be off, Durn. Nothing to be found in this pitiful lot."

The Derzhi riders galloped past Aleksander and me on their way back to the road. I was almost ready to breathe easy again, when the last rider slowed, reversed direction, and walked his mount around us. I kept my head down and my knife moving. Aleksander did the same. After a moment the rider, the fair-haired young noble, moved on after the others, and we both glanced after him. We could see him clearly now. "Hadeon," we said as one.

"We've got to get away from the caravan," I said. "This young lord is not stupid. He saw the Prince's leg and crutches before I covered them. Once he thinks about it, he's going to be back. Then you'll die, W'Assani. If he believes you know where Prince Aleksander is, he'll force you to tell him." Of all the damned bad luck to have the proud young Mardek be the one to see Aleksander's grotesque leg.

"And where do you propose we go?" said the woman, pressing a damp cloth to a cut on her lip.

"You paid me to get you out of Karn'Hegeth, not to die for you. Not to have my whole trade ruined." The wagon was a mess. At least half of the lengths of colored fabric were ripped, stained with blood, or dropped into the muck where the horse and donkeys had been watered. The spilt bones were no matter, save the fox bones and tails that were safely tucked away with Aleksander's sword. W'Assani needed the fox tails to prove the value of her stock. But she needed her life to enjoy her profits.

"We go to the Bek," said Aleksander. "Sovari is waiting in Tanzire. We just leave the caravan early—tonight instead of tomorrow."

"We must go now," I said. I could not speak my urgency. Hadeon had seen Aleksander's damaged leg. He would know. And both Mardek and Fontezhi had messenger birds.

Malver nodded. "Kavel plans to stay here past midday. His chastou are dry and need the time. But everyone is down at the well, so if we leave now, no one will miss us until he reassembles the caravan. If we could just cover our tracks . . ."

"I'll see to that," I said, glad to have something useful to do.

W'Assani was not convinced. She stood in the wagon bed frowning, her hands on her hips. "You can't erase ten leagues of wagon tracks, and there's no wind today. I've seen tracks last for thirty days in summer. So they'll know we ran away and be able to follow us. Better we keep to our story and stay with the others. The emperor can hide in the basket if needed."

"Seyonne can take care of the tracks," said Aleksander, "but I'd advise you to keep your haffai wrapped tight." Then, in a move that surprised even me, who thought I had seen all of Aleksander's surprises, he bowed deeply to W'Assani. "I regret we must disrupt your trade further, madam. Someday, when I am in a better position to do so, I will demonstrate my gratitude more fully. For now I can only tell you that you are as fine a player of deception as I have ever encountered. In fact," he added, standing up again and hitching his crutches under his arms, "I think you should give lessons to Seyonne. Your tricks involve a great deal of blood, but so far, none of it is his."

For the first time in five days, W'Assani was at a loss for words. I didn't think it a common occurrence. Nor did I think it clever to let her see my enjoyment of the scene. While Malver hitched the donkeys and tied the horse to the wagon, Aleksander threw his crutches into the wagon bed and hoisted himself in after them. I pulled off my haffai and hurried down to the well. Nodding respectfully to Kavel, who was supervising the watering of his chastou, I soaked the robe, careful not to get the blood from my hands into the water. The wagon was already pulling away when I ran up the path and threw myself headlong into it. "We can at least clean up a bit," I said, dropping the sopping wad into Aleksander's lap. I sorely regretted the lost chance to wash with the bountiful waters of Taíne Dabu.

We traveled through the dreadful noonday and all through that scorching afternoon, watering the donkeys generously from our filled barrels and taking turns sitting in the sun to drive the wagon. Actually, the other three shared the wagon seat, while I sat on the very back, behind the shade canopy, and spoke the wind. Softly. Just enough to shift the sand and erase our tracks across the dunes. Malver sighted our direction by the sun, conferring constantly with Aleksander, who knew more details about the geography of his Empire than a Thrycian mapmaker. W'Assani took her turn driving, then spent the rest of the time sorting through her stock, stuffing the ruined fabrics into one basket and carefully folding and rolling the rest.

"So, are you shy of driving donkeys?" She stuck her head through the trailing curtain, and before I could answer she had stepped between the wooden struts onto the rim of the wagon box. The desert light had changed from the flat sheen of afternoon into the shifting purple and gold of evening. To the east, the sky had already deepened. Behind us stretched the sculpted dunes . . . a smooth, unbroken sweep of sand.

"I had other things to do." I moved a little to the side, and she sat down beside me, dangling her legs off the back as I was doing.

For a while, she sat in companionable silence, gazing into the desert behind us. Her body moved as we rode, translating the harsh jostle of the wagon into easy grace. As the hour passed I glanced sideways and saw a small frown settle on her brow. I smiled to myself and continued my work. A few minutes more and she opened her mouth, but no words followed. She closed her eyes, then looked again. Finally, just when I thought the question would come, she leaned back against a pile of boxes and propped her feet up against one of the canopy struts, settled, as if she could ride that way to the end of the earth.

"You're not afraid?" I said.

"Do I need to be?"

I shook my head. "Not of me."

"And the one who sleeps?" Inside the wagon, Aleksander was snoring vigorously.

"Nor him."

"Good. I wouldn't want to have my life turned inside out by evil spirits or villain princes."

The stars began to come out. We rode for a long while without saying much of anything.

Later, after W'Assani moved inside to sleep, I decided I had done enough. We were leaving the srif for higher ground—grasslands and wheat country. No one could track us from Taíne Dabu. I stepped over the sleeping Aleksander and W'Assani to the wagon seat and offered to take a turn driving. Malver yielded me the traces, but stayed beside me, sighting the stars to keep us on course for Tanzire.

"Is she your sister or your cousin, M'Alver?" I said softly, pronouncing his name in the Thrid way.

"Mother of earth . . ." The soldier stared at me. Terrified.

"It's all right," I said. "I won't say anything. Not that it would make any difference after all you've done."

Thrid were hired soldiers, mercenaries paid to die in Derzhi wars, skilled at arms, but never trusted. Never honored. Never noticed, except to judge whether they were worth their fee. Never, ever, did Thrid serve in a Derzhi troop, much less command Derzhi warriors. Popular wisdom said that the lowest born man of Derzhi blood would rise to be emperor before such a thing could happen. Except that it had.

"My duty. That's all I've done."

"Why? To hide what you are all these years . . . to serve the Derzhi conquerors . . ." His skin was dark, but not the telltale color of his people. Ordinarily, Thrid were the only race easier to recognize than Ezzarians.

He shrugged and kept his eyes fixed on the rising barrens ahead. "I'm good at fighting. At leading men. And I value my life. Why would I want to leave it in the hands of some Derzhi jackanape who thinks he can pay me enough to go where he daren't poke his spear? I decided to determine my own fate as far as a man can do it."

"But this . . . now . . . this is something more . . ."

He glanced sideways at me. "Aye. A barbarian Thrid might not see so much as an Ezzarian sorcerer can, but I've eyes in my head. Someday I may have sons who want to fight for something worthy."

I nodded and returned my attention to the donkeys. "He is worthy. If we can just keep him alive long enough that he can see his way. I promise you, he is."

We rode on, Malver nudging me back on course as we skirted the last of the towering dunes. After a while I shivered and handed over the traces, saying I was going to retrieve my haffai and bring him a waterskin. As I crawled toward the back, Malver spoke over his shoulder. "Half sister."

CHAPTER 19

Thanks to the water we had taken from Taíne Dabu, W'Assani's donkeys stayed alive long enough to get us to Tanzire, a moderately sized, walled town surrounded by wheat fields and tiny villages, one of which was Vanko's home of Eleuthra. The northern gates of Tanzire stood open, their lower edges buried in weed-choked sand. The thick wooden gates had not been closed for a hundred and thirty years, not since the last remnant of the Manganar royal line had been crushed. A mud-brick tower stood across the broad marketplace from the gate, the remnant of a primitive fortress that had once occupied this site.

As soon as W'Assani had bullied her way past three nosy guards at the gates, Malver jumped off the wagon and slipped into the dim side lanes in search of Sovari. Aleksander and I stayed under W'Assani's canopy while the woman guided her donkeys through the wide dirt street into the town market. We passed at least six mounted Derzhi warriors, all of them of the Rhyzka heged. I thought the Prince would spew steam at the sight of them.

In the way of many towns in the desert regions, the market was a large square, surrounded by two-story houses of mud brick. The upper floors of the houses protruded into the market, supported on brick pillars, so that all around the edges were shady cloisters where sellers could spread their wares. Wagons and carts stopped haphazardly in the open space, where the owners could set up small fences for stock, hammer steel posts into the ground for tethering valuable horses or slaves, or spread canvas canopies to make shade. Ten or more streets led off the market, deeper into the town.

W'Assani hurried off to the town offices to make application to the redyikka—the magistrate who oversaw the market and who would most certainly notice if a merchant failed to register upon entry to the city. Aleksander retrieved his sword and ring from the false-bottomed basket and hid them under his haffai. I sat in the shadows and listened to the gossip among nearby tradesmen sitting together in the shade drinking nazrheel. Much of it was the usual business of family and caravan traveling: news of mutual acquaintances, weather, roads, tariffs, and hardship. But after a while they lowered their voices to where I could catch only some of the words.

. . . Unsettled . . . these new rules from Zhagad . . . How can a man survive, much less make a profit? Monstrous levies . . . on the Suzain road imperial soldiers take half the goods from every caravan . . . whole villages taken for slaves if their taxes fall short . . . all of us in Nyabozzi chains soon enough. Perhaps . . . perhaps not . . . I heard rumor, a name not heard in a year . . .

The voices dropped below my level of hearing, even heightened as it was by skill and melydda. Yet I thought I heard one more word, or perhaps my own mind added it to the whisperings because I recalled the rumors of bandits in Karn'Hegeth. But I could have sworn they said "*lukash.*" *Yvor Lukash* . . . the sword of light . . . Blaise. Was the outlaw band riding again, their truce with the Empire broken by Aleksander's fall? I was on the verge of leaving the wagon to persuade the gossiping men to tell me, when Malver returned with Sovari.

"All praise to Athos, my lord, to see you well." Sovari's words did not reflect his dismay at Aleksander's wretched appearance, but his face spoke volumes.

"Yes, I need some clothes fit to put on before I see anyone, and if you don't have a pot or a puddle or a seep where I can wash this vile stink off of me, I'll strangle you."

"Of course, I'll arrange something. But, my lord, the Bek . . ." Sovari had clearly been away from court long enough to lose the impenetrable mask of courtiers, the polite, incurious veneer that could cover every emotion from murderous rage to driving lust. The good captain did not want to continue. And, of course, Aleksander, skilled at penetrating even the courtier's mask, saw it.

He sighed broadly. "Tell me, Sovari. I'm scarcely expecting heralds or a rose-petal canopy."

"The First Lord will not see you, my lord, nor will he allow a meeting at the Bek stronghold."

"Go on."

"They've told me of a tavern . . ."

* * *

Sovari had taken a room at a bedraggled little inn that was crammed between a tannery and a saddle-maker's shop, its cracked mud walls and weedy stable yard so miserable it didn't even have a name. The copper lantern that hung outside its arched gate was the only way to know that a weary traveler could find a mug of lukewarm ale or a bowl of barley soup or a pallet of straw within. W'Assani planned to stay with the wagon in the marketplace, conduct her business, and protect her goods. Malver stayed to help her with the donkey team before joining us at the tavern. In the back of my mind was the thought to visit W'Assani later after our business was done. Talk a bit. Learn more of her.

We had not been followed to the inn, but I didn't like the room—only the one door and a single, small barred window. I peered out at the waste heaps behind the tannery and decided that the stink was not going to improve very much, even if Aleksander and I were able to wash.

"Sereg, the Fourth Lord of the Bek," grumbled the Prince as he lowered himself to the pallet in the airless room. "What does a Bek fourth do? Probably sharpens harrows for plowmen. Or he's the second lord's idiot nephew. All this cursed way here to meet with a fourth."

Sovari stood by the door, his arms folded, worry lines creasing his rugged face. "Not to excuse their discourtesy, my lord, but I've been here three days, and every morning has seen a new imperial messenger ride in. The Bek—anyone with a grievance against the new . . . against Lord Edik—are likely being watched. They know you're moving."

"Any messenger birds?" I asked. "Any word from Karn'Hegeth?" My hackles had been raised from the moment we rode into the town. The safety of the empty desert seemed far away.

"I've not seen them. But likely any birds would go to the castle at Gan Hyffir, which is still held by the Bek. The Rhyzka have taken over several large houses in town for now; they've at least twenty warriors in the garrison, some with imperial credentials. That's why I brought you such a roundabout way here. Word is the Rhyzka are trying to persuade Lord Edik to give them Gan Hyffir for their sixth. With that they could hold all of northern Manganar."

"I know exactly what they want," snapped Aleksander. "So when is this meeting?"

"Lord Sereg will be in the common room tonight at fifth watch. I'll send the confirmation, then have hot water and food brought." He pointed to folded piles of clothes and two pairs of boots. "My apologies for the clothes, my lord. They're the best I could have made in so short a time. I've four fresh horses in the stable, and I'll be off to set your meeting with the Fozhet as soon as I've given your orders."

"Then we'll see you at Khoura in two days, Captain."

"Two days. I'll be waiting for you, my lord."

Aleksander leaned against the wall. "You've done well, Sovari."

The captain flushed and bowed deeply. "It is and has ever been my honor to serve you, Your Majesty."

"Majesty . . ." said Aleksander softly, after Sovari left us. From the pocket of his filthy haffai, he pulled out his ring and stared at it unspeaking until two serving girls arrived at our door with hot water and food enough for five men. Sovari had done very well indeed.

Once reasonably clean, shaved, trimmed, braided, and dressed in clothes that, though plain, were neither ragged nor bloodstained, Aleksander regained a bit of fire. As soon as Malver arrived, he sent the soldier to retrieve his riding boot, and when the time came for the meeting with the Fourth Lord of the Bek, Malver informed the nervous noble that his rightful Emperor would meet him, not in the tavern common room like a skulking thief, but in the yard behind the tavern, mounted, as was fitting for a Derzhi warrior on the front lines of a battle. I was uneasy at the choice of venue, but the yard was dark, tucked away from the street, and had no windows looking over it but our own. And, indeed, Aleksander was more mobile on a horse.

The posturing did little but service Aleksander's pride, for the Bek fourth lord, neither idiot nor tool sharpener, but the first lord's scholarly youngest son, offered nothing more than had Lord Vassile of the Mardek. The Bek would honor the wishes of their late Emperor and see Aleksander crowned, but they would not fight for him unless he brought evidence that they would not stand alone. Though his family would neither harbor Aleksander nor give him men, horses, or supplies, Lord Sereg himself seemed intrigued with Aleksander's promise to restructure the order of the Derzhi hegeds.

"Did you hear him?" said Aleksander. "The owl-eyed twit said my actions of the past two years as my father's surrogate had given him ideas on how the Empire might be governed differently, split into regions, each with a powerful prince to counterbalance the strength of the Twenty." We were walking slowly back to the tavern from the stable, the Prince's face tight as he deliberately put weight on his booted leg. "I couldn't even make one son," he added bitterly. "What makes him think I could breed five full grown?"

"Did he say anything of bandit raids?" I asked. I had listened to the meeting with only half an ear, trying to watch the street, the yard, and the maze of dark alleyways for anyone who might be looking for a red-haired Derzhi with an imperial ring and a riding boot.

"Bandits . . . no. He said only that matters were getting worse by the hour for the minor houses. New horse levies on top of doubled taxes and conscription of half their heged troops for the borders, right when Edik gave their land—my land—to the cursed Rhyzka. It would serve Edik right if the Yvor— Holy Druya, have you heard something of your outlaw friend?"

"Just gossip." But I wondered. I had induced Blaise to halt his raids as a concession to Aleksander. But if slave taking and the other cruel burdens of the common people were getting worse, Blaise would not sit still for long. My steps slowed, and as I watched Aleksander hobble through the back door of the shabby tavern, I began to consider defeat.

I could not stay with the Prince forever. Was it foolish for me to continue this journey, when what strength I had left might better be saved for a more serious struggle that I alone could face? Was I staying for Aleksander, for the elusive promise of his feadnach, or was I just too cowardly to face my own future?

Distracted, worried, I wasn't paying enough attention to the night. But because I lingered at the edge of the dark stable yard weighing possibilities, I heard the whispers from the shadows by the tannery wall and the light footsteps running away. Two pairs of them. *Damn!* I dodged a stack of empty ale barrels, knocking them tumbling, and leaped over the broken cart frame and rusted stovepipe that were piled at the edge of the yard. I turned left by the tanner's wall, stepping lightly over scrap heaps, only to trip over a wooden staff thrust across the narrow alley right where it entered the street. The one who held the staff tried to bring it down on my head, but I rolled, leaped up, and was on his back before he could raise it high enough. My scrawny assailant wriggled and poked and bit my arm, but I held him tight and dragged him back into the dark alley, casting a futile enchantment toward his escaping companion. I had not seen or touched the runner, and so my working would do little more than slow his steps as he ran to tell what he had seen.

"Where is he going?" I said, snarling at the sullen boy pressed hard against the tannery wall with my arm across his throat. "Who will your friend tell?"

"I won't—"

"Don't think you can lie to me or hold back what I want to know," I said harshly, letting my eyes flare blue. I could imagine how strange and fearsome my eyes would look. Of course the boy, who was no more than thirteen, could not realize that my anger was directed more at myself than at him.

"The first m-magistrate is his uncle," squeaked the boy, spittle leaking from the side of his gaping mouth.

"And who is the magistrate's lord?" No hope that he was Bek's man.

"Lord M-Miron."

"Rhyzka?"

The boy nodded and slumped to the ground, shaking fiercely, tears streaking his dirty face as my knife pricked his belly. I could have threatened him with all manner of torments to force his silence or to counter his friend's tale, but he was already blubbering.

So I ran back to the tavern and burst into the room, catching Aleksander just as he was pulling out his braid. He frowned. "Where have you—?"

"We've got to run, my lord. I was careless. Right now some stupid boy is telling a Rhyzka magistrate about what he saw in the stable yard behind the tavern. I'd swear they weren't there while you were talking with Sereg, but we can't risk it. We'll hope it takes some time for them to come looking."

Aleksander reached for his haffai and pulled himself to standing. "I've no wish to sleep in this rathole anyway."

"I'll saddle the horses," said Malver, starting out the door.

Ten minutes later, we rode out of the tavern stables. No sign of a hunt as we rode through the almost deserted streets. Slow. Agonizingly slow. Our horses' hooves were already loud on the hard-packed dirt; we dared not draw notice by our hurry. But as we approached the market district, I knew something was wrong. The market in a desert town never truly slept. Too many things needed to be done in the cool night hours between the last of the evening shoppers and the first of the morning. Yet the dark square was illuminated by only a few flickering braziers, and the silence was oppressive.

Aleksander felt it, too. Just at the point our narrow street opened into the market, he reined in, pointed to his ear, and then to me. I passed the back of my hand before my eyes and listened. Smelled the dry air that hung in the dark streets. Tasted the silence. Men were waiting in streets just off the square . . . a goodly number, ten or more. I heard their breathing. Shallow. Ready. I smelled the oil on their blades and the nervous sweat soaking their shirts. If we rode into the marketplace, we were going to have a fight. How had they gotten into place so quickly? The boy's tale could not have set this in motion.

I jerked my head toward the market and held up ten fingers, indicating five on the east side, five on the west. Then again three or four more at the gates. Caution demanded that we abandon W'Assani and find a stealthier way to leave Tanzire. But Aleksander pulled back his haffai to expose the hilt of his sword. At the Prince's gesture, Malver relaxed and exposed his own sword. Aleksander signaled that Malver was to go straight for W'Assani. The Prince and I would stand between him and the waiting Derzhi; then we would all make for the gates together. Aleksander cocked his head at me, waggled his elbows, then raised his eyebrows. I grinned, shaking my head, and drew my sword. As he split the night with a Derzhi war cry, I followed him into battle. No wings tonight.

Bursting out of the lane, we made it more than halfway across the square before the first warrior reached us. Aleksander disarmed him with a single stroke and howled in victory. W'Assani's wagon was parked just past the middle of the square, about two-thirds of the way to the gate. At least she should be well awake by now.

We were woefully outnumbered. Soon I was engaged with two warriors at once, one on either side, and not making much progress with either of them. Aleksander was somewhere to my right, battling a large man whose horse bucked in terror when the Prince's sword cut him. Aleksander's mount kept steady as he wheeled and struck. *Keep your seat, my lord,* I prayed. *Fall off and we're done for.* But I had little time to worry about the Prince. A huge blade whistled over my head, and I came near falling myself. Fighting on horseback was out of my experience; demons did not use cavalry. Gods of night, if only we had Sovari. I stabbed at a charging warrior and wrenched my arm as he slipped sideways from his mount. Every stroke of my sword had my side screaming.

Using my left hand to haul on the reins and keep my mount steady underneath me, I raised up in the stirrups and slashed at an attacking Derzhi. From his vociferous oath, I gathered I had cut him, but I was too busy countering another man's blade to look. *Duck. Slash again. Hold this one. Counter. Yes. The rhythm's there. Just find it. Be still, you stupid beast. How can I get the feel of this if you're running out from under me?*

"Seyonne!" While keeping my hand occupied with one fighter, my mind engaged in convincing another man that snakes were slithering up his back, and watching Aleksander dispatch a massive Derzhi who was aiming to slice off his arm, I cast a quick glance behind me. W'Assani was mounted. Blade in hand, she was holding her own with a slender Derzhi, smiling as she fought, her lean body strong and agile. Malver, his sword in one hand and his long dagger in the other, skewered a warrior lunging for my back.

"My lord!" I cried. "Time to go!" Past time.

Aleksander dispatched one more opponent, then began his retreat, circling, slashing, always in control. His boot stuck out awkwardly, and one of the Rhyzka warriors struck at it. But the sword hit the steel rod and glanced away, and Aleksander ripped the man's shoulder, laughing.

I beat off another attacker and bent my mind to enchantment . . . wind . . . sand . . . not the easy shifting to cover our tracks, though not a paraivo, either. Just enough to obscure our attackers' vision and allow us to make a graceful retreat. A bit more in reserve. *Ready . . . split the gale and hold it. Almost to the gate.* Newcomers ran for the walls, but we were already through the gates. With an explosion of melydda, I released a blast of contrary winds that dug out the last of the sand piled against the gates and, with a thundering crash, slammed them shut in our pursuers' faces.

"I *will* find out how you do that!" shouted W'Assani over the roar of the wind, wagging her long finger at me.

I nodded. Something to look forward to. Promising.

We had only a few scratches among us and were ready to set out on our way victorious, but our smiles died unborn when we looked back over our shoulders and saw what had been left for us to see. A wooden beam had been mounted atop the city walls, and from it a man hung by his feet. Just as with those in Karn'Hegeth, his lips and nose had been cut off, and his shorn braid tied to his tongue. He was dead, at least. His belly was ripped apart until he could have had nothing left inside. An imperial sash dangled from his neck.

"No!" Aleksander's cry of anguish could have been heard in Zhagad, and it was all I could do to restrain him.

So that was how they had known to lie in wait for us . . . and why they had not known where to find us. Sovari had yielded the one secret, but held the last. They had sent spies to every inn to search us out, the clumsy boys to the poor place where we were housed, never expecting to find the heir to the Empire meeting his subjects in the squalor of a tannery yard.

"We have only minutes, my lord," I said, my voice harsh in the sudden silence. "Make his sacrifice worthy. We must go now."

But we weren't fast enough, and in my distraction, I had failed to hold the wind as firmly as I held the Prince. From the walls came a volley of arrows, flying true in the still air. From behind me I heard one make a solid hit . . . and then another. I whirled to see W'Assani twice struck, slumping in her saddle. Malver reached for her, only to have an arrow slam into his back and another and a third until brother and half sister toppled in a grotesque embrace onto the barren earth. So much for victory. And promise.

"We have to go," I said, struggling to rein in the creeping . . . no, the raging darkness. "They're dead. All of them dead."

CHAPTER 20

Aleksander and I rode the paths of Manganar and Azhakstan for the rest of that summer, hiding, running, seeking shelter in herdsmen's shacks and caravans, in villages and alleyways and stables, as the Prince tried to find a Derzhi lord willing to shelter or support him. I tried to act as intermediary as Sovari had done. With some effort I managed to alter my features to be more Derzhi-like, but no one would trust a stranger, and I never got past a steward. We dared not commit Aleksander's presence to writing, for Derzhi lords did not read, and scribes were notorious for selling information. With no one to trust with his messages, the Prince had to risk approaching the houses himself. Twice he found the heged strongholds taken over by representatives of the Twenty, and he left without revealing his identity. Twice he was rebuffed completely. Five lords granted him an interview, but gave the same answer as the Mardek and the Bek; they would not commit to Aleksander without evidence of other heged support. Once we had to fight our way out of a walled garden and barely survived it. Yet the Prince would not give up. He was grim and driven, speaking little save of how to get from one town to the next, constantly seeking news of houses he thought most likely to support him, stopping only long enough to keep our horses living.

Though there were more than twenty prospects yet to approach, we were rapidly running out of time. Not only had we lost Sovari and Malver and W'Assani in the debacle at Tanzire, but also most of the funds that Kiril had supplied. By the end of the summer we were dreadfully bedraggled and eating lean. We could scarcely muster a decent set of clothes for Aleksander to wear when meeting a heged lord, and he refused to wear a haffai lest they think he was hiding something.

Two weeks after our flight from Tanzire, Aleksander had discarded his riding boot. Every time we got off our horses, whether in city or desert or village, he would walk for at least an hour, working to recover his strength and flexibility. By the time our plight got desperate, he had thrown away his crutches and used only a single walking stick. The healing had been straight and clean, and I had no doubt that he would recover full use of his limb, but what should have been a reason for rejoicing was only a reminder of everything he had lost.

"Perhaps it's time to contact your cousin again," I said one night as we walked up a desolate track behind Andassar, the village where we had been hiding for the past few days, waiting for the First Lord of the Naddasine to return from Zhagad to his nearby castle. "We can't let Avrel feed us anymore. Marya told me their village taxes are due in ten days. They've four months until their winter harvest is in, and I don't know how they're going to eat until then."

"I don't want Kiril dead, if he's not already. But we'll leave if you wish. Eat grass if we need to. Go back to the desert and hunt."

The argument was always the same.

"We can't go into the desert," I said. "We've nothing to feed the horses, and we can't afford to buy anything. If the horses die, we're afoot, and although you're progressing well, I'm not sure you're ready to walk to Vayapol. And we can't get into a city because we haven't bribe money to get us past the gates. Illusions of money never work; people handle it too much, look too closely. In a town of any size, I could scribe for wages, but only for someone who doesn't question a scribe who looks like a beggar and smells worse. I could do any number of jobs, but the only people who can afford to pay anymore are Derzhi, and no one would hire an Ezzarian with a slave mark on his shoulder. My lord, I understand your urgency, but it's time for you to stop and think."

I hadn't meant to go so far. Perhaps what drove me to it was the view of the pitiful village just below us, the tiny hovels set in the midst of fertile fields of potatoes and barley. The twenty men and women of Andassar worked without respite to produce two crops a year of barley and one of potatoes, harnessing themselves to their plows because they had no beasts of burden, forbidden to hunt the abundant game of the nearby hills because it belonged to their lord. Yet the entirety of their crop could scarce pay their new tax levies, and if we were still here ten days from this, we would witness the harsh result.

Everywhere we traveled we saw the evidence of Edik's rule: markets with no goods a man could afford, caravan owners forced to sell their chastou, beggars everywhere, fighting each other over scraps, and slaves . . . gods have mercy, I had never seen so many slave caravans. The Veshtar, the desert tribe who considered slavery as their god's rightful punishment on weaker souls, flourished in the service of the Nyabozzi, the heged who controlled the trade in slaves. Meanwhile, the lords of the Twenty rode unashamed in splendor—silks and jewels, gold trappings on their horses, perfumed litters for their women—and unchecked in their arrogance of power. No town but had its shriveled heads or corpses on display. No region but had villages burned. No alehouse gossip but told of assassinations, theft, and willful cruelty untouched by law. And no women, girls, or fair youths, lowborn or high, were safe if a lord of the Twenty fancied them.

"How can I leave it, Seyonne?" Aleksander paused at the top of the rise and leaned on his olive wood stick. The gold and red sunset seared the sky behind him. "Do you think I'm doing this for myself? Because I miss silk sheets and servants and fine horses?"

"No, of course—"

"Every corpse you see hanging in the cities is dead by my hand. Every new slave is chained by my failure. In one generation I have destroyed what my grandsires built over five hundred years, and every beggar's hand is pointed at me in accusation. How can I stop?"

Guilt is a cruel taskmaster. I had tried to make Aleksander see the truth of his empire, teach him to take responsibility, but I had never meant the lesson to destroy him. I leaned my back against a finger of rock that pointed accusingly at the heavens and rubbed my eyes that felt like the sands of the desert were permanently embedded in them.

"You've not been sleeping. Weeks, it's been." He cocked his head at me and raised his eyebrows as he always did when he wanted to ask things he knew I would not answer.

"I've got to go, my lord. Soon." The ravaging of the world seemed an eerie reflection of the war being fought in my soul. Denas yet raged, demanding that I go to Kir'Navarrin and insisting that I yield to him at the moment we crossed the gateway. So forceful was his will to speak, that it was all I could do to contain him. But I feared to loose his bonds, to risk my self-control just when I needed everything I had to face my dreams. For my night visions, too, had taken an unnerving turn. Every horror we saw in our travels, I revisited, not once, but a hundred times each night. Every cruelty I had experienced in my life, I lived again and again. Sometimes I was the victim. Sometimes I was the perpetrator. Sometimes, most frightening of all, I meted out punishment to those who did the terrible deeds, and I savored the unholy execution of justice. I could no longer bear my dreams, and so I had learned to wake myself up the moment they began. Nyel's doing, certainly. He had admitted as much. I needed to find an answer to it while I could still think straight, while I could still control my own soul. "I don't want to leave you, but—"

"You've suffered enough for me. Go when you need to go."

And what would he do then? Push on alone. I motioned him back to his exercise. "Not yet. Soon, but not yet." I didn't want to think about my own journey.

We had not planned to hide in Andassar. Marya, a stocky young woman with a crooked spine, had found us in the hills above the village, just as I was about to butcher a wild pig. She had wandered close while gathering herbs and quail eggs, and though I intended to remain hidden from the villagers, I wasn't about to let go of the pig. Aleksander and I hadn't eaten in two days.

"Are you mad, stranger?" she cried. "Would you bring the lord's wrath on a whole village for a runt of a pig?"

"Not mad. Just hungry," I said. "And why would the lord care about a wild pig?"

"Taking game in these hills is forbidden since the Gorusch baron became overlord. Naddasine used to let each Andassar man take one boar or deer a season, but this Gorusch lord sends keepers out every few days to look for signs of poaching." The pig, as if sensing its imminent release, set up a squealing. "You'll have a village man maimed for the kill, if you're not found to own it."

Sighing, I released the pig, sat back on the grass, and watched it trot away at astonishing speed. "Then tell me where I can find something else. I'm going to eat this nasty shirt of mine if I don't come up with dinner. I've naught to pay but work, and I've a friend with me."

"Here." She tossed me a wild plum from the heavy basket she

carried on her hip. "Bring your friend to the last house in the village. I'll feed you."

Marya had insisted that we move in with her and her husband Avrel. Only in the past year had the two become self-sufficient, allowing them to move out of Avrel's father's house and into their own mud hovel. "It's Avrel's bees," said the woman proudly, pointing to the cone-shaped clumps of mud up a gentle grassy slope from her home. "Avrel went to Vayapol once, and spoke to a man in the market who had fat jars of honey, and he learned about bees. And he thought that the meadow here might be a fine place for them, with the clover that comes after the rains and holds for so long in summer. The man in Zhagad wouldn't tell him how he got the bees to stay, but Avrel watched the wild things and learned it of himself."

The young couple had no children as yet, but Marya was confident that Panfeya would bless them soon, now they were housed within their own walls. If the village could but pay their levies this year, all would be well, for Avrel was planning to make more hives and teach the other villagers to care for bees, so that next year they could pay the entire levy in honey.

We told the villagers that Aleksander—I named him Kassian—was a dispossessed kinsman of the Naddasine. A wastrel, I hinted, come to his first lord to petition for reinstatement into the family. They looked on him with awe, a Derzhi in such sorry state as to seek shelter in their village. But they held a better opinion of the Naddasine than other Derzhi, and before a day had passed were offering Aleksander advice on how to approach the old first lord when he returned from Zhagad.

"Respect," said Kero, Avrel's father. "Naddasine has always been one for respect. Not groveling. He don't take to a cowardly mien. But I can stand up boldly and say, 'Here is your share, my good lord,' or 'I've taken my boar this day, my good lord, and none else,' and he will listen with gravity and say, 'Well-done, goodman Kero, or 'A fine kill, fellow,' as if I were a proper man. This Gorusch, though . . . The Emperor, curse his—pardon, Lord Kassian—the Emperor sent his own troops to take the Naddasine lands, and all their houses but this one, and give them to these Gorusch. My cousin serves in old Naddasine's house. She says his sons fear for his life."

"To hear that a Derzhi first lord fears for his life at the hand of the Emperor," said Aleksander to me later. "Even after all this,

I cannot fathom such villainy. Edik is a plague upon this land. If I could do it, I'd cut my arm to let out any drop of my blood common with his."

The last remnants of day were fading as we started back to the village after our difficult conversation, and I sent Aleksander ahead, for I needed to relieve myself. A short while later, as I started down the slope, I caught a glimpse of green in the dying light, a hint of fluttering color just up the hill to my right, brilliant color that had no place in the drab surroundings. I scrabbled over rocks and weeds around the side of the hill, and found her waiting.

"My lady, who are you?" I said, scarcely daring to breathe lest she vanish. "What are you trying to tell me?"

Always before, her gaze had been serene, radiant with affection and concern. But on this night, her gaze did not settle, and her hands were in constant motion, rubbing, kneading, and clasping each other. It wrenched my heart to see her so anxious, though I had no reason for such emotion.

Her lips moved, but I could hear only half the words. ". . . be careful . . . beloved child . . . the Twelve weaken . . . perhaps best not to challenge unknowing . . . worse than I thought . . ." She glanced over her shoulder as if someone were coming up on her from behind. "Come to the gamarand wood. Whatever happens, I beg you come." And then she was gone.

"Wait!" But she had vanished as completely as the daylight. *The gamarand wood* . . . So I was right to think she came from Kir'Navarrin. And yet she was not just a being of light as were the rai-kirah I had known in Kir'Vagonoth, nor was she like one of the physical bodies that demons shaped from their memories of true life. Her form was natural and fully human, and the light that shone from her was more like the feadnach I saw in Aleksander than anything of demons. What was stranger yet . . . a vague sense from our first encounter now grown to surety . . . I knew her. But for my life, I could not say how or why or who she was. Did Denas know her? Was she luring me through the gateway to give him a chance for victory?

I sat on the hillside for an hour, peering into the night, hoping she would come again, afraid of such mystery yet longing to relive it, to understand it, to hear again the words that were already slipping away. . . . *Beloved child* . . . Was she speaking of my son? I closed my eyes and prayed Verdonne, the forest mother, to keep him and his foster mother safe and well.

When at last I gave up my vigil, I quickly became aware of other doings stirring the night air. The smoky scent of torches. Burning grass. Faint cries of grief and fear. Gods of night, what was happening? Silently I sped down the path toward Andassar. The wailing grew louder, and soon I saw the fire—a high mound of baskets in the center of the village. Grain—half a year's harvest—consumed in towering flames.

Marya stood rigid in front of her house, staring at the fire. She had one hand over her mouth and one hand wrapped about her middle. Other women knelt weeping, a few with children clinging to them. Two village men lay dead beside the burning harvest, but no one else was about. No strangers. No living men. No Aleksander.

"Was it thieves, Marya? Raiders? Have the men gone after them?"

She shook her head, and the bleak terror in her eyes told me it was much worse.

"Tell me, Marya. You must tell me everything. Who was it?"

"Derzhi. Gorusch men come for taxes—"

"But your levies weren't due for ten days yet."

She wrapped her arms about herself, shivering in the cool, dry night air. "They said they'd heard we were giving grain to bandits and had come to secure the lord's shares. They made us bring it out, but the count was low. We'd thought to give potatoes and two jars of honey, but they never let us tell it. They said we'd have to send four of us—two men, two women—for hostages until the levy was paid. Kero and Valnar protested that we still had ten days."

She didn't have to tell me more. The Derzhi had killed the two who dared speak out, burned the grain, and taken all the men instead of only four hostages.

"My friend . . . Kassian . . . ?"

Her eyes were wide with shock. "All of them. The soldiers said they would be slaves. Avrel . . . oh, holy Dolgar, my Avrel . . ."

I gripped her arms. She was now shaking violently as the truth settled upon her. "Which way have they gone, Marya? And how many? I can help them, but you have to tell me everything."

Summoning her reserves of strength, Marya gave me every

detail of the raid. Two Derzhi warriors and three common soldiers had come, armed with swords and knives, but no spears or axes. Five village men were taken, plus two boys aged twelve and fourteen, and Aleksander. The prisoners had been roped together by hands and neck and herded down the dry streambed toward the Vayapol road.

I ran for the grassy nook where we had hobbled our horses. The beasts were gone, of course. No Derzhi thief would leave a horse behind. But I pulled away a pile of rocks and found Aleksander's sword and ring still safely hidden. I crammed the ring in my pocket, belted the Prince's weapons around my waist beside my own sword and dagger, then turned my mind to sorcery. A quarter of an hour later, I took wing.

I found them quickly, not difficult for my falcon's eyes to spot the yellow flame of octar-soaked torches. Their ankles hobbled, the prisoners could not move fast, though the soldiers lashed and swore at them. The two boys were in the front, the younger one weeping, both completely naked in the cool night as they stumbled down the rocky gully between two mounted Derzhi. Their hands were roped to the warriors' saddles. Behind the boys came the village men, two by two, barefoot and stripped to their breeches. One man was bleeding severely from a gash over his ribs and being helped along by his terrified brother. Bringing up the rear were Avrel and Aleksander. Aleksander was limping slightly, leaning on Avrel's broad shoulder, his face equal parts blood and fury. Across the Prince's shoulders were deep lash marks. How often in those early days in Capharna had I wished to see him thus.

One Derzhi rode on either side of the prisoners, and the two common soldiers followed behind. The third soldier was nowhere in sight. I fluttered low across the column and then again. On my second pass I caught Aleksander's notice, and when I circled and flew over yet again, he nodded, a fierce grin showing from underneath the blood.

"Look," said one of the Derzhi, pointing at me. "The Emperor's bird."

The true *Emperor's bird,* I thought, and streaked down the ravine to find the best terrain for my plan. There. A few hundred paces farther on, the hills to either side of the ravine got steeper and closer together, and the course of the streamlet curved sharply left. That would do. I flew farther down the hill toward the Vayapol road hunting the missing guard, needing to learn if this was a small raiding party or part of some larger sweep and to judge the time I had to carry out the rescue.

Gods have mercy . . . I discovered more than I bargained for. The fifth rider had emerged from the mountain path and was racing into the open, toward a blot on the night that made my stomach constrict long before I saw anything but pricks of torchlight against the darkness. You always smelled it first—the stench of fear and filth and desperation. And then you heard the drone of moans and weeping and muffled prayers, punctuated by soul-rending screams. I did not need to see the horror in order to name it. A slave caravan.

The soldier halted beside a sentry, pointing back the way he had come. I flew on past him, out over a broad meadow lit by massive bonfires. Facedown upon the ground lay at least a hundred men and boys roped together. One by one they were being detached from the others and taken to Veshtar smiths who seared the crossed circle into their shoulders with a red-hot iron and sealed steel bands around their wrists and ankles. Veshtar slavers in striped haffai then cut off their hair and chained them to the others newly readied for market. A small detachment of Derzhi in Nyabozzi colors guarded the encampment.

I had to get Aleksander and the others free before they reached the meadow. I flew back up the ravine and settled on the rocks above the path. The prisoners' column reached the gap between the narrowly spaced rocks. Good. The warriors on the sides had ridden ahead, so that they were separated from the two soldiers at the back. None of the riders could have the whole column in sight. I would take the two at the back quickly, then cut Aleksander's bonds and give him his sword. He would be waiting for me. I forced everything out of my mind but my own form . . .

. . . Bird . . . sleek of body, broad wing, long tail, taloned hands . . . release the form and consider the shape of your desire . . . your own body . . . the one honed by years of training: fighting . . . running . . . the warrior's body, not that of the bird, save in only one thing . . . wings . . . wide, thin, strong . . . and hold your barriers no matter the cost, for you need your own wit and soul to do this . . .

In one long interval of fire and nausea I made the shift from bird to man, then stood heaving, readying myself to shape wings. But before I could begin that change, a black cloth was dropped over my head, and I was dragged off my rock with someone's arm uncomfortably tight about my throat and something uncomfortably sharp poking into my ribs.

CHAPTER 21

"Over here! Look what I found sneaking about in the rocks." The intense whisper was somewhere behind me. Understandable, since my hooded face was smashed firmly into the ground. The attacker's knife was still threatening my ribs. "What'll we do with him?"

"If he twitches, kill him. We've got to go on. This is too good a chance to miss."

Lost in my uncomfortable transformation, I'd not heard the footsteps come up behind me, and now precious time was passing while I sorted out my confusion . . . and my shape . . . and the identity of my captors. *All right, no wings.* So I had only my human self to work with. My frantic human self. *Kill the bastards now, while they're not expecting it.* Quieting my anxiety so that my senses could work, I felt the position of the knife and judged the man's posture—half straddling me, knee in my back, his left hand twisting my right arm behind me. Holy gods, I wished he wouldn't do that. Easy enough to dislodge for all that. *How many others?* The second speaker was a few steps away. And another person behind him. I reached out with my hearing and all my senses. Three. Four . . . Damn, there were twenty or more of the newcomers! Twenty caravan sentries? And why were Derzhi sentries whispering?

"Look here. Look at his sword!" My captor was yanking my weapons from their sheaths and tossing them aside. "Derzhi bastard . . . who are you?" Oddly enough, he was speaking to me.

While I tried to comprehend, his companions were slipping silently past us. Soon I heard a few muffled blows nearby. More shuffling steps. Hushing noises. A suppressed choking sound. Snuffling, as if someone were weeping. Whinnying horses quickly silenced. A great deal was going on in the dry streambed . . . and very stealthily. They were attacking the slave takers.

I was so profoundly astonished and engaged by this turn of

events, that it was almost as an afterthought that I managed to cast an illusion on my captor's knife—something I had been working on since Tanzire. The weapon should soon feel as hot as if it had just been pulled from a blacksmith's fire. When the man dropped it with a quiet curse, I twisted myself around, and came near breaking his arm as I flipped him onto his back. I did everything by feel, a skill I'd often needed when I fought demons. But when I pounced on top of him, pressed his own knife to his throat and ripped off my stifling hood, I almost started laughing. His face was stained black with coal, and from jaw to brow across each cheek was painted a white dagger. *Yvor lukash* . . . sword of light. My captor was Blaise's man.

"Go ahead, Derzhi scum," he whispered bravely, clearly offended at my grin. "The others will see to you, whether I'm dead or no." The accent told me he was Kuvai. The bravado said he was approximately seventeen.

"My friend, we have some talking to do," I said, bending low to speak quietly. "If you look carefully, you will notice that I am no Derzhi. In fact, I think we're here for the same purpose."

"Not likely," he said sullenly.

"Who's commanding? Farrol? Gorrid? Blaise himself? Are they going after the caravan?"

The boy recoiled and clamped his mouth shut. I jumped to my feet, retrieving my own weapons and Aleksander's before tossing the paralyzed youth his knife. "Go on and join your comrades. Stay healthy, and I'll be along to help."

He crept backward slowly, his eyes on me, as if he couldn't quite decide whether to attack or run. Happily for me, he ran, and I could go back to the business of shifting. Once I had shaped my wings, I drew my sword and took flight, pleased that I'd not have to fight this battle alone.

Strangely enough, the column of prisoners was still moving down the rocky defile. If I'd not seen the four soldiers lying dead in the shadows, I'd have been more worried. The riders flanking the prisoners wore Derzhi cloaks, easily recognizable from a distance, but they had pulled up the hoods to shadow their faces—faces stained black and painted with white daggers. A skilled observer might also have noted that the prisoners were walking more easily than before, their rope hobbles cut, and though their hands still appeared bound and linked to each other, I had no doubt that they could easily pull the knots apart. The prisoners were needed only for the approach, to get the first outlaws past the waiting Veshtar sentries.

The raiders' plan was obvious. While the larger number of the band held back in the scrubby trees and rocks where the defile opened out onto the road, the four disguised outlaws rode with the men of Andassar into the middle of the encampment hoping to surprise unsuspecting guards and free enough slaves to be of help. The terrain could hardly have been worse for their plan. Once their fellows had revealed themselves, the lurkers would have to charge across a wide expanse of the road and the open meadow, right into the arms of the alerted sentries.

Though the detachment of Derzhi warriors guarding the caravan numbered no more than eight, the common soldiers another eight, and the Veshtar slavers perhaps twenty-five, I had no illusions about the outlaws' chances. Both Nyabozzi and Veshtar were ruthless and expert at killing, and they were guarding their lord's property worth thousands of zenars. Blaise's fighters were devoted and courageous, but woefully unskilled.

Aleksander remained in the prisoner's column. He would have realized the flaws in the plan immediately, and with his limited movement, he had no business in a fight on foot. But he would know, too, that any hope of success would be dashed if the fifth soldier spied out the ruse too soon. And if any of the prisoners stayed behind, the game was up. I saw the Prince glancing upward, scanning the night sky. He was waiting for me. Foolish. We were all foolish.

The outlaws herded their "prisoners" through the line of Veshtar sentries. Just as the last rider passed, a bearded Veshtar slapped the outlaw's horse on the rump and called out to another sentry, "*Vysstar haddov Derzhina*!" The disguised outlaw must have panicked; he drew his sword clumsily and swung at the Veshtar. His inexpert movement cost him his life; the young outlaw slid from the saddle, almost cloven in two by the Veshtar's curved sword.

Fool! I swore as the alarm was raised. The sentry's words meant only "good Derzhi rump." Wings spread, sword raised, I streaked down from the sky as two more of the disguised outlaws fell. Aleksander was shoving the villagers to the ground as they stood gaping at erupting chaos. The outlaws burst from their hiding place across the road, drawing the attention of the guards long enough for me to swoop close and toss Aleksander his sword and Avrel the Prince's knife. My own dagger I gave to a wide-eyed Dorgan, another village man who was trying to shield the two naked boys with his broad arms. "Stay low and follow me out," I shouted. "Get any freed prisoners to come with you." After a short, fierce skirmish, I dispatched a Veshtar who had attacked me, unfazed by my spread wings. The Veshtar believed they lived in close proximity to evil spirits, so the appearance of a winged warrior was no more to them than a realized expectation. They assumed that every man would someday encounter such a being.

Mounted Veshtar rode through the churning mass of slaves, shouting at them to remain facedown on the ground, lashing at them with steel-tipped whips. The smiths waved torches at any unfortunate who tried to get up; two screaming captives were in flames. But while the main body of Blaise's men engaged the Derzhi and the Veshtar sentries, other outlaws wielded axes furiously, hacking through ropes and chains, yelling at the dazed prisoners to turn on their captors. One of the Andassar men grabbed up the sword of a fallen Veshtar and joined the outlaws, slicing the ropes that bound the prostrate slaves.

While I ducked a slashing blow and flew up and around to drag a Nyabozzi rider from his saddle, Aleksander dueled with a Veshtar. At first I couldn't see how the Prince was managing to stay upright, but as my opponent leaped to his feet, I caught a glimpse of Avrel, his broad back steady at the Prince's left shoulder, supporting Aleksander and protecting his vulnerable side. I could not watch for long, for the unhorsed warrior was a skilled fighter. I battled the Nyabozzi, beating him back again and again until he tripped over a bleeding slave and fell to the ground. Then a swarm of freed prisoners disarmed him, and I was no longer needed.

I shouted to the remaining Andassar men to send their charges after me, and I fought a way through the converging Derzhi and led the stumbling group across the road. Then I took wing, circled, and went back for Aleksander. He refused to budge, drawing the snarling warriors to himself as dead meat draws flies. So I fought on, too, letting the fever of battle mute the pain in my side, indulging myself in blood and death until the night was won.

* * *

By the time the moon rose to illuminate the broad meadow, the three surviving Nyabozzi were chained together and had white daggers painted on their chests. The dead prisoners were buried, the dead slavers left lying in the grass. Every Veshtar was dead.

Most of the captives who could travel had already fled. Those too injured or sick to return home were being carried up the hill to Andassar, where they might have a few days to recover. The men of Andassar would return home, too, but they knew their time of safety was only a matter of days. They would have to abandon their village, for the three surviving Derzhi would bring down the wrath of the Empire on their mud hovels. Several of the villagers were injured—the one man who had been wounded back in Andassar had lost a good deal of blood—but they were all alive.

Some among the survivors wanted to execute the three Derzhi, but the commander of the outlaws had spread the word that it was forbidden.

"What kind of fools are these not to finish them?" asked Aleksander as he sat on the rocks at the opening of the defile, binding up a gash in his right arm. "When Edik learns of this battle, every village within a league will be destroyed no matter what. But these three Nyabozzi will never let this go. They'll hunt your Yvor Lukash and these villagers to the netherworld to avenge such a defeat. Not to mention carrying tales of the winged warrior." He glanced up at me.

I was standing nearby, slumped over a rock, still sweating and nauseous from my long-held shifting, trying to talk myself out of a retreat into the rocks to vomit and take a nap. I needed to speak with the outlaw commander as soon as he had time. I didn't recognize his or any of the painted faces that moved through the thinning crowd, encouraging, soothing, hurrying the prisoners to move on before anyone came looking for the missing caravan. "Blaise forbids them to kill unarmed men," I said.

"He wasn't always so generous. Not until he met up with you."

I took over binding Aleksander's arm. He was no good with his left hand and was making a mess of it. "Actually I'm sorely tempted to stick a knife in those three," I said. "We buried twenty-three prisoners, some no older than those two." I nodded to the two pale Andassar boys who were wrapped in borrowed cloaks and their fathers' arms. "The Veshtar had already gelded every boy in the caravan." That was why no Veshtar survived. The satisfaction that I could now control and direct my rage palled only slightly when I looked on the carnage I had wrought.

"Bloody Athos."

I finished with Aleksander's arm and had wandered off in search of a suitable branch to serve him for a walking stick, when Avrel came to the Prince and bowed. "Good Lord Kassian, I cannot leave without expressing our gratitude."

"Thank these Lukash men," said Aleksander brusquely, "and my companion, wherever he is, the one with the extraordinary abilities." Neither man could have seen me in the scrubby trees just behind the Prince. "I was rescued just as you were. And you had already kept us from starving."

"Your friend . . . the avenging spirit . . . I know not what to call him. Arago is a simple man's name, but the one I saw this night is not a simple man, and surely he has no need of a poor man's thanks." Avrel shook his head. "But you, my lord, had no cause but your own safety. The spirit would have taken you away from our battle, yet you stayed and fought with us. We of Andassar are privileged to have sheltered you. No wonder the gods send you a guardian spirit. May they ever light your way." He bowed deeply and started back toward the other villagers.

"Avrel!" The man turned at the Prince's call. "You were a fine left leg."

Avrel smiled, bowed again, then ran after his friends who were starting their long trudge home.

"Your reputation as an avenging spirit will never grow to what it should be if you continue puking up your guts after such a show," said Aleksander when I tossed him a sturdy stick, retreated behind his rock, and proceeded to do just that. "Here come your outlaw friends."

I wiped my mouth and forced my stomach back in place just in time to greet the tall man with the painted face who was walking slowly toward us. Beside him was the youth who had taken me captive and five other outlaws. To my astonishment, their swords were drawn. Aleksander growled and his hand flew to his weapon, but a warning movement of the commander's hand stayed him. "Who are the two of you?" The young leader was very nervous.

"That hardly seems the way to greet my friend here who

saved your rebellious asses this night." Aleksander did not react well to having a sword drawn on him. "One who could likely—"

"I think the commander is just being cautious, Kassian," I said, preferring the Prince not recount my abilities that never seemed to live up to people's expectations. "We are strangers, and I happened to mention to the young fellow there that I knew Blaise and Farrol. They don't like those names bandied about, I would guess."

"Indeed you've hit upon the matter," said the commander. Blood soaked his shirt from a gash in his shoulder and dripped down his cheek from a cut on his forehead. "You fought against the slavers . . . Yet you are Derzhi. And you, Ezzarian"—he nodded at me—"clearly you are an extraordinary sorcerer, yet you ride with a Derzhi. What am I to do with you? We cannot permit you to go free, knowing what you know. Yet our orders are—"

"Cannot *permit* us to go free. You stupid, arrogant imbecile! You allowed Nyabozzi slavers to go free." Aleksander waved the stick I'd brought him, and the outlaws drew closer, menacing.

"Kassian, please!" I said sharply. I didn't think the Prince appreciated the severity of the nervous young commander's dilemma. "Commander, I know the hard truths of outlaw life. I know that you are telling yourself that your oaths must not be swayed, even by such service as we have done this night. But those I've named would not be at all pleased if you harmed us, even if it were possible for you to do so. And this sorcery you noticed . . . does it not merit a word to your leader? I think he would be dreadfully unhappy if he knew you had crossed an Ezzarian with such a talent as mine. Don't you agree?"

I would have sworn the man turned pale under his paint. Not all of Blaise's outlaws were allowed to know that he and a few others of his kind could shapeshift. From the shape of his eyes, I suspected that the commander was himself an Ezzarian, perhaps one of the children born like my son and Blaise. But the man said naught of that. "I'm sorry. Truly sorry. But we must protect our leaders. I cannot permit a Derzhi to go free with the knowledge you—"

"Then take us with you," I said.

"Impossible!" Aleksander and the commander said it together.

"Naddasine returns tomorrow," growled the Prince.

I ignored him. "Bind our eyes if you wish, Commander. Believe me when I say, I understand your problem, but I promise you that the Yvor Lukash will have your balls if you harm either me or my friend."

"To take prisoners to our camp is forbidden," said the commander like a runner who, though doubting his stamina, yet forces himself to the end of the race. "For an Ezzarian, we could perhaps make an exception, but never for a Derzhi."

I stood up, and for one single moment, I let the demon blue of my eyes flame and my demon's pale gold light flicker at the bounds of my skin. Even Aleksander edged backward on his rock. "I insist."

I hated frightening people. The lesson had been taught me early, and was one of the most vivid of my childhood.

Using melydda to tease, annoy, and bully others was certainly a part of being a child in Ezzaria, though quickly abandoned as one became immersed in the serious business of training for the demon war. Yet, on one occasion when I was some eight or nine years old and had not yet fully realized what my gifts were to be used for, I got into some mischief, locking another child in a barrel and terrorizing him with the illusion of bears pawing at it. The other child had done me an injury—I never could remember exactly what it was afterward—but I felt quite justified in taking such cruel revenge.

Drawn by the child's screaming and the noise of my illusion, my father came running down the forest path. As soon as he was in sight, I stopped, of course. My father extracted the child from the barrel, comforted him, and sent him home. Then he crouched down beside me and said, "Unfair, Seyonne. Unjust to raise your hand against one who cannot fight back on your terms. Did you even think?"

I started to regale him with the particulars of the dispute, but he raised his hand and said, "I am going to get into this barrel, and I want you to do again what you did to Wyyver. Exactly the same."

I was horrified. "But I could never—"

He laid his hand on my mouth and said, "But you did. Now, do as I say, and for just the same length of time as you did it to him." He climbed in the barrel and made me lock down the cover with my melydda, until he could not push it out. I caused the barrel to shake and roll and splinter, accompanied by bearlike roaring, just as I had done to the child. By the time the roaring and shaking stopped, I was weeping at wreaking such humiliation on the man I honored and loved above everyone in the world. My father had no melydda. This was the first time I had ever considered that I had the power to do him such cruelty. When he crawled out of the barrel, I threw myself in his arms, begging his forgiveness and swearing I would never again use my gifts for such ill purpose.

"I believe you," he said, and pressed me to his pounding heart.

But, of course, intimidating Blaise's men was far preferable to killing them or whatever else it might have taken to persuade them not only to leave both of us living, but to take us back to their camp. I admired their courage for confronting me at all.

Aleksander was furious with me and threatened to stay behind, especially when we were required to yield our weapons.

"The only way they're going to leave behind a Derzhi who knows Blaise's name is to leave you dead," I said. "Of course, I could probably scare them into leaving you alone, but I won't do that unless you ask me politely." I knew the likelihood of his doing that. "Do you really imagine you'll get to see Naddasine after this? Even if the old man is alive, he'll not dare meet with you. You've nowhere else to go."

Aleksander knew these things. He was not a fool. I only wished his stubborn heart would not require me to say them so bluntly.

We were given our horses, and once I had helped the Prince mount up, we were separated, Aleksander to ride near the front of the party under the watchful eye of the commander and I with the riders at the back. Sixteen outlaws made up the group, every one of them injured. Several I doubted would ever fight again; four more were wrapped in their cloaks and laid over their mounts. For two others, there had not been enough pieces left to take home. We rode for several hours, and my guess about the young commander was proved true; I felt his subtle workings that moved us through the ways as Blaise did. Before we could have traveled a tenth of the actual distance to such a landscape, we set out across a wide srif, the dunes unmarked by any recent passing. I saw Aleksander glance about curiously, but he would not deign to question those who rode beside him, and he soon sank back into brooding.

Before very long, the commander called the party to a halt and said the time had come to cover our eyes. "I'm risking my own position to take you in," he said in answer to my reassurances of goodwill and Aleksander's mumbled invitation to kill him first. "And I cannot guarantee your safety once we arrive. No matter what power you possess, someone will take you down if you are judged a danger to our cause. Do you understand that?"

"We understand," I said. "We give our parole, do we not, Kassian? We'll not use anything we see or hear against the Yvor Lukash or his cause."

Aleksander spit into the sand.

The commander drew his sword and laid its point on Aleksander's belly. The moment hung breathless, until Aleksander glared at me and nodded curtly. Of course, I could have prevented any harm. I could have prevented this last humiliation, too. But serving his pride would only prolong what must come.

They tied scarves around our eyes, dropped bags over our heads, and then, with a gracious apology to Aleksander, took our horses' reins. The commander knew enough of Derzhi custom to realize the insult of forcing a warrior to ride without control of his own mount.

Within a quarter of an hour, we were winding upward along a steep, hard-packed trail. The smell of dust and tarbush soon yielded to cedar and pine, and then to grass and wild lavender. A pleasant coolness settled on my skin, a fine mist that tasted of dawn . . . and I'd scarcely begun relishing the wonder of it before our horses were brought to a halt. A number of people were watching, but voices were muted and activities paused as I helped Aleksander dismount and laid his hand on my shoulder to support him. He yanked his arm away.

"This way," said the commander. "Our leaders are waiting."

We were led across a flat stretch of ground, Aleksander limping slowly beside me. Hands forced my head down, and I understood why when my shoulders brushed a fabric doorway and I smelled the damp canvas of a tent. A large tent, as I could stand up easily and my senses told me there were at least five people already inside.

"Here they are, as Jinu reported," said the commander. "I can only plead my case by saying that without these two fighting alongside us, we would have lost far more than six of our own. Perhaps failed altogether. And, as Jinu will have told you, the Ezzarian presented incontestable evidence that he is . . . more like some we know than an Ezzarian of the ordinary sort. I'm not sure we could have killed him."

"I didn't think you would approve of that," I said, wishing I could think of something more clever to greet my unseen friends. "I hoped not, at least."

But before my wit could blossom further, all words died upon my lips, for when our hoods and blinders were removed, neither Blaise nor Farrol was there to greet us. The tent was quite large, crammed with baskets and bags of flour and grain, jars of oil, and other supplies for a large encampment. In the center was a long table with maps and papers spread on it, and several men and women bent over them, some seated, some standing, all of them glancing up as if we had interrupted a critical discussion. Only one of them did I know . . . the one to whom my captor deferred and whose dark eyes grew guarded and wary at the sight of me. Elinor.

CHAPTER 22

What do you say to someone who last saw you raging in madness, savagely destroying another human being? *Sorry* seemed quite inadequate. *I'm all right now* was not exactly true. *You don't need to be afraid* would be presumptuous. And here I was, stained with blood again, and reeking of death and enchantment. Elinor's friends would likely have informed her how the winged Ezzarian had killed more than three quarters of the Veshtar by himself. *In the service of her cause*, I told myself. *To save her raiding party that would have perished but for Aleksander and me*. Nonetheless, I found myself voiceless in front of her, unable to look her in the eye, unable to ask the questions that crowded my tongue at the sight of her. *How does he fare, mistress? Does he grow well? Is he happy*?

Elinor's voice was composed when she broke the stunned silence. "You've done exactly right to bring them here, Roche. Blaise would be most distressed if this man and his friend . . ." Her voice drifted away for a moment. "Everyone, leave us," she said crisply, jumping to her feet. She hurried her company out of the tent, snapping orders. "Roche, find Blaise. Wherever he is, get him here now. Give your report on the raid to Farrol; I'll hear it later. And tell Farrol to double the guard at the perimeter—on the chance you were followed. Jinu, arrange for food and drink to be sent here for our visitors. We must not be disturbed until I say." As soon as the others had left, she spun on her heel. "I didn't send for a healer. Do you need—?"

"I've no desire to impose upon your hospitality," said Aleksander stiffly. "There are many other places I need to be."

"Indeed . . . if you are who I think you are, anywhere you go will see you dead. Jinu said you demanded to come to us."

The Prince could have made a glacier shiver. "This Ezzarian wished to come here. It wasn't my idea."

I needed to introduce them properly. *My lord, this is the foster mother of my child, who is doing her best to undermine what remains of your empire. Mistress Elinor, this is the man who once vowed to slaughter you and all your fellows, but who will, if I can keep him alive against his stubborn efforts, change the world in some way absolutely beyond my understanding. And, by the way, I am still quite mad and getting no better, but I'm somewhat less likely to hack you to bits than the last time you saw me.* The thought had never occurred to me that Elinor would be here.

"Do you have any idea the danger you've brought us?" Elinor whirled on me. "If the Emperor gets wind that this man is anywhere near the Yvor Lukash . . . The only thing that's kept us safe these past months is that the Derzhi are so obsessed with finding him, they've not pressed us too hard. And to bring a Derzhi here into our very heart, one who has ordered our deaths . . ."

"Mistress Elinor—"

"Send me away, then," said Aleksander, cutting me off before I could even decide what I was going to say. He folded his arms across his chest. "Or even better, sell me to my father's cousin. Then you can pay for better warriors, so perhaps you won't set out on these absurd ventures that get people slaughtered—the very people you're trying to help."

The woman leaned forward, her hands pressing on the table, her eyes aflame. "As if *you* are concerned about the people, those you and your Derzhi assassins have enslaved and murdered and driven to desperation for five hundred years. How dare you, of all men, speak of the—?"

"Wait!" I said, wanting to shake them. "Please, my lord, if you would allow me. If we could just begin again . . . I'm truly sorry to come like this with no warning, mistress. I understand the danger, and I'd never put any of you at risk lightly. But time and circumstance have put us in your hands when we've run out of alternatives." Aleksander was ready to burst when I turned to him again. "My lord, Mistress Elinor is Blaise's sister, whose good husband fell at the hands of the Hamraschi as did your father. She has lost parents and friends to the Twenty, just as you have lost so many dear to you. Her brother and her child are in danger every day, just as your wife and Lord Kiril are. Our enemies are the same."

"His sister . . . the one who . . . ?" Aleksander seemed to forget his anger for a moment.

I nodded, my eyes shifting from Elinor's boots to the table to the hanging lantern—anywhere but her face. "Mistress Elinor, you've guessed correctly. I would like to present His Highness, Aleksander zha Denischkar, late of Zhagad and more recently of everywhere his enemies haven't thought to look, including a slaver's harness. By coming here we've placed our lives in your hands, and I ask your patience as well as your protection. We've had a difficult journey and no sleep for more than a day. We need to speak with Blaise, and then we'll leave, if you or he or Prince Aleksander still wish it." Now I had to look her in the eye, else she would have every right to ignore my words. "I swear on the life most precious to us both that my lord Aleksander himself is no threat to your followers. As to other concerns . . . if it will improve your own sleep, you may confine me as you think best." Her dark eyes were not filled with horror, only anger. Good enough. I could live with anger.

Elinor sat on the stool beside her table and propped her chin on her folded hands, the one finger tapping rapidly on the others, the only sign of her agitation. "Blaise should be here soon," she said. "I'll advise him to take the two of you deep into the desert and leave you there." She glared at me, as if I had brought plague to her household, though she no longer wore a matron's apron. Around the waist of her dark blue tunic and skirt, she wore a woven leather girdle with a knife sheath hanging from it, boldly displayed. Her thick, dark braid was bound tightly around her head, save for a few wisps that had escaped and were stuck to her high forehead by the damp.

So many emotions spilled out and gathered in again. Fortunately a soft "pardon, Mistress Elinor" from outside the tent prevented the need for further conversation. Elinor bade the newcomer enter, and a young girl brought in a wooden tray and set it on the table. On the tray were dates, a loaf of bread, a small mound of goat cheese, a clay pitcher, and three cups.

"Thank you, Melia," said Elinor. The girl glanced curiously at the three of us, then left the tent.

Aleksander stood motionless beside me. With no crutch or stick, and his stubborn refusal to use my shoulder, he was probably about to topple over. "May we sit down?" I said. "Until Blaise comes at least?"

"Of course. Eat and drink as you will." Elinor motioned us to the wooden stools where her companions had been seated, but instead we chose the woven mat that lay over the dirt floor.

We were both filthy. Roche had given Aleksander a ragged

haffai as we rode through the desert, but the garment hung open to reveal his bloodstained breeches and lack of shirt, stockings, or boots. He had tied his hair in a knot at the back of his head while we stayed in Andassar, and so it remained, now matted with blood from the battle. I was slightly better dressed, but my clothes were stiff with gore.

The food was good. Neither Aleksander's pique nor my tongue-tied embarrassment in front of Elinor could forestall the demands of hunger, and before two minutes had passed we were eyeing each other over the last date. My belly growled in half-sated pleasure. I could have eaten ten times the amount.

"I can get more," said Elinor, jumping up from her stool as if she had read my mind.

"Only what you can spare," I said. "But we'd be most grateful."

She nodded and ducked hurriedly through the doorway of the tent. She didn't seem to find it necessary to leave a guard with us. I supposed that, for the moment at least, our obvious vulnerability on the most human point of hunger soothed her concerns as to our intentions.

Once she was gone, Aleksander's glance fell on me like a smith's hammer, and not because of an orphaned date.

"I'm sorry," I said quietly when I accepted that he wasn't going to let matters rest until I said something. "This seemed the only reasonable course."

"Was I to have nothing to say about it?"

"You need time and safety to get your leg strong again. You need to stop running for a while, so you can think clearly about what to do next. I can't stay with you much longer. I believe you will find your way, and I want to help you, but I—" Despite my reluctance, the time had come to speak of the siffaru. I ran my fingers through my filthy hair and tried to formulate the telling. "—I have to decide what to do about Kir'Navarrin. I know who's waiting now. The siffaru took me to Tyrrad Nor, and I talked with him."

"You've lost your mind."

"Very possibly." I attempted a smile, though it likely came out weak. "But I believe not. Not yet, at least. I was right about one bit: the prisoner in the fortress is only a man, a powerful sorcerer who can touch my dreams. But everything else— My lord, he is a soul of such complexity, such depth of feeling, such magnificence of power and spirit, altogether different than I imagined." Despite all my misgivings, the feelings poured out of me as strong as ever. "He's dangerous, yes. But I'm half mad to go there and learn more of him."

"Dangerous and magnificent? After a few days of a desert boy's vision—some mind-tangling weed he fed you, no doubt—my ever-cautious friend is 'half mad' to stick his head in a noose? No wonder you wouldn't tell me."

Something struck the outside of the tent softly, and a group of laughing children came to retrieve whatever it was. Only when their bubbling merriment had receded into the workaday noises of a busy camp did I go on. "What I experienced was not just a vision. Whatever Qeb's gift or his herbs, my own power worked with it to take me to Kir'Navarrin. I spoke with the prisoner, walked with him, heard his story. I touched the wall that holds him. And I believe that perhaps I can—" Impossible to speak of it. "I told him I'd come back. He's muddling my head, so I don't know if I dare confront him. But if I decide that's where this path leads, then I need to get on with it while I can, while I have some hope of success."

"I told you to go if you needed." Behind the echoes of anger and bitterness and humiliation was true concern. "But I think you're risking your soul to do it."

"Well, if so, you'll take care of it, right? Back in Drafa you promised me that you'd not let me live a monster, and I have infinite faith in you."

"Even for you, that's a bad joke. So when will you go?"

"I won't leave you alone."

"And so you think to abandon me with people who despise me?"

I grinned. "When has that ever bothered you?"

He snorted and snatched the last date, just as Blaise hurried into the tent. "Seyonne! Stars of heaven, I've been worried about you." I jumped to my feet, and he clasped my hands, probing my depths with a gaze so intense I could not meet it. Between his scrutiny and Aleksander's, my skin felt raw. "When I heard what happened in Zhagad . . . and after . . . Are you all right?"

"Surviving. In control." I smiled and moved out from between him and the Prince. "You remember Prince Aleksander."

Blaise's lean face grew wary, but he displayed no evidence of Elinor's hostility. He bowed slightly. "Of course."

Last time these two had met, Blaise had pledged fealty to the Empire and agreed to halt his raiding, thus allowing Aleksander to avert civil war. In return, Aleksander had revoked his orders condemning the riders of the Yvor Lukash to death and had taken the first steps to change the prerogatives of slave owners. They had made these concessions, not in deference to each other, but because I had asked them to. Now I needed them to build that same trust with each other.

A noise from the rear of the tent interrupted the delicate confrontation. "Linnie?" said Blaise, peering into the stacked clutter of baskets and bags.

Elinor emerged from the shadows unabashed, carrying a basket of bread and cheese. Clearly she had been eavesdropping. Though I was uncomfortable at the thought of her hearing my confession to Aleksander, I couldn't blame her. "Blaise, we can't have him here," she said, jerking her head toward Aleksander. "We've no right. We've sworn to the others—"

Blaise laid a hand on her shoulder. "Let's hear him first." He fixed his attention on the Prince. "What is it you wish from us, Lord Aleksander?" he said. "I hope you've not come to enforce the oath I gave you. Circumstances have changed, and my purposes can no longer lie fallow." Blaise's tone was not hostile. Only clear.

I stilled my tongue. Aleksander's charge had been valid. He needed to speak for his own life.

The Prince shifted awkwardly to get up from the matting, refusing my offered hand. "Circumstances have indeed changed," he said once he'd gotten to his feet and returned Blaise's stiff bow. Even leaning on the table, he was half a head taller than Blaise. "Many things have changed. This damned Ezzarian keeps insisting that I think about what I'm doing, but, unlikely as it seems for anyone who knows me, I've done a great deal of thinking these past months. You are an outlaw who has made secret war upon this Empire, who has disrupted its stability and helped bring it to the brink of ruin. I will not argue justice or right, for men may agree upon a cause while disagreeing about its cure. Indeed, I want nothing from you"—the Prince paused and took a deep breath—"but it appears I must ask anyway. I seem to have misplaced my empire, and so I'm in need of sanctuary. My own people will not have me. So what of you? Will you take me in?"

Blaise's disposition was sublimely serene. I had always envied him that. Passion and reason had found a healthy balance in him, shepherded by an inner confidence that inspired faith and a generous heart that inspired love. But as Aleksander spoke, the hand Blaise had laid so soothingly on his sister's shoulder tightened. Anger, indignation, and disdain played across the outlaw's hollow cheeks and angled eyes in those few moments. But in the end, he nodded and said, "You may stay and share our provisions for as long as you have need. I look forward to further discussions of these matters."

Elinor shook off her brother's hand, dropped her basket of food on the brass tray, and left.

Blaise moved to follow her, but checked himself abruptly. "Rarely do I dispute my sister's judgment," he said. "She's far better than I at weighing consequences. I hope I don't regret this."

Blaise himself walked us across the vale of Taíne Keddar, a blue-green gem in the midst of desolation. Besides feeding off of the deep clear well for which it was named, the high, grassy basin caught whatever moisture was baked out of the surrounding leagues of desert and returned to earth in the form of daily afternoon showers. Groves of fragrant cedars and gray-green olive trees graced a rocky garden of grass and flowers, locked that morning in a watery haze.

Blaise told us that the valley was one of two, nestled high in the rocky spine of the Azhaki wasteland. The legend of two lush, hidden valleys had flourished among the desert peoples for hundreds of years, he said. But the location was so remote, and access so difficult, that no one had been able to say for certain where they lay or even that they existed at all. With his ability to change into a hunting bird and travel where he would, and needing exactly such a place to hide his followers, Blaise had found it.

I was astounded at the number of people abroad in the damp morning. Men and women hurried here and there, hauling wood and water, and carrying baskets of bread from a squat brick building. From the tantalizing smells wafting overhead, I guessed the building housed common ovens. Children chased goats and chickens, carried pails of milk, and led horses to a wooden shed that rang with a blacksmith's hammer. Men were smoothing logs and hammering together a small house to join the scattered mix of old and new dwellings of stone and wood. A number of canvas tents were set up in the lee of a rocky prominence, one of them the headquarters we had just left.

"Sorry I can offer no better accommodation. We're a bit short on roofs at the moment," Blaise said to Aleksander as he led us down a path through an ancient olive grove to a small stone hut. The place was no more than a single windowless room with a dirt floor and a wooden roof—built for storing olives, I guessed. "But this . . . I thought you might be willing to put up with the cramped space in trade for privacy. Seyonne can stay with Farrol and me, or sleep in the barracks, whatever the two of you decide. And we can give you clothes. You both look like you need a change. They won't be fine—"

"No need to keep apologizing." Aleksander leaned on the door frame and surveyed the dismal little shelter. "I'm fully aware of my position and have no expectations. Though I would appreciate boots if they're to be had. I'm unsteady enough without rough ground tripping me up."

Blaise nodded. "Seyonne, you remember Cafazz. He can help with boots. And Sufrah rules the food supplies as before. But this evening . . . and every evening . . . I'd like you to eat with me."

I protested, sure that Blaise was forgetting the awkwardness of forcing our company upon Elinor. "We can do for ourselves," I said. "We've been accustomed to it for a while now."

But he wouldn't hear my excuses. "I think it would be wise," he said, "for many reasons that you can likely come up with for yourselves. Everyone in the valley knows of the Derzhi and the Ezzarian shapeshifter by now. Many know Seyonne and trust him. But I've no doubt that half my people have guessed your identity already, Lord Aleksander, and none have any reason to love you. If you are to be accepted here, then they must see that I consider you no threat." He smiled ruefully. "My companions are quite protective of me. A few of them tend to be a bit overzealous." He entirely understated the matter.

In the hour after Blaise left us, Aleksander took charge of our accommodations, mumbling that he might as well learn to be useful. He found a stick of olive wood to hold himself up, a leafy branch for sweeping out the stone house, and a stand of dried grass to gather for pallets. While he took care of these tasks, I went off in search of water and whatever might be available in the way of clothes. I met several acquaintances from my sojourn with Blaise in Karesh, and though they had surely heard of my mad rage on the night of Gordain's death, none seemed particularly afraid of me. Wary, certainly, especially of my companion. They didn't ask about him directly, but danced about the subject. *You've brought a friend back with you, eh? A Basran someone said . . . Heard it was quite a fight at Andassar. Your friend seemed to know his way around a sword . . . We've missed your sword training, Seyonne. Will you be staying long enough to start it up again? Or perhaps this companion of yours has other ideas . . . ?*

I thanked them for their help; I took back an armload of breeches, shirts, leggings, towels, cups, cloaks, two blankets, a water jar, a sharpening stone, and a pair of boots I thought might fit Aleksander. But in answer to their probing, I said only that I had known my friend a long time, that he was recovering from a severe injury, and that we would stay at least a few days until he was more mobile. All other questions I deferred to Blaise.

As I started back to the olive grove with my load, light footsteps raced down the path behind me. "Master Seyonne! Is it really you?"

I peered around the stack of clothing, precariously perched on top of a water jar, and saw a pair of bright blue eyes shining beneath an unruly shock of blond hair. No wariness here. No fear or holding back. "Mattei! Holy stars, lad, you're as tall as me."

"Cafazz told me you were here." The boy grabbed the water jar from under my stack and hoisted it on his shoulder. "I'm learning to sword fight now. I've ridden on three raids already—more sneaking than fighting, but it's coming. Now you can teach me proper."

The Kuvai youth's greeting was as fine a welcome as I'd had anywhere. Outside of Blaise and Farrol, Mattei was the only person in the outlaw band whom I could truly call a friend.

Five years previous, a Derzhi baron had decided to divert the water from Mattei's village well to make a pond at his Kuvai estate. For daring to question the order which would leave the villagers' crops and animals parched, Mattei's parents had been tied together and burned alive in their own house. Blaise brought a raiding party to stop the execution, but arrived too late. But he found the ten-year-old boy huddled in the root cellar, where he'd hidden, forced to listen to his parents screaming as they died. For the next four years, the boy had not spoken a word.

When I'd come to live with him in Karesh, Blaise asked me to teach Mattei some fighting skills. Blaise believed that if the boy could learn to defend himself and others, it might help heal the terrible wounding that kept him silent. Beset with grief and guilt and soul-sickness after my journey of revelation, I could scarcely bring my own self to speak, but I agreed and began teaching Mattei the rudiments of hand combat. The boy was quick, strong, and ferocious, though his eyes were an abyss of pain as he fought.

One evening after several weeks of practice, I told Mattei of Kyor, the boy of his own age who had died following my command to bring Blaise to the gateway of Dasiet Homol. I told him how I blamed myself for Kyor's death, though my hand had not held the knife that killed him. But I said that, although it was very hard, I was coming to see that I had given Kyor a duty and a purpose, and that I should not regret his ending. Kyor had saved Blaise's reason, and all the good that Blaise had done and would do was a gift Kyor had given to the world. Perhaps, I said, Mattei's parents had died, not blaming their son for hiding in that root cellar, but rejoicing in his safety and the thought of all the good he could do in the world.

Together Mattei and I walked into the wilderness that night, and I showed him how Ezzarians built a ring of holy fire. I explained how we felt close to the gods when we knelt within it, as Verdonne had done in her long siege trapped between heaven and earth. When our fire blazed high, I prayed aloud for wisdom and strength, and asked the gods to comfort Kyor and tell him of the good that had come from his sacrifice. And Mattei, breaking his long silence, whispered his own prayer for the gods to tell Nasia and Rudolf that he missed them terribly, and that he would strive to be their worthy son. We had both begun a healing in that ring of fire. Mattei's excitement at my arrival, and the smiles and bantering that followed him as we walked through the camp, told me he had come farther than I.

On our way across the trampled grass of the open valley with my supplies, I saw Blaise and Elinor galloping off together toward the south end of the valley. "They seem in a hurry," I said.

"Just off to see the old ones, I'd guess," said the boy.

"Old ones?"

"Oh!" Mattei flushed as scarlet as the ajilea flowering in the grass. "I thought Blaise would have— We're not supposed to talk about them, even among ourselves. I'm sorry. But I'm sure it would be all right if I told you. Blaise honors you so—"

"No, no. I don't want you to speak of things you've been told not. Don't worry about it. Blaise will tell me everything he wishes me to know."

I had Mattei leave the water jar at the edge of the clearing by the stone hut, saying I'd come back for it. "I'll introduce you to my companion another day," I said. "He could use a good friend. He's lost his home, seen his father and friends murdered, and heard people crying out and been unable to help them. It's going to take awhile for him to learn to live with it. Right now he really doesn't want to talk to anyone."

"He's in his quiet time," said the boy.

"Aye," I said. "That's exactly it."

CHAPTER 23

All of Taíne Keddar was subdued on that first afternoon, not just Aleksander. The six deaths in the raiding party had cast a shadow over the outlaw settlement, and most of the afternoon had been devoted to the burials. The Prince and I spent several jars of water, two towels, and a goodly while cleaning ourselves, then took a few minutes to visit the burial site of each of the fallen. Derzhi tradition bade a warrior honor those who had died fighting at his side, even if he didn't know their names. Understanding how little Aleksander would be welcome, we did not intrude upon the funeral rites, but arrived just after and stayed just long enough to toss a handful of dirt on the grave and salute the fallen rider with our swords. This duty done under a barrage of silent stares, we retreated to our stone hut and slept.

Just after sunset, I walked up the path toward Blaise and four other men who stood beside a healthy blaze outside one of the larger tents at the valley's edge. The evening breeze was damp after a brief shower, and I welcomed the prospect of a good fire and a hot meal, if not the uncomfortable society that was sure to accompany them. Aleksander was slow in getting his new boots back on, so he'd sent me on ahead, saying he would catch up.

A short, solidly round man was stirring a pot hung over the fire, but when he caught sight of me, he thrust the spoon into someone else's hand and raised his arms in greeting. "Seyonne! Spirit's flesh, it's fine to see you." Before I could get out a word, he was across the wide expanse of trampled, muddy grass, thumping me on the back, almost toppling me to the dirt in his enthusiasm. "The instant I heard the tale of the winged Ezzarian, I knew it was you come back."

"I'd wondered if you were hiding from me," I said, unable to restrain a grin at Farrol's clumsy welcome. Ever since I had helped save Blaise's reason and salvage his own grim future, I had suffered no more enthusiastic devotion than Farrol's.

"Nah. Just running Blaise's everlasting errands. With the size of our company, there's no end to it. And more folk come to us every day."

He put his arm around my shoulders and was practically dragging me toward the group by the fire, but before we got so far, I pulled him to a stop, took his hands, and examined them. They were wickedly scarred, and two fingers on his left hand were curled stiffly. He wiggled them, as if to demonstrate that he had some use of them. "I never had a chance to thank you, or to find out about your injury," I said. "You saved—"

"I'm a bumbling oaf," he said, pained sobriety dousing his exuberance. "Got a fine man killed and came near leaving myself a cinder because I didn't know what I was about—first sending assassins after Blaise and then not knowing how to control the fire. But we did what we could, eh? It's all a man can do."

"You had no way to know, no reason to expect what happened. But I'll never forget what you did. Never."

"Have you seen him?" Farrol lowered his voice, as if the ones by the fire might be listening.

I shook my head. "Elinor's not too happy about my being here."

"She's got a number of—"

"I don't blame her," I said, rushing ahead, not wanting him to feel he had to defend her. "I just can't bring myself to ask it yet. Don't even know if I should. But just to hear a word of him . . ."

Farrol's broad face was filled with sympathy. "He's well. A fine lad. Talks your ears numb when he gets after it. Runs and climbs and keeps healthy. Bright as sunlight on snow."

I could not speak my relief and gratitude.

Aleksander limped out of the grove just then, and I waited for him to reach us. "My lord, this is Blaise's foster brother Farrol. Farrol, this is—"

"I know who he is." The round man's jaw thrust itself out like the rocks that edged the valley. "If you weren't with Seyonne, I'd introduce myself with a sword in your gut. Prayed for the opportunity to do that since I was a boy."

With a stare that could have frozen a volcano, the Prince spread his empty hands wide as if inviting the man to do exactly as he said.

"The Prince is here under Blaise's protection as well as mine," I said hurriedly. "We've a great deal to learn from each other. Perhaps we'd best get to it."

Farrol turned his back and walked away.

I glanced at the Prince as we followed Farrol across the meadow. His face was stone. Indeed his expression did not change during that whole evening, and he said nothing beyond the most necessary politeness as we ate and listened to Blaise and his friends talk about the raid on the slave caravan and those who had died.

In addition to Blaise and Farrol, Roche, the commander of the caravan raid, shared the supper pot. Out of his paint, he was a stringy, pockmarked Ezzarian of twenty-five or so, born demon-joined like Blaise and Farrol. As Blaise questioned the young commander about the problems with the raid, Roche cast side-long glances at Aleksander and me, as if we might contradict him or laugh. He told how the Veshtar had fought more fiercely than he expected and how the Nyabozzi had been able to react to the surprise without a pause. Indeed, anyone setting out to fight the Derzhi and their allies should have known better what to expect, but neither Aleksander nor I offered any comment.

Gorrid, a squat, muscular Ezzarian in his mid-thirties, whom I had met briefly in Karesh, returned my greeting with a hostile glare and spat on Aleksander's boots. His position made clear, he proceeded to ignore us both, neither addressing us nor acknowl-edging my abortive attempts at conversation.

The last of the company was a bearded Suzaini named Admet. Admet was clearly not a warrior. His long robes draped over a se-verely twisted back. He had the pleasant, outgoing, and authori-tative manner of a merchant, and while Blaise and Roche discussed the raid, he stared with unembarrassed curiosity at the Prince and me. As the general conversation moved on, he asked us a few polite questions. Had someone found us a place to sleep? Did we need weapons or clothing or blankets? Had we in-juries that needed tending? Once these exchanges were com-pleted, he turned back to Gorrid and was soon laughing with the other man over some private amusement.

Farrol served out the supper of flet, a thick mush of boiled millet stuck together with pig fat and flavored with onion and scraps of meat. A poor man's staple, it sat heavy in the gut, but would hold a man through lean days. As we ate, the talk turned back to outlawry, with Gorrid and Admet berating Blaise for poor scouting, insisting that better knowledge of the terrain was needed before commencing such large-scale ventures. I felt, rather than heard, Aleksander's snort of disdain. No one else seemed to notice—except perhaps Admet, who flashed a sharp glance our way.

Elinor was not present, and no one mentioned her whereabouts. I listened to the conversation with only half an ear, preferring to let my mind dwell on a child as bright as sunlight on snow, who ran and climbed and talked ears numb. Aleksander and I took our leave early, thanking Blaise and Farrol for the meal and returning to our beds without so much as a word between us.

As Mattei had recognized, the next weeks were indeed Aleksander's quiet time. I had brought him to Taíne Keddar to heal and think, and he worked diligently at the physical healing, at least. He was off before I woke in the mornings, trudging up and down the hillside tracks to strengthen his leg. Sometime near midday, he would return to the hut, build a small fire, and make himself a cup of nazrheel. Then he would grab flatbread and honey or fruit and take it with him out to the grassy spots between the olive trees, where he would bend and squat and stretch, working to regain his flexibility. I assumed he was also doing a considerable amount of thinking during this time, but he shared none of it with me. When we were alone together, most often at night as we lay on our grass pallets in the stone shed, I tried to draw him into conversation, telling him what tidbits of news I had learned. He listened without comment, but did nothing to prolong the conversation. He was not rude or sullen, only distant, withdrawn from the intimacy of the past months, as if I were already departed on my long-delayed journey.

Because Aleksander occupied so little of my time, I tried to make myself useful around the encampment: helping with the building and hauling, cleaning the kill brought back by hunters, whatever was needed. I saw little of Blaise during those first few days and nothing of Elinor. From Mattei I gathered that Blaise's sister was also one of his chief lieutenants, well respected among the company. Elinor and Admet, the Suzaini with the twisted back, set the timing of the outlaw ventures and chose the targets from the reports of scouts and sympathizers throughout the Empire. Unlike my earlier sojourn with the outlaw company, I was not invited to sit in on the sessions where they planned their activities, nor was I asked to teach the men and women fighting skills or sword work. I understood their feelings. How could I be trusted when I kept company with the living symbol of everything they detested?

After a few days I took up running again. Rising early as he did, Aleksander would throw himself on his pallet and fall instantly asleep as soon as we returned from Blaise's fire. I was increasingly shy of falling sleep, however. My dreams had not abated, and rather than spend an unsatisfying night repeatedly waking myself up, I would run the length and breadth of Taíne Keddar under the stars until I dropped onto my pallet like a dead man.

Not long after our arrival, as Aleksander and I were seeing to our horses in the common pasture, a man rode into the valley with news. The Prince and I joined the hundred people who quickly gathered to hear the appalling tale. By the Emperor's order, every village within ten leagues of Andassar had been burned, the man reported. Every field had been salted, every beast slaughtered. What few souls remained in the villages had been killed or sold. "What of the local lord?" said Aleksander, ignoring the surprised gawking of the crowd, who drew away from him when they realized who stood in their midst. "Did you hear news of the Derzhi Lord Naddasine?"

"I did," said the rider, clearly not understanding who was asking. "The Naddasine first lord was accused of harboring the Kinslayer, for the tale had got back to the Emperor that the missing Prince was seen near Andassar. The old man was gutted and hanged as a traitor in Zhagad. The rest of the lot—his five sons and three daughters—were rounded up and given to the Veshtar."

"Given? Enslaved?"

"Aye. Imagine it! Derzhi nobles sealed into slave rings. Though I'd say if they were only enslaved, even to the Veshtar, they got off lucky."

Aleksander shoved his horse's lead into my hand and walked away. No one who looked at him at that moment would have noticed anything out of the ordinary, but I had touched his cold hand and felt its trembling.

Every evening Aleksander and I walked the path through the gnarled olive trees to share Blaise's food and fire. On the fourth evening of our stay, Elinor had joined the dinner company. She served a pottage of beans, carrots, and onions, and nodded politely when I thanked her. Later I saw her frowning, eyes narrowed, as I talked to Gorrid and Blaise about how Aleksander and I had come to be in Andassar and get involved in the raid on the slave caravan. I told myself not to worry so much. Time would reassure Elinor that neither Aleksander nor I was a threat. As to the past . . . I knew I could have done nothing more to save Gordain, and that the horror I had wrought on the namhir was but a product of my madness. There was no need to feel guilty whenever I was around her. But of course I did. Such feelings are not subject to reason. She was the guardian of my child, and I longed to see him. I wanted her to think well of me.

As the others grew accustomed to our presence, conversation flowed more freely. Those who gathered at Blaise's fire spoke of politics and hopes, of worries about supplies, of questions of geography, or of their small victories of the past months—the brutal overseer replaced when his lord's almond harvest mysteriously vanished, or the peasants who had used their own lord's wheat to pay their village's crushing tax levy. The lively discussions provoked a number of arguments. Every person in Taíne Keddar fought for a different reason, some benevolent, some vengeful, some that were little more than a preference for creating havoc over following anyone else's rules. While Blaise was the soul of the Yvor Lukash, infusing even the most mundane concern with the eloquence of true passion, Elinor was its head, her intelligent questioning leading the others to think beyond the limits of their education and experience. To see her argue Gorrid, the fiery debater, into confessing that it was probably useful to have one person to govern, rather than letting every man do as he pleased, or to watch her nudge the shy Roche into demonstrating his facility with verse, was unexpected pleasure.

Though I enjoyed listening to the exchanges and occasionally found myself tempted to offer an observation, I rarely did so. Elinor carefully avoided any repeat of our initial confrontation. She was polite, but cool, accepting the Prince and me, I believed, only because it was Blaise's wish. But my active participation in the group seemed to force her behind a wall of reserve, depriving the whole company of her delightful conversation. So unless directly invited to add my comment, I took my pleasure by watching and listening.

Aleksander remained aloof, never speaking beyond an occasional "well enough" to Blaise's inquiries as to his health and comfort. He always sat to the side, out of the firelight. Sometimes he watched the group of comrades as they talked and teased and argued, prodding one another to be better and wiser. Sometimes he kept his back to them, facing out into the camp where other men and women clustered around other cook fires, their laughter and serious talk blending with the distant bleat of goats and the calls of night birds. I worried about him, but he had closed me off along with everyone else, and I could find no word or deed to open the way again.

On one evening when we had lived in Taíne Keddar almost a month, Farrol asked me how to enchant a fire to burn brighter and longer, and I was taking him through the rudimentary steps, working at the difficult task of dissecting an action that had been second nature since I was seven. "No, the word is '*felyyd*,' which means flame, not '*flydd*,' which means damp," I said when the supper fire hissed and almost went out, and then flared up hugely, threatening to melt the iron pot hanging over it. "And you don't say it aloud."

"But when I just think it, nothing happens . . . not even when I think the right word," said Farrol, his round cheeks drooping. No one could portray an image of dejection as could Farrol.

I smiled at him despite my frustration at being unable to explain something so simple. "Well, you see that's the difficulty. You can't just *think* it. You have to *feel* it, express it with melydda rather than thought or tongue. That's the secret to simple enchantments. I'm sorry I can't explain it better."

We'd been at it for almost an hour, and by this time Blaise and Roche were engaged in the lesson with little success but great good humor. Gorrid was trying to boil chicken bones for soup, and he kept grumbling at us to leave off, for he was either being singed by soaring flames or having to throw more sticks on the fire to keep it from going out. Admet, the Suzaini who had no melydda, sat on a log and laughed at us all. Eventually, the fire took on a slight silver-edged cast that told me someone was getting close to success, but I couldn't figure out who it was.

Only Elinor and Aleksander remained aloof. Elinor sat in the light of a lantern, intent on some sewing project. Aleksander sat expressionless at the edge of the group, his chin propped on his fists and his eyes half closed.

"Linnie, why don't you try it?" said Blaise, after Gorrid threw down a lid in exasperation when a sudden geyser of sparks threatened to set his arm afire. "You were taught some of this. Perhaps you'll have better luck."

"Why would I want to do such a thing?" she said, glaring at me as if I had made the suggestion. "Fires burn as they will, and one learns to control them with fuel and air. Only a fool cares about such tricks of magic."

"This 'trick' can keep you warm if you've limited fuel," I blurted out, caught off guard by the vehemence of her retort. "Or allow you to sleep safely when you're desperate and there are wild creatures about, or enable you to eat or to cleanse wounds when you might not otherwise. Only a fool would refuse to learn what could save a life." During my last two years in Ezzaria, I had fought continually with those who believed that sorcery should never be used to serve human purposes, but only to further the demon war. I thought I had left my resentments behind, but clearly I was wrong.

Elinor's cheeks flamed scarlet and her lips tightened as she returned to her sewing. Our exchange had quenched the playful mood like a cold rain.

Idiot. Could you have insulted her more directly? Hoping to recover lost ground, I tried to make a lesson out of the dispute. "It might seem foolish to keep a fire burning if you don't need it right away, but if you've no means to make one at all, sometimes it's the only answer. To strike a new fire from nothing is far more difficult. Try it . . . here . . ." I grabbed a wad of tangled grass from the tinder basket and set it on a flat stone. "Alter the image in your mind—first see the grass, taste its dryness, smell it, and then consider the spark, quick, clean like the prick of a knife, the heat, the first smoke—and use the words *diargh inestu* instead of the other."

I felt the sputtering flickers of enchantment, and heard the others muttering. *Cold . . . it just leaves me cold . . . can't find it . . . Quiet, dolt. Feel it, don't say it . . . I'll never get it . . . Impossible . . .*

I fixed my eyes on the little wad of grass. To set it alight on the damp stone without touching it would be very difficult. But that was the beauty of sorcery, of course, the art of it . . . to combine the imagining, the tale of the senses, the deep-rooted understanding, and then to loose the warm flood of melydda . . . just enough, shaping it with the word. I closed my eyes and breathed the words *diargh inestu* . . . oh, gods, I never tired of it . . .

"Damn! Who did it?" said Farrol, sitting back on his heels and staring at the tiny golden flame consuming the wad of grass.

Blaise smiled and raised his cup to me. "Our master, of course. Can't you feel it? We creep along the ground while he soars." Which was truly strange for him to say, who could change himself to a bird with a single thought.

I moved away from the fire and sat down on a thick log next to Aleksander, allowing the lesson to lapse. Soon Gorrid was ladling his broth into the wooden bowls stacked beside him, and Roche began passing them out. Elinor abandoned her sewing and brought out bread and cheese.

Though I tried not to let her see me staring, my eyes followed her as she moved around the circle. I was surprised by the implication that she was capable of wielding melydda. When the Ezzarian elders had rendered the cruel verdict that Blaise was demon-possessed and must be left in the forest for wolves to devour, their parents had taken the two children and fled Ezzaria. In the ensuing years, Blaise's parents had given up all use of melydda, terrified that Blaise's "demon" might someday use it to wreak havoc upon those who fought the demon war. They surely would have insisted that seven-year-old Elinor abandon her short years of experience, too, and the ability to control melydda dwindled away with prolonged disuse. Had she recovered it somehow? What other mysteries lay hidden within her?

As we ate, Blaise and Farrol laughed over their magical attempts and speculated on what they might have to do to create other magical workings. Elinor shook her head at them, unable to resist a smile at their teasing, and even sour Gorrid forgot his hostility for the moment and snorted in good humor at the pair.

"You enjoy teaching." Elinor stopped in front of me, offering to refill my bowl and to speak to me at the same time, a gesture of truce that was not lost on me.

"Yes." I fumbled my bowl and spilled the dregs on my breeches, cursing my thick head for not coming up with something clever or interesting to say that might prolong the conversation.

Elinor, her gaze fixed on my bowl, dipped her ladle in the pot and carefully replenished my dinner. "Evidently you're decent at it. Mattei often helps me with Evan."

One would think my bowl had been transformed to beaten gold, for my eyes would no longer leave it. "Mattei is a fine young man," I managed to get out.

"Yes."

Elinor refilled Aleksander's bowl and moved on to the next man. I considered drowning myself in the steaming broth.

After a while, Admet began talking quietly to Roche and Gorrid about a scouting report he'd gotten from a contact in Syra, a mining town east of Zhagad. He seemed to have forgotten that Aleksander and I were sitting right behind him. ". . . and she says the shipments go out regularly every fourteen days. Danye's heard there's a larger one than usual going out five days from now—a levy wagon. The mine garrison is just twenty warriors—ten for each half-day watch. They keep only four warriors at the mine entrance, and six down inside. By the time they pull off extra to protect the shipment, that might leave only five or six warriors in all, plus the overseers and mining stewards. What's even better—they've dammed a stream above the mine, put in a sluice gate that they open to wash the tailings to get the last bits of gold from them. Famarn says it would take no more than an hour to breach the sluice gate and leave it to flood the works. Wouldn't that set the cursed Derzhi baron on his ear? The Danatos would have to forfeit their levies for ten years, and the worst slave pit in the Empire would be left unusable."

"How many would we need to send?" said Gorrid.

"No more than twelve or fourteen. Two to breach the sluice gate, four to hold the entrance. Six to take care of the inside guards and get the slaves out before the water—"

Ever since Admet had begun, Aleksander had been shaking his head. "You'll never do it," he said, interrupting the Suzaini's assessment. Though the Prince spoke quietly, almost to himself, the whole group fell silent and stared at him as if they'd forgotten he could speak. "You'll bury more than six this time. Every one of you will die. And the slaves with you."

"What's that?" said Blaise.

"Danatos and his gold mine—the richest mine in the world. Do you think because he's a Derzhi that he's also stupid? Do you think because he's a mindless villain whose own mother has denounced him, that he would fail to consider such an obvious ploy? It's no wonder you change nothing in this world with such naive heads devising your strategies."

Gorrid jumped to his feet. "You would love us to fail, wouldn't you? Derzhi bastard—"

"Danatos works over seven hundred slaves in his mine," snapped Aleksander, "most of them chained to the rock. They live and die in there. It would take you half a night to free them. And the sluice gate . . . even if you managed to kill the warriors inside the mine, plus the guard and the miner who work the sluice gate, you'd have to deal with the watchpost just across the ravine from it. Not five people outside Danatos's garrison know the exact location of this watchpost, and the warriors' families are held hostage against their revealing it. The post is manned with three archers every hour of every day, and they would not miss the heart of a thief at the sluice gate were it twice the distance, for Danatos's archers are the finest in Azhakstan. He pays them in gold from the mine, which means their hostage families live very well indeed. And it's true there may be only twenty warriors in the mine garrison, but Danatos never provisions less than a hundred and fifty warriors in his keep. Once the alarm is raised, it would take perhaps half an hour to have every one of the hundred and fifty waiting outside the mine . . . but you would never make it out to face them, for the Derzhi warriors inside the mine would already have closed down the air passages and suffocated every living being in the mine—you, the seven hundred slaves, and themselves. They have sworn upon their father's swords to do so, and anyone who thinks to fight a Derzhi must understand that they will do what they have sworn. I would send no warrior of mine on such a mission unless I wanted him dead." Aleksander drank the last of his soup, tossed his bowl on the stack of them, and then stood up as if to leave.

"What are we to believe of you, Prince?" said Admet, the softness of his Suzaini accent not hiding his intensity. "The Danatos are your own kind. For half a year you have been pursuing Derzhi alliances. You could well be trying to protect them."

"I could be," said Aleksander. "Go on and try it then." He started across the grass toward the olive grove.

"Wait," called Blaise. "A moment, Lord Aleksander. Do you know where this archers' watchpost lies?"

The uneven footsteps paused, and after a moment the answer came from the shadows. "I do."

"And do you know how the alarm would be raised?"

"A bell hangs on the cliffs above the mine. Two watchers stand where they can see the mine approaches, which are lit by octar seeps that burn day and night. The watchers never sleep."

"Lord Aleksander, would you ride with us to Syra?" Blaise's quiet question grasped the night and held it by the neck. Lost in my personal confusions, I had missed something of tremendous importance, something extraordinary, but Blaise had not.

"The Danatos hold the mine at Syra by grant of my great-grandsire, given in thanks for repelling the invasion of the Empire by Edusian barbarians, who ravaged every land they touched. Only ten warriors of the Danatos heged survived that battle. Every other was slain. I am my father and his father and his before him; how can I steal back my own gift?"

"Perhaps they have forfeited your gift," said Blaise. "Perhaps they have themselves become the Edusians, ravaging our land."

Months of running and hiding, of a world ripped apart, of life turned inside out, of pain and grief, guilt and exhaustion at last found expression in Aleksander's anguish. "The warriors to be killed in your venture are Derzhi . . . my own people . . . my brothers. I am responsible for them. For the Danatos. For all of you. And yes, for the seven hundred who are chained to the rocks inside the Danatos mine. Do you think this is a game where I can choose sides and upend the board if I don't like the outcome?" Aleksander was not speaking to Blaise or me or anyone else. Only to himself.

"Think on it," said Blaise. "Choose. We go in five days."

CHAPTER 24

Five days. Five days to decide whether to turn against the Empire he had thought to rule. Once committed, there would be no going back. For a prince of the Derzhi to attack a stronghold of the Twenty, to ride out of the darkness and slay Derzhi warriors . . . the word would sweep through the Empire like a paraivo. And there would be no hiding. Aleksander would never paint his face. He would braid his har and ride like a Derzhi prince were Edik's warriors awaiting him at the mine with a noose in hand.

I walked back to the hut in the olive grove that night, determined to breach the wall that had sprung up between Aleksander and me. But he was neither there, nor sitting out under the trees, nor anywhere that I could find him. I sat in the doorway of the hut waiting, unable to take pleasure in the brilliance of the full moon, the towering cedars down the vale beyond the grove, or the scent of wild lavender hanging on the soft night. In my hand I twirled Aleksander's olive-wood walking stick. He had discarded it a few days before, saying I could burn it if I wished.

At some time I drifted off to sleep, for I was stretched across the doorway and the moon had almost set when the hand shook me awake. He was crouched beside me, a dark shadow against steep-angled moonlight behind him. "Seyonne. Are you awake?"

I banished disturbing dreams of mountain prisons and gamarand woods, and sat up, uncomfortably aware of the aching stiffness that seemed to have taken up permanent residence in my back and knees. "I'm completely awake," I said, yawning. "Waiting for you."

He stood up immediately and strode across the clearing to the nearest olive tree, only to spin on his heel and come right back. "I need your help."

"That's why I'm here. Whatever you—"

"I need to send a message to Lydia." He crouched down beside me again. "You've got to do this for me. She trusts you."

"Of course I'll do it. Whatever—"

"She must appear before Edik and petition him to dissolve our marriage."

"What?"

"This is what you'll say to her . . ." He permitted no questioning or discussion. Instead, he gave me the words to tell the wife he adored that he no longer loved her, that he would as soon be wed to a jackal as to a woman who failed to defend him before his enemies, and that he had found a more satisfactory woman to share his bed—one who would give him sons.

"My lord, she'll never believe it. She knows you better than you know yourself."

"Then make her believe it. Enchant her, swear at her. Remind her of how I sent her away, of how I shamed her in front of everyone in Zhagad. You said 'whatever I needed,' and I need this as I need nothing else in this world. She must not be my wife one hour more." He had not taken five days to decide.

"Will it keep her safe?"

"Gods of night, I pray it will. I should have done it months ago, but I couldn't, not while—I couldn't." Not while there was hope of stepping back into the life he knew. He paced back to the olive tree and broke off a clump of the fleshy green fruit, then stared at it as if he weren't quite sure what it was. "Perhaps she's done it already. That would be the best of all. But she is so everlastingly stubborn . . ."

"Have you considered telling her the truth? Letting her decide?" Ysanne had not trusted me with the truth of our child's demon birth. I still felt the bitter hurt of it.

"Of course, I've considered it. But I'll not have her dead for me. Anger will keep her alive."

There was no dissuading him, and I could not muster the conviction to thwart his will. Perhaps this was the way things were meant to fall out. He had yielded everything, as Qeb had foretold. Surely this deed must be the ending of it. *To be willing to cut off your own flesh, though it be your very heart.* "I'll do my best," I said at last.

"You'll fly . . . or something magical . . . ? I hate to ask it, but the time—"

I stood up and gathered my cloak and sword belt from the hut. "I'll get Blaise to guide me. Traveling his ways, we can finish it tonight."

"Tonight?" His strangled response was that of a man who believes he has steeled himself to have a limb removed, only to discover the ax already hanging over him. "Good. Tonight, then. Make her believe, Seyonne. Make her hate me."

Blaise understood my mission and its implications without long explanation, and he agreed to leave immediately. "Three hours hard riding to get there," he said. We would arrive just before dawn.

The easy part of the mission to Zhagad was getting inside the walls. The spires and arches of the imperial city were just taking shape in the gray light when Blaise and I left our horses in the care of a feebleminded hostler. Outside the walls of Zhagad, a city of castoffs had grown up, built by those too poor, too diseased, or too unsavory to be allowed inside the imperial capital. We hurried through its narrow lanes until we found a deserted corner where we could shift to birds' form without being observed.

"You first," said Blaise. "I'll watch."

"Just don't watch *me*," I said.

After the requisite uncomfortable time, I perched on a broken barrel, and Blaise inspected me in the dim light. "A reasonable job," he said, his face looming large in my sight. "Still a little beaky. Your tail feathers should be longer, and you've left too much white in the breast. Haven't you ever taken a close look at a falcon?"

I yelled at him to stop talking and get on with it, which, of course, came out as a totally unintelligible *kek-kek-kek.* He laughed and crossed his arms upon his breast, and in less time than it took me to *think* about transforming, a brown and white hawk fluttered down the alleyway before me.

Aleksander had told me where to find the Marag town house, an imposing pile of finely cut stone, nestled up so close to the palace grounds, its balconies overlooked the Emperor's gardens. Blaise and I flew over the courtyards and walkways, keeping an eye out for guards, especially archers who might be idling away the early hours by taking shots at passing birds. Smoke was rising from the kitchen chimneys, and servants were already dumping wash water into the stone planters and carrying baskets of folded linen from the washhouse into the residence. Aleksander had said that Lydia's apartments looked out on a water garden—a maze of stone steps and sculpted walls, tiled troughs and pools that were filled, sprayed, and spread with an unending flow of water drawn from the deep limestone wells under the desert city. The place was easy to find. In the quiet of the morning, the splash and trickle of the water was unmistakable, accompanied by the chittering of a thousand small birds who rose in a cloud of annoyance at the invasion of a falcon and a hawk.

We circled low over the garden, and I examined the balconies and doorways, debating whether to fly inside the house and search for the Princess, which would leave me in a vulnerable spot while shifting back to my own form, or to shift first and go hunting as a man. The latter would have its own dangers. But the decision was made unnecessary. In the corner of the water garden nearest the house, two women were seated on a small patch of grass beside a pool that shimmered with gold in the morning light. One, fair-skinned, with long, elegant bones, was draped in a voluminous white shawl against the cool morning. Her damp red curls were spread over her shoulders as if to dry in the morning sun. A book lay open in her hand. The other woman wore a servant's plain brown tunic and skirt, and the loose white scarf preferred by traditional Suzaini women, covering the hair and the lower part of the face, leaving the eyes scarcely visible. The two were intensely engaged, the serving woman bent toward her mistress, pointing out something in the book. It appeared that the Princess Lydia was learning to read, a skill most Derzhi disdained as a menial task akin to cleaning or sewing or selling trinkets in the market. Useful, but unnecessary for a race of warriors.

While Blaise perched in the limbs of a lemon tree, I settled on a flagstone path in a secluded part of the garden and shifted back to my own form. Waving a hand at Blaise, I hurried down the winding path, hearing the art of the master gardener in the changing texture of sound as I passed: a splattering fountain, a soft, hissing spray, a gurgling brooklet. In moments I was peering into the lady's courtyard from behind a dripping wall. With no sign of watchers and only the one servant, the situation was as good as I could expect. And so, prepared for every reaction from tears to knife throwing, I stepped out from my hiding place, went down on one knee, bent my head, and cleared my throat. "Your Highness, I beg a word with you."

The serving woman jumped to her feet. "Who are you? How did you get in here?"

"Ways lead both in and out of any maze," I said. "I bring an urgent, private message from the lady's foreign friend." The "foreign friend" was indeed my own self, the designation Lydia had given me when we were working to save Aleksander from the Khelid and their demons.

Oddly enough, my words elicited a sharp in breath, not from Lydia, whose only reaction was a perfect, fragile stillness, but rather from the veiled serving woman, who quickly bent down to confer with her mistress. I did not spy on what was said, and I remained about twenty paces away, hoping to seem less threatening. As the serving woman retreated and settled herself at a discreet distance a quarter of the way around the pool, the Princess said, "Come."

I stood up again and moved a few steps closer. "May I speak freely, my lady?" I said softly.

"The answer depends on what news you bring," she said, meeting my gaze. The fire in her great green eyes told me that her fragility was but an illusion. This woman was the Empress-in-waiting that I knew, Aleksander's worthy sparring partner. "My waiting woman will signal us if anyone intrudes. But be warned. I do carry a knife."

I crouched down beside her, speaking low so that no one could have heard us, save perhaps the brown and white hawk that now sat on an almond tree beside the pool. "He lives, madam."

"And you think I care about the despicable, rock-headed tyrant?" Only one who understood Lydia's temper and her passion for her husband would have recognized the moment's true emotion—the shallow breath exhaled, the quick swallow, the book tossed aside by fingers no longer clenched.

"Indeed, madam, I believe we yet share that particular affliction, although once I give you his message, your feelings may rightly change." I hated what the Prince had asked of me.

She hunched her shoulders under her capacious white shawl as if the day had grown bitter. "Then perhaps you had best get on with it, lest I be tempted to think his sending you, of all messengers, is one of his usual sneaking ploys to regain my favor. How many exiled wives are brought messages by one that rumor names a god?"

"Ah, my lady—"

"Did you know that Edik fears that rumor more than anything? That a winged spirit favors his rival?"

I could allow no such distractions. No matter my own

sympathies, I had to give her Aleksander's words just as he had said them. And then I would have to leave her without any word or gesture of my own that might dilute their cruelty. He had made me swear it, knowing that I disagreed with him on the matter. And so instead of telling her how he had clung to thoughts of her in his pain and how desperately he needed to know she was safe before he could embark on this dangerous venture, I stared at the expanding fish rings on the pool and reminded her that Denischkar heged tradition gave Aleksander the prerogative to take a new wife if the first was barren. As the terms of the marriage agreement drawn up between their houses stated that Lydia would submit to Denischkar custom, Aleksander could also command Lydia to do his will in every matter. Therefore her husband was requiring her to petition the Emperor publicly for a dissolution of marriage. "He regrets the necessity to force you to this," I said. "But he will not have his new wife be second to a woman who cannot be trusted to defend his interests."

"Does the ass think I will believe that he found a new woman willing to put up with him?"

"He insists that you believe it, madam. He says that he has no more time for childish games with you. If you did not believe him in the spring when he banished you from his house and his bed, then you had best come to your senses."

Lydia's pale cheeks flushed, as if the sun were rising there instead of in the east. "And if I refuse to do his bidding and step aside?"

"Lord Aleksander will send the petition to the Emperor and the Council of Twenty himself, along with notice of the breach of the marriage agreement between his father and yours. Your father will be disgraced by your disobedience to his sworn word."

"Edik will laugh at him and burn his petition. What does he care for Aleksander's wishes? And why would my father care, for that matter? No one would hold him accountable for me."

"My lord cares nothing for Prince Edik. But he requires the matter to be made clear to others in the imperial court," I said, "so that both his supporters and his enemies will see that he is committed to the succession. He prefers you handle this unpleasant task by your own doing, as he has no wish to ruin your father and brothers whose support he would like to retain. But you are in his way, and he *will* have you removed."

The waiting woman's hidden eyes seemed to be fastened upon

her own book, but Lydia's slight gesture had the servant up and hurrying to her side.

Lydia glanced up at me and said with remarkable coolness, "Tell me one thing, Seyonne, is his leg healed?"

Startled by the change of subject, I saw no reason to answer other than honestly. "Straight and whole, madam. He has thrown out his last crutch. I saw him running for the first time just yesterday." A few steps only, but a small triumph. A bitter triumph.

"Well, you may tell the lord of kayeets and scorpions and shengars that he may run off a cliff on his repaired leg, and take this 'new wife' with him. As you will see, I have no intention of stepping aside for anyone." The Derzhi Princess gave her hand to the serving woman, who helped her stand, allowing the billowing white shawl to fall to the sides. And then did the world lurch off into an entirely new direction. Aleksander's wife was most assuredly, most obviously, and most immediately not barren.

"Oh, my lady . . . my dear lady . . ." This was as far as I could get for several moments.

"Damn, damn, damn all cursed men . . ." All of a sudden Lydia was fumbling at her gown. Her efforts were fruitless, and the servant had to produce a kerchief for the Princess to dab her eyes. ". . . and damn this vile condition that makes one into a child again. You will not tell him there were tears, Seyonne. They are not for him, anyway, but only a result of this same malady that makes my feet like those of chastou and my skin like a grinding stone."

Indeed her proud demeanor was not diminished by her tears, though she had every right and reason to weep. I could not imagine the strain of her position. Knowing that the least whisper of the child to Edik would see both her and the babe dead. Hearing nothing of Aleksander in the months since he lay so ill in Drafa, save that the Emperor's men were scouring the Empire, vowing to see him dead in the most dreadful ways. Completely uncertain of the future, save that the danger would be worse with every passing day.

"Lady, if we had known . . ." No, I couldn't tell her. Not yet. I could not unsay what I had sworn to say, though all was made irrelevant by the truth. Lydia could not appear before the Emperor to dissolve the marriage, not for something more than two months, but assuredly less than three. And even then, an infant was much more difficult to hide than a pregnant belly, unless you sent the babe away, as my child had been sent away. "We must get you out of Zhagad, Your Highness. You and the child are in grave danger."

"And where would I go? To my husband, who has made his position with regard to me so clear? I think not. The mere fact that he was wrong will not remedy what he's said. So where else is there to go? I am not the most useful of women to be put in a cottage somewhere to fend for myself. Though clever enough, no doubt, the learning might be difficult for the child, and I will not risk that. No, I think that behind my father's walls is as good as I can do."

"No, my lady. You must believe me. You and your child are safe nowhere in this Empire; you are wise enough in the ways of the world to understand that, and soon the danger will increase a hundredfold. If you wish this child to survive, then you must go with me, or prepare to remain here while the babe is hidden elsewhere."

"I'll not be separated from my child."

"I thought not. And so we must find you a refuge, the sooner, the better. I know a place—"

"Is he there?"

"Yes, for the moment. But many others live there as well." I was talking to her back now. "Neither the journey nor the destination will be comfortable. It's a poor place, but the best I can offer."

"If the cursed Prince can live there, so can I. When do we go?" As always, she took my breath away.

I glanced up at the brown and white bird soaring across the tiled roof. "I need to discuss this with a companion. Can you ride at present, my lady?"

"By choice, no, but by necessity, yes. Not fast."

"We'll leave at dusk. I need to make arrangements for an extra horse and water, then I'll come back for you. You'd best not be seen riding through the streets, so you'll need to walk as far as the south gates. But how we're to get you through them, I don't—"

"I'll get her through the gates." The serving woman spoke with startling authority. "She'll be safer with me. We'll meet you outside the south gates at dusk, ready for hard traveling. I will be accompanying the lady, so bring transport for me as well."

"Madam?" I addressed Lydia, though some elusive element in

the veiled woman's speech held my attention on the servant rather than the mistress.

"As she said," said the Princess.

"You must not be recognized," I said. "This will be very dangerous. You should wait—"

"I can take care of it," said the veiled woman. "Can you still trust no one but yourself, cocky boy?" Now I knew what had teased at my ear. Her accent was Ezzarian . . . and she was laughing at me.

I shook my head in disbelief. "Catrin?"

"*Tienoch havedd*, Warden. Greetings of my heart, my first and most prized pupil." My friend and mentor lowered her veil, held out her arms, and drew me into a fierce embrace.

CHAPTER 25

Catrin, a member of the Ezzarian Council that administered the demon war, stepped outside the boundaries of Ezzaria only in the rarest instance. But I could not stay in the garden long enough to find out why she happened to be playing waiting woman to the banished Princess of the Derzhi. Considering that the last time I had seen her, she had been consenting to my execution, the story would likely take more than a moment's telling. And considering the words this normally reserved woman whispered as she clasped me to her breast, I wasn't sure I should be in any hurry to hear her tale. "Holy Valdis give you strength, Seyonne."

I returned her embrace stiffly, unsure of what it meant, unsure of my feelings about a friend who had left me to die. But I had to postpone any exploration of Catrin's heart or mine.

Danger stalked the Princess even within the Marag house, so the women reported. The Emperor had sent his own man to reside with the Marag to intercept "any who might harass or threaten the noble, distraught lady wife" of his "murderous cousin." Lydia spent most of each day in seclusion, walking and sitting in the garden only in the earliest morning when no one was about. Only her father, brother, and two loyal servants knew of the coming child . . . and my mentor Catrin.

Leaving the women with a sufficiency of warnings, I slipped back into the garden and transformed. Blaise and I returned to our alley outside the walls, and I told him what had come about. "We need to get the Princess to Taíne Keddar," I said. "Every moment she remains in Derzhi hands, she's in mortal danger. She has nowhere else to go."

Blaise sat against the alley wall, his face in sunlight, the rest of his body in shadow as the sun crept higher over Zhagad. "Are you trying to get us all killed? You and your royal friends are like a plaguey corpse—like to draw all sorts of vermin after you. No, the lady cannot stay at Taíne Keddar. But"—he raised his hand to quiet my protest—"there is another settlement. I'll have to ask permission, but I don't think they'll refuse me. It's a better place to birth a child and at least as safe." He pulled a biscuit out of his pocket and eyed its unappetizing gray color. "Though safety and comfort are not in great supply anywhere at present."

We spent the rest of the day acquiring two more horses. We had nowhere near enough money with us for this unexpected expense, and no man who valued his skin would consider stealing horses in Zhagad, so the acquisition was a matter of great delicacy, involving strong drink, a game of ulyat, and a bit of enchantment. Once we had the horses, we acquired extra waterskins, along with provisions for a two-day journey and an emergency childbirth. Remembering Vanko's dead infant, I could not shake the imagining of Lydia's being brought to term beforetime on a journey in the desert.

In late afternoon Blaise flew back into the city to watch over the two women as they made their way through the streets. My changing was too slow to be of much use in an emergency. He would fetch me only if I was needed. I sat on a stone wall outside the gates, twisting the horses' tethers about one sweaty hand and snapping the dry twigs off a thorn tree with the other. I hated waiting.

Mounted guards bulled through the teeming crowds, raising more memories of the trouble at Karn'Hegeth. Slaves lit the torches at the fortresslike gates. When a flood of poorly dressed men and women spilled out from the cavernous opening—servants and laborers of too little use to be housed in a noble's palace, and not permitted to stay within the city overnight—I sat up, alert. Among the coarse and weary crowd were two veiled women in brown robes, plodding and pushing a small barrow piled with baskets.

I was ready to leave my post and join the two women when a brown-and-white bird swooped low over a rangy, bearded man shouldering his way through the crowd. A dark blue cloak hid his hands and his dress, the cloak's hood shadowing his face. He was only a few steps from Lydia's back. With a harsh cry the bird soared up and circled over my head, then dipped over the man again. He didn't need to tell me twice. I dropped down from the wall, wrapped the horses' tethers about the thorn tree, and slipped into the crowd.

I purposefully averted my face as Catrin and Lydia passed by me. The blue-cloaked man edged closer to their backs as they moved slowly down the road, Catrin craning her neck looking for me. I shoved my way through the stream of people until I was just behind him. He reached toward the veiled Princess.

"Excuse me, sir," I said, grabbing his outstretched arm and drawing him close, where he could feel my dagger poking under his ribs. "I think we need to have a word in private."

The man muttered a curse and tried to wrestle away. Growling, I pricked him harder and nudged him toward the roadside. If I could get him into the darkening lanes of the outer city, I could whack him on the head until we were well away. But he would not cooperate, and luck was against him. One of the mounted Derzhi rode within ten paces of us. My prisoner snarled and raised his arm. "Your hon—" I rammed my knife upward, silencing his betrayal. Before he could fall, I sheathed my knife and grabbed him with both arms. His head lolling, blood trickling out of his mouth, I draped his arm over my shoulder and staggered drunkenly toward the side of the road, dragging him away from the alerted Derzhi. *Careful. Not too fast.* I maneuvered the body toward the spot where I'd left the horses, and then draped him headfirst over the wall, as if he were vomiting. Snatching the reins from the thornbush and keeping myself out of sight between the beasts, I quickly distanced myself from the dead man.

The crowd began to thin as people drifted off into the dim, smoky maze of tents and shanties. Only a few wagons were left to push on down the desert road along with a handful of mounted travelers, a shepherd with a small flock of goats, and a tinker's caravan. Blaise was now walking just ahead of me, beside the caravan. Some twenty or thirty paces ahead of him were the two brown-robed backs, hesitating as the other travelers passed.

I shoved past the goatherd and his flock just as the first alarm was raised inside the walls of the city. Whether or not they were after Lydia, the alerted guards would find the dead man in moments. "Shifter!" I called quietly, not wanting to bandy names about. Blaise whirled around. "We'd best lift our feet!"

Blaise grabbed the horses while I went after the women. I touched Catrin's arm, just as her bewildered eyes settled on me. Together we drew Lydia out of the traffic. "Catrin, my lady Princess, this is our guide," I said as Blaise caught up to us with the horses. "We must be quick."

I made a step with my hands, and with Blaise and Catrin helping to lift and balance her, we hoisted Lydia smoothly onto her mount. Blaise boosted Catrin up easily, and then the outlaw flung himself into the saddle and led us into the darkness. "Not too fast," I said, though the rising clamor from the direction of the gates demanded that we run. We spurred the horses to a gentle walk as we passed the tinker's caravan. A horn sounded from the walls. Men were shouting—a loud warning yell, likely the dead man being discovered.

Blaise's power swelled into life, his enchantments as visible to me in that darkening night as the rising moon. Though our steps were deliberate, the smudged lights of torches and lanterns dwindled quickly into pinpoints of yellow, sprinkled among the sharp-edged stars. We rode without conversation for well over an hour, our ears and thoughts fixed on the road behind us, Blaise first, then the women, myself at the rear. Hooves pounded the hard-packed road, but no one came near us.

About the time the last faint vibrations of pursuit were drowned out by the dull urgency of our own mounts, Catrin turned in her saddle. "Seyonne, we need to rest soon."

"No," said the Princess. "I can keep going."

I nodded to Catrin and rode forward to Blaise. "Are we well away?" I said. "It's not been long, but I can't sense anyone behind us anymore."

Blaise's eyes were like coal pits in his white face, and sweat beaded his brow. "Another quarter of an hour," he said, his voice rasping. "I'm trying to take us faster."

"A little while longer and we'll be out of danger," I said, dropping back beside the women. "Then we'll stop and rest for a bit. We'll be able to go easier the rest of the way."

The Princess's face was scribed with all the ferocity and determination of her Derzhi ancestors. As I returned to my trailing position, Catrin slowed, matching her horse's pace to mine. "He's the one Fiona told us of," she said quietly, nodding at Blaise. "The one born . . . possessed?"

"Yes." Catrin's scarcely suppressed discomfort erased the remembered warmth of her greeting. I released the tight hold I had maintained on my demon eyes since recognizing her, exposing the blue fire behind their normal black coloring, lest somehow she had deluded herself into believing that I'd not done the deed for which she had condemned me. "He's been demon-joined since birth," I said, "a good and honorable man who is a throwback to what our race is meant to be. The enchantment you feel from him is saving our lives." The words came out harsher than I intended.

"Give me a little time, Seyonne. I'm trying to understand." She held her reins stiffly. After one uneasy glance at my face, she kept her eyes fixed on Lydia's back.

"What are you doing in Zhagad?" I asked, ready neither to apologize nor to forgive as yet.

"Seeking you and Fiona," she said. "The only place I knew to start was with Prince Aleksander. When I heard the stories of the winged rescuer, I knew you must be with him, but, of course, that didn't help me find you. So I sought out the Princess and used the 'foreign friend' ruse to get in to see her. After speaking to her for a little while, learning what kind of woman she is, I believed the Prince could not abandon her forever. Sticking close seemed my only hope. They're well suited, aren't they?"

Catrin had traveled with Aleksander and me on the journey to Parnifour and our confrontation with the Lord of Demons. Taking over her grandfather's role as my mentor, she had worked doggedly to help me prepare for my part in that battle. I owed her an open mind at least.

"Theirs is a match designed by the gods," I said.

"All this business of chastising her in Zhagad, taking a new wife . . . he's trying to protect her."

"Yes."

We halted soon after this. Lydia was sagging with exhaustion, and for a while I was afraid we mightn't be able to get her off the horse. "Monstrous, clumsy cow," she said as Blaise and Catrin helped lower her to the ground beside the tarbush fire I had blazing. "I've won every horse race I've ever ridden, and now an hour's plodding has me weak as a new-dropped foal."

"We'll get you something to eat, my lady," said Catrin, wrapping a cloak about the Princess's shoulders. "You'll feel better after that."

"If I could just have some nazrheel, I'd be better," said Lydia. "Give me the things to make it so I don't have to get up again, then you can go off with Seyonne. All these months you've been so anxious to speak with him."

"I'll take care of the lady," said Blaise, looking more himself now we had stopped. "You two go on, if you like."

I stood up and immediately felt three pairs of eyes staring at me. My shirt was stiff with the stalker's blood. My right hand and wrist were covered with it. I hadn't even noticed.

"You caught my signal, then," said Blaise, breaking the awkward silence. "I thought the man was up to no good. Are you injured?"

"I'm fine," I said. I wasn't going to explain myself for protecting them. "Catrin, do you want to walk or not?"

Catrin rose and looked from me to Blaise. The outlaw bowed to the Princess and handed her a waterskin to hold. "My name is Blaise, madam . . ." He began to pull supplies from a small pack.

And so Catrin and I were left to walk out the knots in our legs . . . and those in our long friendship. I felt her start to speak several times as we walked away from the cheery fire and into the starlit dunes. But she couldn't seem to manage it.

"You needn't be afraid of me," I said at last. "I'm not looking for revenge, and, although I have one living inside me, I am not a demon. Everything Fiona told you—about our history, about the demon world, about the sundering when our ancestors split our souls apart—it's all true. But I didn't kill Tegyr or—"

"Seyonne, Ysanne is dead."

I shook my head as if she had spoken a question instead of an answer. Those words did not fit together. I walked on, up a steep-sided mountain of sand that pulled at my knees and ankles.

Catrin trudged doggedly beside me, taking two steps for every one of mine. "She was partnering with Hueil, a student of Gryffin's who had come along amazingly well and passed his testing some three months before. We'd lost so many others, and Ysanne was determined we'd not lose Hueil, so she would let no other Aife weave for him. We don't know whether Hueil was taken captive, or injured in the combat, or if he would not or could not yield the fight and get out, but Ysanne didn't close the portal. She held more than three days. Hueil never came back, and Ysanne never woke."

My feet kept moving. My blood kept flowing. My lungs kept squeezing air in and out. But everything else in the world slowed to a halt. *Ysanne. Dead.* Up and up the towering dune, slogging through cascading sand, unable to speak, unable to think of what the words meant, as if the sand were seeping in through my eyes and ears and pores, as if it were filling my stomach and my lungs, clogging my mind, drowning me. I stumbled to the crest and stared out upon the vastness of the desert. Empty. The world was empty. A giant's fist squeezed my chest, but I could not cry out nor could I weep. The sand robbed me of breath and tears.

Only after a long while standing in the cold night wind did I become aware of Catrin standing beside me, unmindful of the gusts that whipped her dark hair about her face. "For the first few months after Dasiet Homol, the demons were quiet," she said. "Some of us whispered that perhaps Fiona had been right. Perhaps the demons didn't need human souls anymore. No one dared speak your name. Ysanne would not allow it. She was pursuing corruption with a vengeance, as if to ease her own soul of what we had done to you . . . to justify it. Many began to bridle at her harshness. But then, a few months ago, Searchers began sending stories of new demon possessions, worse than anything we had seen in years—dreadful deeds, virulent madness, horrors in line with our worst experience."

Catrin's tale forced my paralyzed mind to engage. Demon possession should have ended with the move to Kir'Navarrin. That was one reason for opening the gateway . . . so the rai-kirah could reclaim a semblance of life and not have to send the hunters into human souls to harvest what they could of physical sensation and memory. Unless . . . A few of the demons had been left behind in Kir'Vagonoth. The mad ones. The cruel and vicious Gastai hunters who had held me captive for eight months, tormenting my mind and body to the brink of ruin. A few of the other rai-kirah had stayed behind to guard the mad ones, until those who passed into Kir'Navarrin could discover how to heal their cruel brothers. What if the mad Gastai had gotten loose to hunt again?

Catrin urged me to sit down. Bereft of will, I obeyed her, and she settled beside me, pulling her brown cloak tight against the chill. "The hiatus had given us time to bring on a few of the student Wardens faster, and so when the messages began to come from the Searchers, we believed we were as ready as we could be. But the fighting was terrible. For the first month, the young Wardens were forced to withdraw from every conflict. At the same time we began to lose Searchers, Comforters, and messengers, more than fifty—almost everyone we've sent into the world. Then we started losing Wardens, too. Their Aifes said they didn't die."

"Taken captive," I said numbly. "Fallen into the abyss. Gods have mercy . . ." The agonies of my captivity in the pits of the

Gastai still haunted my memory. Now other Wardens were being forced to endure the horror I had known, but without my experience, without the glimmer of truth I had possessed, without the elusive hope of escape that Fiona's faithful vigil had provided me. "How many lost?" Dread settled on my shoulders like an iron yoke.

"All of them, Seyonne. Three captive. Two more severely wounded. Two dead. Two Aifes dead before Ysanne, one left possessed. Each part is bad enough, but if you step back and look on the whole, matters are much worse. As near as I can estimate, all of it happened at the same time: the Emperor's murder . . . and the new demon assault . . . the collapse of the Empire . . . our Searchers dead and the Aifes, and the Wardens dead or captive. Do you understand, Seyonne? Ezzaria is in shambles, and everything we have feared is coming to pass. We've lost the demon war."

The demon war lost . . . Unthinkable. And the Empire . . . Ezzaria . . . Ysanne . . . "Why in the name of the gods have you come to me?" I said. "You must think this is my doing." What else could they believe?

"I cannot ignore that possibility. And, yes, I am afraid of what you've become." Catrin put her hand on my chin, pulled my face toward her, and forced me to look at her. "But whatever you are, I also believe that the soul I know as Seyonne yet lives. You've not asked me the names of the young Wardens taken captive."

"The names?" I could not imagine what she was thinking. What would it matter?

"Hueil, Olwydd . . . and Drych."

"Drych!" The name split the night like a flashing sword. "He survived . . ." By the end of the day I had opened the gateway to Kir'Navarrin, the young Warden, my own student, had been the only living witness to my deeds. But he had been too injured to give testimony, and so my wife, the Queen, had condemned me to die.

"Yes." Catrin's dark eyes filled with tears, rare for this woman of determination and duty. "For days after your escape he lay near death, and insensible for weeks more. But when he woke at last, he told me everything about that battle. How you warned him about Merryt and saved his life. How you tried so desperately to save the others. We thought the demon had corrupted you, made you kill your own brother Wardens, and all the time you were trying to save them and us. Oh, Verdonne's child, Seyonne, you saved us all, and we came near killing you for it."

"Did Ysanne know?" The hope flared like a last spark in the ashes.

Catrin shook her head. "She would not have listened, and Drych would have been judged corrupt and shunned or exiled. I advised him to keep silent until the time was right. I'm so sorry."

But the right time had never come, and so Ysanne had died believing me her enemy, believing that my corruption had unleashed this terror on the world. Catrin was unsure of me even yet. What if they were right?

My friend and mentor took my hands. "We need you to tell us what to do, Seyonne. You and Fiona. Ysanne never named another kafydda, which leaves Fiona as our rightful Queen. After Ysanne died, Drych testified before the Council. Some believed him. Some didn't. But we gathered enough support that the others in the Council have sent me to find Fiona and bring her home. I took it on myself to find you as well."

"Blaise can fetch Fiona," I said, wrapping my arms about myself against the cold. "And I'll go for Drych and the others. I won't leave them there." Not in the abyss of Kir'Vagonoth. But before I could risk that dangerous journey, I had to take the other. First to pass through the gateway into Kir'Navarrin and wrestle my demon, and then to face the prisoner of Tyrrad Nor and find out what, in the name of the gods, I had done.

CHAPTER 26

We arrived at Taíne Keddar in early morning. Though Blaise had worked hard to take us the shortest possible route, our frequent stops for Lydia to rest prolonged our journey through the night. Blaise, his face lined with fatigue, was slumped in the saddle as we crested the last steep rise to the rim of the valley. "A thousand paces down that way," he said, nodding his head down the track and clearly reaching deep for the words. "Two boulders the size of a house. Off to the right is a small track that leads to a cedar grove. Stay there. I'll send someone with food." He waved off our concern at his condition. "I'll be all right. I've got to get permission to take the lady where she needs to go." He didn't say from whom, but transformed and flew away.

We dismounted in the cool privacy of the cedar grove, and Catrin rolled up her cloak to make a pillow for Lydia, who was so tired her tears flowed freely, despite her fiercest efforts to control them. With hard riding, concern for the Princess, and fighting off sleep, Catrin and I had found no further time to talk.

In truth, I had been locked in my own thoughts, trying to conjure Ysanne's face on the day of our wedding, or on the day we knew she was with child, or as we exulted in our first victory in demon combat. But all I could envision was her expression the last time I had seen her—the horror and revulsion when she recognized demon fire burning in my eyes.

And so I had abandoned useless grieving and reviewed my actions of the past four years. Was I wrong to have brought the rai-kirah out of Kir'Vagonoth? Had I put the pieces of Ezzarian history together in error? Had my ignorance and pride brought ruin to three worlds? And my naive confidence after the siffaru—thinking that somehow I was wise enough or pure enough or strong enough to transform a monster when I had no idea of his power . . . what kind of fool was I? I came to no new conclusions, save that I had best stop thinking or I was going to paralyze myself with guilt. Whether I had to reverse what I had set in motion or merely travel the road until its end, the answers I sought were only to be found in Kir'Navarrin. The time had come.

Half an hour after Blaise left us, young Mattei came trudging up the hill to our resting spot bringing a basket of fresh provender, a wineskin, and a stout, competent healing woman named Corya. Mattei took our horses to feed and water them, while I introduced Corya to the women.

Corya wasted no time. She shoved some fruit and cheese into my hand and waved me away. "Off with you now, sir, while I see to this young woman. Though this is not the most comfortable of bedchambers, we need to make sure mother and child have weathered the journey well."

"I am the daughter of a Derzhi warrior," said Lydia, her dusty face streaked with the white tracks of her tears. "A night's journey on a horse cannot harm me or my child." She glared at me accusingly. "You'll not let the cursed prince see this damnable weeping? You'll say it's sand in my eyes or sun glare. Of course, there's no need for me to see him at all. A little rest and I can ride again. Your kind friend will take me to this other place, and I won't have to see him."

"Gracious, woman, if a little salt water is the only result of this adventure, then there's no man of any race can give you grief," said the healer. "Even a poxy Derzhi."

"Ah, you don't know my poxy husband! He could give such grief to a glacier, it would melt to defend itself. Why is there no Derzhi woman god to repair this beastly condition? My husband is a priest of Athos, and he and his god are two of a kind, making all of us miserable who live unshielded. And Druya . . . a bull. What use is he?"

Corya chuckled and stroked the Princess's red hair with her strong hand. "In Thrid some worship a woman god who eats her men. But she's done nothing for us mothers, either, as she lets the bastards get her planted before she kills them. You needn't fret, though. It's all over soon enough, and we who've done this before will always know how to care for you novices." Before one could blink, Corya spread out a clean blanket, allowed me to delay my departure long enough to help shift the Princess onto it, then draped our cloaks from cedar branches to create a screen. "Mistress . . . Catrin is it? Perhaps, as the lady is comfortable with you, you would stay and keep her company?"

I told the women that I would stay close in case they needed me; then I strolled across the slope and climbed up to an outcropping rock where I could sit and view the full expanse of the valley while munching on sour plums and goat cheese. The steeply angled light carved the rocks and trees into deep relief, transforming the grass into velvet and the pools and stream into burnished gold. Tiny figures of people and animals moved soundlessly through that remote landscape, their identities and emotions and imperfections masked by distance. A few hours of such isolation, I thought, away from the unceasing demands of pain and grief, love and desperation, and perhaps I could grasp some sort of clarity.

But the settling peace was soon broken when a kite screamed, diving for its breakfast on the rocks just below me, and footsteps crunched on the graveled approach to my eyrie. Surprisingly, the one who spoke to my back was not Catrin, but Elinor. "Blaise told me what's happened," she said. "The Prince is with Gorrid and Admet in the command tent, working on plans for the raid. If you wish to join him to give him the news, I'll stay with the Princess until she can travel the rest of the way. My brother will take you and the Prince to visit the lady this evening."

"That may not be necessary," I said, glancing over my shoulder.

"I don't understand."

"I may not tell Aleksander she's here . . . or any of it. I haven't decided."

"Decided? What right have you to decide such a matter?" So much for our game of civility. Her nostrils flared and her voice broke with passion and indignation. "Even a Derzhi deserves to know he has fathered a child before he faces death. Have you come to believe what everyone says of you? Only gods play so cruelly with people's hearts."

Somehow the simple directness of her accusation forced my grief and foreboding into painful focus, causing them to erupt like the molten heart of a volcano that has found the point of weakness in the mountain's rocky cap. "I am not a god!" I shouted, leaping to my feet. "I make no pretense of it. I am so far out of their favor, I don't think I can ever find my way back again. Look at me." I thrust my hand into her face. Blood was crusted in the cracks of my skin and under the nails. "There is so much blood on my soul that it leaks out of my very skin. I killed a man last night without thinking twice about it, because I suspected he was a threat, and I was afraid. I killed seventeen Veshtar at Andassar . . . some of them long after they were any threat to their prisoners . . . because I hated them and what they do. I may be half mad with what I've done and what I've yet to undertake, but I do know the horror of it and feel it and fear it. I *am* human, Elinor, so don't tell me what is cruel and what is not." She stood her ground, her lovely face tight and hard, affirming my self-judgment, though skeptical that I might give fair assessment of cruelty.

"Aleksander is my friend. I've had to watch him yield everything of meaning to him, to see him learn hard and terrible lessons about the world, lessons that you knew by the time you were ten. Yes, he is a better man for the learning, but that makes it no easier to see someone you love in such pain. And now, if I tell him that this one thing so precious is not lost, then how will he face losing it all over again? I have faced that very truth—on the night I first saw my child in your arms and your brother told me of the doom of madness that awaited him. Since that day I have done everything in my power to repair this broken world, but I'm afraid my deeds have destroyed me and everything I value, so don't tell me how cruel I am to consider sparing my friend one grief."

I started down the hill, leaving her in possession of the rocks. But I was not yet halfway down, when I reversed course and climbed up again, far enough that I could see her standing where I'd left her, the wind tugging at her shabby blue gown, her eyes squeezed shut, her graceful, capable hand pressed tightly to her mouth. Now I had expended a bit of my rage, I had gained a small part of the clarity I sought. Of all things, I should recognize fear. Perhaps saying the painful words aloud would ease this dread that was gnawing at her generous heart.

"I will not take Evan away from you, Elinor," I called up to her. "Not ever. My son is the only scrap of innocence left in this world, and I would suffer anything to keep him safe and loved and ignorant of the terrors that I know. His mother is dead. He is yours. Now I've given you everything I can. Leave me be."

In the end, I decided that I could not hide the truth from Aleksander, no matter what the painful consequences. Elinor was right. A man embarking on such a course had a right to know the stakes. But I was not going to *tell* him. He would fly into a rage and curse Lydia's stubbornness and contrive some way to avoid the temptation of seeing her. So, late that afternoon, when the Prince found me avoiding sleep in the cool dimness of our hut in the olive grove, and posed the expected question, I carefully sidestepped the answer. "I told her everything, my lord, just as you said it. She didn't take it well."

"Damn her stubborn heart. What did she do?"

"You needn't fear. Her decision is final enough. She's already let Edik know her position." I jumped to my feet and herded him up the path toward Blaise's tent. "Now you and Farrol are done with your business, Blaise is waiting to take us somewhere. I'll explain everything after." Then my duty would be done, and I would take my leave of him.

Our destination was the second of the two hidden valleys—Taíne Horet, Blaise called it. The light was failing as Blaise and Aleksander and I paused high upon its southern wall and looked down on a broad expanse of grassy meadows centered by a small lake. Though rockier and less forested than Taíne Keddar, the valley was thickly settled. From the number of fires popping up in the dusk, it appeared that hundreds of people lived there. Large numbers of sheep and goats grazed the pastures, and we could see at least three distinct settlements.

The largest lay at the western end of the valley. Spread across the rocky meadows were wooden outbuildings and animal pens, while the village itself was tucked into the shelter of three broad, shallow caves in the cliffs of the valley wall. The second settlement lay amid the stands of cedar and olive trees in the eastern valley. Smoke rose from a scattering of wooden houses with roofs of woven branches. An array of large tents pitched on the northern side of the valley, including one expansive tent at the center, composed the third settlement. From that central tent flew a banner wholly unknown to me, a dragon with a serpent in its mouth.

"Taíne Horet is the less hospitable of the two valleys," Blaise told us as we rode the steep narrow trail. "But also the more remote and difficult to find. I explored the region for three days before I flew high enough to discover it. They call this ridge 'the shield wall' and for good reason. You can stand anywhere in Taíne Keddar and swear that there could be nothing behind the cliffs." A slow grin bathed his tired face. "It would have taken you considerably longer to get here if you weren't with me, even if you could have found the path yourselves."

"How long have you had people here?" I said, amazed to see the numbers that made their homes in such a place.

"Well, you see, they are not 'my' people. They settled here long before I came . . . very long indeed. That's why I ask permission before I enter or bring guests. And that's why we must dismount and approach respectfully"—Blaise swung his leg over his gray's back and dropped to the path—"except for you, Lord Aleksander. They will expect to see a Derzhi riding. Their customs are as long held as your own."

Mystified, I dismounted and followed him down the steep trail. As we descended through a jumble of massive red boulders and stunted pines, Blaise and I in the lead, Aleksander behind, we were confronted by three sentries: a brown-bearded Manganar bearing a spear, a Suzaini who carried a curved sword and wore a yellow haffai, and a gangling Thrid youth, who had his bow drawn, an arrow nocked and aimed at my heart.

"Greetings Therio, Vunaz, and . . . is this you, L'Avan? I've not seen you in half a year, lad. I hope you've had good hunting." The sight of Blaise softened the fierce expressions on the three, but their weapons stayed ready as they peered around the outlaw, trying to get a glimpse of who was behind him. "You must have just come on watch. I was here earlier and told M'Assala I'd be back with two others." Blaise gestured at me. "This is my good friend and teacher, an Ezzarian who holds his name private as is their custom. We've brought one for whom you have been waiting a very long time. This, my friends, is Lord Aleksander Jenyazar Ivaneschi zha Denischkar, Firstborn of Azhakstan." Blaise stepped aside and held his hand out toward Aleksander. At their first glimpse of Aleksander, the three wary sentries squared their shoulders, fixed their eyes straight ahead, and raised their weapons, not in threat, but in salute. Aleksander and I exchanged a quick glance of confusion.

"*Aveddi*," said the Suzaini, bowing his head as he spoke. "We are honored beyond telling that this day has come as we stand watch. The old ones will rejoice at your coming."

"Old ones? *Aveddi*?" I whispered to Blaise, watching Aleksander acknowledge the honor done him with a gracious nod and a gesture that clearly invited the sentries to resume their watch.

"You'll see," said Blaise, satisfaction at the exchange of courtesies illuminating his face. I saw then that part of his tiredness had been apprehension at this encounter . . . whatever it was. He started down the path as before, leading his horse ahead of Aleksander. From behind us a powerful voice intoned a chant that pierced the evening air, triumphant, rebounding from the shield wall and the surrounding cliffs, "*Pas maru se fell marischat, Aveddi di Azhakstan.*" I didn't know the language of the Suzaini singer. His echoes still rang across the valley when the Thrid joined in with the same melody, but in his own language . . . and then the Manganar, also in a dialect unknown to me. Their song might have been drawn from the very bones of the earth.

"What do they sing?" I whispered to Blaise.

"They say, 'Comes our defender from out of the desert, the *Aveddi* of Azhakstan.' The Firstborn. It's a chant older than the Empire." Blaise pointed down into the valley. "Those who live here have no use for the Derzhi Empire, but they've been waiting a very long time for one particular Derzhi. I think their wait is over."

Old ones . . . older than the Empire . . . the defender from the desert. Gaspar's stories . . . A glimmer of understanding flared, like the first spark struck in the depths of a cave. "You've taken a great risk, I think."

Blaise wrinkled his long face in wry humor. "Don't say that! I don't know that I would ever have brought him here solely on my own judgment. Your faith is what's persuaded me."

I slowed my steps to let Aleksander catch up with us, thinking to tell him what the singers had said. "My lord, the words—"

"I know." He did not look down at me. Rather his gaze roamed the valley as if he might see the future written in the fire and shadow. "Can you find me some salt? In a hurry? If you would . . . as in Drafa, but three portions." He glanced at Blaise. "Three?" Blaise nodded.

I remembered Aleksander's gift to the old women as we left Drafa, following the ancient Derzhi custom for a noble to give salt to those who sustain him. Even with so little understanding of the night's unexpected ceremony, I suspected that his instinct was correct. So I withdrew into the shadows, wrestled myself into the form of a falcon, and flew off in search of salt. By the time I returned, transformed, and found Aleksander again, he was sitting on the grass with a circle of Thrid, deep in a torchlit grove of cedars.

As I slipped from the shadows to sit behind him, the Prince drained a wooden cup and passed it back to an old Thrid. Blaise was sitting between and slightly behind Aleksander and the old man, translating for them. The talk was of little substance . . . ceremonial greetings and tracings of lineage . . . but as I listened and observed the old man, I realized that he was someone of great importance. I had never seen anyone with so many tattoos. Every mezzit of his dark skin was marked with lines and sworls of ink, even his shaven head. The narrow strip of white cloth wrapped about his loins, his several bracelets and a wide necklace of ivory beads . . . hundreds of beads . . . covered more of the marks. Thrid fathers wore a tattoo for each of their children, and they hoarded their wealth—their legacy for their children—in ornaments of prized ivory. This man clearly had many children . . . or perhaps he was a father to many not born of his body. More than two hundred years had passed since the people of Thrid had fallen under the yoke of the Empire. Was it possible that a Thrid chieftain still lived in exile, here in the heart of the desert?

Wondering, astonished, I almost forgot my errand. But when the old man and Aleksander stood up, I quickly retrieved three small bundles from my pocket—salt cadged from Blaise's quartermaster and tied into small squares of linen torn from his kerchief—and pressed them into the Prince's hand. He snapped his head around and nodded at me. In his bleak face was the first inkling of hope I had seen in half a year.

"*Na salé vinkaye viterre*," he said, opening his hand to the old man. The Thrid took the tiny bundle, smiled, and bowed deeply to Aleksander. *Salt gives life its flavor.*

Aleksander mounted his horse and in the company of Blaise and the old man and at least twenty Thrid, he proceeded slowly across the valley toward the sea of tents. I followed, staying out of the way, watching as the Thrid bade him farewell and a group of young Suzaini came to greet him. The three sturdy warriors, wearing striped haffai, long curling mustaches, and beards woven with red, white, and orange beads, escorted the Prince to the large tent with the unfamiliar banner where waited a powerfully built man of middle age. The man himself was unadorned, save for the beads in his elaborately curled beard, but three white-robed women stood beside him, each of them wearing such a weight of silver that I wondered they could stand. His wives. The three impressive young men who had greeted the Prince were most likely this man's sons. From the deference of the rest of the crowd—those who brought us silk cushions, platters of dates and sweet cakes, and steaming pots of fragrant tea prostrated themselves before our host—the implications began to sink in. This, too, was a man of considerable rank. Was it possible? The Suzaini had been one of the earliest conquests of the Empire, more than four hundred years in the past. After a century of rebellion and resistance, the warlike Suzaini nobility—the palatines—had been exterminated . . . so everyone thought.

Again Blaise served as translator. Aleksander was welcomed to the man's tent, offered refreshment and smoking pipes filled with aromatic herbs. Two hours and thousands of words later, the Suzaini kissed Aleksander on each cheek, bowed, and presented him with his own knife. Aleksander offered him the bundle of salt and the blessing that completed the gift.

After all this, it was no surprise when the Suzaini dignitaries escorted Aleksander to the village tucked into the western wall of the valley. And I could have conjured the image of the white-haired Manganar who stood with a hooded falcon perched on his gloved wrist, waiting to greet the Aveddi. The old man was straight and broad-shouldered, and his long trousers, full-sleeved, knee-length white tunic, and colorful woven belt were exactly thôse that you could see on old tapestries depicting the Manganar tribesmen who had surrendered to the imperial conquerors. All of the Manganar men and women who stood in the circle of firelight wore this most traditional of garb, and with it the *gualar*, the woven, many-pocketed wool garment that dropped over their heads, family identification woven into its colors and patterns. But the broad-shouldered man with the white hair, introduced as Yulai, wore a gualar of pure white, the color that was the combination of all colors, telling us that Yulai's family was the combination of all families. The white gualar was the symbol of the kings of Manganar.

I sat on the rocky ground behind Aleksander as he accepted the hospitality of nazrheel and spiced apples and listened solemnly as Yulai recounted the story of his ancestors' flight from the conquering Empire. Yulai's son, a middle-aged man introduced as Terlach, sat on the old man's right, quietly observing, while a weathered, sweet-faced old woman called Magda sat on his left, pouring the tea and freely interjecting her additions and corrections into the history. A crowd of Manganar men and women sat and stood in a circle around the Prince and old Yulai, listening and laughing and making comments of their own. The hour grew late. The heat of the fire left me drowsy, and as I examined Yulai's falcon, now settled on a wooden perch beside the old man's place, I wondered what it would be like to transform into my falcon's shape and try to speak to the bird. Perhaps it could tell me what all this meant.

Just then, a slight disturbance broke out in the ring of listeners to one side of the old man. A small child ran into the firelight and threw himself first into Magda's arms and then onto Yulai. Yulai rubbed his head affectionately and asked who let him stay up so late. "Mam said," chirped the little boy. "Say 'good dreams,' Goda." *Goda* . . . grandfather.

"Good dreams, little one," said Yulai smiling. "Now off with you."

Yulai set him on his feet and gave him a little shove, but the child was suddenly struck shy by all the people and turned slowly, staring at the ring of smiling folk. Evan. My tongue was poised to beckon him, but in the same moment, he streaked across the grass toward someone across the ring from me. As Elinor gathered him up in her arms, our eyes met, her dark gaze throwing down a challenge I could not interpret. Was Evan's presence an accident, a taunt, a gift? She disappeared into the gathered Manganar, and her posture demanded that I follow her and find out. But I didn't trust myself.

From the moment Catrin had told me about the terrible events in Ezzaria, the sounds and sensations of ordinary life had begun to dull and fade. Ysanne was dead, and to accept that truth would take me no little time. Yet grief had not created this distancing; I had grieved for Ysanne years ago, while we lived together and grew apart. But all through the day just past, my mind had been besieged by visions: of prisons and demons, of the frozen winds of Kir'Vagonoth, of Gaspar and Fessa bound to the tree, of Sovari hanging on the walls of Tanzire, vultures gnawing his entrails . . . and of the Madonai sitting at his game board. The images consumed me, more vivid than the world I walked. And so throughout this magical evening, though immersed in events of historic dimension, I felt no more a part of them than if I were watching Avrel's bees buzzing purposefully about their hive. I didn't belong here anymore. My duty was elsewhere. The only thing that might soften my resolve was my son. I could not allow it. Three young Wardens lay in torment, waiting for me to save them.

I wrenched my eyes back to the fire, and my mind back to the conversation. ". . . received a guest into our house this day, Aveddi," said the old man, beaming. "As is our custom, our guests are treated as our own family, honored and protected as our own sons and daughters, fully sharing in our prosperity or our lacks. I understand that this visitor is of special concern to you, so I wish to reassure you as to my goodwill. You need not fret as you embark upon the course you've chosen."

A puzzled Aleksander nodded politely. "I thank you, Lord Yulai, but—" Whatever the Prince was going to say was lost in that moment, for Lydia appeared just beyond the ring of firelight, leaning on Blaise's arm. She stood behind Magda, among the women and children of Yulai's family. A dark, flowing cloak masked her condition, half hidden as she was in the shifting shadows. Her red curls were piled atop her head, and her pride adorned her as no ornament of gold or silver could have done. But the only color in her face was the rosy reflection of the firelight.

Aleksander stood up slowly. His remarks were addressed to the Manganar, but his words and his eyes were only for Lydia. "Again and beyond all courtesy, I thank you, Lord Yulai. I could ask nothing more . . . nothing more . . . than your shelter and protection for my wife. My only wish has ever been to see her safe, for I love her as holy Athos loves the earth and honor her as the stars give deference to the moon." He did not go to the Princess, constrained, perhaps, by lingering pride or perhaps only by the delicate ceremony of the night, the cascading levels of deference and position and honor, but he held out his hand to her. She tipped her head in cool acknowledgment and stayed where she was. Aleksander flushed and withdrew his hand, bowing stiffly before fumbling at his pocket to pull out the last bundle of salt.

Old Yulai looked curiously from Aleksander to Lydia, but his wife whispered in his ear, and his wrinkled face settled into sympathy. "The hour grows late, Aveddi," he said. "We have much to discuss, but it has waited a number of years and will wait a few hours more. My house is your own this night. My man Daneel will be waiting to show you quarters . . . if you should need him."

Aleksander forced his gaze away from the Princess and presented the bundle of salt to the Manganar, clearing his throat before speaking. To the blessing words he added, "I will be honored to accept your hospitality, King Yulai."

The old king rose and dismissed the assembled friends and dignitaries, and the crowd melted quickly into the night. With a last bow to Aleksander and a kiss of the hand and a kind embrace for Lydia, Yulai and his wife followed their attendants toward the stone houses. Blaise whispered in the Princess's ear, then came to join me. "I think we'll have to leave them to sort it out," he said. "I told her we would wait for a while."

But Lydia would not need our service again that night, nor would Aleksander. The Prince bounded across the ring of firelight toward his wife, but stopped short before crossing the full span of their separation. Instead, he dropped to his knees, bowed his head, and spread his arms. He did not have to wait long for his answer. Lydia stepped out of the shadows and laid a hand on his red hair. Then she reached for his chin and lifted his face to see the wonder that was waiting for him.

"When do you plan to go?" said Blaise quietly as I spun on my heel and walked briskly toward the pond.

"As soon as you can get me there," I said. "I need you to fetch Fiona. Catrin has urgent news for her, and I need to speak with her before I go, learn whatever she can tell."

"I can't do it tonight," he said. "I'm done for. And I would think it well you had a night's sleep, too, before such a journey. But in the morning . . ."

"In the morning," I said.

CHAPTER 27

On the morning Blaise and Catrin and I arrived at Dasiet Homol, the gateway to Kir'Navarrin, I was hearing uncomfortable echoes of the Drafa oracles in my head. Aleksander had yielded everything, stripped himself bare. His powerlessness had indeed transformed itself to strength. Had he also found himself a new kingdom in the desert, as Qeb had envisioned, right when he was setting out to bring down his own empire? And if the boy's seeings proved true, then what of Gaspar's? That was the uncomfortable thought.

To strike terror into the hearts of those you love is a difficult thing, Gaspar had told me. Certainly, Aleksander, Blaise, Catrin, and my acquaintances among the outlaws had feared my madness, but they seemed to have come to terms with it. My horror of what humans could do to each other did not mean I would exterminate them. I intended to stop Nyel's games.

Yet every step toward the line of white pillars that stretched north and south across the hills of southern Manganar increased my feeling of separation from the world I knew. *To give name to the nameless and to stand across the fathomless gulf from the light* . . . I couldn't decide whether the ache in my gut was terror or anticipation . . . and that was profoundly unsettling.

"When did Fiona go to Kir'Navarrin?" asked Catrin, peering through the pairs of towering pillars into a dappled evening very different from the brown noonday in which we sat waiting for Blaise and Fiona. Behind us the ranks of pillars spanned a quarter of a league of dry, rocky grasslands, almost to the southern mountains that marked the boundary of Ezzaria. Though we sat near the northernmost pair, we could see a mirrored image of the pillars before us, set on greener slopes dotted by clumps of trees and ponds that reflected evening light.

I kneaded my scalp, as if my fingers could loosen my thoughts from the dark places where they seemed fixed. Almost two days since I had slept, the night just past no better than the previous day. Every time I dropped off, I had to wake myself again to escape dreams that left me nauseous and shaking. "I think she's been there about six weeks this time," I said. "Blaise first took her through a few months ago. He says she planned to stay longer, but took ill after a few weeks. The rai-kirah know nothing of human diseases, so she came out to visit a healer. A few days at Taíne Keddar, and she was ready to go back. Blaise comes here every few days and opens the way just in case she wants to come out again."

A herd of dune-runners wandered up the hillside to our left, only to take flight when they noticed us, leaping over a dry gully and disappearing over another hill. I pulled flatbread and cheese from a cloth bag and laid them out on the grass, then stared at them as if I couldn't quite remember what they were for. I couldn't stomach the thought of food. My skin was buzzing with too little sleep. My tongue felt thick and my movements awkward, not quite in my control.

"Is she safe?"

"She didn't tell Blaise much—only that she was observing and learning all she could about the rai-kirah and how they live. She claims to feel as safe there as anywhere in this world. There are no monsters. No fighting." Only the danger in Tyrrad Nor, which seemed to span every world.

"All these years, I've worked with Wardens, teaching of portals and walking other worlds. To know that I could do so myself . . ." Catrin's initial astonishment at the opened gateway had settled into bemused observation. Ezzarians had always lived with wonders. "I would probably be disappointed were I ever to go. It couldn't be half so strange as all the things I've imagined. From what we see here, the place seems quite ordinary."

"It's very much like Ezzaria," I said as I peeled a small sour orange and laid it on the cloth bag beside the bread. "A river the size of the Dursk runs just there behind that line of hills, and beyond it a forest of oaks and maples that extends all the way to the mountains—high, snowcapped peaks like those around Capharna and Dael Ezzar. It rains every afternoon in summer. But at night, you would know it's not our world. The starlight is almost as bright as our full moon."

Catrin broke off a piece of bread, but paused before putting it in her mouth. "I thought this was to be your first time through this portal."

"It is." The first time. The important time. The time when everything would change.

She tossed the bread back onto the cloth and laid her hand on my knee. "Seyonne, you're trembling. Tell me why you're so afraid. I told you I'd not run away."

I pulled away. "I don't have time to explain, Catrin. I need to talk to Fiona and get on with this. I'm afraid I've waited too long already. I need to be with him."

"With this demon? I thought he was already—"

"I just need to go." I didn't want to talk about the one who was sitting at his gameboard waiting for me. "Don't keep asking."

I knew I ought to tell Catrin about Nyel. She, whose practical wisdom had kept me thinking straight in the last two difficult years of my warding, might help me make sense of my duties and my future. Yet even at that moment, seeing the world on the brink of chaos and believing that it was Nyel's doing and somehow mine as well, I could not banish the image of the Madonai in his awesome beauty. To speak of such a vision or of my hopes and fears would be akin to running a knifepoint down my belly and pulling open the skin to expose what lay underneath.

Catrin withdrew her hand. "I don't understand it. How can you be so changed, yet still be the man I know?"

"I am *not* the man you knew"—I jumped to my feet and walked to the very brink of the gateway, willing Fiona and Blaise to hurry—"and I never will be again."

At last! Blaise was walking down a dusty white road beyond the gateway in company with a small, sharp-faced young Ezzarian woman wearing men's breeches. Her dark straight hair was cut short, and she carried a pack on her narrow shoulders.

"Master!" Fiona trotted up a short slope and through the pillars, and then took my hands, her solid grip telling me all the things she was uncomfortable expressing in words. She was very thin, even more so than I remembered, and despite the momentary spot of color from her hurry, she was as pale as the pillars themselves. "Is this an illusion or is it truly Mistress Catrin?" she said, raising her eyebrows and tipping her head toward my mentor. "I never thought to see her in company with such corruption as we two."

Fiona might be awkward with sentiment, but she was not shy of her opinions. She had been the plague of my life for more than a year before we began our journey in search of my son and demons and truth. Then she had saved me, first by keeping open a portal during my months of imprisonment in Kir'Vagonoth, and then by snatching me out from under Ysanne's knife, condemning herself to exile from the land where she had thought to be queen.

"She's come for you more than me," I said, forcing a smile and lifting Fiona's heavy pack while she pulled her arms out of the straps. "You only make friends with rai-kirah instead of inviting them to move in." Fiona was the only one I had ever been able to joke with about Denas. Perhaps because she wasn't afraid. When Fiona set her mind to something, even if it was faith in a flawed Warden, she was relentless.

Fiona flopped down beside Catrin, digging a thin leather-bound book and a waterskin out of her pack. She took a long pull from the waterskin, coughing a little as she wiped her mouth and looked up at Catrin. "Why are you here, Mistress? You've ever been one to push the boundaries of obedience, so I understand, but in such a matter as corruption . . . after allowing the Queen to bleed your friend almost to—"

"Tienoch havedd, Kafydda," said Catrin, softly.

"Kafydda?" Fiona's eyes grew wide with disbelief. "I thought that title ceased to have meaning in the same hour the Queen declared that I no longer existed. Or have you forgotten?"

"The Queen is dead."

While a shocked Fiona listened to a brief version of Catrin's tale, I tried to keep myself from interrupting them, from shouting at them that nothing mattered unless I got to Tyrrad Nor with some semblance of my own mind and was able to convince Nyel to stop playing his games. I paced around the fire, the pillars, and the women. *Savor this time*, I told myself. *Listen to the birds, feel the air. Smell the sweetness of the dry grass. An hour from now, you may detest the scent of sage and wild mustard. You may enjoy radishes and bad poetry, ice storms and women who pretend weakness to attract men.* What would it be like to become someone else, to have another's preferences and memories indistinguishable from my own? How would I reconcile conflicting desires? Do I like music or not? Do I run or walk? What is my name? A thousand small battles every hour.

Blaise sat on the grass watching and listening, his arms around his long legs. His patient demeanor was belied by the urgency of a reminder. "We can't take too long to decide who's going where," he said softly, the moment that Catrin ended her story. "It's only two days until the raid on Syra."

Fiona interrupted him with a fit of coughing, deep spasms that racked her small body. "I'll be all right in a few weeks," she croaked, waving off our concern. "I think I've figured out this illness, along with a few other things." She drank from the waterskin, then looked up at me. "So where are you going first? To rescue Drych or to Tyrrad Nor?"

I jerked my head toward the gateway.

She nodded. "Do you have time to listen? I've always planned to go with you on this journey, but now . . ." Her gaze flicked to Catrin.

"You're needed at home," I said, feeling a wave of relief. I didn't want anyone to go with me. "I'm glad they've come to their senses so far as to send for you. What I need to know is whatever will help me in Tyrrad Nor. I just need to understand what I might find there."

"Understanding—I don't think I can help you with that," said Fiona. "I can only tell you what I've seen . . ."

For the next two hours, as the sun on our side of the gateway crept high over the line of pillars, and the sun on the other side yielded to a moonless night, the young Aife recounted her travels in Kir'Navarrin. The rai-kirah had ignored her for the most part, seemingly uninterested in humans now they were home. Once through the gateway, they had dispersed throughout the land, seeking their names, and families, and homes—all the knowledge and memory that had been ripped away along with their physical life when our ancestors decided to split off a portion of their souls from their bodies for fear of the prisoner in Tyrrad Nor.

"Of course, they've not been able to take up their lives as if they'd never been interrupted," Fiona said, "but I would find small groups of them walking together, laughing, talking, swimming in the lakes or crafting boats for sailing, hunting game, feasting, every manner of occupation. Sometimes I would see only their forms of light—radiantly beautiful, just as you described them, Master—and that surprised me, as I thought once they lived in Kir'Navarrin they would shape bodies all the time. A few of them would come and travel with me for a day or two before going on about their business. One named Kryddon, who said he knew you, was especially interested in my studies, as he was trying to do something the same—to understand what had happened to the rai-kirah and why, and to determine how they were going to live in the coming years. They're not recovering quite so fast as they expected, but they're still learning . . ."

Learning was the essence of the matter, of course. The rai-kirah would never regain a true physical existence. Their own bodies were long dead. Their hope had been that by living in the rich and marvelous land of Kir'Navarrin, rather than the frozen wastes of Kir'Vagonoth, their enchanted bodies could satisfy their physical yearnings and reclaim their lost memories.

"Kryddon was very excited that he was close to remembering his name, and even more so because he'd remembered he had a brother named Sirto, and he was off to search for him. And he said to tell Denas . . . you . . . that Vyx was still wrong about fruit and birds. He said you must give them a try when you come and settle the argument once and for all." She grabbed a piece of the peeled orange, popped it in her mouth, and looked up at me, awaiting an explanation.

"They always argued about food," I said, impatient at the digression. "Kryddon and Vyx . . . about what would be worth eating if they could taste what it was really like. Vyx said that roasting birds would be a waste of time, but that roasted fruit would be a delicacy worth savoring. Denas hated it when they talked of such things. He detested being so dependent on flesh to tell him the truth of the world, and despised himself for craving food and sleep and . . . everything. He would prefer to give up eating altogether." As ever, it was strange to speak so of Denas when he was inside of me listening, when we would soon be one being instead of two. "So they're able to use their senses properly when they shape their bodies?"

"So they say. You've given them such a gift, Seyonne. They hold you and Denas in such honor, you cannot imagine it."

"I'm glad things worked out." Good to know that between Blaise and my son and the rai-kirah, something worthwhile had come out of all this, no matter what the future brought.

But Fiona's tale was not done. "I learned all this on my first visit," she said. "Even then Kryddon mentioned that a few of the rai-kirah had stopped looking for their families. Some didn't even seem to be interested in finding their names. He didn't understand it. Names would make them whole, he said, bind their forms of light to forms of flesh so they could truly live."

She leaned forward as if to reinforce her telling. "When I went back a few weeks ago, things had changed a great deal, even in the short time I'd been away. I would walk for days and see no one. Houses sat half built. Fields that had been newly planted were growing wild. Few of the rai-kirah that I did see were wearing bodies, and even their forms of light seemed less . . . substantial. Colors that had been so vivid now seemed pale. I sought out Kryddon again, and found him sitting beside a stream in a meadow, still in his body, but not quite holding it together. Parts of him—legs or face or torso—would shift into light form, but then he would stroke the grass or dip his hand in the stream, and his body would be complete again. I asked if he had found his brother, and he said he wasn't sure. I could scarcely induce him to talk. He had not yet remembered his own name, but he was more worried about the other rai-kirah. Most had decided that physical bodies were too taxing, he said. Sleeping, that's what they didn't like. He was having a hard time with it himself. They would wake up more tired than when they started, therefore many of them had stopped shaping bodies to avoid it. But stopping didn't seem to help anymore. They were all so tired, and some seemed to have disappeared altogether. No one knew where they'd gone."

"He's using them," I said. "Now they have bodies and sleep, he can touch their dreams, too, and being so close to him . . . when they're in this state . . . he wants their strength for himself. Somehow he can take it from them." Fiona looked at me oddly, and I realized I was talking to myself. I was finding it difficult to concentrate on her tale. "What of the prisoner, Fiona? Did they say anything about the one in Tyrrad Nor?"

She shook her head, having to get through another fit of coughing before she could go on. "On my first journey, I asked about it," she said. "Of course I did. No one knew who or what was in the fortress. They weren't even sure where the place was, except that it was high in the mountains beyond the gamarand wood. They wouldn't go into the wood. Said they couldn't remember anything about it, save that it was a holy place, a terrible place, and such things were best left undisturbed until they remembered. But you needed to know, so I couldn't just leave it—"

"You went there!" I crouched in front of her, working to keep from grabbing her shoulders and shaking the words out faster. The woman in green had bade me go to the gamarands.

Fiona nodded, illness and fatigue dismissed in the excitement of her telling. "All during my stay I was trying to find evidence, something to prove or disprove what we thought happened." She spoke to Catrin. "Our ancestors lived in both worlds. The mosaic taught us that. But for some reason that we don't completely understand—something to do with Tyrrad Nor and a prophecy—they decided that it was too dangerous for them to live in Kir'Navarrin any longer. Those who lived here—the builders, we've called them—chose to destroy all their works, so that no one would remember Kir'Navarrin and try to go back. But from what Seyonne was able to tell me, the ones who lived in Kir'-Navarrin on the day the magic was done just walked away from their towns and villages, left their gardens and fields, dropped their tools, left their books open on their tables. I hoped to find some of it—villages, artifacts, artwork, something. But I found nothing save bits of walls and hearths still standing here and there, until I went into the gamarand wood."

She was speaking to me again. "I explored it for days. The feel of that forest . . . I can't describe it. Such a sad place and so beautiful. No signs that anyone ever lived there and no rai-kirah. I was about to give up, when I came on a stone tower, covered so thickly with moss and vines I thought at first it was a tree, huge and impossibly old. But on looking closer, I found stonework under the moss. I've never felt anything like that stone . . . warmer than it should have been and oddly textured . . . almost as if it were alive. But there was no door anywhere, and I thought I would go mad to get inside. Finally I remembered your vision of Vyx pressing himself into the prison wall, and I thought perhaps I had to push myself through it. Three days it took me to work out the enchantment. It took everything I had and a bit more besides, but with words of opening and passage, I eased myself through. Inside the tower, everything was perfectly preserved: furnishings, dishes . . . You must go there yourself. I've drawn a map . . ." She tore a page out of her journal and gave it to me. "It's where they planned it, Seyonne. They sat in a high room in that tower, a room where you can see the peaks of the mountains, and they decided what they had to do. They wrote it down on scrolls of parchment in a language I can't read, but they drew pictures, too, so I could guess what they'd done."

"The split, you mean. Where they planned the split."

"No. Long before that." She opened her book to another page and showed me her sketches of the drawings she'd seen. "Everything was neat and tidy, and the scrolls were laid out on a table with a fresh candle beside them, as if ready for anyone who got through the door spells to examine them. I didn't dare bring them out of the tower; think how old they must be. Seyonne, it's where they planned the prison."

Of course, I recognized what was depicted in the detailed plans. I had walked those ramparts in my dreams. I had explored that garden and touched that bounding wall in my siffaru. Fiona had copied down the text, too, and like Fiona, I was unable to read it. But unlike Fiona, I recognized some of the words. *Madonai, Kasparian*, and *Nyel* were interspersed throughout the text.

"Can you translate this?" asked Fiona, watching me.

"No." I gave it back to her. "Anything else?"

"One more thing," she said. "The strangest of all. High on a shelf, dusty and out of the way, I found a small wooden box. Inside was a cube of black stone about the size of my fist. A word was engraved on it. I'd not have thought one simple word was all that important until I decided to record it with the rest of these things. Seyonne, I couldn't remember it long enough to ink the pen. I'd look at the stone again and repeat the word in my head, but the moment I took my eyes away, it was as if I'd never seen anything. I tried to copy the word blindly, fixing my eyes on the stone, but nothing showed up on the paper. No matter what I tried, I could neither speak nor write nor remember it. So you'll have to look for yourself to see if you can make any sense of that."

Fiona talked awhile longer . . . of encounters with the fading rai-kirah, of her illness that began on setting foot in Kir'Navarrin and worsened each day that she remained, preventing her from any attempt to ascend the massive bulk of the mountain beyond the gamarand wood. She had concluded that humans were not meant to live in Kir'Navarrin, and I knew it was true. Knew it with certainty. Before very long, her narrative trailed off. "You're ready to go, aren't you? Halfway there already, I think."

The three of them were staring at me as I paced in circles

about them, my arms wrapped about my gut as if I were cold or injured, or as if I could hold onto my soul if I could only get a tight enough grip on my body. "He's waiting for me," I said. "I promised him I'd come back. You need to understand about him. He's not what we've thought." The words sounded feeble. Hurried. Meaningless, without the story that went behind them. These three were friends I loved, but they were wasting my time. All my dilemmas and uncertainties and speculations had vanished like windblown smoke. I needed to go.

. . . to stand across the fathomless gulf from the light . . . the one of darkness . . . Oh gods, have mercy, what was I doing?

I stopped my pacing and stepped away from the three of them, and just as if they had fallen off the edge of the world, I no longer sensed their presence. Only the presence waiting beyond the portal was real—the portal and the world beyond it that loomed larger than the landscape around me.

"Seyonne, what's wrong?" The voice might have come from the bottom of a well.

"Who's waiting?"

"Maybe you should stay awhile. Tell us what's happening to you . . ."

Beware, fool! This is the moment of danger! Listen to me . . . With boundless rage, this new voice screamed at me inside my head, smashing through the walls of my enchantments.

Yes, danger. Danger from Nyel's unknown power. But danger, too, from inside myself—my own corruption. Ezzarian tradition taught that allowing a demon into one's soul could cause us to lose the demon war. I had done so, and we had lost. I could not ignore the possibility that all my newfound certainties were wrong. *I cannot listen to you,* I said. *I have important things to do.*

. . . I must remember . . . give me the time . . . we need to know . . . yield to me . . . give way. You will prevail in the end. This soul is yours and will ever be. Yield.

I cannot yield, I said. *I can't take the chance*. I needed all of myself for this venture. *We'll remember what's needed*, I said. *If you question, I'll find the answers*. I forced Denas silent once again . . . for the last time, I hoped.

Only one last thing to say, one matter of importance dredged up from the fading remnants of my past life like a gemstone dug out of the sand. "Tell Aleksander I didn't want to wake him this morning. Tell him . . . my faith is stronger than ever. I believe he will change the world."

"Seyonne, wait!"

"Stop him!"

With a sweep of my hand, I batted away their feeble attempts to stay me. Instead, I turned away from everything I knew and walked into the land that was my true home.

CHAPTER 28

I stepped past the first pair of pillars. The fury in my head fell quiet, as when a storm passes overhead. I braced for the onslaught beyond the eye. Nothing. I kept walking.

Past the second pair. The night was warm and profoundly still. No stirring of wind or night bird's cry. No creature rustling the grass. No rai-kirah anywhere that I could detect. Above me sprawled a dome of stars, an array so brilliant that the shadows of the pillars lay across the white dust of the path as sharp-edged rectangles.

When would it begin? With every step between the ranks of white pillars I expected it . . . the fire, the pain, the struggle for control, the horrifying certainty of invasion.

By the time I had traversed the length of the gateway, through the sixty pairs of pillars that were the reflection of the ranked columns in the human world, the smudge of light that marked the portal was no longer visible behind me. Before me, the silent countryside was bathed in starlight. Stands of gigantic trees in full leaf stood here and there, absolutely still in the silvered light, as if their very growth was suspended for the time. The ponds that lay in the hills and meadows might have been breeding pools for stars.

I stepped past the last pair of pillars. Still nothing.

I gazed out across the rolling landscape, yet every sense was turned inward. What was my name? *Seyonne, of course*. No hesitation. No confusion.

How old was I? *Thirty-eight*. Could that be all?

Who was my family? *Gareth, a gentle man who loved books, a tenyddar, required to work the fields of Ezzaria because he had no melydda, slain by a Derzhi sword on the day I became a slave. Joelle, a Weaver, the powerful protector of our settlement in southwestern Ezzaria, dead of fever when I was twelve. Elen, bright and loving elder sister, dead, too, struck down too young as she tried to defend our land from the invading Derzhi . . .*

Slowly, carefully, I released my breath. Despite the warm night, I shivered as would a man afflicted with ague. My palms were dripping—blood, not sweat as I discovered when I unclenched my fists and examined my hands. My own hands. I could tell the tale of each scar: the knuckle graze from a slip of my first knife, the ragged tear made by a razor-edged dragon wing in a long-ago demon combat, the callused ridges about my wrists from slave rings, and now these bleeding gouges made by terror . . . My scars. My tales. My blood. Mine . . .

. . . yet truly, there was more.

Beyond the pools and grassy hills, a dense forest stretched before me to the horizon. The river beyond the forest was called the Serrhio—the Bone River—because of its white rocks. The mountains beyond the river were called Zethar Aerol, the Teeth of the Wind. At one time, this path of crushed white stone beneath my feet had led . . . where? A town? No, more like a village, yet not even that. We hadn't clustered together like humans, but had spread our houses throughout the countryside, for we could travel easily—fly, if we wished—to find anything or anyone we needed. We, the rekkonarre who made our home in this land. Knowledge of the world I walked was neither wrenched from reluctant hands nor yielded grudgingly to serve a common need. Mine, too, these things.

Just above the western horizon was a pattern of ten stars, the Harper we had called it in my youth—not my time of growing in Ezzaria, but seasons spent here. I had always been fascinated by the stars, and in the space of five minutes, I named fifty of them and located the wanderers: the blue Carab, seen only in autumn, and Elemiel, red companion to the sun, showing itself only near sunrise and sunset, and Valagora, the brightest object in the sky next to the moon itself—the larger moon that existed here in Kir'Navarrin, my home. I knelt down at the edge of the path and scrabbled feverishly in the thick grass until I could scrape up a handful of dirt. I squeezed my hand around it and inhaled its rich aroma, evoking an inner understanding that told me I was three days' walk from home . . . and anger rose from my depths and thundered through my veins like the spring torrents from off the mountains. Lost for so long in the dark and frozen wasteland, deprived of the dome of stars, of this sweet-scented earth . . . so much lost . . . stolen . . . torn away in fire and jasnyr smoke. I had never wanted to believe that we were bound to flesh . . . despicable, cowering, always hungering flesh—

I wrenched my thoughts away from this uncomfortable path, emotions that had entwined themselves in my blood and bone. What was my name? *Seyonne*. Who was my family? *Gareth, Joelle, Elen, Ysanne, who had been Queen, Evan-diargh—dead, all of them dead, save the child who was dead to me for I had given him away . . . and . . .* No further answer came to me. Good. *Knowledge is welcome. Nothing more*. But I hungered for more, like a beggar who arrives at last at the alms gate, only to hear the bar falling into place inside the door.

So, make the best of new knowledge. I needed to plan my course: go to the gamarand wood and investigate its mysteries, find the rai-kirah and discover why their life was failing, learn anything and everything that might help me understand the one I had come here to face. Why was I the only one who could free the prisoner in the tower? Why was I so sure that I could moderate Nyel's hatred, when I knew so little of its cause and so little of his power? He could not be trusted. What was the nature of his prison—the wall and the gamarand wood? The answers I craved were waiting for me here—and power, such melydda in this land, flowing into me with every breath, every step, through every sense, its force building like a dammed-up river . . . waiting . . .

So, what might I already know of the danger in Tyrrad Nor . . . I, who remained Seyonne, yet knew more than Seyonne? Gingerly, I pushed open the doors of remembrance. I knew everything of life in Kir'Vagonoth, of my thousand years of bitter exile, but beyond that, from the time before the split, the time here in my . . . yes, *my* own true life . . . very little. A few names, a few images unrelated to my fundamental questions. We had traveled the ways as Blaise did. We favored unleavened bread. Those who lived in the far north raced wind boats that skimmed the surface of frozen lakes. A child's naming day was in his twelfth year of life. No answers. No stores of knowledge about Nyel or the prison or prophecies or reasons. What I found were the scraps and castoffs left behind in a herdsmen's camp when the people had long moved on.

Disconcerting. Perhaps I was still holding back, masking the important things in my fear of the demon-joining. Tentatively, carefully, not daring to believe that I had passed the moment of greatest danger, I relaxed the internal barriers. Silence. Stillness.

No raging demon. No hidden knowledge of Tyrrad Nor. No answers. Whatever remained of Denas was already a part of me. Everything else was lost. I knew what Gordain must have felt when he first woke to see the void where his leg had once been.

I struck out across the hillside through grass as high as my knee and down a slope toward one of the pools. My throat felt like sand. I dropped to my knees and dipped my hands into the still water, swirls of blood disturbing the pure reflection of the stars as I scooped out great handfuls of water and doused my fevered head and poured it down my throat. Only as I tasted the flat metallic trace of blood in the water did I think of what I was doing . . . washing my bloody hands directly in the pond and drinking the same water . . . forbidden by Ezzarian law for a thousand years lest we come to revel in the taste of blood and filth and thus allow a demon into our souls. I yanked my hands out of the pool, and as the ripples settled, my face came into view, a dark reflection that blocked out a portion of the stars. Nervous, apprehensive, yet driven to discover what I had become, I peered into my own eyes, using my Warden's sight to look past the blue fire and into the darkness beyond. Into the abyss . . .

I started laughing then, wrapping my arms over my head and pressing my forehead to the cool grass. The truth was waiting there inside me. Vainly I tried to retreat, to force my mind back to the world I had just abandoned, to forge a stronger link that might hold me to my purpose. But my own investigations would have to wait. Nyel was reaching for me even now, my eyes and thoughts drawn to him as a blooming flower bends to face the sun.

You said you would come back to finish our game. Are you ready? The voice was everywhere—inside, outside, in my mind, in my ears—the voice of my dreams.

Of course not, I said, kneeling on the silver-kissed grass, as the tide of inevitability swept me onward. *Who could ever be ready to game with a god?* Not I, whose prideful resolve to save the world on my own terms had left me vulnerable to his seductions. Whose very strength had played into my enemy's hands. While struggling to bind Denas, I had allowed Nyel to take such a grip on my heart and mind and soul that to deny him would tear me asunder. I could no more refuse his summons than I could cut off my own hand.

He laughed, not unkindly. *Come, then, and we will talk awhile before we play.*

I folded my arms across my breast and transformed, then flew across the dark and silent land to Tyrrad Nor. He was waiting on the ramparts of the night, as I had always known he would be.

CHAPTER 29

"Did you sleep well?" The cool, damp tartness of a fall morning poured through the open doors and windows as I walked into the room and Nyel raised his glass to me.

"I appreciate your indulgence of a night without dreams," I said, selecting a cup of fragrant tea from a sideboard laden with every delicacy that one might desire for a morning meal. We were in the same room as before—the high-ceilinged room with the tall windows overlooking the garden, the mantelpiece carved in the form of man and woman, and the game board set before the cheerful fire . . . waiting for me. "I had forgotten what it was like to really sleep."

"Now you are here, I can converse with you face-to-face. In the meanwhile, I had to make my points as best I could. You were so everlasting slow in coming back."

His pique had shown more forcefully at his initial greeting, when my feet had touched the ramparts on the previous night. This morning his chiding was more of a reminder than a reproach, a positioning, setting the groundwork for our relationship. He was feeling more expansive and satisfied on this morning. I was here. That's what he had wanted all along.

"Several matters needed my attention," I said. "An inordinate number of problems have cropped up everywhere of late."

"And still you lay these problems at my feet."

I watched his deep, clear eyes, so striking in his gray-bearded face. He knew very well of my beliefs and my hopes . . . and my fears . . . all so foolishly revealed in our first encounter. I would have to do better at keeping my counsel. "I stand here drinking your tea. I wear no weapon."

Indeed my own weapons and the grimy clothes I had stripped off the previous night had vanished before morning. I had waked in the vast bedchamber to find a copper tub of delightfully hot water sitting ready in a patch of sunlight. For the first time in months I could enjoy myself by getting thoroughly clean. But gnawing disdain for such self-indulgence, as well as impatience to get on with whatever my host had in mind for me, spoiled my pleasure and had me out of the bath quickly. Laid out on my bed were linen undergarments, dark breeches and hose, a silk shirt of forest green, and vest and boots of pale leather as soft as a child's cheek, even a dark green ribbon to tie back my wet hair. And beside the clothes lay a sword and a dagger and a wide leather belt with beautifully tooled sheaths for each weapon. The sword was fine—a long, tapering blade of gleaming steel, a comfortable and elegant grip of metal rings, suitable for one or two hands, and a simple rounded pommel, substantial enough to balance the long blade. The guard was slightly curved, and both pommel and guard were chased with silver in a pleasing pattern of vines and leaves. The dagger was similar, simple in design, perfect in balance and edge. I did not strap them on. To wield a weapon of Nyel's giving would surely be an act of significance that I could not yet fully comprehend. Best to leave them where they lay. And, indeed, who were they to be used on?

Nyel answered that question without my asking. "Of course, you have no need for swords and daggers here. But knowing how you value your training for your human enterprises, I thought you might enjoy superior weapons," he said, taking up a plate of bread and sausage and carrying it to a table that sat beside the open doors to the garden. His evocation of the word "human" carried only a modest level of disgust. "Come now. Eat. Share my hospitality, and then we'll have Kasparian come and show you about my fortress. I'd like to think you'll stay for a while. Learn. Listen. And only then decide on your future . . . and mine. I've been waiting a very long time for you."

"Until we resolve our differences I have nowhere else to be." For myself, I was not feeling particularly expansive. "However, I would appreciate a quick resolution."

"Quick, eh?" Nyel stabbed a knife into a sausage and examined it before taking a bite off the end. "And when you've done with the lunatic Madonai, you think to go back to your human master and serve him again? Be his instrument of war? Save him from the consequences of his own human—Ah!" He tossed his knife and its savory burden onto his plate. "Not a good beginning. I told you we would talk first."

I took up a slice of smoked fowl, three oatcakes, and a handful of strawberries and joined him at his table. "I'll answer your questions when you answer mine," I said. "The only difficulty is choosing which one to ask first. Something about three imprisoned Wardens in Kir'Vagonoth, or the assassination of an Emperor, or perhaps an inquiry related to the homecoming of the rai-kirah, who are not finding Kir'Navarrin to be a long-lived solution to their problems. They're afraid to sleep. You *do* know they've come back here?" I dived into the food as if I were in no hurry for answers. Posturing. We might have been boys strutting our wooden weapons before each other. Only his had a steel edge, I feared, while mine was but bark and splinters.

He grimaced and ran a thumb over his knife hilt. "All right, all right. Fair enough." Though I kept my attention on my breakfast, I felt his old young eyes linger on my face for a while before settling to his plate. I experimented to make sure I could still breathe after the pressure of his scrutiny. He picked up his knife and cut off another bit of his sausage, but toyed with it instead of eating. "I think I used up all my stores of polite conversation a very long time ago," he said gruffly. "With so much to say between us, so much to learn, to teach, to understand, I find it difficult to speak of the weather—which looks to be fair until late today—or the food, which, as you see, is nothing remarkable."

"Everything here is remarkable," I said, finishing off my unremittingly bland but quite adequate meal. "My own presence not least of all. Before you do with me as you will, I would like to understand the fundamental question. Why am I here?"

"I told you before—"

"—that I alone had the power to set you free. That's what you said."

"And it's true." The sausage might have been stuffed with diamonds, for the intense attention he was giving it. Subtlety, it seemed, had gone the way of polite conversation.

"But that *was* not and *is* not the answer to the question," I said. "Your aim is not to be free. You would never have allowed me to see your hand in the world if that was your objective. Somehow you've caused these horrors, and you've made them live in my mind until I forbid myself to sleep, until I've begun to see them before my eyes every minute of every day. You've infected me with your own madness, so that I can't even remember which of the vile deeds were my own, but I know that in the past few months, I have done things I would once have considered reprehensible." Elinor had seen it, and Catrin, and Aleksander, and they had tried to tell me that I was not the man they knew. "Three worlds are on the brink of chaos," I said, "and I believe you are responsible. You know I cannot and will not share your hatred of humans, and so I could never set you free—not feeling as you do. I must assume that I'm here for some other reason."

A gust of wind through the open window flapped the long draperies and toppled a vase of flowers that sat between us, spilling a puddle of water that raced for the edge of the table and dribbled onto the patterned carpet. Nyel picked up the flowers and threw them out of the window. "So you will force me to say it before you could possibly understand." He leaned back in his chair and folded his arms tightly across his chest. "Laugh if you will. I want to give you a gift."

I was a very long way from laughter. He looked away quickly, but I had already seen the welling tears. Not for the long-dead Madonai. Not for Kir'Navarrin. Not for freedom lost or a wasted life. His tears were for me. My bones and blood ached with his grief, as if they understood truths that my mind did not. I was at a loss, all my anger, fear, and resolution made insignificant in an instant. "Tell me, Nyel—"

"Since you're so impatient to know everything and be away from here, we'll get on with it," he interrupted brusquely as he reached for a slab of bread and began spreading butter on it. "Go fetch Kasparian. Straight back from the main doors and then down the gray stair into the heart of the castle, and you'll find him in his workroom practicing his sword work. Tell him I need his hand. Go on, then." He took a huge bite and waved me off, keeping his eyes on his food.

I rose, bowed, and left him, more confused than ever.

The castle was larger than it appeared from the outside and quite beautiful throughout. The furnishings were spare and elegant like Nyel himself. The staircases were wide and graceful, the rooms large, with high ceilings and tall windows to let in light and air. Clerestory windows of colored glass gleamed in the morning sun, casting jeweled beams of red and blue and green about the vast spaces. Tyrrad Nor was not a fortress built to repel an enemy or punish a criminal, but a palace to house a lord. Its rooms were crafted with care and comfort in mind, and its defenses were not thick walls and arrow slots, but pervasive enchantments. I was not a ghost this time, and though distracted with the mysterious emotional interchange just ended, I could feel the thrum of power in the air like the charge before a thunderstorm. As a matter of curiosity, while I paused and gaped at a lovely sculpture garden that extended as far as I could see to right and left, I cast a small enchantment. A soft breeze stirred the flowered vines that hung from pillars and trellises, wafting the scent of roses and lilacs past my nose. No alarm bells rang at my working sorcery within a prison built to contain it. No one came running. No doom fell upon me.

I walked on through another passage that opened onto a well-stocked library and a music room furnished with harps and viols, with gleaming brass horns of every size hanging on the walls, and a silver flute laid carefully on a brass music stand, not stacked and jammed in boxes and shelves as in the cluttered rooms of my palace in Kir'Vagonoth, but arranged neatly, ready for use by someone who knew what they were. Five broad, red-tiled steps led me downward into a vaulted cloister that skirted a fountain court, and just beyond it, I found a wide gray stair spiraling downward. The passage seemed to lead down under the castle, so I was surprised to find it funneling me toward an arched glare of sunlight. Caution aborted further exploration and held me in the shadowed passage, for I heard the unmistakable clash of steel—at least three swords beyond the arch. Harsh breathing. Muttered curses. A muffled groan. A grunt of triumph. I peered around the brick pillar.

One man sprawled facedown on the fine gravel of a sun-drenched courtyard. You didn't need to see the white ribs exposed by a gruesome wound to know that he was dead. Casting grotesque shadows on the whitewashed walls, two other swordsmen circled in deadly combat—one of them the tall Madonai, Kasparian. A thick-set, leather-clad man swung ferociously at Kasparian, only to have his blow aborted in shivering power by the Madonai's blade. In one smooth motion Kasparian brought his heavy sword around swiftly into an upward counter-cut, striking at the swordsman's weak side before the man could set up an effective guard. Blood welled from a gash in the man's side. Only because he had staggered off balance from the abrupt end of his own forceful attack did he avoid losing an arm to Kasparian's strike. He recovered quickly and came after the Madonai again, his face a mask of dour certainty, not yet ready to yield to sure defeat, leading Kasparian into another exchange that left the Madonai bleeding heavily from his left arm.

The two of them were masters of the art. With maneuvers devoid of excess movement or posturing, they stepped smoothly from one brutal closure to another, until a sweating Kasparian took advantage of his adversary's overextended stance and swept a cutting blow that came near severing the man's thigh. The swordsman cried out and toppled to the ground.

Kasparian kicked the man's sword away, turned his back on his fallen opponents—the one already dead and the one quickly bleeding out his life—and began to wipe the blood from his long, wide blade with a gore-smeared cloth. Before I could blink, the dying man had pulled out a dagger and, against every possibility, raised it high and let it fly toward Kasparian's back. Incapable of judging right or wrong in the combat, I cried a warning, sure it would come too late, but Kasparian swung around and blocked the flying weapon with his half-cleaned sword. The dagger glanced off the blade and spun through the sunlight . . . and vanished before it touched the ground, as did the blood-soaked victims. The explosion of power almost knocked me off my feet.

"They were enchantments," I said aloud, though it was for my own enlightenment I spoke, certainly not his. "Creations, like the servants."

Kasparian looked me over and snorted in contempt. "You are as blind as you are weak." He went back to his cleaning.

"Nyel bids you come," I said.

The big man carefully wiped the crevices beside the guard and sheathed his weapon. Another mystery. The blood did not vanish with the corpses. These "creations" were not wholly illusions, then. "He's taking you out already?"

"Taking me out?"

"It's not my place to explain." He stripped off his bloodstained shirt and threw it to the dirt, then doused his head and arms and shoulders with water from a spewing fountain set into one wall of the courtyard. When the blood was washed from his left arm, only a thin scratch remained of his severe wound.

"I should think your place would be whatever you please after what you've done," I said, even while staring at his arm. How many times over could I have used such healing power. "You've given your life to serve—"

He spun on his heel and grabbed the front of my shirt, pulling me to within a hand's breadth of his face. "Do not tell me what I've given, human spawn!" he said. "You can have no concept of it—even now that you have taken on this broken remnant of a true being. I never had any use for you before, and now you come here in this mockery and I am expected to give way to you. I, a Madonai, his *attellé*. I would trade five thousand lifetimes in this prison for one moment's freedom to repay your treachery."

"Take your hand off me," I commanded, knowing with unexplainable surety that to react less severely to Kasparian's insolence would be to invite yet another danger I was ill prepared to face.

Droplets of water fell onto his fiery cheeks from his gray-streaked hair, rolling down into his mustache and beard. He was a portrait of fury, unless you looked close enough to see the pain in his eyes. Nyel's gift, whatever it might be, was not for him, nor were the old Madonai's tears. And I, ignorant of his grievance, did not even know enough to say I was sorry.

He shoved me away and snatched a tan shirt that hung on a peg embedded in the wall. With long strides he led me out of the sunny courtyard, throwing the garment over his wide shoulders. *I know him*, I thought, with quick, confusing insight, *the "I" that is not Seyonne*.

I also noted that, as soon as we walked into the shadowed passageways, the sunlit arch behind us was transformed into a very ordinary doorway with a dim and cavernous room beyond it. Was the courtyard no more real than the combatants? The blood had not vanished, though.

Nyel was waiting at the game board. "I told you he would come, old friend. Your doubts are proved unworthy."

Kasparian bowed stiffly. "So he has shown willingness to consider your offer?" He had not behaved so formally on my ghostly visit. This tension between the two was new.

Nyel fingered the obsidian king that sat well defended in one corner of the board. "I thought to show him first . . . one venture . . . and then explain more fully. How can he choose without seeing? You will assist me yet again, good Kasparian?" This question bore so much more than words—the essence of Kasparian's grievance. I was right in the middle of it and had no hint of the reason.

"I am ever yours to command, my lord."

Nyel nodded graciously, offering Kasparian dignity, if not the substance of whatever it was the big Madonai craved. Kasparian pulled a third chair close beside the table, facing the fire, as Nyel waved me to the empty seat opposite him. "Come, lad. Don't be nervous. I'm not going to corrupt you further. Perhaps you'll have a new view of matters before we've done. I am prevented from wielding power on my own—a condition of my confinement—but I was left one source of amusement. As you've guessed."

"Dreams," I said, lowering myself to the wooden chair opposite Nyel and to the right of Kasparian, all speculation as to these undercurrents erased by the promise of enlightenment. "You can shape dreams."

"My jailer was intelligent enough to realize that to live a Madonai's full lifetime without any contact with the world was cruelty far beyond death. And he was never cruel . . ."

Nyel's eyes were so deep and so dark—blue and black become one rich color—that as I sought for understanding, I felt myself sinking into their depths, cold and clear as blue-black water, engulfing me . . . The room, the fire, the daylight fell away behind me. I had no sense of danger, or perhaps it was that every breath of my life was fraught with danger in that hour and this journey was nothing different. If I was to learn, then I had to let Nyel show his hand. This was the path I had chosen . . . *for good or ill, for death or life*, Gaspar had said.

And so I let him take me deeper yet, the icy touch of the dark water on my skin pricking my senses awake . . .

. . . A blast of bitter wind almost tore my fingers from the edge of the cliff. The clouds were on top of me, ragged, ripped with the wind and lightning. If it began to rain, I would be done for. Slowly, my shoulders on fire, I hoisted myself up . . . one mezzit . . . two . . . A bit more and I could risk moving one hand, reaching for the stump of twisted pine just beyond the rim. My broken legs dangled in useless agony into the chasm . . . no help there . . . Every breath was a fiery lance. The howling from below me . . . oh, holy gods, they were waiting for my fall . . . don't look down . . . don't listen . . . The wind blew dirt in my face, wafting the stench from below . . . devouring the last of the light . . . Another gust . . . tugging at my dead legs. Hurry . . . Fingernails ripped . . . a slip . . . the dirt so loose . . . spatters of rain . . . A glimpse downward where the howling grew louder . . . triumphant . . . The pits . . . the abyss . . . pain unending . . . dark-

ness unyielding . . . forever. The dirt began to crumble beneath my hands. The stump of pine shifted farther away. I clawed at the earth. No! Oh, holy mother, please don't let me fall. I'll go mad in the darkness . . .

"Go on, lad . . . help him. It's what you wanted to do instead of coming here." The urgent voice drew me out of the vision. My hands still trembled, the wind still whined, and the howling still had my blood cold, but I could no longer feel the loosening edge of the cliff. "And well you should help, knowing that your own people have caused his torment. They sent him to this place. They caused this war for fear of me and have resisted the truth all these years, making matters worse, sending the poor Gastai back to Kir'Vagonoth over and over until they went mad from it."

"What is this place?" I said, my voice shaking with the fear and pain of the desperate man as I watched the wind whip the crooked pine. "What's happening? What do I do?"

"Summon your power. Become his waking shadow. My jailer has bound me to this fortress, and so I can only observe and speak and counsel. This boy needs no counsel. He needs your hand, your strength, your care. He is on the verge of yielding his soul, and you, of all men, know these pitiful creatures that hunger for him. Do not condemn him to this perverse joining. Use the power you have been given."

I struggled with confusion, half in, half out of the vision. "This is someone's dream."

"A poor prisoner's dream. One of your own. You can help him, fight for him, take him where he never thought to go. But with caution always. It is so easy to break a mind if you reveal too much of yourself. Exactly as you learned in your training; those you helped never could know that a battle had been fought in their soul."

One of my own—a Warden in the pits of Kir'Vagonoth, clinging to his soul, dreaming his last dream of light. If I could help him . . .

"Set loose your power. To save him you must give all of yourself . . . no holding back . . . no allowing fear to cripple you as you have done in the past . . ."

With no more idea what I was doing than a youth pursuing his first love, I summoned my melydda . . . and unleashed the flood.

My power had been building since the moment I stepped through the pillars of Dasiet Homol, and the torrent surged through my body and soul, through limbs and loins and heart, such grandeur, such harmony, such glory at my beck that I cried out with the awe and joy of it. I was newborn in that moment, a being of power who could live in dreams, who could cross the boundaries of worlds with my thoughts, who could shape enchantments so glorious as to burst the heart.

This is but the beginning, lad. You are still bound to earth and flesh, but I can set you free. If you but say the word, everything will be yours as was ordained from the beginning of time.

I would hear him. But I had things to do that could not wait. I closed my eyes, touched my power, and embraced the Warden's fading dream.

CHAPTER 30

"Take my hand," I said, stretching out as far as I could manage on the clifftop. "I won't let you fall." Through the murk I could see only his pain-filled eyes and the hands that clawed at the crumbling earth. "It's all right. I'm here to help you." Yellow lightning split the growing darkness, and the ground shook with thunder as the clouds released the deluge. "We'll get you out of this." With one more extension, I touched his fingers. A flare of hope in his despair and he lunged upward, catching my finger-tips just as I clamped my left hand on his wet wrist and heaved. "Now, hold on tight," I said, gritting my teeth against the pull of his weight. He held . . .

. . . and I opened my eyes to frigid darkness.

What expression of words or images can conjure a moment of perfect horror? No matter what the mind's true voice professes, when you smell and feel, taste and see the stuff of your worst nightmare, it is difficult to believe you are not living it. Absolute darkness. Bitter cold. The stench of human blood and waste, and the acrid residue that torture leaves on unwashed skin. A floor that has no more substance than the unyielding midnight en-veloping body and soul. For one terrible instant I believed that the past year had been but a delusion and that I was still captive in the pits of Kir'Vagonoth. But then I felt someone beside me, sobbing quietly in the darkness. I recognized that anguish: the hopelessness of pain that never eased, of feeling reason guttering like the flames of a spent candle.

"Don't be afraid," I whispered, laying one hand on his hud-dled back and another on his arm to keep him from scrambling away in shock. His skin was cold and damp with sweat, and he was quivering like a frightened animal. "I've come to get you out."

"Who's there? I dreamed . . ." A trembling hand touched my arm, then recoiled sharply. "No one there. No one. A trick aren't you? The devils' trick." Through the palpable darkness, I felt him retreat into himself and begin rocking back and forth—the prisoner's comfort and the madman's. "I won't tell you anything. Do as you will." Even in this dreadful place, I could smile. I recognized the voice and the determination. Drych.

"Hush, stubborn lad, I'm no trick. Seems you're not an easy man to kill. Last time I saw you, we were in another vile predicament, but we both survived it."

The rocking stopped, and soon I felt the cold hand again, fumbling about my shoulder and then my face, until it rested on my left cheekbone, where I wore the Derzhi scar. "Master . . . is it you? Oh, gods, please be real . . . oh, holy gods . . ."

"It's all right," I whispered, gathering the trembling Drych into my arms as if I could shield him from one more moment of fear and pain if I could but get enough of myself around him. "I'm quite real, I think, though some questions remain as to how I got here. Can you walk?"

"N-not sure." His teeth chattered so violently he could scarcely speak. The pits were buried beneath the surface of Kir'-Vagonoth, not so bitter as the windy landscape above, but carved from ice, nonetheless, with no scrap of softness or comfort to ease the brutal cold.

"Let's get you on your feet." I draped his arm across my shoulders and hauled him up. A quickly muffled cry told me that his injuries were not confined to his dreams, but I dared not cast a light to examine him or keep him one moment longer in that place. I had no idea of how long I could remain with him on this magical journey or what power I might possess to fend off his captors.

"This way," I said, steadying him as we walked, using my senses and the memories I had inherited from Denas to choose our direction through the stinking nothingness, trying to ignore the surety of demons lurking nearby. We climbed a short sloping way, and I soon felt a hard surface beneath my feet, rather than the formless uncertainty of the pits.

To walk out of the pits of the Gastai was no easy matter for either the demons or their unlucky prisoners. You could wander forever, yet have strayed no more than ten paces from where you'd begun unless you had been told the secrets of the ever-changing passages . . . or happened to be the one who had devised the confusions of enchantment that kept the mad ones locked away. And so I had done in my thousand-year exile, trying to protect my people from their degenerate brethren—I who had made my home in Kir'Vagonoth, not I who had been imprisoned here.

My head came near splitting from the effort of thinking in such ways. How stupid, attempting to keep separate all the memories that insisted on jumbling themselves together. Though I had given Denas no time to remember his life before the split, all his knowledge and experience of this world lay at my beck. Become part of me at the moment of our initial joining, a thousand years were mine every bit as much as my childhood in Ezzaria or my years of bondage to the Derzhi.

Piercing howls like the cries of the zhaideg, the desert scavenger wolf, broke out behind us. Drych faltered, moaning softly and sinking toward the ground, trying to shrink into a knot. "They'll not have you," I whispered, gently forcing him up again, trying to move him faster through the dark emptiness as the soul-shriveling noise grew close. "I swear to you."

A quarter of an hour of hard going and I sensed a solid wall looming in front of us. I felt my way along it, searching the brittle edges and rough joinings for the exact spot, speaking the finding words until the cold stone gave way beneath my hand and we almost fell into a narrow passage. I urged Drych deeper into the warren until the hunting cries grew faint again, and we came to the seal of power that kept the first door hidden from those confined to the pits.

"Close your eyes. No one can see us here, so I'm going to make a bit of light." Only a little, lest I sear his eyes, deprived of light for so many months. The muted gray gleam illuminated a small, circular chamber hewn from ice and stone. Drych leaned against one wall, his head bent almost to his knees, fighting to get enough air while taking only the shallowest of breaths. His emaciated body was bruised and crusted with filth, blood seeping from deep lacerations on his face and back and chest. Claw marks, it appeared. One eye was scarred shut—burn scars—and he held his left arm clamped tightly to his body.

"Two others," he said between gasps, his good eye squeezed shut. "Don't know where. Or even if they're living. Demons tried to make me tell their names. I might have done it; gods forgive me, I don't even know."

"You've done your best. You've not yielded your own name, so I would guess you've not yielded anyone else's, either."

"Olwydd is so young, Master, barely nineteen." Drych himself was no more than twenty-three, though he must be feeling as old as time itself, I knew, after half a year in the pits. "I heard him screaming long ago. Ages ago. Such horrid screams." Tears rolled from his closed eye, streaking his filthy cheek. "I don't think he could be alive."

Damnable dilemma. The howling, though distant, had not stopped, and I well knew the dreadful vengeance the mad demons would inflict on any remaining prisoners. Yet, since I could not understand the terms of my presence or the method of my departure, I dared not risk vanishing before helping at least one of them out. If safety was to be found in Kir'Vagonoth—and despite my swearing, there was no assurance of that—then I'd best get Drych to it. "I'm going to take you out of here first," I said. "Find you some help. Then I'll try to come back for the others. If I can't do it, it will be up to you, as soon as you're able." Of course, first I had to make sure I remembered how to get *anyone* out of the pits.

The chamber appeared to have no doorway save the one we had come in. But I knew another opening existed, one that led to a steep stairway and into yet another chamber with a portal to the outside world. *Concentrate . . . think . . . remember . . . back to the time when you finally realized that the mad ones could no longer be allowed to roam free and you shaped this place . . .* I traced the threads of memory until I found the right words, and then, with a surge of melydda, I unmasked the seal, a tangle of frosted light set into a frame of ice twice my height. To my dismay I found the seal in tatters—the traces of colored light thin and faded, the enchantments weak or broken. Any of the villainous Gastai who had a dram of sense remaining would be able to walk right through the door. And where were those who should have been maintaining it, the healthy rai-kirah who had volunteered to stay behind and guard this passage? Another job to do before I left Kir'Vagonoth: seal this opening and find someone to guard it. But first things first.

"Come on, then. Just a little more and you can rest." I got Drych up the steps and into another chamber, quite like the last, save for a raised black square of stone in its exact center. "Hold onto your stomach," I said, taking firm hold of the flagging Warden and getting him onto the black stone. "This will be a bit unsettling."

At my invocation—a demon word that meant "proceed"—we were plunged into a nauseating blur of whirling gray. I pushed forward ten difficult paces. With the eleventh, Drych and I stepped into a snowy wilderness. A blast of frigid wind laced with sleet slammed into us, staggering my companion, raking our exposed skin, threatening to suck the air from our lungs.

Kir'Vagonoth was the place of our thousand-year exile, a sunless wasteland of constant storms, of unending winter, of savagery and despair that we had shaped into a semblance of life. We had made beauty even in such a place as this. We had survived. With a howl louder than the mad Gastai, the wind tore at my hair and my shirt and spit snow into my eyes, but I would neither cover myself nor bow before it. Rather I let it scour my face, relishing its brutal power, allowing it to feed the pride and anger that threatened to burst the bonds of my flesh. We who had survived here were the true beings, yet we had been discarded like scraps of putrid meat. How had such a travesty come about?

"M-m-master . . ." Drych was clothed only in the ragged remnant of a tunic, and the moment's exposure to the wind had him shivering uncontrollably, his lips and nose quickly taking on the dead white of frostbite.

What had I thought to do with the man? I was here by virtue of his dream, our contact made into flesh by my power and Nyel's gift. I had no idea of my limits, but logic and instinct told me that they would not encompass taking another being of flesh back with me to Kir'Navarrin. That meant I had to find out if any rai-kirah survived here besides the mad ones, and if so, to persuade them to care for Drych until an Aife could open a portal to let him out. I needed to find Vallyne, for her power and my castle would be the last stronghold in Kir'Vagonoth. No time to consider the discomfort of such a meeting; poor Drych was freezing. Shaking off my distractions, I shifted quickly to my winged form. "Let's see if we can find a bit of shelter."

As if slammed by the wind, Drych fell back against the wall of ice that housed the portal and the gate to the pits and dropped to his knees, his battered mouth working without success to form words, and his dark eyes staring at me with such awe as if he'd seen the heavens open up to swallow him. I couldn't understand it. He had seen me winged in our last battle and had heard the stories of my change since he was a beginning student. But when I reached out and said I'd carry him for a while so we didn't have to slog through hip-deep snow to find a place to hide him, I realized that more had changed than wings.

I was on fire, or at least had taken on the appearance of it. Golden light enveloped my entire body, which seemed still to be my own save for a slight increase in bulk and the absence of familiar scars. I could judge these things quite well, as I was now naked save for a sword belt of pale leather. Even the slave mark on my shoulder had vanished. I touched the left side of my face . . . no, that one remained. The scaly imprint of falcon and lion on my cheekbone was still cold and dead, as was the long, knotted scar on my right side. But the other marks were gone, and the rest of me was quite warm, despite the radical change in dress.

I shrugged. "I must have done something different in my shifting." But that wasn't it. As I hefted the wretched, speechless Drych in my arms and took flight, I considered my shape and tried to slough off the glaring oddities—or at least reshape some clothes—but I could not find the pattern. It was as if instead of imposing an enchantment, I had removed it, as if I wore my own true form and had forgotten the steps needed to modify it. But to investigate such a matter while battling the wind was impossible, burdened as I was with the awkward weight of the young man, and peering through the murk in search of familiar landmarks. *First things first.*

I flew above the snowy landscape hunting for the houses built by the strongest of the rai-kirah. Though most had been abandoned when we left Kir'Vagonoth, they should still stand to mark the way. Confusing. I couldn't find any of them. At last, a broken tower poking up from the snowfields drew me closer to the ground, and I discovered ruins buried under ice and snow. Staying low, I followed a path that told of long months of progressive war and destruction. Eventually I came to the Rudai city, the sprawling shell that we had built in imitation of the cities the Gastai saw on their sojourns in the human world. The towers, temples, walkways, and houses had stood dark and deserted for uncounted years, and remained so—what little of them still existed. The city was rubble. I flew onward, over the long, low workshop buildings where the Rudai circle had shaped everything from chairs to poultry, from gowns to wine to frost-carved roses that did everything but grow. All were now gutted and filled with drifted snow. War had passed over all of this land. Had anything . . . anyone survived it?

Apprehensive, I flew on toward the castle I'd had built to house both friends and enemies—friends so I could protect them, enemies so I could watch them. One of my enemies had been left behind when we abandoned Kir'Vagonoth—Gennod, who had tried to force the joining with the human . . . me . . . and lead the opening of Kir'Navarrin himself. He had intended to destroy the Ezzarians and free the prisoner in Tyrrad Nor. But I had outmaneuvered him and left him imprisoned in the pits with the mad Gastai.

When I saw and felt and heard a whirlwind of darkness on the horizon where I should have seen ice towers piercing the clouds, I thought of the broken door seal on the pits. No Gastai could have wreaked such havoc on all we had built here. Only a Nevai—one of our most powerful circle—could have done so. Gennod was free.

A little further and I glimpsed the castle towers above the whirlwind—one, two, three, at least, still intact. From inside the dark wall of the storm I heard the howling din of full-scale demon battle. "I knew this was too easy," I said to Drych. "Hold on." I gathered speed and streaked through the storm, penetrating the black wall. In the murk were beasts of every kind, changing shape even as I passed, clawing each other, flying, wrestling on the ground, their fur or scales or wings whipped by the circling wind. I dodged a dragon's blast of fire, barely missed having my legs sheared off by razor-edged wings, and then flew high to avoid a pair of bearlike creatures that tore at each other with steel claws. Three slavering wolves charged again and again at a breached wall where a single rai-kirah wearing a human form was trying to keep them back. The defender would not last long without help.

Up and over I flew. Poor Drych whimpered softly as I shot almost straight down into the clear eye of the whirlwind. Half of my castle lay in ruins. What remained was still marvelously beautiful, its icy facets transforming the fires of destruction into jewel-like iridescence. On its highest battlement stood a figure of silver light, her radiance extending a shield of power to protect the citadel. Her golden hair flew free in the wind, and her white gown might have been a creation of swirling snow. As I circled and set my feet on the ice, her green eyes widened in wonder and touched me with true fire.

"My love," she said. "Oh, my dearest love, how is this possible?" Surprise and disbelief must have shaken her composure. She would never have permitted such warmth to show had she been given warning of my coming. Her greeting bore no remnant of the fury of our last meeting—when she had cursed me yet again for abandoning her in favor of duty. We had known my choice would mean losing myself in a human soul, and she had sworn never to forgive me. So many years we had loved—

I wrenched myself away from these disturbing thoughts and emotions, the demon's most private memories . . . and instantly felt shamed. Somehow in this dreadful place where Denas had lived and fought and raged against cruel fate, the true horror of what I had done to him for the last year of his existence struck home. I had walled him up in a prison of silence. To crush these last whispers would be murder, as surely as if I had taken my Warden's knife and plunged it into his heart.

And so I put aside my own guilt and discomfort and set free the buried memories of Vallyne and unfulfilled love, allowing them to flood over me. I touched her face and saw her probing hunger. *Oh, gods, a thousand years . . .* But though her gaze searched deep for the passion to match hers, hollow memory was all that remained. All I had to offer was admiration, respect, and the traces of the enchantment she had laid on her captive Warden. I had killed the part of me that might respond. She needed to know the truth.

"I am not the one you think," I said, unlocking our gaze and crouching down to ease Drych to the ground. "No matter this aura I happen to have acquired. Or rather I am he, as we knew would happen, but I am myself as well. Mostly myself." The only thing more difficult than defining my state of mind in my own head, was trying to explain it to anyone else—even to Vallyne with whom I had discussed the implications of human joining for a hundred years.

Vallyne folded her arms across her breast and bit her lip, smiling in resigned amusement. Then she walked around me slowly, examining every aspect of my flesh in minute detail. I wondered if the ridiculous rush of blood to my cheeks would be as obvious beneath the gold light I wore. Unlike the immodest Derzhi, Ezzarians usually kept themselves clothed. "You wear the color well," she said at last, "though your body is not quite so beautiful as the one you . . . Denas . . . wore in your time here." Only then did she look me in the eye again, genuine pleasure almost hiding the depths of her sadness. "I am happy to see you, friend Seyonne."

"And I you, Lady," I said. "I've come seeking sanctuary for my young friend here, and your aid in retrieving two of our brothers who still languish in the pits. Will you grant us your favor?"

"You've no need to ask for whatever I have," she said, shrugging off painful truth and shifting her attention to the dazed Drych. "Welcome, friend of my friend." She crouched down beside the young man and extended her hand. He was staring awestruck at a rai-kirah wholly at odds with his training and experience—a being of light, color, and beauty that seared the heart, as unlike the monsters who had fashioned his torment as the soft breezes of Ezzaria were from the storm around us. Remembering my own first glimpse of Vallyne, I guessed he was no longer noticing the cold. "I've already summoned someone who'll get you warmed and fed," Vallyne went on. "I regret that our hospitality has so sadly lapsed. No dancing at all. Quite limited sustenance, and we daren't ride out for pleasure. No charming, ever-confused guest such as this one"—she nodded her head at me and widened her eyes in teasing—"to read for us. And this—" She waved her hand at the wild darkness that spun around the castle. "Sadly, I might be feeding you in this hour, only to leave you starving and frozen again when the time vessel next empties itself."

"Gennod let them loose. How was he capable of it?"

Vallyne flushed. "I'm afraid those you left here to guard were not such good jailers. We thought someone would come back for us, but no one did. And with no word of when we might expect it . . . Have you so soon forgotten the craving, my love?" Her voice was scarcely audible above the storm. "We hungered so. Don't blame us."

"Someone thought to let a few Gastai go hunting." To feed on a human soul and bring back the experiences and sensations to share with those remaining in this wasteland. "And the hunters returned worse than ever."

"Indeed so. Though we don't understand why."

"Dreams," I said, thinking aloud, putting the evidence together at last, understanding how Nyel had been able to touch the rai-kirah all these thousand years. "Rai-kirah living in Kir'Vagonoth cannot dream. But when the Gastai possess a human soul, they dream, and those dreams can be changed . . . touched . . . by the one in the tower, just as my dreams were touched. All these years we Ezzarians have believed that we made the demons worse by our combat, but it was never our doing. It was his."

"His? So you've gone there . . ."

"It's complicated," I said, and then took refuge in the problem of the moment. "Gennod's wearing you down."

"We'll hold. Though I would not refuse a few more warriors were they available. *You* look quite capable."

"I've come here by a means I don't quite understand," I said. "That's why I'm not sure I can get my three young friends out of Kir'Vagonoth as yet, and I'm not sure how long I can stay—" An earsplitting screech and a burst of flame drew us to the edge of the battlement. The graceful turret of the outermost tower splintered under the assault of a monstrous bird, sending great shards of ice whirling into the storm. The fragments glinted silver and gold and blue in the firelight, dusting towers and windows and the three of us with new frost.

The bird's head and long neck were that of a serpent roughly the diameter of a large tree, its body the size of a house, and its small eyes glowed red; only a demon of considerable power could shape such a monster. "Gennod," Vallyne and I said together.

Two slightly smaller birds with sharp talons and hooked beaks flew out of the broken tower. They were certainly more agile than the serpent bird and ferocious in their defense, but they stood no chance, as the wingspread of the giant bird was so much larger. Even as we watched, one of the smaller birds raked the monster's back with its claws. The serpent's tongue whipped out and caught the harrying defender, who disintegrated in a burst of purple fire. The second defender shot high into the churning sky, then plummeted toward the serpent bird, talons fully extended. The monster's wings swept the air with such force as to flip the smaller bird upside down, the heavy wings slamming into the helpless defender and crumpling its lighter frame. Colored light oozed from the broken bird like living blood, beginning to take a humanlike form, but before it could reshape itself, the dazed rai-kirah was swept away by the dark whirlwind.

With a scream of triumph and a flick of its ropelike tongue, the serpent bird returned to its assault on the tower, shattering first one and then another portion until all that remained of the graceful structure was a glassy mountain of blue-gray ice far below us. Then the bird rose into the air, circled lazily about the castle, and laid its red serpent's eye on Vallyne.

Freed from the momentary paralysis induced by the duel, I ran across the frosted battlement. "Someone will come for you, lad," I shouted over my shoulder. "Heal well and save your brothers." *And you, glorious Vallyne, live forever!* Without breaking stride, I leaped up to the merlon and into the churning air, yanking the sword from the sheath at my side and spreading my golden wings. Drawing melydda from my blood and bone, I summoned the wind to my service and soared upward toward the monster.

CHAPTER 31

A sharp edge bit into my hand, threatening to slice through to bone, and I loosened my grip on the hard, angular lump. What inept sword maker would leave such a ridge on a sword grip? Even as the stench of burning feathers and seared flesh yielded to scents of roses and tea and wet grass, and the harsh screams of dying monsters gave way to the hiss of quiet rain, the laceration on my palm stung more fiercely—a tether drawing me out of battle and storm. I opened my hand and stared. The black warrior . . . the obsidian game piece.

"I had more to do," I said. "The gateway to the pits . . . the two other Wardens . . ." I set the piece carefully on the game board, forcing my hand not to tremble—my quite ordinary hand with its familiar scars. My bones ached. My shoulders felt raw; the seepage from my throbbing left thigh was surely blood. My right side felt as if a spike had been driven inward and upward into my lung. At least I was clothed again; nonetheless, I felt vulnerable—flaccid, weak, as if half my blood had been drained away.

"Your dreamer must have fallen asleep," said Nyel from across the game board. "You cannot remain with him once he sleeps again and begins a new dream."

I could not take my eyes from the patterned game board, for in the trickery of light and dark, of pattern and form, I could still catch glimpses of a silver brilliance that pierced whipping clouds to give me heart, of long, difficult hours of combat in my golden form, slaying the serpent bird just when I had begun to fear that I could not. "His waking shadow," I said. "Made flesh from his dream."

"The *vietto* is the rarest of enchantments, even among the Madonai. Passed from master to *attellé* if the student's power is great enough. If the student's heart is generous enough. If the student's soul is rich enough to weave it with wisdom."

"I need to get back to my sword practice." Kasparian shoved

his chair away from the table. "You've no need of me anymore." His heavy footsteps echoed through the silent house. The voiceless servants came in and stoked the fire and closed the garden doors against the splatter of rain and the rapidly cooling night. Night. I had been in Kir'Vagonoth an entire day.

"The *vietto*. This is how you traveled to the human world," I said, looking up at my companion as the last vision faded. "You and your friend Hyrdon, who didn't want to be a god."

Nyel was leaning back in his chair, sipping a glass of wine. "It took me quite a while to realize that I had taken flesh in a true world and was no longer part of a dream, that my deeds in that realm were true events, not just a passing vision. Who could imagine such a thing? I told myself it was dangerous to meddle, foolish to become involved with beings so ephemeral. But I could not stay away from the forest people. They lived in beauty, just as we did here, and I could not understand how they bore such hardships—hunger, disease, and early death—yet remained so in love with living. I tried to care for them, teach them whatever I could that might ease their way. As time passed, I decided to choose only one of them at a time to be my dreamer. Things get very confusing when you touch too many different minds. And indeed you remain somewhat . . . attached . . . to the person who brings you through. On your recent adventure, for example, you would have found it difficult to stray too far from the young man. You felt the bond with him, well beyond your shared experience of torment."

True. All true. "Why did I take on this altered form . . . the light . . . the sword? Is that part of it? I couldn't shape myself the way I wanted."

Nyel rose and walked to the table in the middle of the room where carafes of wine and ale stood ready for his choosing. He refilled his glass, filled a second one, and brought it to me. A few stray red droplets fell toward the game board, vanishing the moment they touched it. "This enchantment is of the Madonai, not the rekkonarre. With the *vietto*, the enchanter becomes the physical expression of his power. His every other form is but a shadow of this one. And so this was your true Madonai form—a warrior's form, it seems—that tried to show itself. It would always be the shape of your greatest strength, though you surely could have changed to whatever you wished had you understood how to do so. But you are bound to human flesh, and so your transformation was flawed, incomplete." He settled in his chair again and ran a finger along the smooth edge of the game board. "The pain and weariness you feel now are the cost of your human birth, as is the truth that you cannot do this thing of yourself. You needed me to guide the enchantment for you . . . and you needed Kasparian, of course, because the one who stole my name also stole my ability to initiate such workings or, indeed, to accomplish any save this one."

Another piece slid into place. "You can speak in dreams and shape them to your design," I said, "but you can't travel through them anymore."

"Correct. I was able to follow and observe you in your glory this day. But I could not have come to your aid had you needed me. My jailer intended for me only to observe." Amusement glanced across his face along with the echo of his grieving. "He would not be pleased to know I had learned to shape or speak in dreams."

So that was why Kasparian had let himself be imprisoned with Nyel. Without his *attellé* to initiate the enchantment, Nyel would have been without even the small amusement his jailer had left him. His jailer . . . his son, if the god story was true. A fitting explanation for his edge of bitterness.

"What of Kasparian?" I said. "He was allowed to keep his name." I needed to understand about names.

"Kasparian was . . . and is . . . limited enough that it was not necessary to cripple him. He has no power over dreams. Forgive him his faults. He is a good man. Truth is often the cruelest torment."

I stood and walked away from the game table, sensing I was at the verge of some discovery, yet so tired that it might pass without my notice. "I thank you for your gift, Nyel. The young man I rescued was my own *attellé*. At least he is free of torment now. He has hope of getting home and some measure of safety, as do the others left there—both human and rai-kirah." Gennod was dead; I could not argue with the satisfactory outcome, though I believed Nyel the entire cause of the problem. "You're quite confusing me."

Was all of this designed to demonstrate the power of the Madonai? If so, the designer had accomplished his goal. Beneath the mantle of weariness and the remnants of my intoxication, I could feel both the pulsing enormity of my own melydda and the clear and poignant understanding of my lack. I possessed such power as I had yearned for throughout my life, but my human hand could wield only a portion of it. Was that his objective? Was this growing hunger I felt gnawing at my soul a punishment for my ancestors' fault? *Truth is often the cruelest torment.*

I pushed open the garden door that the servants had closed, allowing a wind-borne spray of rain to bathe my face, hoping it might prick my mind awake. Nyel came to stand at my shoulder. We were exactly the same height.

"Did you think this small grace was what I planned to offer?" he said. "Did you not hear what I told you? I've not brought you here to tantalize you with things you cannot have."

What had he said as I fell into his eyes? *This is but the beginning, lad* . . . "You said I was bound by earth and flesh, but that you could set me free." The old man's gaze compelled my attention. "What did you mean?" My stomach felt hollow, anticipation bordering on terror.

"Of all the rekkonarre you have the heart and the wisdom to use the *vietto*. You think me mad, and indeed I confess it. I have lived too long. My griefs have festered into bitterness and misjudgment. I, too, have done things that I would have considered reprehensible in my youth. You've seen them. But you can make matters right again . . . Is that not everything you have ever wished to do?" He grasped my shoulders and forced me to look into his eyes, and with a love I could not fathom, they begged me to believe him. "I wish to free you from the cost of your compassion. I can change you, unbind you from all that holds you back, allow you to repair these horrors I have done. You will be as you are meant to be, and I will die unburdened of my sins. Can you comprehend what I offer? I will make you Madonai."

A simple matter, he told me. Because I was newly joined. Because of the power I could bring to the working. My mind and soul, the joining of Seyonne and the demon, would remain as they were now. Only the nature of my body would change . . . still flesh and blood and bone, but purged of those elements that hindered my easy movement through the portals of dreams, free of the scars that interfered with my transformation to a being that would feel neither pain nor weariness, cleansed of the frail heritage that prevented full use of my melydda. I would be able to touch dreams at my own will and become flesh through them, to fight unhindered for those things I believed were good and right, or to teach, as had ever been my truest pleasure.

"You were not born to watch events from the side, to let others take the lead, to lose your strength and die when you have scarcely begun."

Oh yes, and I would live for uncounted ages of the world. An aging warrior in my own world, I was but an infant in the span of a Madonai lifetime.

"You see the burdens of such a choice. To remain apart—for you could not allow such power to be skewed by trivial concerns or personal feelings. To live so long and to be the only one—indeed these are difficult, as I can attest. But as you grow in your own power, you can do this same for others you find worthy of our name. The Madonai race will be reborn in you. The balance of the worlds will be restored."

But I would not be human. Nor could I live in the human world again. That had been one of the Madonai's problems. Humans could not live in Kir'Navarrin; as Fiona had seen, they sickened quickly. Nor could Madonai exist for more than a short time in the human realm. They had built the first portal between the worlds, but could not use it. Only the rekkonarre—my people fully joined—could live in both worlds. Only those Madonai who possessed the secret of the *vietto*, who could take on flesh through enchantment and dream, could exist in the human world as often as they wished, for as long as their dreamer could stay awake.

"You could care for humans, if you judged it wise. Better than you have done thus far. Though I cannot mentor you in wisdom or in judgment, I can teach you much of power." Think about it, he said. No need to rush. At every step I could choose until the last when it was done.

"Come, come," said Nyel, shutting the garden door, reining in his eagerness so tightly that only the slight flush of his cheeks yet spoke of it. "You don't have to decide tonight. You're tired and wounded—bleeding on my carpet. Go up to your bed and I'll send Kasparian to tend your injuries. Tomorrow, we'll talk again."

I walked slowly through the quiet house. Always so quiet. I did not go straight to my bedchamber, but walked up and down the corridors and stairs, past paintings and statuary, workrooms and kitchens, courtyards and sitting rooms and sleeping chambers. I stood on a high balcony and stared at the stars, then wandered inside again, in and out of more rooms. I saw none of them. All I could see was Drych—sick, broken, wretched Drych—alive. All I heard was the infusion of blessed hope in his voice when I had proved myself real.

Who could imagine such a gift? Melydda unbounded. And freedom—from pain and filth, from petty, senseless rules, from endless bloodshed and sorrows I could not heal. Exactly what I had always wanted—to make things right. When I wandered into my room at last, I did not light the lamps that stood ready, nor did I snuff the single candle and fall onto the soft bed. Rather I sat on the bare floor in the corner, knees drawn up, my arms wrapped around my legs, and my forehead resting on my knees. Only in the hour of my demon-joining had I felt so frightened. The prisoner of Tyrrad Nor had offered to make me a god, and I could think of no reason to refuse him.

Kasparian found me there. He brought a bundle of linen strips and a basin of water with steam curling out of it. "The master says you are injured. Let me see." Without touching the candle to the lamp wicks, he set the corner ablaze with light.

"I've no need for your help." I wanted no company, no intrusion on the chaos of my thoughts.

"Do you think I'll poison you? Cripple you? Take petty vengeance in the guise of healing?"

"No." I was certain of that, just as I was certain he would like to do so.

"Where is your wound?" Whatever his reasons for doing Nyel's bidding, they had nothing to do with wishing me well.

"Tell me," I said, "did I offend you at some time, or is my only crime that your master is offering me what you hunger for and believe you deserve? You know I can't remember." As he seemed determined to hover over me whether or not I wished it, I stretched out my bleeding leg.

Kasparian drew his knife and slit my breeches. An ugly gash on my thigh oozed blood and the serpent bird's sticky black venom. Only now that I saw the wound did I realize how wickedly it hurt. The Madonai began to sponge it clean with the hot water, and I pressed my back to the wall.

"I am forbidden to speak of the past," he said as he worked.

"You possess strength of enchantment that I do not. One may chafe at such a matter, but it changes nothing."

He reached out and dragged a chair close by my left hand. "Grab onto this and the chest on the other side and hold still. We need to get this poison out, or you'll lose all feeling in this leg." Indeed my toes tingled ominously at the end of my throbbing limb. While my bloodless fingers gripped the carved seat of the wooden chair and the brass handles of the clothes chest on my right, Kasparian, with the skill of a surgeon, used his knife to enlarge the wound and allow the blood to wash the black vileness out of it.

The prospect of a body that could fight without pain was extremely attractive at that moment. I needed to think of something else as he blotted, squeezed, and swabbed. "If you could wield this power, Kasparian, shaping dreams and traveling through them, what would you do with it?"

"Better for all that I never have such power."

"But if you did?"

His answer was not at all what I expected. "I would remove those you brought back to this land—send you and them back to your cursed world—and I would seal the last gate forever."

Not set his master free. Nor himself. Nor wreak the vengeance that I yet believed was Nyel's true desire. "But the rai-kirah somehow make him stronger," I said, "and clearly he wants me here. I thought you loved him."

He washed the last blood and venom from my leg with uncomfortable vehemence. "You know nothing of love."

I wondered if he was right. Surety in any matter was a thing of the past. "I could use some advice," I said. "I don't know what to do."

His head remained bent to his work. I could not see his face, but only his long dark hair, thick and threaded evenly with iron gray. "You should question," he said softly, winding the clean linen about my thigh along with some enchantment that eased the most acute discomfort. "Seek answers beyond this house. Love speaks with many voices." He tied off the bandage with a yank that made me wince, then gathered up his materials.

"I'm sorry for whatever came between us, Kasparian." Such antagonism was not developed at a distance.

He shot me a glance of purest hatred. "Save your sentiment.

You are the most despicable of beings, and I will curse your name until the end of time."

At some time I crawled out of my corner and into the bed. Thus do fear and mystification often yield to more mundane concerns. The floor was very hard. I could easily become spoiled with sleeping in a bed again.

My dilemma was not resolved by sleep. When sunlight crept through my windows, I washed, but in some childish show of truculence, I ignored the fresh shirt provided and put back on the bloodstained one of the previous day. I contemplated the weapons that were again laid out for me, but turned my back on them and went downstairs. Unready to face either of the Madonai, I was relieved to find myself breakfasting alone. Though fiercely hungry, I ate lightly, forcing myself away from the table and its inexhaustible supplies of meat and bread and fruit before anyone else showed up.

The day was brilliant, the kind of clean-washed morning that can only come after a rain. The sunlight and sharp air drew me outdoors, and, my wound already on its way to healing, I headed for the path that led up the mountainside. I had always sought clarity on mountaintops. But as I crossed the garden, I caught sight of the black wall. Kasparian had advised me to seek answers beyond the house, and despite his hatred, his recommendations were not carelessly given. Could he have been telling me to cross the wall?

The wall's surface was not so damaged as I remembered, only crazed with a network of threadlike cracks, like pottery with an imperfect glaze. As when I had come there in the siffaru, I laid my palm on the stone, carefully probing the enchantment of the wall, hoping to feel its shape and consequence, and so to learn of it. Somehow I expected the wall to be cold—enchantments often had that effect, as if they drew the substance from the artifact they touched. But the black stone was, in fact, quite warm, far warmer than the stone benches that stood nearby in the sunny garden.

I yanked my hand away. I would have sworn the stone had moved . . . bulged . . . swelled, perhaps, around my fingers. At the same time I was stricken with such riotous emotion that I threw my head back and laughed even as tears streamed from my eyes and terror burst from my skin in acrid sweat. A fearful thing, this wall. A wondrous thing.

I tried to clear my mind before I touched it again, but to no avail. As I brushed my hand along its flawed surface, faces came alive in my mind, and with them the continuing barrage of sentiment: a woman with startling blue eyes, a man with a bald head that shone like polished leather, a heavy-browed man who carried a giant bow and laughed until the earth rumbled, a round, pink-cheeked young woman of serious mind, a fair-haired young man—oh, gods, I could not remember his name, but in some long-ago time beyond the barriers of memory, he had been my dearest friend in all the world. More of them . . . ten, eleven . . . the twelfth place unfilled . . . No. I was wrong. One more face appeared—a wry, narrow face with a well-trimmed beard, who grinned at me over his shoulder, then vanished in a blaze of blue and purple and swirling gray green. Vyx. Though every face was familiar, he was the only one of them I could name, the only one who had been with me in exile in Kir'Vagonoth. Twelve places . . . Vyx had always intended to come back here. His choice had not been a whim of the moment. Were the others the same, friends of mine who had given everything to keep this wall secure? *Damn your stubborn pride for destroying any chance to remember more. You should know these people.*

I walked in the sunlight beside the wall, dragging my hand along it, fumbling in the many-roomed house of memory where such friends should have been safely tucked away. Halfway around the garden, I stopped abruptly. A single, deep crack split the black surface from ground to top. Though ugly and gaping, the crack had not yet broken completely through to the outside. My finger traced the jagged split. Was someone else waiting to come and fill it? I feared not—twelve seemed "right" somehow, complete—and yet I would not wish this wall in anyone's future. A terrible fate. All these things I knew, but did not know.

"Explain it to me," I said, sitting on the damp ground beside the wall, leaning my back on it, closing my eyes, and turning my face to the sun. "One of you come and tell me, so I'll understand what you did. I've got to know if this gift I'm offered is the grace you've earned or the very act that makes your sacrifice a waste."

I sat there a long time. I summoned the faces one by one and twisted my mind into knots trying to retrieve some memory of them, but I uncovered very little. The young man I'd called my dearest friend loved sleeping in the open under the stars and swimming in the deepest pools of the world—staying for weeks in the deeps, shifting himself to make it possible. The serious young woman had bested me in some contest of wits, and I had resented it very much. The bowman was a superb hunter and a merciless taskmaster, both loved and hated by everyone who knew him, and he had taken my friend and the serious girl and me on some magnificent adventure that entirely escaped my memory.

Of course I remembered more of Vyx than any of the others, for I had lived with him in exile. But he should never have been in Kir'Vagonoth. I could not shake that conviction . . . which made no sense at all. No one had planned that we, the rekkonarre, would split ourselves into two beings. And why would any one of us have been exempt from the price we had paid for the prophecy—the seeing that had induced us to forsake Kir'Navarrin and destroy ourselves?

As in Kir'Vagonoth, I felt the shame of what I had done to Denas. A man of strength and duty who had known fully what he was doing when he took my hand and yielded his own life. Though his voice was silent, I once again vowed to heed whatever of him remained in me.

When I gave up at last, no nearer to a resolution, I lay back on the grass and embraced the peace of noonday. A gold-brown bird soared high above the mountain, graceful, majestic as it caught an updraft and held almost perfectly still for a moment, poised on the cusp of the wind before disappearing behind the peak. The bird led me to think of Blaise, and then of the other friends I'd left behind in the human world . . . the real world as I thought of it. They seemed so irretrievably remote, almost as distant as those whose faces I envisioned when I touched the wall. Yet the wall had been here for hundreds of years, while Catrin, Fiona, Blaise, Aleksander—

I sat up with a sudden start. The fifth day. If time ran anywhere near the same in the two worlds, this would be the day of the raid on Syra, the day when Aleksander's world changed for good or ill, for life or death. I should be there. I might manage easier to walk on the star Elemiel, I thought, so impossible was the distance between Aleksander and me and so unyielding the tether that bound me to Tyrrad Nor. Were he to be on the other side of that wall, I doubted I could have found my way to him.

But then, of course, I remembered Nyel's offer and the promise that it gave. Perhaps I *could* be there. And that led me to consider Nyel's hatred of Aleksander and the Madonai's ability to influence dreams. With an explosion of dismay, I leaped to my feet and ran for the castle, yelling for my host.

"What is it, lad?" He stood on the wide steps beside the garden, just outside the doors to his sitting room. His old young eyes were red-rimmed and tired, and the creases alongside them were deeper than I'd noticed before.

I stood on the garden path at the bottom of the steps. "Tell me of your crimes in the human world, Nyel. Did you shape a Frythian assassin's dream? Did a Rhyzka bully abuse his child wife to death because of you? Where was your hand in all this trouble?"

"Why does it matter? You know I have no love for humans. I confess it freely."

"Do you know what's happening today? Have you manipulated someone, done something to make it fail?" I was on fire with my conviction. Somehow he was going to get Aleksander killed.

He shrugged. "I can only share your dreams and visions, not read your thoughts to learn of your affairs. And I keep no tally of the other dreams I touch. I seek out dreamers that are interesting. So many dreams are fragments or too odd or of too little substance to be useful. But, yes, I've found fertile ground in these warring Derzhi. They are everything I despise, and I take great pleasure in confounding them." He started for the door.

"Send me there," I called after him.

He paused, but did not turn. "Where?"

"To Aleksander. To Syra. If you care for me as you say, if your gift is meant for good, for love, for the world's hope—and my heart believes you, Nyel, though my reason screams at me to be afraid—then I beg you do this for me. Let me help them. I won't ask again. Afterward I'll choose yes or no, but if you fail me now, I swear the answer will be no."

"You threaten me over this human wretch!" He whirled about, and if the brow of an angry god could launch thunderbolts as storytellers claim, so his would have done.

"No. Not threaten. Never that." And "never" was the truth. Even in my fear of what he had done, I could not bear the thought of harming Nyel. "But I've told you of my belief in Aleksander's destiny. If you allow him to be harmed, then I can't believe you fit to judge your gift good or evil, right or wrong. If you wish me to make things right, to substitute my judgment for your own, then you must begin now and not only when I allow you to make me other than human."

He was quivering in his wrath, his presence swelling until I felt it loom as huge as the mountain itself. I was ready to take wing should he burst with his fury as I feared. But as the moment slid past us, he turned for the door again, merely human-sized. "I will not send you to this prince, nor to the rekkonarre who flies with you. Someone else. A stranger."

"As long as it is someone who wishes this venture to succeed." *No tricks, old man.*

"You will remember that you are still vulnerable. I would not have you dead."

"I will return here and settle this." Fully aware of how vulnerable I was, no matter which side of the dream I walked, I climbed the steps and entered the game once more.

CHAPTER 32

The desert was littered with corpses . . . vultures feeding . . . The birds glared at me as if I were intruding on their private amusement. The broken bodies were chained together and facedown, save for a few . . . the naked boys . . . turned so you could see what the birds had done with their razor beaks . . . the mutilation . . . though now the children were dead, the savage ruin of their manhood was only another twist of the heart. Too late . . . too late . . .

"This is the one you want?"

"Yes. This one." We had touched a number of dreams, some fearful, some incoherent, some wholly unrelated to the coming events, but this one . . . Surely this dreamer had seen the slave caravan at Andassar to shape this horrific image of what might be discovered on the Syra raid.

"And you choose this path freely?"

"Yes, yes. Get on with it."

"So be it."

I waded through the bodies, thicker now, piled one upon the other . . . knee high, everyone dead. "This time we'll save them," I said. "This time . . ." Over my head now, blotting out the sun . . . the choking stench . . . and so dark . . . down, down underground and everywhere were more slaves . . . all dead . . . Where had he gone, the dreamer? Down deep into the cave . . . There . . . hacking at the chains, cursing as his blows shattered the iron links, only to have them flow back together like slips of tin in a smith's fire.

"Hello!" I called.

The man whirled about and raised his ax. Smoking tears streamed down his face, eating deep grooves in his cheeks. His face was not familiar, but, then, who dreams of his own face? I blocked the descending blow; what would happen if he killed me in his dream? "I've come to help. Wake up." He looked puzzled and reached for my extended hand . . .

Brutal heat pressed me to the gritty rock. I blinked my eyes, trying to clear my head of the transition, carefully not moving anything else until I had a better idea of my surroundings. The desert, most certainly. The red rock under my nose felt like a baking oven, and though my head cast a long shadow to my left, the sun, whether rising or setting, drew the moisture from me. Further to my left, at something of a distance, were more rocks, jagged pinnacles of red, walls rippled like the dunes, but pressed hard together by the years. The ocher cast of the light falling on the rugged cliffs told me it was afternoon. Cautiously I rotated my head without lifting it, until I could see to my right.

Sharp steel pricked my neck, and a boot smashed down on my hand as it flew instinctively to my weaponless belt. "Who are you?" The nervous man with the high-pitched voice did not sound like anyone I knew.

"A friend. Can I sit up and introduce myself before you break my fingers?"

"Slowly. And stay on the ground. Put your hands on your head." The timbre of his voice signaled no moderation in either his ferocity or his sincerity. Obediently placing my palms on my hair, I sat up and turned around to face him. No, not familiar. A stranger under his black-and-white paint. Perhaps he had only heard stories of the raid on the slave caravan at Andassar, to set him dreaming so vividly. His dark beard and ringlets strung with beads named him a Suzaini, and his sleep-heavy eyes blinked at me in uncertain recognition.

"I'm a friend of Blaise just arrived here to help," I said. "You've probably seen me at Taíne Keddar, or perhaps . . . did we meet three nights ago at Taíne Horet? I was with the Aveddi." He could be one of the Suzaini palatine's men. One of the palatine's sons who had escorted us to the great tent . . . yes, the proud bearing hinted at it.

The brawny young man withdrew his sword, but did not sheathe it. He held the weapon with a practiced hand, but the nervous excitement that gave edge to his voice and tension to his movements suggested that he had never faced a true battle. "How have you come here?" He glanced uneasily down a steep track that seemed to be the only way down from the flat red rock on which I sat. "Why did no one signal me that you were on your way up?"

We had an awesome vantage from the rock, and as I peeked

over my shoulder, I saw what the man had been sent here to watch. Far below us, a fortress had been built right into the side of the cliffs. "Perhaps someone was dozing off in the heat," I said. "Maybe they noticed that I'm not armed and didn't look inclined to push you off the rock." I jerked my thumb at the fortress. "I'd recommend you get your head down and your weapon out of the sun or you'll have someone less friendly than me up here."

I suspected he flushed under his paint as he dropped into a crouch. With a wary eye on me, he sounded the harsh chucking cry of the cave swallow. Only when he heard an answering call from down below did he relax a bit, cram his sword back into its sheath, and stretch out on his stomach to resume his watch.

"I've come to take a last look around on behalf of the Aveddi," I said. "Make sure everyone's ready. Have you seen anything?"

"Naught. All's been properly quiet since well before dawn." One might have thought the young man had ordered it that way by his own watching.

He was correct that the fortress showed no signs of alert. No signs of life at all. Not even those it should have. "You've seen no servants? Herdsmen? Hunters?" The fortress fronted a dry, steep-walled gorge. The water stores would be deep inside the citadel, where it delved into the rock, but most of the garrison's supplies would be brought in by caravan. And if a hundred and fifty men lived here as Aleksander claimed, then surely there would be small herds—goats for milk and sheep or pigs for fresh meat—kept back in the shady nooks of the rocks, where springs or seeping moisture allowed sparse grazing. Either that provender or fresh kill from a hunt would be brought in at least once a day. "It seems very strange that no one's brought supplies to so large a garrison."

The young Suzaini glared at me, swelling in indignation. Evidently he heard a personal reproach I did not intend. "Indeed, sir, my eyes betrayed me only for a flea's heartbeat. The sun scarcely moved in the time. The Aveddi says a hundred fifty are housed here, and I respect his word, though were it not for his saying, I would mention otherwise that the fortress is oddly quiet for so large a force. So—they've not a sign that we're here, and the Aveddi will smite them with his mighty arm should they show a nose once we've got into the mine."

At only the slightest expression of my amusement at this earnest pomposity—I had taken great care not to smile—his wounded pride sagged into misery. His heavy brows came almost together in distress. "Truly I am shamed at my laxity, sir—and Gossopar surely punished me with the most dreadful dreaming. Last night, good Admet agreed that my friend Jakor could take this post at sunset, so that I could join the Aveddi in his first riding—to represent all Suzai on this glorious occasion. You've not come to tell me I have to stay here all night? I've waited my whole life to get into a fight. Jakor is a good boy and will wind his horn if the Derzhi garrison rides out."

His yearning to strike a blow was so vivid that my own fists clenched. *You remain somewhat . . . attached . . . to the person who brings you through*, Nyel had said. I sighed and smiled at the eager fellow. "No, you're to come with me, and you'll not have to wait until sunset. What's your name?"

"Feyd al Marsouf de Sabon ak Suza, sir. Anything I can do. Anything—" Suza was the ancient name of the vast lands east of Azhakstan. Only its Derzhi conquerors had named it Suzain—"little Suza," the first of so many humiliations.

"I'm Seyonne. You must learn to trust your own seeing, Feyd. The Aveddi relies on your skills to confirm or counter his information. If all he wished to hear were his own words, he would not have sent you. Now, go fetch this Jakor and his horn."

While the young Suzaini scrambled down the track, I peered over the edge of the rock and passed the back of my hand before my eyes. With every sense I could bring to bear, I examined the Derzhi fortress. Though the distance was great and the fortress walls were thick, by the time my dreamer returned accompanied by a stubby youth who carried a curved bronze horn, my head was ringing with warnings. Feyd's instincts were right. No warriors were inside that fortress. I knew it as I knew my own name.

"Be alert, Jakor," I said as I grabbed Feyd's black shirt and shoved him right back down the path. "Stay down and stay awake."

The thought of leaving Feyd behind never occurred to me, though traveling in bird shape would have been much faster than negotiating the hair-raising, one-boot-wide goat track to get down from the rock. And to explain to the small party of Suzaini raiders how I'd gotten up the wicked thing without anyone noticing or why I needed to borrow one of the group's horses to be on about my business was deucedly awkward. "You'll understand everything later," I said to Feyd as we mounted up and set out westward, leaving his small troop scratching their heads. "We just need to get to the Prince—the Aveddi—or to Blaise as quickly as we can. The Danatos warriors are not in that fortress, and someone had damned well better find out where they are. Tell me what you know of tonight's plan, Feyd. I want to make sure you've got it clear." Being "attached" did not mean I had to tell him everything.

"The commanders entrusted their plan to me when they honored me with this post," said the young nobleman proudly as we rode through an interconnecting maze of narrow sandy-floored gorges. Twilight had already reached these shaded rifts, the red walls so high you could see only a ribbon of deep blue far overhead. "Blaise alone will take on the archers at the watchpost, and remain there on guard to see that they're not replaced. Farrol and three others are to silence the watch on the mine entrance just after the watch change at sunset. That leaves six hours until the next guard change. As soon as Farrol's signal is given, the Aveddi will lead Gorrid and Roche and five others to take on the guards in the mine and clear the way for the rest of us to come in and free the slaves. At the same time Admet will lead three fighters and Pherro the water worker to the sluice gate to open and ruin it so it cannot be repaired. It was my father's advice to bring Pherro, who devised the water system at Taíne Horet. The Aveddi shows great wisdom. Have I said the plan rightly?"

"Well-done," I said, my mind racing faster than we could ride through the twisting gorges. "It's good to rehearse a plan in your mind before the time comes."

"May I speak freely, sir? One matter troubles me. As you know him so well, perhaps you can tell me if I have mistaken the Aveddi's intent."

"Certainly. With me you are free to question as you will. It does you credit to speak up."

Feyd dropped his voice as if the breeze might waft his voice to Aleksander and again risk his participation in the night's doings. "Some of these outlaw fighters are—holy Gossopar save us, sir—they are women. We never thought the Aveddi would accept it, as Derzhi seem to understand the proprieties. The good Blaise has these odd ideas—and we have great affection for Blaise—but we thought— The Aveddi says he will accept all who raise a sword in faith and honor, but perhaps he might be saying this only to respect Blaise's wish on this occasion and so it would not be necessary to reconsider our own positions for the future. Can you explain the Aveddi's mind?"

I laughed and thanked Gossopar—or whoever else might be in charge of the mystery I lived—that I was riding to Aleksander's side on this night. "The Aveddi grows in wisdom every day, Feyd. Watch him and learn." I spurred my horse faster through the towering rocks. "Now turn your talented observations to something else. What might need to be different about our plan if the Danatos were prepared for our arrival?"

Feyd's brow creased ponderously. "I suppose they would alert the archers and those who watch the mine entrance, which would mean great danger for Blaise and Farrol."

"No," I said, letting my own thoughts feed on his. "Think. If those two initial ventures fail, the signal to go ahead will not be given and the rest of us will never show up at the mine. If the Danatos's only objective is to protect the mine, that would be enough. But if they've been warned of this raid, then they're going to be determined to catch whoever's planning it, don't you think?"

Feyd was quick. "Of course! Then the Danatos might let their own watch be taken, even the archers, to deceive us."

"Exactly. Once Blaise and Farrol have taken their targets, everything will go forward. Our leaders will be drawn out . . ." And Aleksander and seven others were to enter the mine first. What if there were a hundred and fifty to greet him inside the mine instead of only a few guards and overseers? No. The mine would be too cramped for so many. The warriors inside the mine would be alerted, but the main body of the garrison would be waiting to close in when the outlaws showed themselves. I explored every other scenario I could devise and discarded it almost as quickly. "So how can we see if my fears are justified without jeopardizing our surprise?"

"We cannot search every rift and cave around here for the garrison. There are hundreds of places men can hide. That's what makes our own plan work."

"Tell me, Feyd, do you know where the archers' watchpost is?"

"Yes, sir. Not far from here. But Blaise won't be there yet."

"Show me the archers. If I can get near enough to see who's

at the watchpost without revealing myself, we'll have an idea of how much we need to worry." It would be less trouble than finding Blaise. My shapeshifting friend could be in any one of a hundred places at the moment, and he might be in no danger at all.

We had perhaps two hours until sunset. A short distance further and we came to a break in the cliff wall, where several side rifts came together, much as a number of streams join to make a wide river. The cliffs were pockmarked with caves, and to my surprise, instead of taking me up one of the steep tracks like that back at his own watchpost, Feyd led me down another flat-bottomed gorge, plodding along, peering into holes and behind rocks, unsure of himself. After a few hundred paces, he dismounted and led his horse into a low cave.

I followed him, protesting. "This post would be high in the rock. I thought you knew—"

"Did you not hear the Aveddi's tale of this place?" he whispered, looking at me askance. "I thought you were his beloved friend."

"I had to go away for a few days," I said. "He didn't have a chance to tell me."

Feyd pointed deeper into the cave. "If I've found the right place, then just there past the bend on the right, we should find a chute—a narrow, angled passage that leads steeply upward. The Aveddi says that if you climb this chute all the way to the top—a considerable way, he says—and then step out on the ledge and ease around it to the left without falling to your death in the chasm, you'll come on the archers' watchpost. I don't know how Blaise is planning to come at it, or how you're to get close enough without letting them see you, but I said I'd show you and so I've done." His broad chest stretched a little further.

I ought to have given Feyd a lesson in too easy trust—he seemed to take my word in any matter. Perhaps our "attachment" was working both ways. He was proud and foolish, good-hearted and inexperienced, and, against all reason and expectation, I would have trusted him with my life.

"You've done well," I said. "I'm not going to endanger Blaise's scheme, just see if I can get a peek. Stay close here. And, Feyd"—I gave him my most serious expression—"do *not* go to sleep. I'd need to report it to your palatine, and he'll have your balls, if not your head, for it. Do you understand?"

Of course, the young warrior could not understand the true

implications of his falling asleep, but I didn't think I had to worry. He hung his head like an overlarge child. "Never again, sir."

"Good." I hurried into the cave, casting a faint light to search for the chute. *Damn!* It would take me a half hour to climb. I would have to change a little sooner than I'd planned. I assumed Blaise was going to get there the same way I thought to do it—fly. Thankful for my newly easy shifting, I shaped my falcon's form and fluttered up the long chimney, then swore at myself that I should have devised a shape more suitable than a large winged bird for the cramped space. But when I emerged in the evening sunlight, I was happy for the broad wings. The "ledge" that was the path around the cliff wall to the watchpost made the goat track down from Feyd's rock look like the Emperor's Road.

Only a few moments more and I had my answer. To my immediate left was the stomach-heaving depression in the sheer cliff that was the archers' watchpost. From a perch on a nearby outcropping, I could look down and across the gaping chasm and see what the post was set here to protect. A sizable stream threaded its way across a broad green shelf, only to have its flow aborted by a rounded earthwork that caused the water to back up and form a small lake. A few goats grazed in the green little spot, and two men sprawled on the grass just beside a rectangular structure of iron and wood that was set into the embankment. This was the sluice gate that could allow the water to flow through the earthwork and into a series of rocky trenches that headed down the mountainside to service the mine. No sign of extra guards or watchfulness at the sluice.

As for the watchpost designed to protect the sluice and its guards, the three men who sat in it were no elite archers whose families lived in gold-endowed luxury. They were not even common soldiers, but ruffians as one might find for hire in city alleyways or lurking in the wake of caravans looking for easy money. One of the slovenly trio was regaling the other with an unseemly story of a Zhagad brothel as the two played at ulyat with chips of rock. The third was pissing down the plunging cliff side and taking bets from the other two on whether he could hit one of the goats with a shot from his bow.

"They've not put you in this crow's eye to shoot, Rakiis," snorted one of the ulyat players. "Until they pay you archer's gold, you'd best not waste your pittance on a fool's gamble."

"Swallow your prick," snarled the bowman as he tied up his breeches and snatched up a bow. His arrow came nearer killing his companions than touching a goat. Exactly as I had guessed. These three were naught but fodder for the outlaws' strike. The Danatos knew we were coming.

A few more questions to be answered before I joined Aleksander. Of primary importance—where was the missing garrison? I made a quick survey of the terrain between the sluice and the mine entrance, which, according to Feyd, was half a league to the west. Surely somewhere I would glimpse the missing soldiers. But I saw no one, and instead of hunting farther afield, I found myself circling back toward the watchpost, the chimney, and the cave underneath it where the nervous Suzaini sat waiting for me. I couldn't leave him behind. *Attached.* Perhaps if I were to change to my own winged form rather than the falcon's shape, I might be able to escape my dreamer's binding, but for the moment I just swore a bit and sped downward through the chute.

Somewhere out of my range of vision, the sun was plummeting toward the horizon. It had taken us far too long to get to this place where the slotlike rift we were traveling opened into another, wider gorge—the spot at which Admet, the Suzaini outlaw with the crippled shoulder, had commanded Feyd to await Aleksander and report on the doings at the garrison. Feyd held up his hand for caution. We slipped off our horses and peered around a great pillar of rock that marked the junction. To our right, two thousand paces down the shadowed gorge, was the entrance to the mine, a large dark blot at the base of the cliff wall, obscured by thick yellow smoke from the burning octar seeps in front of it. Between our position and the entrance, deep wagon ruts and evidence of many horses suggested that the gold shipment had gone out on schedule.

All was quiet, save the birds that screeched and twittered from their roosts in the rift walls. My imagination had to conjure the muffled thud of rock hammers, the creak of wooden ore carts, the curses and shouts of overseers, and the groans of the laboring captives chained in the flickering torchlight under the rock. I was almost sick with my sense of that wretched place and the dangers that hung about it as thick as the yellow smoke.

Somewhere above us was the mine watch, where guards stood ready to signal the garrison should anyone untoward approach the mine entrance. Whoever watched there would be sacrificed, too, I guessed, to draw the outlaws deeper into the trap. And somewhere close would be the hundred and fifty warriors from the fortress. Despite a number of side excursions, including my circling flights in falcon's form, Feyd and I had found no sign of the missing Derzhi as we raced toward the mine.

"I'm going to shift again," I whispered to Feyd. "Don't be afraid."

Poor Feyd had almost shed his young beard when I had come screeching down the chute, flown right into his face, and proceeded to transform into my own shape. But after his initial astonishment, he had accepted my hurried explanation as if he met shapechangers every day of his life. Only his mumbled prayers every time I shifted revealed the depth of his fear and his courage. This change was going to be a bit more difficult for him, I thought. Suzainis had a particular dislike of bats. Unlucky, they said.

"Don't follow me, no matter what. If the Aveddi arrives before I return, it's up to you to warn him. Use my name. Tell him that Seyonne is sure the Danatos have been warned. Do you understand?"

"But I should be with you."

"Only if you can sprout fur or feathers in the next breath. I'll be back, lad. Your duty is here." I was getting the feel of the distance we could be comfortable apart. And so, praying he would stick to his post and neither run away from me in terror nor after me in dream-induced fervor, I considered bats, swallowed my own unpleasant boyhood memories of the creatures, and shifted.

Bats are not blind. So my teachers had told me. But then, neither can they see with as great a clarity as a falcon nor even so well as a sorcerer with or without his melydda to help him. I had thought to enter the Danatos mine unremarked, and that was indeed the case, but I was unprepared for the confusion of sight caused by weak bat eyes and sputtering torchlight and large men moving in and out of patches of unrelieved darkness. Somewhat disconcerting also was the need to hang upside down to do any stationary observations, as my wretched feet were too weak to hold me up. Bats don't perch. Fortunately I could hear very well, else I would have given it up and chosen another form. And eventually I managed to decipher what I was seeing.

Massive beams supported the weight of earth and rock above the mine. The cavernous atrium was lit by torches set in iron holders bolted to the rock, and was piled with barrels and crates, coils of ropes and chains, grinding wheels, and bins of tools. The small two-wheeled carts lined up beside the doors would be used for distributing rations of water and food to the slaves bound within the mine, and for hauling out the gold they hacked from the earth. Under the supervision of a bearded overseer, two slaves were unloading barrels from a large wagon and stacking them. The smell told me that these particular barrels contained octar, not water. A great deal of octar. Two slaves began soaking fresh torches in the contents of one barrel and throwing them into the carts. Three more overseers hovered about a group of some twenty slaves, all strongly built, horribly scarred, and hobbled by short lengths of chain stretched between their ankle bands. The sullen group stood waiting in front of a massive pair of iron doors set into the back wall of the atrium—the doors to the network of shafts that were reputed to riddle this entire ridge. Rumors said the tunnels spanned some twenty leagues or more.

Everything was wrong. From the first moment, I felt it. Smelled it. Tasted it. Why so many barrels of octar? Yes, torches dipped in octar would be the only light inside the mine, but why so much at once? And where were the Derzhi warriors? I fluttered from a corner near the entrance back into the shadows of the cavern, dodging the disgusted swipe of an overseer's hand as I passed close over his head. I saw no one else. Not only were there no extra guards awaiting the outlaws' assault, but there were no guards at all. How could they have left the mine undefended? From their huddled terror and mumbled curses and prayers, I would have thought the slaves were new workers being introduced to this living death. But their scars were old, and even the youngest of them wore the distinctive hunch and permanent squint of mine slaves. And where was the noise? Truly the sounds I'd heard from back in the rift had been my own imaginings, for the mine was profoundly silent, save for the activity I saw right before me.

Slaves were commanded to open the iron doors, and only as two men lifted them from the brackets where they rested did I note the wide metal straps that had been laid across the tight-fitting doors. The mine had been locked. Sealed. Dread gnawed at my spirit. Two other slaves manned the gear wheels at the sides of the doors, and the moment the grinding clamor of the opening doors began, I abandoned my corner and flew through the slowly widening gap.

The cool dry tunnels smelled foul—the stench a familiar one for anyone ever held in close confinement for a long span of time—and they were unremittingly dark. After a few brushes with solid walls, I let my instincts take over and guide my flight by the sound of my own high-pitched squealing. But my instincts led me nowhere that a man or woman of any shaping could wish to be. Nothing lived in those tunnels, nor in the wider rooms I felt expand around me from time to time before narrowing into another passage. Every once in a while, I would come to the end of a tunnel, the face of the rock where the veins of gold lay exposed, ready for the taking, and I would feel them there . . . soft bodies, still and lifeless. Not warm. Not anymore. Everyone was dead.

I fluttered frantically from one passage to another, desperate to find any evidence to contradict my belief. The hobbled slaves were now chained to the two-wheeled carts, dragging them through the dark tunnels and lighting torches along the way, illuminating the buried horror. Seven hundred, Aleksander had said. And only these few souls had been spared, now charged to haul out the dead and burn them. Thus the octar.

Time . . . The sun must be nearing the horizon. I was too slow to explore all the passages, hunting for one body that might still be breathing, something to relieve this vile darkness that enveloped the world and was seeping into my soul. I allowed instinct to guide me back to the mine entrance. No need for me to explore the passages so as to tell the full story. The others would come soon and discover the magnitude of our defeat. Perhaps they would find one who lived—a small victory to wrest from the ruins of the night. For now, I had other duties. The missing warriors. Where in the name of all gods were they waiting?

CHAPTER 33

I emerged from the cave into dusk, the last edge of gold outlining the rim of the cliffs far above me. With only a thought I changed from bat to falcon, stretching my wings to catch every shift of the air, rising and circling wide over the rift and the pockmarked cliffs. No sign of the missing Derzhi. No sign of anyone save the small party of horsemen riding toward the stone columns where Feyd stood, a tiny dark figure waiting for them. Heedless of secrecy or wonder, I touched earth behind the Suzaini, changed to human form, and waited for the horsemen to halt.

"Where's the Prince?" I said harshly, sparing no time for explanations. "I thought he was to lead this assault."

"Seyonne!" Three voices said my name at once—and the three painted faces each revealed something of truth. Feyd's lips murmured an invocation to his god, his expression already reflecting the horror that I knew. Roche's pleased surprise quickly faded into a puzzled frown. And Gorrid . . . was I wrong to think the dislike in his hard eyes was laced with fear?

"There was word of trouble," said Roche. "Lord Aleksander has gone to—"

"Don't tell him anything," Gorrid commanded. "You heard the stories of Dasiet Homol, how the women said he was possessed by some fearful being. We daren't trust him."

I ignored Gorrid. "Roche, tell me where I can find the Prince. Everyone on this mission is in danger. Feyd will witness as to what we've found at the fortress, and in the first moment you step into the mine, you'll know of treachery so foul you'd wish your children blind before they laid eyes upon such vileness. Remember what you know of me from Andassar, from Taíne Keddar, from Blaise's trust. You must tell me where Aleksander's gone. His life depends on it."

In the moment I spoke the words, I knew them true. What could have compelled the Danatos to take such a drastic step—

to murder their own slaves? Only the need to use their troops for something other than securing the slaves, along with a despicable determination to deny the freedom they could no longer prevent. Perhaps they didn't realize how few outlaws were coming, or perhaps there were not a hundred and fifty warriors garrisoned in their fortress. But no matter the numbers or the plan. I could think of only one reason that could inspire greed of such monumental consequence—the prospect of something infinitely more valuable to replace their dead property. The Kinslayer. They were after Aleksander.

Feyd broke in. "The fortress is empty, Roche, and the archers have been withdrawn from the watchpost. It's surely a trap. You must tell us where the Aveddi can be found."

"We got word that there were more warriors at the sluice gate than we thought," said Roche, convinced more by Feyd than me, it seemed. "The Aveddi said I should take command here—to reap the glory in his stead, he told me—and he took out alone to help them at the sluice."

Of course. Stupid of me not to see it. Slaves could be replaced, but the mine could not. The Danatos could never allow the mine to be flooded. And, too, the dark hillsides that opened onto the green shelf and the lake were perfect places for warriors to hide and so to capture their wayward Prince. If they were sure he would be there, if someone had betrayed him, sent him there believing he was needed . . .

"Gaverna," I said to a Basran woman who was one of Blaise's fiercest fighters, "get up to the mine watch. Tell Farrol that only twenty slaves are left living, all chained to the carts. Only four overseers to deal with, no guards, no warriors. Set a watch and do whatever you can to confirm that no one else survives, but make it quick and get out."

"Only twenty—" Gorrid and Roche spoke together, aghast. Gorrid's bronze skin lost color.

"The Danatos decided that their slaves were not to be free," I snapped. "The rest of you—the battle is at the sluice gate. If not for Aleksander's sake, then ride for Blaise; his life is at risk as well." For if Blaise, manning the watchpost, saw Aleksander in trouble, he would surely fly across the chasm to his aid. And if we didn't get there in time, every man and woman of the outlaw party would die . . . except for Aleksander. Aleksander's death belonged only to the Emperor. "And if not for Blaise, then ride for the seven hundred dead."

I turned to my dreamer. "Your fight is waiting, Feyd. Will you come with me?"

Feyd straightened his back and loosened his sword in its scabbard. "Four hundred years ago, on the first day of Wolf's Moon, Parassa, the royal city of Suza, fell to the Derzhi Empire," he said. "On that cursed day, every girl child of Parassa was slain. Every woman was ravaged, bound, and sent to the slave markets of Parnifour and Vayapol. Every boy child was cut to ensure that the noble houses of the Suzai would come to an end, and the men and boys were condemned to dig mines like this under the rocks of Suza. All these years the Suzai have waited for the Firstborn of Azhakstan to return to the desert and make amends for the deeds of his fathers. I will not fail him." He mounted his horse. "Lead us, Master."

With a surge of melydda, I shifted into my warrior's form, and as the last of the sun's gold vanished, my own golden light flared bright, and I took wing.

No perspective of a battlefield can rival a view from the air. As I raced westward, following the dark network of the rifts that would lead me to the green meadow, the sluice gate, and the trap laid for Aleksander, I could see the darker smudge that was Feyd and Roche and the ten riders galloping along the same route below me. The moon already hung over the desert beyond the wall of these mountains, and as I veered to the right over the green shelf, its wavering image was reflected in the evening ripples on the lake. At its northern edge, the level meadow broke over into a steep slope, crisscrossed by a narrow track leading downward to the valley floor.

I caught one glimpse of deceptive peace. Five Derzhi warriors protected the gate, two of them mounted and riding slowly about the rim of the lake on patrol, two standing stiffly, spears in hand at either side of the sluice gate, one tending a fire. Three horses grazed nearby. But at the very moment of my arrival, five riders reached the top of the steep track and shot across the meadow toward the gate and the guards, four painted outlaws led by a Derzhi voicing the wild and throaty war cry of the desert. Aleksander. Four of Blaise's outlaws could never outmatch five Derzhi warriors, but with the Prince at their side, they would believe the balance tipped in their favor . . . except that I knew better.

For the moment I stayed high and circled the meadow, anxiously searching the cracked shoulders of the adjacent ridge, the narrow slots in the cliffs where men and horses could hide until they heard a signal to descend upon the unsuspecting raiders. *There!* Even so high above the ground I felt the quiet tension in the dark gully below me . . . twenty . . . thirty men and horses, surely no more than forty, well disciplined, waiting until the attacking outlaws were fully committed. Of course the Derzhi would believe forty enough to take the Prince and a handful of outlaws. But then where were the rest of the warriors? I assumed that the Danatos, determined to take their prize, had sent all of the garrison into this combat, prepared in case the outlaws got wind of the treachery and sent their entire force to attack the gate. But my search revealed no more warriors, and the clash of steel and angry shouts below told me that I had no more time. The hidden horsemen burst from the slot in the cliff. I circled back, drew my sword, and descended on the line of Derzhi spilling out across the meadow.

Surprise is a formidable weapon in combat, and awe and astonishment are its worthy companions. My wings were fully spread, and my body glowed fiery gold. I killed seven Derzhi before even one thought to aim sword or spear in my direction. Even then I had half of them circling and running into each other trying to see what I was and from what quarter I would come next, while others remained cowering in the gap in the cliff, afraid to face me. But while I reaped the benefits of successful surprise, I saw Aleksander suffering the consequences of the reverse. The five guards who had seemed to be pursuing quiet routine were mounted and battle ready before the outlaw party had crossed half the distance from the edge of the meadow to the lake. Perhaps Aleksander suspected the trap even then, for he tried to pull up, but his four companions were not so observant and rushed on headlong. Not one to retreat at any time, the Prince released his mount, and when the two parties clashed, he was again at the head of the outlaw band.

By the time thirteen of the hidden warriors lay dead beneath me, a few of the troop had recovered their wits and were trying to reform their party. One on one they could not touch me. Three on one kept me busy. Each time I seemed to be in trouble, I thought of the seven hundred helpless souls murdered in their dark prison, and my anger gave strength to my arm and power to my enchantments. Even so, some of the Derzhi slipped away and rode for the gate and the Prince. I could not allow it.

I wrenched out an arrow that had pierced my left shoulder, set the bloody shaft afire, and threw it with such force it pierced the archer's neck. A last sweep of my blade beheaded one warrior and unhorsed another, and I soared upward and flew toward the lake. One by one I cut down the escaping Derzhi, unheeding of their groans and screams. I called up the wind and the water, causing a monstrous wave to climb out of the muddy basin and sweep two horsemen into the lake. Another was trampled when I drove his horse mad with stinging bees.

By the time I reached the sluice gate, Aleksander was engaged with two of the gate guards who were pressing him hard. Two Derzhi were on the ground—one dead, one injured—along with an outlaw missing his head. The remaining Danatos guard fought two outlaws at once, while a man with a painted face worked on the gears and latches of the gate, ducking and dodging the flying weapons and hooves when the battle came too near him.

Aleksander caught his first sight of me. "Great Athos, save us!"

"They're coming for you," I shouted to the grimly smiling Prince, who used the occasion of my arrival to skewer one awestruck opponent while I unhorsed the other.

Aleksander pulled his horse around to look for his next opponent and kicked the unhorsed Derzhi in the head lest the man stab the preoccupied Pherro. "What in the god's holy name have you done to yourself?"

Lungs burning from the heavy fighting, I forced myself to inhale before trying to speak, and even then I could not afford to waste strength on explanations. "At least twenty more coming around the lake. Over a hundred of the garrison unaccounted for." Where were they?

I touched earth between the two struggling outlaws and the remaining gate guard. The Derzhi guard staggered backward and dropped to his knees. Before the gaping warrior could make a god sign against evil, I cut him in half. None too soon. The first rider of the larger party rounded the end of the earthwork, sword raised and heading straight for the Prince. As he blazed past me, I pulled him off his horse and severed his neck. A second rider followed close on his heels. This one swerved to avoid me. The wind rose at my command, and I raised my bloody sword one more time, but before I could take flight, a dark shape streaked screaming across the sky and flew into the man's face. The warrior's mount reared and threw him to the ground, where he lay unmoving. The bird circled once, and after a blurring moment, Blaise was running toward us.

"When I saw the fire—and you—I decided there was no more point in holding the watchpost," he said, staring at me unabashed. "Stars of the heavens, man, what have you—?"

"Get everyone away," I said, still heaving, warm blood dribbling from my shoulder, though I felt no hurt from it. "You were betrayed." I hacked off the head of the unhorsed Derzhi, and then spread my wings, ready to take on the remainder of the Derzhi riders. Feyd and Roche and the rest of the raiding party were riding over the lip of the meadow, and I yelled for them to follow me.

"Seyonne!" Aleksander called after me. Though his command was quiet, somehow my name on his tongue reached me in the grim place where I had existed since I'd seen what was done in the mine.

I held the wind under my wings so as to hover over him, my gold fire bathing his worried face. "My lord?"

"Watch your soul, my guardian. I would not buy my life with it."

"They should not have left the mine unguarded," I said. "They killed them all, my lord. Seven hundred, less twenty they saved to stack and burn the others. I have no mercy left in me."

The battle was joined again a few hundred paces from the gate. Feyd struck his blow for Parassa, for lost Suza and four hundred years of humiliation. I sent Blaise hunting for the rest of the warriors, while I killed again and again. Aleksander fought with deadly success, but only until the first Derzhi dismounted, knelt, and begged quarter. "Not one more drop of blood," he shouted, dashing to every duel, halting the slashing swords with his own if his voice was not enough. "Not one more hair will be touched."

He forced the seven surviving Derzhi to kneel and place their hands on their heads while the outlaws disarmed them and led their horses away. And then he rode before the line of prisoners, back and forth, as if to make sure that each one saw his face—especially those who wore the gold trappings of nobility. One of the kneeling Derzhi spat at the Prince, but Aleksander stayed the hand of the Manganar raider who raised his hand to strike the man. "Rope these seven together. While we take care of our fallen, they will gather my brothers and bury them," he said to the raiders. "I'll leave no Derzhi warrior for vultures, no matter his crimes. When the work is done, we'll take the prisoners down to the mine and see how they should be judged."

As the prisoners set about the grisly task, and the raiders stripped the bodies of weapons and tended to their own dead and wounded, I touched earth near the Prince. Everyone withdrew hastily, leaving us alone in the center of the battlefield. "You need to find out where the rest of the garrison is waiting," I said. "Your prisoners know. Did you see the smug looks on their faces?"

Aleksander dismounted, crouched down beside a fallen Derzhi, and began cleaning his hands on the man's ripped cloak. "Of course, I saw it. They expect me to torture the information out of them, but I won't. They'd die before they told me—or near enough. If things are going to change, then it must begin now. I want these seven to carry the tale of it to Zhagad." Before standing up again, he rolled the dead warrior to his back, closed the staring eyes, and straightened the cooling limbs, laying the man's sword on his chest until the outlaws could collect it. "I hoped you would agree." He stood up and faced me square on, his whole posture a question I could not answer; I did not yet know who or what I was.

"Then we'll have to learn what we need to know some other way," I said, yielding the point. Reluctantly. Abandoning wings and light, I shifted back to my own form, rubbing my head to try to clear the muddle.

Aleksander nodded, satisfied, and then he mounted and rode off toward the others, encouraging the outlaw fighters, ignoring the scowls and curses of the Danatos warriors, watching carefully to see that they did not break their parole. Impatient at the delay, I stood at the top of the embankment, where I could see, trying to find the missing piece of the night's puzzle. Blaise returned after a while, reporting that he saw no evidence of the other Derzhi. "Perhaps the garrison has been reduced," he said, sitting down on the grassy hillock and offering a waterskin.

I sat next him and took the cool leather pouch. Only as I drank did I realize how thirsty I was. "It doesn't make sense," I said. "They can't be sure we'll go back to the mine. We've no reason to but to help the last twenty before they're thrown on the pyre with the dead. But if not here and not at the mine, then where else could they be planning to hit us?"

"Gods of night, would they do that? Burn the living?" Blaise paused before taking another swig from the waterskin for himself.

"There is no evil one human will not work on another," I said. And no betrayal. Who had told the Danatos that Aleksander was coming?

"Blaise!" Roche called from the sluice gate. "Pherro says he's ready to open the sluice."

Blaise glanced at me as he stood. "Have a care, Seyonne." He dropped the waterskin in my lap, then slid his way down the steep embankment toward the gate and his men. "We've got to make sure Farrol has everyone out of the mine first," I heard him tell Roche. "I'll go find out. When the Aveddi starts down, he wants you and Pherro to stay behind . . ." They walked off together, leaving me to solitude and worry.

Who was the traitor? Despite my suspicions, I could not accuse Gorrid just because he hated Aleksander. Everyone at Taíne Keddar bore some grievance against the Prince or his father. The matter of the slaves was the biggest stumbling block to pinning this villainy on one of Blaise's people. No matter their feelings about Aleksander, none were callous enough to jeopardize the outcome of the raid for personal vengeance. This was not some angry outlaw running to the Danatos unthinking. Someone had conceived a plan. That eliminated Gorrid. He was not a complex thinker; he hated Aleksander, but he hated the Derzhi even more, and his loves and hates would always define his actions. So who was it? I could not leave this world until I knew, if I had to prick young Feyd to sleeplessness for three days.

The last vestiges of daylight faded from the sky, my friends and enemies left indistinguishable in the murky borderland of night. My senses were tuned with every scrap of power I could muster, listening for hoofbeats, for muffled voices, for harness bound with strips of leather to mute its telltale ring, for swords and knives being carefully unsheathed. The missing warriors were poised to cut our throats, but where? I riffled through the exchanges of the day. Through Feyd's recitation of the plan. Through the meeting with Roche and Gorrid outside the mine. Through weeks of listening to the outlaws at Blaise's fire at Taíne Keddar. In the fifth time over, I knew the answer.

"Roche!" I said, slithering down the embankment and calling to the quiet young Ezzarian as he helped a group of his men and women load up the sizable pile of confiscated Derzhi weapons by tying them to backs and belts and saddles. "Who scouted this raid?"

The dark-haired man buckled a fine leather sword belt atop three others around a Kuvai woman's shoulder. "Admet," he said. "After our bungling at Andassar, he said he wanted to check the terrain for himself, so he came out here three days ago to see to it."

"And who was with him?"

"No one. Easier for one to keep hidden."

"Alone? But he can't travel the way you do." Admet was human, not a joined Ezzarian.

Roche glanced about noting who was in earshot. "Did no one ever tell you the location of Taíne Keddar? That was the beauty of this plan. The valley is only a few hours' ride—for anyone—from Syra." He shook his head. "That's why we thought we could get so many slaves away safely, because with Blaise, Gorrid, Brynna, Farrol, and me taking them through the ways, we could have had them in Taíne Keddar in half an hour." The young Ezzarian pulled another sword belt from the pile, jerking on it impatiently when the long sheath caught in the tangle. "No, Admet came on his own to do the scouting, and he was right in every point. I suppose we fouled it up some other way this time."

Admet. And Feyd had said that Admet was to lead the fighters to the sluice gate. "Have you seen Admet tonight?" I asked. "Maybe he can give me some idea as to whether the garrison was in place that day or if they've moved out since." Or how the Danatos got wind of the Prince . . .

Roche took a bundle of knives from a stocky youth who had rolled them in a dead man's shirt, and he stuffed them into a saddle pack. "He brought us word of the extra guards at the sluice, but then Brynna took him back to Taíne Keddar to help make ready for the slaves. Admet can't fight you know—not with his back the way it is. He was a slave himself as a child. The Derzhi broke him. Left him crippled."

And so a great deal became clear. "So he guided the four fighters to the sluice . . . and then he came to fetch Aleksander."

"That's right." Roche called after me as I turned to walk back up the embankment. "It was good you were here, Seyonne. You saved us again."

I just shook my head. Seven hundred dead.

Admet, the wily Suzaini strategist. A complex thinker. A man who might believe he could punish Aleksander while somehow managing to rescue the slaves. Gods . . . that was it. He'd made a bargain with the Danatos. *We'll hand over the Kinslayer, but you'll allow us into the mine . . . leave it unguarded. We'll trade one man for seven hundred. And you'll get to keep the mine, for we'll set the trade at the lake and leave before breaking the sluice gate*. The Prince alone was to be taken. Not the other fighters.

But the Danatos had been wilier than Admet. *We'll take the Kinslayer, and we'll leave the mine unguarded, but you'll never take our property. We'll kill them first. We'll take the prize and leave you nothing . . . nothing . . .*

"No!" As the pieces settled into position, I was appalled at the image I had built. Of Admet hating Derzhi so much that he believed them stupid and could not distinguish one from another. Of the Danatos first lord, denounced by his own mother for his continuing dishonor, swearing to abide by the agreement, while planning from the first how to twist it to his advantage. Of Admet riding home after his clever bargaining, smug in his success. And of some Danatos spy who followed the broken Suzaini on his human path . . . all the way to Taíne Keddar. First ensure the capture of the Kinslayer, and then wipe out the Yvor Lukash. Seven hundred slaves were nothing. For this, the Emperor would yield them half the Empire.

Mad with rage and terror, I shaped wings and shot into the sky, crying out for the others to abandon their useless tasks and follow me. I knew where the remaining Danatos had gone.

CHAPTER 34

Taíne Keddar was in flames. The houses and tents were already ash, the ancient olive trees but dark, twisted scars on a sky of garish orange and red. By the time Aleksander, Blaise, and the other riders crested the encircling ridge, I had surveyed the valley and found it devoid of life. Flames licked at a few dark forms lying here and there amid the burning fields and groves. Everyone else—the attackers, as well as those who lived in the valley—had disappeared.

"Where would they go?" I screamed at Blaise over the roar of the flames, knowing—terrified—what he would answer. Ash swirled lazily in the torrid air like enchanted leaves that vanished at a touch. A pine exploded into flame just behind me.

"Taíne Horet," he said. His bony face was distraught, his serenity shattered as he pointed to the path that wound through a stand of burning trees and led deeper into the mountains toward the old kings' stronghold. Aleksander slammed his heels into his horse's heaving flanks before the word had left Blaise's tongue. I was the only person ahead of him.

Whether it was Blaise or I who worked the enchantment to speed us through the rugged terrain, I never knew. The riders did not slow as they passed the hacked remains of the settlers' rear guard, but thundered after me as they had since I told them of my terrible suspicion. No man or woman of the raiding party but had a child or lover, kinsman or friend among those in the valley. I could not think of Evan. Anger already ruled my arm, and I needed to keep some semblance of reason.

The Danatos had many hours' head start on us, but when we hit their backs, they had only just collapsed the first ring of Taíne Horet's defense. Their rear guard was positioned in the rocks and trees at the base of the ridge. Halfway down the descending path, Aleksander silently motioned his meager troop into a wedge, set himself at the apex, and gave the signal to charge. I soared from the heights and flew in just ahead of him. My first victim was still wide-eyed and gaping as I shoved his warm body off my sword and smashed another man in the face with my bare foot. Two other warriors fell back at the sight of me, the light of my Madonai body coloring their pale faces sallow. Roche rode up and skewered one of them in the back, and I spun in the air and swept my blade, taking the head of the second man. Enchantments lay in my hand like a second sword that night, impossibility and distance and bone-deep weariness of no more import to me than gnats to a mountain.

The battle was a bloody one. Between the raiding party, the remaining Yvor Lukash from Taíne Keddar, and the people of Taíne Horet, we had superior numbers. But most of Blaise's people were city-bred poor or peasants, strong, but untrained in combat, or freed slaves, trying to substitute vengeance and spirit for the weakness of their broken bodies, or old people, or children; there were a great number of children. And the others—the Manganar, Thrid, and Suzaini who dwelt in Taíne Horet—had hidden in these rocks for decades, hoping, waiting, planning, and training; but their enemies had been images from history, not superbly trained warriors wielding swords and spears with ferocious precision.

Indeed the Danatos fought as if possessed by the mad Gastai. They believed their prize very close—power next to the Emperor's own—and they recovered quickly from our surprise assault. The outer ring of warriors, so easily penetrated by our initial attack, hardened into a wall of steel, threatening to close about our wedge. They held us at bay while their lines pressed forward, orderly, methodical, scouring the valley, pressing men, women, children, goats, donkeys, and horses before them, killing any person who resisted.

Aleksander, seeming to be everywhere at once, molded and shaped his sixteen fighters, teaching and encouraging them even as he threw himself against the Danatos lines. But the Derzhi ranks refused to break. Our riders were too few, and when the Danatos' inner ring had captured or slaughtered those within their grasp, they would turn and crush our pitiful band like a lion's great paw smashing an annoying dog.

I strove to protect both Aleksander and Feyd—I could not afford to have my dreamer slain—and I killed any Derzhi within reach of my blade. Always I kept my eye out for Admet. I had not told the others of my suspicion, but I had sworn to myself that he would go on trial before I left the human world. If he had done what I believed, he would die for it.

"We've got to get through," Aleksander shouted up at me as I slashed at a warrior threatening his back. It was difficult to see in the dark, the only light the wavering glare of the fires the Derzhi set as they passed. "Can you find us a way?"

"Done," I cried. "Roche, you've got the Prince's back."

I shot upward to look about, trying to make sense of things through the smoke and screams and flailing weapons. The three camps were in chaos, the sentries and guards who yet lived barely managing to hold their own as they retreated. The people of the valley hadn't enough horses to mount their defense, and the mounted Derzhi swept through the slow-footed fighters like fire through dry grass. Fifteen or twenty defenders fell for every Derzhi. I flew the length of the Derzhi front, trying to find some small gap, some weak spot where the ranks of disciplined Derzhi might be breached, hoping to discover some firm center where Aleksander might rally the frantic people and take advantage of his numbers.

A force of some twenty to thirty Thrid charged out of the burning groves to attack the Derzhi left flank, only to see half their number cut down in the first engagement. I showered the Derzhi with sparks I gathered from the fires, enabling a tattooed woman to rally the Thrid fighters. Soon, more joined her, and she began to form up a small line of resistance. I flew on.

Several of the Yvor Lukash fighters were trying to make a stand near the Suzaini encampment. The Palatine Marouf—Feyd's father—was off at the front of the battle. A small party of Derzhi had outflanked them and now threatened to wipe out their families. A Suzaini woman lay on the ground unmoving, bloody and exposed, and an old woman sat in the dirt wailing, trying to cover the pitiful remains with hands and skirts. Other women, responsible for their husbands' wealth, were trying to retrieve their children and their hoards of silver before a similar fate befell them.

A fresh wave of Derzhi swept out of the darkness, driving the Yvor Lukash fighters and the panicked women away from the Suzaini tents. A blood-smeared youth leaped out from behind a bush and slashed wildly at a Derzhi rider who was bearing down on a woman carrying two small boys. The youth didn't see a second Derzhi ride up behind him, sword raised.

"Mattei, behind you!" I dived into the fray, shoving my young friend to the ground and stabbing at the attacking warrior, while using my wings to sweep Mattei's target from his rearing mount. "Stay back, lad," I cried as the unhorsed warrior scrabbled quickly to his feet. A few strokes later and the Derzhi choked on his own blood and fell to earth, trying to prevent his entrails escaping through the gaping hole I'd left in his belly.

I spun on my heel. Mattei was staring at me as he crept backward over the rocky ground. I reached out my hand to haul him up, feeling like smiling for the first time in hours. "Come on," I said. "Let's get you someplace less dangerous." But my simple gesture scribed his young face with mortal terror, and uttering a whimper, he scrambled to his feet and ran off into the darkness.

"Mattei, wait . . ." No time to go after him. I had to hold back the attacking Derzhi while the Yvor Lukash fighters got the Suzaini women away.

Another sweep of the front showed me that the Thrid woman had positioned her fighters securely among the trees, and her archers and bold swordsmen had slowed the Derzhi advance and stretched the enemy's lines. A small victory, but the best prospect I'd seen. I raced back to Aleksander and Blaise, who were being sorely pressed by a Danatos second lord. The Derzhi noble was screaming at his men that the Kinslayer was among them.

"Go left!" I shouted, pointing the Prince toward the Thrid. "W'Assani's people hold the way."

While I used fire and sword, wind and terror to prevent the Derzhi from closing ranks behind him, Aleksander fought his way toward the valiant Thrid. A half an hour later, a path of fallen Derzhi behind him, he broke through into the heart of the battle. From the center of the valley a murmuring tide of sound swelled to drown out the screams and shouts and the roar of the flames. "Aveddi!" The cries echoed from the cliffs, and soon the very shape of the combat changed. Outward pressure from the center halted the Derzhi advance, and before another hour had passed, the rear guard began to fall back toward the hills. Once there, they had to deal with me.

Every hour that I fought in my golden form I felt stronger. Yes, I was tired. Yes, I had a dozen bleeding gashes and punctures. Yes, I still felt a tearing fire in my side whenever I raised my right arm. But with every passing moment, my reactions grew faster, my strokes more powerful, my movements quicker and more sure. I had been born to wear that form of light, to fight such battles, to use the power I had been given to protect those who needed it. I could sense the slightest movement behind me, and I could hold a part of my mind outside the combat, using it to ready my weapons of enchantment. I could see with such clarity—the fighters at my hand, the shifting lines of combat, the dark, surging mass of Blaise's people. The bony outlaw himself was leading the right, with the two Manganar Yulai and Terlach beside him. The Thrid woman held the left, and in the center stood Aleksander, the Firstborn of Azhakstan, his red hair flying, fighting with the measured fury of a king defending his citadel. Behind his sword my child was safe, as was his own, but only if no Derzhi left this valley with the tale of its location. *Let them fear me*. And so I gave myself willingly to combat, and killed every warrior my hand could reach.

Everything wore the varied colors of blood—the dark, gore-soaked earth beneath my feet, my naked flesh smeared with red and rusty brown, even the rocks above and beside me, flushed with the scarlet dawn. Quiet had descended on the valley, but I hadn't noticed, for the battle raging in my veins had only now found its final release. I yanked my sword from the twitching body at my feet, then dropped to my knees and made sure of him, driving my knife into his heart. "Not my son, you bastard," I said, the hoarse whisper that grated in my throat all the sound I could muster. Blood matted his dark beard and his striped haffai. His sword hilt slid from his limp hand, and I kicked the weapon away when I stood up again, as if to be sure he could not rise from the dead and bring more treachery into the world. "Never him."

"Holy gods, Seyonne, what have you done?"

I whirled about and saw them standing there—Blaise, the stunned accuser, cradling one arm, his paint half washed away by sweat and blood, and gray-faced Elinor, her blue skirt stained and torn, a well-used sword at her side, her hand steadying her wounded brother. Elinor gazed at my last victim expressionless, as if the burden of horror that she already wore could not accept yet another portion. The sight of her there, in such a state, set off a firestorm in my soul.

"Tell me!" I bellowed. Flames burst from my hand and sword, and the two stepped backward, almost tumbling down the steep path. I summoned the dregs of my strength to restrain my fury. "Please tell me . . . Evan . . ."

"He's well," said Elinor. "Safe with Magda. Safe."

Blaise was still staring at the dead man in the striped haffai. Heavy footsteps brought Roche and Gorrid to join him, their tired faces glazed with shock and dismay. And behind them, surveying the sea of corpses around me until his gaze rested on the dead man at my feet, came Aleksander.

"The devil has murdered Admet!" screamed Gorrid, drawing his sword, his face becoming a mask of hatred. "How many others of our own have fed his blood thirst?"

Aleksander reached out and stayed the outlaw's arm. "You cannot challenge him, Gorrid," he said softly, stepping in between us. I held my weapon at the ready, the pounding of my blood vibrating the fouled blade in rhythm with my heart. "Look around." No fewer than forty Derzhi warriors had felt my sword as they tried to escape the valley. The Prince nodded his head at the dead Suzaini and raised one eyebrow. "Will you tell us why?" His voice was calm and steady, but in his amber eyes . . . He was afraid of me.

With a word and a thought, I shifted form, feeling the light go out of the world along with my golden radiance and my strength. Indescribable weariness settled in my bones. My body felt gray and heavy, my clothing restrictive, my senses crippled and dull. I tried to form an answer, the fewest possible words to tell them of Admet's prideful, treacherous bargain. But my tongue was confused, as if accustomed to another language, and my mind could not seem to shape the evidence into a sequence they might understand. As I struggled to speak, yet another man came staggering up the hill. The curling hair and beard named him Suzaini, and his broad shoulders identified him as Feyd well before we could see his face.

Feyd's breath was ragged when he stopped beside Admet's body. My dreamer's wide, dark eyes flew to mine.

"The betrayer," I said, those two words all I could manage.

Feyd seemed to understand. He closed his eyes and said, "Gossopar forgive him. Such shame for Suza." The young man wavered for a moment, and then gathered himself and bowed to me. "My honor is yours forever, holy lord." Before he could come up again, he fell face forward into the dirt. I glimpsed a ragged, bloody hole in his back just as the world vanished.

* * *

"Did you accomplish what you set out to do?" The question came from an infinite distance. I had only to open my eyes, but the slightest movement felt like dragging myself through a sea of mud. "Come, Kasparian, bring him wine. Human bodies are not meant for this."

"I had to kill him," I said, shoving away the wine cup being pressed into my hand and resting my forehead on the cool glass of the game board. My lips were not trying to answer Nyel's question, but the questions left on the tongues of my friends. "He was running away, half mad with guilt. He would have betrayed you again—I saw it in him—to justify himself." I had not slain Admet solely in anger, nor had I wreaked unthinking vengeance. I had given him a chance to explain, to tell me how he had never meant to cause the horror he had unleashed. But all he'd done was curse Aleksander and me, and say that we had killed the seven hundred in the mine and the uncounted dead of that night's battle. Admet had sworn to bring down Aleksander no matter what he had to do to accomplish it. Even then, despite the demands of vengeance and fury, I had not struck him until he drew his sword, vowing to kill me . . . and then do the same to my son. Gods of night, how did he know about Evan? I didn't think Blaise had told anyone of my kinship to Elinor's foster child. And now . . . *fool* . . . Why hadn't I found out before I killed him?

"Of course you did what you thought was right." The voice was closer now, just across the table from me and not unkind.

The cost of the night's venture would be dreadful. We had won a victory in name only, wrested from such a vile and monstrous defeat. The war we had begun would be long and terrible, and my friends would have no time to plan, no time to prepare, no place to hide. Aleksander could not fight it alone.

I shoved my chair back from the little table and stood up, noticing in passing that it was raining again in Nyel's garden. The movement had my wounds clamoring for attention, and I had to grab the table edge to keep from collapsing from sudden dizziness. The thigh wound of the previous day was reopened. Between that and my shoulder, I had lost a good deal of blood. "Please, if you would have hot water sent to my room, and medicines for healing. And bandages. I've no wish to trouble Kasparian this time."

"It will be done."

I hobbled to the doorway and leaned on it for a moment, my back to the room and Nyel. "When can we begin?" I said.

A moment's silence. "It will take me some time to make preparations—a moon's turning. Perhaps twice that. Then we can proceed as rapidly as you wish, every step your own choice." No unseemly eagerness marred his speech. I appreciated that.

"I must go back to help them," I said. "They're too few and too unskilled."

Of course I could walk back through the gateway to the human world and serve Aleksander in my mortal form, but I dismissed the thought the moment it passed through my mind. What man, offered sight and strength and freedom, could live a blind and crippled slave? I believed Nyel would keep his promise and allow me to act freely. I had made my own choices as I fought, and any judge who witnessed the entirety of my actions at Syra and Taíne Horet would say I had done only what was needed to save my friends from disaster. Truly there was a price. There was always a price. I had seen it in Mattei's face . . . and in Aleksander's.

"There is a great deal that you can learn as you wait." Nyel didn't understand.

"I can't wait until I'm changed. I need to go back as soon as they're ready to fight again. That will be days, not weeks."

I glanced over my shoulder. Nyel was staring at me, weighing his answer. He dearly wanted to refuse. *So choose,* I thought. *Turn me down and force me to leave this place*. Truly at that moment I could not have said what I wanted him to answer. But my aching body knew.

"Though I believe you'd do better to delay your return to the human world until we can rid you of your inborn flaws, I'm willing to accept your sense of urgency. Your judgment must prevail . . . as you informed me so clearly." No, he had not forgiven me for using his own words against him. I should take that as a warning. But I wasn't really afraid. He knew he'd won, and his quibbling was for his own gratification, not my discomfiture. "I will send you back through dreams as you require. The experience will allow you to develop your skills. But I'll not have you become more entangled with these humans, just when you should be learning the detachment proper to one who will hold such power. You will exchange speech only with your dreamer, no other human, until you are Madonai and can do as you please. Will you accept this condition?"

"If it's the only way I can continue," I said.

"The only way. If you cannot live without human thanks and glory, or if you must depend on a human voice to command you, then you are not worthy of my gift."

"And so tomorrow you'll help me explore dreams so I can choose where and how I'm to go back? I don't know if my last dreamer yet lives."

"As you wish. Tomorrow. And in the meanwhile, I'll prepare to set you free."

CHAPTER 35

How rarely humans consider the other world that lies alongside the one we walk. Not a separate physical world like Kir'Navarrin or Kir'Vagonoth, but the plane of existence that every man and woman and child inhabits for a portion of every day—the world of dreams. A place where any man can work magic or any woman fly. Where events can repeat themselves over and over again, allowing us to examine every nuance. Where fantastic creatures live, and we see colors the sunlight cannot show us. Where we can walk with terror and test our mettle, yet withdraw in safety, with no more consequence than racing hearts and pillows damp with sweat. We've learned to fear the world of dreams, thinking of it as a place where madmen dwell, and yet I've heard it said that those who fail to dream can themselves go mad. Perhaps that was the source of my madness. My dreams had not been my own for a very long time.

"Halloo! A fine afternoon, is it not?" Nyel's cheerful greeting halted my steps halfway across the garden, well before I reached the wall. Exhausted from the events at Syra and Taíne Horet, I'd slept the day and night around. And finding no one about when I finally abandoned my bed, I had decided it would behoove me to stretch and walk a bit before beginning whatever business awaited for the remainder of the day. As long as I was outdoors, I'd thought to try again to understand the mysterious structure of Nyel's prison. Despite the rigors of the previous day's combat, my mind and body felt fresh and rested, and I hoped I might muster more insight into the puzzle of the wall than on my last attempt. I even dallied with the idea of changing to my winged form . . . my "Madonai form," Nyel had called it. Perhaps strength and melydda could reveal more of the wall's nature than my limited human perceptions. The light glinted brightly from the wall as if the black stone was newly cut and polished.

"A fine afternoon," I said, pausing while Nyel caught up with me. His steps were brisk and sure on the gravel path. A breeze stirred my damp hair, and despite the cloudless sky, I shivered beneath my linen shirt. Autumn was coming to Kir'Navarrin. Though the grass and foliage were still luxuriant, here and there among the trees I caught a glimpse of gold or red, sometimes a single leaf, sometimes a small branch, arrived early at the culminating glory of its season. How was it that the most perfect of seasons was the precursor to the cruelest? I hated winter.

"Is it your injuries kept you abed so late? Do you need Kasparian to tend you?" The Madonai examined my clean clothing with an air of distaste, as if looking for fractured bones poking out or unseemly spots of leaking blood.

Irritated by his rude inspection, I started walking again, though I soon found myself following his course instead of my own.

"Your remedies seem quite effective." Indeed that was far short of the truth. I had dressed my wounds after leaving Nyel the previous afternoon, and when I examined them again upon rising, I found most were near healed already, only the most severe, the gashes in my thigh and shoulder, at all troublesome.

"Clearly you are experienced in caring for yourself. When you didn't come down this morning, I sent Kasparian to make sure you had not died in your bed. He reported you still snoring." He turned off the main path abruptly and led me into a rectangular enclosure bounded by tall hedges. In the center of the small patch of lawn sat a white-latticed arbor overgrown with trumpet vines. Though the grass and hedges and vines were still summer green, the yellow-orange trumpet blossoms were overblown, limp and wrinkled. "Yesterday you seemed eager to learn more." He motioned me to sit in one of three graceful white chairs set in the shade of the arbor. A small table sat in the middle, and on it were the game board and the black and white pieces.

"I am certainly eager," I said, "but not so much as to rush forward completely unprepared. When gaming with a master, one should make no move without wits. I needed the sleep."

"Of course. I want you to feel comfortable with your decision," he said, easing himself into the chair opposite me. "Today you'll just explore dreams. Not move into them. Not shape them. Only observe. That's what you want?"

I nodded. So much to learn. How did you follow the progress of a war through dreams? How did you find the dreamers you desired out of the countless souls in the world? How could you judge your timing and make sure you arrived at the critical points? And once those things were sure, whether traveling by my own power or by Nyel's grace, how would I decide where my help would make the most difference? "I've a great number of questions," I said.

Without warning and without greeting to either of us, Kasparian strode into the garden and flopped his huge frame into the third chair. Sweat beaded his broad face, and fresh blood spattered his white hose. He had been sparring again.

"Let's have no questions right now," said Nyel, his eyes not wavering from my face, ignoring the grim and graying Madonai as if he were nothing more than one of the rasp-voiced jays that had boldly moved from tree to grass to table, investigating us. "Experience the lesson, and then ask what you will. In your previous ventures, I have taken you into only one dream at a time. This time, you wish to see them all. Do you choose this freely?"

"Yes, of course."

"Attend me well . . ."

I gave myself willingly to the exercise, noticing, as the world began to slip away, that the season had begun to change in Nyel's eyes as well. Interlaced with the springlike glory of his youth and the summer's abundance of his care for me, I felt the thin steel edge of winter. Even one day removed from the events at Syra, my hasty decision suddenly seemed ill considered . . . until I closed my eyes at Nyel's bidding and discovered the world of dreams . . .

Chaos. Cricket's chirp . . . roar of forest's burning . . . the cracking of the earth's own heart . . . smearing scarlet, emerald, glaring yellows . . . sun scorching, exploding into a sky of fire, scalding ocean . . . soaring music, flutes and viols . . . mellanghar droning . . . birds . . . thousands screeching . . . sobbing . . . longing . . . Baking bread . . . roasting meat . . . Bells ringing, tolling . . . Storms . . . of biting sand . . . of crashing ocean and lowered sky . . . drenching torrents . . . Sweet skin . . . smooth . . . coarse, wrinkled . . . flaking away . . . yielding, rotting, punctured, bleeding flesh . . . The wild, eternal hunt . . . galloping . . . slavering jaws . . . ripping teeth . . . wailing, nauseating, maddening . . . and falling, falling . . . Stabs of bitterness . . . roses, sweet hay . . . Despair, dread, soul-searing joy and terror . . .

"Let go, boy! You do not have to experience each one. Hold back. Observe. Let them flow as they will, but not through you. Not unless you choose." The dry voice was deep inside my head, its intimacy cutting through the clamor.

Panting . . . gasping . . . chest constricted with pain, my overwrought heart was hammering to escape my ribs, lest it burst from incapacity. I was being swept along by currents of sensation, tumbling out of control, on the verge of weeping with the assault, choking, drowning.

A firm hand grasped my own. "Anchor here. Control it. Take the time to clear your mind and look again."

Desperately I sought refuge in sensory isolation—an exercise I had perfected in captivity. Only when I regained my composure did I release my senses, allowing them to function only as I commanded. Soon I was drifting in the teeming ocean of dreams, and then floating above it, able to watch the patterns forming and re-forming themselves beneath the surface like reflections in a dark glass.

"Better?"

"Better," I whispered, in awe of what I could see in the dark, satiny swells: a man being chased by wolves . . . a woman exploring a tall house with no floors, only bare beams, unable to remember what she was searching for . . . a child tumbling off a horse . . . falling . . . falling, much farther than from saddle to earth . . . With no more than my desire, I traversed a wide swathe of ocean and viewed an endless variety of dreams. Lengthy stories and minute fragments, many of no more duration than a heartbeat. Only a few worth study at any one time.

"Pause above one that interests you and reach beyond it, as if you were casting your net into the sea to catch up this vision. Draw your net together and explore the mind beyond it . . . shape the dreamer. When you are skilled, you will be able to see the dreamer's surroundings and circumstances, perhaps catch a glimpse of his life."

These things were far more difficult than Nyel's vague instructions implied, even for one accustomed to walking the portals of human souls. By the time he had coaxed, advised, and taunted me into one small success—conjuring the hazy impression of a grizzled donkey driver who plied the long and boring road from Vayapol to Karesh—I felt as though I'd fought another battle.

"Enough for now," said Nyel. "Human flesh is not capable of more. We can try again tomorrow."

But I had no intention of stopping the lesson so soon. "Another," I said. "And, yes, I choose this freely." Again, I flew over the patterns floating in the deeps. Three more dreamers came to life by my hand: a shepherd in a highland meadow, dreaming of a pliant village maid, a woman racked with nightmares of a monstrous birth, and a slave enduring another night of torment and loss. With the third I began to get the feel of space and time, the uneven texture of the deeps. I could touch the dreamers beyond the floating visions, and imagine that when I was truly proficient, I would be able to bypass the entangling dreams and see only the landscape beyond.

By the fifth day of Nyel's instruction, I was in control. I could now see the human world spread out before me . . . distorted, obscured, dim, and colorless behind the vivid flotsam of visions, but enabling me to identify towns and cities and landmarks to locate my dreamers. Though Kasparian struck the spark, and Nyel worked the dream enchantment called *vietto*, I had learned to harness my own melydda to my efforts, sorting through the manic eddies of the dreamworld. And from the texture of dreams, I could discover the days and nights and seasons of the world, its plagues, famines, and battles, the nuances of pleasure or torment.

On the tenth day Nyel taught me the art of shaping dreams—gathering the image and imposing my own design. "Always with care," he said, "for you are touching the soul as intimately as is possible for a mortal being." As well we both knew. Why else was I sitting in his garden preparing to abandon my human self? "Look here," he said, "in this desert place I've found a typical woman's dream, a mother's dream . . ."

Searching . . . searching . . . through the crowds that grow denser with every passing moment. Where is he? Lost . . . wandered away . . . Music playing across the field . . . pipe music that he loves. Hear the laughter . . . of course, it's he . . . unharmed, unafraid . . . but all these people are crowding in between us . . . Push through. Hurry. The toothless beggar laughs at my plight . . . the old women pawing over dead things. "Ours are long gone," they say. "Rotted in the ground. Why should you have one living? Barren crow . . . losing the one given you."

"Child! Come back to me!" Hurry. The music fades . . . Hurry!

"So ease her search. You can do it. Part the crowd. See? Yes, that's it. You can get to the pipers first and hold the child for her, so he won't wander away . . ."

The dark-haired child stands beside a cart, where, within a framed box, two dolls dance, moved by sticks held by the piper's wife. The boy stands on his toes to see. I gather the small body into my arms, lifting him onto my shoulders, so he can watch the dancing dolls.

"Child, where are you?" The call comes from behind us, and I turn so the mother can see her boy safe on my shoulders.

"He's safe here with me," I call, hoping to ease her worry. "I've got him."

I can't pick her out among the myriad faces of the crowd. Everyone looks worried and frantic, and there are so many . . . But as I wave a hand, trying to catch her eye, her voice screams out, "No! Not you!"

. . and the dream faded from the ocean.

"Some human fears you cannot ease," said Nyel, and we went on to another lesson.

On the fourteenth day, I encountered Aleksander.

I had been searching for my friends in the unsettled dreams of Azhakstan. They would have had to move away from Taíne Horet, regroup after the disaster; no matter how many Derzhi I had killed, simple reason said that the valleys were no longer safe. Others would have been told of the refuge in the desert. But neither Aleksander nor Blaise would wait too long to strike again.

I drifted over the silken waters, observing the play of light and color and form. The landscape I explored was desert and night. So many dreams, fearful, anxious dreams—the night before a battle. I paused. This one . . . how could I fail to recognize the soul where I had lived for three days so long ago? I bent down and touched the waters with my mind's finger, watching the ripples roll outward as I permitted my senses to embrace his dream. *Galloping, racing . . . the choking sand billowing in waves, obscuring the quarry . . . only a white tail visible through the storm, braided as the Basrans braid their horses' tails. No glimpse of the rider . . . the child . . . too small to ride alone . . . too small to be lost in the desert . . . hurry . . . faster . . . dead men and women on every side . . . more and more of them . . . From the paraivo emerges a stark image, a man hanging by his feet, rats feeding on his ripped belly as his body sways in the wind . . . his amber eyes alive . . . unable to scream, because of the red braid tied to his tongue. The biting sand becomes a hail of arrows . . .*

"I'm coming!" My cry was unintended, but his fear was so great, his intent so unshakable . . .

"No! You will not!"

Abruptly the visions fell away, leaving me hanging over the table heaving, as if my entrails had been drawn out through my eyes. A dull crash across from me was accompanied by the sound of splintering wood.

"I gave you no leave to speak to him. I told you I would not send you to this charming beggar who uses you like the slave you were. What courage does he show, hiding his petty blood feuds behind a Madonai warrior?"

My eyes came into focus to see Nyel, red-faced, standing across from me. His white chair had toppled to the ground, cracking one of its delicate arms.

"I was not going to him," I said as soon as I recovered from the sudden change. "If you remember, I don't know how as yet. And I intend to honor our bargain. But once changed, I *will* go." Silly to leave these things unspoken. Nyel had won a great number of points, but the outcome of our joust was still in doubt. I could not waste time dissembling.

"I have hopes your judgment will improve by the time you are Madonai."

"In a few hours, I'll wish to return to the human world," I said. "To a different dreamer, if you insist, but in the flesh as we agreed. I'm healed and rested, and they're going to need me today." Aleksander was not waiting until the refugees were settled, but was riding for Tanzire. A small target, but a symbol. Those who slaughtered Sovari, Malver, and W'Assani would recognize its meaning, would spread rumor throughout the Empire, all the way to Zhagad's palace. And I needed to be part of the talk, I knew. Lydia had told me how Edik feared the tale of the winged warrior more than anything—the speculation that the gods protected Aleksander. Aleksander would need every advantage he could muster, even tales and rumors.

"How can I send you to serve this human prince as I prepare to make you Madonai, your smallest finger worth more than the entirety of his life?" Nyel's trim gray beard quivered.

"I do thank you for this gift," I said. "I wish I understood more of your aims. What am I that you should give so much to me?" The ever-present question.

He didn't answer. Just turned his back and stomped away.

Kasparian picked up the broken chair and slammed it upright. "You are in a combat above your head, boy," he said through gritted teeth. "You, of all warriors, should know that any hold can easily be reversed." He didn't elaborate, but crashed through the shrubbery and disappeared. Some unlucky opponent—real or illusory—was going to suffer that afternoon.

Nyel's fury was unsettling, evoking the memory of my own mad rages, like a scent or a taste can raise long-buried events. A potent reminder not to lose all caution. Yet I also chose to see it as a measure of his generosity in allowing me the freedom to act against his own desires. I was not deluded into thinking him entirely benevolent, but neither could I believe him insincere in his efforts to give me something magnificent.

I could have explored the world of dreams for the next few hours, perhaps picked my dreamer and learned more of Aleksander's plan. But the exploration was itself exhausting, so that even if I had been in control of the event, I likely would have deferred my curiosity until I took flesh through the dream. Instead, I stood in the clear space of the tiny lawn and began the kyanar, stepping through the movements to prepare myself for battle. Slow. Focused. Calming. As long as I wore this human body, I would maintain the habits that had served me well. And when I shifted—my skin prickled with anticipation, with hunger for the golden warmth and strength and the fiery melydda that would flood my veins—I, Seyonne, would remain in control.

CHAPTER 36

Aleksander's face was ruddy in the firelight. "We need a way to neutralize the watch and get through the gates. Our informants say the Bek lords are locked in the cellar of the guard tower near the northern gates. The southern gate tower is the stronger defense, and the barracks are right beside it, but they don't want to parade the prisoners through the town once the gates are open tomorrow morning. Too easy for stray Bek warriors to disrupt the executions. So they've made it easier for us. Once we're through the gates, we can surprise the guards and, if we don't take too long about it, have the prisoners out before the next guard change. Then we'll join Terlach and Marouf to take Gan Hyffir. So . . . I understand that some of you have the talent to get inside, take down the watch, and get the gates open . . . is that right?" The Prince stood in the center of the small group, looking from one face to another as his fingers tapped the hilt of his sword. "That would make things a great deal easier."

The ten men and women in the circle shifted uneasily and looked at Blaise, who was sitting on the sand, his right arm bound tightly to his chest. "Ordinarily, that's my responsibility," he said. "I think I can—"

"Indeed you cannot." The woman came from out of the night behind the circle and handed Blaise a cup before sitting down beside him. Elinor. Her hair was braided and bound up around her head. The flames made her skin glow like burnished copper. "Unless some god has magically knit the bones in this arm, you're not going to be able to fly or even defend yourself, much less take care of eight or ten Derzhi warriors. Someone else will have to do it. Gorrid, I know your easiest form is a zhaideg, but you've shifted to birds before. Roche has never had success with birds, and Brynna is at Gan Hyffir."

"I won't," said Gorrid, stretching out his legs, folding his arms across his chest, and leaning back against a saddle pack, as if to distance himself from the others in the huddled circle. "I won't risk my neck for any thieving Derzhi nobles. Let them all hang."

"As I said, I'll not hold it against anyone who wishes to stay behind," said Aleksander. "But the Bek are not your enemies. They are a family of great honor that does not deserve what's going to happen tomorrow. If we can set them free, they'll listen to what we have to say. And if we can give them back Gan Hyffir, they'll hold this region and bring others to our cause. You need to understand . . ."

"Tell them," I whispered as I elbowed my companion and shoved him out from behind the tent where we were crouched in the deepest shadows of the desert night.

"My lord Seyonne will open the gates of Tanzire," said Feyd as he stepped into the circle of firelight. Eleven startled faces turned to the young man who bowed respectfully to Aleksander. "He would be very pleased if you will permit him to take on this duty, Aveddi."

Aleksander's sharp gaze quickly searched the shadowed encampment. "Seyonne! I knew he'd come. Where is he?"

"He came to me this night . . . in a dream," Feyd stammered, his ivory skin flaring deep red as everyone stared at him. The young Suzaini's broad chest was bare but for the strip of linen wrapped about his shoulder, covering the laceration in his back. In fact, other than the bandage and a great deal of curling black hair, he wore only the short, loose undergarment called "fenzai." Once recovered from his astonishment at finding me in his tent as well as his dream, and having listened carefully to what I required of him, Feyd had insisted on dragging me immediately to the meeting where the Aveddi and his leaders were finalizing the plan for that night's venture. He had been so eager to be of service, he had forgotten to put on his haffai, an excruciating oversight for a modest young Suzaini.

"Came to you in a dream . . . is that possible? Has he been able to do this before?" I could not see Elinor's expression, but her voice was troubled.

"Not to my knowledge," said Aleksander. "But now, I would swear I've seen him in . . . Gods, who knows what's going on with the man? Tell us about him, Feyd."

"Of course, Aveddi. I was dreaming of my father—Gossopar protect my sire on his mission this night—and in this dream, as my good lord father chastised me for my wounding in our last battle, the Lord Seyonne prevented me setting my father's beard on fire. The Lord Seyonne expressed to me his deepest regards, Aveddi, and his unyielding faith in you. And the same for Blaise and Mistress Elinor and all the company, and he assured me that he will stand with us in all our ventures as far as is possible for him to do."

"Go back to bed, Feyd. You're still asleep," Farrol called. "Your father's beard is safe from you this night."

A few others laughed with him. *I'd be happy for the sorcerer to come along, as long as I don't have to be too close to him . . . I dreamed of my mother-in-law last night. Will she be in Tanzire, too? . . . Saved my life at Andassar, and at least twice at Taíne Horet . . . thankful he's with us . . .*

"How can you speak lightly of this cursed Ezzarian?" Gorrid leaped up from the sand. "If he does come, he'll likely slaughter more of us as well as our enemies. Do you so easily forget our brother Admet?"

The accusation hung in the air like smoke on a windless night. It was left to Blaise to answer. "If Admet betrayed us at Syra, as Feyd claims—"

"Admet could never betray us to the Derzhi. The traitor was someone else. Someone who loves them, who thinks Derzhi pigs can be 'honorable.' " Gorrid glared at Aleksander. "This cursed godling Seyonne murdered Admet to hide the treachery, not to avenge it."

"You may accept my word as I have given it to this company," said the Prince in the quiet voice that was his most dangerous, "or you may challenge me as is the right of any man, but you will not impugn Seyonne's honor, nor use the incident to divide us. Whatever Seyonne did, he did with reason and justice. I will believe that until someone brings me clear evidence otherwise." He beckoned Feyd closer to the fire and turned his back on Gorrid, as if daring the angry man to strike. "Come, Feyd, where is Seyonne? I need to talk to him, to tell him our plan."

Go on. Say it as I told you, lad. I pulled back behind the tent, leaned my head against the warm canvas, and listened.

"For the moment he chooses not to communicate with any human in the ordinary way, my lord. Even you should not expect it. But he says he will be with you and do whatever is needful."

"I see." A moment's pause and then I heard Aleksander pivot on his heel. "Well, we must take him at his word, then, no matter how or when he chooses to speak it. Seyonne will open the gate. Roche, Petra, Cawsho, and Denys will come with me."

"May I be permitted to ride with you also, my lord?" said Feyd nervously. "I should be at the gate . . . at Tanzire . . . I believe . . . if you would allow me the honor."

There was a brief silence. "I heard good reports of you from Syra and Taíne Horet. Your wound is not a problem?"

"It is well healed, Aveddi."

"All right. Ride with me. I need to learn more of you, I think." Good. Aleksander was putting the pieces together at least a little. I wanted to keep Feyd at Aleksander's side. There seemed to be no strict limit on the distance allowed between me and my dreamer; we just grew increasingly anxious the farther we stretched our bond. If I was going to concentrate on my business, I needed him close.

"Blaise, you'll see to the reserves, then?" Aleksander was still at work.

"We'll have five wait at the first break of the dunes in case you need help," said Blaise. "Gar, Katya, Bertram, Yori, and myself. Farrol will lead the rest of the fighters straight to Gan Hyffir."

"You? I thought that was settled."

"I promised Linnie I'd go no farther than the dunes," said Blaise, his unaccustomed grumbling attesting to the frustration of his injury. "One of us should be there, just in case someone needs to get away in a hurry. I can do that much at least."

Departing footsteps and side conversations told me that the group was breaking up. Aleksander continued to review his plans and would do so until they rode out. Every man and woman would know exactly what was expected in the coming hours, and Aleksander would know exactly what to expect of them. He was a masterful commander. "Mistress Elinor, I trust you to implement your arrangements for the horses."

"Mattei and Gerla have five extra horses fitted with weapons, water, and the clothing and banners you requested," said Elinor. "They should have arrived at Tanzire just after the gates closed at sunset, and will be camped outside the walls with the other latecomers. The gate guards are very strict about the closing. Gerla grew up in Tanzire and knows the town, if you should have further need of her. They'll be expecting you at first watch, ready to see to your mounts as you go inside. If you've nothing more for me tonight, I'm needed back in Zif'Aker."

"Of course. Thank you, Mistress. The boy is better?"

"Much better. It was just a childhood fever."

Fever. Evan. *Say more.* My mother had died of fever, and other people I'd known in Ezzaria. Children. Were fevers not worse in children? But the stream of the night flowed onward.

"Gorrid!" The Prince called a little louder. "Perhaps you could accompany Mistress Elinor back to Zif'Aker. Capable though the lady be, two pair of arms and eyes are safer, and we cannot afford to lose either of you. Unless there is anything else . . . ? Safe riding to all. May all of our gods stand with us in this night's work."

Shuffling footsteps approached my position—two men talking low. I ducked into Feyd's tent and awaited the young man's return, drawing darkness about myself in case Aleksander thought to poke his head in looking for me. *Are you satisfied, old man? I'm hiding from him.* Though perhaps it was as well we could not speak. I was confident in my decisions, but not yet ready to lay them out for scrutiny by those who could not possibly understand.

And Evan . . . ill. I pictured him as I'd last seen him, standing wide-eyed in the firelit circle of old Yulai's camp . . . running to safety in Elinor's arms. It was all I could do to refrain from following Elinor back to him. *It's not the time*, I told myself. *Not yet. Someday.* But if I were to be a Madonai . . . what then . . . ?

A large body bulled through the small tent opening. "Lord Seyonne!" The 'whisper' was loud enough to wake a tree.

"Will you please lower your voice? *No one* is to know I'm here."

"The Aveddi asked me privately of your whereabouts, just as you predicted. But I answered just as you told me. He didn't like it when I said you would accept no private messages from him. He was ready to walk away, but then he stopped and asked if you seemed 'well' and 'easy.' I said that you seemed quite healthy and had no particular difficulty with any matter that I could see, if that was what he meant by 'easy.' My lord suggested that if you had made at least one bad joke in all your speaking, then such would signify that you were 'easy,' and he wouldn't worry so much about you. I thought for a moment, and then I described how you had said you threatened a number of times to haunt his dreams, but had decided that mine were 'less pompous and more artful.' I wasn't sure this was what the Aveddi meant, but he laughed most robustly and seemed satisfied. Is this permissible to report, sir? Since he was addressing me and not sending any message to you, I thought it would be acceptable to repeat it in your hearing." Feyd's pale bulk filled the dark tent, along with the smell of his dried sweat and the scented oil he used to curl his hair and beard.

"Yes. It's all right." Out of all expectation, wrapped up as I was in fear and mystery of such magnitude, I felt like laughing, too. But I had no wish to insult Feyd's zealous obedience. "Thank you, Feyd. Thank you very much. But no more. As of now, my words are only for you, and I must hear only your own thoughts and observations in return. It is a condition of my presence." I had agreed to speak only with my dreamer and had already stretched the meaning of my vow.

"Of course, my lord, I understand. Our holy god Gossopar went through many trials as he ascended to his power in Kalliapa Gran. He once had to remove every hair from his body with fire—even that in the most private of his nether parts—and stay smooth-shaven in that manner for a year. To be forbidden speech with one's comrades, even in time of battle, is perhaps less torment, especially if you have the hair of a Suzai!"

"Indeed," I said, no longer able to withhold a smile at my dreamer's earnest comforting. "Though Ezzarians are notoriously sparse of hair, I would not welcome such a trial."

However, I did not welcome this trial, either. Feyd excused himself from further conversation, as his custom was to offer prayers to his god as he arrayed himself for combat. And so I huddled in his tent and listened to the sounds of the outlaw band preparing for battle. Along with creaking leather and metallic echoes of blades and harness came the nervous laughter, the last reminders of position and tactics, quiet encouragement, the generous assurances of manhood and courage and faithfulness, shared solace over fallen comrades, all the human intercourse that was now forbidden me. A number of people passed along messages to be sent back to loved ones with Elinor, and I silently passed along my own. *For you, my son. If I can do this thing . . . make the world whole and healthy for you . . . Whatever is necessary to make it so, I will do.*

Heavy footsteps paused just on the other side of the tent wall.

"Your sister is right, you know," said Aleksander quietly. "Stay out of action until you're fully healed. Believe me, I understand how it leaves your gut in a tangle to stay behind."

"I've never had to send them into this kind of danger without me."

"Despite my multitudes of faults, which were duly noted and gossiped about, the courtiers in Zhagad forever praised me as bold and brave because I insisted on riding out with my warriors on a mission. They didn't understand that I took the easier path. We've a long siege ahead, Blaise. You'll have more chances than you could ever want."

"The gods ride with you this night, Lord Aleksander."

"I wish I understood— Would you walk with me for a bit? I'd like to know a little more about a few of the men. This man Feyd, for one . . ."

I could have shifted form and gone with them to eavesdrop further on their conversation. But even such a one-sided "entanglement" seemed a violation of the spirit of my agreement. A month or two, the Madonai had said, and then I could do as I wished. Until then, if the condition of my presence was isolation, so be it.

In the months since our escape, the powerful Rhyzka heged had gotten their wish and moved one of their lower-ranked lords into Gan Hyffir, the last holding of the Bek heged. The Bek first lord, taking a lesson from the dreadful punishment wreaked upon the Naddasine, had not protested directly to Edik, but rather withdrawn into Tanzire. From a small town house he had tried to maintain his dignity, his tenants, and his purse strings by continuing to manage the Gan Hyffir farms and find markets for their wheat. He had proclaimed loudly that his generous Emperor, though desiring a well-made fortress for his powerful Rhyzka allies, could surely not have meant for either a Derzhi noble or his loyal tenants to starve. But old Bek's restraint had not saved him. The first lord, his three sons, and one son-in-law had been scheduled for execution, their women strongly encouraged to take poison. The Bek warriors remained quartered at Gan Hyffir, but were stripped of their yellow-and-blue Bek scarves and conscripted directly into the Emperor's service under Rhyzka command. Aleksander planned to change all that.

When the Aveddi and his riders set out for Tanzire, I flew with them in falcon's form, high above them in the moonless night, so that Aleksander would not guess that I had been in his camp. I would abide by the agreement. Indeed, self-isolation had served me well when I was a slave. But detachment did not require me to insult my friends.

Blaise had us within sight of the walls of Tanzire a mere half hour after Aleksander's signal. I left the party then, and flew ahead to open the way.

Tanzire slept. Perhaps my new-learned skill with dreams was what told me that it did not sleep peacefully. Sovari's bones no longer hung from the ramparts, nor were there any visible remains of W'Assani or Malver left upon the desolate land outside the walls, but I felt the three restless spirits close that night, and I had no doubt that Aleksander would feel them, also. "We will remember you with more than blood," I said as I perched upon the very post where the faithful guard captain had been so grotesquely displayed. "But tonight blood will be paid." I shifted to my true form, and, one by one, I settled silently behind each of the Rhyzka archers on the wall. I touched each man on the shoulder and let him turn and gape at my wings and golden light. Then I killed him, saying, "This for the faithful Sovari," or "This for the noble Malver," or "This for the glorious W'Assani." When all was done, I touched earth and unbarred the gates that I had loosened from the sand so many months ago. Without benefit of cranks or gears or even the wind, I shoved them open just enough to let the raiders in.

Easy to see what had been planned for the lords of the Bek on the morrow. Across the wide expanse of the marketplace stood the ancient guard tower, and between the tower and the gates, five gibbets stood waiting. They occupied the very spot where W'Assani's wagon had been abandoned, and where we had fought our way out of the city to meet crushing defeat when we thought our victory won. I would allow no repetition of that horror on this night.

Outside the walls was the motley sprawl that sprang up outside of any closed city. A few small fires marked the travelers' camp, and the quiet sounds of restless beasts and wakeful children hung in the still air. Two young merchants lounged by a muddy trough watering their string of horses.

The stars slogged relentlessly along their night's path. Seven horsemen rode out of the desert, slowly, as if tired from long journeying. They merged easily into the drowsy camp, and soon the slight wrinkle their arrival caused in the fabric of the night was smoothed again. Only from my vantage could one see the seven dark-clad strangers slip through the open gates a short time later. They looked up as they passed below me, of course, and I raised my hand in greeting, but did not go down to meet them.

I remained on the walls, making sure that no one came to close the gates, to replace the guard untimely in the mud-brick guard tower, or to bother the two young merchants who seemed to have acquired a few more beasts than they had brought to the watering trough. Only a suspicious eye would have remarked that the two had saddled the string of horses they'd told their fellow travelers were to be up at auction the next morning.

In less than half an hour, the first two raiders slipped out of the alleyway beside the guard tower. The rest soon followed, along with five new companions—the freed prisoners. Almost done. But the group had only just passed the waiting gibbets when I heard urgent hoofbeats from the direction of the guard barracks. Another betrayal? More likely some signal not given, some report not made. Whatever the reason, we needed to be away.

Sword drawn and ready, I shot downward and touched earth at the far edge of the marketplace, where the guardsmen would emerge from the dark street and into the open. Aleksander, who was bringing up the rear of the rescue party, left the others and hurried toward me across the expanse. "What are you doing?" I held up one hand to stop him and pointed my sword in the direction of the approaching danger. Though he could not yet have heard the horsemen, he reversed quickly in his tracks and called to the others, "Run!"

He heard the pounding onslaught soon enough, as well as the terrified cries of townsmen who peeped out of their shutters and observed my blazing form as I raised a towering whirlwind of sand. Once I had the wind churning, I could not judge time, for I was fully occupied with some twenty Rhyzka warriors.

How long to hold? I ducked a slashing blow from a Derzhi horseman and brought up my sword in a counter. Three, four blades at once. *Long enough for them to get through the gates, onto the mounts that Mattei and Gerla have ready, and far enough away that pursuers won't know their direction.* Not too long, though. I couldn't hold twenty indefinitely.

But I got caught up in the battle, in the challenge of opposing so many. Each time a party threatened to break free of me, I lashed out with another blast of flaying wind and called down a rain of fire. The horses screamed and reared, and I laughed when I got them so tangled they could not pull away from each other. "Not so fast!" I bellowed, and pounced on a determined warrior who was heading for the gates. I lifted him out of the saddle with one arm and threw him to the ground. Not gently. Ducking two blows, I stabbed upward to catch one of the attackers, yanked the other from his saddle by the leg, and managed to snatch a glance at the gates. No sign of my friends. The uncomfortable tightness in my chest told me that my dreamer was well out of the city.

How long has it been? A spear grazed my back in the sensitive area where my wing joined my flesh. Fortunately it did not penetrate deep, but only gouged a stinging hole and fell away. I spun in the air and saw three arrows, two spears, and at least ten blades headed my way. *Long enough.* Soaring upward, I pounded the gates shut with a final burst of enchantment. Then I abandoned Tanzire and sped through the desert night toward Aleksander and the besieged Bek fortress.

CHAPTER 37

I had fought at Tanzire much longer than needed. By the time I made my way to the squat, cheerless fortress of Gan Hyffir, Aleksander had taken charge of the battle begun by Feyd's father Marouf and Terlach, the son of the Manganar king. Before the assault, Brynna, one of the demon-joined Ezzarians, had slipped unobserved into the fortress and opened the way for two more of Blaise's people. The three of them had made their way into the guard barracks and told the Bek warriors that a new leader from the desert—a Derzhi lord who was favored of the gods and was called the Aveddi, the Firstborn of Azhakstan—was coming to reclaim Gan Hyffir and prevent the unjust execution of their lords. And so, at dawn, when the Manganar and Suzaini troops struck, the Bek rose up inside the fortress and threw open the gates.

This is not to say the battle was easy. The Rhyzka were well disciplined and outnumbered us three to one. A determined troop of archers occupied the highest tower of the fortress and rained down death on our fighters. In the space of ten heartbeats three arrows narrowly missed Aleksander, who was riding back and forth along his front lines, trying to keep his inexperienced troops from falling back under the barrage. I took care of the problem. The archers were well protected by Rhyzka swordsmen, but it was only a matter of time and work to clean them out.

Blood flowed freely that morning, but by the time the sun hung at its zenith, Aleksander was embracing the Bek first lord and his sons, and introducing them to the commanders who had retaken their stronghold. Together the Prince, Marouf, and Terlach ushered the Bek through the gates to the cheers of Bek warriors and the odd company of Manganar and Suzaini fighters and painted outlaws of the Yvor Lukash. The symbol of a flaming arrow, the Bek banner that Aleksander had brought as a gift to the beleaguered heged, flew once again on the ramparts of Gan Hyffir. Above it flew another banner. Many were asking whose crest was a woven pattern of gold, red, and yellow that looked like a sun rising over a field of golden grass. I knew, though I had seen it only in books of history and lore. It was the royal crest of Manganar.

As my blood-fever cooled, I circled over the battlefield like one of the vultures, watching the victors care for their wounded, lay out the dead as their customs specified, and round up Rhyzka prisoners who knelt waiting, hands on heads. The fortress stood on a rugged hilltop, and the battle had spread over the flanks of the hill as the Bek drove the Rhyzka out of the castle and into Aleksander's arms. From the wide vantage of the cloudless sky, I glimpsed the flash of a raised weapon in the folded rocks at the base of the hill and heard a faint cry . . . and then another. No one else in the milling, exhausted aftermath of battle seemed to notice.

I drew my sword once again, dived, and touched my bare feet to a shelf of warm sandstone. While one Derzhi stood guard, a second Derzhi raised his sword above the head of a kneeling Thrid. Three other men had already met the fate that awaited the captive. The two Derzhi wore the colors of the Rhyzka. I neither challenged nor warned the executioner, just knocked away the upraised sword and kicked him in the head, dropping him on his backside. A wave of my weapon discouraged the other warrior from making any move . . . or perhaps it was the sight of my wings unfurled or all the blood on my golden skin. The Thrid man looked up, trembling, and I jerked my head toward the fortress and the battlefield. He bowed, grabbed his horses, and ran.

I had every intention of shepherding the two Derzhi back to the first Bek warrior I could find, but the one sitting on the ground, a thick-chested, youngish man with the puffy eyes, coarse skin, and red-veined nose of one much older, shot me a glance of such malevolence that it stopped me in midmotion. Though I was not threatened in the least by human hatred, his vicious demeanor caused me to look at him more closely. That's when I noticed his earring. Derzhi earrings often designated heged rank, the size, materials, design, and gemstones combining to allow easy distinction of a first, second, or third lord from a lowly tenth. We had heard that the Rhyzka sixth was the resident of Gan Hyffir, but this man was of much higher rank . . . the second lord of his heged. The second lord of the Rhyzka was the first lord's son, which meant his name would be Bohdan, the brute who had taken his ten-year-old bride named Nyamot and used her to death.

We were likely a strange sight for those who stood on the battlefield or on the ramparts of Gan Hyffir—the naked, blood-marked warrior with wings leading a man, also naked, by a neck halter. When he fell, I dragged him until he could get up again. It had been the hardest thing I'd ever done to keep from mutilating him. I had stripped and bound him, my knife poised over the flaccid weapon he had used to murder a child. As is the way with brutes, his courage deserted him quickly, and he screamed and begged and wept. Mercy did not stay my blade. Rather this matter was so charged with significance that I could not deprive Aleksander of its resolution.

And so I kicked and prodded Bohdan onward toward his proper judge. By the time we reached the fortress gate, an expectant crowd had gathered, including Aleksander and the Bek lords. I touched earth, forced Bohdan to his knees with a yank on the halter, and passed the rope to a puzzled Lord Sereg, the Bek fourth whom Aleksander had met in Tanzire. Then in Aleksander's hands I laid the Rhyzka tef-coat and the bloody earring I had ripped from Bohdan's head. "What's happening with you, Seyonne?" he said, studying my face. "What's all this?"

Without a word I summoned the wind and flew upward, circling about to hover over the Prince and his prisoner. Having no answer from me, Aleksander shifted his attention to what I'd brought him. He touched the earring, and I saw the change when the understanding came. His fist clenched about the earring, and he raised it high with a blood-chilling cry of triumph. I did not stay to watch his resolution. I trusted him to act with wisdom . . . more than I trusted myself. And indeed, I had other matters on my mind. I returned to the battlefield.

Feyd was walking beside his father as the Suzaini palatine spoke to his fighters, healthy and wounded, and heard each man's report of his role in the battle. The bearded noble berated each wounded man, encouraging him to combat the weakness that had led to his injuries and demonstrating his expectation that in the warrior's next trial, the man would strive to triumph over such imperfection. As the father and son walked away from a cluster of men who were preparing a dead fighter for burial, I touched earth and nodded respectfully to Marouf.

"My greetings to you, most holy one," said the Suzaini noble, bowing deeply, his eyes flaming in wonder. "What service may I offer you?"

I did not answer, but only beckoned Feyd.

"Honored father," said the younger man, "my lord Seyonne has need of me. May I be excused from your side to accompany him?"

"Of course. Certainly. I am pleased that my son is of use to one so favored of the gods." The palatine glanced from side to side as gawking fighters moved close to see and hear. His voice rose a bit louder. "Holy warrior, you honor the house of Sabon and inflame the glory of Suza by choosing one of our own as your companion. For so long our history has been diminished . . ."

"Horses," I murmured to Feyd, and the young man scurried off as I heard out the nobleman's few moments of rhetoric. I was dreadfully impatient, but to listen respectfully was little enough to do for a proud people who, in the span of a few centuries, had been reduced to a caricature of themselves. Every Suzaini back grew a little straighter as Marouf spoke.

When Feyd returned, mounted and leading an extra horse, I nodded wordlessly to Marouf and to the small crowd who had gathered. Then I gathered the wind and took wing, motioning Feyd to ride after me, thinking that to change to human form right then would diminish what small gift I had given the Suzaini. And though it precluded much conversation, once we were away, it just seemed easier to fly. "I need to go to Zif'Aker," I called down to Feyd. "Lead me there." As in everything, Feyd did as I commanded.

"Ride into the settlement and tell everyone the news of the raid," I said, leaning heavily on a dusty lemon tree and looking down on Zif'Aker, a dry little valley in southeastern Azhakstan that was Blaise's new hiding place. Shifting to human form when we had come within sight of the bleak encampment had been a mistake. My side ached fiercely, and every bone felt like lead. Clothes felt awkward and stiff. "Take your time about it. Are you sure that's the right tent, the third from the end?"

"I'm certain of it. And what shall I do once I've told them of our victory?" Feyd's eager young face showed no lack of will, though he had dismounted slowly and lost his footing several times as we descended the steep hillside toward the lemon grove that overlooked the latest resting place of the refugees from Taíne Keddar and Taíne Horet. He was tired, too.

"Go to bed," I said. "You'll have done good service this day."

"You'll be gone when I wake tomorrow, won't you?"

I smiled and touched his broad shoulder. "Only for a while. Keep yourself safe, and I'll be here when you need me again."

"I've no experience of sorcery, save this strange traveling with the good Blaise and his kind," said Feyd. "Will you ever explain this to me?"

I fixed my eyes on the small figures far below me, hurrying about their evening tasks in the dusky gold light. "No," I said. "I probably won't. But don't think it any lack in you. I am very grateful for your companionship."

"To serve you is my honor, holy lord, and I could wish for no more." His weary steps receded, back up the hill to where his horse was waiting.

Holy lord . . . I wished they wouldn't call me that. Absentmindedly I rubbed at my leather vest, trying to ease the soreness in my shoulder and wishing I could reach the middle of my back where my shirt was sticking to the seeping spear gouge. One advantage of fighting naked—your clothes couldn't irritate the injuries. I pulled off the vest, threw it on the ground, and tugged at my shirt until it came unstuck.

About the time the sky had faded from bronze to deep gray-blue, I saw the shadowy horseman ride into the settlement, and the inevitable lamps and torches gather around him like fireflies about a rain puddle. I shifted to falcon's form, flew down the hill, and circled the crowd. A glimpse of the tall, slender woman near the center set me at ease. Soon thereafter, I pulled aside a flap of canvas, ducked my head, and walked into Elinor's tent.

The space was not large, scarcely enough for two pallets, a pile of leather saddle packs, and a small wooden chest. A strip of leather brushed my face as I stepped in. High above the chest hung a flat tin plate with a candle set on it. The candlelight revealed a sword belt hung from the roof pole, sheath and weapon well out of reach of a small child. The child himself lay sleeping on the pallet, his dark lashes resting on rose-gold cheeks, one fist drawn up under his chin, the other clutching a threadbare blanket. Only when I passed my hand over his face to rest on his dark hair did I feel the soft stir of his breathing. He was warm with bed and blanket, but not fevered. I took a deep breath, as I had not since I'd heard the word fever.

A breeze found its way through the tent flap, causing the candle to flicker. I should leave before Elinor returned, but I could not will myself to move. So I sat beside the rumpled bed and watched my son sleep, trying to keep my thoughts at bay lest they somehow sully his innocent dreams.

"What's going on? Who are—? Seyonne!"

The exclamation jolted me out of that peaceful confusion that is just beyond thought, yet just short of sleep. I blinked in the sudden brightness. Feyd must have drawn out his storytelling, for on the tin plate hanging above the wooden chest, the gasping candle flame floated on a puddle of wax. The brighter light glared from a battered oil lamp in Elinor's hand.

My hand still rested on Evan's head. Only as I felt Elinor's eyes on me did I notice the dried blood under my nails and in the creases of my skin. I quickly withdrew my hand. Was I forever to be steeped in blood when I encountered Elinor?

"What are you doing? Is he all right?"

Shaking my head and holding out empty hands, I stood up to go. I doubted Elinor truly wanted words from me, and even if I were permitted to speak, she would likely not believe the things I wished to say. And so I turned for one more look, a glimpse of beauty to fill my memory and of innocence to fill my soul, and then came near jumping out of my skin when a hand touched my back.

"You're bleeding." It was not quite an accusation.

I shook my head again and waited for her to move out of the doorway.

"Let me look at it. The others will be back soon, and from what Feyd says, the healers will be busy." She took down the tin plate, blew out the failing candle flame, and hung the lantern from the hook on the roof pole. "I didn't know gods could bleed."

What use was there to protest, even if I could do so without speaking? We had fought this battle already. And indeed my human flesh betrayed me. Even copper-colored Ezzarian skin would reveal such throbbing heat as I felt in my face.

Evidently Elinor misinterpreted my heightened color. "All right, I'm sorry. That wasn't fair. I never know what to say to you, Seyonne. You frighten me . . ." This modest overture left me completely off guard, and so I did not resist when she took firm hold of my arm, spun me around, and pulled up my shirt. ". . . and yet—Stars of night!"

Not a pleasant sight, I knew. Not with a raw, seeping wound right in the middle of a slave's legacy of scars. I quickly yanked the tail of my shirt down again, held up one hand to signify that she needn't say or do anything else, and with the other I moved her aside so I could get out of the suddenly sweltering tent. I did not meet her gaze, nor did I look over my shoulder to see if my back was truly on fire where her hand had so gently brushed my horrid skin.

Somewhere between Elinor's tent and Feyd's, the world went dark and disappeared.

When I dragged my heavy eyes from the game board, Nyel and Kasparian had already moved to the far side of the room and stood talking quietly together. I did not wait to hear what they might have to say. Outside the wide-open doors, the moon was high, the night cool; the garden smelled of late summer herbs and drying leaves. Though I was physically tired, I had no desire to sleep. Food had been laid out on a table in Nyel's sitting room, but I wasn't hungry, either. I needed air, solitude, and time to think.

I wandered down the gravel paths in the silver light and forced myself to go through it all again—the reasons I had to undergo this change. I had eased Aleksander's dream-spoken fear by telling him that I would help him. And his chances of success were so slender, so impossible, that he needed every advantage I could bring him. Yet who could explain the consequences of even so benign an interference? What if my comfort had made him less cautious? What betrayal would he have felt, what loss, if I had failed to keep a promise so rashly given in the intimacy of his dream? And then there was the bloodshed. I had killed without remorse to protect those I loved, and would do so until they were safe. Truly I had no need to explore my reasons for accepting Nyel's gift of power; their safety was everything. But experience told me that the human world would never be perfectly safe. Would I ever be able to stop killing?

Nyel was right to insist on my isolation. Already the power I held was immense and my hunger for it almost uncontrollable; even as I thought of it my breath came short and my body spasmed with the desire to shift, to shed my constricting clothes and feel the surge of melydda. Yet what dangers did I risk, tangling such power with love and anger and fear? And could I bear the cost?

Yes, that was the difficulty. I had known every kind of pain of both body and mind, yet seldom had I felt such piercing hurt as I had just experienced. My back yet burned with the touch of Elinor's hand, a human hand that spoke more eloquently of kindness and forgiveness than any words. Was I willing to relinquish such contact? Could I do such a thing and remain whole? Perhaps this was the hard lesson Nyel was trying to teach me whenever his eyes filled with tears: that the price of power and destiny was certain to be pain and loss on a scale with his own.

As I walked the paths of Nyel's garden, lost in such uncomfortable musings, I began to feel nauseated. At first I thought that fear and moral discomfort were upsetting my empty stomach and making my hands clammy. Or perhaps the illness was some delayed response to the night's hard fighting. When I began to feel dizzy and feverish as well, I thought the symptoms must be a reaction to the wound in my back. Maybe the injury was worse than I thought or the weapon had been tainted with poison. I decided to return to the castle.

For the first time in an hour, I glanced up to get my bearings and realized that I was on the verge of walking straight into the wall, right at the point where a jagged line marked the crack in the stone facing. Though its position was correct and the shape of the inky crack familiar, the flaw appeared narrower than before, and the tracery of smaller lines extending from it no more than surface imperfections. Curious. But I could not pursue an investigation on this night. I felt near collapse.

I reversed course and staggered toward the lights of the fortress, only to find the wave of sickness receding as quickly as it had come. By the time I reached the path that led to the steps, I felt hale again. Even the gouge in my back no longer nagged at me. I stopped for a moment and stared at my hands. Dry. Steady. In fact—I stepped into the light and turned them over to be sure—the scars on my hands had vanished, including the callused ridges about my wrists left by Derzhi slave rings. A quick examination told me that all my other scars remained where I expected them. But every mark on my hands was gone.

I was still unsettled when Nyel walked out onto the broad

porch. His straight, slender form was cast into silhouette by the brightly lit doorway behind him, leaving his features in darkness. Which face did he wear this night? His voice sounded youthful as he called, "Are you not tired, lad? Or hungry? Do you not need a bed after such a grueling adventure?"

"I don't want to sleep yet."

"Then let's talk." He walked down the steps past me and across a small lawn, settling onto a stone bench that overlooked a pond. On the still black water floated the yellowing leaves of pond lilies. Though his back was to me, I could hear the old sorcerer clearly. "Tell me about your son."

A chill that was no remnant of my brief illness danced across my back. Why was I so sure Nyel wished me well? "My son is none of your concern."

"Everything of your life is a concern to me. Did you think I didn't know of the child? I first learned of him when you lay dying, and now I've seen him through your eyes. A beautiful boy. What hopes you must have for him. You need have no secrets from me."

Easy for him to say, who had a treasure house of secrets. "Perhaps I'll tell you of my son when you tell me of yours." His son . . . his jailer.

In the space of a heartbeat, winter settled on that autumn garden. In frigid silence Nyel rose and walked away, abandoning his questions and mine.

CHAPTER 38

Over the next weeks I had no time to consider either the unsettling exchange with Nyel or the inner questioning that had preceded it. Nyel did not mention my son again and showed no further signs of displeasure. I continued my work with dreams, though only for an hour or two a day. Nyel said he needed time to prepare for the enchantments that would effect my change. He gave no hints as to the timing, method, or duration of that event, only promised once again that I would be given a choice at every step. Mundane occupations like eating and sleeping seemed to demand less and less of my time, but the hours were filled to bursting, nonetheless. Though he did not respond to my particular questions, Nyel made sure I did not lack for answers.

He set me to reading his library of scrolls—histories of the Madonai, their tales and poetry and learnings. Theirs had been a rich life, pondering the mysteries and beauties of the universe. A life of adventure, exploring their wide and varied world from mountaintop to ocean's depth, vying with wild creatures of varieties not known in my own world. A life of study, examining the growth and change of animals and plants, the marvels of weather and storm, the nature of color and art, the nuances of music and its effect upon the soul. Days of reading and I had touched but a particle in the vastness of their knowledge.

In other hours, my mentor provided certain enchantments for me to try—the simplest ones that did not require the full power of a Madonai. With Kasparian to initiate the working and Nyel to guide me, I spent one entire day exploring the world within a tree. Floating in the veins of life that threaded its body, I traveled from root to trunk to branch to stem to leaf. I walked the rings of growth that told its history, of years of drought and plentiful rain, of fire and storm and blight. Sitting within the green world of a single leaf, I experienced the pulsing, infinitesimal unfolding of its growing; I felt the sun's hot caress upon my back and tasted the liquor of life. I emerged from the enchantment awed with its power, beauty, and mind-stretching understanding. The smell, the taste, the feel of that tree, the life that set it apart from every other, had become such an intimate part of me that I could truthfully say, *I am oak—this one of all oaks in all worlds.* I could have spoken its name if tongue and lips could have articulated such a word.

"Was it well-done?" said Nyel, his gray brows knitted together, his old young eyes probing as I sat on the grass under the canopy of that tree, lit by the double-sized moon. "I cannot follow you into these places as I can through the dreams. Such workings are forbidden me." Forbidden—because his name had been taken away, the conduit of the soul that enabled the use of power. A dreadful thing, to strip a man of his name, so that even those who knew him would forget, all encounters and relationships fading like dew at noonday. When the person died, all trace of his existence would die with him, wiped from the scrolls of history as if he had never been.

"Well-done. Very well," I said. "No matter what else happens between us, Nyel, I thank you for this. I never imagined . . ."

"To experience the infinite varieties of life . . . yes, I thought you'd like that. Every journey such a wonder. Beauty and complexity to grow the mind and enlarge the soul. And all of it waiting for you," he said, smiling, the first genuine pleasure I had seen in him since my return to Kir'Navarrin. "I can teach you a thousand more such workings. I've waited so long to share them with you."

As in our first encounter, his smile transformed him. But unlike the first time, I did not drop my eyes. Rather I tried to probe that figure of beauty and wisdom and power much as I had explored the oak, to travel the paths of his thoughts, to unravel the mysteries of his intentions. But I had not the power, and the vision soon faded. Nyel was but a lean, gray-haired man with marvelous eyes, eyes that were filled with kindness and love and long-held sorrow.

I told myself that he was mad, and so these things I felt from him were surely some false creation. But I was a Warden, trained to see and feel the truth within the soul, and he was not false. Everything he expressed was reflected in me, as if I were a mirror of his heart. And so I was forced back to the question. "Nyel, please tell me why I'm here. Why me?"

His smile vanished, and he would not answer.

* * *

Every few days, between my studies and enchantments, I would traverse the ocean of dreams and return to Aleksander by way of my dreamer. The Bek rescue and Gan Hyffir raid had been successful, a needed victory, a tale that would take on its own life and spread throughout the Empire. The Prince had sent Bohdan to Edik just as I had delivered him, naked and bound. At risk of their own lives, four warriors of the Bek had pledged to throw the brute at the Emperor's feet, leaving Edik with a cruel dilemma. Would he give Bohdan up to the Hamraschi, risking his alliance with the powerful Rhyzka, or would he refuse his Hamrasch allies their blood price, risking the same vengeance that had fallen on Aleksander? Along with Bohdan, the Bek warriors presented Edik with one more gift—a falcon's feather. No one in Zhagad would fail to know its meaning. The Denischkar falcon was in flight. Aleksander was coming.

Gan Hyffir was a foothold, but a precarious one, and its winning left Aleksander with his own dilemma. The battles at Syra, Taíne Horet, and Gan Hyffir had cost him no less than fifty of his best fighters, as well as more than a hundred and fifty others dead. Though the Bek were a valuable ally, they brought no more warriors to Aleksander's side, for the small Derzhi house had agreed to take on the difficult task of retaking northern Manganar, with the understanding that they were to train Yulai and Terlach's Manganar troops to fight beside them. They would need every man they could muster to withstand the Rhyzka, not to mention whatever retribution Edik sent from Zhagad. Unless he found more fighters quickly, Aleksander would run out of soldiers with his war scarcely begun.

The answer was Blaise. Aleksander asked the shapeshifter to take on the task of recruiting fighters to the cause. The move was brilliant. Blaise's strength had always been his passion and commitment rather than his sword arm or his strategies, and now he carried word to the Manganar and Suzai and Thrid that the Aveddi had raised the banner of their lost realms and fought shoulder to shoulder with their own lords. Over the next weeks, as I watched the ragtag bands of ironmongers and shepherds, drovers and farm girls arrive in Zif'Aker, all of them both terrified and determined, I knew that Blaise had found his proper calling.

As for more skilled recruits, the Prince devised a plan for that, too. Lord Sereg, the well-spoken and intelligent Bek fourth lord, had chosen to remain with Aleksander. Before many days had passed, Sereg and Roche were off to speak to the Mardek in Karn'Hegeth, to the Fozhet in Vayapol, and to the other minor houses who had promised to support Aleksander if he could prove that anyone else was with him. Sereg himself would stand as the proof, while carrying the message that Aleksander was fighting not for the throne of the Derzhi Empire, but for a newly forming vision of the world.

While Blaise and Sereg expanded his army, Aleksander took up raiding again, causing Derzhi nobles and their henchmen many a nervous night. Everything he knew of politics and grievance throughout the Empire he used to choose his objectives. We kidnapped tax collectors, not the cruelest of their ilk, but ones who could be convinced by fright, mystery, and a touch of royal persuasion to forego their exorbitant overcollection, thus easing the burdens that caused local merchants to starve out their poorest customers. Rather than attacking individual slave caravans, we hit the three trading centers in the desert that spawned them, thereby disrupting the vile traffic between the more recently conquered territories and the heart of the Empire. We raided a Veshtar camp where spies had reported the sons and daughters of the Naddasine were kept in cages. From my perch on a spit of rock overlooking the bloody remnants of that battle, I watched Aleksander oversee the release of two hundred slaves, offering his own hand to gaunt scarecrows who could scarcely move and his own waterskin to walking corpses half mad with thirst. Secret grain stores, disputed lands, an armory owned by a divided family, a horse merchant hoarding prize breeding stock . . . all the tenderest spots in the Empire were ripe targets.

I joined the raiders on most of these ventures. Whenever I traveled in the dreamworld and sensed a raid was imminent, I asked Nyel to send me to Feyd. The Madonai always resisted my petition, insisting that I wait until I took my "proper form" to reduce my chance of injury. "Is this foolish path your free choice," he would say, "or is this more piteous begging from this human princelet who cares naught for your wounding? Wait but a little while, and you will be stronger than you can imagine."

"Yes, this is my choice. I accept the risk, because the risk of not going is far worse."

No matter how I wheedled, coaxed, or railed at him, Nyel

refused to tell me when or how my change would come about. He would not "soothe the impatience of a short-lived species" by rushing a working of such complexity. And so I buried cravings and curiosity by continual work to increase my imperfect strength and power.

At no time in those long months did I speak to any human but Feyd. Though I assumed such restraint would be difficult, I soon became accustomed to it. My dreamer would tell me the night's plan and, if there was clear need of my skills in some part of it, I would dispatch him to Aleksander with my intent to take on the task. Otherwise, I would appear at the scene unannounced and do whatever was needed most, sometimes ensuring the victory, sometimes holding back the enemy so that the Prince and his fighters could escape, for by no means did they win every skirmish. With my help, they avoided the most severe consequences of defeat. No matter Nyel's constant opposition or my own growing impatience with the war, I could not abandon my friends.

I was sorely tempted to find a dreamer in Zhagad itself and take down Edik or the lords of the Twenty to speed the progress of events. But my place was at Aleksander's side. My Warden's oath, that human-wrought fetter still fixed at the core of my being, bound me to protect and nurture one who bore the gods' mark, and so I would do until my last breath.

At first Aleksander questioned Feyd about me and tried to send me messages along with his plans. Whenever I appeared at his side, he would grin and raise his eyebrows as he had always done when trying to probe my private mysteries. But as the weeks passed and I remained aloof, he gave up trying to bridge the distance between us. If circumstance permitted, he would greet me with a slight bow. No smile. No greeting. No expectations. Soon, even the bow became less frequent. My presence was appreciated as happy chance, like good weather or favorable terrain, but Aleksander no longer tried to direct my actions or outguess me, any more than he could manipulate wind or desert. I felt a certain freedom, no longer bearing the burden of his concern and curiosity. And if I felt a faint twinge of regret as he laughed with Farrol or huddled with Elinor and his commanders over a map, I promised myself that everything would be different as soon as Nyel got on with his business. Meanwhile my power grew, as did my craving for it.

* * *

When not fighting or studying, I walked and ran and climbed the mountain path, trying to keep my body loose and take my mind off my compulsion to shift. On one day almost four months from my arrival in Kir'Navarrin, I glimpsed Kasparian hurrying through the passageways and followed him. His dour expression told me he was off to practice his fighting again.

"Have you some dry place to work?" I said, matching his long strides. "I could use some exercise." The weather had turned foul a few days before, Aleksander had not needed me, and after enduring two rainy days of idleness, I was ready to tear down the castle with my teeth.

After a dark stare that clearly indicated he would prefer to use me for his day's victim, he said, "Come along if you will." He hurried down the broad stair deep into the bowels of the castle, halting at the arched doorway where I'd found him on my first day in Tyrrad Nor. The door opened onto a cavernous darkness. A wave of his hand lit fifty torches, revealing a long, narrow room so vast the Frythians could hold their famous jousting tourneys inside it. The low ceiling was supported by ranks of stone arches that ran the length of the room on right and left, further narrowing the space. At the far end was a long bench with a variety of weaponry laid out on it—swords, knives, and spears of various weights and edges, bows, arrows, and lances, quarterstaves, cudgels, and whips, and every variety of shield and protective clothing. A well-stocked armory for a man who had no opponents save illusions.

"Madonai were not always a peaceful race," he said, as if he'd heard my unspoken questions. "We grew beyond it, but some of us chose not to lose the skills. There were always beasts to deal with, many of far more sophistication than those of your world." As Kasparian arrayed himself in leather armor and whetted the edge of a massive broadsword, he told me Madonai stories that I had not found in Nyel's library, of wild hunts and armies of beasts, of manlike creatures who drank blood, of creatures of fire whose touch incinerated the soul. "Now I pursue only one quarry," he said.

A surge of enchantment and we stood in a field of tall grass extending to right and left and before us in gentle dips and swales to a distant horizon. White-hot sun glared from a silvered sky. Astonished, I whirled about and found the columned room still stretched out behind me, though its angles were skewed, its edges blurred like the portals of my demon warding. Five armored figures took shape between me and the chamber doorway.

"I would advise you to arm yourself or hide until I have them all occupied," said the Madonai.

Stepping backward from the severe landscape, I felt the shift from hot, dry wind to cool stone and hard floor. I lifted a leather vest down from a hook on the wall, hefted a few of the weapons, and started to buckle a scabbard about my waist. But Kasparian's stories had taken my mind elsewhere. I had no desire to join his battle. I saw enough true killing.

So, as the five warriors spread out and moved toward the sunlight and Kasparian, I slipped into a deep corner of the shadowed colonnade, intending to take my leave of the arena. Kasparian went on the attack, moving faster than any two-legged creature I had ever seen. By the time I set out for the doors, I had to step over one of his opponents who had crawled under the colonnade after a blow to its belly had all but ripped it in two.

"Mercy . . ." I was halfway to the door when I heard the agonized whisper, almost drowned out by shouts and the clash of swords. Back in the darkness, the still form lay curled about its grotesque wounding. What illusion was so real as to beg release when out of the earshot of its creator?

I hurried back to the fallen warrior and dropped to my knees. "Who are you?" I said, tugging at the leather helm. "What are you?"

Fair hair, drenched with sweat, spilled over my hands, and the movement must have jarred him from the brink of death, for he spasmed and groaned, throttling a scream.

"Gods, I'm sorry." I brushed the hair back from his pain-ravaged face and my mouth fell open in horrified astonishment. "Kryddon?"

The rai-kirah's fading blue eyes widened for a brief moment, and he struggled to speak. "Friend Seyonne, noble Denas . . ." With impossible strength his hand gripped my shirt and dragged my face down to his. Blood bubbled from his lips. "Save yourself. Go to the Lady. We're dying . . ."

Before I could question him, his hand fell away, and I felt the unsettling jolt in the universe that always resulted from a rai-kirah's death. What was happening outside the black wall? How did Kryddon happen to be caught up in Kasparian's enchantments? I had believed that Nyel was taking power from the rai-kirah in Kir'Navarrin through their dreams. Were Kasparian's morbid entertainments involved, too? And who was Kryddon's "Lady"? Was it possible she wore green and lived in the gamarand wood? But I had no opportunity to ask my questions, for Kasparian settled in for a long night of sparring, and Nyel was nowhere to be found. Nyel allowed no talk before our scheduled hour of dream work in the mornings, but I vowed to get answers right after.

On the next morning, however, my intention came to naught. Human dreams told me that serious plans were afoot in Aleksander's war, and so I stepped into the human world instead.

CHAPTER 39

"The Aveddi says that he will set his foot in every captive land before he goes to Zhagad," said Feyd that night as we sat on a windswept knoll overlooking Aleksander's base camp, "and he will raise the banner of that land and see its rightful defenders given the chance to hold it." As had become their habit for larger or more intricate operations, Aleksander's troops had made a staging camp close to their target to rest their horses and snatch some sleep before making their assault. This gave the joined Ezzarians time to bring more fighters from the growing number of camps scattered through the Empire. With Blaise traveling the Empire spreading news of the Aveddi, and Roche taking Sereg out among the Derzhi, only Gorrid, Brynna, and Farrol were left to guide Aleksander and all his fighters. To everyone's surprise, including his, Farrol had become Aleksander's right hand, learning the art of command from the Derzhi he had once despised.

"Why venture this now?" I said, puzzling yet again over Aleksander's choice of Parassa. The heart of ancient Suza had died on the long-ago day of the Derzhi conquest, when all its residents had been killed or enslaved and the last stronghold of the Suzai palatinate razed. But the city's situation on the eastern flanks of Azhakstan, where the wide and shallow Volaya River created a ten-league-wide strip of fertile ground stretching all the way from the northern mountains to the oceans beyond the eastern wild lands, was too valuable to lie fallow. A new city had grown up from the ruins. "Though I know he wants to give your people this gift, it will cost him dearly. Even more when he has to leave your father and his men to hold it."

Feyd offered me a portion of the dried meat he had pulled from his saddle pack. I shook my head. I hadn't eaten in three days, but I wasn't hungry. It didn't seem strange anymore, just as I no longer kept count of the scars that vanished after each of my forays through the portal of dreams. Something about changing back and forth to my Madonai form was eliminating them, I supposed. Only the two—the slave scar on my face and the knife scar in my side—were ever visible on my true form, and apparently my human flesh would soon be the same. Good riddance to all such annoyances.

"It was a sudden thing," Feyd said, wrenching a bite from the leathery strip and chewing it slowly. "We were going to take the water sources near Karn'Hegeth. The Aveddi thinks the Fontezhi might put a stranglehold on the water in retaliation for our attack on their grain stores. But then, two days ago, Roche brought Lord Sereg back to Zif'Aker, and they conferred with the Aveddi and Farrol for an hour, and immediately the Aveddi changed our plans. He said that a new garrison was being sent from Zhagad, and the commander was bringing orders to burn out the entire lower city without warning the people who live there. The Emperor commands a new racing drome be built on the site for horse races and such like. But everyone knows that Parassa has been fertile ground for the Yvor Lukash and his message. The Emperor wants to punish any city that sends us fighters."

"But these things are happening everywhere. Why start with Parassa? Why risk so much and with such a sketchy plan just when he's building his ring around Zhagad?" I peered down at the quiet camp. No fires cheered the night; only a few lanterns and the brilliance of a half-grown moon revealed the dark forms of some seventy men and women along with their horses. Some of the raiders were asleep, some in quiet conversation. Every once in a while, someone would stare up at where we sat. I had already shifted and so was easily visible at the top of the hill. I could watch more effectively and think so much more clearly in my Madonai form. But on this particular night, my attention would not stay on the watch. The image of Kryddon's anguish would not leave me, and I felt uneasy and angry and irritated at everyone—Nyel, Aleksander, and even Feyd, who seemed more and more timid every time I came to him. I was sick of fighting, yet I could scarcely hold back from flying over the next ridge to Parassa and destroying the fools who ruled it. Short of such immediate release, I wished that I could understand Aleksander's reasoning. Why didn't he hit the fresh troops the moment the old garrison had gone? Had anyone thought to warn the people of Parassa? "Are you sure you've been told everything?"

Feyd's mouth was still full of meat, and he swallowed hurriedly. "The Aveddi says that secrecy is paramount on this mission.

That's why he brought so few fighters and why he will give detailed orders only as we proceed." He raised his strip of meat to his mouth again, but lowered it without taking a bite, wrinkling his brow and fixing his eyes on the ground. "Knowing that I speak with you, the Aveddi has been most careful that I am given all the information that our commanders are given. Everyone knows that I am privileged far beyond my unworthy fighting skills. Sometimes my father is not told so much." He wiped his mouth and offered me his waterskin, but I shook my head again. "They treat me as if I am a priest."

My attention had been fixed on the camp for the past hour, as if I could wring Aleksander's thoughts out of the night. But the wistful strain in Feyd's words forced me to attend the young noble at my side. My gold light reflected in his eyes and made the silver beads woven into his hair and beard shine—full regalia for a son of Suza come to fight for his homeland. Weeks had passed since I'd even considered his odd position. "Would you like me to find someone else, Feyd? I know it's not easy being set apart from your comrades. I've never asked you—"

"Oh no, holy lord!" His ivory skin flushed, and his dark eyes grew wide. "I am honored to be in your service. Privileged beyond all men. Every day I thank holy Gossopar for sending you to our aid, and I pray him to lift this darkness from you and draw you into the light at his side."

"This 'darkness'? Why do you say that?" I was on my feet without knowing how I got there, yelling at my dreamer, though his words were all innocence and my sudden fury unreasonable. Insolent beggar. "I am not the one of darkness! I make my own choices and will always—"

"Pardon, my lord." Feyd threw himself prostrate at my feet, which only served to infuriate me the more. "Please, holy lord, forgive my foolish tongue. I am but an ignorant man, unworthy to consider the workings of the gods. Chastise me as you will for my offense."

"Why do you speak of gods and darkness? Tell me what you mean." The fighters in the camp likely heard my bellowing, as the day's disquiet came boiling out of me. "Answer me!"

Feyd spoke in a tremulous whisper. "Because you are with us through the night, holy one, coming always with the close of day. You live in my dreams; I feel you there . . . see you there, majestic in your fortress in the realm of night, even when you choose not to manifest yourself to me in flesh. And even when your presence in our world lingers into daylight, the night enfolds you. This dark burden of your trial, of your sorrow that even the Aveddi himself does not understand, cloaks your deeds in terror as if your glorious light is but a deeper darkness. Forgive me, holy lord. Clearly I am wrongheaded and see falsely."

I fought for control, barely restraining my hand that was raised to strike him for his mewling cowardice . . . for his fear. Why should he fear me? I was not his enemy. And, of course, even as I voiced that claim, the absurdity of my upraised hand with angry flames shooting from the fingertips was not lost on me. "What do you see in your dreams that makes you fear me?" I asked, forcing my hands together behind my back. "I fight at your side. I shed my own blood in your cause just as you do. Tell me, Feyd."

Though his words were muffled by the ground, each sounded clearly like a lash striking flesh. "You stand upon the ramparts of a mountain fortress, holy lord. Always it is night, and the wind lifts your black cloak and fills your wings. But in my dream they are not wings of light, holy one, and your face is terrible, as when you are in battle. Please forgive me, lord . . ."

Of course. I should have expected nothing else. Hating . . . despising . . . my own fears that were exposed by the young man's honesty, I nudged him gently with my foot. I held my voice quiet. "Feyd, stand up. Now. Come on."

Slowly, trembling, the young man got to his feet, his eyes cast down.

I spoke a word of enchantment, waited a moment, and then lifted his chin. His eyes were closed. "Look at me, Feyd. Come, look at me."

Reluctantly, he raised his eyes, which now reflected only moonlight, no Madonai brilliance.

"I am a man, Feyd. A sorcerer, not a god. I am not holy. Far from it. Truly I need whatever help I can get, whether Gossopar's or that of a brave Suzai warrior whose fighting skills are not at all unworthy. But neither do I come from the darkness."

"Of course, ho— Of course." His eyes fell to the earth again, and he did not raise them as we sat down on the grass, and I took up my watch. Neither of us spoke again.

When I saw the stirring in the camp below us and heard Aleksander's command, I shifted back to my Madonai form, uneasy with it as I had never been. Feyd bowed to me and mounted his horse, ready to follow Aleksander into battle.

"Go with Gossopar, my friend," I called after him.

"And you, holy one," he whispered. Perhaps he thought I couldn't hear him.

To survive this night we were going to need Gossopar and any other god that might be available. Parassa had a Derzhi governor, usually a low-ranking noble of a major house, and a garrison of a three hundred Derzhi warriors. When assigned to Parassa, the governor would bring a small troop of personal warriors of his own house, but the responsibility of the city garrison rotated through the hegeds every half year, as Parassa was considered an immensely undesirable posting. Though prosperous, the town was of little strategic importance, located far from the frontiers and on only one minor trade route. And the Suzaini had been pacified for so long and were so widely dispersed throughout the Empire, rebellion was of little concern. No glory could be found in Parassa, and no amusement in a dull farming town so remote from court life.

Though the garrison numbered only three hundred and the governor's party perhaps fifty more, Aleksander was mad to think he could stop the burning, much less hold the city afterward, with only Marouf, his forty eager Suzaini fighters, and thirty Thrid. Perched atop a ruined watchtower and looking down on the dark city as Aleksander revealed his plan to his commanders, I was even more convinced of his foolishness.

"We take the citadel first," said the Prince, pacing briskly in front of Marouf, Feyd, Farrol, Gorrid, D'Skaya, the tattooed Thrid woman who had developed into a formidable commander, and two men I didn't know. "Only the governor and his personal troop occupy the citadel tonight. The governor will give the signal to begin the burning as soon as he hears that all is ready. The garrison is to be deployed about the entire lower city, so they're spread thin . . . and we'll make sure the governor's signal is never given. Marouf and I will take the front gates of the citadel, just as at Gan Hyffir. Once the alarm is sounded, D'Skaya will give the defenders just enough time to surge to the front gate, and then she'll hit them from the rear. Hardile, you and Soro will follow me. Farrol will hold the reserve, twelve men, at the customs house halfway between the citadel and the lower city—just in case someone from the garrison decides to break discipline and ride to the governor's defense. Gorrid will patrol the citadel periphery to intercept any messengers trying to sneak out."

Though temporarily in falcon's form so I could listen without detection, I had a clear view of our dilemma. Parassa was not a closed city, so the gates were no obstacle. Kill a few guards and we were in. But the governor's citadel was at one end of the city, high on a bluff, far from the smells and diseases of the river, while the lower city that we had come to protect was sprawled for half a league along the waterfront, separated from the more prosperous quarters by a narrow finger of the river. To bottle up the governor and his guardsmen while preventing the garrison from torching the poor quarters would require splitting Aleksander's troop into two pitifully inadequate forces. Even with my increased strength and melydda, I could accomplish neither task alone. Surely Aleksander knew that.

"Once we've taken the citadel," Aleksander continued, "we'll join Farrol and use the customs house for our base as we deal with the garrison. Handling the garrison warriors will be easier than you believe. Remember, they're likely uncomfortable with what they've been told to do. Just stay alert and follow my lead. Remember that if anything happens to me, Farrol will be in command." He stopped and faced each one of his commanders. "Kill *no one* and allow your fighters to kill no one who does not challenge you. Is that clear? Swear to me that you understand this."

All of them swore as he asked, and with handclasps and shoulder grips and wishes of good fortune, they mounted up and headed back to their waiting fighters. Aleksander was the last to go, perhaps because Feyd was waiting beside his horse. "Aveddi, if I might . . ."

Aleksander looked down at the earnest young Suzaini. "He is here tonight?"

"Indeed, my lord, I believe he is."

"Gods, Feyd, convince him to talk to me. I need to explain all this. Some matters are too dangerous for anyone—even you—to know."

Feyd answered as I had instructed him. "He chooses not, my lord, and this will not change for a time yet. But if you tell me what part you need him to play this night—"

"I need him not to slaughter every blighted warrior that holds a sword! I need *Seyonne's* eyes and *Seyonne's* wisdom. That's what I need. Tell him that. Otherwise he can fly off somewhere else and do as he damned well pleases."

Feyd stood openmouthed as Aleksander rode away, and then he glanced uneasily to the top of the ruined tower. "I heard," I said as I shifted form, illuminating his pale skin with the golden light that his human eyes perceived as darkness. "You've no need to repeat it." Likely Feyd thought the words would burn his tongue or perhaps that I, the one of darkness, would cut out the offending organ. "Shall we see if we can find something useful to do?"

Clearly Aleksander's proscriptions had nothing to do with the defenders in the citadel. The fighting was fierce, and the Prince did not object when I eliminated the soldiers dropping hot balls of tar on top of him or the warrior who nearly decapitated Marouf. When the short, fierce combat seemed under control, I went searching for the Derzhi governor and found the soft, balding man cowering in a wardrobe. Leaving him trussed and gagged, his satin breeches fouled from his fright, I flew out over the walls in falcon's form to see why in Verdonne's name the garrison had not rallied to the governor's defense. Surely someone would have heard the sounds of fighting. It made no sense.

I circled the citadel and spied someone running through the tightly shuttered streets, away from the citadel and toward the lower city. Sword and vest named him a soldier. Not Derzhi . . . I swooped low, only to see his dark outline blur and resolve itself into the form of a zhaideg. Gorrid! Only the surly Ezzarian shaped himself as the scavenger wolf. Where was he off to? He was supposed to prevent any Derzhi messengers passing the citadel gates.

Gorrid loped across one of the stone bridges that spanned the Volaya tributary, then into the streets, skirting the palatial customs house where Farrol hid with Aleksander's reserves. Farrol's watchers must have missed him.

The lower city was as dark as the pits of Kir'Vagonoth, and the only sounds marring the stillness were the slop of the river backwaters under the docks and the occasional shriek of a gull. One might think the people had smothered their children and animals to keep them silent. The zhaideg trotted about the dark periphery, slowing as he passed the still figures, the soldiers standing poised and ready for the signal that their murderous ring was complete. Amid the stink of gutted fish and decaying vegetation, I smelled octar-soaked torches and straw bales ready to be lit. Along the riverbanks every quay and dock was guarded. Boats drifted away from their moorings, sagging low in the water, holed to prevent their use for escape. Demonfire . . . this was not to be just a cleansing, but a slaughter.

The zhaideg bypassed three boxlike warehouses along the waterfront before slinking close to a fourth. Faint lantern light shone through the shuttered windows, and Derzhi warriors guarded the cavernous doors. The wolf paused in the shadows and with a blur of enchantment reshaped itself into Gorrid. To my dismay, he walked up to one of the Derzhi guards, spoke a few words, and was quickly escorted inside.

Treachery! I dived from the sky, but the door had been shut firmly behind Gorrid, and it took me a frustrating eternity to find a way in. I lit on a windowsill, nudged open the shutter, and fluttered through the dank maze of stacked crates and barrels toward the cluster of lights at the far end. But I was too late to hear anything. Everyone was shouting . . . calling . . . laughing. Spirits of darkness, what sort of creatures laughed as they set out to slaughter their own kind? The warehouse doors swung open, and two riders spurred their horses to a gallop, one turning to the right, the other to the left, both of them bearing lighted torches. Gorrid stood watching the rest of them, a small troop of Derzhi . . . some twenty or more . . . race through the gaping doorway and onto a road that would take them straight to the customs house, where Farrol was waiting and where Aleksander would be joining him at any moment.

"Bastard!" I screamed as I shifted. "Traitor!" I kicked the startled Gorrid in the face as I flew toward the door. He toppled to the dirt, blood spurting from his nose. I circled and swept my sword delicately across the back of his thighs, relishing his scream. Hamstrung, he could go nowhere until I came back to question him. Then I would kill him. For the moment, I had to stop what was about to happen. In less time than it took to think about it, I beheaded the first rider before he could signal the waiting soldiers to fire their torches. By the time I swept the second rider from his saddle with his spine severed, he had left three torches burning behind him. But either I had begun moving faster than I had ever moved or the three Derzhi sentinels were inexplicably slow, for they had not shifted from their positions when I snuffed out their torches and their lives in the same instant.

A quick circle from a greater height, and I saw the trap ready to spring. Aleksander was already crossing the bridge to the lower city, accompanied by only five men. He must have left the rest at the citadel. What in the name of the gods was he thinking? The troop of Derzhi would arrive at the front of the customs house at exactly the same time Aleksander reached the back.

Weaving an enchantment that I had never before attempted, I sped downward toward the pillared customs house. I flew through the open galleries near the roof and into the vaulted vastness where the outlaw reserves sat mounted and waiting for some signal they were needed. "Get them out!" I screamed at Farrol, who spun and gaped at my sudden appearance as I touched earth beside him. "Whatever you do, keep Aleksander out of here." I grabbed his shoulders and shook him. "Do you understand me? Keep him out!"

"Seyonne, wait . . ." Farrol tried to catch my arm, but I shoved him away and shot upward out of his reach.

"Keep them out or they die with the black-hearted Derzhi." Already the stone walls were quivering as the enchantment flowed from my hands into them.

Quickly Farrol yelled at his men to vacate the customs house and bar the Aveddi from entering. They needed no encouragement as I laid my hand upon one and then another of the columns that supported the roof, and cracks appeared in the massive stone cylinders. But the stubborn Farrol did not follow his men. Rather he stood in the center of the room and called up to me, a sturdy, round man of good heart, never temperate in either opinion or action. "Seyonne, don't do this. It's all right." Hooves thundered up the road toward us from the city. Falling dust dulled the sheen of sweat on his round face. "Gods of night, Seyonne, it's his *cousin* . . ."

Even as I touched the last pillar, as dust and shards of marble and plaster showered from the shuddering vaults, the word lanced through the storm of madness. The secrecy . . . the strange plan . . . the dangerous matters . . . *kill* no one *who does not challenge you . . . Handling the garrison warriors will be easier than you believe* . . . Aleksander had known these warriors would be no challenge. *His cousin* . . . Kiril. The Parassa garrison were Kiril's men.

What had I done? Kiril . . . Aleksander's dearest friend, his brother in all but parentage, a piece of his heart . . . and twenty others of his command racing here in laughter to greet their Prince, their Aveddi. And just below me was Farrol . . . foster brother to Blaise and Elinor . . . the man who had saved my son's life . . . stubbornly risking his own to prevent my killing innocent men . . .

With an ear-shattering crack, one of the columns shattered, crumbling in a torrent of rubble. The roof and walls groaned in agony. The great doors at the front of the customs hall burst open, and I had to choose—the one or the twenty. "Run, Farrol! For the gods' sake, run!" I spread my wings and dived for the doors, bellowing my warning. Another crack behind me, and another, and the roaring rumble of an avalanche. Before me rearing horses, screaming, men crying out in terror as I swept them backward and made myself into a wall of fire to keep them out. One man died, trampled by a frenzied horse, and then another when he was split open by a toppling cornice. At least two more lay on the ground when the living had retreated into the night. Only then did I summon the wind and turn back to the hellish scene of my creation.

The sky was raining stone. One by one the pillars snapped as I dodged the toppling slabs and the unending cascade of brick and mortar. Only moments and the whole structure would collapse. My working had been excellent, a model of destruction. My own light reflected on the swirling dust was the only illumination, and to hear anything above the noise was impossible. But even as the sky fell, I searched. A jagged portion of the ceiling caught one wing, pinning it to a broken column. Rips in my wings were excruciating, but I felt nothing as I yanked it free and left a ragged tear. The falling stones glanced off me like pebbles off a mountainside as I plowed through the piles of rubble, hunting for any sign of movement. "Farrol!" *Sweet Verdonne, let him live.*

He lay beneath a slab of the ceiling, a curved panel painted with the likeness of customs officials offering tribute to the Emperor. I wrenched the massive piece away and gathered his broken body in my arms. As the wall beside us crumpled with a roar, bringing down the remainder of the roof, I soared upward toward the cold stars, crying out my agony of shame. I could not remember how to express human grief. My Madonai eyes seemed incapable of tears.

CHAPTER 40

The storm raged over Tyrrad Nor, a howling, bitter wind stripping the garden to its twiggy bones, a driving rain turned to sleet with the night. The first harsh taste of winter had come to the mountain, although the lands beyond the black wall still basked in mellow autumn.

Icy droplets rolled down my naked back, each one a lancet of fire on abraded skin. I knelt in the corner of the castle ramparts and fought to keep from crying out. Never had I known such pain, not even in the pits of Kir'Vagonoth. *One more try. Just one more . . . say the word . . . make the shift . . . fly . . .*

"You're wasting your time." The newcomer might have been deposited on the exposed heights by the storm. The whine of the wind and the howling protests of my body had disguised his coming, but I was so far gone in my misery, I felt no surprise. What man beset by demons is surprised when one of them appears in the flesh? "Haven't you learned enough yet?" Kasparian's expressionless comments came with a proffered towel and cloak.

Ignoring his outstretched hand and its promises of comfort, I hauled myself up onto the gap in the stone wall overlooking the abyss of storm and night. Weak-kneed with exhaustion, I invoked my melydda yet again. I was determined to be away, to leave this place of seduction, of deception, of corruption. Yet, to my disgust, even though I stood at this point of abdication, I still craved the sensations of power. *First the word. Then comes the first flush of enchantment, the breathless pleasure as blood and bone and muscle feel its touch, the stretch, the pulsing growth as the wings begin to unfold . . . it is what I am meant to be . . .* But again my shoulders ripped apart, flayed, raw flesh on fire, exploding agony in every scrap of my being. In moments I was slumped in the corner once more, a quivering heap of wretchedness.

"It's the prisoning spells." He spoke as if I were a mewling child.

Naked and groaning as I was, curled up in a ball, head bowed to the sleet and storm, anyone might think the same . . . or recognize me as an arrogant fool driven to despair by guilt and horror. I could not even call upon my gods. I was dreadfully afraid that they, who had given me gifts beyond mortal imagining, had watched me turn them all to murder. Afraid that they would peer into my soul and see that I could not weep.

"Give it up before you're naught but an ugly mess on the garden walk. You can initiate no enchantment in Tyrrad Nor."

Kasparian's assertion made no sense, even to a mind dulled with pain and self-loathing. Of course I could use power in Tyrrad Nor. On the first day of my return I had called up a wind . . . and after . . . yes, Nyel and Kasparian had initiated the enchantments, but I had used my own melydda to shape them. "I am not a prisoner here," I croaked through chattering teeth. "I came here of my own choice. I can leave of my own choice." A foolish claim when I had been trying to leave for more than half a day—to climb over the wall, to shift my form and fly from the garden, from the mountain crags, or here in the rain from the ramparts of my nightmares, stripping the clothes from my back in an attempt to free the power that would not come. Always failing, each time left in greater torment than the last.

"Where is it you think to go?"

"Away." Reason had no claim on me that night. Going had nothing to do with destination, everything with origin and movement and change. I could no longer travel my present course. For good or ill, for death or life, Gaspar had said, but the path of my choosing had led only to death and corruption. *Warriors make mistakes. We have to live with them and accept our limitations. Guilt is self-indulgence.* Nyel was not the only mentor who had tried to teach me that lesson. But the deaths at Parassa were more than a mistake. Enough was enough. "Why can't I shift?"

"No Madonai can initiate his own enchantments within these walls, save myself, who was considered too weak and useless to be a threat. Even I cannot cross the wall." The ice wind froze my hair and circled my limbs with its razor fingers, but it was the truth in Kasparian's words that made me shudder. "And truly, you have very little power as yet. What you have used in the human world is dross."

My throat tightened. "I am not Madonai. We've not even begun . . ."

But Kasparian's unsmiling laughter told me differently.

Was it possible? Nyel had repeated the question so often I'd not heard it: *Do you choose freely?* Every time I'd gone to Aleksander. Every time I'd learned a new enchantment. Oh, gods, every time . . . a step along the way. Thus, the lack of appetite, the waning need for sleep, the vanishing scars . . . One of my hands flew to my face and felt the rough deadness of the slave mark, while the other clutched my side, and for once I was glad of the familiar ache. "It is not done. Not yet."

There had to be one more step, at least, one more offer that I would hear, knowing, and could refuse. So that I would not murder all my friends in frenzied madness. So that I would not become the thing I feared. So that I would not stand atop these ramparts and destroy the world.

"To inherit true Madonai power you must submit one last time. But your body is Madonai as much as it will ever be. For now, you, too, are bound by our prison. These last flaws are retained by your own weakness—your human memory—and will fade with time. Once your journey is complete"—he shrugged—"you may have power enough to break the infernal wall or you may not. But then there is always dream traveling." The dagger of his bitterness twisted in my gut.

"He said that at every step I could choose . . ."

". . . and so you have chosen." He dropped the cloak over my hunched shoulders and the towel onto the paving. "The servants will bring hot water to your room whenever you decide to leave off this pitiful display."

My forehead rested on the paving. Perhaps the pressure of cold stone might ease the pounding in my skull. I thought Kasparian had left the ramparts, for the night felt empty, as if the wind and the darkness had devoured every soul in the universe. But as I wrapped my arms about my belly, words spilled onto my back, scarcely distinguishable from the freezing rain. "I would recommend you seek advice before you refuse him the last step."

Seek advice. Would that I could. Would that there was someone who might listen and understand and tell me what to do. But the only advice I heard was my dead father's gentle remonstrance. *Unfair, Seyonne. Unjust to raise your hand against one who cannot fight back on your terms. Did you even think?* Even with such poignant memory, tears would not come.

When a pale sun rose in a winter-blue sky, I was still huddled in the corner of the ramparts, sure of nothing but that I would throw myself wingless from the tower of Tyrrad Nor before I would accept another gift from Nyel. No more game playing. Oh, I did not blame him. If he had told me from the beginning that my participation in his enchantments was the mechanism for my change, I would have chosen no differently.

Unjust. Unfair. To thrust the power of a Madonai into a human conflict. That was the sin of my arrogance: to believe that strength and honorable intentions justified such violation of the world's ordering. *Your strength will be your downfall*, my demon had said. And so it had been. Nyel had warned me that the entangling of human emotions and Madonai power was dangerous. Now I had seen the consequences of detachment and could not stomach them. So, as I gathered the cloak about my clammy flesh and descended from the ramparts of my prison, I told myself I'd best prepare for a lengthy stay in Tyrrad Nor. If the only possibility of escaping this prison was to follow my current path to its end, abandoning what scraps of my human self remained, then I would never leave.

Clean clothes and a tub of steaming water were waiting in my room, as Kasparian had promised. I soaked for an hour and then fell onto my bed, forcing my body into a sleep it no longer needed.

A full day passed before I allowed myself to wake. After bathing and donning the clothes that were laid out for me, I paced the castle corridors. I needed to get my blood moving. The day was uninviting. Windy. Dull. I did not avoid Nyel, but neither did I seek him out. Confrontation would come soon enough. He knew all that had happened at Parassa and how I felt about it. His attempts at comfort when I had first emerged from the disastrous venture had been quite sincere, voiced in his kindest and most reasonable tones. But I had desired no consolation, especially that which told me such mistakes were the result of my improper fawning over a race of liars, that by caring too much for those who were not worthy, I corrupted my own judgment. Innocent people had died at my hand. Curse the devil's soul forever, I had murdered my friend.

I wrenched my thoughts to present and future. What did it mean to be neither human, nor rekkonarre, nor fully Madonai? I tried a few enchantments as I walked through a courtyard of hissing fountains: summoning a wind, casting a light, shaping a minor illusion in the way I had always done it. But the words and spells I had learned in Ezzaria had withered away. Like dry riverbeds, their familiar courses were devoid of that which gave them life. The failure left me dry and incomplete, as I had been in my slave years. The gift of sorcery that I had carried with me since my birth had been transformed into something new, a furnace laid with glowing embers that pulsed with the beating of my heart and roared into life whenever I shaped wings. Knowing full well the likely outcome, I breathed upon the embers and tried the spells again . . . and in moments I was clutching a fluted column, trying to stay upright until invisible bludgeons and axes stopped shattering my bones. The Madonai core existed, but was inaccessible. Nyel had insisted that I would wield my own power when I was wholly changed, but had promised nothing if I stopped short of that.

And so what of my third part, the human part? I returned to my room, picked up the knife that had been laid out for me at every waking and dragged the blade across my left arm. I scarcely felt it. Blood welled from the thumb-length gash, but slowed to a trickle in only moments. By the time I grabbed a discarded towel to blot it, the wound was already half closed. It appeared that if I remained as I was, I could live a very long time with frustrated desire and limited occupation. A most dangerous combination.

Where did Kasparian think I was to get advice? Certainly not from Nyel, who did nothing but confuse me. Nor from the bitter Kasparian himself or his silent servants. If I could not cross the wall, I could not question the rai-kirah, themselves victims of this perverse power, or make my way to the gamarand wood, where, so visions and the dying Kryddon had told me, enlightenment awaited. What of history, then? Was there some writing that might tell me what I was or how to reverse what had been done? My restless feet took me to the fortress library, a warren of rooms housing thousands of books and scrolls, maps and drawings. But a few hours flipping through brittle pages and unrolling fragile manuscripts only to find more spells I could not use and adventures I could not share left me with such craving for melydda I could scarcely breathe. I was so cold. So empty. And the embers within me pulsed, waiting to fill me with warmth and light. Only a few hours into my rebellion, and I was on the verge of capitulation.

"Weak-willed murderer!" I threw an armful of ribbon-tied rolls to the flagstones. Before the dust and fragments of shattered parchment had settled, I was striding down the broad stairway and out of the front doors, inhaling deeply, trying to gauge the best path to set off running. Perhaps exercise would dull the hunger for today. Would it suffice for a thousand years or more?

I started jogging toward the wall, thinking to take the longest path around the edge of the garden and up the track that ascended the mountain. The closer I got to the wall, the more unsettled my stomach became. Now I understood the sickness I had experienced on the night after the battle at Gan Hyffir, just as I understood why Nyel never walked near the wall. The "prisoning spells," as Kasparian called them, would be designed to keep a Madonai away from it. But I continued on and ran the circuit of the wall and the mountain path three times before deliberately dropping to the damp turf at the base of the wall. "Go ahead," I said, settling my back against the cracked stone. "Do your worst."

I expected to feel the full impact of the binding enchantments when I touched my back and head to the wall. Indeed a dull ache crept into my muscles and streaks of red light pierced my eye sockets, distorting the weak daylight. When I closed my eyes to will away the discomfort, however, I was distracted by more visions of the Twelve Friends—those who existed somehow within the enchanted barrier. The images left me wondering again how they had crafted this prison and why. I ought to know. All of them had been my friends in that distant life. Had I helped design these very enchantments that threatened to tear me apart? A fitting irony that I had destroyed the part of me that might have remembered how to break through them.

These considerations led me to think of Fiona and her discovery—the tower in the gamarand wood where the Twelve had planned this fortress. How had Fiona described it—the tower without a door? *Smooth and warm . . . stone that was alive . . .* This wall could be described just the same. *I pushed gently,* she had said. *Eased myself through, using words of opening and passage.*

I leaped to my feet and faced the wall. Laying the flats of my hands against the warm stone, I pressed gently, and as before, the stone seemed to swell about my fingers. But when I tried to weave words of opening and passage, my throbbing discomfort exploded into agony. I held as long as I could, convincing myself that I felt some softening beneath my fingers, some movement, some release, but I soon fell to my knees, retching. Empty and sick, I gripped the edge of a deep crack to push away from the wall, mumbling, "I'm sorry, Lady. All of you, forgive me." And the stone swelled up around my hands and drew me in . . .

Eternal grayness . . . daylight filtering through the pores of the black stone. Chill, airless solidity as when you walk into a tomb. The warmth of the wall was a sign of those who existed here; what they themselves experienced was unyielding cold. I reached out my hands like a blind man and felt the fluttering softness of their touch, like moth wings propelling me on my way through the grayness. "Tell me who you are," I said as I moved through them. "I can't remember. Can you show yourselves? Tell me what to do." I reached out to touch their minds, but discovered only living stone. So many years. So grim a duty. Voices long faded. Yet even in the cold and silent grayness, I felt no hatred. Not for me, not for the prisoner they were there to confine, not for the world that had forgotten their sacrifice. A last firm shove on my back—I would have sworn I heard the faintest echo of Vyx's laughter, he who had come late to his post . . .

. . . And I opened my eyes to a small, neat room. The curved walls were undecorated, save for a single window that looked out upon a woodland of yellow trees, alive with the twitters and whistles of wrens and robins and orioles. The gamarand wood, and beyond it, the mountain of Tyrrad Nor. This was Fiona's tower.

"Hello?" My call was only for form's sake. The still air had already told me that no one was there.

A table of pale wood stood in the center of the room, fifteen backless stools drawn up around it. Laid out on the table were pens and ink, a pewter pitcher half filled with fragrant red wine, fifteen wine cups, and the scrolls Fiona had transcribed—the drawing of the fortress and the manuscript. Language was no longer a barrier. A quick perusal of the manuscript told me nothing that I did not already know about Tyrrad Nor: its size and shape and accoutrements, its barricade of spells. The black stone was slightly more mysterious. I opened the wooden case and read the word scribed on the stone: *Kerouan*. Unlike Fiona's experience, closing my eyes or looking away from the stone did not erase what I had just read. I traced a finger over the word, wondering, then dropped the stone in my pocket. If I found someone to ask questions of, I could ask this one, too.

I descended the curving staircase. What would I do if I found no one in the wood? Though I had spent a frenzied night attempting to leave Tyrrad Nor, now I was beyond the wall, I had no idea where to go. Find my way to the gateway, I supposed. Or see if any of the rai-kirah survived; my body's change might prevent me living in the human world again.

As I opened the lower door, I laid my hand on the tower wall and closed my eyes. The warm stone softened at my touch. *A lonely vigil*, I thought, as I envisioned a sour old woman's ruddy face. *You don't even have the comfort that there are others beside you. But the birds are here, at least*. Whoever she was, she had loved birds better than men or women. I greeted her and thanked her, and then stepped out into the forest of gold.

Marveling, I touched a pair of the twining yellow trunks, one rough, one smooth, a single tree at root and spreading crown, yet always a duality. The smooth trunk birthed the dark green leaves that turned to yellow fire in autumn, as well as the white blooms of spring; the rough trunk curved about the first, protecting it, producing the liquor of life from water, sunlight, and its own nature to feed the crown and root. The branches were bare, the fading brilliance of leaves and blossoms a carpet beneath my feet. Through the tangle overhead loomed the mountain's granite knee, and high above me sat the thin girdle of black stone that was the wall. The steep angle and lowering clouds prevented any view of the fortress behind it. Good. I didn't want to see it ever again.

The forest had fallen still when I stepped out of the tower. No sound of bird or insect marred the palpable silence. The air was cool on my cheek, and the scent of old leaves and damp earth filled my nostrils. And more . . . traces of intelligence pervaded the woodland, the unmistakable residue of sentience. The vibrant threads were so distinctive, I could name them neither human nor Madonai, but I could surely name them.

"He loved you, didn't he?" My voice jarred the quiet. "You're the one." The mortal maiden chosen by a god.

No one answered, and I walked on, the trees shaping my path. Though my instincts bade me flee, only one way was open to me, every other blocked by drooping branches or fallen trees. I would clamber around them only to find myself trudging uphill again, back toward the fortress and its cruel temptations. "Let me go, Lady," I said to the wood, "or give me answers." The breeze riffled my hair and fingered my cheek softly. "I cannot grieve. I don't know how anymore." Somehow I believed that she was listening. "Is it because I'm neither one nor the other? He is Madonai, yet he still feels. He loves me, and he grieves for me as the sun mourns for the earth that it can never touch. Why? I've let him blind me, cripple me, make me everything I despise, and yet I cannot hate him for it. If I don't understand, how can I know what to do?"

Silence. I turned downhill again, swearing under my breath. Faced with yet another blockage, I raised my hand and summoned melydda, but was instantly on my back with a stinging bruise on my face. The blast of power had been breathtaking and from no source that I could see. I mumbled an oath, making sure my hand was still attached to my arm. "All right. All right." I stumbled to my feet and followed the path chosen for me.

Now, with every step, the sweet woodland smell became more tainted with the acrid scent of ash, of freshly charred wood and burned grass. A few more steps and I emerged from the trees. The Lady was seated on a rock overlooking a scorched vale, stark black skeletons of gamarand trunks. The steep rock face across the burned vale was stained dark red, as if some horrific carnage had taken place nearby, splattering it with blood. Wisps of smoke still curled from a few thick stands of trees, while the breeze stirred the hot ash and scattered it on the Lady's green gown and dark hair like gray snowflakes.

When her luminous gaze came to rest on me, I sank to one knee and bowed my head. "My Lady Verdonne," I whispered. Why had it taken me so long to understand who she was—the one who stood between the god and the human world, the forest maiden who had been made immortal? Not a goddess, but a woodland, a boundary between light and darkness, trying to shield both humans and rekkonarre. My day within the oak had taught me of the immortality of a forest—unless it burned so hot that its seeds and roots were destroyed, unless its home ground was made sterile by flames. "Forgive my blindness, Lady. Help me see my path."

"Can I command you to be other than you are?" Her chin rested in her hand, and her voice was as much a part of that woodland as the rustling leaves. "Perhaps then this business would be easier, for I would not care what became of you." Her sigh was the breeze that shifted the layers of ash. "For so long I've believed that if you could but find your way here again, we could devise a way to hold him. But never did I think your journey would be so filled with pain. How can I ask more?" She rose and came to me. Her hand touched my shoulder and drew me up, and another on my cheek lifted my head to look on her. Her bronze skin was shaped by fine bones, and her spare features, the burnished glow of her hair, and the faint lines about her eyes spoke more of mature wisdom than blooming girlhood. She reminded me of Elinor. Only the immensity of her presence named her far, far older than my son's foster mother. "Ah, beloved, what am I to say to you?"

"I'll stay here a prisoner if need be," I said. "Or I'll walk back through the gateway and into the desert to live a powerless hermit. I'll take my place in the wall, if that is necessary. But I cannot take another step along his path, though I go mad with it." And I would go mad. I knew I would. "Just help me understand, Lady. Command me." For so long I had tried to control my own future. Whatever life and fate had put before me, no matter what pain my choices cost me, I had insisted on shaping the event to my own design. Now I was tired of choosing. No more of it.

She put her arm through mine, and we strolled along the edge of the burned forest. "We've so little time. It's enough to make one shake the World's Tree until its roots break loose!" Jerking me to a halt almost immediately, she bent over to brush the choking ash from a young gamarand. As she wiped her gray-smudged fingers on her green mantle and propelled me forward once more, she shouted in the direction of Tyrrad Nor. "May its fruits bruise your balls, Madonai, and its trunk bash your hard head!" She punctuated her outburst with a bone-bruising squeeze of my arm. I jumped a little and gaped at her. She crinkled her lovely face into a rueful smile. "What is it? Do our people no longe swear by the World's Tree?"

Swear . . . In that crystalline moment, the name that I ha bandied about for thirty-eight years assumed the shape of human woman instead of a goddess—a human woman who, afte more than a thousand years of guardianship, could still rail i good-humored ferocity at what fate had brought her. I could no help but grin. "My lady . . . our people swear by your name!"

Amused resignation danced on her face. "I suppose tha makes as much sense as a tree. The powers who truly shaped th world must be accustomed to odd guises."

So small an exchange, so trivial to ease a man's awe and des peration. Yet it drew me back to our business, too, for Ezzarian also swore by the name of her son . . . the jailer. But it was wit rational need and no longer with panicked frenzy that I phrase my request. "Tell me the story, Lady."

"First, look up there." She pointed to the wall. "Look closely." For the first time in a long while I called upon my Warden' senses, the human skills of far-seeing and sharpened hearing tha were nothing of enchantment, only long training and practice The entire outer surface of the wall was crumbling, as if some one had taken a battering ram to it.

"Three days ago the wall was almost whole," she said. "It wa an astonishing sight, for our enchantments have been on th verge of failure for many years. Even when Vyxagallanxchi too his place a year ago, his gift—the last of the Twelve—wa quickly used up. But in the last few months the damage has bee reversed, the cracks sealing themselves, the wall reabsorbing it broken pieces." She paused and fixed me with her gaze. "Do yo know why?"

I shook my head.

"Because of you. Because of his love for you. And perhap because of yours for him."

The day shifted, as if the sun's great eye had blinked. "Bu now it's broken again," I said, swallowing hard to keep my nerv ous stomach in place. "What's causing it to fall apart?"

"You know the exact events more than I," she said, resumin her pace, drawing me along in her wake as a ship guides a floa ing leaf. "On the day of our wedding, my husband gifted me wit the heartbond of the Madonai, and so I am one with his joys an sorrows, though I rarely know their cause. I know he travels i dreams, and I know what he's learned to do with them—my fault, I'm afraid, for it was my suggestion to leave the breach in his bonds that has caused the world such distress. I can see the visions he creates, and so I learned of you—the cause of his great joy. I tried to reach you, to warn you, but I've nothing like his power, of course, even contained as he is— "

"—and I would not listen either to you or to this rai-kirah that's joined with me; I shut him out, silenced him before he could remember." I had destroyed him with weapons forged of my lifelong fears, of the need to control my own destiny, of my reluctance to allow anyone—my wife, my friends, and especially a powerful and angry rai-kirah—access to my soul.

Her red-gold cheeks deepened in color, and a wind of sadness wafted through the woodland, shifting the fallen leaves. "You must not blame yourself. Never, never do that. There is too much weight in these matters to think they hinge upon a single pivot. Every deed we do, every happenstance, even our own sense about what we've done and seen—all have their places in the great puzzle of the world. Just tell me what's happened in these few days, and then I'll explain more. To understand what must be done, you need to see the past more clearly. If it cannot be from your own remembrance, then it must come from me."

And so we walked the forest paths, through the trees and out again into another desolation of ash and smoke, while I poured out the story of my bargain with Nyel and its terrible consequences. I told her of my inexplicable reliance on his good intentions and my foolish belief that if I could not save him, I would at least be able to kill him. "But I know now that such a deed is inconceivable," I said. "He has me in such thrall that my hand could never raise a weapon against him, even if I knew what one to use. I fear for my soul, Lady. And if I lose it, the world will suffer." Astonishing how the very act of speaking such perilous truth can soothe its mortal dread. Or perhaps it was only the Lady and my belief that she could forgive me anything, even to the destruction of the human race.

We had come to a slow flowing stream, a ribbon of floating gold, and we sat on the leaf-strewn earth beside it. She drew up her knees and hugged them. "He believes you will refuse him. That's what's happened to the wall. All his hopes, both for good and evil—for he is truly mad and cannot see the difference—are bound up in you. And without hope, he is lost again, and we are all in danger. The wall will fail."

"I have been a naive fool," I said. "To let him do this to me—"

She laid her hand on my knee and leaned forward. "No, no! Do not doubt your own mind, dear one. Everything you've seen of him, everything you've felt of his goodness, is absolutely true. When I waked beside my father's fire to see the one from my dream sitting beside me, those glorious eyes gazing at me in wonder and curiosity and no small portion of lusty interest, I first learned the meaning of beauty and love and kindness. For twenty years I learned nothing other from him. Oh, we argued. Everyone would tell you of it. He was strong-willed and proud and used to having his way. And I was my father's only daughter and very like. But our disputes were always rooted in good humor, and our delight in each other, both body and mind, soon mended them. Everyone who knew him—Madonai, human, and rekkonarre—felt the same. No one in any world has been better loved than he who dwells in Tyrrad Nor or more deserving of it."

She withdrew her hand and laid it in her lap, staring at it as if it were a part of someone else, not quite belonging to her own body. "Even when his people began to die, things did not change between us for a long while. He would come to me and lay his head in my lap as I sat beside our fire, telling me who had sickened that day and who had died, and of his endless investigations to discover the cause of their decline. I would wipe his tears and tell him news of the children. Seventeen of the rekkonarre dwelt within a day's walk of my hearth fire. Though he came always in the night, he would often linger into the day, so that he could spend time with our own son."

Son. The word was like a spark of lightning over distant hills, a portent of the coming storm.

"The children were the joy to balance out his grieving," she went on. "Imagine the horror of this early death for the Madonai. Think of how we feel when a youth or maiden dies—far worse than for an infant death, because a youth or maid of twelve or fifteen summers has begun the journey, brought joy to her family or strength to his village, but has yet to realize the full promise of life. So many things undone, untried, unknown. Such was this for his people, for a Madonai who has lived only a few hundred years is but a youth. Now think of a plague that takes our young people one by one, the most generous and most joyful first—for those are the Madonai who first mated with humans. When the younger ones were dead, the elder tried to make children, too, and then the elders, too, began to die. All in the matter of a heart-beat in the span of their long lives. Why did my love not die with them? He didn't know. Was it because he was the first? Because he was the strongest? Because he loved to travel through my dreams and had never stepped through the gateways in the flesh? More and more he remained in his world, pushing himself to find the reasons and the remedies, giving everything he had to make things right again. When he stopped coming to me, I tried to send messages, and I tried to go to him. But he would neither see me nor would he see our son, for he had found his answer and could not bear it."

I dislodged a snag in the stream, where a charred limb had stuck in the earthen bank and caught the drifting leaves, holding them until the mass had turned black and clogged the flow. The rotting mess swirled and broke apart, moving away slowly until the golden stream ran free. "He told me he planned to destroy the gateways," I said, "and because it would have prevented the rekkonarre from spending time in both worlds, thus dooming them to madness, he was called a child-slayer."

"Kasparian told him that story when his mind was still quite fragile. To know the whole of it would have destroyed him again when he was only just recovering. I've no way to know how much he remembers now." Verdonne clasped her hands in her lap. "My husband was going to destroy the gates. That's true. But the danger to his people still existed. He could not destroy the enchantment, the *vietto* that had brought the Madonai to our world in the first place, could he?" And so the storm broke.

"He came to me in the night," said the Lady. "Lay with me as he had not done in a year, weeping every moment even as he pleasured me beyond mortal imagining. When we lay sated beside my hearth fire, he reached for his tunic and pulled out a jewel, a diamond that could have been a star brought down to earth in his hand. His body would take fire with golden light when his power was flowing. On that night, the jewel grew golden, too, so that his tears reflected its light, and I asked what was this working that grieved him so sorely. 'It is the answer,' he said as wailing rose from the forest, first from one direction and then another. The sky darkened with the sound as if clouds had covered the stars. The night bled. And he lay in my arms with his jewel and his tears, as the wailing rose from ever more distant settlements.

" 'What terror is abroad this night?' I said. 'Why do you lie here weeping and do nothing?' Never had he failed to answer our distress, giving everything of his heart, of his labor, and of his power to ease our human travails. But on that night he just gathered me in his arms and stroked my hair, and sobbed that no one suffered or was afraid. He'd seen to that, he said. I felt him quivering, cold sweat on his forehead and his breast. Soon he rolled to the side, groaning, still clutching the jewel, and I saw he was in terrible pain. 'Love, what is it?' I said. 'Make it stop.'

" 'I cannot,' he said. 'I tried to find some other way. Truly, my darling one, I tried. But it is my people. Unless I do this, I'll have killed them all.' But, of course, that's exactly what he was doing to the humans and the rekkonarre . . . killing them all and taking their pain and fear into himself to ease their way into the realm of death."

"And who stopped him?" I said, knowing the answer even before she spoke it.

"You did, my darling—the son he cherished beyond all telling. When you woke from your sleep at my call and challenged him to end the slaughter, he could not bring himself to slay you. For love of you, he shattered his jewel before it was spent. And once he broke the spell to stop the killing, the guilt of his race's ruin and the pain and fear of ten thousand dead tore his mind apart."

CHAPTER 41

Nyel. The Nameless God. My father. Mine and not mine . . . for even when my flesh and spirit knew and believed and witnessed to my mind that Verdonne did not lie, my soul clung to the gentle man of books and earth who had sired me in Ezzaria. Gareth of the line of Ezraelle was my soul's father, not a proud, tormented Madonai who had tried to exterminate the human race. No matter that he had sought to ease their way into death, the Madonai had chosen slaughter to remedy a grievous tragedy. And because he had been a good and honorable man, he had gone mad from it.

His son had become his jailer and lived on until the split that had sent the rai-kirah into exile and the human sorcerers back to Ezzaria. And though his physical body had died a thousand years in the past, that son still lived, an inseparable part of me.

"So what are we to do?" I said. The day's false warmth had fled, and I hunched my cloak about my shoulders, turning away from the rising north wind so I would not have to look upon the fortress and the wall and a future that terrified me.

"Give him back his hope."

Such a simple, pleasant phrase to describe a nightmare. I turned on the Lady, such fear and anger rising up in me that my body quivered. "Let him make me a monster to follow him? I cannot do it." For I could see his strategy now. Yes, he wanted his son strong and powerful, a true Madonai . . . a god. But he also wanted me ruthless, free of the weakness that had caused him to fail. No wonder he hated Aleksander. No wonder . . . holy stars of night, no wonder he wanted to know more of my own son. "You're telling me to give up my human soul. Don't you understand? I've seen what I'll become. I can't do it."

The Lady's calm reason was terrifying. "You tried to contain his power with your enchantments, and for a very long time you succeeded. But the Twelve are tired, fading, and no Madonai are left to give themselves to the wall. Our friends paid a terrible price to allow him to live, hoping that someday his madness would heal and that he would again bless both worlds with his love." Verdonne laid her hand on my arm, trying to soothe my agitation, strolling through the yellow trees as if we were discussing the weather or the price of flour in the market.

She told me how I—Valdis—had no more been able to slay my father for his crime than he had been able to hurt me, and so I had designed a way to contain his power. Twelve Madonai—out of so many who loved him, I'd had to choose—had allowed me to weave their essence into a wall, for pure Madonai power was all that could hold him. A thirteenth had become the tower guardian to provide the way in and out of the fortress. Verdonne had paid the price, as well, bound to this forest forever, giving it her strength and living with its pain. And then I had woven enchantment that stripped my father of his name. I had led him into the fortress and soothed his raving terrors, for it was to be a very long while until his mind regained any semblance of balance.

"Before many years had passed, the rekkonarre began to forget the prisoner, just as you intended when you took his name," she said. "The Madonai were long dead, save for Vyxagallanxchi. Verdonne and Valdis and the Nameless God became the stuff of myth. But every day you saw the fortress was a knife in your heart, and as your father regained this show of reason, you were afraid the love you bore him would weaken your resolve. That's when you and Vyx decided to destroy your own memories of him. You came here and told me what you planned, knowing that you would forget me, too."

Time slowed to a crawl as my fingers wrapped around the black stone in my pocket. "But I recorded his name, didn't I? So that if he were ever to recover—"

"Vyx wrote it. He put it under an enchantment so that no one but you could read it."

Vyx had not been one of the rekkonarre, but my tutor, my protector, my mentor, a young Madonai devoted to me—his half-human *attellé*. Vyx had remained with me through the long years of forgetting, through the frightening time of the prophecy when I had been persuaded that if we didn't take drastic precautions, a winged shapeshifter was going to set the Nameless God free to destroy the world—not remembering that the one we feared was my own father. After we who remained—the rekkonarre, the builders—had worked the enchantment that split our souls, Vyx lived with me through exile in Kir'Vagonoth, remembering only that someday he would have to return to a black wall in Kir'-Navarrin to complete his life.

Truth and awe had sapped my fury. "If we cannot rebuild the wall, then what—?"

"The time has come for him to die, beloved. Let his devotion to you be our last remembrance of him. You could try to slay him now as you are, challenge him in some 'honorable' combat or destroy him in his sleep. But we have no way to gauge his true strength save by the wall, which says he is stronger than we would wish. With Kasparian to aid him in taking power from these poor shadows that inhabit Kir'Navarrin, the risk of his victory is too great. But the only way he can make you fully Madonai is to gift you with his own power, weaving it with that which was born in you. He cannot create Madonai sorcery anew, only transfer it, and at the moment of his yielding, he will be at his most vulnerable."

Nyel was not my true father. I did not owe him a son's loyalty. But Denas . . . Valdis . . . was a part of me, and if I was to live with myself, I needed to tread carefully in these matters. "What if I don't kill him, Lady? What then?"

Our path had led us back to the tower. Verdonne pulled aside a vine and laid her hands on the stone, smiling sadly and murmuring something that was beyond my hearing—a greeting to the tower guardian, I thought. Then she lifted her gaze to mine. "Perhaps nothing. He may yield you his power and fade away in his fortress, content that he has done everything possible to redeem his sins. Perhaps with the strength you bring to this completion, you will then be able to leave the fortress and do as you will. But he has had a very long time to consider his plan, and my husband was the most intelligent, most powerful of his kind, which is saying a great deal. It is possible that he could revoke his gift if you failed to live up to his expectations and complete his dreadful work." She took my hands in hers. "Fix this duty in your mind so that you will not forget your purpose amid the magnitude of your change. You must finish what you've begun. Accept his gift and take his life while he feels the joy of the giving."

Truth weighs heavier than other words, my soul's father had once told me. It bears a substance of its own, like an ingot that comes from the forge glowing, yet unmalleable. It rings clear like crystal when tapped, shines like silver beside lead. "And if I do this," I said, scarcely able to form words for the constriction in my chest, "who will contain me?"

"You will find your way. You are a man with two noble spirits, one that I know as I know my own heart and one that I have only glimpsed. What my son could not do alone, you, the stranger, will enable him to accomplish. The true powers of earth and sky have brought you to this place, forged you, shaped you, honed you. I trust them. And I trust you, my son and my friend."

There was no more to be said. In only a matter of moments I had passed through the tower wall and climbed the stairs to the quiet room. I carefully placed the black stone back in its wooden box. Kerouan. The Nameless God. I looked out through the window at the bright woodland, and then stepped across the fathomless gulf.

"You confound me!" Nyel's hand was poised above his game board, halted in midmotion at my declaration. "After your unhappiness of these past days, I assumed—"

"I would be grateful if you would stop 'assuming.' I am not a child. You can allow me to make my own decisions, and you needn't hide the difficult bits. I understand the consequences of my choices, have accepted them freely, and will do so until the end. I was unhappy because I killed innocent men, forced into it because my friend Aleksander refused to trust me fully. And then I discovered that I cannot walk through these walls, because you have already begun my change. Clearly you don't trust me, either. What man, Madonai or human, would not be 'unhappy' to discover that the two souls he trusted above any in the world could not reciprocate?"

"I have been, perhaps, overeager in my gifting."

An understatement of the case, to be sure, but as near to an apology as I was likely to hear. "So will you do as I ask?" I said.

Nyel carefully replaced the game piece—the white warrior king—onto the black-and-gray board. He rose and walked briskly to the windows, clasping his slender hands behind his back. "As you wish. I will send you to a new dreamer with the same conditions as before. But now to satisfy your need for truth: this venture, whatever your purpose, will be the last step of my working, save for the full gifting of power. When you return you will be Madonai, body and mind. Your human frailties will be eliminated, but not without cost. Certain portions of your past . . . memories, feelings . . . will have faded."

"As my scars have done? Kasparian says that even these two that remain may vanish in time." I helped myself to a glass of wine, marveling that my hand was steady. "Perhaps you've allowed them to stay to remind me of human perfidy." Let him make what he would of my bitterness. I was interested only in his answer.

"Ah, you are indeed perceptive. These two blemishes . . . rascally difficult to erase. Their roots delve so deep. We've scarcely begun your education—so many, many lessons to be learned—but we've no need to rush, and reminders will be valuable." He whirled about, his face alight as if the moon had risen in the southern sky beyond his garden windows. "Everything of your human past will be altered in the moment of your change. Not lost, but made remote, as if it belonged to someone else, like a story told you in your youth. Without some mitigation, such a drastic shift of mind would be frightening, I think, and I would not have you feel that I've stolen your life. So I've allowed these last physical anchors to remain until you can release them yourself, along with the painful memories they represent."

Gods have mercy, he was proud of his plan. He was doing me a "kindness." I breathed a little easier and, behind my folded arms, kneaded the ache buried deep in my side beneath the "blemish." A flimsy plan had come to me in the hours since I had returned from the gamarands. A dreadful gamble with incalculable stakes. And I would not be able to depend upon myself to make the proper moves; the very thought made me queasy.

"Good enough," I said. "I just want to be done with the business. Leave me the reminders. I'd rather not be drawn into stupid plans like this last one . . . gods, their ignorant, foolish schemes. All it would have taken to prevent this disaster was for Aleksander to entrust his plan to the intermediary I had chosen. What arrogant stupidity. I thought he had learned better."

"You are a tool they use for their own purposes," said Nyel. "What friend forces his comrade into violating his conscience?"

Night settled on the mountain, the day's clouds scattered with the north wind. The clearing weather left the air cold, and the stars that popped out of the blackening sky were hard-edged like glass. As Nyel summoned Kasparian to send us into the world of dreams, I paced and fidgeted, grateful at the Madonai's occupation that allowed my thoughts to focus on my dreamer and what I was going to say.

Before I had composed half the words I needed, Nyel returned with Kasparian in tow. The bullish Madonai's dislike burned steady as he arranged the chairs about the game table. Verdonne's revelations had explained Kasparian's hatred and jealousy. How bitter to see your master bestow his gifts upon your jailer . . . upon one who was not born Madonai . . . upon the son who had not loved his father as well as the *attellé* who had given up everything to share his master's exile. How unjust must fate appear to such a one.

Kasparian lit a candle as we settled around the table. A spider crawled up the pillar of wax. Nyel, his lean face eager, had the enchantment poised on his tongue, and before the first drip of wax had slumped down the candle, engulfing the struggling spider, I was floating above the sea of dreams.

She was only dozing. The trail of her dream was so faint and so quickly passed that I came near missing it. But explosive enchantment had possessed me from the moment of Nyel's touch, and I would not have failed to take the path of my desire had her dream been the length of a snowflake's life in desert noonday.

"Seyonne!" Elinor pressed her back against the lemon tree, sleep startled from her dark eyes. "What are you doing here?" Her aspect was wary, but not cowering, which spoke everything necessary about her courage. To wake from an afternoon drowse and see a man standing over you clothed in naught but a sword belt and garish light could be nothing but disconcerting, especially when the last you'd heard of him was that he had brought down a building to crush your foster brother's head. Unfortunately I was not going to ease her mind on that afternoon.

"I've come for my son. It's time for him to live with me."

I might well have struck her. She leaped to her feet, face flushed, all uncertainty dismissed. "You gave me your word!"

"Things change," I said.

"You said you would suffer anything to keep Evan safe and loved and happy," she said. "I believed you."

"And so I will do. Where is he?"

"Look at yourself, Seyonne! You'll frighten him. You frighten all of us now."

"Do you doubt me, too, Mistress? What more must I do to

prove myself?" We stood face-to-face on the steep, dry slope overlooking the crude tent settlement where I had last visited my child. The sun angle was low, the world streaked and splashed with red-gold light that no one would mistake for darkness. "I will not discuss this. It's time Evan learned of me and of his rightful place in the world."

Her graceful jaw grew hard. "And what would he learn? We don't even know what you are anymore. Even the Prince fears you've changed into something other. How can I hand over my child to one who—?"

"Evan is *my* child. He should be with me, not running about the desert with a band of miserable outlaws in the middle of a human war. With your stupidities and your ignorance, you'll all be dead within the year." I gathered a wind to fill my wings and took a step toward the tall woman. "Do not doubt my intent, and do not test me. Remember Parassa."

Her bold flush had faded, but she neither backed away nor withered under my glare. "None of us will forget Parassa. Was it not Parassa where your blind blood thirst killed my brother Farrol—a man who called you friend and crippled Gorrid—a man of honor and faith who has sacrificed his personal vengeance to serve your Prince? Where seven of Lord Kiril's men fell at your hand because you would not lower yourself to speak to the Aveddi? What makes you think you are fit to care for a child?"

True. All true. Her accusations stung like the tail of a whip. And now I was to violate the one vow I had thought inviolable. I was to put my child in danger. But I knew my friends, and nothing else would make them believe . . . "Tell me where he is, or I'll burn every tent in this camp to find him." My voice thundered through the dusty air, threatening to crack the rocks and split the trees. "I'll wring the necks of your people one by one if you try to keep him from me."

"Fires of heaven." At last she began to believe.

I swept my wings and took flight, circling about her like a vulture over carrion, shouting so that all in the settlement below would hear me. "Where is my son?"

"All right, I'll show you." She picked her way down the slope, stumbling a few times in her hurry. However, she did not stop thinking. "You'll take him to Kir'Navarrin?" she said, calling up to me.

"It is his home. His right."

"You'll need someone to care for him. He's so small . . ."

"I can conjure servants to see to his needs." I swept my wings again, swirling the dust around her.

"Conjure servants . . ." She squinted up at me as if trying to see through my skin, and then she shook her head. "Don't you understand? He's afraid of strangers. It's usual for children of his age. You can't—"

"He'll learn."

She slipped on a patch of loose rock and almost lost her balance. Her breathing ragged, she stopped for a moment to test her footing and scan the slope for a safer route. The people of the encampment had started to gather, shading their eyes against the last sunbeams and staring up at us. "No matter what you've become, you cannot be cruel enough to take a child away from everyone and everything he's ever known."

"Do not tell me what I can and cannot do! Am I still a slave? Everyone tries to set my course, telling me do this, do that, hold back, take care, you must, you must not. But things will be different now. I have found my true home, my true form. I have inherited such power as you cannot imagine and will have scarcely come into my prime long after you and these human creatures are dust. I wish my son to inherit my father's legacy. And I *will* have the boy out of danger. Damn your insolent—"

"And are there no dangers in your new realm?" She interrupted my bellowing, her gaze unwavering.

An arrow of fear pierced my wits as if shot straight from Elinor's eyes. *Careful. Careful.* I had planned to say these things—to make her fear me. But power was swelling my shoulders and my chest and my loins, was stretching my wings, threatening to distract me from my purpose. I was ready to lash out at her in ways I never intended.

Brutally, I forced myself to concentrate. I would be changed only when I returned to Nyel, when my dreamer slept again. *Keep to the plan. Nyel is watching* . . . "I am not unreasonable. You may send one person with him." Unless I could make this plan work, my child was safe nowhere.

I soared upward before she could answer and flew toward the settlement. As Elinor ran the last steep descent, I furled my wings and touched my feet to the dusty road a few hundred paces from the gathering crowd. I folded my arms and turned my back to them.

Behind me, shuffling steps and low murmurs gave way to a firm tread and familiar voice. "Speak with me, Seyonne." Aleksander's footsteps stopped at a considerable distance.

I fixed my eyes on Elinor and said nothing. Only a few moments later, when the woman ran breathlessly down the road to join him, did I turn to the Prince. The crowd had parted to let him pass, and he bore himself as a king confronting a messenger from an unknown realm. Feyd stood behind, his head bowed where I could not see his face. Was the Suzaini youth shamed that I had come to someone else or was he hiding his relief? Beside the Prince stood a stone-faced Blaise, holding my son. Evan was looking at me curiously, a finger stuck in his mouth as he clung to the bony Ezzarian.

I forced my attention to Elinor. "Who will accompany the child?" I said, taking up as if there were not a hundred new witnesses to our conversation.

Elinor looked from me to the others and back, beads of sweat glistening on her forehead. "Seyonne has come for Evan," she said to the others. "He wants to take the boy to safety in Kir'-Navarrin." Her words spilled out quickly, shutting off the protests that Aleksander and Blaise had ready. "He is . . . adamant . . . so there's no use arguing. Please don't fuss. And someone must go with them so Evan won't be afraid. I'm going to go."

"Linnie, you can't," said Blaise, biting back his fury. "You heard Fiona tell us of her sickness. You wouldn't survive for more than a few months."

"We'll face that when it comes," she said.

"I'll go," said Blaise. "The boy is comfortable with me, and I can—"

Elinor shook her head. "You're needed here; the Aveddi depends on you, and the future of this Empire is more important than any one of us. Besides, Seyonne charged me with Evan's care. I will not abandon my child."

"As you wish." I nodded to Elinor as if the others had not spoken. "Make what preparations you need. I will require your brother to escort you through the gateway of Dasiet Homol to the tower in the gamarand wood. Once there, he will open the way as Fiona described it, but only you and the child will proceed to the room at the top of the tower. Be warned that I will permit no deviations from my commands. In the tower room, you have but to request entrance to the fortress, and you will pass through. Is all clear?" Elinor nodded, and I continued. "This is for the child's safety. For his future. Fathers must do what is necessary for their sons, and sons must know their fathers and remember them."

"Linnie . . ." Blaise's plea was to no avail. Elinor kissed him and said he needed to see to horses and water while she gathered up Evan's things.

I walked away from the crowd to wait, deliberately ignoring them again. Their hostility was like a bitter wind, and I felt the furtive movements of hands to knives and swords. When the first boot moved in my direction, I whirled about and snarled, filling my wings and shooting fire from my fingers.

"Off with you," said a quiet command. "You've not skills enough to face him." When the crowd withdrew, I turned away again, watching the moon climb off the eastern flank of the valley. Soon only Aleksander stood behind me; I felt his eyes hot on my back. "Talk to me, Seyonne. Or must I call you some other name? Where is my friend . . . my brother . . . the man who saved my life and my soul and taught me how to use them? There are things I would tell him, news he would be glad to share."

I made myself stone . . . or as near to it as a shapeshifter dares go.

"I need to know if my friend intends to return, for I sorely need his help and his wisdom. But only his." Steps brought him closer. "I understand what happened at Parassa. Everyone understands—even Blaise. Holy Athos, Seyonne, I hold no blame to you that I don't hold to myself. More live because of you than died because of you. But it can't happen again. Please, let me know that you hear me."

But I did not turn, and I did not speak, and, after a while, he walked away.

Within half an hour, Blaise brought the horses. While others loaded bundles and waterskins on the saddles, Aleksander stood to the side. Soon Elinor came to me, carrying my wide-eyed son in her arms. "Is there nothing I can do to persuade you to wait awhile?" she said. "Until he is a little older and can understand what's happening?"

"Only if you can assure me that this war ends today." I paused for a moment, glaring at her. "I thought not." I made sure my voice could be heard by all. "You may inform any who are interested that since he cannot trust my judgment, I no longer serve your Aveddi, but only my own purposes. You are correct that I am not as I was. But I'll not abandon this world to chaos and confusion. I will continue to aid in this conflict as I promised, and I will expect all agreements and compacts with me to be similarly upheld. Humans are renowned for breaking faith. I still wear two scars that remind me of it every hour." I pointed to the two that remained.

I believed I felt a change in Aleksander . . . a caught breath . . . a stiffening back . . . a grave surety. But I was not looking at him, so I could not be certain. *Faith.*

I flew high, watching as Elinor and Blaise held a last hurried conference with Aleksander, made hasty farewells to the rest of the assembly, and set out riding through the moonlit desert, their forms blurring on occasion as Blaise worked his magic. Elinor leaned forward in the saddle as if riding into battle, the wind catching tendrils of her long hair and whipping them across her face. Evan rode in front of Blaise, the man's body a shield around the sleepy child. Near moonset the weary horses plodded up the hill to the Place of the Pillars, the twin ranks of white stone that stretched moon shadows across the grass. Blaise built a small fire. As her brother began the work to open the gateway, Elinor wrapped Evan in a blanket and held him in her lap, rocking him slowly. I sat atop a distant pillar and watched them, weaving an enchantment of drowsiness and casting it over the woman.

My choice was made for Evan's safety. For all of them, so I told myself, though the cold sweat that trickled down my spine spoke of doubt. For Evan to be secure, I must put him in danger, trusting Elinor to shield and comfort him through whatever was to come. But I had been wrong so many times, had misjudged so sorely, and my craving was so great that it could be clouding my judgment. These seeds I sowed could be the very kernels of destruction. The prophecies that had shaped my people's history had described a dreadful ending. A square of stone from a mosaic portrayed one possible future of my deeds as unrelieved blackness, and to touch that palm-sized square was to feel the despair of the world. But I clung to Gaspar's words. *You must walk the path you've chosen. For the light to triumph, there must be darkness.* An old man's rambling was my hope. Not my sword arm, not my senses, not my insights or intelligence or experience. Only a desert-born vision, a woman's courage, and a prince's strength and faithfulness.

Elinor's head began to droop. I inhaled the clean, sweet air of the human world, and as the woman settled beside her child to sleep, I turned away and embraced the darkness of my dreaming.

What must it feel like for the shore when the ocean's tide rolls out? Teeming life withdrawn. Ceaseless activity stilled. The land's edge washed clean, only flotsam and jetsam remaining to be withered by sun or picked at by birds. Ponderous weight removed, and the essence of sand and rock left exposed to bask in the day's warmth. Glorious simplicity. So I felt when I stood up from Nyel's game table no longer human.

I stretched out my arms and examined them. *Both hands present, forearms ridged with sinew, elbows, broad shoulders . . .* nothing to disturb the eye. Nor anything to restrict further examination, for I stood halfway between the fire and the garden window, unclothed save for my sword belt. Outdoors it was snowing. *Legs whole and well formed.* I did not glow golden in this realm. *Chest. Little hair . . .* I'd never had much. *The knotted white line just below the ribs on my right side speaks of unfaithfulness, mistrust, betrayal, ignorance. Belly. Loins. Yes, still male, too, all parts intact. Wings . . .* a thrill in my gut when I felt them tightly furled against my back. Was I to be winged forever? Everything accounted for. My hand touched the left side of my face . . . *brutality, cruelty, despair.* These scars were like drips of acid touching pleasured skin. I would be rid of them as soon as I knew how. And I knew . . . by all the world's wisdom, I knew so much already, now the tide of pain and ugliness had receded and left me Madonai.

Other eyes were examining me. Young old eyes alive with exultation. The old man stood beside the frosted window, his face reflecting the hearth fire. Not smiling yet, for there was still the final gifting to accomplish once he was sure of me. His hair seemed grayer and his lean face dry and soft, as though the robust flesh beneath his skin had already turned to dust.

I spread my arms wide and bent my knee. "My lord father, I am as you have made me. Teach me as you will. You know my hunger."

No longer could we maintain secrets of the heart. His joy and triumph were as exposed to my viewing as my own desires were bared to him. Yet I was in the more vulnerable state. I was an artwork newly created from a malformed original, and the artist yet maintained his control over my shaping. Indeed, as he walked across the patterned carpets of dark green and red, his midnight eyes locked to my own, I felt his breath blowing on the fire within me, nurturing the white-hot flame that was scouring my soul and memory, cleansing me of the impurities of my hybrid birth. I was starving for fuel that only he could give, the power that would transform this flame into a holocaust. I gave no consideration to what was being destroyed, only to the magnificence that would remain.

From behind me came a loud crack. Kasparian had snapped a stick as thick as my wrist and thrown it on the hearth fire. He snatched another stick from the basket and then drew his knife, and began to shave long slivers of wood from the dry stick with the ease of slicing cake. The splinters fell onto a pile on the clay-colored hearth tiles at his feet.

My father's eyes never left me nor did my own stray from his face for long, though the image of Kasparian's hungry knife now lay atop my mind like a thin coverlet, a distraction. My own dagger, sheathed in finely tooled leather, lay heavy against my bare flank. Ironic that Kasparian's interruption should remind me of it. The devoted Madonai would be appalled.

"So at last you have answered your own question," said my father. "When I first discovered you among the shadows in such bitter exile, I wanted to tell you then of your true identity. But you were so full of anger—rightly so—and you had so little memory of your heritage. Not enough to build on."

"And I refused to dream in Kir'Vagonoth," I said, gasping for air enough to speak beneath his smothering attention. "I hated taking on flesh, and so you had no way to speak to me."

"No matter. I was so proud of your strength and grace. And then you found the other, your human partner, your match in every way. How the powers of the universe have blessed us, my son, after so long an agony to send this good Warden to save us both. When I learned how you planned to join with him, I decided to do whatever I could to bring you here, giving you some hint of your rightful place in the world. You needed to understand that I bore you no ill will. Far from it. I wanted to give you everything." My father laid his hand on my cheek, leaving every nerve, every muscle, every fiber of my body awake and quivering as if a knife blade had traced their shape. "Still, I could not let myself believe you would forgive me, and so I laid these petty traps and snares. You've seen more clearly than I. And now I am humbled by your trust . . . to bring this child of your body to live here." He withdrew his hand, and I leaned forward trying to hold the connection. But he folded his arms across his green-shirted chest and did not seem to notice. "And so we come to the culmination. You are a vessel, prepared to receive a gift unlike any given since—"

"Please, Father." I could scarcely hear his words for my raging hunger. Without his power to complete my own, I was little more than a withered husk, incomplete, unviable, an aberration, born not of nature but of enchantment.

He laughed and opened his arms, spreading his cloak wide as if he had wings of his own, transformed in that instant to the young god who had sired me. "Open your heart, Valdis my son, and receive what you need of me."

The sight of his broad chest, exposed and vulnerable, led my hand to my knife hilt. Somewhere beyond the tumultuous madness of my desire lay the certainty that this was a moment that would never come again, a moment of safety, of necessity, of duty. But I could not kill him. The being named Kerouan had once been beautiful and holy, and even now he wished me only good. He was my father. I loved him and could consider no demand of duty that would do him harm. A fading voice within me affirmed this resolution, insisting that violating this conviction would be my own surest road to corruption and madness. *Faith*, said the voice. *It all comes down to faith*. And so I let the moment pass and fell into a blue-black sea. The Nameless God embraced me, and I was filled.

CHAPTER 42

"There's three persons come to the garden," said the conjured servant, a plain-faced woman who looked as though she might dissolve in the storm wind that raked the castle ramparts. "They say they're here at your command, Lord Valdis, though they do not address you by your proper name."

I stopped in mid-stretch. My shoulders were tight after three days of nasty winter weather, and though I had no intention of flying off into the howling wind and sleet, I had come to the open heights where I could extend my wings and flex them properly. I could shape the wings at will, and thus had no reason to retain them all the time, but I felt unsettled, cramped, incomplete when I went too many hours without. Wings were the outward expression of my power, the first enchantment that I could initiate on my own.

"Three?" That wasn't right. "I commanded that a woman and a boy pass through the tower portal."

"Indeed, my lord, they are a woman, a male child, and a man who claims to be their protector. Master Kasparian says that the man, like the child, carries a true being within him."

Blaise. The name came instantly. One of the rekkonarre. A good man, but disobedient. I had no use for him here; he did not think my child belonged with me. "Take the woman and the boy to the quarters I've had prepared. Make them comfortable with food and dry clothing, and bring them to my father's study an hour from now. The man may stay in the garden and freeze or return the way he came, as he chooses. He is forbidden to shapeshift here or to proceed beyond the garden. Have Kasparian see to it."

Kasparian knew my orders. He was to prevent interference by my human acquaintances, but he was not to harm them. Once I could command my own power in this world, I would rethink the prison and its barriers and its occupants. And that time would come very soon. Only three days since my father had transferred his power to me, and already I could feel it swollen like a snow-fed torrent in spring.

For the moment, the binding spells I had created so long in the past left me unable to initiate any Madonai enchantment, save my own body's shaping. I, too, was dependent on Kasparian. But, unlike my father, I could do very much as I pleased once the first spark was struck even by so dull an edge as my father's *attellé*. Only crossing the wall was impossible. Any enchantment that my father could teach me, I could shape and wield once Kasparian had given it life, and I had confidence that I would control the wall itself once my strength had grown enough. I had plenty of time. I *would* be released from this confinement.

As for my father . . . I wasn't sure what I was going to do about him. He was still mad. Humans and rekkonarre had rightly feared him all these years. I understood his power, his deeds, and his reasoning—and the flaw that had torn him apart. He had done his best to cure me of that weakness, not so that I could carry out his slaughter as I had so foolishly feared, but to enable me to make reasoned judgments without going mad. Free of human sympathies and confusions, I would be able to sort out problems that only a Madonai had the power to address. Time would tell how well he had done.

I finished my stretching, watching the ice crystals form on the leading edges of my wings, pleased to note that even the sensitive membranes were not bothered by the cold. Just as I started down the tower stairs to my apartments, a loud screeching broke out beyond the battlements. Retracing my steps and peering over the wall, I saw a large brown-and-white bird struggling to fly toward the fortress from the direction of the garden. Its valiant efforts were doomed to failure. Besides the constant buffeting of the wind, the bird was caught by a rope of light tossed from Kasparian's hand. The harder the bird fought, the tighter drew the noose about its neck.

"I told you that you are forbidden to approach the castle in any shape whatsoever," shouted Kasparian above the bluster of wind and the indignant squawks of the bird. With a few snaps of the rope, he had the bird back on the ground, where it quickly reshaped itself to a bedraggled man who knelt clutching his neck and gasping harshly.

I jumped up and onto the merlon. "Perhaps we need to illustrate the penalties for disobedience," I called down to Kasparian as my wings filled and my cloak flapped and billowed. "Stake him out in the garden until tomorrow midnight."

The man Blaise gawked stupidly as I stepped off the ramparts and spiraled downward on the storm wind to stand over him.

"I've no wish to harm you," I said to the kneeling man, touching Kasparian's hand and casting the spell that would prevent the captive rekkonarre from shapeshifting throughout the coming day. The man groaned a little as his bones felt the binding of my enchantment. "But I am not to be trifled with. You will tell your fellows when you return to your world."

Blaise tried to speak, but Kasparian jerked on the rope and left him choking. I caught the air and soared upward. The man seemed very small as Kasparian dragged him away.

I returned to the tower stair and my own business, shaking off the damp while unshaping my wings. Once in my apartments, I donned gray breeches, boots, and a loose shirt of black silk, and I tied back my hair with a silk ribbon. A short time later I joined my father in his study.

"So your boy is come," said my father, using one finger to move a piece on his game board. He had scarcely stirred from his chair by the fire since my change, claiming that the years weighed heavy on him now that his essence was so diminished. Not wishing to seem greedy or presumptuous, I had not pressed for a clearer estimate of his condition. An undeniable peace had soothed his edgy humor, though indeed the transfer of power seemed to have left him vulnerable to his declining body. But the threads he cast into the world and into my soul even now were no weakling wisps. Any who discounted my father from the game of power before he breathed his last would rue the miscalculation. "Does the child know you at all?" he asked.

"No more than I knew you when first I came here," I said. "But that will change. By the time he is grown, he will remember nothing but his true home and family, unusual as we are." I bowed slightly and smiled.

"You need to find some way to placate Kasparian," he said, chuckling. "He threatens to step on the mite without remorse if the boy gets in his way."

"I've already spoken with Kasparian. We've come to an understanding." In exchange for his tolerance, I had promised the Madonai that he could stay with my father no matter how I chose to control Nyel in the future.

From the hallway sounded footsteps and a quiet whispering. A servant held the door, and through the opening we could see the boy hanging back, clinging to the woman's dark blue skirt. She stooped down to speak to the child for a moment, and then straightened, took him by the hand, and led him into the study. Neither showed any sign of fear as they crossed the room. I nodded my approval to the woman. The child gaped about the spacious room with its shining lamps and ornaments, his dark eyes growing wide at the sight of the black and white game pieces that glittered in the lamplight.

"May I present my son Evan-diargh?" I said, bowing first to my father and then to my son. "A proper introduction will have to wait until I know him better myself." The child, paying no mind to either of us, pulled loose from the woman's hand and wandered forward, stopping halfway between the woman's position in the center of the room and the alluring game table. He eyed my father, judging, I supposed, whether to risk proximity to the stranger in order to gain access to the intriguing shapes so near the old man.

"Here, lad," said Nyel, taking one of the small rounded warriors from the game board and rolling it across the carpet to the boy's feet. The child snatched it from the floor, smiled shyly, and stepped a bit closer to the table.

"Evan," said the woman softly, and the boy quickly retreated to her side, poking one finger in his mouth while clutching the ivory warrior.

"And this is Mistress Elinor," I continued, "who has cared for my son since his birth."

"One of the rekkonarre," said my father. "But lacking her true being. Pity."

"And who and what are you who presumes to pity my birth, sir?" said the woman. She spoke quite boldly for one whose hands were clenched into bloodless knots at her side.

"In this place I am called Nyel for lack of anything better," said my father with a great sigh. "The names given to me in the human world, you know better than I. As for *what* I am, a tired old man is the most accurate description. One who has seen his fondest wish fulfilled and is deciding what lesser pleasures to enjoy for his waning days. You have clearly done good service in the nurture of this child, and so have no need to fear me or my son." Nyel laid his hand on my arm.

"Your son . . ." The woman glanced sharply from Nyel to me.

"The matter is too complicated to explain," I said, clasping my hands behind my back. "And is none of your business. Are your quarters adequate?"

"For a prison," she said, emboldened, no doubt, by my father's gentle air. The more fool she, if she underestimated him.

"You are not confined to your rooms," I said. "My son may roam where he pleases in the castle and grounds, excepting only the private apartments of my father and his companion, Kasparian. Kasparian also has a sparring arena just below this center part of the fortress. The arena is a dangerous place for a child. I have commanded Kasparian to keep it locked, but it is your responsibility to keep the boy away from it. You will accompany the child as is necessary to teach and care for him. You will find no dangers here beyond those of any house with stairs, towers, and windows—far fewer than where you were. Fewer than in any human dwelling of my experience."

She would not be cowed. "Yet you cannot deny that we are confined."

"*You* may leave Kir'Navarrin at any time, Mistress."

That silenced her impudence for the moment. She knew very well that she would leave alone.

The boy was tugging at the woman's skirts, whispering, "Mam. Mam. Can we go home now?"

The woman laid a hand on his head, quieting him. "I beg you excuse us, good sir, but I should put Evan to bed. We've traveled a long way. If you will accompany us, Seyonne, I'll show you how he likes to be put to bed. If you're to care for him in the future, you'd best learn."

My father chortled in delight and rocked back in his chair. "Indeed, my son, I believe you've brought a determined spirit into this house. And I thought the *child* would be the most interesting visitor we've seen in a millennium." He waved his hand at the three of us. "Go on. Go on. Indeed, lad, you should learn what she has to teach. When she sickens or dies or decides that her loyalties are to her own kind instead of this boy, we'll not wish the child's habits disrupted."

Irritated by the woman's presumption and my father's encouragement of it, I bowed curtly to my father and gestured the woman toward the door.

The woman murmured quietly to the child as we climbed the

curved stair, pointing out the bird-shaped carvings on the staircase, telling him not to scrape the game piece on the polished wood, and dragging him away from the fountain on the landing before he tumbled into it. Her words and actions were directed to the boy, but her eyes kept flicking to me until I was tempted to see if some unsightly growth had appeared on my forehead. When she hesitated at the convergence of four corridors, I indicated the way, and we soon arrived at my son's apartments.

The main room was large and would command a fine view of the gardens. Shelves lined one wall, filled with toy ships and balls, books and paper, and sticks of coal to draw with. Under the wide casements stood a clothes chest stocked with new shirts, breeches, undergarments, and boots of the proper size. A conjured servant was just laying out a supper of cold meat, apples, and toasted bread on a small, low table. While I stood in the doorway watching, Mistress Elinor sat on the rug beside the bedroom fire and helped the boy change into a well-worn nightshirt pulled from a traveling bundle. I considered leaving. I had no interest in bedroom rituals; servants could learn such things and carry them out when the nursemaid was dead or gone. Yet I stayed, listening and watching.

". . . But this is your new house . . ." said the woman, when the child popped up from her lap and tried with pokes and shoves to stand her up, demanding to go home. ". . . and it is a very nice house with many new things to see. Here, have some supper. You've not eaten in ever so long." She pulled the boy onto her lap, coaxing him to try a bite of cold fowl. He shook his head, but accepted a square of toast, watching the servant make up the small bed that stood against one wall.

The bed prepared, the plain-faced serving woman picked up several cloth-wrapped bundles that lay by the outer door and pointed to a smaller doorway off to one side. "I'll put your things in your room," she said to Elinor.

"Leave them, please. I'll be staying in here."

"Your room is next to this. Not so large, but sufficient." The servant was of Kasparian's creation and bidding, and so, of course, quite expressionless and unintelligent.

"As I said, I'll be sleeping in here with my son."

"But you've no bed here for sleeping, and I'll not be moving any furniture without I'm told by Master Kasparian."

The human woman shrugged and shifted her attention back to

the child, picking up the dropped toast. Clearly the argument was concluded, though the simpleminded servant who disappeared through the door with the traveling bags did not understand who had won.

I admired strength in a woman, though I knew better than to trust the one who possessed it. As I crossed the room to join the woman and boy by the fire, my hand rubbed the nagging reminder on my side. This woman must be taught to bend; she claimed my child as her own.

"Hello, Evan. May I join your supper?" I said, bowing to him slightly.

The child buried his face in the woman's breast. Of course any child was fearful of new circumstances and unfamiliar faces. I seated myself in an armchair a few steps away from the two, thinking that perhaps he would be less shy if I were not so tall. Taking an apple and a knife from the table, I cut off a thin wedge and offered it to the boy. "I'm pleased you've come to live with me, Evan. I've been waiting a very long time for us to be together." A very long time. I looked into the past to review the course of our separation and was appalled at what I could remember of it—a legacy of rampant ignorance and fear, injustice and cruelty. I recalled an image of this woman staring down at a crippled man who had been dreadfully mutilated and other humans hacked into bloody refuse, and her face as she blamed me for the carnage—

The boy snatched the piece of apple from my hand.

"Say thank you to"—the woman looked over at me—"what should he call you? He still thinks of Gordain as his da."

Gordain. A human man, not even rekkonarre. "You will speak no more of Gordain to my son. I would not have him mourn a human. In a Madonai house, the male parent is addressed as 'Fyothe.' The closest human word would be 'Papa.' "

The woman nodded, burying any retort, as well as the questions that came so clearly to her tongue. She would not even know the term Madonai. "Evan, say, 'Thank you, Papa.' "

The boy squirmed and murmured something like, then buried his face again while beginning to nibble at the bit of apple. I cut off another wedge. "I will not tolerate your teaching him to fear me." I made sure my tone was nothing that would frighten the boy.

"Seyonne"—the woman lowered her voice, glancing sidewise

at the doorway to the adjoining room—"we need to talk privately."

"With regard to . . . ?"

She examined my face carefully, perplexed and hesitant, all her bravado fallen away. "Give me a sign, Seyonne," she whispered, pleading in a most pitifully human way. "We thought—The Prince was sure— After what you said about promises and faith—"

The servant returned and began to bank the fire for the night. The woman glanced at the servant's back and spoke in a normal tone again, though her face had not lost the probing worry. "Your somber manner surprises me. Prince Aleksander says you are prone to telling bad jokes at awkward times such as these."

I could not understand her strange manner. "I find little humor in anything human, Mistress Elinor. My experiences in your world belie any inclination toward it." The servant left again. I jumped up from my chair, unable to sit still. The woman's comments unsettled me, as if a spark had shot from a too close fire and stung my forehead between my eyes. I hated the sensation. "And do not presume. As I've told you before, I am not the man this human prince knows; I have discarded that part of my existence. You are a servant, remaining here by my forbearance, and I would advise you to remember it. You should address me as Master Valdis."

A certain brightness deserted the woman's face, as when the last vestige of the sun's disk slips below the horizon, leaving the actual daylight little changed, but its quality irrevocably altered. She began to rock the boy slowly, laying her cheek on his dark head as his heavy eyelids sagged. "Valdis," she said. "The name of the Ezzarian god. I thought you disdained the role of god."

"Ezzarians have no concept of what or whom they speak."

"Then tell me, Master Valdis, why is it so important that Evan should be moved here now, and so quickly? We've tended him well, kept him from harm, loved him as is a child's right. The war has moved farther from our settlement, and so there is no immediate threat to his safety. You've had little time to spend with him in the past, and if you continue your participation in the Aveddi's war, that will likely not change. What do you think is going to happen in the human world that you no longer trust us to protect the boy?"

I tossed the knife and the remains of the apple onto the table.

"I wish my son safe. I don't remember exactly why I felt it necessary to move so quickly."

"You don't remember?" Her head popped upright. "Four days ago you threatened to kill two hundred people if I didn't get him here immediately!"

"But that was before."

"Before what?"

The woman was a morass of impertinent questions, but I knew that daily life would be easier if we remained on reasonable, if proper, terms. So I answered her. "Before my change. Before I became wholly Madonai." Explaining would have been easier, of course, if I had known the information she wanted. But, as with so many pieces of my discarded existence, the logic behind my actions was hazy. "I believed quite urgently that my son should be here with me, but I don't recall the entire chain of reasoning that led up to that belief. I was still human then. Human 'reasoning' is inextricably entangled with human emotions, and such convoluted paths are difficult to recapture now that my body that generated and supported those emotions has changed so radically."

"Your body has changed . . . not human . . ." Her bewildered expression was but another annoying question.

"I am now Madonai, as are my father and Kasparian, although they were born and I was gifted . . . transformed. The rekkonarre—you and the rest of your race—are the product of human and Madonai mating twelve hundred years ago, a grievous mistake that has corrupted the world. In me, my father has remedied that mistake. Do you see now?"

"I'm beginning to understand. And now you are . . . changed . . . in this way, you remember only facts from the past—events, decisions, names—not how you felt about them or why."

"Whatever else was involved in my decision, I will likely remember it later. Not that it matters. My son's proper place is with me, not in some human war camp at risk of slavery or mutilation, or cruel, wasteful, useless death—these damnable human plagues. He will be raised as Madonai, and when the time comes, I will give him the gift that my father has given me."

The woman pressed her lips together, stroked the child's hair, and shifted him onto her shoulder. Her gaze did not leave my face.

Now that her questions were mercifully silenced, I took my leave. "The child sleeps. I'll see him in the morning." I felt her eyes still fixed on me as I walked out of the door.

Disliking the murky confusions the woman raised, I returned to the ramparts, shaped my wings, and leaped into the air. Unfortunately, battling the storm wind and the annoying limits of the cursed wall did not silence the fool woman's question. Why had I brought the boy here so soon and so fast?

Indeed I had told her one part of the answer. My soul revolted at the thought that my son might someday wear scars like those on my face and my side. And the boy was rekkonarre, thus would need to spend time in both worlds. But not yet, so why was his presence so urgent?

A second part of the answer was surely that bringing Evan here would convince my father of my intent to complete my change. And so it had done. But a fortress prison housing a mad Madonai and his two companions was not a rational choice for raising a child. Until I could break the wall and decide what to do about my father, having the boy here held its own dangers.

Which meant there was a third part to the answer, and that one, to my head-bursting frustration, I could not remember. And so I twisted and dived in the wind over the mountain, letting the storm batter my body and monopolize my attention.

When morning came, cold and overcast, I bathed, dressed, and resisted the urge to make my way immediately to my son's chamber. He was still half human. He would be sleeping or breakfasting. I needed to go dream traveling, and so I met Kasparian in the library, the room I had chosen for my own study. But no sooner had the sullen Madonai sat down at the worktable and begun his enchantment, than I pushed his hand away and dismissed him. "We'll do this tomorrow," I said. "I need to reconsider my objectives in this war."

Before a quarter of an hour had passed, I was watching from a tower window as the woman and Evan walked out into the winter garden, bundled in cloaks and scarves. The child ran from pond to statue to frozen fountain, laughing and teasing, climbing and hiding and running. The woman was always there to pull him away from the frozen ponds, to brush the snow from his clothes before it could melt, to help him down when he had climbed too high, to laugh with him when he bumped a tree trunk and showered the two of them with snow. Soon they wandered deeper into the garden, where I could no longer see them. Before I could decide whether to go out and join them, I heard a terrified wailing.

I sped through the castle, shaping my wings and taking to the air the moment I was out of doors, following the sound to its source. The woman stood on a snow-covered knoll, clutching the sobbing Evan. Though I saw no blood, no hurt on the boy, no evidence of broken limbs, the woman's cheeks were also streaked with tears. Only when I touched earth beside them did I grasp what distressed them. Down a short incline the man Blaise lay on a flat section of the lawn, faceup, his limbs bound and stretched between four stakes. His garments were stiff with ice, his hair and brows frosted, and he was shivering violently. The rope of light still circled his neck, preventing him from speaking.

"He will not die," I said. "His punishment lasts only until midnight. He will be very cold, but perhaps he will remember to obey my commands." Snow drifted from the heavy clouds.

Pressing the sobbing child to her shoulder, the woman walked slowly down the slope until she stood only a few paces from the prisoner. "How can you do this? Blaise is your friend. He helped save you from despair. He has loved and cared for your child—"

"—and I have saved Blaise from madness and preserved his life countless times. But does that give him leave to violate my home? Does appreciation for past deeds oblige me to allow him opportunity to steal my child away?" Why was reason so alien to human thought?

"Seyonne is truly dead, then," she said, shifting her gaze from the shivering man to me. "This change that has transformed your body has also destroyed your heart."

"Indeed," I said, looking down at the man and feeling nothing. "I believe that was the point."

The weather worsened all through that day. I had Kasparian watch to ensure the man did not die or lose a limb to frostbite, and at midnight I went myself to set him free. What pain he suffered was likely the result of restored circulation and cramping muscles. But the discomfort was evidently considerable, as his eyes glistened with tears as he watched me unbind him. Unfortunate, but necessary. I gave him my hand, and he stumbled to standing.

"Tell your fellows," I said.

He nodded, pressed his bony hands to the black wall, and vanished.

Evidently the incident served warning enough to still the woman's combative nature. Her font of questions dried up, and her attempts at familiarity ceased. Only her unrelenting observation was left to irritate me. Unfortunately, the child was bothered enough by the memory of Blaise's punishment that he would neither leave his room, nor engage with anyone but Elinor. In order to confront this distancing before it festered into fear and to ensure the woman did not encourage it, I spent most of Evan's waking hours with the two of them, delaying yet again my return to the human war.

For a day after Blaise's release, the boy would pursue no activity, no matter that I had a set of gaming pieces made for him, and some magical toys: a small wooden horse that galloped about his chambers, and a palm-sized sailing ship that flew upon the air. I had the woman stay back while I gave him his food, but he would not eat. By evening I deserted their company, exasperated. But after a glass of wine and an hour's running, I regained my perspective. Gods' teeth, the boy was not yet three years old and had witnessed a close acquaintance in considerable discomfort. He was not afraid of me, only of the harm that had come to his friend. I climbed the stairs again, thinking to bid him good night. A quiet voice came from the room, and I paused in the doorway to watch and listen.

". . . He would carry his boy on his shoulders in the bright mornings, and they would walk through the green forests, and over the green hills, and into the fields." The woman was sitting on the edge of the small bed, and the child was curled up in his blankets listening. "And there the man would dig in the soil and teach the boy of plants and roots and growing things, of worms and mice and . . . what else?"

"Rabbits!" said the child.

"Rabbits, indeed. And as they worked the soil and planted seeds, the man would tell his boy stories of rabbits and their life in their burrows—"

"What tale is this you tell?" I blurted out, feeling a sudden pain like a knife's point behind my eyes.

The woman tucked the blanket around the child, not taking her eyes from the small, worried face. Her answer was spoken in the soothing rhythm of the storyteller. "It is the story of Evan's family, of his grandfather, I believe. But perhaps I am incorrect about that. I learned it from my brother, who learned it from . . . one who knew it well. It has been Evan's favorite since he was a babe, the only tale sure to quiet him when he's upset."

I could not stay. I was near blinded by the pain in my head, and it was all I could do to keep my voice steady. "Tomorrow. I'll come again tomorrow."

Once back in my own chambers, the pain receded quickly. After all, I was Madonai.

The morrow was little different. The woman watching. Evan skittish. Myself playing the fool to gain the favor of a child. Ludicrous. On the next day I returned to my studies in the library. My father taught me enchantments to control the movements of water. Much more satisfactory. I looked in on the boy in the evening, and he bowed quite properly when I entered his room. I returned his small courtesy, and then sat with him while he ate a reasonable portion of broth and bread. I sailed his wooden ships on the air, but he did not try to play with them. None of the three of us said much of anything. When the woman began preparing the boy for bed, I bade him a good night and left.

On the next day I went traveling in dreams and found the human war quiet. Forces were mustering in northern Azhakstan, near Capharna, the Empire's summer capital in the mountains. Capturing Capharna was a logical step for the Prince to take, but a massive one, requiring considerable preparation. Disappointing. I had been hoping for a fight.

For the remainder of that day and through the next, I could find no occupation to settle me. Was I already going mad from my confinement? The air felt brittle, the shivering world on the verge of crumbling. I could neither sleep nor concentrate on studies or enchantments or exercise. My father's concerned inquiries were constant irritation. "Is it not enough that you made me?" I snapped. "Must you think and feel for me, too?" I screamed at the woman to stop staring at me or I would strangle her, and then cursed myself for losing my temper at a nursemaid. What was I waiting for?

On the afternoon of the fifth day from Blaise's departure, I learned the answer. As I paced an inner courtyard, Kasparian brought the news that a human man was waiting in the garden, demanding to speak with me. As if the key had been fitted into its proper lock, all the jarring edges within me settled into place. The red fire of sunset shot through the lowering clouds like a crack in the sky as I took wing and settled upon the ramparts of my fortress. Of course he would come. The wheels of inevitability had turned, shifting us all into position.

"My lord," I said. "What can I do for you this evening?"

He looked up, the amber of his eyes visible even from my high perch, his red hair taking fire with the dying sunlight. "I've come to keep my promise, Seyonne. Shall I come up there to kill you, or do we finish it down here?"

CHAPTER 43

"Tell me who you are." He leaned against a barren ash tree in the snowy garden, appearing as easy as a shengar settled under a tar-bush in desert noonday. I was not deceived. His hand rested on his sword hilt.

"Can you not use your vaunted skill to judge me, Prince?" I had flown down from the tower, unshaping my wings once I stood on the steps that overlooked the garden. I did not wear a weapon as yet. My visitor hardly frightened me. His vest and breeches of thick, padded leather and the boots that reached to his thigh spoke of serious caution on his part; he hated such protective garb. I knew a great deal about this man.

He shook his head. "For this matter I cannot trust instinct. Nor even Blaise's word. Not when it is Seyonne's life in the balance."

I laughed and swept a broad bow. "I thank you for your caution, my lord. But I can put your mind at ease. I have Seyonne's knowledge, memory, and form, but his body is now Madonai, not human, and I am no longer subject to his emotional confusion. The part of him that served you"—I touched my left cheek—"that scrubbed your floors of vomit, wrote your letters, and guarded your back, is no more." I drew my cloak about my shoulders. Without the wings I felt the cold. "Tell me, what is Seyonne's crime that you, who purport to be his friend, would slay me? Has he mislaid your crown or failed to wipe your feet? Perhaps he has shed too little blood for you that you thirst for his." What kind of fool is so beguiled by strength and charm and leadership—truly Aleksander had those in abundance—that he translates them into the kind of bondage I had served? How stupid I had been to think this prince could bring reason and order to the human world. "Why are you here?" I said.

Kasparian appeared at my side, my sword belt laid across his arms.

The Prince did not move, but I felt the subtle shift in readiness ripple through him. "I made Seyonne a promise, and I never break faith with a friend. Do you not remember?"

From the time I had run to Zhagad to warn Aleksander of assassins, my thinking had been clouded. I owned all of "Seyonne's" memories, just as I remembered my thousand years in Kir'Vagonoth and the pitiful smatterings of my life before the split that sent me there, yet I could not remember half of my dealings with Aleksander for the murk of human sympathies that surrounded them. But enough was clear. "I recall a number of promises. A promise to disembowel me if I failed to deliver a message to your guard captain. A promise to slaughter every Ezzarian should I attempt to return to my home. And once, I think, you swore to cut off my hand if I did not drop my eyes from your face. I'll not drop my eyes, Prince."

He cocked his head. "So tell me—who was it came to my camp eight nights ago and stole away my counselor and her fostered child?"

"Ah! Is that my offense?" I took my sword belt from Kasparian and leaned toward him in mock severity. "Summon the woman immediately, Kasparian. We need her sharp eyes to bear witness to my good heart." The Madonai bowed and disappeared inside the fortress doors as I buckled on the wide belt of soft leather and strapped the scabbard to my thigh. "Ask her who I am," I said to Aleksander. "She can vouchsafe that I have maltreated neither her nor the boy, and then you can explain why you would kill me for claiming my own child. I recall you mentioning a number of times that I should leave you to your own fate and spend more time with him. Was there some promise involved with that?"

Though I quipped and cut at him, I searched my mind for reasons. Yes, on my visit to retrieve the boy, I had reminded the Prince of promises and faithfulness, but as a warning against this very kind of perfidy. Aleksander had called me his friend and brother, and now he was here to kill me. Humans knew nothing of faith.

"This vow is of longer standing," he said.

Kasparian soon reappeared on the fortress steps with the woman. The boy was not with them, a wise choice on Kasparian's part. I would commend him for it later.

At the woman's arrival, the Prince sloughed off all pretense of ease. He moved toward the steps, his eyes fixed on the woman's grave face. "How fare you, Mistress? And the boy?"

"Master Valdis and his father are all courtesy," she said, dipping her head to me. "Evan and I are well-provided for."

No further words were exchanged, but she shook her head slightly and, for one fleeting moment, the Prince's ruddy complexion lost color. "So be it," he said softly, and shifted his gaze to me. "If you plan to use your sorcery to prevent me, Master . . . Valdis . . . then do so now, for I do swear that I will take your life this day." Watching him and listening, one might almost believe he could do it.

"Your time and place are well chosen," I said. "At present, unless I carry Kasparian here in my scabbard, sorcery profits me little in this realm. But I do not fear to face you on mundane terms, Madonai to human. As you've brought no war steed, I will even forego my wings." Whatever the mystery of this determined blood lust—how did he think to benefit by slaying the one who had brought him to the brink of a new kingdom?—I relished the prospect of a fight. Too much concern with children and women threatened to sap my developing strength. "So where shall we test ourselves, my lord Prince? We can duel here in my garden and my fortress, but my knowledge of the terrain would give me unfair advantage. Kasparian can create us any venue we choose in his sparring arena—desert, forest, wilderness, familiar to us both or strange—much like the portal landscapes I've described for you. And you needn't fear that he will build me an advantage. I am the only being he despises more than human princes."

"I don't care where we fight. Only that I fulfill my bond."

I considered the problem. "Perhaps we should start where all this began . . ."

I drew Kasparian aside and described what I wanted, allowing him full access to my memory of the place. He departed, and I motioned to the Prince and the woman. "Come along then. By my child's head, you have nothing to fear until I draw my sword. And you, too, Mistress. I would have you witness that I fought him fair." As I led them into the heart of the fortress, they followed at a distance, talking quietly. I did not eavesdrop. Their concerns were none of mine.

To begin a duel cold is an awkward thing. In my Warden's days I had entered combat in a state of studied calm, but always imbued with the fire of righteousness and duty. Of late my arm had swung with vengeance and anger and other feelings that my mind could name, but no longer comprehend, remote sensations, like an unpleasant taste lingering in my mouth. Blood should be shed for reason, not passion. And yet, when I jumped lightly onto the square wooden platform in the barren courtyard of Kasparian's devising, reason was not enough to draw my hand to my blade.

Kasparian had done well, even conjuring the bitter wind that had broached the gray walls of Capharna's slave market courtyard on the day I had stood naked and chained on display for my new master. The ground was pitted and puddled with frozen slush, and the iron loops set into the walls for attaching slave chains still spoke of degradation.

I could see neither Mistress Elinor nor Kasparian. Somewhere in the fortress they would be watching . . . as would my father, too, I guessed. All his feelings about humans had coalesced in his hatred for this prince. He would not wish to miss my triumph.

The Prince's demeanor was admirable. He wasted no time and lost no focus at walking from a buried passage in Tyrrad Nor into the replica of a long-ago winter's day in his empire's summer capital. His face was as stark and barren as the walls, and his gaze was only for me. He drew his sword and dagger and attacked.

Reluctantly I drew my weapon. "You must explain this vow you service," I said, countering his first blow and shoving him away after a brief closure. "My father has freed me of human weakness, which means that even this despicable venue gives me no lust for personal vengeance."

Another brief, violent exchange. Every sinew of Aleksander's body was prepared. Every part and portion of his being was intent on his movements and mine, but he was not yet fully committed. His strokes were quick and light and precise. He was feeling me out. Was he not yet sure of his purpose?

In the center of the wooden platform was a post and crossbars to which the living merchandise at auction was bound for inspection. I danced backward, using the structure to separate myself from the Prince. "A matter of honor is it not, to tell a man why you plan to kill him? But then, what do human princes know of honor?"

Aleksander moved slowly to his left, leaving the post out of the way again. "I promised Seyonne that if ever he became the dread being of his visions—the monster he believed would destroy our world—I would slay him. I hoped the changes we saw in you were but for show, some tactic in a war we could not see. I prayed that you knew what you were doing, and that at any moment you would tell me a bad joke and show me how you had saved us all yet again. But then you took your son . . . brought him to this place you feared . . . into this danger . . . and I knew . . ." He circled slowly to his left, and his fingers shifted slightly on his sword grip. "The curse of Athos be upon this fortress and whatever power dwells here who has done this to my friend . . ." And with a savage cry he fell on me with a blow that could sever a thousand-year oak.

Madonai though I was, the bones of my right arm came near shattering at the meeting of our blades, and I dropped backward off the auction block to give myself a moment to recover. But I had scarce swiveled into position and yanked my dagger from its sheath to join my sword, when he leaped across the wooden platform and unleashed his steel on me again. One blow and then another and another, not a heart's pulse between them. Around the wooden block, up and over, from wall to wall we fought—or rather he attacked and I defended—until I was backed against the rusty iron gate. To my salvation, the gate swung open, and our battle moved into the cobbled slave market, surrounded by cheerless walls, low roofs, and guard towers that mimicked those of the Derzhi mountain city in all save living inhabitants. The afternoon was gray, the heavy clouds pregnant with winter. A dirty blanket of melting snow lay over the deserted stocks and pillories, and long icicles hung like frozen daggers on the ragged awnings and stone facades.

The Prince drew me into a high counter, then spun about and aimed to take vicious advantage of my vulnerability, but I retreated once again, saving myself from a blow that could have sliced through my rib cage. I stumbled backward through a blacksmith's shed, tripping over a pile of leg irons and chain. Reluctance and curiosity fell victim to necessity as I countered Aleksander's ferocious assault again and again.

Through the slave market gates and into the city streets we circled and scrambled, and only when we reached a wide bridge over a half-frozen river did I have an instant to consider strategy. The Prince's thickly padded vest was restricting his movements, a flaw that I had already exploited. A scratch on his neck was bleeding, and another on his forearm. And so he yielded the advantage of his relentless fury by pausing at the bridge gate to remove the vest. He should never have done it. When he came after me again, I was ready.

Aleksander was strong, and his skill, speed, and endurance were legendary among his warrior people. Our fighting skills were well matched; either one of us could prevail. But my Madonai body would not tire, nor would minor woundings deter me. Aleksander was young and fit, but he was human. And so I would let him continue to attack for as long as he could stand up, but I would lead him and tease him and bleed him, and when he was half dead from it, I would kill him.

I turned and ran across the bridge, taunting him, shouting to be heard over the ice-clogged torrent of the river. "Come, human, take me if you can!"

He gave chase, splashing through the ankle-deep slush of ice and filth in the narrow streets of the poor quarter. Every few hundred steps, I would halt and allow him to engage me, not too close, but yielding him five hits for every scratch I put on him. Then I would duck and dodge his next blow and run away, up and down the refuse-strewn alleyways. By the time I stopped again, my nicks and scrapes had faded, while the Prince looked as though he'd run through steel brambles. I laughed and let him come at me again.

At one stop, as we circled like two dogs eyeing the same piece of meat, he started talking. "Elinor says you answer to the name of your god Valdis. Is it so?"

I spun to meet his lunging step, left a dainty blood streak on his cheek, then stepped back. "I am everything that remains of Valdis and his memories, and I possess the power that has been waiting for him since his birth. If humans view Madonai power as the sign of a god, then that is their own limited vision."

Circling. "And this prisoner you've feared . . . this sorcerer . . . you call him father . . . the Nameless God . . ." He feinted left, then swept another powerful blow to my right.

My counter drove him backward. His back slammed into a tenement wall, loosing a small avalanche of ash-grayed snow upon his head. "My father was once the greatest of the Madonai," I said. "He has made me Madonai, too, gifted me with his power—"

"—and his hatred of humans. You told me of that." He brushed his face with his sleeve and spit the snow from his mouth, never lowering his guard.

"I do not hate humans. Neither do I care for them. I have been freed of such weaknesses so I can make reasoned judgments." I lunged forward and pressed him with a series of intricate moves that left him bleeding in ten places.

But he did not lose focus. He beat off my attack until we both stepped back. "Yet your care, your compassion . . . was always more effective than your sword. Don't you see that? Fiona could tell you. Blaise, too." He waved his sword to the scene around us. "Here in this very place you once stopped me from razing the poor quarter of Capharna. You were always watching me, and on that day I began to see things through your slave's eyes. I hated you for forcing me to see."

I glanced at the ramshackle warehouses and mean dwellings on every side of us. Indeed I recognized the place. A Derzhi heged had wanted to burn out the quarter and all its poor inhabitants to build a palace. Aleksander had refused them. On that same day in this street, the Prince had commanded a servant to give me a cloak and shoes against the freezing wind.

For one brief moment, I thought I had missed a move, and his dagger had caught me behind the eye. But I had no wounding. Why did my head keep hurting so these past few days? Was some spell carried by the woman and the Prince? *Nonsense. They have no power.* I tried to concentrate. "Do you think to distract me with sentiment, Prince? Remember, I have none."

Dismissing the piercing discomfort, I lunged, staved off his dagger with my right foot, and ripped my knifepoint across his chest. His quickly muted oath punctuated our conversation, and blood stained the ragged tear in his shirt. I smiled and danced away. He resumed his attack. I dodged a ferocious strike and took off running. We had been fighting for two hours, but I felt as fresh as if I had just stepped onto the field.

Through the streets and back across the great bridge I led him, up the causeway toward the palace where I had been his slave, and then back toward the city marketplace. Our clashing steel and grunting efforts were the only sounds in the ghost city save the river and the wind gusting weakly from the heavy clouds. I began to question his tactics. He would feint a blow at my legs, his favorite target when dueling, but strike at my neck and shoulders—

a reasonable ploy, but becoming predictable. He was tiring, perhaps not thinking clearly. I led him and teased another bloody hole in his sleeve. He looked like a juggler in his tattered garments, striped with red. Blood flowed freely from the shallow chest wound, a deep cut in one leg, and another gash in his left forearm.

A flurry of blows and another chase through the gloomy afternoon. The Prince drove me backward into Capharna's vast central marketplace, through abandoned stalls and into a potter's booth, knocking over tables stacked with bowls and cups and painted jars that shattered on the ice-slicked paving. I backed away into the center of the square, beckoning him as a drover calls his mule, only to be brought up short by some obstacle, a pedestal of stone. I tried to slip left around the shoulder-high block of marble, but a wood-vendor's wagon was in the way, piled high with sticks and logs and staves. Before I could go the other way around, Aleksander attacked again.

"Why do you bring me to this place of all of them?" he said, panting with his efforts. Yes, he was tiring at last. But still foolishly confident. He closed the gap between us, sweeping my sword aside, closing in and aiming his dagger at my heart. For one moment we grappled, a knot of straining muscle and damp skin and edged steel. Even tired and bleeding, he was as strong as a Makhara bear. "Oh, gods, where are you, Seyonne? I don't want this."

He was too close; his left hand was pressing my right arm up over my head, exposing my side. Feeling suddenly vulnerable, I gathered my strength and shoved him away. I was Madonai. No human could best me. As he stumbled backward, crashing into the wood wagon, I kicked his sword out of his hand. It skittered under the wagon. I dodged about the pedestal and backed away yet again, taunting him to charge me, daring him to turn his back on me and crawl under the wagon to pick up his sword. He held back for one moment, bent over, his fists on his knees, and breathing harshly. My shirt and hands were sticky with his blood. Soon I would take him. Soon.

I gave him a moment to recover. No need to run too far ahead now. No need to rush. While he caught his breath, I glanced up to the bronze statue that topped the pedestal—a dying Derzhi warrior, slumped beside the corpse of a mythical creature called a gyrbeast. In the counterpart of this very statue, back in true

Capharna, had my people hidden an enchantment that had led the two of us to their place of exile. At the feet of this dying warrior, Aleksander and I had begun a journey . . .

My eyes fell to his blood on my hands. Like the glowing iron that had seared the slave mark on my face, so came the white-hot pain behind my eyes once more. The wounds of my flesh were already closing, but this one . . . oh, gods of night . . . this one . . .

. . . a journey through a frozen forest . . . a steaming pool and a white-haired man with a staff . . . a lion shape streaking through the woodland, bloodied . . . torchlights flaming in the night . . . four slave rings broken, lying in the grass . . . a fortress of strength in the midst of desolation . . . the life-giving waters from a fountain of joy and light . . .

Like the gasping Prince, I could not breathe, could not speak. What weakness had been left beneath my skin? For that moment I felt powerless, and I staggered backward, trying to focus my vision through the glaring ferocity of pain. Powerless when I needed strength . . . *Powerless.* As if one ray of dying sunlight pierced the lowering clouds, as if the knife blade behind my eyes ripped open a pall of darkness to reveal one spark of life, so came a shattering truth. *Tell me who you are*, the Prince had said, and for that single moment, I knew the answer.

"I am my father"—the cry burst from me as the Prince snatched a thick branch from the wood wagon, heaved a ragged, sobbing breath, and charged—"and his father before him." My sword was high, ready to slash through the human warrior that rushed toward me, bearing death in his hand. But my weapon did not fall . . . not for the moment's breath that made it too late, when the wooden club smashed into the scar on my right side, and I could no longer move.

Nerveless cold radiated from the fiery explosion in my side until half of my body was numb. My arm fell limp; my sword clattered to the paving. My right leg folded underneath me, and, even had I the strength to do it, there was nothing to catch hold of. When my left elbow struck the ground, my knife went flying, and then my executioner was kneeling at my side. Through the haze of shock and pain and flying snow, I could see his dagger poised above me and the white blur of his face, anguished, as if he were preparing to cut off his own flesh . . .

"No!" The mountain's root beneath us shook with Nyel's wrath. If I could have sharpened my blurring eyesight, I would not have been surprised to see the earth crack and molten rock spew forth in that moment. But as it was, I saw only the nauseating result as the stones and structures of Capharna sagged, shifted, and reshaped themselves into the stone floor and columned vault of Kasparian's torchlit arena. Three forms took uncertain shape a few tens of paces away—Nyel, Kasparian, and the woman. Only Aleksander was held motionless, a solid center to the blurring universe, as unmoving as the bronze statue, though his eyes were living, and tears rolled down his blood-smeared cheeks. I lay crumpled in the dirt below his abruptly halted knife, fighting for breath, not sure my heart was still beating.

"No human will touch this misbegotten weakling, this sniveling creature I have called my son." Nyel's face appeared in the spinning maelstrom, his skin flushed, his mouth contorted, and his eyes . . . the gods save us all . . . his eyes wearing the hard glitter of madness. "What are you?" He was near spitting with disgust and loathing as he stood leaning on Kasparian's arm looking down at me. "You—a Madonai—have allowed a human to defeat you. Whether from intent or your own incapability, it is all the same . . . this shame . . . all my hopes . . . our history. I gave you everything. You were to bear the glory of the Madonai upon your shoulders, and now you lie here groveling before this human worm. You have ever been his slave, groveler, and only an old man's foolish desire saw you else."

The clouds had gathered again. The pall had sealed itself. I could not say what I had done or why, but I tried to assert control of my body, so that perhaps I could still determine my own fate. "Wait, Fyothe . . . Father . . ."

But one half of me was dead, the other lost to weakness for the moment. I could not yet move, and Nyel would not listen. "You are unworthy of my gifts. Vile, human-tainted flesh . . ."

I knew what was coming. Nyel had only one answer to raging disappointment, and it had ever been death. Fear had no power over me, and so it did not much matter which of them, human or Madonai, did the deed. Regrets without shape flitted through my head as Nyel's quivering hand snatched Aleksander's knife. I closed my eyes, reached for clarity, and awaited the cold steel . . .

But the harsh cry that echoed from the vaulted ceiling, that pierced the shadows behind the ranked columns to either side of us, that shook the foundations of the world, was not mine. I blinked open my eyes to discover a stone-faced Kasparian lowering Nyel gently to the earth.

"What have you done, *attellé*?" whispered Nyel.

"You were going to kill your son in anger, Master. The deed would have destroyed you."

Necessity overcoming incapacity, I struggled to my knees and saw the knife hilt protruding from Nyel's chest, and Kasparian rising to his feet.

"Kill Valdis? Never . . . never could I do such a thing." Nyel's voice was weak, but did not quaver. "How could you think it? I gave everything to spare him—my freedom, my life, all the others—every Madonai dead. I have made him a god."

Never before that hour had I seen such clear evidence of Nyel's madness or the subtlety of it . . . how he could shift from virulent loathing to reasoned hurt with no deception, no contrivance of manner. Far, far more dangerous than a monster is the honest madman. And I had once thought to set him free.

His hand reached out weakly. "Valdis? Where are you, lad? Remove this traitor's knife. It pains me."

"I'm here," I said, dragging the weight of my half-dead body to his side. I knelt over him and considered the weapon. The knife had been carefully positioned. Once the blade was removed, even Madonai healing would not be fast enough to stanch the flow of blood. The Nameless God would die.

I laid my hand on the dagger hilt and looked into his old young eyes, no longer wild and dangerous, but bleak. Resigned. He knew the consequences of his death. He had no name. No one in any world would remember him beyond this day.

"I wanted to teach you more, my son. So much for you to learn." He laid his hand on my arm, searching my face. "I have loved you beyond all others in the world. You will remember me?"

But what he asked, I could not give. Even those who had lived with him and talked with him would forget. I would forget. "As I am, I can neither love you nor grieve for you," I said. "You have cured me of it. I will leave you behind as I have forgotten my human loves and griefs." My head was clear again. I was as Nyel had made me.

Nyel's hand gripped my bloodstained shirt. "But you will be strong, free. You can do as you wish. Force Kasparian the traitor to help you remember; surely he'll not forget me. He is Madonai, my *attellé*. Command him."

Kasparian was standing behind me like one of the stone columns. At this he walked away. He kicked Aleksander's knife, fallen from Nyel's hand, all the way to the wall, and, with a ferocious snap of sorcery, he freed the Prince of his paralyzing enchantment. Aleksander sat back on his heels, coughing and shaking his head. The woman hurried to his side, knelt beside him, and began to bind his injured arm with her cloth belt. His blood still smeared my hands.

I watched the two of them and felt nothing. No pain behind my eyes. No gaping wound. No comprehension of the determination that racked the Prince's face or the hand the woman laid softly upon his shoulder. Only reason served me anymore. Only reason. Forever. I turned back to the dying Madonai. "Perhaps I can offer something that will serve us both. I have a bargaining chip you cannot imagine." I bent down to his ear and spoke my terms.

"No!" His weak protest was almost unhearable. Dark blood welled from around the knife. We did not have long. "I will not."

I had no passion with which to beg. Only reason. "As you have loved me, Madonai, love me now," I said. "Each of us will get what he desires. I will be as I am meant to be. You will not be forgotten."

"My good and glorious Valdis, do not ask me . . ." But I did not relent, even to this pleading, and at last, as the death rattle robbed him of speech, he gave in.

"Kasparian," I said. "If you please. One last service for your master."

It seemed, at first, as if the old sorcerer might refuse. But he was incapable of denying Nyel for long. So he knelt on the dirt beside us, and when I told him what was required, he showed the first sign of astonishment I had ever seen from him. "When it is done, you will set the Prince free," I said. "He may take the woman and the child and go about his business."

Kasparian nodded, laid one wide hand on Nyel's head and one on mine, and then struck the spark of Madonai enchantment as only he could do within the precinct of Tyrrad Nor.

When the deed was done, I imagine that he leaned toward the dying Madonai and spoke softly, saying, "My good master Kerouan, rest well and know you will be remembered and honored until the end of my days." But I could not claim truthfully that I heard him say it, for I was screaming with such pain as I had never known, as my power was stripped away, my mind turned inside out, and my body forced to remember what it was like to be human.

CHAPTER 44

I longed for the flame. It was so tiny, a wisp of gold flecked with blue, so distant from the dark and lonely place where I existed, but I had such hope that it might warm me. Sometimes it grew larger, and I would hear hissing, sputtering whispers that tickled and teased at my hearing, but refused to shape themselves into words. *Patience. Patience. Listen long enough and you will hear . . . if they are truly words and not just the echoes of dying dreams.* A fearsome thing, that flame. What might its light expose? Perhaps darkness, cold, and silence were better. Sometimes it winked like a cat's eye. And though I dreaded the revelations of its light, each time it flicked out, I cried out in despair that it might never shine again.

My cries made no sound, of course. My voice had been used up long ago, screaming. For a very long while, I had known nothing but chaos. Profound darkness. Rootless terror. Agony without form or focus. But at some time I had crawled onto this desolate shore, and here I sat, shivering, hoping, afraid, bereft of sense and memory, watching the distant light. *Patience.*

"If we could just take him home, where there's sun, and life, and food with substance that is not enchantment. I can get so little down him; he's wasting away."

"We daren't take him out of here, Linnie. He could die from it . . . or worse. Stars of night, it's only your word that prevents the Aveddi killing him. If we only knew what really happened, what he was, what he is. Will this Kasparian tell you nothing?"

"I think he grieves. He sits by that game board day and night, never sleeping. At least he sustains us. I believe that if he chose, the servants, the food, everything would disappear . . ."

I could not open my eyes for the brightness. And though the whispers had at last taken form, their shapes were drawn with such pain, I could not bear listening. Nor could I decipher the meanings as yet, only that I did not want to know. I turned and fled back to the darkness.

"Why won't he wake up, Mam? My ship won't fly anymore. He'll make it fly."

"I don't know, child. Perhaps he needs to sleep for a while yet. He's very ill."

"He said he would teach me to make it fly when I was bigger. Will you teach me?"

"I wish I could, but I need more teaching myself. Here, come sit with me beside him. No, it's all right. He would never hurt you. He loves you very much, more than you will ever know, I think . . ."

". . . swear he's better. Closer. His left hand moved yesterday when Evan started climbing on the bed."

"Linnie, you've got to go back. Your cough is worse, and I see no change in him at all. I'll stay. Or Gorrid—he's offered to take your place."

"We've discussed this before. I won't leave without Evan, and I'm not taking Seyonne's son away from him."

I stood at the brink of the light again, undecided, shivering. I could come now, of my own will, to the place where the veil of fire filled my vision and the darkness was behind me. *Patience. The heat is still too intense*. But as I turned to leave, something small and soft reached through the veil of fire and touched my cheek, smearing a spot of dampness.

"Don't cry" came the whisper. "Mam will take care of you. Go back to sleep."

I went, but not quite so far as I had thought to.

"My lord, you must persuade her to go back. I don't know where in the name of the stars she came by this infernal stubbornness."

"Perhaps it runs in the family. You've got your own measure of it. You say she's well?"

"Kasparian's concoction has helped her a great deal, but I don't trust it . . . or him; he still refuses to speak with us. And she won't leave without Seyonne."

I had learned to recognize the difference in the voices, to think of them as different minds expressing themselves. A very basic concept, but the best I could do.

"Athos' balls, he's naught but bones." The newcomer stood very close, smelling of sweat and horse and leather. It surprised me that I could picture horses and leather and know what they were used for. I could almost visualize the speaker himself. His every word was packed with images, as if he were an entire world all unto himself. "You've seen no sign of change?"

"I'm no good at looking. I see what I hope to see—a twitch of an eye, something I think is a smile, especially when the boy is close. Linnie's worse than me about it. That's why I dragged you here. You're the one to say if we dare take him out." This speaker came often. Kind. Worried always. He loved.

I was waiting for the other voices, the two that were with me all the time. The ones who spoke to me, sometimes with words, sometimes with touch, strong and sure or soft and teasing, prodding me to move, beckoning me to venture farther into the flame.

"Aveddi! It's been too long."

There. Better. Just the sound of her made me warmer. And he would be nearby—the small one who told me stories, who whispered secrets that made even less sense than the other talk, who bounced and jostled until the woman told him to settle or she would send him away, but in a tone that told me and him that she would never send him away. The small hand slipped into mine. "It's Uncle Blaise has come," he said, tickling my ear, he was so close. "And he's brought the 'veddi Zander. Do you want some milk? Mam said not until she's talked to Uncle Blaise and Zander. It's very important."

Milk was good. Cheese would be better. But I was happy to listen, too. Perhaps this time something would make sense.

"Mistress! I'm glad to see you well," said the horseman. "Every day for two months I've wanted to come, but Capharna would not lie down for us."

"But now you've won it, all gods be praised, and Blaise tells me that your cousin has taken Vayapol. I want to hear everything, and I would guess Seyonne does, too."

"Seyonne! Has he—?"

"He's not spoken, no. And he's not yet opened his eyes." I felt her move close. A scent of winter air and wood smoke. A cool hand on my brow for one brief moment. Sweet breath feathering my skin as she spoke. "But I watch him as we talk, and I believe there's sense in him. And if he's here with us, then he cares about what you have to tell."

The one who smelled of horse and leather came closer, too. A massive presence. "And you truly believe he is Seyonne and not the other?"

"My lord, did you not feel him with you on that day?"

"I hoped for it until the end—of course I did—but what I felt was his sword. I've got the scars to prove it. There was no mistaking his intent, Mistress. It was no friend I fought."

"Certainly you're right. The change I saw was only for a moment. But for that moment, it was so clear. If you'd not been half dead yourself, you would have noticed." Secrets were bursting from this woman. I clung to her voice, believing she held the key to my future. "He let you take him, Aveddi. I'm sure of it."

The child began tugging at my hair. Damn! A painful, scraping yank indicated an inexpertly wielded comb.

"Sorry," he whispered, and began again. No one seemed to be paying him any mind.

"He gave himself the name of the Ezzarian god," said the horseman. "But Blaise saw him—I saw him—as the very image Seyonne described to me from his dream, the sorcerer who despised humans and would see us all in torment—the one he feared."

"And he was that sorcerer. No mistaking it. But he was Seyonne, too, no matter what he claimed or believed. Remember what he said just before you struck him down. Think of the words. The exact words."

" 'I am my father, and my father before him . . .' " The horseman's voice trailed away. I wanted to retreat into the darkness, to run from the wounding, but the child had taken my hand again, and I had not the strength to pull away.

The woman broke the silence. "He was staggering as he said it, and holding his head. I had seen him do that once before, on the night he heard me telling Evan his father's stories. And then, what did he do? He raised his sword against you, and every law of combat, every evidence of that day—your condition, his strength, his skill—tells me that you should be dead, Aveddi. Only you're not. Which father was he was invoking in that moment?"

"I need to think on it, Mistress. I swore to him—"

The child bounced and jerked away. "Mam. Mam, we're hungry. We want cheese and milk."

The talk changed after that, first to food and drink, and then to tales of war. The horseman—the Aveddi—was preparing for a dangerous battle, and I found myself drawn into the complexities of the plan he laid out. The names of places and people appeared as small gray voids as his voice led me through the map of his tale, but as the time passed I saw them take shape in the landscape unfolding in my mind: Kiril, Gorrid, Bek, Naddasine, Mardek, Capharna, Vayapol, Karn'Hegeth, Parnifour . . . Zhagad. Aleksander.

". . . But even if I can take Edik alive and put him on trial, as Blaise suggests, who can I get to sit as judge? Who has the strength, the power, and the neutrality to make it honest? I won't see this new world birthed in vengeance, but everyone is caught up in the war . . ."

The new world. Someone was needed to mete out justice to end the old order so the new could take its place. Such a one would need to be fearless, stubborn, above reproach, uninterested in the spoils of power and able to convince the weary thousands of it. I knew someone like that, if I could but remember the name . . .

The talk went on around me, the easy talk of friends in hard times, the subdued laughter that makes no attempt to mask the sorrow and worry that exist alongside it, but only to balance and soothe and witness to ongoing life. The woman spooned milk into my mouth and shooed the child away, lest he bounce it all out again. But my mind was off racing, hunting for the name and considering the consequences. Yes, that was it—the answer he needed. I was bathed in fire.

Come on out. I imagined the boy just behind me, shoving me forward. *It won't hurt. I promise. Mam will take care of you.*

"Evan, what are you dreaming, child? Eat your supper." The talk went on. The clatter of dishes, a soft laugh.

The small hand nudged me again. *Come on, Papa.*

"Fiona."

The room fell silent, and I had to force my eyes open to make sure anyone was still there to hear. The effort to speak was so great that I saw no use in wasting it. But they were there, the four of them sitting at a round table lit by candles. I was propped up in a chair by the hearth, a red blanket laid over my lap.

"What was that?" The three adults spoke as one. "Did you say something Blaise . . . Linnie . . . Aveddi?" The child was intent on carving a block of cheese into giblets with his small knife.

"You need Fiona. To judge." My voice was little more than a whisper, but it might have been a lightning bolt, for it loosed such a storm of words and questions and solicitations that no hurricane could rival it.

Aleksander reached me first, leaping over a chair and then kneeling on the floor in front of me, the better to examine my face. "Seyonne?" he said. His gaze was raw. Bleeding.

"My father . . . is Gareth . . . of the line of Ezraelle," I said, reaching deep for the right words, able to push them out only slowly with long gaps in between. "And if you don't stop mooning about, my lord, these people will start to think you have a heart." A very bad joke.

One might have thought the sun had taken up residence in that cold room.

I was infernally weak. And no wonder to it. Nyel's changes to my body and mind had taken almost four months of enchantment to accomplish, and all had been undone in a single instant. So devastating was this reversal that for more than eight weeks I had lain in unmoving stupor, losing almost a quarter of my weight. Aleksander's blow to my side had taken its toll as well. My right arm remained almost useless, only a slight prickling in my fingertips hinting that the limb was alive. I had to hold it close to my belly with my left hand to prevent it dangling at my side or flopping on the bedclothes like a dead fish. It would take some getting used to. As for my mind, both knowledge and memory seemed intact, though distant, which left my speech slow and hesitant, and my thinking easily confused.

From that first night of my awakening, Elinor seemed to understand what I needed, shushing Blaise and Aleksander every time they began to question me and insisting that they allow me some breathing time. "Come back in seven days," she said. "I'll have him ready to go home."

After much argument to which I was not privy, the two men returned to their war and Elinor went about her own business. In the next days she spoke to me only of mundane things: Was I comfortable, was I hungry, did I wish her to continue exercising my arm as she had done when I was insensible? She had seen such weakness mended, but only if the limb was not allowed to wither. Now that I was awake, she said, I could move everything else myself.

Somewhere I found the words to say that I would appreciate her help very much. "I've not been truly asleep," I said, unable to look beyond her scuffed boots. "I know all you've done for me—"

She would not let me continue. Rather she straightened my blankets and went off to call the servants to bring supper, dismissing my verbal fumbling. "Time enough for such talk later." And so, other than feeding me, exercising my arm several times a day, and providing me the means to wash and relieve myself, she left me very much alone with my thoughts. I needed that, but I looked forward to the hour of our exercise. I had grown accustomed to her touch.

Evan, whether warned by Elinor or following his own intuition, played quietly with his ships on the floor at my feet, making noises of ocean, birds, and sailing men. I never tired of watching him.

I spent a great deal of time in a chair by the window, looking out on the snow-covered garden and the ring of black surrounding it, not thinking so much as gathering thoughts for future consideration, letting the events of the past months and years ebb and flow around me. Outside of this room, this small island of vibrant life that Elinor and Evan made for me, the fortress was silent and empty. I could grieve for Kerouan now, and for the universe, which had lost such beauty and grace and power as he had once been. On one winter afternoon, a great slab of the wall gave way and collapsed into the snow. So the Twelve, too, knew their long vigil was ended. I wept on that day. Though unable to articulate the sorrows that welled from me, I would not suppress or discount them. They were mine as surely as was my grief for Ysanne and Farrol and all the others.

By the day Aleksander and Blaise returned, I could stand up without immediately toppling over and even take a few shuffling steps when supported. "You're not going to carry me," I said, fumbling with the fastening on my cloak, wishing they would look away and not see how awkward I was left-handed. "I will walk out of this place on my own feet."

"And if we should find you in a heap on the path, will we be allowed to scrape you up?" said Aleksander, slipping his shoulder under my dead arm just as my weak right leg wobbled, threatening to give way.

Blaise hefted one of Elinor's green cloth bags and scooped up Evan, who had managed to escape Elinor's hand and climb onto a table. Elinor took the other bag and led us out of the room and down the stairs, past the two expressionless servants who had brought us food, drink, and whatever was needed for more than two months. When I looked back over my shoulder, the man and woman were fading out like morning haze.

Aleksander was all for heading straight out the front door, but I shook my head. "He saved my life and has seen to our care. I can't leave without a word."

The Prince waited at the door while I stepped into the sitting room, supporting myself with a table edge. As Elinor had said, Kasparian sat at the game table by the hearth fire, his elbows propped on the table beside the gleaming black and white game pieces, his head resting on his hands. His long brown hair, threaded with gray, hid his face, while the carved figures supporting the mantel gazed down at the room in solemn unconcern.

"I'll not thank you for my life," I said, concentrating to find the words I wanted and get them out in a reasonable time span. "I don't deceive myself that you did any of this for me."

He did not acknowledge my presence. I didn't expect it.

"I do thank you for sustaining my child and his mother. That was driven by your own goodness of heart, not by your love of Kerouan. Even so, I know you would rather not hear anything from my lips." No disagreement from the still figure. "But I wanted to ask you one more boon. Someday, when I can get about again, and I've had time to think about what's happened, I'd like to come back here and speak with you. I was foolish and destroyed the memories of this life—Valdis's life—my life. I want to remember. As I promised my father. May I come?"

After a long stillness, he spoke, still not looking at me. "You've naught left, do you? Not a scrap."

Glancing behind me to see no one listening, I answered. "No."

"You'll go mad with what you've done."

"Perhaps. But at least I won't be dangerous. May I come?"

"I'll be here."

I turned my back on the last of the Madonai and hobbled to

the front door, where Aleksander waited in a beam of winter sunlight. "Are you all right, Seyonne?" he said.

Blaise, Evan, and Elinor were already halfway to the wall. I nodded toward the black barrier. "As soon as I'm past that, I'll be fine."

They took me to one of Blaise's hidden settlements in the thick forests of the Kuvai hills, an encampment of some fifty war refugees, none of whom knew me. I shared a ramshackle cottage with a deaf-mute named Kesa, and I learned how to speak with gestures. As I could use only one hand, it was good he was not talkative. I felt as though a castle tower had fallen on me, scattering the bits and pieces of mind and body across the world's landscape. Every human engagement was a journey to find the proper pieces and fit them together again.

Fiona came to visit me in Kuvai as soon as she got word of my return. She wore the gold Queen's Circlet that I had last seen on Ysanne's brow, though she snatched it off as soon as the cottage door closed behind her, leaving the two of us alone.

"Put it back," I said. "It fits you well."

"Gaudy thing," she said, twirling it in her fingers. "You don't mind?"

I did not speak, but only shook my head, not wishing my voice to betray some lingering sentiment that might put the lie to my true belief. Fiona would be a worthy queen.

Sitting beside me on my bed, she told me how they had recovered Drych and Hueil and poor lifeless Olwydd from Kir'-Vagonoth, of her acceptance of Aleksander's offer to sit in judgment of Edik and the Derzhi, and of her belief that it was time for Ezzarians to reveal ourselves and the history of our demon war to the world—a monumental step and irreversible. "I think you've infected me with your disease," she said. "Here I am, risking everything I know, just because I think it right. A number of our countrymen and women think I'm mad to do it."

I kissed her hand and told her that Ezzaria was blessed to have her. Our old charge was not done—the mad Gastai still took souls—but Drych and Hueil had come back with ideas of joining forces with Vallyne to control the demons in Kir'Vagonoth, making our demon battles a thing of the past. Ezzaria would need to change.

Fiona did not stay long on that visit. I still tired easily and was not yet ready or able to explain all that had happened to me. But before she left, I asked her to examine me, to look deep with a sorcerer's seeing so that all might know—and so that I might be reassured—that naught was hidden. Though hating to intrude on me in that way, she did not hesitate. She knew her duty. When she was done, she embraced me fiercely. "Welcome back, my friend," she said. "Your demon is still a part of you and will ever be, but your soul is entirely your own." For the first night in more than two years, I slept easy.

Elinor took up residence in a nearby cottage, and Evan spent most of every day running back and forth between us, hiding, climbing, teasing, an everlasting exasperation and delight. As I grew stronger, Elinor and I spent a large part of every day together, making shoes and clothes for him and nursing him through scrapes and scratches. Our relationship was awkward. I tried to let Elinor know that she need not feel obliged to spend further time in my company. If she was worried about leaving me alone with Evan, I would accept whomever she might select to be with us. She dismissed my offer, saying that she preferred to see to things herself. And then she added that, as long as we were spending time together, she might as well continue to exercise my arm. Over the winter months, the prickling in my fingers spread to the whole limb, and I began to hope that I might regain its use.

In truth I had no greater pleasure than watching Evan and Elinor together. Indeed, I took equal pleasure watching the mother as the child. Elinor's countenance was a subtle canvas, a background of intelligence, illuminated by patience and compassion, touched lightly by her moods and humors. The left corner of her mouth twisted upward at a childish folly. Her brow dipped and her eye widened slightly when listening to a small boy's tale of wonder. Her red-gold coloring deepened just a bit when she chased him laughing through the Kuvai woodland.

At first I held back, content to watch them, scarcely even speaking, save in answer to a direct question. My speech was halting and awkward, and I would often come across dead spots in my memory, causing me to stop in mid-sentence while I groped for a word or idea. Elinor noticed this, of course, and after a few weeks, she quietly insisted on a new exercise. "I think you should hold an hour's conversation with me every day. How will you ever be able to teach Evan the things he needs to learn from you, if you can't get out five words in an hour?"

We met every afternoon while Evan slept. She would work my arm, and we would talk of ordinary things. Of food and weather. Of people in the village. Of the war. Of Evan's needs and behavior. Occasionally of our own childhoods. Safe ground. By midwinter I was so much improved, she had me teaching Evan the lore of trees and forest, saying that he should learn from me those things that were of such importance to Ezzarians. Even then we did not give up our hour. Though I wondered where words might take us if our conversations were ever to wander farther afield, I held to the familiar and mundane, refusing to risk her discomfort or displeasure. The imagining was pleasant, though. Very pleasant.

Beyond this, I ate and slept and walked when I was strong enough, and ran when I was stronger yet. As soon as I could manage, I helped the villagers haul wood and water and clean the meager kill their hunters brought in, and I listened to their music and their god stories as they sat by the fire on the long winter nights. I shared their hunger for news of the Aveddi and rejoiced with them at the tales of his safety, his valor, and the victories he won. The vicious heart had gone out of Edik and his henchmen, so the fireside gossip said, the turning point having come soon after the victory at Parassa. The despicable Emperor was holed up in Zhagad. It was only a matter of time until the war was won. Even the gods saw victory at hand, so an old woman told me, for they no longer felt it necessary to send their winged spirit to aid the Aveddi Aleksander.

Aleksander came to me as often as he could throughout that winter and spring. Blaise would bring him whenever events allowed the time. While Blaise visited with Elinor and Evan and his other friends in the settlement, Aleksander would lean back on the rough walls of my house, drink wine, and ask advice or talk about his plans and strategies, his commanders and troops. Once or twice, he fell asleep. On one spring midnight, as he applied ground yellowroot to his feet that were tormented by bootrot, he spoke of his uncertainty as to his place in the world once the war was won. With the lands of the Empire returned to their rightful owners, he believed his day as a ruler was over and that his best hope to escape vengeance would be to seek the protection of one of the old kings. "I've thought to offer service to Yulai," he said. "D'Skaya has said she would have my arm in Thrid, but the jungles would grow mold on me, I think. Look what a wet spring in the northern marches has done to my feet! Manganar has deserts and will likely occupy a good share of Azhakstan after the war. And Manganar warriors ride horses, while the Thrid fight afoot. My legs don't like marching."

"Your destiny still awaits," I said, smiling as I passed him another packet of the powdered roots. "You'll find your way. I have faith in you. More than ever."

He knew exactly what I meant by this, and as ever when he thought of our duel, he grew somber and tried to ask forgiveness. I did my best to reassure him. He had kept faith as I had counted on him to do. In the end he had not needed to kill me as I had intended, but if things had fallen out differently, the world would have been glad of his service.

As to any further explanations, he knew better than to press. Always he would ask how my healing progressed, and I would say, "Improving." He would look at me and judge, and then make some pointed comment: "You need to drink more nazrheel," or "A woman in your bed would be the best exercise for your arm," or "I'll expect a footrace to that oak and back on my next visit, and this time I'll trounce your sorry bones." We would laugh, and he would go, promising to come again when the war permitted. The light still shone in him, brighter than ever.

CHAPTER 45

On the day of the spring equinox, the Aveddi of Azhakstan, the firstborn of the desert, rode down the Emperor's Road toward Zhagad. A white cloak billowed from his shoulders, and his red braid was wound with wooden beads. He wore no adornment that might signify rank, and indeed, he claimed no rank, not even on this, the day of his triumph. On his flanks rode Yulai and Magda, the King and Queen of the Manganar, and their son Terlach; Marouf, the Palatine of Suzai, and his five sons; and W'Osti, the Thrid chieftain and his war leader D'Skaya. On the Aveddi's immediate left rode his cousin Kiril zha Ramiell, leading the first lords of more than fifty Derzhi families, along with the Yvor Lukash, his face painted black with white daggers, and a tall woman, her face painted likewise. On the Aveddi's right rode his wife, Lydia, carrying their infant son on her back as the women of the desert have done since ancient days. The child was yet unnamed, for his father was at war, and Derzhi custom forbade naming a child in wartime, lest the child be marked with death.

And, yes, just behind the Aveddi rode a man in a gray cloak, a slender man that few could name, his black hair showing signs of gray. Though he wore no weapon and seemed quite ordinary, many of the Aveddi's company watched him warily. I had asked to observe the day's events from the gate tower, pleading lingering illness, but Aleksander would not hear of it, saying that any man who was running three leagues through the Kuvai hills every morning could not claim weakness. He wanted me with him.

Behind this noble vanguard rode five thousand men and women from every corner of the land. Uncounted thousands more stood along the roadside, hung over the city walls or out of windows, or lined the streets within the royal city. No musicians or jugglers or dancers were performing. No hawkers or vendors plied their trades with paltry tokens of celebration. This day was solemn . . . a day of judgment and witness.

Awaiting the Aveddi on a hurriedly built dais at the gates of Zhagad stood a small figure dressed in a green gown, a circlet of gold banding her forehead and her short dark hair. I smiled as I noted her almost imperceptible fidgeting. Fiona had worn men's clothing for most of her life; she hated skirts. On either side of her stood a man dressed in a dark blue cloak trimmed in silver, each carrying a silver knife sheathed at his side—the two young Wardens, Drych and Huiel.

As the Aveddi's party approached the gates, Fiona stepped forward and raised her arms. Slowly, from the sand to either side of her, rose twin white poles, and from them banners unfurled, white, sewn with the likeness of a dark green tree, a silver dagger, and a small oval mirror—the Queen's banner of Ezzaria, which had never flown in view of the world outside our borders. Tears pricked my eyes.

"Greetings to this noble assembly from the Queen and the Mentors' Council of Ezzaria." Her voice could be heard by every man and woman present—striking even deeper awe into the onlookers. "What seek you at the gates of Zhagad?"

"Tidings of justice, gracious Queen," spoke Aleksander, "and our lands' peace."

"Then hear me, honored petitioners," said Fiona. "The tyrant Edik, whom we have judged guilty of crimes too numerous and too terrible to speak on this fair day, is dead by our device, as are the First Lords of Hamrasch, Rhyzka, Nyabozzi, and Gorusch, who have carried out the tyrant's wickedness upon the people of your lands. Seven and forty lower-ranking commanders and nobles we have judged to have deliberately and murderously executed the tyrant's will, and upon these accused we have placed a bane of sorcery. They have been sent forth upon the roads of this land impoverished, forbidden to have contact with their kinsmen, forbidden to settle in any place for more than a day, their magical bonds preventing all speech and hearing until the day they are adjudged repentant for their deeds or they are dead. Those who wish to see them punished should refrain from a moment's pleasurable vengeance. Rather watch them live and learn of what they've done. As you have recommended, Aveddi, the remaining nobles and common soldiers who have participated in these crimes have been dispersed and given our parole, enjoined to seek the forgiveness of their countrymen by word and deed, lest they too be subject to our penalties. We have marked their names and will be watching."

Fiona spread her arms and touched the shoulders of her Wardens. "Know this, petitioners," she said. "For a thousand years my people have given of themselves to ward human souls from demon ravaging, yet we neglected the true demons that live here in our world, even those who tormented our own brothers and sisters. Never again, Aveddi. We swear to you and to this mighty assembly that from this day forward, we will be vigilant."

As the crowd murmured its wonder and approval, Aleksander nodded and motioned Yulai and Marouf and W'Osti forward. "Then my mission is done, Lady, and I yield the leadership of these forces to those whose rightful place it is." He held out his hand to his wife, and they withdrew their mounts behind the three rulers. But Fiona held up her hand to stay him, and silenced the swelling voices of the crowd.

"You have come here today as a war leader, Aveddi, forswearing all state beyond victory in the name of these who follow you. You have raised the banners of these rightful rulers as they reclaim sovereignty of their own lands. But what of Azhakstan itself? For five hundred years, the Derzhi kingdom of Azhakstan has perpetrated crimes against these brother kings and their subjects. And before the sun sets on this day of judgment, the matter of your own history must be considered. You were once the voice and hand of a cruel empire, sharing in the miseries it created, heir to its tyrant's throne, and so you, too, must submit yourself for sentencing. What say you all, noble kings and princes?"

Shouts of agreement rang out from every side.

Fiona gave Aleksander no opportunity to protest. "If you accept your culpability in these matters and yield your future to the wisdom of this company, then dismount, Aveddi, and stand before me, as a sign to us that you indeed abjure rank and privilege and right of birth."

Aleksander hesitated only long enough to lay his hand on that of his wife and on the head of his sleeping son. Then he slipped gracefully from his steed and walked forward, only the set of his jaw and a slight flush betrayed any ruffling of composure. The crowd gasped as one as he unsheathed his sword, and breathed again when he laid it across Fiona's outstretched hands. Though his head was unbowed and his lean form towered over Fiona, any observer would know which of the two was supplicant.

The young Queen nodded in satisfaction, and her voice soared through the bright morning. "The Ezzarian Council has considered the matter of Aleksander, once heir to the Derzhi Empire, and has taken counsel from these assembled lords of Manganar and Suza, of Thrid and Kuvai and Fryth, and all the lands that the Empire once claimed, and we have spoken with these noble Derzhi who have pledged life and honor to right the wrongs of the past. Aleksander Jenyazar Ivaneschi zha Denischkar, have you anything to say in your own defense?"

Aleksander shook his head.

Fiona nodded and continued. "Because the Derzhi have broken the ordering of the world, so must the Derzhi repair it. Because the Derzhi have stolen their neighbors' wealth, so must now the Derzhi return their good service to these same neighbors. And as the Derzhi have assaulted their neighbors, so must they now stand in their neighbors' defense. To repair and serve and defend, so must Azhakstan be strong and capable of bearing such responsibility. Therefore, the Council has decided that the Derzhi Kingdom of Azhakstan will stand, with boundaries as writ in this map from ancient times before the bloat of empire. As repair for past injustice, the Kingdom of Azhakstan shall claim no seat of power, no royal capital; Zhagad and Capharna will now be as any other city, with no restriction and no preference in trade or residence. The imperial palaces will be sealed by my hand, their continued existence a reminder of greed and tyranny. And to rule this kingdom, an Azhaki king or queen shall be named by the Derzhi tribe's good counsel and serve with the consent of the neighboring rulers, the candidate's own strength and wisdom to be his or her only recommendation."

Fiona pointed toward Kiril and the Derzhi, and so forceful was her query, I thought flame might shoot from her fingertip. "Noble lords of the Derzhi hegeds, who say you all should be the First of Azhakstan to lead you in this service of redemption?"

As one voice, the Derzhi lords cried, "Aleksander!"

Then Fiona swept her arm across the multitudes and cried out, "And you who are owed this service and defense, would you have this Aleksander, the Aveddi, firstborn of Azhakstan, become your Protector?"

And the ayes rang out in thunderous splendor, echoing across the desert, joined with shouts of "Aleksander!" and "Aveddi!"

Fiona nodded. "So be it. We render this judgment: Aleksander zha Denischkar, at dawn tomorrow, if you be willing, you shall be anointed and crowned King of Azhakstan and Protector of the Living Kingdoms, charged to spend your remaining days, not in aggrandizing your own realm, but in rebuilding and defending these which you have helped rebirth." She offered Aleksander his sword. "Will you serve, Aveddi?"

Aleksander reclaimed his weapon, and in a voice as clear as the desert morning and as strong as a paraivo, gave his answer. "I will. By mighty Athos' head, I will."

The cheering could have been heard all the way to Kir'-Vagonoth.

And so came the time for me to look to the future.

In the mild evening of the day of judgment and witness, Aleksander asked Fiona and me to accompany him to Drafa, where he would keep vigil in the holy city on the eve of his coronation as had been the custom of the ancient kings of Azhakstan. Qeb stood waiting by the tamarisk grove, unsurprised as we rode out of the desert, his sightless eyes as brilliant as the starlight. As he led Aleksander to his cave, a solemn, wide-eyed girl-child of six or seven years guided his steps.

After Sarya and Manot had their fill of smiles and weeping at our return, and a quick approving assessment of Fiona, the two old women took up a guard beside the cave entrance, and Fiona and I strolled through the ruined city. We talked of Catrin and Hoffyd and their child, expected any day, of old Talar and her new school of forest lore, of friends and pairings, weather and trees.

But Fiona was not one to shy away from more personal conversation. As the hour grew late and we crested the rise, dragging our fingers over the fallen stone lion, she looked up at me expectantly. "And now of you, my friend and mentor. How are things with you?"

"Improving overall," I said. In most ways, at least, that was true. Time and quiet living had done me a world of good. "Having the chance to be with Evan has been the best medicine."

"And his mother, too?"

I glanced quickly at Fiona to see what she was asking. Few

things could make my face hot anymore, and I kept telling myself that Elinor should not be one of them. Despite the pleasantries of the last months, some things were impossible. "I could ask no better loving for Evan," I said. "And she has helped me immeasurably. Did you note that I can hold a wineglass now? And speak a whole sentence without forgetting who and where I am?"

To my relief, Fiona's question was innocent and quickly past. "It's fine to see your arm stronger, and that you've put on enough weight to cast a shadow. But back in Kuvai, when I examined you, you said that you might need something from me later, and I had the notion that it might be something important. Is there anything I can do for you before I go home?"

My steps slowed with a burden I had explained to no one and wasn't sure if or when I could. "Only one thing. Someday . . . I'd like to come back to Ezzaria."

She burst out laughing, but sobered quickly when she looked at my face. "Why ever would you need to ask?"

"Last time I heard, I was forbidden on pain of death to return. You've seen for yourself that I am demon-joined. And you don't yet fully understand what I was those months in Tyrrad Nor or what I could have become."

She pulled my head down and kissed the top of it. "Gods above, foolish man, I trust you beyond anyone I know. Ezzaria is your home. We will be honored by your coming."

I was gratified by Fiona's trust and acceptance, but I came to the conclusion that I could not take advantage of it. Not yet. I yearned for Ezzaria's green embrace, the peace and healing I believed existed in its hills and forests. But I could not abandon my child and his mother. This decision was not based solely on my desire to remain near Evan, but on hard reality.

The world had changed from top to bottom. Aleksander was a king without a palace, and would need to learn how to live and work within the bounds of his new role. He would spend a great deal of time outside of his own kingdom, seeing to the borders and the safety of those he served. His wealth was now limited to his personal holdings in Azhakstan, and he had already asked the lords of the Mardek to determine how to divest him and other Derzhi of the houses and lands they could no longer afford. Kiril was to be the commander of the young King's troops, charged with retraining Derzhi warriors to be defenders and not conquerors, and Blaise was no longer the Yvor Lukash, but Aleksander's First Dennissar, the King's personal representative to the adjoining kingdoms. Blaise's outlaws were returning to their towns and villages; everyone who had depended on the outlaw band for sustenance was going to have to find a place to live and new means of support. That included Elinor. Our refugee encampment in Kuvai was already half deserted, so I'd heard.

On the road from Drafa to Zhagad on the morning of his coronation, Aleksander had asked me to remain with him as his First Counselor. "Athos knows, I need someone to help me figure out how all this is going to work. It's not exactly the living I offered you four years ago, but you'll never want. And as it's all your doing, it seems only fair that you should haul about with me to see it finished."

I told him I would think about it. And so I had, and about Evan and Elinor and Ezzaria as well.

On a late afternoon, five days after Aleksander's coronation, I knocked on the door of a modest dwelling in the outer ring of Zhagad with a brace of chickens hanging over my shoulder. Blaise, Evan, Elinor, and several of Blaise's outlaws were temporarily housed with a dye maker, the father of one of the outlaws, who still wept with relief every time he saw his daughter walking openly about the city, wearing a badge of valor granted by the new Azhaki king.

"I've brought dinner," I said when Elinor opened the door, "courtesy of Yulai and Magda."

Elinor expressed surprise to see me. "Blaise staggered in an hour ago," she said, pointing to the body sprawled across one corner of the hot little room, snoring profoundly, "but he fell asleep while taking his boots off. He said he's been talking for five days straight, and that the King looks to go five more without stopping. I assumed you were with him." Gingerly she took my proffered fowl. "Shall I cook these or are you going to join the snoring?"

"Chickens are hard to come by right now," I said. "It would be a shame to waste them. But first, I'd like to talk with you a bit about—"

Evan barged into the room just then, insisting on showing me a new sling that Roche had made him for his third birthday. "Mam said that you will show me how to use it properly. I am to use the very smallest stones, and call out before I let one go, and never, ever, ever use it inside a house." His blue-black eyes were wide and solemn as he pronounced the rules. Elinor's wry expression, along with a pile of broken pottery sitting on the table, told me the source of his solemnity.

"Those sound like very good rules," I said. "And it looks to be a fine sling. When the day cools a bit, we'll go out and try it."

While Evan regaled me with unending chatter about Roche and the sling and his small disaster with Dyana's favorite pot, Elinor shrugged and took the chickens out into the courtyard behind the house to clean them. All through the cooking and eating, as I held Evan on my lap and showed him how to hold his sling, as I listened to the exuberant conversation of the dye maker and his family, and laughed as they made jokes about Blaise's trumpeting snores, I watched Elinor move through the noise and heat of the cramped house with quiet humor and grace. When the shadows were long across the city, the dye maker's family set off for the market to drink nazrheel and listen to the day's gossip. I took Evan into the courtyard and spent an hour laughing and dodging his small leather pouch as it whirled about his head and showered us with pebbles. When the boy and I had collapsed on the paving, spent with our efforts and good humor, I noticed Elinor standing in the doorway of the house watching us.

"You wanted to talk," she said.

Evan's head was bent over his pebbles as he began arranging them carefully by color and size in the cracks of the paving. Though he took no notice and concentrated on his private game, I stroked his dark hair. "I heard this morning that Aleksander had asked you to travel with Blaise—a dennissar in your own right—but that you had refused him. I assume you understand what it meant for him to offer—the respect he has for you—"

"—and that I'm a woman. Yes, I understand. And I was honored. But I told him I wished to live quietly for a while. A child should not grow up knowing only war and politics."

She said nothing more. Just stood there. Waiting. She didn't make things easy.

"Yes. Exactly so . . ." What was it I had come to say? It seemed so feeble. So presumptuous. ". . . and so I thought . . . you'll need some way to live wherever you plan to settle . . . and I could find work as a scribe, perhaps, now my hand is working better . . . so I could be close by . . ."

"But the Aveddi relies on you. His First Counselor, I've heard. Will you not roam the deserts with him?"

Her manner was impassive, curious, while my face was surely as hot as the aforementioned deserts. "He can come wherever I happen to be or call on me as he wishes. I'll always answer his need. But I've no more yearning to roam the deserts than you do, and some things are more important even than Aleksander and his kingdom." I pushed a pile of black pebbles toward Evan's hand and watched his small fingers place them in the cracks. "Unless you tell me not, I'll go wherever you go."

"And what if I say I choose Parnifour or Hollen or some other place far from Azhakstan . . . far from Ezzaria? Would you truly go there and do scribe's work to keep us?"

"I will do whatever is necessary. I told you that before. It has not changed."

"Aye, so you said"—a change in her voice drew my eyes upward to meet her own—"and so you have done."

So much spoken in those simple words. Faith. Trust. Understanding. A generous spirit . . . waiting. Her utterance opened a door in my heart and gave me a glimpse of possibility. I searched her strong and lovely face and saw nothing to contradict my hearing.

Quickly I packed Evan's fist full of pebbles, hefted him onto my shoulders, and stood up, praying he would stay occupied and quiet for a little while. "Mistress Elinor, would you honor me by walking out this evening . . . to the market . . . for a cup of nazrheel?"

She tilted her head as if giving the matter due consideration. Then she nodded. "Perhaps we need to take up our conversation exercises again. This would be a fine evening for it." Her mouth curled ever so slightly at the left corner.

Before I could so much as get across the courtyard and take Elinor's arm, a barefoot, yawning Blaise walked out of the dim house behind her and, without a single word, snatched a giggling Evan from my back and disappeared back into the house. One might have thought he was standing there waiting for the opportunity.

Our conversation exercise wandered slightly farther afield that night; Elinor wanted to know all about Ezzaria and what it might be like as a place to raise a shapeshifting child. We would need to discuss a great deal more as the days passed, but the evening's conversation was pleasant. Exceedingly pleasant.

Seven days after the Day of Judgment, and six days after Aleksander's coronation, I stood in the evening light at the top of a towering dune awaiting the King of Azhakstan. He had sent word that he was determined to ride out on this evening, to take one hour away from advisers, petitioners, stewards, and job seekers, and that he would appreciate the company of someone who didn't want him to *do* anything.

I was smiling when he rode up the dune, his red hair flying, for I had just spent an afternoon with Lydia and young Sovari Lydiazar Aleksandreschi zha Denischkar. Life would never be dull for the royal family of Azhakstan. The tiny boy's hair was fiery red, and after giving me a toothless grin charming enough to melt stone, he took up yelling louder than a chastouain prodding his balky beast through the desert.

Aleksander slipped gracefully from his white horse and whispered whatever command ensured the beast would stay patiently where it was left. Part of his own special magic. "Holy Athos, I had to threaten everyone with hanging to get them to stay behind. You haven't let anyone slip you a petition just in case you saw me, have you?"

"Not a one. Perhaps I could come up with something, though."

He groaned and motioned me to walk with him across the crest of the sand until we were out of sight of the haffai-clad guards clustered at the base of the dune. The empty desert stretched out before us, splashed with purple and gold. As we slipped and slid our way to a second crest where we could see no one and hear nothing but the quiet stirring of the wind, his shoulders relaxed and he sighed in pleasure. "Here, let's sit for a while. I need this."

He spread his cloak on the sand and settled there, leaning back on his elbows. He cocked his head as I sat beside him. "You're not going to stay with me, are you, Seyonne?"

I laughed and shook my head. "How can you tell so quickly? We haven't spoken in almost a week. And I only just decided."

"This time I cheated. Fiona told me you were talking of going to Ezzaria. And something's been troubling you since you came back—no wonder that. So, will going home remedy it?"

Of course Aleksander would be the one to notice. I scooped up a handful of the warm sand and let it trickle through my fingers. "I hope."

"Tell me, Seyonne. You owe me that. I came a gnat's eyebrow from killing you, and you insist that you intended it, though you knew it would be a deed that would haunt me the rest of my life. You took your son to that place not knowing how things would fall out. That tells me the magnitude of your fear, and that you have accomplished some dreadful task that we ordinary folk will likely never comprehend. Whatever happened between you and the old man before he died brought you back safely, and I thank the everlasting gods for it. But you are my friend and brother, and I would know what grieves you."

He was right. I owed him everything, and so, against all intent, I told him everything. As the purple shadows lengthened across the dunes, I spoke of Kerouan and Valdis and Verdonne, of traveling in dreams and the bargain that allowed me to participate in his war, of the crumbling wall and my unquenchable craving for sorcery. I told him of my dilemma: how I could neither allow mad Kerouan to keep his power nor risk him recouping it from me in displeasure, how I could not slay the old sorcerer and keep the power myself without ensuring my own corruption, certain that if I violated my demon's warnings while I possessed the unfettered melydda of a Madonai, I would become the tyrant to end all tyrants. ". . . and so I had to take the power and die with it. Your promise was my only hope, and dragging Evan into danger and trusting Blaise and Elinor to witness to my change were the only ways I could think of to convince you. Thanks to Kasparian, we were given another choice. And in the end . . . seeing you and Elinor there . . . thinking of Evan . . . I had enough memory of my true life and enough reason to know that I did not want to continue without feeling. I could see no point to such an existence, no matter how long. Unlike Kerouan's expectation, I would have felt no satisfaction in killing you or any human. So I told him I would give him back his name, if he would take back what he had given and die with it . . ." My voice trailed away much as the sunlight was fading from the sky.

"And you were left— Oh, mighty gods, Seyonne. You have no melydda."

I brushed the sand from my hands and from my boots. "Not a

scrap." I tried to smile it away. "It feels a bit more final than before, when I was a slave. But you never know." The loss itself was bearable. I had lived powerless for many years. But it was very hard that I would never be able to show my son how to enchant a light with his fingers or to fly with him through the heavens and catch him if he fell. "I appreciate your concern, but you mustn't worry. My father lived a blessed life without melydda. I'll not spend the rest of mine mourning a gift that most people never dream of."

"Like lost empires?"

I grinned. "But you'll not rot in some Thrid jungle, either."

"Indeed." He sighed and twisted his face into a rueful grimace, still laced with worry about me.

Only one sure path to get him off this morbid sympathy. I had told him so much; I might as well tell him the other thing. "As long as you are dredging up my deepest secrets, I've one more to confess."

"Which is?"

"I walked out with a woman last night. Just walked, talked a bit, nothing else. But last summer you made me promise to tell you whenever the great day came."

Aleksander stared at me in wonderment and then exploded into laughter, flopping onto his back and clapping his hands to his head.

"I didn't think it was all that unlikely," I said, a bit miffed at the level of his hilarity.

"Athos be praised," he said when he finally regained control of his humor. "She finally got you to look at her and not just the boy. Gods, you didn't take him along with you when you walked out?"

"Blaise watched him," I said, wondering if I would ever be able to surprise Aleksander with anything short of the destruction of the world. "And what do you mean 'got me to look at her'? She's despised me for a year."

We talked into the midnight hours, Aleksander shooing his worried guards away with a message for his wife and another for his aides, saying that business could wait until sunrise. At last, as the moon settled onto the silvered desert, our conversation slowed, and, knowing our hour had long passed, we stood to go. I watched from the crest of the dune as he sprang onto his horse and started down toward his kingdom. He looked back once and raised his hand. "Be healed, my guardian, and happy."

And I called after him. "Be wise, my king, and glorious."

Before another week had passed, Elinor, Evan, and I set out for Ezzaria. Blaise left us at the border, the rocky cleft that would lead us over the mountains and down into the green and sheltering forests. He would have led us all the way to my destination, the nameless settlement where my mother, the Weaver, and my father, the farmer, had taught me how to live, but I wanted to savor every step and introduce Elinor and Evan to every rock and tree along the path. We took a week to travel the rest of the distance, and never had I known days of such peace and delight.

Now midsummer has come and gone, and on this starlit night I sit alone beside a steaming pool, deep in the forests of Ezzaria. The pool is very like the one in Dael Ezzar, where my old mentor helped me rediscover the melydda I believed lost in my years as a slave. Today I tried to step into the scalding water, calling on my senses to protect me long enough to endure immersion, a good first lesson in preparation for true sorcery. For the fiftieth time, I failed, though I think perhaps this failure was slightly less abject than the previous forty-nine attempts. Faith links the senses to one's power, so Galadon taught me. And so I must have faith that someday the rains will fill the dry watercourses of my soul, allowing that part of me to live again. Tomorrow I'll come back and step into the pool once more. Or perhaps the day after.

Meanwhile my days are filled with quiet joys. I've begun to teach my people of our beginnings and to write down the story, so we will always remember. Come autumn, I'll return to Kir'-Navarrin and have Kasparian tell me more.

Blaise reports that some of the rai-kirah who remain in Kir'-Navarrin are shaping bodies again, though a number have bade farewell to their comrades and walked into the gamarand wood. The rai-kirah say that these have unshaped even their light-drawn forms and returned their true being to the land. The tower has crumbled to dust, and no one has seen anything of the Lady. The woodland thrives.

Catrin and Hoffyd's black-haired daughter, Chloe, was born demon-joined. Two more Ezzarian children have been born since Chloe, and they, too, are whole. Elinor looks to become our newest mentor, telling these parents stories of Blaise's and Farrol's childhood, and preparing them—and me—to manage childish shapeshifting. Elinor and Evan remind me every day of the richness of life, and I regret no choice that I have made. But after my experiences of the past few years, a man cannot but consider . . .

Had I given up the chance to be a god, to learn answers that those of us born in the human world have yearned to know since the beginning of time? Was Kerouan himself a god in the days before his madness? And if not Verdonne and not Valdis and not Kerouan, then whose hand has shaped us? And if not in Tyrrad Nor, then where are the gods and how are we to learn of them? I contemplate these things as I walk these beloved hills and forests and struggle to learn again from the beginning. I have found no answers as yet.

But, of course, in the end, the exact truth of it doesn't matter. My child and his mother hold me fast in their love, and I am set free to think and remember. I think of Blaise, sharing his sublime and passionate wholeness with the hungry world. I remember Sovari and Malver, W'Assani and Galadon, Farrol and young Kyor, and, yes, Ysanne, too, offering life itself to sustain us. I watch Fiona, determined and stubborn, guiding my beloved Ezzaria into a new service. And I imagine Aleksander, riding his desert kingdom, bearing the weight of our lives and safety upon his strong shoulders, sheltering us all under his mantle of light. It is, after all, tales of strength and honor and purpose that reflect the true glory of the gods, no matter who they are and where they may reside.

Verdonne was a beauteous woodland maid, a mortal, who caught the eye and heart of the god who ruled the forest lands of earth. The lord of the forest took Verdonne to wife, and she bore him a child, a fair and healthy son named Valdis. And the mortals who lived in the lands of trees rejoiced at the alliance between their own kind and the gods.

The forest god grew jealous of the love the woodland people bore for Valdis, angry at the thought that this boy—half mortal—might someday steal his throne, and the god plotted to kill the child and all the mortals who loved him so. The grieving Verdonne, unable to persuade her husband of Valdis's guileless nature, sent the boy into the sheltering trees to save him, and she herself took up a sword and set herself between the god and the world of mortal men.

Verdonne battled with the god all the years as their son grew to manhood. The cruel god stripped his wife of her clothes to shame her, melted her sword to taunt her weakness, and burned the fields and forests around her so that she would have no sustenance. "Yield," bellowed the forest god. "I will not sully my sword with mortal blood." But Verdonne would not yield.

The elemental spirits, who ordinarily care nothing for the affairs of gods or mortals either one, watched as the mortal woman challenged the mighty god. They marveled at her courage and took pity on Verdonne. They gave her sunlight as her cloak when the god took her clothes, and thunder and lightning for her weapons when he melted her sword. They gave her rain to wash her wounds, wind to bear her up, and fire to sustain her.

"Yield," bellowed the forest god. "You are mortal, and when you die I will have my way. You have no hope." But Verdonne would not yield.

Then came the day when Valdis reached his manhood and laid his strong hand upon his mother's shoulder. Verdonne smiled and stepped aside, and Valdis wrenched his father's sword away and stripped his father of his power. But instead of keeping these things for his own, he laid them at his mother's feet. "You have shown your people the selfless strength and faithfulness of a true sovereign ruler. These are rightly yours."

Verdonne ruled the sweet forest lands until she grew tired, for her body was mortal. But Valdis honored her and made her immortal, and even unto this day she rules the forests of the earth and he remains her strong right arm.

Valdis built a magic fortress, a prison furnished with beauty and comfort, and because Valdis would not be a father-slayer, he locked his immortal father away in that fortress. And the young god took his father's name from him and destroyed it, so that no man or woman could invoke it ever again. But woe to the man who unlocks the prison of the Nameless God, for there will be such a wrath of fire and destruction laid upon the earth as no mortal being can imagine. And it will be called the Day of Ending, the last day of the world.